FURTHER CHRONICLES OF FAIRACRE

FURTHER CHRONICLES OF FAIRACRE

BY MISS READ

ILLUSTRATED BY J. S. GOODALL

Comprising

MISS CLARE REMEMBERS · OVER THE GATE
THE FAIRACRE FESTIVAL · EMILY DAVIS

MICHAEL JOSEPH
London

MICHAEL JOSEPH LTD
Published by the Penguin Group
27 Wrights Lane, London W8 5TZ, England
Viking Penguin Inc., 40 West 23rd Street, New York, New York 10010, USA
Penguin Books Australia Ltd, Ringwood, Victoria, Australia
Penguin Books Canada Ltd, 2801 John Street, Markham, Ontario, Canada L3R IB4
Penguin Books (NZ) Ltd, 182-190 Wairau Road, Auckland 10, New Zealand

Penguin Books Ltd, Registered Offices: Harmondsworth, Middlesex, England

Miss Clare Remembers first published by Michael Joseph 1962
© Miss Read 1962

Over the Gate first published by Michael Joseph 1964
© Miss Read 1964

The Fairacre Festival first published by Michael Joseph 1968
© Miss Read 1968

Emily Davies first published by Michael Joseph 1971
© Miss Read 1971

First published in one volume as *Further Chronicles of Fairacre* in Penguin Books 1985
Published in one volume as *Further Chronicles of Fairacre* by Michael Joseph 1990
© Miss Read 1985, 1990

A CIP catalogue record for this book is available from the British Library

ISBN 0 7181 3361 7

Printed and bound in Great Britain by Richard Clay Ltd, Bungay, Suffolk

CONTENTS

MISS CLARE REMEMBERS

To my Father
with love

He who, in the vale of obscurity, can brave
adversity, can behave with tranquillity and indifference, is truly great.

OLIVER GOLDSMITH
The Disabled Soldier

PART ONE

CAXLEY

I

A finger of sunlight, wavering across the white counterpane, woke Miss Clare from a light sleep.

The old lady lay for a while, without moving, watching it tremble like water across the bed and down the uneven bulging wall of her cottage bedroom.

She knew the time without troubling to turn her head to consult the china clock which ticked busily on her bedside table. Her own easy waking, and the strength and direction of the sunbeam, told her that it was a little before six o'clock on this June morning.

And there was no need to get up, thought Miss Clare, with a little shock of pleasure. Each morning, since her retirement from schoolteaching, this tremor of elation had stirred her waking moments. To be freed from the tyranny of the clock, after so many years of discipline, was wholly delightful. Almost every day of her working life Dolly Clare had resolutely thrust the bedclothes from her as the clock struck six. The habit of years dies hard, and still she woke at the same time, and rose very soon after, but with the blessed relief of knowing that, at long last, her time was her own.

She lay now, frail as a bird and very still, beneath the light covers, listening to the early morning sounds. Above her a starling chattered on the chimney pot. To thwart just such nest-builders she had prudently had wire netting stretched across the mouths of the chimneys, and now she could hear the starling's claws and beak plucking the wire and making metallic music. Far away a cow lowed, and farther still a train hooted imperiously as it rushed towards London. Miss Clare could have slipped back easily into slumber again.

But suddenly there came the roaring of a motor-bike kicked into life. The clock vibrated in sympathy, and Miss Clare sat upright.

'That's Jim off to work,' she said aloud. 'Time I was up.'

The motor-bike thundered by, shaking the old lady into wakefulness.

'And this is the day that Emily comes! Plenty to do today!'

She put back the bed clothes and thrust her bony legs towards a patch of warm sunlight on the rug. Miss Clare's day had begun.

It was strange, thought Miss Clare, half an hour later, moving methodically about her small kitchen, how little Emily Davis knew of the important part she had played in her own life. For almost seventy years now she and Emily had been friends. For several years they had taught side by side as pupil teachers, and when their ways had parted, weekly letters, lengthy and beautifully penned, had sustained their affection. No matter how long their partings, on meeting they fell together as sweetly as two halves of an apple. Now, in old age, the warm friendship had an added quality, for the knowledge that it must end before long quickened their love for each other.

They had first met under the steep slated roof of Beech Green school, when Emily Davis was seven years old and Dolly Clare a forlorn newcomer of six. Standing now in the kitchen, her brown breakfast egg poised in a spoon above the saucepan of bubbling water, Miss Clare looked back across the years and saw the scene as sharply as if it had all happened that morning.

It was the same kitchen that she and her mother had left to make their way to the nearby school. It was a wet Monday morning in March and the Clare family had moved into their new home on the Friday before. Two hours earlier Francis Clare, Dolly's father, who was a thatcher by trade, had set off to work, pushing before him a little handcart containing his tools. Upstairs lay Dolly's sister Ada, two years her senior, and smitten this morning with a timely cold and a violent cough which meant that school was out of the question for her. Envying her from the bottom of her heart, Dolly set out for the unknown, clutching her mother's hand.

'Don't you stir till I'm back, Ada,' called Mary Clare, her face tilted up to the bedroom window. 'I shan't be ten minutes.'

She hurried off so briskly that Dolly was forced to run to keep up with her. Her mother's hand was hot and comforting through the cotton glove. The child had need of comfort. New black boots pinched her toes and rubbed her heels. Her long tartan frock, decently covered with a white pinafore, bundled itself between her legs as she ran along. Her straight yellow hair had been strained to the top of her head and tied there so tightly with a black ribbon by her over-anxious mother that she could feel the skin over her temples drawn upwards in sympathy.

But her physical pain was as nothing to the ache in her heart. Fear of the ordeal before her, the entry alone into a strange and possibly hostile world was bad enough, but even this was less than the misery which had gripped her since the move from their old home at Caxley. This was the third day of grief for young Dolly Clare, the third day of mourning for her lifelong companion, her other half. Emily, her rag doll, had disappeared during the chaos of moving day, and for her young mistress the world was in ruins.

The road to the school was muddy and rutted deeply where the cart wheels made their way. This morning rain lay in long bright bands on each side of the rough flints in the centre of the lane. Other children were making their way to school, shabby satchels or plaited rush bags containing their dinner bumping on their backs. They looked curiously at breathless Dolly, scuttling at the heels of her mother, and nudged each other and whispered as they passed. Dolly was glad when they clanked over the door scraper and entered the high schoolroom.

Mr Finch, the headmaster, was a solemn figure in black with a silver watch-chain drawn across his waistcoat just on a level with Dolly's throbbing temples. The room was very quiet, and a number of children were already in their desks sitting very prim and upright, but with their eyes fixed unwinkingly upon their new schoolfellow. Dolly was too overcome to return their gaze, and looked at her new boots already splashed with chalky water from the lane.

'Yes, sir, she's already been to school at Caxley,' her mother was saying. 'She can read and reckon, and is a good hand with a needle.'

'Date of birth?' asked Mr Finch sombrely.

'Tenth of April, sir, eighteen eighty-eight.'

'And her full name?'

'Dorothy Annie Clare, but she's called Dolly, sir.'

'I will tell my wife. She will start with her.'

'I've another girl to come. Ada, sir, she's eight, but in bed poorly this morning.'

'Very well,' said Mr Finch with a note of dismissal in his voice. Taking the hint, Dolly's mother gave her daughter's cheek a swift peck and disappeared homewards, leaving her younger child as lonely as she was ever to be.

She stood on the bare boards of the schoolroom trembling from her tight black boots to the top knot on her head, fighting against tears and longing for the comfort of Emily's hard stuffed body in her arm. But Emily had gone, even as her mother had gone, and though in an eternity of time, when the great wall clock struck twelve, she would see her mother again, yet Emily had gone for ever.

The figures in the desks wavered and swelled as the hot tears pricked her eyes.

'You can sit by Emily for now,' said a woman's voice above her head. She found herself being led to the further end of the long room. Emily, Emily! The word beat in her head like a bewildered bird trying to get out of a closed room. In her present dream-like condition it seemed possible that she might be advancing to meet her long-lost familiar again, although the dull ache at her heart counselled otherwise.

She found herself in front of a double desk. At one side sat a grave dark child, with black hair smoothed from a centre parting to fall into two long plaits. Her eyes were grey and clear like water and her smile disclosed a gap where her two front milk teeth had gone.

'This is Emily,' said Mrs Finch.

It wasn't, of course, to Dolly Clare; but the smile was engaging and the grey eyes reassuring. And, amazingly, the stranger was called Emily!

Tremulously, through her tears, Dolly smiled back, and the friendship began.

Buttering a finger of toast on her breakfast plate, Miss Clare mused on that far-distant meeting with the second Emily in her life amid the misery which had engulfed her in the schoolroom. That such 'old, unhappy, far-off things' should have the power to prick her into acute feeling so many years after, made the old lady marvel. Yet, she told herself ruefully, she had difficulty in remembering the name and aspect of a friend's house she had visited only three days earlier! Memory played queer tricks as one grew old.

Emily's face at seventy was far more difficult for her to recall than that seven-year-old's which flashed so vividly upon her inward eye. As for the earlier Emily, who had shared the first six years of her life, why, Miss Clare could see her more clearly still. She could see the brown painted curls, the wide painted eyes and the dented nose which had suffered much banging on floors and chairs. She could smell the stout calico of which she was made, and see the quilted bodice and green-striped long-legged drawers painted upon it; and she could feel e 'en now the delicious scrunch of the hard-packed wood shavings with which she had been stuffed. The sharply indented waist could be spanned by little Dolly's two joined hands, and the legs and arms were prickly at the ends where the calico had worn thin. There was something infinitely reassuring about the smell and weight of Emily as she leant drunkenly against her. No possible harm could befall anyone, thought young Dolly, if Emily were there.

For Emily was the good spirit of the home and, young Dolly felt sure, her blessing embraced Father, Mother, Ada and every living thing in the little house at Caxley where it had all begun so long ago.

2

In 1888, the year of Dolly Clare's birth, Caxley was a compact, thriving market town. Its broad main thoroughfare was lined with lime trees and behind these stood shops and private houses built mainly of good rosy brick and weathered tiles.

Here and there, a Georgian front was decorated with grizzled grey bricks known locally as 'vuzz-fired' or 'gorse-fired'. There were several handsome doorways, some hooded, some with elegant fanlights above the well-kept paintwork, and the general impression was one of solid prosperity. Travellers from London, journeying westwards, had paused at Caxley to change horses, or to eat or to sleep, for countless generations and had gone on their way refreshed. There was warmth and beauty in the rose-red aspect of the town and a bustling hospitality among its prosperous tradespeople which won the affection of many a stranger.

The broad High Street narrowed to a stone-built bridge at its western end and crossed a river which wound its placid way to join the Thames. Beyond that, on rising ground to the north, a few cottages constituted the outskirts of the market town, and among these was the four-roomed house belonging to Francis Clare and his young wife.

What the hurrying stranger did not see as he took the highway beyond the handsome bridge was the poorer part of Caxley. The river made its way round the southern part of the town in a series of wide loops. Here was an area of marshland dotted with a few ancient cottages. As the town grew during the nineteenth century, several mean streets were built also on this marshy wasteland by speculators. They were slums within ten years of their building, liable to flooding in the spring and damp from the rising mists for the rest of the year. 'That marsh lot', as the townspeople called them, were scorned, pitied or feared by their more prosperous neighbours, and children from respectable homes were warned against venturing into those narrow streets after dark.

Here lived the humblest of Caxley's citizens. From these dank dwellings, very early each morning, issued the old crones who cleaned steps or scrubbed out shops, the labourers on nearby farms, and those employed in digging a new way for a branch line of the local railway. More often than not there were children left behind in the homes to get what poor breakfast they could before setting out to school. The Education Act of 1870 meant compulsory schooling, and the pennies to pay for it were hard to come by in many a marsh home, and handed over grudgingly on a Monday morning.

But though poverty and hunger, aches and pains were common in these mean streets, conditions were not as stark as in the industrial towns further north and west. Very few children went barefoot and very few older people were callously neglected. Caxley was small enough to know its people, and a rough and ready charity did much to mitigate real need. Though little was organized officially for the relief of the poor in the town, yet shop-keepers, the local gentry and the more prosperous citizens were generous to those in their employ or who were brought to their notice as being in want. This casual and spasmodic generosity had something to commend it in a small community, for the feckless and improvident had small chance of waxing fat at others' expense, while those truly in need were given help. It would take some years before the conscience of the town as a whole was roused by the sight of 'the marsh lot' and their dwellings, but meanwhile they were accepted as 'the poor man at the gate', and an inevitable part of the social structure of any town at that time.

The marsh people themselves frequently said how lucky they were. The parents of some of them had taken part in the bitter riots earlier in the century. The marsh dwellers knew all too well true tales of the starving farm labourers who had marched to demand a wage of half a crown a day, in the winter of 1830. The fate of these unfortunates at their trial, when sentence of death was recorded against many and others were transported as convicts to Australia, was fresh in their memory. Consequently, although their own conditions were deplorable, they considered themselves more fortunate than their predecessors, sharing, to a small extent, the growing prosperity of the latter part of Queen Victoria's long reign.

Perhaps those who felt the pinch most at this time were the small tradesmen, the clerks and the shop assistants, too proud to seek charity, and keeping up an air of respectability with precious little to maintain it. There was a great company of such people in Caxley at that time, dressed in neat, dark attire, much darned and much pressed, whose pale faces spoke of long hours and poor nourishment, and whose main anxiety was not so much the serious difficulty of living on their small wages as concealing their difficulties from those about them.

Francis Clare and his wife were of this company. To be sure, Francis's round face was not pale, for his outdoor occupation gave his a weatherbeaten aspect, but Mary's wore a pinched and sallow look. It was she who bore the major part of their poverty, making each penny do the work of two, and depriving herself so that Francis and the two little girls should benefit.

She had been in good service before her marriage, employed as a general maid in a farmhouse some miles west of Caxley. The farmer and his wife were hard-working and kindly. Despite the low conditions of agriculture at that time, and the recent disastrous harvest of 1870, yet there was wholesome food for all the household produced there. Outside, the logs were stacked in hundreds, sawn up by the farm hands when the weather was too cruel for fieldwork. Coal was cheap and was bought by the truck load. The farm carts trundled to Caxley station once a year bearing sacks of corn, and brought back enough coal for the winter instead.

At Michaelmas the pigs were killed, salted and jointed and hung in clean muslin from the beams in the kitchen. Strong beer was brewed, in an enormous copper, from home-grown barley, and provided a nourishing drink for the men. There was milk in abundance, and butter was made once a week, Mary herself turning the churn more often than not. All the bread, the massive pies and puddings, were made from home-ground wheaten flour. Vegetables and fruit were picked fresh each day from the garden, and the farmhouse kitchen seemed always to be filled with the fragrance and the clatter of cooking.

Only when night came and the oil lamp glowed on the kitchen table, a round pearl of light in its milk-white globe, did the bustle die down. Then the single men, who lived on the premises, and the farmer and his wife, with Mary, quiet as a mouse in the corner, would settle round the fire or at the table, and read or talk or take out the mending basket, until the yawning and nodding began. Then the young men would say their good-nights before stamping across the cobbled yard to their bothy above the stables, and Mary would climb up the creaking stairs, candle in hand, to her windy little room under the roof. Finally, the farmer and his wife would rake through the fire, put up the massive fire guard, shoot the heavy bolts on the doors and make their way to bed. By ten o'clock on a winter's night the farmhouse would be wrapped in silent darkness, and the only sounds to be heard would be the snort and stamp of a horse beneath the bothy, or the croak of a startled pheasant from the spinney.

All too soon, it seemed to young Mary, the morning would come, and she would hear the carters taking their horses across the yard, the rumble of heavy wheels and the rhythmic squeak from the pump handle in the yard as the farm hands set about their work. Soon, she too would have to clamber from her truckle bed to rekindle the great kitchen fire, the first of many jobs.

The days were long and busy. Mary learnt
how to keep a house clean, to cook and to sew.
The farmer and his wife were childless and
treated Mary with affection. She was a docile
girl, willing to learn and fond of her employers.
Life at the farm was hard but happy, and no
doubt she would have been content to stay there
for many years had Francis Clare not crossed her
path.

He was twenty years of age when first she saw
him. He came in the early autumn, with his father,
to thatch the six great ricks of wheat and barley
which stood majestically in a nearby field. His

hair glinted as brightly as the straw among which he stood and his
blue eyes appraised Mary as she carried an earthenware jug of beer
to the thatchers. The two men were at work there for a week, and
Francis made no secret of his interest in Mary.

Later that autumn he came again, this time alone, to repair the
thatch on one of the barns. He appeared so often at the kitchen
door, and Mary seemed to have so many occasions to cross the yard
to the barn during his stay, that she was sorely teased. The farmer
and his wife liked young Francis. He and his father were known for
miles around as respectable and honest workers. There was no reason
in the world why Mary should not welcome the young man's
advances. There would always be work for a thatcher, they told
each other, and they could not keep a good girl like Mary, now
almost twenty and as pretty as ever she would be, on a lonely farm
for ever.

By Christmas it was generally understood that Francis and Mary
were 'keeping company'. Now Mary's needlework was for her
trousseau and her bottom drawer. The farmer's wife, when sorting
out her linen or her crockery, would say:

'Here, my dear, put that aside with your things. 'Tis a bit shabby,
maybe, but it'll prove useful I don't doubt.' Later, Mary was to
count these casual gifts amongst her dearest possessions.

On Michaelmas Day in the following year Mary was married
to Francis and the young couple went to live in the little house
on the outskirts of Caxley. They paid a rent of two shillings a
week to the baker in Caxley who owned the property. Francis

had ten pounds in savings, and Mary had five new golden sove-
reigns, a wedding present from the farmer and his wife. There
was plenty of work to be had. Francis owned a fine set of thatching tools and had abundant strength and skill to use them. Queen
Victoria had reigned for almost fifty years, England was beginning
to enjoy prosperity, and Francis and Mary, young and in love,
prepared to be as happy as larks as the year 1885 drew to its
close.

Mary Clare's first home was one of a pair of cottages close to the
road which ran northwards from Caxley. Francis's own home lay
less than a mile away, and his parents were frequent visitors.

A narrow strip of garden lay between the road and the front
door, and the little brick path was edged with large white stones.
This tiny patch Mary claimed for her own and busily planted pinks
and columbines and a great clump of old-fashioned purple iris to
flower the next year. A moss-rose already flourished by the gate,
and still bore a late bloom or two when Mary arrived at the house
as a bride.

The front door led directly into the main living-room of the
house, and behind this was a small scullery. A box staircase led from
the living-room to the main bedroom at the front of the house, and
a narrow slip room, above the scullery, which was really nothing
more than an extension of the minute landing, constituted the second
bedroom.

It was a small house, but enough for the young couple, and they
arranged their few pieces of furniture to the best advantage and
were well content. Mary's taste was good. Her own home, a farm
labourer's cottage, had been humble but beautifully clean and neat,
and at the farmhouse she was accustomed to seeing solid pieces of
well-made furniture, and well-designed utensils of copper and wood
in daily use.

She spread the scrubbed deal table with a red serge cloth in the
afternoons, when the midday meal was done, and enjoyed the sight
of a white geranium in a pot set squarely upon it. Round the edge
ran fringed bobbles which were to delight her little daughters in the
years to come. On the mantelpiece stood bright tins containing
sugar, currants, tea and salt. The rag rug before the hearth was of
her own making, and the fender and fire-irons of steel were polished

first thing every morning with a small square of emery paper, until they shone as brightly as silver.

Their only regret was the smallness of the garden. Only a few yards of light soil stretched beyond the back doors of the two cottages.

'Not enough to keep us in potatoes,' said Francis, 'let alone a bit of green stuff.'

He planted onions, carrots and a row of cottagers' kale, and set down some old flagstones near the back door for Mary's wood and iron mangle to stand upon. This done, there was no room for anything else in the garden.

To have to buy vegetables seemed shocking to the young couple, and certainly an unnecessary expense. As the first few months went by Mary was appalled to find how much it cost to run even such a modest establishment as their own.

Not only vegetables, but meat, eggs, flour and fruit, which had been so abundant at the farm, and which she had hitherto taken for granted, now had to be bought at the shops in Caxley High Street or at the market. Despite her care, Mary found that she frequently had to ask Francis for more housekeeping money, and she began to dread the look of anxiety that crossed his face when she told him that she had no money left in her shabby purse.

For the truth of the matter was that Francis was even more discomfited by the cost of married life than his wife. Although there was always thatching to be done, yet it tended to be seasonal work. After harvest, when the ricks needed to be thatched, the money came in well; but in the winter time when bad weather made work impossible, a thatcher might go for weeks with no earnings.

Francis was beginning to find, too, that the customers who had employed both his father and himself now tended to ask his father alone to do their work. It had been agreed between them at the time of Francis's marriage, that they would set up separately, and it was only natural that the older man should be asked first to undertake those jobs which he had done for many years. There was no doubt, too, that Francis was not as skilful or as quick as his father. He began to find that he had a serious rival here, and though they were outwardly as devoted as ever, yet Francis could not help feeling that his own trade was decreasing steadily while his father's prospered.

He took to going further afield for work, and set out very early to any job he had been lucky enough to get. Clad in thick clothes, wearing heavy hob-nailed boots and leather leggings, he trudged off before daybreak during the first winter, along the muddy lanes to the north and west of Caxley. He had built himself a little hand-cart in which he pushed the tools of his trade, his shears, roofing knife, eaves knife, twine, and the bundles of short hazel strips, called sprays in those parts, which were bent in two and used as staples to hold down the thatch.

There were many hazel thickets on the chalky slopes around Caxley, and Francis had permission to cut from several of them. Mary used to enjoy these outings to collect the hazel sticks, and never came back without a few flowers or berries from the woods to decorate the window sill. Later she used to help Francis to slice the sticks and to sharpen each end so that the straw would be pierced easily.

Despite the pinch of poverty, the two were happy, although neither of them enjoyed living so near to a town, and Mary missed the boisterous friendliness of the farmhouse. Although she did not admit it to her husband, she found life in the cottage lonely. Her immediate neighbours were an aged couple, both deaf and quarrelsome, who had rebuffed her innocent countrybred advances when she first arrived. She was too timid to do more, and knew no one of her own age in Caxley.

Consequently, she was obliged to fall back upon her own resources during the long days when Francis was away from home. She scoured and scrubbed, cooked and sewed in the little house and worried constantly about making ends meet. She was determined not to lower her standard and become like 'that marsh lot' who lived within a mile of her own doorstep. She had lost her way among those dank streets one day when she was exploring the town, and had been distressed and frightened by the dirt and violence she saw there. In the first few months of married life Mary adopted an attitude of proud respectability which was to remain for the rest of her life.

In the summer of 1886 their first child was born. The baby arrived during one of the hottest spells in August, a small, compact child, fair like her father, and as neat and beautiful as a doll. Francis and Mary were delighted. She was christened Ada Mary and throve from the first.

'But it's to be a boy next time' said Francis, bouncing his little
daughter on his knee. 'Must have another thatcher in the family or
who's to carry on when I'm past it?'

'I'll see what I can do,' promised Mary.

But it was not to be. When Ada was rising two, a fat toddler
already tugging the fringed bobbles from the red tablecloth, a second
daughter arrived.

It was an April day. This second birth was more complicated
than the first, and Mary had paced the little bedroom all day,
watching the showers sweeping across the window and drenching
the primroses in the tiny front garden.

It was early evening when the baby was born. The showers
suddenly stopped, and the sinking sun lit up the room with golden
brilliance.

'Open the window,' whispered the mother to the old woman
who acted as midwife.

The cool breeze carried with it the fragrance of wet earth and
spring flowers. On the glistening rose-bush a thrush sang his heart
out, welcoming the sun after the storm.

''Tis a good omen,' pronounced the old crone, returning to the
bedside. 'That'll be a lucky baby, just you wait and see.'

'But it's a girl?' cried Mary, tears of weakness springing to her
eyes at the thought of Francis's disappointment when the news
should reach him.

'That don't matter,' replied the old woman sturdily. 'That child
be blessed, I tell you, boy or girl. And the day will come when
you'll remember what I told you.'

Mary need not have worried. Francis welcomed this second little
girl as warmly as the first. Although she had not the beauty, nor the
lusty strength of Ada, she was equally fair, and very much quieter
in temperament.

One Sunday afternoon in May, when all the lilac was in flower
and Mary's clump of irises hung out their purple flags, the Clare
family, dressed in their best clothes, carried the baby to the parish
church. She wore the same long christening robe which Ada
had worn, a garment of fine white lawn, made by Mary, covered
with innumerable tucks and edged with hand-made crochet
work

Mary felt a glow of pride as she handed this elegant bundle to the vicar at the font.

'I name this child Dorothy Annie,' intoned the vicar sonorously, and dipped his finger in the water.

3

Memories of her first home crowded back to Miss Clare as she cleared her breakfast table in the kitchen at Beech Green. To be sure, she thought, the things that one would have expected to see most clearly escaped her. The faces of her mother and father, the aspect of the home outside and the simple geography of its interior, the view of the lane seen through the wooden palings of the gate, and even the appearance of her sister Ada at that time, evaded her memory.

And yet there were other things, objects of no particular merit or beauty, whose feel and smell — and taste, too, in some cases — she recalled with a thrilling clarity after all these years. The white stone nearest the wooden front gate, the first of the row leading to the door, was particularly beloved by little Dolly. It rose to a substantial knob, large enough for a small foot to balance on, and so afforded her a better view of the world outside the front garden. At the foot of the knob was a hole, about two inches across, which held rain-water to the depth of a child's finger. It glittered in the whiteness like a grey eye in a pale face, and gave the stone its individuality. Sometimes the child propped a flower in this natural vase, a daisy or a violet, and once she had dropped in one of the scurrying wood lice which lived beneath the shelter of the stone. The pathetic attempts of the creature to climb out, and her own remorse when it died in the hollow of her palm, were never forgotten.

There was, too, a certain knot in the wood of the back door whose satin smoothness Miss Clare could still feel on her finger tip. Below it a drop of resin had exuded, sticky and aromatic. These two fascinating lumps, one cold and hard, the other warm and soft, within an inch of each other, were a source of wonder and joy to the child. Nearby was the handle of her mother's heavy mangle, white as a bone with drenchings of soap and water, and split here and there so deeply that a child could insert tiny leaves and twigs and make believe that she was posting letters.

Other memories were as fresh. Miss Clare recalled the slippery coldness of the steel fire-irons beneath her small hand, the delicious stuffy secrecy of hiding beneath the table, and the sight of the red bobbles quivering at the edge of the tablecloth. She could still feel the mingled love and terror which shook her when her father held her high above his head near to the oil-lamp that swung from the ceiling, and the roughness of his coat and the prickliness of his cheek.

But clearer than any of these early memories was that of Emily the doll. Heavy, ungainly, battered, but ineffably dear, the look, smell, feel and taste of her rag doll flashed back across the years to Miss Clare. Her home and her family might be hidden by the mists of time, but the image of Emily shone still, as splendid as a star.

With the arrival of her second child Mary Clare found her life busier than ever. Throughout the summer of 1888 she struggled against an overpowering weariness. As was the custom at that time, the young mother had fed her first baby for over a year, and prepared to do the same with the second. But poor diet and the constant nagging worry of making ends meet had taken their toll. Little Dolly's progress was slower than her lusty sister's had been, and Mary faced the unpleasant fact that she would have to stop feeding the child herself and undertake the expense of buying milk for its consumption. It was a bitter blow.

With the coming of autumn Mary's spirits sank still further. Now came the added expense of coal, oil and candles, winter boots for Francis and warmer clothes for the children. She spoke despairingly to her husband, and he did his best to cheer her. His was a resilient nature, the open air blew away his cares, and he had no idea of the intensity of his wife's misery cooped up in the little house with her babies and with nothing to deflect her mind from the cares around her.

'You let me do the worrying, gal,' he told her with rough affection. 'I guaranteed to look after you when we was wed, and I'll do it, never you fear!'

He gazed round the lamp-lit room, at the firelight glinting on the polished fender and the black pot which bubbled on the hob sending out wafts of boiling bacon. Upstairs his daughters lay asleep, bonny and beautiful. He could see no reason why Mary fretted so.

'We may be a bit short – but that's only natural. We're in no debt, and now the harvest's in there's work aplenty for me. We'll be able to put something by this winter, for sure, then one day we'll be able to get somewhere further out in the country to live. Be better for you up on the downs, I reckon.'Tis lowering to the spirits, living near the marsh here.'

Mary did her best to be comforted. She had not the energy to point out the drawbacks of the little house, nor did she want to appear dissatisfied with the home that Francis had provided. Compared with 'the marsh lot' they were superbly housed, but the autumn gales had lifted several slates from the roof and had driven rain into the bedroom through the gaps. The window frames had shrunk with age and fitted poorly, and many a keen draught whistled through the rooms. There was no damp course, and the walls of the scullery glistened with moisture. The strip of matting which Mary spread on the flag-stoned floor there was dank and smelt musty.

Francis was a handy man and cheerfully undertook household repairs. It was as well that he did, for the baker landlord in Caxley took no interest in his property at all. He knew, though his tenants did not, that the pair of cottages was to be demolished within a year or two to make way for an extension of the railway line already being prepared from Caxley to the northern part of the county. He did not intend to spend another penny on his houses, and told Francis so flatly when the young man timidly approached him.

'What d'you expect for two shilluns a week?' growled the baker. 'A palace? And how far d'you reckon two shilluns is going to go when it comes to putting a new set of slates on the roof? You wants to come down to earth, me boy. If that ain't grand enough for you, you knows the answer.'

After this encounter, Francis was even more determined to move house as soon as he could find somewhere that he could afford. Meanwhile he and Mary stuffed the cracks with folded paper, and Francis borrowed a ladder and did a little rough thatching here and there among the slates of the rickety roof, to keep the worst of the weather out.

Mary stuffed long strips of sacking with more straw, and put these sausages along the foot of the outside doors which let in the fiercest draughts. They were makeshift measures, but they helped to make the little house more habitable, and gave the young couple a comfortable glow of self-reliance, despite their poverty.

'Where there's a will there's a way!' quoted Mary, ramming a draught-stopper hard against the lintel

'We'll find somewhere by the spring,' promised Francis, glad to see a momentary return of her spirits.

But his brave hopes were doomed to be dashed The winter of 1888 still lay ahead, and worse troubles than poverty were to visit the Clares' home during those bitter months.

One November morning, soon after his encounter with the landlord, Francis Clare was at work for another landlord, more zealous than his own

His employer on this occasion was a man called Jesse Miller, who farmed several hundred acres of land lying between Beech Green and Springbourne He was reckoned to be a hard man of business but a good master to his men He had more conscience than many of his fellow farmers at that time, and saw to it that his men were housed well To be hired by Jesse Miller at the Michaelmas hiring fair in Caxley meant hard work but above average living conditions, as the local workers knew well.

Francis was busy thatching a long row of four cottages, and expected to finish the work by the end of that particular week. The day in question was clear and sparkling, and from his lofty perch Francis had a fine view of the distant downs, a soft blue hump against the bluer sky. A clump of elm trees at the edge of Hundred Acre Field had turned a vivid yellow, and reminded Francis of the sprigs of cauliflower, stained with turmeric, that were to be found in his wife's home-made piccalilli.

The sun was overhead, and his stomach told him that it was dinner time long before the clock on Beech Green church struck twelve. He descended the ladder and fetched his satchel from the handcart.

Seated on a bank, at the rear of the cottages, he enjoyed the warm sunshine on his face. He undid the knot of the red and white spotted handkerchief that held his meal and took out a generous cube of fat boiled bacon, the heel of a cottage loaf, and a small raw onion.

He ate slowly, paring the food into small pieces with his old worn clasp-knife. A tame bantam sidled closer as the meal progressed, looking with a sharp speculative eye at the feast. Now and again Francis tossed her a crumb which she pecked up swiftly, and afterwards she would emit little hoarse cooing noises, half purr and half croak, in the hope of further largesse.

He heard the click of a gate at the front of the cottages and guessed that one of the men was coming in for his midday meal. The appetizing smell of rabbit stew from the end cottage had tickled his nostrils most of the morning. Only one other cottage was occupied that day, by an old lady whose son was working on a distant quarter of the farm. Two younger women from the other two cottages had gone together by the carrier's cart to Caxley market.

Although Francis Clare knew pretty well all that was going on in the houses upon which he was engaged, he made it a rule to be as unobtrusive as possible. His father had taught him the wisdom of such conduct many years before.

'People don't want you prying into their affairs,' the old man had said. 'You be enough nuisance anyway, sitting atop their roof days on end. And there's another side to it. Say you gets chatting one day, come the next the women'll come chatting to you when

you wants to get on – or. worse still, asking you to chop 'em a bit
of firing or mend the clothes line. You keep yourself to yourself.
my boy, and get on with your own job.'

It had been good advice, thought Francis, putting the last piece of
bread in his mouth, and leaning back for a brief rest. He closed his
eyes against the dazzle of the sun. The food made him content and
drowsy, and for two pins, he told himself. he could doze off. But
the days were short, there were still a few yards of roof to thatch,
and he must get back to the job. He stood up briskly, brushing the
crumbs from his thick corduroy trousers, observed the while by the
attentive bantam.

He was halfway up the ladder. emerging from the shadow of the
cottage into the bright sunlight on the roof, when the accident
happened His heavy boot slipped on a rung. he lunged sideways to
catch at the roof, missed his hold, and crashed to the ground, with
one leg trapped in the ladder which fell across him.

The noise brought the labourer and his wife running from their
back door, and the old crone, who lived next door, hobbling after
them. They found Francis, with his eyes closed, blood oozing from
a gash at the temple, and his left leg bent at an unusual angle, and
still threaded through the ladder.

''E be dead!' said the old woman flatly. She took off her apron
calmly and began to spread it over the unconscious face of Francis.

With some exasperation her neighbour twitched it off.

'Give 'im time,' begged John Arnold roughly. ''E's winded, that's
all. Cut back and get a drop of water. gal,' he commanded his wife.

Francis Clare came round to feel the sting of cold water upon his
forehead. the blue sky above him and an overpowering smell of
rabbit stew blowing upon his face from the anxious countenances
that bent over him.

'Take it easy, mate,' said John Arnold kindly 'You bin and done
a bit of damage to your leg We'll lift you inside.'

'You looked dead to me,' quavered the old lady. She sounded
disappointed. 'Cut down like grass, you was. White as a shroud. I
said to John 'ere: '''E's dead!'' Didn't I then, John? I thought you
was, you see,' she explained, her silver head nodding and shaking
like a poplar leaf

The journey from the hard earth to the rickety sofa in John
Arnold's living-room seemed the longest one of Francis's life. He

lay there with sweat running down his ashen face, listening to the three making plans for him.

'I'll run up to Mr Miller. He'll know what's best, and meantime you get on up to Doctor's and see if he be home to his dinner,' said John, taking command. 'And you, granny, bide here with the poor chap and see he don't move. Come 'e do, he'll have them bone ends ground together or set all ways. That wants setting straight again in a splint, but us'll do more harm than good to meddle.'

He turned to Francis and patted his shoulder encouragingly.

'Don't fear now. We'll be back afore you knows where you are.'

'But you haven't had your dinner!' protested Francis weakly, looking at the plates which steamed upon the table.

'That don't matter,' said John heartily, and disappeared through the door, followed by his wife who tugged on her coat as she ran.

Francis heard their hurrying footsteps fade away and thought how good people were to each other. John must be hungry, his wife had spent all the morning preparing that savoury dish, yet not a flicker of reproach had crossed their faces at this interruption. Their only concern was for his comfort.

The old lady had turned a chair sideways to the table and sat with one elbow on the scrubbed top, gazing at him with dark beady eyes.

Francis smiled weakly at her, but his head throbbed so violently and he felt so giddy that he was unable to talk to her. He closed his eyes and listened to the whisper of the fire in the kitchen range and the rhythmic wheezing of the old woman's breathing. Within two minutes he had fallen asleep.

The doctor could not be found. He was still out on his rounds, rattling along the country lanes in his gig, and not likely to be back until well after dark, his wife said.

Francis was carried back to his home in one of Jesse Miller's carts. A bed of straw and sacks lessened the jolting, but the deeply rutted road caused many a sickening lurch and Francis could have wept with relief when the cart stopped at his gate and John Arnold went in to break the news to Mary.

For almost three months Francis was unable to go to work, growing more anxious and dispirited as December made way for January and the weather grew more bitter. It was now Mary's turn to comfort, and this she did as well as she could.

Lack of money was their immediate problem, for with the bread winner useless nothing came into the house. Francis's father came forward at once and insisted on doing his son's outstanding work as well as his own, handing over the money to Francis and waving his thanks aside. Francis and Mary never forgot their debt to his parents, and the two couples were more closely knit by this misfortune than ever before.

The kindly farmer and his wife, from whose house Mary had been married, heard of her plight and sent a bundle of mending for Mary to do weekly, and paid her for it very generously. The carrier's cart brought the mending, and a big basket of vegetables, eggs and butter as well, and such kindness warmed their sad hearts during that cold winter.

Sometimes, in his blackest moods of inaction, Francis would brood on the unjust state of affairs which cast a man still further into despair when he needed help most. He was grateful to his father, to his friends and neighbours, but he did not want charity. Somehow or other he ought to be able to ensure that a certain amount of money came into his home to keep his wife and babies while he was off work. People talked about it, he knew. It was to be a long time before such theories were put into practice; and meanwhile Francis and his wife had to endure hard times.

In later years Dolly Clare was to hear her parents talk of that black winter, the first of her life, as the time when they had been driven to the verge of despair.

But time passed, the spring came, and Francis limped about again, burning to get back to work. Mary's spirits rose, Ada played once more in the little garden, and the baby lay there too in its wicker bassinet, gazing at this bright new world and finding it good.

4

The baby's first birthday was celebrated by a family picnic in the woods which bordered an expanse of common land north of Caxley.

After the bitter winter, spring was doubly welcome. It was unusually warm. Primroses and anemones starred the leafy mould underfoot, and early bluebells, still knotted in bud, were already to be seen. Mary and Francis breathed in the woodland scents hungrily as they rested on a mossy bank with their backs against the rough comfort of a beech tree.

The battered baby carriage was drawn up near by, its occupant deep in sleep. But Ada, rosy and sturdy, scrambled joyfully over tree roots, plucking the heads from flowers and gathering twigs, feathers, acorn cups, pebbles and any other fascinating object which caught her excited eye.

'Wouldn't it be lovely,' said Mary dreamily, observing the child's happiness, 'to have a little house of our own in the wood. Or better still, just on the edge of it, on the common.'

Francis smiled at her fancies.

'We'd soon be hustled off, I knows,' he told her. 'No better'n gipsies, we'd be thought. But you take heart, my dear, one of these fine days you shall have a little house away from Caxley and the throng.'

With the sun above him, the warm air lifting his bright hair, and his family closely about him, Francis felt his strength renewed. He had been back at work for some weeks, and although his injured leg was still weak he found that he could get through a day's work steadily. Although money was scarce, to be busy again raised the young man's spirits. In a month's time, he told himself, his leg would be as good as new. In fact, it was never to be quite as strong as its fellow, and Francis walked with a slight limp for the rest of his life.

Mary stirred from her day-dreaming and began to unpack the food from the basket. Ada, breathless with her exertions, came up to this interesting object, and flung herself down beside her mother.

'I wonder where we'll all be this time next year,' said Mary, holding a loaf to her chest and looking across its crusty top to the distant common. 'D'you reckon we'll have that little house by the time our Dolly's two years old?'

'That we will!' promised her husband stoutly. 'Just you wait and see!'

But Mary was to wait for another five years before hope of a country cottage came her way, and little Dolly was to celebrate several birthdays at Caxley before making her home in the Beech Green cottage which would shelter her for the rest of her long life.

★

It was in Caxley, therefore, that Dolly Clare spent the first for-
mative years of her life. The lane outside the cottage gate was dusty
in summer and clogged with mud in the winter. The child watched
the carts and waggons, the carriages of the gentry and the tradesmen's vans, rumble and rattle on their way, raising dust or churning
mud, as they travelled to and from the town. The diversity of the
horses fascinated her. Ada loved best the shiny high-stepping carriage
horses that trotted proudly past, and would call excitedly to her
little sister when she saw them approaching:

'Come quick, Doll! Quick, you'll miss 'em!'

But Dolly's favourites were the slow-moving patient great cart
horses whose shaggy hooves stirred vast clouds of dust as they plodded
towards the market town with the farm waggons thundering behind
them. There was a humility and a nobility about these powerful
monsters which tore at the young child's heart in a way which she
could not express, but which was to remain with her always.

The two little girls reacted differently to many things. To go
shopping in the High Street or in the market square was a delight to
the volatile Ada. To the quieter Dolly it was sheer misery.

'Ada! Dolly!' The urgent summons from the house in their mother's voice would be the prelude to this ordeal.

First they had to endure a brisk rubbing of hands and faces with a soapy flannel wrung out in cold water. Then came swift and painful combing of hair with a steel comb which seemed to find out every sensitive spot on little Dolly's scalp. Both children had curly hair. Ada's sprang crisply from her head, but Dolly's was softer and fell in loose curls, later to form ringlets. Ada endured the hair-tugging stoically, chattering the while about what she would see and what she wanted her mother to buy.

'Hold still, child!' Mary would command. 'And hush your tongue! Us'll be lucky to get a good dinner from the shops, let alone sweeties and dollies and picture books!'

Dolly's eyes filled with tears of pain during the combing despite Mary's endeavour to handle her gently. She knew it was no pleasure for the younger child to go shopping, but there was no one to mind her and the two must perforce accompany their mother everywhere.

At last they set out. Sometimes Dolly was pushed in the rickety perambulator, but its days were numbered, and more often than not she would struggle along beside her mother's long heavy skirt, clutching it with one desperate hand, or holding on to the stout shopping basket which her mother held. Never for a moment did she let go. The thought of being parted from her mother was too terrifying to be borne.

Ada, on the other side, leapt and gambolled as gaily as a young goat, greeting friends, pointing out anything which caught her eye – a lady's pink parasol, a gleaming carriage door with a crest on it, or a pig squealing in a cart, covered with a stout net, and resenting every minute of its journey to the market.

Caxley High Street was always busy. It was a thriving town which served a large area, and the shops always had far too many hurrying people in them for little Dolly's liking. Customers pressed up to the counters to be served, assistants scurried back and forth filling baskets, weighing out sugar, fetching lumps of yellow butter on wooden pats, and slapping them feverishly into shape on the marble slab behind the counter.

Important customers usually waited in their carriages outside the shop while their menservants bustled to and fro carrying parcels, and the proprietor of the business himself fetched and carried too, leaving his premises to pay his respects at the carriage side. Sometimes a horseman, not wishing to dismount, would shout his order to someone in the shop. Out would race the shop boy at top speed, the parcel would be stuffed into a jacket pocket, coins would jingle, and the horse would clop-clop off down the street again.

The bustle was the breath of life to Ada. She scrambled up on the high round-seated chair by each counter, bouncing with such zest that her lofty ill-balanced perch frequently tipped over. From here she watched, with eyes as bright and round as a squirrel's. She loved to see the butter patted, and its final adornment with a swan or a crown from the heavy wooden butter-stamp. She delighted in the scooping of currants from deep drawers with a shiny shovel, and the see-sawing of the gold-bright scales and weights.

But Dolly, crouched between the counter and her mother's skirt, was in no mood to relish these joys. Bewildered by the noise, hustled to one side if she ventured forth, and half-suffocated by the people who pressed and towered around her, she longed for the time when her mother replaced her purse in the deep petticoat pocket beneath her voluminous skirts and they could make their way out into the street again.

Of all the shops, Dolly dreaded most the butcher's. The headless carcases, split down the middle to disclose heaven knew what nameless horrors in their sinister depths, were frightening enough The poor dangling hares, with blood dripping from their noses to the sawdust on the floor, were infinitely worse. To see them flung on to the butcher's block and to watch his red hands wrenching the skins, with a sickening tearing sound, from their bodies was even more terrifying to the child, and the final awful tugging to release the head had once caused her to be sick upon the sawdust, thus bringing upon herself the wrath of her mother and the butcher combined.

But the most appalling experience, which happened all too frequently was the purchase of half a pig's head. This useful piece of meat was very cheap and very nutritious, and Mary Clare often bought it for the family. Dolly watched, with fascinated horror, the whole head placed upon the butcher's block. The eyes, small and blue in death, seemed to look at her. There was something pitiful and lovable about its round rubbery nose and the cock of its great waxen ears. When the butcher, chatting cheerfully the while, raised his cleaver, Dolly squeezed her eyes shut and gritted her milk teeth, remaining so until the ominous thudding had stopped. She had never been able to keep her eyes closed long enough for the butcher to weigh, trim and wrap the meat, and so endured each time the ghastly sight of that cloven head, brains, tongue and grinning teeth exposed by the butcher's onslaught.

Mary, delighting in her purchase and making plans for several meals from it, never knew the repugnance which little Dolly felt. The child could not go near the basket which held this horror, shrouded in newspaper, and was careful to walk on the other side of her mother on the return journey. For Dolly, this was only the beginning of her misery. The pig's head would float, she knew well, in a basin of brine for hours to come, on the floor of the scullery, and every movement would set it swivelling slowly, while one blue eye cast a cold malevolent beam from its watery resting-place.

'Don't pick at your vittles,' Mary would say two days later, when she placed a plate of boiled pig's brain before her younger daughter. 'Look at Ada gobbling up hers! You be a good girl, now and clean up your plate.'

'That's right, my little love,' Francis would say jovially. 'Thousands of poor children 'ud give their eye teeth for a plateful of brains like that. Why, I wager there's plenty down the marsh would like 'em!'

For all unhappy little Dolly cared, as she pushed the revolting things about, the marsh children could have them. Memories of the butcher's shop, the strain of living with half a pig's head in the house, and meeting the reproachful gaze of that one fearsome eye, completely robbed Dolly of any appetite. Her parents' concern was an added burden, yet how could she explain her revulsion?

And so the pigs' heads continued to appear and to cast their shadow over young Dolly's existence. It was small wonder that shopping in Caxley High Street presented so little attraction for the child in her early years.

Although Dolly's heart sank when her mother slammed the gate and turned left towards the town, it rose with equal speed if she turned to the right, for that way lay the fields, woods and gorsy common land which were becoming so dear to her. That way led to her grandparents' home. Most visiting was done on a Sunday, when Francis was free.

During his enforced idleness, and as soon as he could hobble as

far, it had become a habit for the young family to spend Sundays
with the old people.

'At least they'll get a good feed,' old Mrs Clare had told her husband. 'That baby don't appear too strong, for my liking; and it takes
Francis out of himself to leave that chair of his now and again.'

'Don't overdo it,' advised her husband. 'They don't like to feel
they're having charity, that pair, and good luck to 'em. Besides,
they won't want Sundays booked here for the rest of their lives.
Invite 'em as much as you like while things are bad – but you ease
up a bit when our Francis is back at work.'

By the time the little girls were four and six, the Sunday visits
were occasional treats. One particular Sunday remained vividly in
Miss Clare's memory.

It was a day of high summer. The family set off clad in their Sunday best. Francis wore the dark suit which he had bought for his wedding, and Mary's lilac print was drawn back into a bustle showing a
darker mauve skirt below. Three rows of purple velvet ribbon edged
the skirt, and on her head was a neat straw hat with velvet pansies
to match the underskirt. Both frock and hat had been a present from
her generous employers at the time of her wedding, and were kept
carefully shrouded in a piece of sheeting on working days. Dolly
thought her mother looked wonderful as they set off, and told her so.

'Has Queen Victoria got a hat like that?' she wanted to know.

'Dozens of 'em,' laughed her mother, flattered nevertheless by
the child's admiration.

'Not as pretty,' maintained Dolly stoutly. Her own clothes did not
give her as much pleasure. Her two petticoats, lace-edged drawers and
white muslin frock had been so stiffly starched that it had been
necessary to tear them apart before arms and legs could be inserted.
Now the prickly edges dug into her tender flesh, and she knew from
experience that the lace on her drawers would print strange and
uncomfortable patterns on her thighs from the pressure against
grandma's horsehair sofa. Tucked under one arm she held Emily,
wrapped in a piece of one of her own old shawls. She was the least
well dressed of the party, but not in her mistress's eyes. She was heavy
too, and Dolly was obliged to hitch her up every few yards.

But these minor discomforts were soon forgotten in the joys of
the walk. They crossed a stile and made their way across a meadow
high with summer grass. Some of the bobbing grasses stood as high

as Dolly herself and she saw, for the first time, the tiny mauve seeds quivering at the grass tips. Ox-eyed daisies and red sorrel lit this sweet-smelling jungle that stretched as far as the small child could see. Above her arched a sky of breath-taking blue where two larks vied with each other in their outpourings.

In the distance the six bells of Caxley parish church chased each other's tails madly. A warm breeze, scented with the perfume from a field of beans in flower, lifted Dolly's hair, and she became aware, young as she was, of her own happiness in these surroundings. Sunlight, flowers, Mother, Father, Ada and dear Emily were with her. Here was security, warmth, love and life. Nothing ever completely dimmed that shining memory.

At grandma's house there were different joys. There was an aura of comfort and well-being here which the child sensed at once. The furniture was old and solid, unlike the poorer machine-made products in her own home. The old couple had inherited well-made pieces from their families, and the patina of a century's polishing gleamed upon the woodwork. These sturdy chairs and chests had been made and used long before the commons were enclosed and their self-supporting owners became poor men. The difference in the two homes was eloquent testimony to the revolution which had split a nation into classes. Although the young Clares might consider themselves fortunate when they compared their way of life with that of 'the marsh lot', yet the fact remained that they were as poor. Francis's parents were the last inheritors of an older England where a man might live, modestly but freely, off his own bit of ground.

After the greetings and the Sunday dinner were over, the grown-ups settled back to rest and talk and the two children were told to sit up to the table to play.

'I'll take off your sashes, so they don't get crushed,' said their mother, undoing Ada's blue and Dolly's pink one. It was good to expand, free of their bindings. The sashes were eight inches wide and four or five feet long. Made of stout ribbed silk, they were considerably restricting when tied tightly round - a well-filled stomach. Dolly watched with relief as her mother rolled them up, smoothing them on the table to take away the wrinkles.

Ada was given a picture book, but Dolly had her favourite object to play with – a square tin with pictures of Queen Victoria on each side. It had been bought at the time of the sovereign's Golden Jubilee,

the year before Dolly's birth, and had held tea then. Now it was
grandma's button box, and Dolly was allowed to spill out the contents across the table and count them, or form them into patterns,
or match them, or simply gloat over their diversity of beauty.

There were big ones and tiny ones. Buttons from coats and caps,
from pillowcases and pinafores, from bonnets and boots, cascaded
across the table. There were buttons made of horn, bone, cut steel,
jet, mother o'pearl, linen and leather. Dolly's fingertips, as well as
her excited eyes, experienced the gamut of sensations roused by
handling the variety of sizes, textures, colours and shapes which
were held in the bright button box.

As she bent over her treasures, scraps of conversation floated to
her from the grown-ups.

'Found a house yet, my boy?'

'Not that I can afford, Dad.'

'You won't find anything much cheaper than you own, I'd say.
Take my advice and stay on a bit till you've built up the work again.'

'Things aren't too good. Straw's scarce.'

'Ah, there's not the wheat grown. Old George Jackson, shepherd
to Jesse Miller, was in here this week. He's got more sheep than
ever before. He gets twelve shilluns a week, he tells me, and two
pounds Michaelmas money. He's not doing so bad.'

'And gets it regular, too,' said young Francis, with a hint of
bitterness in his voice.

The women talked of clothes and bed-linen, meals and children.
They seemed, to Dolly, to talk of nothing else, unless it were of
illness and death, and then it was in low tones meant to keep such
things from attentive young ears.

At last the time came when the buttons must be swept from the
table back into the jingling tin. Dolly followed the two women
into the kitchen and watched the preparations for tea.

Bread and butter at grandma's was quite different from that at
home, for here the bread was cut very thin and buttered very
thickly. Home-made plum jam could be spread upon the second
slice, too – the first must be eaten plain – whereas at home one
either had bread with butter on it or bread with jam, never both.
Fingers of sponge cake followed the bread and butter, the top
sparkling with a generous sprinkling of sugar.

The children had milk to drink from mugs with a pattern of ivy

leaves round the rim, but the grown-ups
had tea poured from a huge brown teapot which wore a snug buttoned jacket
to keep the tea hot.

Grandma's tea was kept in a shiny
wooden tea-caddy with a brass lion's head
for a handle on the lid. When this was
lifted, Dolly saw first two bowls filled
with sugar, each settled securely in a hole
At each side of the caddy lay a long
polished lid with a small black knob.
When these were lifted they disclosed the
tea, China on one side, and Indian on the
other. This tea-caddy was an unfailing joy
to Dolly, and when later it came into her possession she treasured it
as much for its intrinsic beauty as for its associations.

After tea the little girls' sashes were re-tied, their hair combed
and their hands and faces washed upstairs in grandma's bedroom.
The thick eaves of the thatch jutted out beyond the windows and
made the room seem dark, despite the golden evening.

Then came the moment which was to stamp this particular
Sunday as a day of perfection as clearly as the morning walk through
the meadow had done.

The old lady opened a drawer in the chest by the bed and took
out a piece of red flannel.

'For Emily,' she said, giving it to Dolly.

The child unfolded the material slowly and with some bewilderment. It proved to be a cloak with a hood, exactly the right size for
the doll.

Dolly was speechless with joy. She could do nothing but throw
her arms round her grandmother's knees and press her flushed face
against the black silk of the old lady's Sunday frock.

'Well, what do you say?' said Mary with increasing asperity. But
Dolly could say nothing. With trembling hands she unbound the
shawl from Emily's heavy body and dressed her in her new finery. She
looked even lovelier than her mother had looked that morning, and
far more splendid than Queen Victoria on the side of the button box.

'I made it out of my old petticoat' said grandma, as they descended the steep stairs. 'There wasn . enough for the children, and

I thought Dolly'd like dressing-up her
Emily.'

Farewells were said and kisses given.
Still no words came from Dolly,
overwhelmed with good fortune, but
the ardour of her kisses was gratitude
enough for the old lady.

Dolly carried the resplendent Emily
all the way home, and Francis carried
them both for the last part of the
journey. Windows and roofs were
turned to gold by the sinking sun. The
drop of water in the white stone by the gate gleamed like a jewel.
From the height of her father's comfortable shoulder Dolly looked
down upon the rose-bush, its flowers as blood-red as Emily's new
cloak.

The scent brought memories of the bean-flowers' fragrance and
the smell of crushed grass in the summer meadow. The ox-eyed daisies,
the red sorrel, the rose-bush, and the pansies nodding on her mother's
bonnet, seemed to whirl together in a dazzling summer dance.

Dizzy with happiness, dazed with golden light, at last Dolly found
her tongue.

'Lovely,' she sighed, and fell instantly asleep.

5

Soon after that golden day, Dolly started school. Ada had been
attending the church school at the northerly end of Caxley for over
a year, so that the younger child had heard about teachers and classes,
sums and slates, and marching to music.

It sounded attractive, and though she dreaded leaving her mother,
yet the thought of Ada's company was supporting. She was, too,
beginning to look for more than the little house and garden could
provide in interest. Her mother was usually too busy to answer
questions or to tell her stories. Her father was much more of a
playmate, but he was seldom there. With Ada away at school young
Dolly was restless, and when, at last, she was told that she would be
accompanying Ada, the child's spirits rose.

She was dressed with particular care that first morning. Over her navy blue serge frock she wore a clean holland pinafore. With a thrill of pride she watched her mother pin a handkerchief to the pinafore, on the right side of her chest, conveniently placed for use in 'Handkerchief Drill Time' which, as Ada had explained frequently, came just before morning prayers and appeared to rank as rather more important. It made Dolly feel important, one of a fraternity, and she wore this emblem of enfranchisement with deep satisfaction.

Her mother sat her on the table to lace her little black boots and tie the strings of her bonnet. The red bobbles on the tablecloth joggled as she wriggled in excitement. Ada, already dressed, jumped up and down the path between the open front door and the gate, looking out for Esther, an older girl, who took her to and from school. This morning she wanted to tell Esther that her sister was coming, and her mother too, and that Esther need not wait for them.

Esther was a tall thin child, with a long pale face and prominent teeth. She looked perpetually frightened, as no doubt she was. Her father was a heavy drinker and violent in his cups. He was a ploughman, but at this time when so much arable land was being turned over to pasture, he had been put to sheep-minding, hedging and ditching, mucking out stables and cowsheds, and other jobs which he considered beneath him. Had he realized it, he was fortunate to have been kept in work at all by his hard-pressed employer. With the influx of cheap grain from the United States and Canada, prices for English wheat had dropped so disastrously in the last few years that he, and many like him, had turned to grazing in the hope of recovery. That, too, was to prove a forlorn hope within a few years, as frozen meat from Australia and New Zealand, and dairy products from Denmark and Holland poured into the country. It was small wonder that men who had spent their lives on the land now uprooted themselves and took their strength and their diminishing hopes to the towns. Others, like Esther's father, too stupid to understand the significance of the catastrophe, either suffered in bewildered silence, watching their families sink and starve, or sought comfort in drink or the militant succour offered them by the evangelical churches.

Transition is always hazardous and distressing. The working people of rural England at that time were largely untaught and trusted the gentry's guidance. They witnessed the crumbling of a way of life, unchanged for centuries, and distress, resentment and fear harried the older generation. The younger people saw opportunities in towns or, better still, overseas, and thousands of them left the villages never to return. Little Dolly, kicking her legs on the table as they waited for Esther, was to be a mature woman before English farming found its strength again, and by that time machines would have come to take the place of the men who had left the fields for ever.

'We don't want you, Esther,' shouted Ada exuberantly from the gate, as the lanky child came into sight. Mary lifted Dolly hastily to the floor and hurried outside, much vexed.

'Ada! You rude little girl!' scolded her mother. 'You come in, my dear,' she added kindly to timid Esther, 'and take no notice of Ada.'

She picked up three small parcels, wrapped in white paper, and gave one to each child. Dolly and Ada knew that they contained a slice of bread spread with real lard from grandma's and sprinkled with brown sugar.

'There's a stay-bit for you,' she said, 'to eat at playtime. Mind you don't lose it, and no eating it before then, or the teacher will give you the cane.'

Esther put hers carefully in the pocket of her shabby coat, but Ada thrust her own and Dolly's into a canvas satchel which had once been Francis's dinner bag, and now carried such provender, as well as books or a pencil, to school.

'Stay by the gate while I gets my bonnet,' said Mary, lifting her coat from a peg on the door and thrusting her arms into it. Her everyday bonnet was kept on a shelf just inside the cupboard under the stairs. She tied it on briskly. The only mirror downstairs was a broken triangle propped in the scullery window for Francis's shaving operations, and Mary did not bother to waste time in consulting this. She shifted a saucepan to the gentler heat at the side of the hob, locked the front door, took Dolly's hand, and hurried schoolward.

Ada and Esther went before them, the younger child skipping cheerfully, swinging the satchel and quite unconcerned by her recent scolding. She was beginning to be bored by Esther's attentions. Strong and lusty, Ada could have done without Esther's support after the first week at school. Her boisterous good spirits disarmed any possible bullies, and her tough little fists would have attacked anyone foolish enough to molest her.

Esther adored her. To look after Ada made the pathetic child feel wanted and useful. Mary's bright smile and her occasional present of an apple or rough sandwich as 'a stay-bit' warmed Esther's heart. In the Clares' modest home Esther saw all that she wanted most. Mary knew this, and knew too that her young children were as safe in Esther's devoted care as they would be in her own.

Dolly's spirits were high too, as she struggled to keep up with the others. She could hear the school bell ringing in the distance, and looked forward to the delights of sitting in a desk and having a multitude of children for company. If Ada said school was fun, then it must be. For nearly five years Ada had told Dolly what to expect. So far she had never been wrong. Trustingly, she trotted behind Ada's prancing heels.

The bell had stopped ringing by the time they turned the corner and came in sight of the asphalt playground in front of the school. Children were forming lines, and two or three teachers stood in front of them. One had a whistle and blew it fiercely.

'Straighten up, Standard Four,' she shouted. 'Take distance, there. Take distance!'

The children lifted their arms to shoulder level and moved back to make a space. Dolly watched in amazement.

Her mother kissed her swiftly and put her hand in Ada's.

'You stay with Ada, my love, till your teacher fetches you. They knows all about you, 'cos I filled in the form the other day.'

Dolly's eyes began to fill with tears, and her mother dabbed them hastily with the corner of her scarf. Her voice grew urgent.

'There, there now! Don't 'ee cry. The others'll think you're a baby. I must be getting back to cook your dinner, my lovely, and Ada and Esther'll bring you home very soon.'

Wisely, she hurried away, doing her best to smile cheerfully at her woebegone little daughter, who looked smaller than ever against the bigger children ranked in the playground.

'Hurry up, you three!' called the teacher with the whistle, and Mary saw the three children scurry into place. With considerable relief she noticed that Dolly, though pale, was now dry-eyed. She turned towards home realizing, with a shock, that she was alone for the first time for years, and that she would find her house empty.

★

Twenty minutes later Dolly sat in a long desk close beside Ada. There were four children on the narrow plank seat which they shared and Dolly was perched precariously at the end, her boots swinging in mid-air.

Before each child was a fascinating square carved into the long desk top. Although Dolly did not know it then, she was soon to learn that each one measured a foot by a foot, and that the little squares inside were each a square inch. Under her lashes she looked to see if her companions were as interested in their property as she was, but they were old campaigners of several terms' standing, contemporaries of Ada's, and were sitting bolt upright with their arms folded tidily across their backs.

Dolly put out an exploratory finger and traced the lines lovingly. 'Don't fidget, dear,' said Miss Turner, briskly. 'Hands behind backs.'

Dolly attempted to put her hands away as neatly as her sister, but found the position extremely uncomfortable. However, Miss Turner seemed satisfied with the effort, and returned to her scrutiny of a large book on the desk before her, leaving Dolly free to gaze about her.

The schoolroom was long and contained three classes. All the children faced the same way, and all sat in desks holding four.

At Dolly's end of the room Miss Turner faced her two rows of infants. In the middle of the room sat the teacher who had wielded the whistle. Her name was Miss Broomhead, Dolly learnt later, and not unnaturally she possessed a multitude of nicknames, none of them flattering. The children in her class were aged from seven to ten or eleven, and their desks were a size larger than the infants', and had four inkwells spaced at regular intervals, whereas the infants' had none.

At the far end of the room the headmaster, Mr Bond, held sway. He was small and neat, with white hair, very blue eyes, and a sharp tongue. He was a stickler for punctuality, tidiness, cleanliness and obedience. Good work took its place after these four virtues. Very often, as he well knew, it followed automatically, for orderly habits make an orderly mind just as surely as an orderly mind expresses itself in a tidy manner. For the eager, clever child, however, whose mind outstripped his pen, Mr Bond's standards could be heartbreaking. He might do a dozen sums of horrid intricacy and get them all correct. but if one small blot or crossing out marred his page then Mr Bond's red pencil slashed across the whole, and he must perforce copy it all out again under threat of a caning. With the amazing patience and endurance of childhood, these conditions were accepted, and Mr Bond was not considered unreasonable in his demands. In fact, he was respected for his high standards, and in an age which was geared to great efforts for a small return, Mr Bond's methods, harsh as they might seem to later schoolmasters, suited his pupils and prepared them for sterner employers in the future.

Two great fireplaces stood at each end of the long wall facing the children. One stood conveniently near Mr Bond's desk, the other by Miss Turner's. Miss Broomhead, unluckily placed in the middle, had to be content with any ambience cast by a large photograph of Queen Victoria which held pride of place in the exact centre of the wall behind her. The Queen was in her widow's weeds, a small crown upon her head, and a veil flowing from it to her shoulders. One plump hand rested on an occasional table, and her gaze was fixed upon some unseen object which appeared to provide her with no satisfaction. Above the heavy frame were lodged two small Union Jacks thick with chalk dust from the blackboards and soot from the fires.

Directly beneath the Queen stood a glass case containing a stuffed fox against a background of papery ferns and tufts of wiry heather. His white teeth looked very sharp and his glass eyes very bright. Dolly wondered, in her innocence, if she would ever be allowed to play with him. At the infants' end, a smaller glass case held a stuffed red squirrel holding a hazel nut in its tiny claws; and at Mr Bond's end a sinister collection of common amphibians, including frogs and newts, at all stages of development, disported themselves among dead reeds and moulting bulrushes arranged around an improbable-looking painted pond.

Six brass oil lamps, with white shades which reminded Dolly of her father's summer thatching hat, hung from the lofty roof and swung very slowly when the door slammed. Three tall narrow windows, set very high in the wall at each end of the room, provided most of the daylight, but two smaller ones, behind the children, added their share, and a constant villainous draught for good measure Children in the back desks, just below these windows, philosophically endured stiff necks and ear-ache, or used their wits to gain a move to a desk nearer the front.

Almost a hundred children were taught in this one room, and, as Dolly soon discovered, it was amazing how quietly the work was done. Heavy boots on bare boards made far more noise than the voices of teachers and pupils, and when, in the long sleepy afternoons, the bigger children were writing or reading silently to themselves, the atmosphere grew so soporific that many an infant, essaying a wobbly pot hook, let fall both slate pencil and slate, and fell asleep with its head pillowed on the carved square of the desk lid. When this happened, wise Miss Turner let sleeping babies lie, rousing them only when the clock said a quarter to four. Then, with bewildered eyes and one flushed cheek grotesquely marked with inch squares, they would return reluctantly to this world, submit dazedly to buttoning and tying, and so stumble away with big sisters to the haven of home.

School proved much more complex for Dolly than Ada had led her to believe. The parting from her mother affected the younger child severely, although she showed little, and departed docilely each morning holding Esther's hand. She had always been much more dependent on her mother than Ada, and once the older child had gone to school the bond between Mary and Dolly had been stronger than ever.

One incident about this time the child remembered all her life. She came upon her mother sitting by the window one day, holding a needle to the light. She frowned with intense concentration, trying to jab the cotton through the eye. Dolly spoke to her, but so intent was she upon the task in hand, that her mother made no sign, but simply bent closer to the window, her eyes glittering and fixed in awful absorption.

To Dolly the remembrance of her mother s complete mental withdrawal on that occasion was terrifying. Far easier to bear were her brief physical absences to the garden or to the rooms upstairs. But to be so close to one's mother, to put one's hand on her skirt, to speak to her and then find she was not there, and that one was of no more significance than the wallpaper beside her was an experience fraught with terror. It was also indicative, she realized later, of the deep need she had of her mother's affection.

But once she had made the daily parting and was on her way to school, Dolly, facing the inevitable, put her mother from her thoughts. Her new companions were overwhelming. Everything about them intrigued the little girl who had known only a few people until now.

In the first place there were so many of them, and they were so diverse. Her path did not cross those of the bigger children very often, but there was surprise and variety enough in the thirty or so boys and girls whose class she shared.

Much to her relief she was allowed to sit by Ada, but she had been moved to an inside position on the bench, and on her right hand side sat Maud and Edith. Edith at the end of the bench was a nondescript five-year-old, the child of a shopkeeper in the High Street. She was the sort of child who fades into the background of a class, having nothing outstanding to make her memorable. Her hair was mousy, her eyes hazel, her dress was drab but tidy. Quiet to the point of apathy, producing neat undistinguished work, dully obedient, Edith existed at the end of the bench.

But Maud was quite a different matter. To little Dolly, pressed so closely to her, Maud was as strange and foreign as a Chinaman. The first thing one noticed about her was her aroma. A sourish, slightly cheesy smell emanated from her, and this became overpowering when the four jumped to their feet, tipping up the long bench behind them, before marching out to play. This movement seemed to release a bouquet of scents from Maud's disturbed clothing, and added to the basic sourness there would be whiffs of stale frying, paraffin and vinegar. Later in life Dolly Clare recognized these mingled smells as the poignant scent of poverty.

Maud was very thin. She wore a tartan frock meant for someone much bigger and stouter. Her long pale neck, shadowy with grime, protruded like a stem from a flower pot, and the shock of red hair atop might have been mistaken for a shaggy bronze chrysanthemum Her eyes were pale blue and protuberant her wide mouth perpetually open, and she fidgeted and wriggled without ceasing, thus drawing upon herself a rattle of fire from Miss Turner's tongue.

'Sit still over there!' she would command, turning the frosty glare of her glasses upon Dolly's desk. Poor Dolly would flush pink with shame, but the guilty Maud would be unabashed, and giggle behind a dirty hand.

Maud's mottled mauve legs were bare, which slightly shocked Dolly in those days of muffled limbs. Her bony feet were thrust into a pair of broken boy's shoes, so ill-fitting that they frequently fell off, exposing Maud's claw-like toes. She was constantly hungry and never owned a handkerchief. Light-witted (and light-fingered, too, it proved later), Maud was the pathetic product of one aspect of England's industrial prosperity. Her home was in the marsh.

Dolly grew very fond of her. Maud was loud in her praise of Dolly's clothes and her soft curls which she delighted in stroking. Her own rough thatch grew more tangled daily as she scratched her head remorselessly. Dolly accepted the scratching, the smell and the giggling of her neighbour without rancour, but wished she would not fidget so much and draw attention to the bench as a whole. Years later, when Dolly herself was a teacher, she wondered that Maud, and many others like her, had not fidgeted more, plagued as they were with the torments of the poor. Unwashed and tangled hair harboured head-lice, bodies packed four to a bed bred fleas, inadequate diet nourished thread-worms – but not their hosts. One stand-pipe of cold water, in a yard, to serve twelve houses, did not encourage cleanliness. Large families meant exhausted mothers, leading to neglect or despair. When you came to think of it, the grown-up Miss Clare mused, it was a tribute to Maud's resilience that she lived at all.

There were a number of children from the marsh in Dolly's class, and, young as she was, she soon noticed that they incurred Miss Turner's wrath more frequently than the rest of the class. To Dolly's tender heart this seemed monstrously unfair, but in the nature of things this was understandable. Their work was as dirty and careless as their dress. They lacked concentration and energy. It is difficult to attend to abstract things when one is pinched with hunger in the middle and aflame with head-lice at one end and chilblains at the other. Miss Turner was not unsympathetic, but she had a job to do, and had to do it, moreover, under the eye of a vigilant headmaster.

Consequently, she berated the slow, whipped on the lazy with the lash of her tongue, and encouraged the zealous with hearty praise. She was a good teacher, brisk and cheerful, with a rough and ready way of dealing with the offenders, who seemed, to Dolly, almost always from 'the marsh lot'.

One incident, and its sequel, brought home to the little girl the shattering unpredictability of this new world of school. A squeal of pain from the boys' side of the class made them all look up from the pot hooks and hangers they were writing with their squeaky slate pencils. Miss Turner hurried forward to investigate.

'Miss,' whimpered one five-year-old, holding up a quivering forefinger, 'Fred Borden's been and bit me.'

Sure enough, the tell-tale teeth marks were still red upon the shaking finger, and Fred Borden was pink and sullen.

'Couldn't help it,' said the culprit unconvincingly. Miss Turner swept into action.

'By my desk,' she ordered, following the child to the front of the class.

'Put your slates down,' said Miss Turner, obviously enjoying the chance of a practical lesson in behaviour.

'Here's a little boy who likes to bite other people. Should boys bite?'

'No, miss,' came the self-righteous sing-song.

'Only dogs bite,' affirmed Miss Turner severely, turning to the shrinking malefactor. 'And as you seem to have turned into a dog this morning, I shall have to treat you like one.'

Dolly was appalled. Poor Fred! Did this mean he would be beaten? Dolly shook at the mere idea. He looked so sad, and no bigger than herself, that her gentle heart throbbed with pain for him.

Miss Turner bustled to a cupboard and returned with a length of tape. She tied one end loosely round the child's neck, and there was a titter of laughter which grew to a great shout as she motioned to the child to crouch on all fours as she tied the other end to the leg of the desk.

'There, now,' said Miss Turner, red with bending and the success of her lesson. 'You must stay tied up until dinner time. We can't have dangerous animals that bite running loose in the classroom, can we, children?'

'No, miss,' chanted the class smugly.

'Back to work, then,' commanded Miss Turner, resuming her patrolling up and down the aisles. Dolly took up her slate pencil with a shaking hand.

That anyone – especially someone grown-up – could tie up another person like an animal horrified the child. To be sure, Fred Borden, who had feared a trip to the other end of the room where the cane lay on Mr Bond's desk, seemed quite cheerful as he sat on the floor by the desk. But Dolly, putting herself in his place, would have been prostrate with shame. To have sat there, publicly humiliated, enduring the gaze of thirty heartless schoolfellows, would have broken Dolly. In fact, Fred Borden was enjoying the limelight, felt no hardship in missing a writing lesson, and considerable relief at getting off so lightly.

At twelve o'clock he was released, and the children trooped home to dinner. It so happened that Fred Borden and another boy were dawdling along the road as Esther, Ada and Dolly came up to them. The boys turned and spread their arms out to bar the way. They both grinned cheerfully. They felt no malice – this was just a reflex action when they saw three little girls trying to get by.

Esther stopped nervously, too frightened to protest, and near to tears. She lived considerably further than her charges, and time was short. She dreaded being late back to school.

Dolly, still shocked by the morning's experience, felt that she must tell poor Fred of her sympathy, but could not think how to begin

At that moment, Ada went into action.

'Bow-wow! Who's a dog? Who bites? Who's a dog? chanted Ada mockingly.

Fury at her sister's cruelty shook the words from Dolly's tongue. She stepped forward and put one small hand on Fred's filthy jersey. Her earnest face was very close to his.

'I was *sorry*,' she babbled incoherently. 'I was *sorry* she tied you up. She shouldn't have done that. I was *sorry*!'

To her amazement, Fred's grin vanished, and a menacing scowl took its place.

'Shut up, soppy!' he growled fiercely, and with venom he thrust the little girl away so forcefully that she fell backwards into Esther. Fist still raised, Fred followed her.

'What d'you want to hurt her for?' shrilled Esther, finding her voice.

'Because I 'ates 'er!' shouted Fred passionately. 'Because I 'ates all of you! You stuck-up lot!'

And with the hot tears springing to his eyes, he turned and fled down the narrow alley that led to the marsh.

6

One windy March day in 1894 Francis Clare came home from work in a state of high excitement. He blew into the little living-room on a gust of wind that lifted the curtains and caused the fire to belch smoke.

'Well, Mary,' he cried, dropping his dinner satchel triumphantly on the table, 'I've got a house.'

'Francis! No! You mean it?'

'Sure as I'm here.'

'Where?'

'Beech Green.'

'But you've never been to Beech Green today?' queried Mary, still bewildered. The two little girls, playing with Emily on the rag hearthrug, gazed up at him as open-mouthed as their mother.

'No, no. I've been at Springbourne all day, like I said, thatching Jesse Miller's cow shed. He come up while I was working and says: "You the young fellow as near killed 'isself a year or two back and had a ride home in my cart?"

'I told him I was. He's getting forgetful-like now he's old – kept calling me by my father's name, but it appears one of his chaps told him we was looking for a cottage, and he's got an empty one we can have.

'"'Tisn't a palace," he said, "two up and two down, but a pump inside and good cupboards. Take a look at it, and tell me what you think. Two shillings a week rent old Bob used to pay me before he left me to go to work in Caxley. That suits me if it suits you." And he threw the key up to me, and off he goes.'

'Well!' said Mary flabbergasted. 'And what's it like?'

'Nice little place. Next door to Hundred Acre Field. Good bit of garden and handy for the school. I reckon you'll like it. We'll go over Sunday and you shall see it. Ma'll have the girls, I don't doubt, and we can walk it easy in just over an hour.'

It was the most amazing news, and the family could hardly eat for excitement. By the next Sunday, when Mary had seen it and pronounced it perfect, all that remained to be done was to give a week's notice to their landlord and accept Jesse Miller's offer of a cart to carry the furniture from the Caxley home to the new one.

They were to move on Lady Day, which gave them about a fortnight in which to attend to the multitude of domestic details involved in moving house. For the last few days the Caxley home was almost unrecognizable. Curtains had been taken down, cupboards cleared, boxes stood, roped and massive, in the most awkward places, and chaos reigned.

But for all the bustle and confusion, Mary and Francis smiled. At last, they were leaving Caxley. At last, they were on their way to the open country where their hearts had always been.

Hearing their mother sing, as she washed china and stored it in a box stuffed with their father's thatching straw, the two little girls exchanged secret smiles. Beech Green might be unknown to them, but obviously there was no need for apprehension. Beech Green, it seemed, was the Promised Land.

The day of the move dawned still and cloudless. The Clare family was up betimes and the front door was propped open so that the coming of the farm cart could be instantly seen.

Breakfast was a picnic meal that day, of bread and cold bacon cut into neat cubes on a meat dish on the bare table, for such refinements as cooking pots, plates and tablecloths were all packed up.

It had been arranged that Mary and the children should travel on the cart with the furniture, while Francis stayed behind to lock up and return the key to the landlord.

'Jim's going to give us a hand putting our traps in at Beech Green,' said Francis, naming the carter who was to transport them, 'and I should be with you soon after you gets there. We'll be straight afore dark, my love, curtains up and all, you'll see.'

Outside, the early sunshine lit the tiny garden and shone through the open door upon the bare wall of the living-room. Perched on the budding rose bush, a speckled thrush sang his neart out, as if in farewell. It was strange, thought Mary suddenly, that she felt no pangs at parting from this her first home. Here the two babies had been born, and she and Francis had known happiness and misfortune. She had come across that uneven threshold as a bride, and was to leave as a wife and mother, but despite its associations, the house meant little to her. She would be glad to leave it.

There was a distant rumbling, which grew as they listened. Then came the sound of heavy hooves, and Jim's voice.

Whoa there, old gal. Whoa, Bella!'

'He's come!' squeaked the two little girls, flying to the gate. The adventure had begun.

For the next hour or two Francis and Mary went back and forth from the house to the farm cart, helped by Jim who was almost as strong as the massive mare between the shafts. The children tore up and down in a state of wild excitement, getting in everyone's way, until Francis could stand it no longer.

'You two keep out o' this,' he said firmly. 'Play out the back or upstairs where we've done. We'll all be wore out before we starts.'

Ada skipped out through the back door, but Dolly made her way up the echoing shaky stairs to her empty bedroom. It was queer to see its bareness. There were dusky lines along the walls where the bed, the chest of drawers, and the cane-bottomed chair had stood. A blue bead glinted in a crack between two floor boards, and Dolly squatted down to prize it out.

Near her, where the skirting board joined the floor, was a small jagged hole where a mouse lived. Her mother had set a trap many times, but no mouse was ever caught. Dolly sometimes wondered if this were in answer to her fervent, but silent, prayers on these occasions. Each night, kneeling on the hard floor with her face muffled in the side of the white counterpane, she had chanted:

> God bless Mummy,
> God bless Daddy,
> Aunties and Uncles,
> And all kind friends,
> And make me a GOOD girl,
> For Jesus Christ's sake
> Amen.

On the nights when the trap was set, she added fiercely and silently:

'And PLEASE DON'T let the mouse get caught,' before leaping into bed beside Ada, and drawing up the clothes.

Now, she thought, the mouse could have the whole house to live in, and would never see a trap again.

She wandered to the window and looked out into the back garden. Ada was trying to stand on her hands, supporting her legs against the fence. It was strange to think she would never do that again here. Dolly turned to look at the room again. It seemed to be waiting, it was so quiet and eerie. She felt as if she were intruding, as if the place she stood in were no longer hers.

Soon she heard her parents calling.

'Come on, Ada and Dolly! It's all ready now. Let's get you dressed.'

Within half an hour they were off.

Nearly seventy years later, the details of that amazing journey still remained clear in Miss Clare's memory. There had been an iron step, she remembered, to climb on in order to get into the cart. It was shiny with a hundred boot-scrapings, and had a crescent-shaped hole in it through which one had a terrifying glimpse of the road below.

Jim, Mary and the two children squeezed together on the plank seat that ran across the cart. Dolly felt most unsafe, for her feet would not reach the floor. Emily was tucked by her, but Jim said she had better be put in the back.

'Ain't no room for us to breathe, let alone your dolly,' said Jim cheerfully. 'Give 'er 'ere.'

He clambered down again and Dolly reluctantly handed Emily, in her red cape, into his huge knobbly hand. He went to the rear of the cart and propped Emily up in a chair.

'There she be,' called Jim. 'Now 'er's got a clear view of the road.'

Satisfied, Dolly settled down to present delights. The horse's massive brown haunches, moving just below her, fascinated the child. Leather squeaked, brass jingled, wooden wheels rumbled, and the whole cart seemed alive with movement and noises.

A gentle climb, from the river valley where Caxley lay, occupied the first mile or so of the journey. The sun was high now, and from her lofty seat Dolly could see over the hedges into the meadows. They steamed gently in the growing heat, for they were wet from overnight rain.

About half a mile before it entered the village of Beech Green the road plunged down a short steep hill between high banks topped with massive beech trees. It was the first time that the child had seen great roots writhing out of the soil like underground branches. It seemed to make this new world even more strange and foreign.

'Nearly there,' said her mother, putting a steadying arm round

Dolly, so that she did not slide forward on to Bella's great back. 'You'll see your new home soon.'

They emerged from the tunnel of trees and began to rumble through the scattered village. Ada noticed the school standing back from the road. A few children, playing in the dinner hour, watched their progress, and one child waved. Ada waved back energetically, but Dolly was too timid.

Their own house lay half a mile or so further, on the outskirts of Beech Green. Three miles further still lay the village of Fairacre where so much of little Dolly's life was to be spent.

Dolly's spirits rose with every turn of the wheel that took her further from Caxley. The light breeze stirred her hair, hanging now, almost to her shoulders, in blessed holiday freedom. The inevitable had happened at the Caxley school. The propinquity of Maud's auburn tangles had soon led to Dolly's head-scratching, her mother's shocked discoveries, and the tight tying-back of poor Dolly's locks on school days. The feeling of wind in her hair enhanced the delights of the day as the child kept a look-out for the new cottage.

At last a bend in the road revealed it – a snug, thatched, tight little beauty of a house, set behind a thick hedge just quickening to green. The cart slurred to a stop, the noises ceased, and the full quiet harmony of the wide countryside became apparent.

Jim lifted the two children down. He and Mary began to busy themselves with the load, helped by the vociferous Ada. Dolly, as if in a trance, pushed open the small gate and wandered past the cottage to the end of the garden. She had never realized that the world was so big.

Before her, beyond the garden hedge, sloped the gentle flanks of the downs with Hundred Acre Field at the base, and their tops, hazy in the distance, fading into the blue of the sky. Birds sang in the hedges, in the trees, and far above her in the blue and white sky. The happiness which had warmed Dolly in the flower-lit meadow on her way to her grandmother's returned to her with renewed strength.

She felt as a minnow, long held captive in a jam jar, must feel on being released into a brook; or as a bird set free from a cage into the limitless air. This was her element. These criss-cross currents of scent-laden air, spangled with bird-song, splashed with sunshine, flowed around her, lifting her spirits and quickening her senses.

Dolly Clare had come home.

★

Now, a lifetime later, white-haired Miss Clare stood in the same garden, gazing at the same view and drawing from it the same comfort and strength which it had always given. Her hands were full of roses. Some would stand in the small sitting-room, but the choicest would be put beside Emily Davis's bed in the spare bedroom.

The thought of Emily reminded Miss Clare again of the lost doll. It was dusk, she recalled, before the first Emily had been missed. Distressed though she was, little Dolly had been less upset than her parents feared, for the enchantment of the day still possessed her.

'I'll see Jim tomorrow,' promised Francis. 'He'll have her safe, never fear.'

But Emily was not with Jim. She had fallen from the back of the cart and lay face downward at the side of the lane between Caxley and Beech Green. A ten-year-old boy, who had spent the morning rattling two stones in a tin to scare the birds from his master's crop, found her as he went home to dinner. He turned her over with the broken toe-cap of his boot, and snorted with scorn.

'Some kid's old dolly!' he shouted to the wind, and booted it, in a magnificent arc, over the hedge.

It was a week before she was found, and Dolly had shed many tears of mourning. A man, cutting back the hedge, had discovered the sodden doll and taken it to the local shop, where Francis later collected it.

'There, my dear,' he said to Dolly, 'now you can be happy again.'

Dolly took the long-lost doll into her arms, but never completely into her heart again.

Emily looked so different. She had the pale remote air of one who has been ill for a long time. One eye had gone, and though Mary sewed two white linen shirt buttons in place of her former eyes, this only added to the strangeness of the doll in her young mistress's eyes. She cared for her as zealously as she had always done, putting her to bed, tying on the red cloak before taking her into the garden, and propping a cushion behind her back when she sat at table. But the glory was gone.

It may have been that the new living Emily had taken her place. Certainly she had become very dear to young Dolly.

'And still is,' said old Miss Clare, stirring herself from her reminiscences.

The clock struck twelve inside the house, and from the distant village school Miss Clare heard the shouts of children released from bondage.

'I've done nothing but day-dream,' Miss Clare told herself returning from the noonday blaze to the shade of the kitchen. 'Emily will be here before I'm ready for her. But then that's one of the pleasures of growing old,' she comforted herself.

Singing softly, roses in hand. she mounted the stairs to the waiting room.

PART TWO

BEECH GREEN

7

Life at Beech Green was an exhilarating affair, after the confines of Caxley, and made all the richer by the friendship with Emily Davis.

She was a mischievous, high-spirited child, the middle one of seven children. All nine of the Davises lived, as snug and gay as a nestful of wrens, in a tiny cottage as the end of a row of four.

Dolly found her way there before she had lived a week at her new home. There was a happy-go-lucky atmosphere about the Davises' house which enchanted the little girl who had been more primly brought up. She tumbled in and out of their home, revelling in the games, the nonsense and the carefree coming and going of the seven children and their numerous friends.

Emily's father was a gardener at the manor house at Beech Green. He was a giant of a man, with a face as brown and wrinkled as a walnut. Two bright blue eyes blazed from his weatherbeaten countenance, and his laugh shook the cottage.

'My husband's a very larky man,' Mrs Davis would say proudly. 'Likes his joke, and that.'

She was barely five feet high, with a figure so neat and child-like that it seemed impossible that she could be the mother of such a large and boisterous brood. Her energy was boundless. She scrubbed and polished the little house, cooked massive meals, washed mountains of linen, and then knitted and sewed, or tended her flower garden, as a relaxation. Throughout it all she laughed and sang, finding time to play with her children, cuffing them good-naturedly when they needed correction, and seeming, at the end of the day, to be as fresh as when she rose at five-thirty.

Dolly loved Mrs Davis dearly. Her warm and casual friendliness made her feel part of the family, and her self-assurance grew.

In the corner of the cottage living-room sat old Mr Davis, Emily's grandfather. He had been a carter, but now, unable to work regularly, he made a few pence by mending pots and pans for the neighbours. His right hand was encased in a black kid glove, which fascinated young Dolly.

One day, soon after her arrival at Beech Green, the old man caught the child's eyes fixed upon his hand. A soldering iron was heating in the open fire, and between his knees old Mr Davis held an upturned kettle.

'You be wondering why I keeps me glove on, I'll wager,' he grunted.

Dolly smiled shyly.

'Well, I ain't agoing to take it off to show you, me little maid, or you'd 'ave a fright. I ain't got much of me fingers left, if the truth be told.'

He bent forward, breathless with the effort, and removed the red-hot iron from the fire. Dolly, with a thrill of horror, saw how he held it gripped in the palm of his hand. He dipped the iron in a little tin on the fender, and a hot pungent smoke rose from the sizzling liquid.

'I was out in that ol' snowstorm for two days,' said the old man.
'Afore you was born or thought of, that was. In 1881 – getting on
for fourteen year ago. I'd taken a load of hay over to Springbourne
that day, and it was snowing pretty lively as I went. But how the
Hanover I got back as fur as I did that afternoon, I never could tell.
Just this side of the downs I 'ad to give in. I cut the horses loose and
said: "Git on 'ome, you two, while you can." I felt fair lonely
watching them slipping and sliding down the hill, up to their bellies
in snow, leaving me on me own.'

'You should have sat on one,' said Dolly gravely.

'Easier said than done,' grunted Mr Davis, applying his soldering
iron to the kettle. There was silence while he surveyed his handiwork
for a minute or two, and then he resumed.

'The snow was that thick, and swirling around so, them two
horses vanished pretty quick. I could 'ear 'em snorting with fright
and shaking their heads. They 'adn't seen nothing like it, you see.
Nor me, for that matter.

'There I was, and I couldn't make up me mind to stop in the cart
or try and plod on home and risk it.'

'What did you do?' asked Dolly.

'Risked it,' said the old man laconically. 'Risked it, and fell in a
dam' ditch I never knew was there, and 'ad to stop there two days.
I ain't seen nothing like that blizzard before or since. If it 'adn't a
been for the two horses getting back I reckon I'd a been there still.
They never got home till next day, and it took four chaps searching
in turn to find me, it was that cruel.'

'Did you shout?' asked Dolly.

'I was past shouting after the first 'alf-hour,' answered Mr Davis,
holding the kettle to the light and squinting inside it. 'By the time
they dug me out I was as stiff as this 'ere iron. Stayed in bed a
week, I did, and 'ad to 'ave three fingers and two toes plucked orf.
The frost-bite, you see.'

Dolly nodded, appalled.

'I shan't forget 1881 in a 'urry,' said the old man and thrust the
soldering iron back into the red heart of the coals with a deft thrust
of his maimed hand.

The Davises were not the only new friends. Francis and Mary
Clare blossomed in their country surroundings, and the neighbour-

liness which they had missed so sorely in Caxley now seemed doubly dear.

The family had for so long been thrust in upon itself. The next door neighbours at Caxley, cross and aged, had been ever present in Mary's thoughts, and Dolly and Ada were often scolded for making a noise that might penetrate the thin dividing wall. Fear of strangers, and particularly of 'the marsh lot', kept country-bred Mary from making many friends in Caxley. Francis's illness and their pinching poverty were other factors in 'keeping themselves to themselves'.

Back in the country again, fellows of a small community, Mary and Francis felt their tension relax. A move is always an excitement in a village, and by the end of the first long day the family had met more than a dozen neighbours, some prompted by kindness, some by curiosity, who had called to welcome them.

Within a few weeks Francis had the cottage garden dug and planted, and found he had already promised to exhibit something in the local autumn flower show which was to be held at Fairacre. Mary, to her surprise, found that she had been persuaded to join the Glee Club, run on Friday nights by the redoubtable Mr Finch in his schoolroom.

'Us makes our own fun,' Mrs Davis said to Mary. ''Tis all very fine for the gentry to go to Caxley in their carriages for a ball at the Corn Exchange, but us ordinary folk, as goes on Shanks's pony, gets our fun in the village.'

And Mary, with her two little girls safely at school all day, and a husband back at work, was only too ready to join in the simple homely fun of which she had been starved for so long.

Dolly and Ada took to the village school like ducks to water. They had been well drilled at Caxley and found that the work here was well within their grasp. Their classmates were somewhat impressed by the two new girls who had experienced the superior instruction of a town school, and Dolly and Ada felt pleasantly distinguished.

The smaller numbers made school life much less frightening for timid Dolly, and gave Ada greater scope for her powers of leadership. In no time she was the acknowledged queen of the playground, and had all the younger children vying for her favours, and the thrill of 'playing with Ada'. Mr Finch, who hid a genuine fondness for children beneath his pompous veneer, was glad to have such a bright pupil among his scholars, and Mrs Finch, who had some difficulty with discipline, was relieved to find that Dolly was as sedate as she was hard-working.

But the greatest joy for Dolly in this happy new life was the discovery of the infinite beauties in the natural world about her. That first glimpse of Beech Green and the realization that she had found her real home, was repeated daily in a hundred different ways. The walk to school took about a quarter of an hour, and revealed dozens of enchanting things.

In that first spring, Dolly discovered that a bed of white violets grew on the left-hand bank just before the farm gate. They were well hidden by fine dry grass, but their heady scent betrayed them, and the child exulted in the pure whiteness, enhanced by the spot of yellow stamens lurking in its depths, of each small flower. Almost opposite grew a rarer type of violet, almost pink in colour, which was much sought after by the little girls of Beech Green. Dolly soon grew wise enough to keep the news of its flowering to herself.

Nearer the school, the lane was shaded by elm trees which grew upon steep banks. Here Dolly found a pink and fleshy plant, which Mr Finch told her was toothwort. It was unattractive, and reminded Dolly of the pink pendulous sows in the farmyard as they lumbered about among their squealing young. But it had its fascination for the town-bred child, and she felt proud to see it put on the window-sill at school, neatly labelled by Mr Finch's own pen.

There were terrifying things too to encounter on the walk to school. Behind the farm gate, just beyond the violet bed, a dozen grey and white geese honked and hissed, stretching sinuous waving necks, and menacing the child with their icy blue eyes and cruel orange bills. Dolly shouted as bravely as the other children when the geese were safely barred, but sometimes the gate was open, and the geese paraded triumphantly up and down the lane. Then Dolly would scramble up the steep bank, over the roots of the elm trees and the toothwort, and try to gain the safety of the cornfield beyond, while the geese stretched their great wings and ran, hideously fast, creating a clamour that could be heard a mile away.

The geese were frightening enough, but even more disconcerting was Mabel, who lived in a cottage half way to school. She was a grotesque, misshapen figure, almost as broad as she was tall, the victim of some glandular disease which was incurable at that time.

Mentally she was aged about six, although she had been born thirty years earlier, and she played with a magnificent doll all day long. In the winter Mabel was invisible to Beech Green, for she was closely, and lovingly, confined in the stuffy little house by her doting parents. But during the warm weather the pathetic stumpy figure sat in a basket chair placed on the front path. From there she watched the neighbours go by as she nursed the expensive doll.

'Them poor Bells,' the villagers said, with genuine sympathy, ''as got enough to drive them silly theirselves with that Mabel. Got to be watched every minute of the day! But don't 'er mother keep 'er beautiful?'

Cleanliness was a much-prized virtue in Beech Green, and Mabel was held up as a shining example of Mrs Bell's industry. The poor idiot was always clothed in good quality dresses, covered with a snowy-starched and goffered pinafore. Her coarse scanty hair, as bristly as that which grew upon the pigs' backs in the farmyard near by, was tied back with a beautiful satin ribbon. Her podgy yellow face, from which two dark eyes glinted from slanting slits, was shiny with soap, and her fat little legs were always encased in the finest black stockings, with never so much as a pinpoint of a hole in sight.

To Dolly's terror, Mabel took an instant liking to her, and would waddle to the gate, holding up the doll and uttering thick guttural cries of pleasure. Dolly's first impulse was to run away, but her mother had spoken to her firmly.

'You can thank your stars you weren't born like Mabel, and just you be extra kind to that poor child – for child she is, for all her thirty years. No flinching now, if she comes up to you, and you let her touch you too, if she's a mind to! She's as gentle as a lamb, and the Bells have enough to put up with without people giving their only one the cold shoulder!'

And so Dolly steeled herself to smile upon the squat unlovely figure behind the cottage gate, and sometimes put a violet or two into that thick clumsy hand, and admired the doll with sincerity. She never saw Mabel outside the house or the garden, and never understood one word that fell from those thick lips; but when, in three or four years' time, the child mercifully died, she missed her sorely, and could only guess at the loss suffered by Mr Bell, and still more by Mrs Bell, whose clothes line had fluttered daily with the brave array of Mabel's finery.

Looking back later, to those early days at Beech Green, Miss Clare was amazed to think how many subnormal and eccentric people there were among that small number in those late Victorian days. There were many reasons. Inbreeding was a common cause, for lack of transport meant that the boys and girls of the village tended to marry each other, and the few families there became intricately related. Lack of skilled medical attention, particularly during childbirth, accounted for some deformities of mind and body, and the dread of mental hospitals – sadly justified in many cases – kept others from seeking help with their problems. Certainly, when Dolly first went to live at Beech Green, there were half a dozen souls in the neighbourhood who were as much in need of attention as poor Mabel.

There was the boy who had epileptic fits who sat in the desk next to Ada, and was looked upon with more affection than distress by his classmates, as the means of enlivening Mr Finch's boring lessons. There was old Mrs Marble, who gibbered and shook her fist at the children from the broken window of her filthy cottage near the school, and who would certainly have been ducked in the horsepond had she had the misfortune to have been born a century earlier. There was a very nasty man who delighted in walking about the woods and lanes with his trousers over his arm, frightening the women and little girls out of their wits, but excused by the men as 'only happening when the moon was at the full, poor fellow'.

Then there were the three White children, abysmally slow at lessons, but with tempers of such uncontrollable violence that the whole school went in terror of them. How much of this vicious frenzy was due to mental disorder, and how much to their parents' treatment of it, was debatable. It was the custom of Mr and Mrs White to lock their refractory offspring in a cupboard under the stairs where, in the smelly darkness among the old shoes and coats that hung there, they were allowed to scream, sob, fight, pummel the door, and exhaust their hysteria before being let out again, some hours later, white and wild-eyed and ready to fall into their nightmare-haunted beds.

Even the great ones of the village had their sufferings. The lady of the manor, Mrs Evans, whose visits to the school meant much curtseying and bobbing, had one frail chick among her six sturdy ones, and Miss Lilian was never seen without a maid or her governess in attendance ready to direct her charge's wan look towards anything of cheer.

As young Dolly soon discovered, Beech Green had its darker side, the reverse of the bright flower-decked face which charmed the newcomers. But it all added to the excitement of daily living. It gave the solemn little girl a chance to observe human frailties and quirks of behaviour, and gave her too an insight into the courage and good humour with which her fellows faced personal tragedy.

These early lessons were to stand her in good stead, for before long she too would be involved in a family disaster whose repercussions were to echo down many years of her adult life.

In welcoming all that life in Beech Green offered her, in both happiness and horror, the child unwittingly prepared herself for the testing time which lay ahead.

8

The first intimation of the event which was to colour so many years of Dolly Clare's later life was her mother's visit to the doctor in May 1896.

Mary Clare suspected that she was pregnant again, and she viewed the situation with mixed feelings.

'Just got my two off to school,' she confided resignedly to Mrs Davis one morning, 'and then another turns up. All that washing again, and bad nights, and mixing up feeding bottles! Somehow I don't take to the idea like I did, but Francis is that pleased I haven't the heart to tell him it's not all honey for me.'

'You waits till you has seven,' commented Mrs Davis cheerfully. 'Time enough to gloom then, I can tell you. Why, your two girls can give you a hand, and if it's a boy you'll be looked after proper in your old age!'

Somewhat comforted, Mary Clare made her way, one Tuesday morning, to the converted stable in the manor grounds where Dr Fisher held his weekly surgery.

'There's plenty to be thankful for,' she told herself, as she trudged up the broad drive between the flowering chestnut trees. 'Francis is as pleased as Punch, and he's in work again. And this place is far better to have a baby in than that Caxley hovel. It can lie in the garden, and I'll get the washing dry lovely with the winds we get here. And Mrs Davis is quite right about Dolly and Ada. They're big enough to help now they're eleven and nine.'

Her usual good spirits asserted themselves, and by the time the doctor had confirmed her suspicions she was facing the future with more hope. It is always heartening to be an object of interest, and Mary looked forward to many a cosy chat with her new neighbours, as she returned to her cottage.

Francis was jubilant when she told him that evening.

'It'll be a boy this time,' he assured her. 'You'll see, my love. A real fine son to carry on the thatching trade. The girls will be glad to hear the news.'

'They'll not learn it from me for a few months yet,' replied Mary tartly. 'Time enough for them to know when I takes to my bed.'

'If you don't want them to hear it from all the old gossips in the village,' warned her husband, 'you'd best tell 'em yourself before long.'

'Well, we'll see,' said Mary, more gently, recognizing the wisdom of her husband's remark.

The baby was due in November, and the little girls were told one mellow September evening as they went to bed. Mary found it an embarrassing occasion and had steeled herself to it all day. She had rehearsed her short speech a dozen times, and delivered it with a beating heart and a pink face.

'I got something nice to tell you two, my dears. A wonderful secret. God's sending you a little brother next November,' she said, with rare piety.

At last it was out, and she waited, breathless, for the reaction. Dolly sat up in bed, open-mouthed but silent. Ada bounced unconcernedly on to one side and said nonchalantly:

'Oh, I know! Jimmy Davis told me you was in kitten last June.'

Mary's pink face grew crimson with fury.

'The rude little boy!' she exclaimed, outraged. 'I'll see his mother hears of this, and gives him a good box side the ear, too! And I don't know as you don't deserve one, too, for listening to such rudeness!'

Seething with righteous indignation, Mary left her daughters unkissed, and slammed the door upon them. Relating it later to Francis she found her annoyance giving way to amusement as he gave way to his mirth.

'Looks to me quite simple,' laughed Francis. 'You wrapped it up too pretty, and Jimmy Davis put it real ugly, but one way or another, now they know. You go up and say good night to 'em and see how pleased they'll be.'

By the time darkness fell, peace was made, and the thought of a fifth member of the Clare family brought much joy to the four already awaiting him.

Amazingly, it was a boy. Mary's labour was grievously protracted, and the local midwife had been obliged to send for the doctor after hours of effort. Dolly and Ada had spent the night with the Davis household. Somehow two extra children fitted into the nutshell of a house with no difficulty, and they were thrilled to have a mattress on the floor of the girls' bedroom.

At dinner time next day they were told that a brother had arrived and they could go and see him.

'But mind you're quiet,' warned Mrs Davis. 'Your ma had a bad time with him and wants a good sleep.'

They rushed homeward, and the midwife led them on tiptoe to their parents' bedroom.

Pale, and appallingly tired, Mary smiled faintly at them from the pillows. Beside her lay a white bundle, containing what looked like a coconut from the Michaelmas fair. On closer inspection, Dolly could see the dark crumpled countenance of her brother, topped by a crop of black thatch. His eyes were glued together into thin slits, as though nothing in the world should prize him from the sleep that enfolded him.

Dolly was seriously disappointed. She had imagined someone looking like Mabel's beautiful doll, very small but exquisite. But she sensed that this was no time to express her dissatisfaction, and smiled as bravely as she could at her mother before taking Ada's hand and making her way to the door. Before she put her hand on the knob she noticed that her mother had fallen asleep again, with the same desperate concentration as the baby beside her.

That evening the two little girls returned to sleep at their own home. As soon as Francis came in he kissed them heartily, looking younger and more handsome than he had for many a year.

'Ain't he a lovely boy then?' he said to them proudly. 'Ain't you two lucky ones, having a brother after all?'

He led the way upstairs, and Francis bent over Mary and the baby. Mary looked less deathly pale, and smiled at the family, but the baby still slept, snuffling slightly in his shawl.

'You're all over bits,' Mary admonished her husband, as pieces of chaff fluttered down upon the bed from his working clothes. He laughed, and plucked a long golden straw that had lodged in the leather strap around his trouser leg.

'There you are, son,' he said, threading the bright strand through his child's small fingers. 'Get the feel of straw in your hand, and you'll grow up to be the best thatcher in England.'

It was that small incident that gave young Dolly a glimpse of her father's exultant pride, not only in his son, but in his work, and the new hope he now had of an assured future.

The baby thrived and was whole-heartedly adored by the family and the neighbours. His most fervent admirer was Emily Davis. One might have thought that the child had seen enough of babies, but little Frank Clare seemed dearer to Emily than her own young brothers, and she pushed his wicker pram as frequently as his sisters did.

By the time he was sitting up and taking notice of the world around him, the summer of 1897 had come and Beech Green was busy with preparations for the Diamond Jubilee of the aged Queen Victoria.

The local lord of the manor, Mr Evans, had invited everyone to games and a mammoth tea party, and excitement ran high as the great day in June approached. Many people remembered the celebrations ten years before when the sun had blazed upon a nation rejoicing in a reign of fifty years. This time, they said, it would be better still.

In the great world beyond Beech Green there was perhaps not quite the same fervour for the military pomp and processions as there had been at the Golden Jubilee. Many thinking men felt a growing distaste for imperialism, and distrusted 'jingoism', which they suspected inflamed a love of conquest for its own sake. This did not lessen the devotion to the Queen, who by now was an object of veneration to all her subjects. The majority of her countrymen had never known another monarch on the throne, and as the day of the Diamond Jubilee grew nearer, many tales were told of memorable events in her incredibly long reign.

Dolly's grandfather, on one of his visits to see the new baby, brought the remote figure of the great Queen very clearly to the child's mind.

'I was down at Portsmouth once, staying with my brother. August, it was, in the year 1875, and the royal yacht *Alberta* come over from Osborne one day. The Queen herself was aboard, and there was a shocking thing happened. Somehow or other a little yacht got across the *Alberta*'s path and was run down. It sank in no time, and three poor souls was drownded. They told us the Queen was beside herself with distress, pacing up and down in the *Alberta* with the tears falling. Poor lady, she had a wonderful kind heart, and that were a sore and terrible grief to her.'

He presented the little girls with a Union Jack made by their grandmother so that they could hang it from the porch on Jubilee Day. On this occasion he had not brought his wife, for he had pedalled over on his old penny-farthing cycle, an archaic vehicle to which he was much attached. Dolly and Ada watched him remount after tea, and waved the flag vigorously after his retreating figure.

The day itself dawned clear and shining. 'Real Queen's weather again,' people cried to each other as they bustled about. Household chores were done quickly that day to leave time for the preparations for the afternoon fun. In the grounds at the manor long trestle tables were spread with new lengths of unbleached calico for table-cloths, and on these were dozens of dishes of buns and lardy cakes, sandwiches and pies. Maids fluttered back and forth from the house bearing great trays of cups and saucers, tea urns, jugs, spoons and all the paraphernalia of rural junketings.

Dolly and Ada were beside themselves with excitement. All the schools had a holiday, and it was a thrill to wear one's best white frock with one's best black stockings and nailed boots. Their pink and blue sashes were freshly pressed, and Mary had tied hair ribbons to match upon her daughters' curls

Dolly felt very sorry for one family who sat opposite her at the long tea table. They had recently lost their mother, and all the four children, even the youngest who could scarcely toddle, were clad in deepest black. From the crêpe bows which decorated their black hats to the toecaps of their heavy boots the gloom was unrelieved. Even their hands were encased in black cotton gloves which they did not remove even when eating. Under the brilliant blue sky, among the laughter and sunshine, they perched like four little black crows in a row, silent, and suffering the heat in stolid endurance.

After a colossal tea, one of the daughters of the house sang patriotic songs, accompanied by her sister, at the piano which had been wheeled out upon the grass from the drawing-room. Applause was polite but not very enthusiastic, and everyone, including the Misses Evans, was relieved when the real festivities began with the sports.

The Clare family did well, for Francis won the men's wheelbarrow race with the eldest Davis boy in the barrow whilst he did the pushing, and later still, Ada tore splendidly across the field in the girls' hundred yards, sash flying, nailed boots pounding, to win by a short head from the butcher's daughter. Dolly came second in the obstacle race, but was beaten by Emily Davis whose wiry skinniness negotiated ladder rungs and wriggled under tarpaulins with amazing dexterity.

Francis received half a crown, but Ada was delighted to have six yards of the unbleached calico which had recently covered the tea tables. It made stout pillow cases for the family which lasted for many years, and was considered by all to be a practical and most welcome prize.

At the end of the long golden day the little family made its way home. Young Frank slept in his wicker perambulator, and across the bottom was lodged the roll of calico. The lane was warm and scented with honeysuckle from the sun-baked hedges, and the smell of hay, lying ready to be turned when the labourers returned to the fields next day after the holiday, mingled with the other summer scents.

Tired Dolly, clinging to the pram for support, thought she would never forget such a wonderful day. Nothing ever happens in Beech Green,' she had heard people say. No one could say that now, was Dolly's last thought, as her dizzy head burrowed into the pillow beside Ada's. It was the most splendid thing that had ever happened in her young life.

Although Dolly, at nine years of age, was unconscious of the importance of the Jubilee and its times upon her outlook, yet looking back, as an old woman, she began to realize how deeply events and national movements had influenced even such a quiet life as her own. The Queen's celebrations had brought unaccustomed vivacity and loquacity to the country folk around her. Dolly, unusually excited by the stir, learnt more then about England's place in the world, her great men, her victories abroad and the reforms needed at home, than she had ever done before.

From Mr Finch she learnt of the vast areas of the world ruled over by their own Queen. From him she learnt of the Empire, following his pointer as it leapt from one red splash to another across the map of the world hung over the easel. She was told of the courage and military persistence of those who had subjugated the natives of those parts, and the benevolence of the great Queen whose laws now ruled them. She was not told of the feelings of those subjugated, but supposed that they were as happy to be in the Empire family as she was herself. Certainly the most splendid photographs of African chiefs, Indian princes, and the nobility of many far-flung territories taking part in the Diamond Jubilee celebrations, were cut from the newspapers and pinned up on the schoolroom wall where they were much admired by Queen Victoria's young subjects.

From the newspapers too, Dolly and Emily, both becoming avid readers, soon recognized the modern hero. He was a man of action, willing to tear up his roots and leave his country to explore unknown lands, to seek his fortune – in gold, maybe, in diamonds perhaps – to fight bravely, to dominate and to carry the British way of life to the unenlightened. He was a hero likely to be acceptable to boys as well as girls, for he was a colourful figure of wealth and power to those living amidst the pinching poverty of rural England at that time. The lot of the agricultural labourer grew worse weekly The trek to find work in the towns continued More and more white-collar workers struggled along in increasingly drab surroundings. It was small wonder that they craved colour and sensation to add excitement to their lives. The accounts of England's conquests overseas and the blaze of publicity which illuminated her leaders fired many a young man to join the army or to emigrate to those colonies whose exotic representatives marched in the Queen's processions.

The nineties needed sensation. The Diamond Jubilee was an occasion for national rejoicing, not only in the Queen, but in the nation's image as personified by her, proud, beloved, and a world-ruler. It was an image of Britain's greatness which was to remain with Dolly and her contemporaries. It gave them a deep sense of pride which would be needed to sustain them through many a change and the tragedy of two world wars. It gave them too a stability and a faith in ultimate victory which a later generation was to marvel at, deride, but secretly envy.

Later, Miss Clare was to see the follies and mistakes that had accompanied Britain's imperial policy during the nineties, but on that June night, after a shining day of rustic rejoicing, everything seemed wonderful to the little girl, with God in his heaven, the Queen on the throne, and the glory of an Empire everywhere around.

9

The friendship between Emily and Dolly deepened with time. They shared a passion for flowers reading and little children, and were lucky enough to find plenty of each to keep them happy.

The woods on the hill to Springbourne, a neighbouring village on the other side of the downs, were their hunting ground for flowers almost all the year round. They found wild snowdrops, violets, anemones, primroses and nodding catkins while the year was yet young. Later, bluebells and curling bracken fronds delighted them. Foxgloves and campion followed, and then in the autumn, they had the joy of collecting hazel nuts and blackberries, as busily as the red squirrels that darted airily across the frail twigs high above their heads. Even in winter the wood offered treasures for those who cared to seek, and the two little girls would return carrying orange toadstools or lichen-covered branches in their cold hands.

Both children were fortunate too in having parents enlightened enough to give them a small patch of garden for their own cultivation. Most cottage gardens at this time were given over exclusively to the growing of vegetables for the family, and there was real need for this. Consequently, very few children had anywhere to play on their own territory, and fewer still were able to count a yard or two as their very own. Dolly and Ada shared a patch, and Emily had a much smaller one in her own garden. Here the children planted any seeds they could beg, and slips of plants given them by indulgent grown-up gardeners. The result was gay and unusual. Radishes and marigolds rioted together, a cabbage sheltered a clump of yellow pansies, and double daisies tossed their fringes beside mustard and cress.

They were lucky too with reading matter. Mr Finch, for all his pomposity and strictness, was a good teacher, and fostered any talent and interest that he saw. Books from the school library shelf could be borrowed, if brown paper covers were made for them and they were returned within a week. Often he lent a book from his own house, and this was greatly treasured. In this way Emily and Dolly were able to read more recent fiction than the Marryats, Mrs Ewings, and Kingsleys on the school shelf. Rider Haggard, Conan Doyle and Kipling were some of the new authors that the little girls met for the first time, and though there was much that escaped their understanding, the excitement of the stories swept them along in a fever of anticipation and made them long for the chance to see the strange foreign places they portrayed. Young though they were, they too had caught the fever for adventure which quickened their elders at this time, and they mourned the fact that they were female, and so never likely to have the opportunities of Allan Quatermain. Dolly's greatest moment came when Mr Finch presented her with a copy of *Three Men in a Boat*, which remained a favourite of hers for many years, though at its first reading she skipped all the moralizing bits and the descriptions.

There were plenty of children, in their own families and their neighbours', to satisfy their interests, and mothers were glad to trust their toddlers to two girls who were so unusually sensible. Their sorties to the woods were usually in the company of Frank and another toddler or two straggling happily along behind them, or stuffed in an old pushchair and rattling over the uneven path.

'Fresh air's free,' the mothers used to tell them; 'you get as much of it as you can.' And out the children would be bundled, while cottage floors were swept and scrubbed, and the steel fenders and fire irons were polished with emery paper, and everything 'put to rights', as they said, in the few snatched minutes of freedom from their offspring. Consequently, there were always plenty of young children ready to join in games, or to be petted and admired by the older girls.

Looking back, Miss Clare saw how valuable all this unconscious training had been to her work as a teacher. The love of flowers and reading she passed on to many a country child, and her own response to young children, protective and warm-hearted, never failed her.

Friendship with Emily meant less dependence on Ada, and now that the two sisters were growing older, the differences in temperament became even more marked. Ada grew more handsome as the years passed, and her boundless vivacity made her attractive to the boys at Beech Green School as well as the girls. Fearless and athletic, she could climb a tree or vault a fence, despite her hampering skirts, as bravely as the boys, and Ada Clare was known as 'a good sport'.

Francis Clare adored all his children, but his bonny Ada became increasingly dear to him. Mary looked in some doubt upon her firstborn. There were times when she was headstrong and disobedient, and Mary foresaw a difficult time ahead when young men would enter Ada's life.

Sometimes Dolly was frightened by Ada's bold disobedience of her mother; at other times she was grateful for some small rebellion which proved successful and benefited them both. The weekly dosing was a case in point.

As was the custom at that time in almost all households, the Clare children were given a mild purgative, usually on Saturday evening. Francis had been brought up to expect a teaspoonful of a home-made concoction with nauseating regularity. His mother chopped prunes, raisins, figs and dates, plentifully sprinkled them with powdered senna pods and a little medicinal paraffin oil and mixed it together to form a glutinous and efficient purge. It had the advantage of being reasonably palatable and wholesome, but Mary considered 'Grandma's jollop', as the children called it, very old-fashioned, and substituted castor-oil, which she disguised in hot lemonade.

It was Ada who called Dolly's attention to the suspicious oily rings floating on the top.

'Don't you drink it,' she warned the younger child, in her mother's absence. Mary was at first persuasive, then unsuccessfully authoritative, and finally plain cross, as the two little girls flatly refused to drink the brew.

Francis only laughed when she told him.

'Give 'em Grandma's jollop then,' he suggested. 'They like that, so they say.'

But Mary tried another stratagem. On the following Saturday a plate of dates was offered to the children.

'This one hasn't got a stone in it,' said Dolly with surprise.

Her mother, busy ostensibly with darning, said briskly:

'Maybe it's got some grey powder inside instead.'

'That's right, it has,' agreed Dolly.

'You get some dates like that,' said Mary complacently. 'Some has stones and some has grey powder.'

They ate them unprotesting, thrilled to have such a treat as dates, but Ada discovered the trick before the next Saturday. Other children had grey powder administered in this form, she heard from her schoolfellows.

Fruit laxative tablets, called optimistically by Mary 'nice pink sweets', were tried next. Dolly and Ada held them in their mouths, pretended to swallow them and then removed them when their mother was out of the room.

'Put 'em under the table ledge, quick!' whispered Ada, and there for several weeks a collection of sucked tablets grew, on a narrow ledge under the table top, well hidden by the red tablecloth.

At last came the day of open rebellion. Ada refused to take any form of medicine again.

'You'll be ill,' warned her mother. 'It's only taking these pills regular that's kept you and Dolly so fit and well. Your mother knows best now '

'That she don't, said Ada defiantly, tossing her bright hair 'If

you looks under the table ledge you'll see what we've done with
'em all this time. And we ain't come to no harm!'

The pink tablets were discovered, the two little girls sent to bed
in disgrace, and Francis told all when he returned.

He hugged his vexed wife and restored her spirits.

'Well, she've told the truth. Their insides works all right without
a lot of oiling, it seems. Let 'em off, my dear, and save a mint of
money, and temper too.'

Thus Ada's battle, and Dolly's too, was won. These things
happened when Frank was too young to be included in the ritual,
but as soon as he was old enough he was told by his sisters just how
fortunate he was to have escaped such horrors, and how thankful he
should be to those who had smoothed the path before him.

If Mary had a favourite among her three children (and she stoutly
maintained that she had not), then it was little Frank. He was darker
in colouring than the two girls, who took after Francis. The dark
bright hazel eyes that shone so lovingly upon his mother were the
same as her own, and his hair grew as crisply. More open in his
affection than her daughters, Frank charmed Mary by his frequent
hugs and kisses, and many a smack was left unadministered because
the knowing young rogue disarmed his mother with his blandish-
ments.

'Make the most of him while he's yours,' observed Francis,
watching the toddler on his mother's lap. 'He'll break plenty of
hearts, I reckon, before he goes off to settle down and leave you.'

'You won't leave your mum, will you, my love?' said Mary,
dancing him up and down.

Although she had learnt of the advent of the baby with mixed
feelings, the joy which she felt in this boy lay largely in the feeling
of future security which he brought, although Mary herself was
unconscious of this. The girls would marry, Francis might die first:
a son was an insurance against want and loneliness, a joy to her now
and a comfort for her old age.

When, in the autumn of 1899, the Boer War broke out, she
looked upon her three-year-old and gave thanks that he was so
young. Several young men from Beech Green had joined the army
to escape from hard times and to seek adventure. Some were now
in South Africa and Mary knew the anxiety which gnawed at the

hearts of their mothers. She prayed that her Frank would never have to endure the dangers of war, nor she the heartbreaks of those who wait for news.

Christmas that year was a sad one, overshadowed by the reverses of the army in South Africa. At the manor, the Evans family were dressed in heavy mourning for the eldest son, who had been shot from his horse whilst attempting to relieve Ladysmith with General Buller's forces. The village was stunned. This seemed to bring the war very near, and people concerned themselves with the direction of the hostilities with real anxiety. Should General Buller have suggested to White that he surrendered Ladysmith? It seemed a terrible thing for an Englishman to think of giving in. But then look at the loss of lives! Look at poor Algy Evans and the Willett boy from Fairacre and the Brown twins from Caxley! So the tongues wagged, and wagged still faster when they heard that Buller had been replaced by Lord Roberts who had lost his only son in the same battle that took their own Algy Evans.

Queen Victoria was reported as saying at this time: 'Please understand that there is no one depressed in *this* house. We are not interested in the possibilities of defeat: they do not exist.' These brave words were heartening, but did not completely quell the fears that shook her less heroic subjects' hearts.

When Dolly visited the Davis' cottage one day, just after Christmas in 1899, she found it clamorous with dismay. Albert, the eldest son, had just announced that his New Year resolution was to join the army. Some of the family took his part, but his mother hotly attacked him. Dolly watched amazed the change in this smiling little Jenny-wren of a woman to a blazing fury.

'It's always what *you* wants,' she flared at the white, silent boy. 'Thinks yourself a hero, all dressed up in this new-fangled khaki to catch the girls' eyes! What about us? How's the family going to manage with your wages cut off?'

The boy began to explain haltingly, but was overborne. Dolly's heart bled for him as his mother's wrath gradually evaporated into self-pity.

'And what about a mother's feelings? Here I've brought you up from a baby, sat up nights when you was ailing, give you all you wanted, and what do I get in return? You fair break my heart, you do. You can't love me if you treats me like this.' She pulled a handkerchief from her sleeve and mopped the hot tears that coursed down her face. It was the old man of the house who opposed her most bravely. As he shook his black-gloved fist at her, his roars overcame the furious sobbing.

'You let 'un go. He's old enough to know what 'e wants, and you should be proud he's got the guts to want to fight. Don't I know his feelings? I went through the Crimean War – aye, and saw plenty of blood too, my own included, and would've died there but for Miss Nightingale, God bless 'er – and glad to, when we was fighting for the right thing. You women don't know half a man's mind. You try and keep 'im 'ere, tied down to your niminypiminy little ways, and 'e'll 'ate you, and 'isself too, for the rest of his days.

The boy cast a grateful look at the old man, and he continued more softly:

'There, gal, don't take on so. He'll be back before you knows where you are; and you can bet a fortune he won't go no further than Salisbury Plain for many a long day. Let 'im 'ave 'is fling.'

Arguments flew for the rest of that week, but Albert was not to be deflected, and on the first day of 1900 he went to the recruiting officer in Caxley.

Emily and Dolly thought he was a hero, and defended his action enthusiastically. Here, in real life, was a happening as exciting as those they so often read about. Their interest in the war became redoubled, and they pestered old Mr Davis to tell them about his earlier war-time memories, but all his accounts, they discovered, soon turned to eulogizing Miss Nightingale, whose personality had completely ensnared him.

'She's the most beautiful woman alive,' he told them, and the bravest. She never cared how rough or foul-mouthed we was to begin with – she soon altered all that. We fair worshipped her out there, and I see her once not long ago when I went to stay with a brother of mine at Claydon. There's a big house there that the Verneys own, and Miss Nightingale stays there sometimes with her sister. She was sitting with her in the garden and I stood behind a tree and looked at her, and looked at her. I thought to myself: "If ever a lady deserves a rest it's that one." '

His old eyes grew so ardent when he spoke of Miss Nightingale and her band of nurses that Dolly seriously considered the possibility of taking up nursing as a profession as she watched him What

could be more rewarding than to see love and gratitude flashing from the eyes of a soldier? A young one preferably, of course. Perhaps Albert Davis? Though, on second thoughts she did not want him hurt at all. And how becoming a nurse's uniform was! Dolly saw herself tripping lightly up and down a long ward, a veil floating behind her, the idol of her adoring patients. She was enchanted by the idea.

Enchantment ended a few hours later when little Frank was sick that evening and she was sent to clear up his cot. Sousing revolting bed linen in a tub of icy water, she realized, with devastating clarity, that nursing was not for her.

10

During the first year of the new century, the object of prime importance at Beech Green School was a large-scale map showing the area in which the Boer War was being waged.

Each morning, before prayers, the boys would gather round it,

moving the little flags to show the day-to-day progress of the troops
Great was the rejoicing when besieged Ladysmith was finally
relieved on February 28th, and greater still when, after 217 days of
siege, Mafeking too was relieved in May.

Mr Finch was so infected with the national fever on this occasion
that he let the children have a bonfire in the playground, and
watched their wild dancing around it with an indulgent eye.

The most envied boy in the school was one who wore a tie of the
new khaki colour decorated with dozens of tiny Union Jacks. The
war, it seemed, was as good as won, as the summer wore on,
and when, in the autumn of 1900, Lord Roberts and Buller came
home to England, Beech Green felt sure that peace was not far
distant.

'Your boy won't never get to South Africa,' they consoled Mrs
Davis. 'Just a case of Kitchener clearing up the mess, and it'll all be
over by harvest, you'll see.'

At the end of the summer term another excitement occurred.
It was announced that Mr Finch was leaving and would take up
a new appointment in a large school in the county town. This
meant promotion, and his neighbours were quick to congratulate
him.

The children were secretly glad to see him go. He wasn't a bad
old stick, said some, but it would be good fun to have someone
new who wasn't so strict. As one wag put it, in Dolly's hearing:

'Talk about the relief of Mafeking! I reckons it'll be the relief of
Beech Green School when old Finch goes!'

The new headmaster came in the autumn. He was young and
unmarried, but possessed a fiercely possessive mother who ruled the
school house and her son as well.

Ada and the older girls were his slaves from the start. His fair
wavy hair, worn a shade too long by country standards, and his
pale face made him an object of interest and reverence. His clothes
were much less formal than Mr Finch's had been, and he favoured
big floppy ties in delicate pastel colours.

'Proper wishy-washy young feller', was what the men of Beech
Green called the newcomer behind his back. But the women were
inclined to take his part.

'He's just up-to-date, that's all. Very good thing too, to have someone who can teach the children without waving the cane at 'em all day,' they maintained.

His name was Evan Waterman, and he proved to be an ardent churchgoer, much given to genuflection and crossings during the services at Beech Green, which occasioned deep suspicions in the hearts of his Low Church neighbours. The vicar was delighted to have such a devout young man in charge of the school, and his visits there became more frequent and lengthy than ever.

'Lives in the parson's pocket,' grumbled old Davis one day, in Dolly's hearing. 'Don't trust that new chap no further'n I can see 'im! Too good to live, 'e be, mark my words!'

Mr Waterman had not been in school for a week before he told the children that he hoped he need never use the cane again, and to give emphasis to his words he threw it dramatically on to the top of a high cupboard where it lodged among a group of dusty wooden cubes, cones, spheres, and other geometrical shapes which had been undisturbed for years.

The rousing cheer which greeted this display might have warned a wiser man of perils to come, but Evan Waterman simply flushed with pleasure and told himself that he had won a place in his pupils' grateful hearts. Had he known it, it was not gratitude that enflamed those savage breasts, but the thought of a rollicking future where impudence and laziness would go unpunished. The boys winked merrily at each other, quivering with secret mirth. The girls gazed at their new headmaster with rapt devotion. In any case, they had seldom felt the cane, and had nothing to lose.

He told the children that he hoped they would look upon him as a friend, and would tell him of anything that perplexed or frightened them.

'I am here to help you,' he said earnestly, leaning forward in his desk with his pale blue tie flapping dangerously near the inkwell. The red faces of the older boys, choking with suppressed laughter at such antics, he attributed to natural bashfulness. He was determined to put into practice the new ideas in education, and to throw out the repressive methods which he saw had been those used by Mr Finch. To see the children curtseying and bowing to their elders shocked Mr Waterman seriously. The military precision with which the classes stood, turned and marched from the schoolroom to the playground appalled him. In the future, he told himself –

and his astonished pupils – all would be freedom and light, and work would be done for the joy of doing it, not because he said so.

He might have known, poor fellow, that such drastic changes take time, and are bound to be accompanied with much trial and tribulation. Certainly the younger children benefited from this easier régime, and the fear that Mr Finch had aroused in them was never inspired by Evan Waterman's presence in their classroom.

The new infants' teacher, who had taken the place of Mrs Finch, was a robust young woman who cycled from Caxley daily on her new safety bicycle. She was a rosy-cheeked young Amazon, called Jenny North, and the village was quite sure that she would soon conquer Evan Waterman's heart and install herself as mistress of the school house in place of the dragon who lived there at present. This topic kept the village gossips engrossed for quite a fortnight, but – alas for their hopes! – the young woman was 'going steady' with a respectable draper in Caxley, and had eyes for no one else. She looked upon her headmaster's methods with a tolerant eye, but did not hesitate to administer a sharp slap upon her young sinners' legs, when her classroom door was safely closed. She and her charges understood each other well enough, and Beech Green parents soon realized that their young ones were getting on steadily under their new teacher.

About the older children they were less happy as the weeks went by. Gales of laughter and a few shouts could be heard from the schoolroom, where only Mr Finch's stentorian tones had been heard before. Rude rhymes were written on stable walls beginning:

> Old Milk-and-Waterman
> Lost the cane ...

and the little girls came home, bright-eyed, with tales of kind Mr Waterman patting their hands and telling them they were growing up to be very pretty.

Francis Clare was present one day when Ada burst in from school and threw her books so carelessly on the table that they slid across the surface and crashed to the floor.

'Look out, my girl   remonstrated Francis. 'That's your school books, you know '

'Don't matter,' responded Ada carelessly, tossing back her bright hair. 'Mr Waterman says we can do some arithmetic or learn poetry, whichever we like. And he told me not to sit up too late over it, or I'd spoil my pretty eyes.'

She smirked as she repeated the words, and Francis looked at her steadily. Now, at fourteen, in her last term at school, she certainly was pretty, but it wasn't Mr Waterman's place to tell her so, thought Francis with rising anger.

'You don't want to listen to such foolishness,' said Francis. 'And your headmaster should know better than to encourage vanity. Pick your books up, and then go and help your mother.'

When the girls were safely in bed Francis spoke openly to Mary.

'I don't like that chap and I never shall. He's no business to lead them girls on so, and I shall have a word with the vicar about the way he's going on. The best thing we can do, my dear, is to get our Ada settled in a good job and let her leave as soon as it's fixed. No need to wait till Christmas. She's fourteen now and big enough to find a place.'

Mary Clare agreed.

'Mrs Evans was asking for her,' she said. 'It'd be nice to have her handy, and she'd be happy at the manor, I'm sure. I'll have a word with the child.'

'You do that, Mary,' said Francis, 'and I'll give that young feller a straight word or two. There's plenty of talk about him in the village – the work at school is going downhill fast, they say, and the boys just play the goat and get away with it. If you ask me,' continued Francis sturdily, 'a bit of straight-forward soldiering wouldn't hurt that young Waterman.'

The next day Mary broached the subject of going into service with Mrs Evans at the manor. To her surprise, Ada was vehemently against it.

'I'm not being maid to no one,' said the girl violently. 'Why should I be at everyone's beck and call! I knows what it'd be! All the greasy cooking pots would be left for me to wash. All the back corridors and stone floors would be mine to scrub. I'd do the vegetables, and clean the mud out of the sinks, and squash the black beetles and do the flues! Well, I'm not going to, then. I'm going to work in a shop – that's what I want to do!'

'But you'd still be at everyone's beck and call,' pointed out Mary

'And there's only one shop in Beech Green, and that don't want anyone to help.'

'It's Caxley I'm thinking of,' said Ada. 'I don't want to be buried alive in Beech Green all my life. I want to see things going on. There's plenty of shops in Caxley that'd take me on.'

'Well, we'll think about it,' said Mary, taken aback at the assurance of her firstborn. 'I'll talk to your dad tonight and we'll see if we can hear of something.'

Meanwhile, Francis had called at the vicarage and had a few words with the vicar about his new headmaster. To tell the truth, the good vicar himself was beginning to have some misgivings about the new appointment, and agreed to speak to Waterman that week.

'I'm taking my two girls away as soon as I can arrange it,' said Francis as he said his farewells on the vicarage doorstep. 'And you'll find that other folk in Beech Green will be doing the same, sir, unless things alter.'

And the vicar, watching the thatcher's broad back vanish between the Wellingtonias that lined the vicarage drive, sighed heavily. He recognized righteous wrath when he saw it.

To Dolly, now twelve years old, that autumn seemed a time of upheaval and change. She was amazed to hear from her father that he was making plans to transfer her to Fairacre School next term. For her part, she quite liked Mr Waterman, though not with the ardour that the older girls felt for him. Already gaining the cool wisdom that was to be her mainstay in life, the younger child recognized the headmaster's folly as well as his good intentions, but felt sorry that his overtures were so rudely flouted by the boys. She enjoyed his lessons, appreciated his love of poetry and nature, and was beginning to wonder if she too might be a teacher one day.

She knew little of Fairacre except that the school was much the same size as Beech Green's and that it stood near the church. The headmaster had been there for a year or two, had a grown-up family, a jolly, bustling wife, who took the needlework lessons, and shared her husband's passion for the local hunt. They always walked a pair of hounds, which frequently burst joyfully into the schoolroom, and on the days when the hunt met near Fairacre the schoolchildren were allowed to follow on foot. It all sounded happy enough, but it was strange, and Dolly did not like changes.

From her father's manner, though, she realized that the affair was settled, and she made no demur. Ada was found a modest post in the draper's shop in Caxley owned by Jenny North's young man and his father. This stroke of good fortune was brought about by Jenny herself, who recognized a quick bright assistant when she saw one, and knew that Ada's pretty face would attract more business.

It was arranged that the girl should live with Francis's parents and walk daily to the shop in the High Street, not far from the school which she and Dolly had first attended. Sunday was the only day of the week when she could get home, and the grandparents promised to bring her in their old trap or send her with an obliging neighbour.

'But what I really want,' said Ada, eyes shining, 'is a new safety bicycle like Miss North's. Then I could go from here each day, couldn't I, mum?'

'Ah well,' said Mary indulgently, 'you save your wages and see how it goes. I reckon you're a lucky girl to have everything fall out so nice for you.'

The house seemed very quiet without Ada s boisterous presence, and little Frank was promoted to her empty bed in Dolly's room. Dolly was glad of his company, although he was usually fast asleep when she crept up at night, a pink and white cherub with tousled dark curls.

He woke early, and Dolly first discovered her ability to weave stories to amuse the little boy. He liked best one about a naughty child called Tom whose adventures continued in serial form for weeks on end. Years later, Dolly Clare revived Tom's adventures for the amusement of many schoolchildren.

Frank, at nearly four years of age, was increasingly dear to Dolly. She took him with her wherever she could, and was already looking forward to taking him to school at Beech Green after Christmas, when the ultimatum had been given about the move to Fairacre. Now someone else would have to be found to take Frank to school, for Fairacre was too far away for his short legs, and in any case, the teaching which he would get with Jenny North perfectly satisfied Francis and Mary. Time enough to think of Fairacre for young

Frank, they told each other, when he was big enough to go into the headmaster's class.

'And if I knows anything about it,' said Francis, 'there'll be a different headmaster sitting in that chair by that time!' Both parents thought a great deal about their son's future, and Francis was delighted to find that, young as the child was, he already showed an interest in the straw, the knives and hazel spars which one day, Francis hoped, would be the tools of his honourable trade.

They were all glad of the child's gay prattle during that period of autumn gloom, for, besides Ada's absence, other circumstances cast a shadow. The war, which had seemed all but won in September, now took a turn for the worse, and fighting flared up again, on a scattered front, and with renewed bitterness.

As Christmas approached, anxiety grew. On December 22nd it was announced that thirty thousand more mounted men would be sent overseas. Among them, this time, was young Albert Davis, and there was much sadness in the little home. It looked as if the Christmas of 1900 was to be as gloomy as the year before.

The sight of her friend Emily, her face mottled with crying and her eyes puffy and red, brought home suddenly to young Dolly the widespread wretchedness of war, in contrast to the excitement and glory which had so enthralled her a year earlier. She pondered on this new revelation of war's grim side one morning in the Christmas holidays, as she stood by the kitchen copper, watching the clothes boiling gently, the suds sighing up and down like someone breathing. Death was a fearful thing and an ugly one. She remembered the horror of the corpses in the butcher's shop at Caxley, and shuddered. Only that morning she had come across a squashed wren on the road outside their gate – a small round pile of flattened feathers with its tail neatly erect upon it. She had watched that wren, for many weeks, running up and down and in and out of the thorn hedge, and rejoiced in its perky two inches of feathered vitality. And now it lay, stilled for ever, a pathetic scrap, as neat and tidy in death as in life.

To think that men could set out to reduce each other to that dreadful condition made the child feel cold with revulsion as she prodded the steaming linen with the copper stick. It was bad enough to have Christmas overshadowed, to have to endure the loss of Ada's company, to face the ordeal of changing schools, and to see the Davises – and particularly dear Emily – suffer so, without this final overpowering horror of death to torment her.

Later, she wondered if those black thoughts had been something in the nature of a premonition. For, before a month had passed, death was to come very close to Dolly Clare, setting a grim mark upon that little household which even time itself could never completely remove.

11

One morning in January 1901 Dolly awoke first. It was still dark and she could hear her father and mother moving about downstairs getting ready for the day. Usually, young Frank woke when they stirred and insinuated himself into Dolly's bed hoping for more stories.

But this morning he lay heavily asleep, drawing deep snoring breaths that at first amused his sleepy sister.

Wake up, Frank,' she called at length. 'You're snoring like an old piggy!'

There was no reply.

Dolly began to whistle a tune that he called their 'waking up song a modified version of the army reveille, but there was no response from the sleeping child.

She climbed out of bed and padded across the cold ancient boards to peer at her brother. He seemed much as usual, as far as she could tell in the dim light, but when she put her hand on his forehead to push back his hair she found it hot and wet with sweat. Frightened she ran downstairs to the lamp-lit room where the smells of breakfast rose from the stove.

'Frank's bad,' she told her parents, and followed them up the narrow staircase, shaking with cold and fear.

The candles were lit, and Mary and Francis leant over the bed. The child woke and smiled at them, and Dolly's heart was comforted

'He don't look too bad to me,' said Francis. 'Keep him in bed today my love. He's just got a bit of a chesty cold.'

'He will keep taking his scarf off,' said Mary anxiously, 'and it was that bitter yesterday when he was out in the garden.'

She looked at her son closely.

'D'you reckon we should get the doctor?' she asked hesitantly. Doctors cost money, and were not called unnecessarily to the Clare household. Besides, she did not want Francis to think her unduly pernickety, but Frank had never ailed anything before, and this seemed a severe type of fever.

'You let him lie there today,' repeated Francis. 'I'll get home in good time, and if he don't seem to have picked up, we'll send for the doctor then.'

He kissed his womenfolk, bade them cheer up, and set off for work.

Frank slept most of the day, making the same alarming noise which had woken Dolly. Mary Clare's fears were calmed by Mrs Davis, who assured her that her own children had often suffered such symptoms, and a day in bed usually cured them.

'Believe me, my dear,' she told the anxious mother, 'that little 'un's all right. You knows what children are – up one minute, down the next. It's because he's the only boy you're worrying so. You see, tomorrow he'll be fairly.'

But when Francis came home that night he thought otherwise. Dolly had spent most of the day by the bedside, shaken by doubts, and only half-believing the comfort given by Mrs Davis. When she saw her father's face, her terror grew even greater.

'You cut along and get the doctor, Doll,' he said, and Dolly fled through the darkening village for help. Bronchitis was diagnosed, and the child was moved downstairs to a makeshift bed on the sofa, drawn close to the stove where a kettle steamed for two agonizing nights and days.

Mary never left his side for the whole of that time. She sat white-faced and very silent, ministering to the unconscious child's needs, and watching his every movement with awful concentration. When she spoke to Dolly, it was with such tenderness that the child could scarcely bear it.

Dolly was thankful that it was the school holidays and that she could be there to help in the house and prepare the simple meals that, in fact, none of them had the heart to eat. Throughout the time that she worked, she prayed so vehemently that her head

ached with effort. She tried to will God to make Frank better.
Surely, she told herself, He wouldn't let him die! Not a little boy
like that, who'd done nothing wrong! If men at war were killed,
it was understandable, for they knew what they were doing, and
God, she supposed, took some of them simply because men did
die in wars. But there was no reason why Frank should be so sacri-
ficed. Her distracted thoughts followed each other round and round
in a demented circle, and all the time the prayers went up, and
she saw them in imagination, as an invisible vapour rising through
the kitchen ceiling, and then the thatch, and finally the lowering
grey winter clouds, spiralling their way heavenwards to that
omnipotent Being in whose hands the life of little Frank was
held.

On the third night, while Dolly slept above, the child slipped
away, one hand in each of his parents'. He had never regained
consciousness, but there was nothing to show that death was so
close. He gave a little hiccup, and the harsh breathing which had
dominated the house quietly stopped. The silence had an icy quality
about it, and for a stunned moment the stricken parents were
powerless to move.

Then, across the motionless body of their son, their eyes met.
Francis took Mary in his arms, and their bitter grief began.

The day of the funeral was iron-cold. A light sprinkling of snow
whitened the churchyard, throwing the gaping black hole, awaiting
the small coffin, into sharp relief.

In Dolly Clare's memory that day was etched for ever in stark
black and white. The sad little family stood watching the coffin
being lowered into the icy earth. A bunch of snowdrops trembled
upon the lid, as frail and pure as the child within. Clad in heavy
mourning, Dolly remembered that other family she had pitied, so
long ago it seemed, on the sunlit afternoon of the Diamond Jubilee.
The bare black elm trees were outlined against a sky heavy with
snow to come. Black spiked railings round a tomb nearby were
tipped with snow, and from the church porch a row of footprints
blackened the snow where the mourners' feet had passed. No colour,
no warmth, no sunshine, no movement, comforted the spirit at that
poignant parting, and Dolly remembered, with sharp intensity, the
feeling of loss which had shaken her when she had kissed her

brother's forehead, as cold and hard as marble, a few hours before. In the utter negation of death lay its chief terror.

In the weeks that followed, Mary Clare remained calm and unusually gentle with her family. After the first few hours of grief, she showed little sign of her loss The neighbours shook their heads over her.

'She ought to cry, that she ought!' they told each other. 'That poor lamb's been buried over a week and she ain't shed a tear. 'Tis unnatural! She'll suffer for it, you'll see!'

There was certainly something uncanny, as well as heroic, about Mary's composure, but Francis was glad of it. His own tears were too near the surface for him to have endured his wife's emotion bravely.

It was perhaps as well for Dolly that her departure to Fairacre followed hard on the heels of this tragedy. Great was her joy when Emily told her that she too was starting at Fairacre School, and they could begin the new adventure together.

They set off through shallow snow on the first day of the term, Dolly clad in her mourning black and Emily, in gay contrast, in a bright scarlet coat which had once been her sister's.

They carried bacon sandwiches for their midday meal, and an apple apiece from Mrs Davis's store. The clatter of their strong nailed boots was muffled by the snow as they tramped along, and their breath steamed as they discussed what lay ahead.

'I know about half of them anyway,' said Emily, seeking comfort. 'There's the Willets and the Pratts. I've played with them sometimes, and they said Mr Wardle's all right if you don't give him no cheek.'

'But what about Mrs Wardle?' asked Dolly.

'Rips up the sewing a bit,' said Emily laconically, jumping sideways into a fresh patch of snow which invited a few footprints.

'But I reckon they'll both be better than old Milk-and-Waterman.'

And Emily was right. On that first morning, as they sat together among their new school fellows, Dolly took stock of Fairacre School and began to feel the warmth of her surroundings thaw the bleakness which had numbed her for the past few weeks.

A massive fire roared behind the fireguard, and though it could not hope to warm completely a room so lofty and so full of cross draughts, yet it was a cheering sight on a cold January day. Mr

Wardle, warming his trouser legs before it, proved to be a hearty boisterous man who welcomed the newcomers, and bade his schoolchildren do the same.

He was that rare thing, Dolly discovered later, a happy man. Blessed with boundless energy, superb physique, a lively wife and four children now out in the world, Mr Wardle enjoyed his little domain and liked to see those in it equally happy. His recipe was simple, and he told it to the children over and over again:

'Work hard, do your best, and a bit more, and you'll get on.'

Sometimes he put his recipe into a different form and read them a homily about the sin of Sloth, which he considered the most vicious one among the seven.

'If you start getting lazy,' he would say, bouncing energetically up and down, 'you'll get liverish. And if you get liverish, you'll get sorry for yourself. And that's when the rot starts. Use your brain and your body to the utmost, and the Devil will know that he's beaten.'

He certainly set them all a fine example. His teaching was thorough, exact and lively. His spare time was taken up with gardening, walking his hounds for miles around the countryside, training the church choir, and adding to a magnificent collection of moths and butterflies. His authority was unquestioned, unlike that of poor Mr Waterman at Beech Green, and Dolly soon found herself responding to the vitality of this man who could kindle a spark in even the stolidest of his country scholars.

The children, perhaps because of Mr Wardle's example, seemed friendlier than those at Beech Green, and Emily and Dolly, who had secretly feared a little teasing and bullying, found no antagonism. Nor were any remarks passed about Dolly's black clothes, much to her relief. Although she did not know it until many years later, Mr Wardle had already warned his children about Dolly's loss and given them to understand that extra kindness would be expected of them, and good manners most certainly enforced, if his vigilant eye saw any shortcomings.

He was a man whose good heart and good head worked well

together. Quick to recognize a child's vulnerability, he never descended to sarcasm and ridicule to gain his ends. Severe he could be, and when he was driven to caning them the cane fell heavily, but it rarely needed to be used. Work, exercise, fresh air and laughter kept his charges engrossed and healthy; and from Mr Wardle Dolly Clare learnt much of the ways of a good teacher.

About a week after their arrival, on January 22nd 1901, Dolly and Emily sat with the rest of the big girls at one end of the main room, with needlework in their hands and Mrs Wardle's eye upon them.

It was called 'Fancywork' on the timetable, and each child had a square of fine canvas and skeins of red, blue, yellow and green wool on the desk in front of her. They were busy making samplers, using the various stitches which Mrs Wardle taught them. 'Fancywork' was a pleasant change from 'Plain Sewing' which involved hemming unbleached calico pillow slips with the strong possibility of seeing Mrs Wardle rip them undone at the end of the lesson

The room was quiet. The boys at the other end were drawing a spray of laurel pinned against a white paper on the blackboard, and only the whisper of their pencils as they shaded the leaves and carefully left 'high-lights', broke the sleepy silence.

It was then that the muffled bell of St Patrick's next door began to ring, and Mr Wardle, looking perplexed, hurried out to investigate. When he returned a minute later, his rosy face was grave.

'I have very sad news,' he told his surprised listeners. 'Queen Victoria is dead.'

There was a shocked silence, broken only by the distant bell and the gasp from Mrs Wardle, as her hand flew to her heart.

'All stand!' commanded Mr Wardle. 'And we will say a short prayer for the Queen we have lost, and the King we have now to rule us.'

Afterwards, it seemed to the children, the grown-ups made too much of this event, but they were wrong. Their lives were short, and to them the Queen had always been a very old lady near to death. To their parents and grandparents, who had known and revered her for all their lives, this passing of a great Queen was the end of the world they had always known. National mourning was sincere, and tinged with the bewilderment of children who have lost the head of a family, long loved and irreplaceable.

Dolly never forgot Emily's words to her as they crept quietly from the playground that day to make their way homeward.

'Won't Frank be pleased,' said Emily, 'to have the Queen with him!'

It was exactly what Dolly herself had thought when Mr Wardle had broken the news, and the comfort of hearing it put into words was wonderfully heartening. Certainly the shock of this second death was considerably lessened by Emily's innocent philosophy, and the thought of Frank's gain mitigated their own sense of loss.

It was not the first time that Emily had been of comfort to Dolly by her ability to come to terms with the unknown. In the years to come, her child-like simplicity and faith brought refreshment to them both.

Sixty or so years later, Miss Clare, half asleep in the shade of her plum tree, recalled that historic day, and its dark solemnity lit by Emily's touching confidence.

There certainly could be no greater contrast in the weather, thought Miss Clare, watching the heat waves shimmer across the sun-baked downs. In the border, the flaunting oriental poppies opened their petals so wide in the strong sunlight that they fell backwards to display the mop of black stamens at the centre. At the foot of the plant, Miss Clare's tortoise had pushed himself among the foliage, to escape from the June heat which even he could not endure.

She could hear the faraway voices of children at play, and guessed it must be about half past two, when Beech Green School had its afternoon break. Soon Emily would be with her again, as comforting and as hopeful as she had been on that bitter bleak day so long ago.

Miss Clare stretched her old stiff limbs in great contentment, revelling in the hot sunshine and the joy of Emily's coming. Looking back, she saw now that an age had closed on the day that Mr Wardle had called them to prayer, and she who since then had seen many reigns, could imagine the impact which Victoria's passing had made upon her parents' generation.

But for Dolly the twelve-year-old child, that day had been chiefly a turning-point in her own happiness. She could see now, sixty years later, that several things had contributed to the sudden

lightening of her misery. Mr Wardle's infectious vitality, new surroundings, work praised and encouraged, had all helped together to
raise the child's spirits from the depths into which her brother's
death had cast them. The natural buoyancy of youth and time's
healing powers added their measure of restoration, but it was Emily's
homely words which had really set her free at last. It was as though
the Queen had taken Dolly's burden upon herself by entering into
that unknown world where Frank already waited, and fanciful
though the idea seemed a lifetime later, yet it still seemed touching
in the strength and hope it had given to a sad little girl who had
needed comfort sorely.

'Ah! It's good to grow old,' said Miss Clare, contemplating that
pitiful young figure across the years, 'and to know that nothing can
ever hurt you very much again. There's a lot to be said for being
seventy!'

And turning her face gratefully to the sun, she continued to wait,
lapped in warmth and contentment, for the coming of Emily.

PART THREE

FAIRACRE

12

From the first, Dolly Clare liked Fairacre. It was a compact and pretty village, grouped charmingly about its church, unlike Beech Green, which straggled along the road to Caxley. Some of the cottage roofs had been thatched by her own father, since they had come to live near by, and still shone golden in the sunshine. More ancient roofs had weathered to a silvery grey, while others, more venerable still, sagged thinly across their supports and sprouted with green patches of moss and grass.

Not all the cottages were thatched. More than half were tiled

with small tiles of a warm rosy brown which combined with the
weathered brick to give a colourful appearance to the village. A few
large houses, built in the reigns of Queen Anne and the early
Georges, glowed with the same warm colours among their trees,
and little Dolly Clare grew to love the vicarage, which could be
seen plainly from the playground of Fairacre School, admiring its
graceful fanlight over the front door, and the two great cedar trees
which stood guard before it.

Fairacre, in those Edwardian days, was rich in fine trees, planted
to give shelter, no doubt, from the roaring winds which swept the
whaleback of the downs above it. Limes and horse-chestnuts shaded
gardens, and clumps of magnificent elms sheltered the cattle and
horses in the farm meadows. Close by the school, protecting both it
and the school house, towered more elm trees, in which a thriving
rookery clattered and cawed, and several of the neighbouring farms
had leafy avenues leading to their houses. There was much more
ivy about at that time. The dark glossy leaves muffled many a
garden wall and outhouse, and added a richness to the general scene.
When, in later life, Miss Clare looked at old photographs of the
Fairacre she had known as a child, she realized how denuded of
trees the village had become within her lifetime.

She and Emily loved it from the start. Their spirits rose as they
turned the bend and approached the church and school. It was almost
three miles to walk each morning, but the two little girls were
quick to find lifts with obliging carters and tradesmen, and rarely
had to walk both ways in the day. Dolly, who had been so frightened by the size of Bella on the day of the move from Caxley, now
treated these great-hearted horses with affection and complete trust
as she scrambled up from shaft or wheel hub to her high perch
beside some good-natured driver who had taken pity on the two
young travellers.

In all weathers, riding or walking, they traversed the familiar
road. They looked out for the first wild flowers of spring, the pink
wild roses that starred the summer hedges, and the bright beads of
autumn berries. They watched the birds building nests, and could
tell to a day when the eggs would hatch. They knew where a badger
lived, and where a white owl would appear as they plodded home
on a murky winter afternoon. Those three miles grew as familiar
and as well loved as the faces of their mothers. There was always

something new, something beautiful, something strange, to find daily, and the two children learnt as much from their close scrutiny of banks and hedges as they did in the busy classroom at Fairacre school.

As Dolly and Emily neared the end of their schooldays, in the early part of Edward VII's reign, they found that one or the other was frequently called upon to walk from Mr Wardle's room to the infants' room next door in order 'to give a hand', as Mr Wardle always put it, to the teacher in charge.

They were now called monitors, and with one or two other children of fourteen, undertook a number of daily jobs in the running of the school. Numbers thinned after the age of twelve, for those who could pass an examination in general proficiency were allowed to leave, and farmers were eager to employ these young boys now that labour was difficult to obtain. This meant that those over twelve who were left behind were often lucky enough to get closer attention from their headmaster. Mr Wardle looked upon Dolly and Emily as promising pupil teachers of the future, and gave them every opportunity of learning the rudiments of the job under his roof.

Both girls enjoyed their time with the babies. Miss Taylor, a wisp of a woman with two protruding front teeth which were the only outstanding feature of an undistinguished appearance, was glad to delegate some of her duties.

'You take the little boys, dear,' she would say to Dolly, 'and you can manage the girls, Emily, while I hear the big ones read.'

And so, to a background of young voices chanting round the teacher's desk, Emily and Dolly would squat on low chairs by their charges and show them how to write capital letters on their slates, holding small hot hands within their own while wet slate pencils traced uncertainly the mysteries being explained.

Sometimes, when Miss Taylor wanted peace in which to mark sums or tidy cupboards, Dolly would perch on the high chair before the class and tell them one of the stories about naughty Tom which had once delighted little Frank. It warmed her heart to see the joy with which the children listened, and the company and affection of these babies did much to soften the blow of Frank's death.

It was no surprise to the girls when one afternoon Mr Wardle asked them to stay behind to talk about training as pupil teachers. It was a golden June afternoon with the weathercock on St Patrick's ablaze in the sunshine against a clear blue sky. Their schoolfellows' cries died rapidly in the distance, for hay-making was in progress and the children were racing to join their fathers and big brothers in the meadows.

Emily and Dolly stood demurely in front of Mr Wardle's great desk, eyeing the massive brass ink stand and the array of pens.

'Well, would you like it?' asked Mr Wardle after he had outlined the training involved.

'I think I should,' said Emily hesitantly. Her grey eyes were clouded with concentration. A wisp of dark hair cleaved to her damp forehead. Volatile and exuberant by nature, Emily was pondering earnestly on her ability to stick to a course for four years and then to the profession to which it led. She liked children, she liked the idea of teaching them, but would she tire of it? She raised perplexed eyes to Mr Wardle's lively blue ones.

'You'll like it more every year,' promised Mr Wardle, seeing the child's doubts. 'You'll make a very good teacher in time.'

He turned to Dolly questioningly.

'I will,' said the child steadily. She might have been taking her vows, thought the schoolmaster, both touched and amused by the calm assurance with which she declared herself. It was strange that on this occasion the more timid of the two should be so confident. With a flash of insight, he recognized in that moment that he was in the presence of someone who would become a much greater person than he would ever be, and he felt unaccountably humble.

'You're a born teacher,' he said quietly, and turned the key in his desk drawer to bring the interview to a close.

Together the three emerged into the dazzling sunlight.

'Tell your fathers that I have spoken to you about this,' said Mr Wardle, 'and ask them to come and see me. Meanwhile, think it over well. You don't want to spend your whole life regretting a decision. Take plenty of time to make up your minds.'

He watched their figures dwindle into the distance. The heat waves shimmered across the lane, blurring the outlines of their pale print frocks and wide straw hats. One of them, he thought, half-closing his eyes against the brightness, has given her mind to it

already – and her heart and soul too. He only hoped that she would
find as much happiness as he had himself.

Strangely moved and elated, he crossed the shade of his garden
and entered the school house.

In the following September the two girls returned to Fairacre
with the status of pupil teacher. This meant that they helped Mr
Wardle and Miss Taylor, and under their guidance prepared and
gave lessons occasionally, generally making themselves useful. Twice
a week they went into Caxley for evening classes, and occasionally
they attended an extra class, or a demonstration lesson by a qualified
teacher, on a Saturday morning.

Both girls were excited by their promotion. They enjoyed the
trips to Caxley, and knew that they were luckier than most village
children in continuing their education after the age of fourteen. To
be sure, the work expected of them was fairly simple – Arithmetic,
English, Geography, History and Nature Study – only a little more
advanced than Mr Wardle's final lessons with his top class, but it
was stimulating to see different pupils and to be taught by a variety
of men and women.

Francis and Mary were pleased with Dolly's choice of career.
Their shy one, it seemed, was blossoming. Mary helped Dolly to
lengthen her skirts and to dress her soft hair in a top knot in a
manner suitable to her new dignity. Emily's dark braids were now
worn wound about her head, and the two girls spent much of their
time adjusting each other's hair pins. The conversation on the way
to Fairacre these days dealt with fashions rather more than education.

They both longed for 'low shoes' instead of the stout laced boots
which they were still obliged to wear. The Misses Evans, also in
their teens, were lucky enough to wear shoes with straps every day
of their lives, and on high days and holidays, so Dolly heard, they
had real silk stockings to wear with them. They surveyed their own
cotton-clad legs, terminating in the loathsome boots, with acute
disfavour.

On the evenings that they went to evening classes they eyed the
young women of Caxley, who appeared to their unsophisticated
eyes as positive fashion plates. Sometimes a carriage would rattle
past, bearing a beautiful lady, on her way home from a tea party,

wearing one of the delicious large Edwardian hats smothered in tea roses and with clouds of veiling tied beneath the chin. Dolly and Emily gazed with wonder. Would they ever be able to have a hat as adorable as that?

Getting to Caxley was a problem. Mr Wardle took them in on Tuesday evenings when he went to play chess with an old friend, and brought them home again. He owned a small governess cart, and it was a tight squeeze to get even such slim people as Dolly and Emily into it with sturdy Mr Wardle taking up more than half the room. On Thursday evenings they relied on the corn merchant's waggon which had been delivering goods in the Beech Green area all day, but this arrangement had its drawbacks, for the driver was a slow, ambling fellow, and the girls were in a ferment of anxiety until they were dropped at the Institute in Caxley High Street. They returned home in style on Thursdays, for one of the women teachers, the daughter of a prosperous grocer in the town, had the use of her father's carriage and spanked along the lane to Beech Green when the lessons were over.

It was Ada who was responsible for solving this problem of transport in an indirect way. Growing prettier every year, with bright bold eyes and burnished hair, Ada had many admirers. The young men of Caxley were frequent customers at the general draper's where she worked, called in to finger ties or to try on one of the dashing new straw boaters, while their eyes wandered over the pretty assistant. It was no wonder that old Mr and Mrs Clare grew anxious about this wayward grandchild. Despite their protestations, Ada came home later and later in the evening, and they felt powerless to control her. They spoke plainly to Francis about it one Sunday when they spent the day at Beech Green.

The girls had been sent out with a message while the problem was talked over. Francis was greatly perturbed.

'She'll have to live here,' he said firmly. 'Ada's our child, and we must see to her. 'Tisn't right that you should be bothered with her feckless ways at your time of life.'

'We'll see if Mrs Evans can have her there to work,' promised Mary. 'There's no way for her to get to Caxley every day, and maybe she's better in the village.'

The old man looked dubious.

'She won't take to it kindly, that I do know,' he said. 'And, to be fair, the girl's doing well at the shop, and they want to keep her.'

'Well, she can't get there,' said Francis, 'so that's that.'

'Your father and I,' said old Mrs Clare, 'have been thinking about that. You tell them, my dear,' she nodded to her husband.

'If you're agreeable,' said Mr Clare, 'I'd like to buy both girls one of these new safety bicycles apiece. They may as well have their little something now, when they need it, as wait for me to go to my grave and then get a pound or two. What'd you say, lad?'

'I'd say,' said Francis, with feeling, 'that they're two real lucky girls, and Mary and me'd be proper thankful to you.'

Mary was looking a little apprehensive. ''Tis real kind of you,' she said earnestly, 'but – but d'you think they'd be safe? I mean, Caxley's a busy place. They might get knocked down, or run into something if they couldn't manage the machines –'

Francis broke in upon his wife's misgivings.

'I'll see they learn to manage 'em before they goes to Caxley,' he assured her. 'You tell 'em the good news when they comes in, dad, and watch their eyes sparkle! You'll get plenty of kisses for this!'

'I don't want kisses or thanks,' said the old man, although he looked pleased at the thought, 'but they're good girls, and I'm glad to do it for them.'

And so it came about that once again Ada and Dolly shared a bedroom and set off each morning on their marvellous bicycles, one to Caxley and the other to Fairacre; and on Tuesdays and Thursdays Dolly rode proudly into Caxley to the evening classes, independent of lifts and free to come and go whenever she liked.

Only Emily was sad, and that sadness did not last long, for Mrs Evans remembered an ancient bicycle propped in an outhouse and lent it to the girl for as long as she needed it. Pedalling along together, the wind playing havoc with their insecure coiffures and their long skirts, the two friends felt that life could hold no greater joy.

★

Francis Clare was delighted to have both his daughters at home again. His gay Ada had always been his secret favourite, and he was glad of her boisterous presence for Mary's sake.

Since the death of Frank, Mary had become much quieter. She rarely spoke of the child, and shrank from any mention of him by Francis. It was only to be expected, Francis told himself at first. The wound was still fresh and any attention to it gave pain. But as the years passed it seemed unnatural to Francis to remain so silent about the tragedy which had smitten them both so cruelly.

Every week Mary made her way to the grave and put fresh flowers upon the pathetically small green mound. She went alone, and this hurt Francis. She chose her time, when Francis was at work, and when he remonstrated gently with her, the tightening of her lips and stricken look in her eyes were enough to silence him. If only he could thaw her, he told himself, if only she would speak of her grief, then it could make things so much easier for both of them. As it was, he dared not hurt her more, and could only hope that the passing of time would bring them both comfort.

Ada's good spirits lightened the little cottage and Francis rejoiced in her vivacity. What if the boys did look at her in Caxley? Who could blame them? Ada had her head screwed on the right way, thought Francis, and knew how to behave herself. It was only right that she should attract young men at her age, and with her pretty ways. To tell the truth, he was half in love with her himself, seeing again the beauty that had been Mary's in years gone by.

So he comforted his wife when she wondered if they should be stricter with their lively first-born.

'There's safety in numbers, my love,' he said. 'Ada won't do anything silly. She may be a bit flighty. What girl at seventeen isn't? But she'll make some young man a good wife, you'll see.'

He spoke fondly, thinking of the years immediately ahead when Ada would still be a daughter in his house, with the possibility of marriage far ahead in the future. He did not see the flicker of doubt that passed across his wife's face.

13

While Ada enjoyed the bustle of life in Caxley High Street, and felt her spirits lift as she skimmed on her bicycle towards the town, Dolly found quiet satisfaction in the remote tiny world of Fairacre.

The school's setting was sheltered and peaceful. In those days rough turf surrounded the building, with a stone-flagged path leading to the road, and another to the school house. In summer this little green was white with daisies, and the bigger girls showed the younger ones how to make daisy chains with a pin, or a sharp thumb nail. Later, plantains sent up their tough stalks and knobbly heads, and the children used to pluck these and play 'knocking heads off' with skill and energy.

The writhing roots of the clump of elm trees provided more amusement for the babies, who contrived houses and shops in the spaces, and a steep bank which sloped into a field below the trees provided numerous slides in wet or dry weather.

On the grass, under the shade of the trees, stood a bucket of water. This was replenished daily by Mr Wardle, from his own well, and was the only drinking water for the school.

'Tastes a bit funny in the afternoon,' Dolly Clare heard one child say to another.

'Ah! But mornin's it's lovely!' replied the other fervently, obviously grateful for small mercies.

It was Dolly's duty to watch the children during the dinner hour. In the summer, they sprawled on the grass with their hunks of bread with a bit of cheese or bacon to help it down. Sometimes a few radishes or lettuce leaves were added to the meal, when they were in season, and in the autumn plenty of fine apples, plums and nuts were carried to school in the children's dinner bags. Washed down with a swig from the tin mug standing by the 'old bucket', it all tasted good to country children.

In the winter the desks were dragged forward nearer the blazing fire, and the children ate their meal with one eye on a large kettle which lodged on a trivet. Dolly and Emily made cocoa for them all, ladling a spoonful into the cups brought from home and adding a wobbly stream of boiling water from the heavy kettle. There was no charge for this, for years before, in the bitter winter of 1881, the managers had decided to provide this beverage from their own purses, and the kindly custom continued. A jug of milk was sent over daily from the farm near the church, and brown sugar was kept in a great black and gold tin which had come from China years before, to find an alien home at Fairacre. For many of the children the cocoa was the most nourishing part of their meal, for times were still hard for the agricultural labourer, and bread formed the major part of the contents of the school satchels, Dolly noticed.

School began at nine, and ended at four, so that for most of the year Dolly and Emily cycled home in the light. Only at the end of the Christmas term and early part of the Spring one, when the oil lamps were lit from a long taper and shed meagre pools of light upon the children's heads below, were Dolly and Emily obliged to fix lamps to their bicycles and pedal through the dark lane behind the two wavering beams.

Dolly found the work absorbing. By nature she was methodical, cool-headed and patient. The children responded to her quiet ways with trust and affection. But it was for Emily that they showed most enthusiasm. Her quick wits, her humour, and her ready laugh made the children too excitable for Mr Wardle and Miss Taylor's liking. When Emily took a class into the playground to play 'Cat and Mouse' or 'Poor Jenny Sits A-Weeping', the shrieks would penetrate the stout schoolroom walls, and Mr Wardle, intercepting sly grins among his pupils, would stalk forth to call for stricter discipline outside.

'Ticked off again!' Emily would sigh, as they cycled home. 'I wish I could keep them as quiet as you do, Dolly.'

'They can do with livening up,' answered Dolly. 'I think they're kept a bit too meek indoors, and then they get wild as soon as they get outside. But, there you are, that's how Mr Wardle wants it, so we must do as we're told.'

'But just wait till we're headmistresses!' laughed Emily. 'We can do as we like then with the children.'

The possibility seemed so remote to the two young girls that they treated it with amusement. They might teach for a few years, they supposed, and enjoy it very much, but marriage, they felt sure, would one day claim them – marriage to someone as yet unknown, for all the known young men were far too familiar and dull to consider   and then another way of life would begin for them.

And so, happy in the present, and with vague and happy dreams of the future, Emily and Dolly passed the years of their pupil teaching in the long golden afternoon of Edward's reign, with never a thought of the shadows of war which crept slowly but inexorably nearer to their small bright world.

One June evening, about this time, Dolly came out alone from the evening institute in Caxley High Street. Emily was at home with a feverish cold. As she mounted her bicycle she caught sight of Ada in the distance, strolling some way ahead, on the arm of a thickset young man.

Dolly had heard Ada say that morning that she would be late home all the week as they were getting stock sorted ready for the summer sales. Had she finished, Dolly wondered, or had the task been fictitious?

The couple progressed slowly. They were deeply engrossed, and Dolly pedalled equally slowly to keep behind them. There was a look on Ada's face which she had never seen there before. It was a dumb, adoring look, quite unlike the bold flirtatious glances with which Dolly was familiar. The young man's arm crept round Ada's waist and they turned down a side lane towards the river.

Dolly trundled home much perturbed. She had recognized the young man, as he turned, as the son of a local publican. Though the father was respected, it was general knowledge that he had hopelessly spoilt his only child who was allowed too much money and too much licence. Harry Roper, thought the youthful Dolly, must be quite old – twenty-five at least – and Ada knew, as well as she did, that there were dozens of pretty girls, in Caxley alone, who had been as besotted as Ada now was, and who later had regretted their infatuation.

Cycling along the warm lane, with her eyes half-shut against the clouds of gnats, Dolly pondered. It was unlike Ada to lie to her mother. Then again, it was unlike Ada to be so secretive about her escorts. This affair was obviously more serious than the others, and Dolly did not like it.

She decided to say nothing to her parents, nor to Ada. But she was uncomfortably guilty that evening in her parents' presence, and glad to escape early to bed. There she lay, anxious for Ada's safe return, but it was past eleven o'clock before the girl crept upstairs, and by that time Dolly was sound asleep.

This escapade had its sequel, for the next day Francis met a friend who had been in Caxley the night before.

'Saw your girl last night,' he said brightly, his face alight with the pleasure of tale-telling.

'Oh yes,' answered Francis, observing the note of happy anticipation. 'She'd been to evening class.'

'Not this one hadn't!' asserted the friend inelegantly. 'Behind the bar of "The Crown" she was, and served me with a pint, too.'

Francis was completely taken aback, but with a countryman's caution did his best not to show it.

'I must be getting along,' he said, collecting his thatching shears and making towards the ladder.

''Bye,' said the other, setting off in the other direction, well pleased with the encounter.

Francis watched him go, and leant back against the ladder to consider this unsavoury piece of news. He was shocked by more than one aspect of it. In the first place, it looked as though Ada had deliberately lied about staying late for the sale. It also seemed that she was mixed up in company of which he had no knowledge. But worse still was the thought that she had appeared openly in a public bar. This hurt Francis deeply. She had disgraced them all. Francis liked his pint now and again, and enjoyed his local pub, but at a time when drunkenness was rife and the wretched results were everywhere around, the idea of women, and particularly his own young daughters, being seen in a public house, was horrifying. His parents had been strict teetotallers, and he had been brought up to consider public houses as dens of depravity. If word of Ada's escapade ever reached her grandparents, it would be the end of them!

And what was the publican thinking of, to let a young girl serve in his bar? Francis grew belligerent at the thought, and found himself snapping the shears viciously.

'Best get on with my work,' he said aloud to a prowling cat. 'But I'll have a word with that young lady tonight. Maybe I'm too soft with her.'

He mounted the ladder and attacked the straw with unusual savagery.

★

Ada did not trouble to deny anything. She was in a hard, bold mood, off-hand and insolent, calculated to send her parents into a frenzy. Dolly, cleaning her shoes in the kitchen, trembled for her sister. Mary was torn between tears and an overpowering desire to box the girl's ears, but Francis handled the affair competently.

'What's wrong with bringing the young man here?' asked Francis. 'If you like him well enough, let's see him. He'll come if he thinks anything of you.'

'Everyone's against him,' protested Ada, 'and you're the same. You haven't even seen him but you tell me I oughtn't to go out with him. And I don't see why I can't go to his home. He can't help living in a pub.'

'He don't live in the public bar,' said Francis shortly, 'and that's where you were – and serving too. His father could get into serious trouble for that, and he knows it.'

Ada's face flamed scarlet.

'I hates this place! Full of a lot of tittle-tattlers with nothing better to do than make trouble! But they shan't stop me seeing him – and neither will you!'

Francis kept his temper with difficulty.

'See here, Ada. I'm your father and I must do the right thing by my own daughter. You're young yet – '

'I'm nearly nineteen,' Ada burst in, 'and he's twenty-five, and we're going to be married as soon as we can.'

There was silence for a moment in the little room, then Francis spoke gently.

'I'd like to have heard about that from him first. The sooner I see this young man the better, I reckons, and his dad, too.'

'You don't understand – ' began Ada, with a wail.

'Your mother and me has both been in love, you know,' commented Francis dryly. 'We don't want it explained to us. All we're saying is: don't do nothing in a hurry. If you've got any sense at all you'll keep away from him for a bit until I've seen him.'

'Oh, you *old* people!' expostulated Ada, flinging out of the room. Dolly heard the thud of her feet on the stairs and the creak of the bed as she flung herself upon it.

Francis and Mary exchanged hopeless looks.

'Well,' said Francis heavily, 'I'll go and thin my carrots. Need a bit of fresh air after that. Let her simmer a bit, my dear, and then you see what you can do with her. Proper headstrong hussy she's getting!'

'She always was,' said Mary candidly, to her husband's departing back.

The next day Francis made his way to 'The Crown' to see the publican. He did not relish the interview, but it had to be faced, and a steady anger helped his determination. He found his anger evaporating, as the meeting lengthened.

Mr Roper knew nothing, he said, of Ada, although he had seen his son with a girl in the parlour. His wife was about at the time, and he himself was busy with a party of travellers. He had been obliged to go into the yard to arrange stabling for their horses and had knocked on the parlour window and told Harry to attend to the bar. He was as upset as Francis to hear the news, he said; and Francis believed him.

They talked straightforwardly of the affair, and agreed to speak to their children again. If marriage was what they wanted, then Harry would call upon Francis at once.

'But if he's lukewarm,' said Francis honestly, 'you can warn him off. I'm in no mind to lose our Ada anyway, and she'll have plenty of choice.'

They parted civilly, and Francis returned to Beech Green with a more contented mind.

But for Dolly, this family row had particular significance. On the fateful night when the storm had broken Dolly crept to bed, praying that Ada would be asleep or content to lie silent. She herself was in such a turmoil of doubts and fears that she craved nothing but the unconsciousness of sleep.

But Ada was awake and in an ugly mood. She lay in bed watching Dolly undress by the light of a candle.

'I suppose you're glad I've been found out?' she said, speaking low so that their parents would hear nothing through the thin wall which divided the two rooms.

'Ada!' cried Dolly, cut to the quick.

'Ada!' mimicked her sister in a spiteful squeak. 'You know you were watching us – sneaking along on your bike! I saw you!'

'I couldn't help it–' began poor Dolly.

'And I bet you told mum as soon as you got home, that I wasn't sorting stock. Wanting to make me out a liar.'

'And are you?' asked Dolly, with a flash of spirit.

'Yes, I am then,' said Ada defiantly. 'You're driven to it in this mean rotten place. And I don't care! When you're in love you'll do anything!'

Dolly was shocked into silence. With trembling hands she hung the last of her clothes on the back of the chair, blew out the candle, and slid into her cold bed. The dreadful words beat in her brain – words all the more sinister from their sibilant whispering. 'When you're in love you'll do anything!' Lie to your parents? Shout abuse at them? Attack your sister with false accusations? Was this what love did to you?

She remembered Mr Waterman reading poems about love to his callous young pupils. Surely he had told them that love was ennobling and fired people with all that was good and beautiful? Love had not done that to Ada, it seemed.

She summoned all the courage and calm she could amidst the tumult and the darkness, and spoke pleadingly.

'Ada, you don't really mean that. You're just upset. Try to go to sleep.'

Ada gave a hard, harsh laugh. It sounded like the cackle of a jay in the dark room, and it sent shivers down Dolly's spine.

'Don't you soft-soap me! You're a sneak, and I know it. And I mean every word I say. What do you know about being in love anyway? You only got me into trouble because you're jealous – and that's the honest truth, Dolly Clare!'

The vicious whispering ceased as Ada thumped over towards the wall. Exhausted with emotion she fell asleep almost immediately, but Dolly lay appalled and icily awake until the dawn came.

During that long terrible night she came to realize that the rift which had been widening so steadily between Ada and herself was now too wide for any successful bridge. Gone were the days when Ada was always right, when Ada led and she followed, and when Ada - the bright, the beautiful, the brave - could count on her adoration and obedience.

Nothing would ever be quite the same again. The words had been said, the cruel blows given. Dolly felt that even if she could come at last to forgive, she could certainly never forget.

She fell into sleep as the cocks began to crow, and woke, two hours later, leaden-eyed, to a world which had lost some of its brightness for ever.

14

Looking back across the years, as she lay half-dozing in the sunny garden, old Miss Clare marvelled that she should remember that wretched night so clearly. Was it true, she wondered, that she had been jealous of Ada's popularity with the young men? She had not realized it at the time. She had been furious and severely shaken by Ada's spite. But was there an element of truth there which the youthful Dolly unconsciously recognized? Certainly her interest in boys was remarkably small at that time, Miss Clare remembered, and smiled to think of her first 'walking out', which occurred a little before Ada's escapade.

It was, not surprisingly, with Emily's brother Albert. He was now a corporal and a very fine figure in uniform.

When he came home on leave the family made much of him. Mrs Davis, all passion spent, was now proud to show off Albert in his khaki, and basked in the congratulations of her neighbours when he accompanied her about the village or took her shopping in Caxley.

He was a quiet, happy boy, pleased to be back in the over-crowded cottage but secretly a little lonely when the rest of the family were out upon their various ploys during the day. He wandered round Beech Green, leaning on a gate here and there to chat with men gardening or women hanging clothes. He stopped to talk to old school-mates, as they cut back hedges or turned the plough at the end of a long furrow, and felt mingled pride and guilt at the envy which he saw in their eyes.

'It ain't all beer and skittles,' he assured his questioners, almost apologetically. 'Sometimes I reckons you chaps has the best of it.' But he knew he was not believed. To the stay-at-homes, he had the glamour which a uniform and travel give.

To have some purpose for his meanderings, Albert frequently

strolled towards Fairacre to meet his
sister and Dolly on their way home
from school. He was fond of them
both, and a little sorry for Dolly,
whom he considered overshadowed
by Ada. If he had been bolder he
might have approached Ada himself,
but he knew that she was besieged by
young men, and was afraid that he
might be rebuffed. He felt safe with
Dolly, and asked her one day if she
would like to go to Caxley with him

on the next Saturday. Somewhat surprised, Dolly agreed.

It was all very innocent and pleasant. They cycled together to the
town, Albert on Emily's bicycle. It was a blue and white March day
of strong sun and wind. Dolly bought some crochet cotton and a
new hook, a pound of sprats which her mother wanted, and two
ounces of cabbage seed for her father. Albert accompanied her into
the shops, watching gravely over her purchases, and buying some
cold wet cockles in the fishmonger's as a present for the Davis
family's supper.

The fish was put into a small flat rush bag which was secured
with a skewer. As the afternoon wore on it grew dark with damp-
ness and decidedly smelly, but the two were in great spirits and felt
very daring as they took their burden into a tea shop in Caxley
High Street and Albert ordered ices.

'What would you like to do?' asked Albert, as they tinkled their
spoons in the glass dishes.

'I don't really know,' said Dolly truthfully. 'I mustn't be too late
because my bicycle lamp isn't right and anyway I want to wash my
hair when I get back.'

Albert looked a little relieved. He had been wondering if he could
afford to take Dolly to the show in the Corn Exchange put on by
the local Nigger Minstrels. It might have been good fun, but they
would have been late back, and Albert was not sure if his parents
and Dolly's would have approved. Perhaps another time, he told
himself vaguely.

'We'll have a walk in the park,' he said firmly, and called for the bill.

The daffodils were in bud, and they sat on a bench with the fish bag oozing gently beside them. Albert rested his arm along the back against Dolly's thin shoulder blades, and finding that she made no demur, shifted a little closer.

Dolly's silence stemmed from surprise rather than shyness. She did not have the heart to tell the young man that she was very uncomfortable. Albert's arm gave her a crick in the small of the back, and he was sitting heavily on the side of her skirt. Dolly doubted if the gathers would hold at the waist, as the material was rather worn. She leant a little towards him in order to minimize the strain and found Albert, much encouraged, tipping her head to rest on his shoulder.

Her discomfort now was considerable. His epaulette was stiff and dug into her cheek, and her neck was strained unbearably. A cold hairpin, sliding from her rumpled bun, lodged inside her collar and added to her troubles. Albert took her hand and held it very tightly and painfully in his own.

They sat there in silence with a chilly wind blowing round them. A bed of early wallflowers competed unsuccessfully with the damp fish bag for their attention. Dolly, squinting sideways at the daffodils, found her view impeded by Albert's neck and was interested to observe how much larger his pores were than her own. It was a decidedly clean neck, she noticed with approval, and the lobe of the only ear she could see had a healthy glow.

At last cramp began to invade her left foot, and feeling that she could bear no more, Dolly struggled into an upright position. There was a cracking sound, but whether of gathers or stiff joints Dolly could not be sure, and then the two smiled upon each other, Dolly with relief and Albert with affection.

'It's getting very cold,' said Dolly gently.

'Best be cycling home,' agreed Albert, collecting the fish bag.

They pedalled home companionably in the twilight, talking of this and that, but making no comment on their prim embrace on the park bench. Only when they stopped at Dolly's gate were future plans mentioned.

'Will you write to me sometimes when I'm away? asked Albert, looking very young as he screwed and unscrewed Emily's bicycle bell.

Of course I will,' said Dolly warmly.

'And come out again perhaps?' continued Albert.

'Thank you,' said Dolly, a little less warmly.

'Good,' said Albert, and looked as though he might lean across Emily's bicycle and peck her cheek. At that moment Francis Clare opened the door of the cottage.

'Got my cabbage seed, Doll?' he called cheerfully.

'Goodbye,' said Dolly hastily, 'and thank you for that lovely ice cream.'

Pushing open the gate, she trundled her bicycle towards the house. The lamp made a pool of light round her father's familiar figure in the doorway. It was good to be home.

This incident, touching and absurd, had no real sequel for Albert's leave ended very soon after. But Dolly kept her word and wrote occasionally telling Albert about the doings of Beech Green and Fairacre. Her letters were beautifully penned; no blots, crossings or spelling mistakes marred their exquisite pages, and their subject matter was as blameless, for Dolly had no stronger feeling than friendship for the young man and was too honest to pretend that anything more was felt. After some months the letters between them grew less and less frequent, and Dolly heard of his engagement to a girl in Colchester, some time later, with genuine pleasure and some relief.

Meanwhile, Ada's love affair gave Dolly food for thought. After his interview with the publican, Francis tried patiently to get some sense from his defiant daughter.

'I've told you and told you,' said Ada obstinately. 'We're going to get married whatever anyone says.'

'But what if he doesn't want to?' queried Francis. 'Takes two to make a marriage, and he ain't bothered to come and speak to me about it yet, has 'e?'

'Looks to me,' commented Mary, in support, 'as if you're throwing yourself at him. That's no way to go into marriage, Ada.'

'Why should he come here to be picked over and found wanting?' demanded Ada belligerently. ''Twon't do no good to either of us, as far as I can see.'

They could get no further with her in this mood. Francis was perplexed. He disliked the idea of pursuing this young man, but if he refused to come and see him then he supposed he must make some effort to find out the fellow's intentions if Ada's happiness was involved.

'Dammit, Mary!' he sighed to his wife. 'Girls is a darn sight more trouble than boys when it comes to wedding 'em.'

He waited a fortnight, but nothing happened. Ada continued to see the young man, and, short of locking her in her room, Francis felt he could do nothing about it. At length he went again to Caxley and had an uncomfortable session with the publican, his wife and their son.

The young man was ill at ease, but assured Francis that he wished to marry Ada. Harry Roper did not impress Francis. He was thickset, with a surly expression, and had the heavy, dark, good looks which would soon coarsen with corpulence. Francis was amazed that Ada was attracted to him.

There was no doubt, however, that she would be well provided for. Jack Roper, the publican, also had an interest in a flourishing market garden, and he proposed to set up the young couple in a small greengrocery business in the town as a wedding present. So far, he knew, Harry had failed to remain in any job longer than a year. Marriage, and a business of his own, he hoped, would settle his son permanently. At twenty-five he should have sown all his wild oats, and it was time he turned his attention to domesticity and the raising of a family. The Ropers, for their part, liked the lively girl who seemed so determined to marry their son, and felt sure she had the power and energy to direct both her husband and the business.

The Ropers were invited to the Clares' cottage. The two families exchanged civilities, the engagement was announced, and the marriage arranged for the autumn. Mary seemed pleased with matters, but Francis had a heavy heart. It was not what he wanted for his best-loved child.

There was a triumphant excitement about Ada, throughout the weeks before the wedding, which Francis found distasteful.

'She feels she's got the better of us all,' he confided to Mary. 'But what does that matter if she's not truly happy herself? And do that young Harry really want her?'

It was Mary's turn to calm fears this time.

'Our Ada's always known what she's about, and she's chose a solid fellow as'll see she's always comfortable. He loves her all right, never you fret,' she added casually.

Francis was not completely convinced, but this matter-of-fact attitude of Mary's gave him a little comfort. Presumably women knew best in these affairs.

But when he stood beside his glowing Ada before the altar, his misgivings returned. She looked so radiant, so young and so trusting in her white lace frock, standing beside that dark stranger whom he disliked. Behind her stood Dolly, pale and demure in blue, the only bridesmaid.

Francis gave Ada away, feeling as though part of his heart had gone too, and all through the wedding breakfast, which was held in 'The Crown', he felt cold and wretched. With the rest of the party he waved goodbye to the young couple as they drove off in a carriage to the railway station, and was ashamed to find that tears blurred his final view of them.

It was Mary who remained dry-eyed.

Dolly and Emily had just finished their four years' pupil-teaching at this time. Little Miss Taylor at Fairacre School now retired, and Mr Wardle suggested that Dolly might like to carry on. She was appointed as infants' teacher that September, and continued to cycle from Beech Green daily. Emily heard of a post, some miles away at a village on the south side of Caxley, which appealed to her. An aunt lived in the village and would put her up, and she would be teaching children from twelve to fourteen, which was what she had always wanted.

The two friends, who had seen each other daily for most of their young lives, missed each other sorely. They promised to write once a week, and they met occasionally in Caxley or whenever Emily managed to get home for a week-end. Without Emily and Ada, Dolly felt quite forlorn for several weeks that autumn.

But the interests at Fairacre and its school grew more absorbing as the months passed. Mr Wardle and his wife left the village, a year after Dolly began her teaching, and a new headmaster, called Mr Hope, came to live at the school house. He was a shyer, cleverer man than his predecessor, one who loved animals and flowers, and who wrote poetry with some skill and feeling.

Dolly liked him, and his vague young wife. They had one daughter, Harriet, a child of outstanding beauty and intelligence All three, Dolly thought, had charm and uncommon sympathy, but she missed the Wardles' splendid invigorating presence, the hearty good humour and the drive which was essential to stimulate the native laziness of the Fairacre children. She hoped that Mr Waterman's methods would not be repeated.

At first, all went well. Despite his delicate appearance and gentle ways, Mr Hope had the ability to catch the imagination of the children. He was more aware of the progress of the world than Mr Wardle had been. For Mr Wardle, Fairacre and its immediate environs offered all that was needed in interest and amusement. Mr Hope soon made his older children conscious of the exciting changes about them.

He told them about aeroplanes and the pioneers who flew them. He conjured up visions of air travel in the future for his open-mouthed, and slightly disbelieving pupils. With a poet's flair for words he described the great icy wastes at the farthest Poles of the earth, whose mystery and beauty were just becoming known and explored by brave men. He told them of Peary and Shackleton and of Scott, and he made his country children realize that adventure was still to be found.

In advance of his time, the schoolmaster recognized the power of topical news, and photographs from the papers were pinned on the walls to encourage an interest in matters of the day. He was adroit enough, too, to relate these national events to their own small world, whenever possible, and Dolly listened to him one April morning as he pointed out the splendours of a mighty new liner.

'And Mr and Mrs Evans at Beech Green are going to sail in her,' he told them. 'When they come back I shall ask them to come and tell us all about it.'

Dolly had heard that the Evanses were going abroad from Mr Davis, who was their gardener.

'Taking poor Miss Lilian,' he said, 'to see some famous doctor over there. They say he may be able to cure her. Cuts a bit out of your brain, he does, and many a poor soul's found his wits again that way.'

Dolly thought it was brave of the Evanses, to go so far, and hoped that the proposed operation would be successful, for Miss Lilian grew more pathetic yearly, and it was common knowledge that her ageing parents feared for her future when they had gone.

A few days later Mary Clare was delighted to find a picture

postcard on the mat. The postman rarely called at the little cottage, and a picture was far more exciting than a plain envelope.

She held it up for Dolly to see at the breakfast table.

'I call that real nice of Mrs Evans. Written just before they sail, she says, and she's never seen anything so lovely before. Hopes we are well, and Miss Lilian sends her regards.' Mary put the card face upward beside the bread board and peered closely at it.

'You can see the name quite clear,' she said excitedly. '*Titanic*!'

Three days later the village heard the news. The names of the Evans family were not on the list of survivors. It was a stunning blow.

Mr Hope took down the picture of the ill-fated ship, but could say nothing to the children at that time. He was as stricken as they were at the horror which had come so close to them.

The house stood with its blinds drawn for three weeks. The eldest son, known to the neighbourhood as 'Mr Bertie', then moved in with his wife and young family. With him came two or three servants who had been in his employ in London.

Mr Davis gave the Clare family the news.

'There's a new chap coming to be head gardener,' he told them. 'Seems a nice enough young fellow, if you like 'em with red hair, which I don't.'

'And what's happening to you then?' inquired Francis.

'Three times a week,' said Mr Davis, 'and it suits me. Getting a bit long in the tooth these days, and the family brings us in a bit. We'll manage.'

He made his way to the door and then turned to Dolly.

'Keep your eye out for that young chap,' he said, with mock solemnity. 'You can't miss that hair. Just like a sunset it is.'

He opened the door and was gone.

15

It was strange, thought old Miss Clare, that the *Titanic* disaster in the spring of 1912 had brought such unexpected happiness in its wake

Although, at this time, she was almost twenty-four years of age.

she had remained remarkably untouched by love. There were several reasons for this. By nature she was reserved, and in company she was an observer rather than a participator. Ada's tempestuous marriage had made her cautious, and circumstances did not throw many young men across Dolly's path. At home she found that her parents grew more dependent upon her for company, and she herself, tired after a day's teaching and the long cycle ride, was very content to stay at home during the evenings.

She had not been conscious of any gap in her life. Her work, gardening, reading, helping her mother with household affairs and writing to Emily, kept her occupied and happy at the cottage. She took part in the life of both villages, helping with socials and jumble sales, fêtes and church bazaars, and considered her life completely satisfying. She was all the more surprised, therefore, to find how overwhelmingly easy it was to slide into the state of love within a few weeks of Arnold Fletcher's arrival at Beech Green.

They first met when the young man called at the cottage with a message for Francis. Dolly was weeding, squatting down with her back to the gate, and did not hear him approach. She was startled by his voice, and struggled to her feet, much hampered by an old sack which she had pinned round her for an apron.

'You should kneel to weed,' said the young man, smiling upon her. 'It saves your back.'

There was no doubt about who he was. The bright auburn hair, which flamed above his pale bony face, identified him as the Evanses' new gardener. His eyes were of that true dark brown which is so rare in English faces, and they looked very kindly on Dolly's discomfiture.

After that he came often. He had an easy friendliness which disarmed Dolly immediately, and she felt happy in his company from the first. They found that they had much in common. His knowledge of plants and trees was deep, and unlike many gardeners, he was equally interested in wild growing things. He was an avid reader and a cricketer. Beech Green found him a reliable slow bowler and a swift-running fieldsman, and by the end of May he was playing regularly for the team.

Both he and Dolly enjoyed music and Arnold took great pride in a new phonograph which he sometimes brought over to the Clares' cottage. After much adjustment a hollow nasal voice echoed through

the little room: 'This is an Edison Bell record,' and after a short rushing noise, the music would begin. It all seemed miraculous to the listeners, and Dolly first became acquainted with Handel and Bach, whose music she was to love throughout her life, by way of Arnold's phonograph.

It was soon common knowledge in the neighbourhood that Dolly and Arnold were 'going steady', as the villagers said. There was general approval.

'About time that girl got settled,' said Mr Davis to his wife. 'Won't have time for much of a family if she leaves it much longer.'

'Nonsense!' snorted Mrs Davis. 'Who wants to begin a family at eighteen like I did? Dolly's got plenty of sense – and plenty of time too. I shouldn't want to see her with a long string like ours.'

'But I thought you liked 'em!' answered Mr Davis, somewhat affronted by this sidelong attack.

'Case of have to!' commented his wife shortly, pushing him to one side as she bustled by with a steaming saucepan. Mr Davis wisely held his tongue. No point in adding fuel to the fire, he told himself.

Francis and Mary both seemed pleased, but Dolly sensed that her mother's approval was not whole-hearted. Latterly, Mary's manner had been strange. She was at an age when women are the prey of moods and Dolly had tried to be understanding. She guessed that, unconsciously, Mary clung to her last remaining child, and it was this that caused her mother to be cool at times with the young man. Nothing was ever said, and the matter was small enough to be ignored. In any case, Dolly was so deeply happy that troubles could scarcely affect her.

They became engaged later that year. Arnold took Dolly to Caxley where he bought a delicate little ring which she had seen in the jeweller's window and adored at first sight.

'But it's a *regard* ring, Dolly,' protested Arnold. 'I feel more than *regard* for you!'

But that was the ring which she wanted, and as she turned it upon her slim finger admiring the ruby, emerald, garnet, amethyst, ruby and diamond which spelt out its message, she felt that no one could be so happy.

Soon afterwards, in the Christmas holidays, Dolly paid her first visit to London, on the way to meet Arnold's parents who lived in Norwich. She had been by train from Caxley to the county town on a few occasions, but to ride to Paddington was a real adventure, and to see the capital itself an even greater thrill. Very few of the older generation in Beech Green, and not many of Dolly's, had seen London, although they lived within seventy miles of it, for fares were expensive and there were very few holidays.

She and Arnold went by horse bus from Paddington to Liverpool Street. Dolly was appalled by the number of vehicles, most of them horsedrawn, but some motor driven. The speed and dexterity with which the bicycles moved in and out of the traffic made Dolly shudder, and she found the noise worse than Caxley on a market day. The streets too seemed very dirty, and she was interested to see how necessary crossing sweepers were as they brushed a clear way across the road for the ladies to use.

Dolly had never seen anything so enthralling as the ladies fashions in Oxford Street. She admired the wide hats tied on with veiling, the net necklets held up with whalebone which gave their wearers a haughty appearance, and the long sweeping skirts, held gracefully to keep them from the dirt, above neat buttoned boots. The journey to Liverpool Street passed all too quickly.

She was glad of Arnold's protection in that cavernous place of reeking smoke, hooting engines and hustling people, but once the sad poverty of the slums was passed she settled back to enjoy the different scenery of East Anglia. She never forgot her first sight of those wide wind-swept heaths and the magnificent avenues of the Norfolk countryside, with great clouds bowling in from the North Sea, moving like pillars of snow across the vast blue sky.

Arnold's parents were welcoming. They lived in a small crooked road in the shadow of the ancient cathedral. Dolly liked them at once, and was taken on a tour of relatives who lived in the city, and who proved equally friendly. She and Arnold spent three happy days in Norwich, and she grew to love the place more with every hour that passed.

When the time came to return to Beech Green, and the farewells were over, she stood at the train window and watched with regret the last of that lovely and lively city slide behind her.

Arnold, amused at her pensive face, put his arm round her comfortingly.

'We'll come again,' he promised. 'Lots of times.'

But Dolly never saw Norwich again.

Long engagements were common in those days, and Dolly felt no hardship in waiting for her wedding. It was an idyllic time, she thought. She saved as much as she could from her small salary, and bought and made many things for her future home. Friends presented her with linen and china, and Dolly found much satisfaction in her well-filled bottom drawer.

Emily, who was also engaged, to the son of a local farmer, was as busy and as happy as her friend. The two girls had plenty to talk about now when they met, and despite the major distraction of their future husbands, the weekly letters still passed between them. There were things, Dolly discovered, that one could only tell to Emily, no matter how dear Arnold might be, and their shared school experiences made a constant bond.

Fairacre School had its problems at this time which perturbed Dolly. In the January following her visit to Norwich, a tragedy had occurred in the headmaster's house.

Harriet Hope, the only child, had died from the same disease which had taken little Frank Clare. She had been a child of such unusual vivacity and beauty that the blow was all the more cruel. Mr Hope and his wife could not face the village for a week after the funeral, and Dolly coped alone with both classes, glad of the extra work and responsibility which kept her from dwelling on the loss of the attractive child.

When at last Mr Hope returned, he was a changed man. His vigour had gone, never to return, and his duties were undertaken mechanically. Worse still, he began drinking heavily, and frequently arrived in the schoolroom smelling strongly of liquor. It was not long before he began to make an excuse to leave the school soon after ten each morning, and could be seen making his way to 'The Beetle and Wedge'. He returned within half an hour just in time to mark the arithmetic he had set before his departure. But his marking pencil often wavered, and the smell of beer was most noticeable. It was small wonder that the older boys and girls winked and giggled at each other behind his back, and that the parents at Fairacre, torn between pity and indignation, wondered if they should report their schoolmaster to those in authority.

While Mr Hope was out, the door in the partition between the two classrooms was left open so that Dolly could keep an eye on both classes. She took to setting her babies some quiet work in their little desks, for during the headmaster's absence she knew she would have to make several visits to his room. Through the open door she caught glimpses of mischievous dumb show. One wag would pretend to swig from a bottle, another would clutch his stomach and roll his eyes in mock drunkenness, and these capers aroused titters from the rest of the children. It was a difficult time for Dolly, and she found it better to forestall this insolence rather than deal with its effects. Her presence in the room guaranteed good behaviour, for most of the children had been in her hands only a year or two before, and young though she was, Dolly's tall dignity commanded respect.

The babies suspected nothing, and were content to set out their counters and attempt the simple adding up and taking away sums displayed on the blackboard in Miss Clare's clear hand. Sometimes, during those quiet periods when she walked the length of Fairacre

School with all its young scholars in her care, Dolly grieved for the tragedy which was being enacted around her.

Standing at the narrow Gothic window, she gazed at the dazzle of fruit blossom in the school garden, and the grandeur of the elms against the sky. She could see the roofs of the village, the blue smoke spiralling against the background of the distant downs, as blue as the smoke itself. It was appalling to think that a man could throw away such beauty and the security of a home and congenial work for the sake of drink.

That sorrow had driven him to it, Dolly knew well. That same sorrow had broken his wife's health and this added to his own misery. But Dolly could not understand why he gave way. He had so much to lose, and to her mind, there was so much around him to offer comfort and sanity. The countryside alone offered untold blessings of sight, sounds and scent. He had the affection and, till recently, the respect of the children and their parents, and a fine gift of teaching. His conduct was incomprehensible to young Dolly.

What Dolly failed to recognize, because of her inexperience, was that she judged Mr Hope by her own standards. She had a calm wisdom beyond her years, and the ability to stand aside from a problem and assess it rationally. No matter how troubled her heart might be, as it was at the unaccountable attack on her by 'the marsh' boy so many years before, or by the death of Frank or by Ada's sudden vituperation, yet her head took command and dictated the course to take through stormy waters. That a man might be engulfed by the storms, and finally shipwrecked, simply through lack of judgement, was a state of affairs which Dolly could not imagine.

Nor could she realize the state of despair to which a man might be driven so that he was impervious to the world around him. Dolly's quick eye and ear supplied her constantly with a succession of small delights – a field of buttercups, a child playing with an animal, the bubbling of a clear spring in the hedge, the flaming of Arnold's hair in the sunshine. That a man might be stricken deaf and blind with grief, and so be cut off from the mercies of nature's healing, was beyond the girl's understanding, at this time.

After some unhappy months, matters improved a little, for the morning absences ceased and Mr Hope remained on duty It was common knowledge that the vicar, who was chairman of the managers of the school, called upon the headmaster one evening and remained in his house for nearly three hours. After this warning, 'The Beetle and Wedge' saw Mr Hope no more, but he did not stop drinking. He and his wife went out less and less in the evenings. Failing health, and shame at her husband's condition, kept Mrs Hope house-bound, while despair drove Mr Hope to the bottle, which led only to further despair.

So the sad state of affairs drifted on, and it was lucky that Dolly had so much happiness in her love for Arnold and in the bright world around her that she was able to work by the side of the pathetic headmaster of Fairacre School with constant cheerfulness.

An added joy, in the early summer of 1914, was the birth of Ada's first child. Despite her robust good health, Ada and her husband had waited six years for a son, and three miscarriages made them wonder if they were doomed to have no family.

Dolly and Arnold went to Caxley one evening to see the new baby. Harry Roper let them in the door by the side of his shop. The greengrocery business was doing well and, as his father had hoped, Harry had settled down well with his young wife. It was quite apparent, though, that in spite of her youth Ada ruled her husband. It was she who urged him to buy a smart horse and cart and to employ a good-looking young man to drive it on a round. Harry would have been content to let customers come to him. Ada saw that 'H. Roper – Caxley's Finest Greengrocer' went further afield.

Dolly suspected that it was not a very happy marriage. Prosperity had thickened their figures and lined their brows. Harry's native indolence needed to be scourged by Ada's nagging tongue. Material success meant the vindication of her early rebellion to Ada, and she intended to show the world that the Ropers had succeeded. It was an attitude which jarred on the unworldly Dolly, but on this May evening she rejoiced that her sister and brother-in-law should have a new and unifying interest.

Ada lay in a vast brass bedstead, her son in a beribboned cradle at her side. Dolly had never seen her look so pretty.

'Well, there's your nephew,' said Ada, nodding to the swaddled infant. 'And your godson, too, if you like the idea.'

Dolly was much moved. She picked up the warm bundle and

looked at the tiny crumpled face among the shawls. It was more than she had ever hoped for, and it meant a new and happier relationship with Ada which she welcomed gladly.

'There's nothing I'd like more, Ada,' she said softly. The two sisters looked at each other with a sympathy and affection which had been lacking for years. It was as though they were children again, sharing the joy of a precious new present.

'We're going to call him "John" after Harry's dad,' said Ada, at last. 'And "Francis" after our dad. We'll have him christened at Beech Green when I'm up and about.'

It sounded perfect, Dolly told her. She returned the sleeping baby to its cradle, kissed Ada with warmth, and made her farewells.

Arnold, cycling home beside her, noted his Dolly's glowing looks and attributed her happiness to the new nephew. It was good to be looking forward to their own marriage later this year, he thought, for Dolly was now twenty-six and it was time they began a family of their own.

But Dolly's thoughts were of the past rather than the future. In those few minutes with Ada it seemed that some of the comradeship of their childhood had been regained. In the long look which had passed between them, Dolly recognized the old Ada she had always loved, and believed that that brief vision was a happy augury for the future.

16

The marriages of Dolly Clare and Emily Davis were planned for the autumn. There were practical country reasons for this, for Edgar, Emily's young man, would have helped his father to get in the harvest by that time, and could be spared for a few days for the less important job of marrying and taking a short honeymoon.

Arnold, too, would be particularly busy in the Evanses' garden in September, and the cottage promised them by Mr Bertie would not be vacated until Michaelmas Day. He had promised to get the decoration and repairs done immediately, and the young couple expected to be able to live in their first home towards the end of October.

Dolly was so engrossed with household plans and the making of her trousseau that she took little notice of the newspapers and the talk of troubles abroad. She was vaguely aware that a foreign Archduke, with the same name as her father's, had been shot, in a country whose name meant nothing to her. She heard her father talking to a friend about it in the garden one hot June evening, but she was bent double, with her hands thrust among the thorns and fruit of the gooseberry bushes, and her attention was otherwise engaged. This would be the last time, she told herself, that she would pick the crop to bottle for her mother. Next year she would be picking in the Evanses' garden and the fruit jars would stand upon her own white shelves.

All through July, as Dolly spent her last few weeks at Fairacre School, trouble brewed far away. She heard Mr Hope talking to the boys and girls about Germany and her military power. At home Arnold and her father shook their heads, and the names of Sir Edward Grey and the Tsar of Russia and the Kaiser and Crown Prince flew back and forth across the room. Dolly was too happy to worry about such far-off affairs, and it was not until the first day of August that Dolly realized that her own small world might well be shattered by a great explosion outside. It seemed, suddenly, that everyone spoke of Belgium – Belgium's neutrality, Belgium being overrun by the Germans, Belgium who must be helped.

'We wouldn't go to *war*, would we?' asked Dolly, much shocked, one Sunday morning. Arnold had cycled to Caxley for a paper, and it was spread out upon the table with all four grouped around it. The headlines said 'Germany declares war on Russia', and on the same page were the words 'Bank rate rises to 10 per cent.' It all seemed incomprehensible to Dolly, but from the gravity of the men's expressions she realized that calamity was threatening.

'It'll be France next,' said Arnold quietly. 'And we'll have to go in.'

'That be damned,' answered Francis robustly. For him still the French were the enemy. Hadn't his mother told him Bony would get him when he was a boy, even though the Frenchman had been dead for years? Tradition dies slowly in the country, and the idea of spilling his blood for a parcel of Frenchies did not suit Francis Clare.

'And what about Belgium then?' asked Arnold.

'Oh well,' said Francis roundly, 'that's a different kettle o' fish. If the Kaiser steps in there, he's for it.'

'Comes to the same thing,' said Arnold laconically.

In two days' time Arnold's words were proved true, and Dolly, with mounting horror, watched the enthusiasm which greeted Britain's entry into the war. Just as, faced with Mr Hope's tragedy, she deplored his rejection of reason, so now in the world-wide dilemma she was appalled to think that no settlement could be reached between nations except by the idiocy of war. She tried to talk about it to her mother, but Mary shrugged her shoulders, and dismissed the subject with:

'It's the men, dear! They govern the country, and they knows what's best.'

When Dolly retorted that it was a pity they did govern then, if that was what they thought best, she was teased by her father and Arnold.

'Our Dolly's turning Suffragette! Votes for women!' they cried. And Dolly smiled and remained silent, for she knew it was useless to try to explain the fire, kindled by injustice and deep feeling, which burnt within her.

The summer holidays had begun and Dolly had time to think of things. She had planned to return and teach for a few weeks in the autumn term before getting married. On marriage she was obliged to give up her post, for no married women teachers were employed in that area. She was looking forward to earning a little more money before her enforced resignation, to put towards the many expenses of their new home.

Now these long-settled plans were thrown into confusion. Within a week of the declaration of war, Mr Bertie, who was in the Army Reserve, left to join his regiment, and his wife announced that the house would be turned into a hospital. She explained to Arnold that his cottage would be available if he should need it in October, but it was quite clear that she imagined that he too would be in the Army by that time. In this she was right.

Dolly and Arnold discussed their future long and earnestly. Lord Kitchener's appeal for half a million men had gone out, and Arnold was determined to become one of Kitchener's Army without delay. Dolly, though sad at heart, could not help admiring his single-mindedness. He looked upon the war as a great adventure, and something more – a crusade against the evils of subjection. She did all in her power to make his going easier. It would have been wrong, and also impossible, to deflect him from his purpose.

At first, immediate marriage seemed the right thing, but after some cooler thoughts they decided against it.

'It's best if you carry on with your teaching,' said Arnold, 'while I'm away. Something to stop you from fretting. We'll get married a bit later, say, after Christmas. It'll all be over by then, they say, and we can settle down without parting.'

It seemed sensible, and Dolly agreed. And after all, it was only a few months, and maybe Arnold would worry less about her if she were still under her parents' care. Sadly and bravely, the young couple rearranged their lives, and neither spoke of the possibility of mutilation or death, for it barely entered their thoughts.

The next day Arnold and a dozen other young men drove into Caxley to the recruiting centre. Dolly never forgot that summer morning. Harold Miller, son to the man who had let Francis have the cottage so long ago, held the reins at the front of one of his own farm waggons. He was a lusty red-faced man in his thirties, grinning broadly on this unforgettable morning, and thoroughly enjoying the thought of excitement ahead.

The waggon was freshly painted bright blue, with red wheels. Two massive black carthorses pulled it, their coats shining like coal and the brasswork of their harness jingling and gleaming in the sunlight. Two small Union Jacks fluttered from the front of the waggon, and Harold Miller had decorated his whip with red, white and blue ribbons that fluttered in the breeze. It was a brave, gay turn-out, which matched the spirits of the young men riding aloft, and the villagers waved enthusiastically when it descended the long slope of the downs and stopped at Beech Green to collect the recruits.

They were all dressed in their Sunday suits. White collars, or clean white mufflers, showed up the sunburnt country faces, and Dolly thought that they looked as fine a body of men as any in England. They glowed with good health and eagerness. Normally as quiet and docile as the powerful horses in front of them, the thrill of war had woken them to life. Ahead lay adventure, the unknown, hazards to face and battles to win. Now they would see, as such lucky chaps as Albert Davis had seen, foreign parts and foreign ways. They would exchange the confines of home for a limitless new world, and at the heart of each of them lay the encouraging certainty that they were fighting for a right and proper cause.

Dolly, with a pang, thought that Arnold had never looked so happy as at that moment. His red hair glowed above his sun-tanned face. He had one arm round his neighbour's shoulders, as the great waggon rumbled away from the waving crowd, and looked as though he were one of a band of brothers, each as exulting and purposeful as he was himself. She remembered old Mr Davis's words so long ago. No woman could ever know completely the whole of a man's heart.

All through August, Dolly and her mother went several times a week to Caxley Station to help to distribute cups of tea and sandwiches to the troops, who passed through in their thousands to Southampton. Thanks to the British Fleet, the Expeditionary Force was ferried safely across to France in the ten days between 7 and 17 August. Dolly was told that this meant that a hundred and sixty thousand men were carried during that time, and sometimes, it seemed to her, the majority must have come through Caxley Station.

Hot and tired, she cut bread and butter, sliced meat, mixed mustard, tended urns and milk jugs, and carried trays up and down the length of the packed trains in the broiling heat. But she forgot her minor discomforts in the warmth of the welcome she was given by the men. Most of them had been travelling for many hours, but their spirits were as unquenchable as their thirst. To Dolly they looked unbelievably young in their khaki uniform, and had the same air of gaiety that Arnold wore. She waved to each departing train, a long, long monster fluttering with a thousand hands, until it disappeared round the line which curved southward to the sea. Then she hurried back to the trestle tables to prepare for the next train load which would follow so soon after.

Emily helped too, and sometimes Ada left her baby, and spent an afternoon at the station. Harry had also volunteered for service and was now busy putting the shop into order, before he was called up, so that Ada could run it easily in his absence. Arnold and the others who had jolted to Caxley in the waggon, awaited their call-up impatiently, carrying on with their jobs in a fever of suspense. Suppose it should all be over before they arrived?

They did not have long to wait. As news of the retreat from Mons came through at the end of August, Arnold and his friends were sent to a training camp in Dorset.

'It won't be for long,' Arnold promised her as they said goodbye. 'You look out for a nice little house for us to go to after Christmas. We'll have the Kaiser squashed by then.'

He echoed the general feeling of optimism. Despite the ugly sound of the retreat from Mons, it was only a set-back, people told each other, and a chance to prepare for a resounding blow at the enemy. Britain was the greatest country in the world, supported by the mightiest Empire ever known – it was unthinkable that such power could be beaten. Francis and Mary, and many like them, remembering the display of might at Queen Victoria's jubilee, could see no possibility of defeat at the hands of mere foreigners. Dolly had private doubts, but was glad of the robust spirit around her.

At the end of November Arnold had a short leave before going to the Western Front. He was thinner than before, but his face glowed with health and high spirits. He was more gentle and loving than Dolly had ever known him, refused to let her show any hint of sadness, and forbade her to accompany him to Caxley Station on the evening of his return.

She walked slowly with him, in the early twilight, along the road to Caxley, and they stopped beneath a sycamore tree to make their farewells. The bare branches seemed to stretch kindly arms above them, as if in blessing, and at their feet the winged seeds lay on the wet road, a sign of hope and life ahead.

He put a little packet into her hand before taking her in his arms. It was only then, and for a brief moment, that Dolly caught a glimpse of something more than resolute gaiety in his mien. For that one telling second, darkness came into his eyes, a weary hopelessness shadowed his face, as though he knew that he was powerless in the grip of the fates.

Their faces were cold as they kissed, and Dolly's throat ached with the effort of controlling her tears. But when they finally parted Arnold's smile was as warm as ever. He took his cap from his head at the bend of the lane and waved it cheerfully. His fiery head shone with the same bronze glow as the winter sun's slipping below the shoulder of the downs behind him.

When he disappeared from view, Dolly sank on to the damp bank among the writhing roots of the old tree, and let the hot tears fall. She made no sound, but sat hunched silently, tasting the salt drops as they ran over her mouth.

When at last it was dark, she rose to her feet, patting the comforting rough bark of the tree which had witnessed her grief. She never passed it again without remembering that evening.

In the quietness of her bedroom she undid the packet. It contained an oval locket made of gold threaded on a long gold chain. Inside was a photograph of Arnold and facing it a lock of his blazing hair.

She slipped the chain over her throbbing head, and by the wavering light of the candle, surveyed her blotched swollen face and the beauty of the locket which lay cold upon her breast. She was to wear it every day of her long life.

One February day of biting cold, Dolly returned home from school to find an incoherent letter from Arnold's parents, written on a flimsy half-sheet of paper, with the ink blurred by tears. He had been killed by a hand grenade lobbed into his water-logged trench near the Ypres Canal. Three other men had been killed instantly with him.

Dolly's first reaction was of stubborn disbelief. A flame as vital as Arnold's could not be snuffed out so easily. It was all a dreadful mistake. Why, she had had a letter from him only yesterday! She pushed the paper, almost impatiently, towards her mother.

It was Mary's anguished face which really convinced Dolly that the news was true, and later still the rare embrace of her sympathetic father. But for many days she was too numbed to cry. It was as though this tragedy had happened to someone else. She went, pale and dazed, about her daily life. She set work for the children, read them stories, bound up their broken knees and listened to their tales. Francis and Mary, Mr Hope, and all who knew her in Beech Green and Fairacre feared for her reason. There was an icy remoteness about her which frightened them into silence when she approached.

Even Emily had no power to thaw her. During those dark weeks she came daily to the Clares' cottage to do her best to comfort her friend.

'There's nothing you can do for me,' Dolly told her gently. 'Don't be sorry for me. I don't feel anything at all.' She was touched by Emily's staunch devotion and felt almost guilty that she should be so calm.

'Sometimes I think,' she told Emily one day, 'that my heart was killed at the same time as Arnold's. Only my poor dull head works now.'

It was a small incident a week or two later that snapped Dolly's chains and released her grief. Every morning she fed the birds which came to the doorstep of the cottage. Among them was a robin, bolder than the rest, who came so frequently that the Clares' cat ignored it. But on this particular morning the cat, who had been watching the proceedings from a window-sill, leapt suddenly upon the robin, killing it at a blow, and returned immediately to the window-sill where it yawned indolently.

Dolly was shaken with fury at this wanton attack. This robin had been hatched in the damson tree in the garden. She had watched its parents, day after day, feeding their young. Their efforts had brought up the little family, all of whom had gone, except for this one. The Clares had thrown him crumbs daily, and Francis looked for his company when he dug in the garden. His clear piping and bright eye had cheered the wretched winter.

That such abundant vitality should turn to half an ounce of dead feathers, with the stroke of a paw, was horrifying to Dolly. Tears of pity and rage shook her as she lifted the victim. Its breast was the same colour as the hair within her locket, and it was this that made her tears fall faster. Now the full realization of her loss gripped her. A blow as cruel and as senseless as the cat's had robbed Arnold of life and her of joy. The paroxysms of grief continued unabated all that day to be succeeded by a week of such black and hopeless despair that Dolly longed to die.

Only then did she understand the pitiful state of those who could find no comfort. She could understand now the depths of Mr Hope's despair, his rejection of a world which could offer him no solace. Never again, in her young arrogance, would she despise those who failed to interest themselves in the bright world about them. There was no bright world for those in the pit.

It was a long time before Dolly herself could clamber slowly from it and seek the light again.

17

The war ground on mercilessly. Now there was a grimmer spirit everywhere, for it was obvious that victory would not be easily won. Fighting was going on in all quarters of the globe, but it was the losses on the Western Front that meant most to the people of Fairacre and Beech Green, for it was there that almost all their men were fighting.

In April 1915, while Dolly still groped her way to normality, the new weapon of gas was used at Ypres, where Arnold's broken body shared a grave with ten others.

Dolly never forgot the horror with which she heard this news. It was followed almost immediately by a message from Emily's Edgar, who was out there.

Dolly was with her when his postcard arrived. It said starkly: For God's sake send me a gas mask.' Bewildered and shocked, the two girls looked dumbly at each other. What was a gas mask? Where could you buy one? How could you make one?

With no time to lose they fashioned a thick pad of cotton wool which they bound with tape, adding more tapes to tie it round the head. They tried it on each other, and in normal times would have laughed at the ludicrous sight. But it was too gruesome an affair this time for laughter.

They packed it up, with a hasty loving note from Emily, and Dolly and she cycled to Caxley to catch the last post. The lanes and fields were brushed with tender green, and the downs, ineffably peaceful, brooded over all. It seemed unbelievable to Dolly that, within hours, the parcel they carried so carefully would be in another world where there were no trees left, no birds to sing, but only grey mud, guns, and suffering men.

It was gas which ended Edgar's war service. At the end of May he returned to England, a gasping, coughing shadow, and was sent to a hospital on the south coast. For months Emily made the long anxious journey each week while the young man struggled back to life. It was now Dolly's turn to be of comfort, and she marvelled at the endurance of Emily's slight frame and the light of courage that shone in her clear grey eyes. Although she taught all the week at Springbourne, where she was now headmistress, and worked increasingly hard at home, she still undertook the week-end journeys with unfailing hope.

Dolly, at Fairacre School, thought how little the war had changed it. Unlike Springbourne, its headmaster had not gone to war. Mr Hope's repeated attempts to join up met with failure through ill-health. He could best serve his country by staying at his post, he was told. He grew shakier and more morose as time went on, and the morning visits to 'The Beetle and Wedge' were resumed. Dolly could not help hearing the gossip that flew about the village, though she herself preserved silence, steadfastly refusing to be drawn into discussions about her headmaster.

Two evenings a week she stayed late at the school with a party of local Red Cross workers. They sewed, knitted and packed parcels under the lamps swinging from the lofty roof, while the news of husbands and brothers and sons far away was exchanged. The women were extra kind to Dolly at this time. Her tragedy touched them, and they felt great admiration for her increasing care of the children.

'Carries that school along alone these days,' commented one.

'She's the one that should be head there.'

'They don't learn much after they've left Miss Clare,' agreed another.

Certainly Dolly had enough to do. The school was growing. A family of Belgian refugees contributed five more children, and there were several Londoners who had been sent to stay with local relatives to escape the bombing attacks on the capital. Dolly enjoyed their fresh outlook, and, remembering her own apprehension as a newcomer to Fairacre school, tried to make them particularly welcome. Now that so many men were away, far more women went out to work. A munitions factory on the outskirts of Caxley employed a number of Fairacre mothers, and Dolly passed them each morning as they cycled into work. To her mind, they looked happier and healthier cycling along together in all weathers, than they had when they were cooped up in their cottages. Many of them were tasting independence, and the pleasure of earning, for the first time in their lives. This emancipation would not be lightly thrown away when the war was over.

The food shortage, which so seriously affected the towns, was not apparent at Beech Green and Fairacre. Dolly was made aware of their good fortune one day when she was throwing maize to the chickens in Mr Hope's garden. A boy from London watched in amazement.

'We 'ad that for dinner up London,' he told her disapprovingly. 'My mum'd give you what for if she saw you doin' that.'

Dolly realized that the rebuke was a just one. Certainly they were short of such things as sugar and sweets, but corn, vegetables, fruit and even butter, were plentiful in the quiet little world of Fairacre. They had much to be thankful for, thought Dolly, beginning once more to find comfort in the work she loved, and the ever changing natural beauty about her.

Life could never be quite as sweet again. A vital part of her had died, it seemed, with Arnold's going; a part which beauty, work or the love of friends could not replace. But from these sources came a measure of comfort for which she was humbly grateful. She learnt, at this time, the invaluable lesson of finding happiness in little things, and by picking up small crumbs of comfort as she went about her daily work nursed her damaged spirit back to health.

In the summer of 1916 Dolly was looking forward to Emily's wedding. Edgar was still an invalid, at a convalescent home not far from his first hospital. Emily made her weekend journeys regularly, and the plans for the long-awaited marriage were all ready. One of the farm cottages was waiting for them and Edgar was expected to return to light duties on the farm at Michaelmas time.

The two young women spent many evenings together making curtains and covers for the new house. Dolly's pleasure in the preparations was occasionally clouded by her own sense of loss, but she was careful never to let Emily know her feelings. She was sincerely glad for her friend, she was fond of Edgar, and looked forward to being a frequent visitor to the little home when they had settled in.

One sunny evening she had arranged to meet Emily at the empty cottage to help her measure the floors for lino and rugs. Edgar's farm lay beyond Springbourne, in a wide valley, hidden by the swell of the downs from the villages of Beech Green and Fairacre, and hard by the larger farm of Harold Miller. As Dolly Clare pushed her bicycle up the steep chalky path from Beech Green she thought of the varying fates which war had brought to the men of that district. While Arnold lay dead, and Edgar broken, Harold Miller went from strength to strength, and had just been commissioned on the field, she heard, at Thiepval. He would be a gallant fighter, she felt sure, remembering his tough smiling face as she had seen it last as he drove his comrades to Caxley in the brightly-painted farm waggon. How many more would come back with just such honours, she wondered? And how many would share Edgar's and Arnold's fate? Accompanied by such pensive thoughts, she rode down the other side of the downs and made her way to the cottage.

The door was open, but there was no welcoming cry from Emily. Dolly stepped in and saw her sitting, dazed, upon a wide window-sill. In silence Emily handed her a letter. Dolly read it slowly in a shaft of evening sunshine which fell through the little window. The only sounds were the fluttering of a butterfly against the pane and the distant bleat of sheep on Edgar's farm. It said:

Dear Em,

I don't know how to tell you. I don't expect you to forgive me. But I can't marry you. There is a nurse here who looked after me all the time. I love her very much and we are getting married as soon as we can. I have tried to tell you before, but never managed it.

Em, I am sorry, but you will meet someone much better than me. I don't deserve you anyway.

Your loving,

Edgar.

Stunned, Dolly slid on to the window-sill beside her friend and put her arms round her. She held Emily's head against her shoulder. They sat in dreadful silence, while Emily's slight frame shook with sobs, and her tears made a warm wet patch on Dolly's print blouse.

After a time, Emily straightened up and looked dazedly about the room. She folded the letter carefully, tucked it into her wide belt, and stood up. She dried her eyes, smoothed her hair, and went from the empty room through the front door.

Dolly followed her, torn with grief and fearful for her welfare. The evening sun had turned everything to gold, and glinted on the key in Emily's hand.

Dolly watched her close the door of the house which was to have been her home. She turned the key resolutely in the lock and thrust it, with the letter, into her belt. Then she looked steadily at her friend. Her clear grey eyes were swollen with crying, but were as brave as ever. They lit with sympathy as they observed Dolly's stricken state, and she came to her friend and kissed her soundly.

'It's her house now,' she said firmly. 'Edgar's made his choice. I'll abide by it.'

Without a backward glance she mounted her bicycle and the two friends rode slowly, and with heavy hearts, back to Beech Green.

Dolly often thought, later, that Emily's lot was far harder than her own. She was fated to live for the rest of her life within a mile or two of Edgar and his wife, cloaking her feelings before all who knew the sad story. Public knowledge of one's affairs is a factor of village life which can cause annoyance. Sometimes it can cause tragedy, but sometimes it can be a source of strength. The sympathy which flowed to Emily, as a result of Edgar's marriage to another, did not show itself in words, but she was conscious of much kindness and was grateful for it.

Dolly never forgot Emily's reaction to this blow, and the turning of the key upon her hopes with such swift resolution. She had come to terms with the situation as decisively as she had so many years ago, when she had heard of Queen Victoria's death and saw in it a comfort to little Frank Clare, in a world unknown. It was her acceptance of fate, which Dolly admired. She seemed to bear no rancour towards Edgar, and refused to discuss his future wife.

'What use would it be,' she said one day to Dolly, 'to try and hold Edgar against his will? I don't want a marriage like that.'

But not many women, Dolly thought, would have felt that way. Some people wondered if Emily Davis were heartless, and if her love for Edgar had waned during the long months of waiting. But Dolly knew it was otherwise.

In the years that followed, Emily never passed the house that might have been her own, if she could help it. She would walk a mile further, along a winding lane, rather than take the steep path beside the cottage, and when, by chance, she and Dolly came across Edgar one day, resting beneath the sycamore tree where she had said goodbye to Arnold, Emily's sudden pallor told more than words, and the look in her eyes reminded Dolly of the stricken gaze of some dying animal. As she knew only too well, time would bring merciful relief from pain, but it would never cure the cause.

The visits of Ada and her children did much to cheer them all at this time. John Francis, Dolly's godchild, was a rampageous two-year-old when his sister was born, and Mary and Francis were the most indulgent grandparents.

Ada drove over in a smart governess cart from Caxley whenever she could spare time from the business. Harry seemed to be enjoying the war. He was fighting in Italy, and wrote cheerful letters home about the lovely country, promising to bring Ada there for a holiday when the war was over. His opinion of his Austrian enemies was low, and of his Italian comrades in arms not much higher, but he gave Ada to understand that Harry Roper was equal to coping with all difficulties. In truth, Harry quite liked his freedom again. His naturally buoyant spirits had been kept in check by Ada who had seen that any excess energy was harnessed to the business. Now he had a free rein, and Harry was to look upon his years with the army as one of the happiest times of his life.

Ada was now a very prosperous matron. Dolly marvelled at her extensive wardrobe, the children's expensive toys and the lavish amount of food which she generously brought to her parents' cottage.

Francis gloried in his Ada's success. Mary seemed less enthusiastic. It was the children that roused her spirits. It seemed as if she became young again when they tumbled about the cottage floor or called from the garden.

For all Ada's ostentation and finery, which jarred upon Dolly, yet she was warmly welcome. Despite the differences in temperament, the two sisters were fond of each other, and the children were a strong uniting bond. Harry's absence meant that the family saw more of one another. It was a comfort to Dolly to share the responsibility of her parents' care, and she hoped that Harry's homecoming would not sever the ties which had grown stronger during the war years.

At the beginning of November 1918, a jubilant letter came from Harry Roper describing the taking of an island called Grave di Papadopoli in the middle of the river Piave. He had helped to build bridges over which the Italians poured to victory, splitting the Austrian army in two.

'Now the way's wide open,' wrote Harry exultantly. 'With Austria down in the mud, we make straight for Berlin!'

The war news from all quarters was as cheering as Harry's. Mutiny had broken out in the German Fleet at Kiel, the Americans had cut the German eastern and western forces by taking Sedan, and the Allies were pursuing the enemy on the Meuse. The news that Foch was meeting German delegates, to arrange an armistice, sent the hopes of everyone soaring. On November 11, Harry Miller of Beech Green, with five other local men, entered Mons with the victorious British army, while the bells of that shattered town played 'Tipperary'. Early on the same morning the Armistice was signed, and fighting ended at 11 a.m.

In Caxley the rumours flew round that Monday morning. Someone said that the news had been telephoned to the Post Office. Flags began to appear on buildings and the bell ringers hurried to the parish church. But no official confirmation was forthcoming, and it was decided to wait a little longer. The market place and High Street began to fill with excited crowds.

At half-past twelve official confirmation of the Armistice was posted in Caxley Post Office and the town's suspense was over. The bells pealed out, the Union Jack was hoisted on the Town Hall and flags of all nations sprouted from roofs and windows. Monday's meagre war-time ration of cold meat was ignored while Caxley rejoiced.

At Fairacre, Dolly heard the news from Mr Hope, during the afternoon. One of the children had brought a collection of French and Belgian postcards to show her. His father had sent them regularly – beautiful objects of silk with fine embroidery showing flowers and crossed flags of the Allies. Dolly was holding them in her hand when Mr Hope burst into the room.

'It's over!' he cried, his face alight. 'The war's over!'

The babies looked at him in amazement. They remembered no other kind of life. War had always been their background. His excitement was incomprehensible to them.

He called the school to attention, told them the news and then gave a prayer of thanksgiving. School ended early that day, and Dolly rode home through the grey November afternoon with much to think about. Rejoicing, for her, was tempered by Arnold's loss, but she felt overwhelming relief at the ending of suffering and slaughter.

Now the sons and lovers, the husbands and fathers, would come home again, and the village would have young men to work in the fields and to laugh in the lanes. Now the girls and wives and mothers would find happiness, glad to have someone to share the joyful responsibilities of home life.

But not all. How many cottage homes, Dolly wondered, mourned today when all the world was gay with flags and bells?

Over forty years later, old Miss Clare felt her eyelids pricking at the memory of that distant day. She knew now the price that the parish of Beech Green had paid.

Twenty-six names were carved at the foot of the stone war memorial, now weathered to a gentle grey. In the neighbouring parish of Fairacre seventeen young men had died, so that over forty men had been taken from the thousand people who made up the population of the two parishes. Miss Clare had known them all, and could never be reconciled to their loss. She honoured the high ideals of sacrifice and patriotism which had illumined the path of these young men, but the tragic pity of it all overcame her other feelings.

In the years that followed, poetry became a source of joy and comfort to Miss Clare, but the loveliest songs sung by the young war poets who were her contemporaries, moved her so swiftly to weeping that she could not bring herself to read them often. 'The heartbreak at the heart of things', as one of them wrote, was too poignant for Miss Clare's generation ever to forget.

In the heat of the June sunshine Miss Clare's old fingers strayed to the locket. She bent her white head to look at it. It was thin and smooth with years of wear, and its glitter had mellowed to a soft golden sheen. But inside, the dear face of Arnold Fletcher was still clear and unlined, and his bright hair had no touch of grey. For Arnold and his comrades would never grow old.

18

Outwardly, Beech Green and Fairacre seemed to change little in the years after the war. Two bungalows were built on the road between the two villages, but no other new houses for some time. Most of the men returned to the villages, but some, unsettled by the last few years, took this chance of leaving the country and moving town-wards.

Harold Miller was now in charge of the farm at Springbourne, as his old father had died during the war. He found himself so short of men that he decided to sell several of his outlying cottages, including the Clares'. Francis was given the first chance to buy it for the sum of two hundred pounds. The family spent several evenings in earnest discussion, and finally decided to purchase it with the savings of a lifetime.

'Well, I never thought to live in a house of my own,' declared Mary proudly. 'Now we don't need to fret about paying the rent every week.'

'It's to be yours when we re gone, said Francis to Dolly. 'Ada's well provided for, and this place don't mean much to her, and never did.'

He looked through the leaded panes at the trim garden and Dolly saw the pride of possession light up his face.

'And if you was hard pressed,' he continued, 'you could always sell it. Or say you got married,' he added, somewhat doubtfully.

'We don't need to think about that for a good few years,' replied Dolly. 'You'll enjoy it for another twenty or thirty.'

Ada and Harry bought a house about the same time. Living over the shop, Ada said, was downright common, and if they didn't have a place on the hill on the south side of Caxley, like all the other people who had done well, their two children would never be able to hold up their heads. Harry, delighted to be back and to find a flourishing business and money in the bank, agreed readily. Within a year they were installed in a brand new house with HARADA in curly chrome letters on the oak-type front door.

Emily too had moved. She had been acting head teacher during the headmaster's absence on war service, and was appointed head when he moved to a larger school. A little house went with the post, and as her father had died, Emily persuaded her mother to leave the cottage where she had reared her thriving family and live at Springbourne with her. Mary Clare missed her good neighbour sadly, but sometimes made the long walk over the hill to spend an hour or two with her.

Fairacre school had its changes, too. Private warnings to Mr Hope had been of no avail. The man was now a physical wreck and the work of the school suffered badly.

One spring morning he came into Dolly's room looking vaguely bewildered.

'I'm leaving Fairacre,' he said abruptly. 'I had my notice this morning.'

Dolly was not surprised, but she was sorry that he was going. There were many things about the man that she liked, and change was always distasteful to her.

'The managers suggest that I have a holiday for a month or two,' went on the headmaster, 'and there will probably be a vacancy for me in Leicestershire.'

Dolly guessed that this opening must have been suggested by Miss Parr, one of the managers of Fairacre School, who had relatives in Leicester. Privately, Dolly thought Mr Hope was lucky to get anything. She suspected that he would have an assistant's post in the new school, and in this she was right.

He left at the end of May, and Dolly wondered who would be the next occupant of the school house. Fairacre School was very much bigger than Springbourne so that a man would be appointed. For the last few weeks of term Dolly and a woman supply teacher from Caxley coped with the school between them, and in September Mr Benson arrived.

The first thing that Fairacre noticed about the new headmaster was that he had a car and a wireless set. The car was a Ford T model with a beautiful brass radiator and brass headlamps, and the wireless set was the latest type with a superior gadget to hold the cat's whisker above the crystal.

'Go ahead sort of fellow,' commented Mr Willet to Dolly Clare. Young Mr Willet had been badly wounded during the war, and was making a modest living as caretaker to the school and by growing vegetables and plants for sale in his own flourishing garden. He was clearly impressed by the new man, and so were all the other males from six to sixty, Dolly observed, for such is the power of things mechanical.

He had other interests besides the car and the wireless set. He had served with distinction in the R N A S and had travelled widely. In the few years he was at Fairacre he reminded Dolly of Mr Hope in his younger days, for he had the power to fire his listeners with his own enthusiasm. He was a great supporter of the League of Nations, and tried to explain its world-wide task to the children who only knew the small world of Fairacre.

'There will never be another war,' he promised them, many and many a time. 'This war was the war to end all wars. Now we shall use reason to settle arguments between nations.'

He bought many magazines and papers for the children from his own meagre salary. He found that they read these far more easily than books. Arthur Mee's monthly *My Magazine* was a great favourite, and Dolly remembered the frontispiece to one of the issues very clearly. It showed a little girl, barefoot and in a pink tunic, opening the golden gates to a new world where all was peace. It was typical of the ardent hope of a war-shattered world. 'Never again!' was the cry, uttered in all sincerity.

The new world certainly seemed a happy place in the years that followed. Fairacre did not boast any bright young things of its own, but its inhabitants were pleasurably shocked to read about those who painted the big cities red. The *Caxley Chronicle* reported the dancing of the Charleston at the Civic Ball in the Corn Exchange, and some of the older generation felt that the age of decadence had arrived.

There was certainly an air of gaiety about which reached even to such leafy retreats as Beech Green and Fairacre. It was a daily wonder to wake to a world at peace, to know that one's menfolk were home again, that the guns thundered no more, and that life could be relished for the good thing it was.

An enterprising firm in Caxley started a bus service during the twenties and this made a world of difference to those living in remote villages. Twice a week, on Thursday and Saturday, it was possible to ride from Fairacre through Beech Green to Caxley by bus, and there to shop or meet one's friends, or even catch another bus to the giddy pleasures of the county town fifteen miles away. The older people, whose cycling and walking days were over, were enraptured by this new wonder, and Mary Clare became a regular passenger on Thursday mornings

'Proper old gad-about you're getting these days!' teased Francis, but he was glad to see Mary with this new interest. Now she could go to see Ada and the children much more often, and though she sometimes wondered if she were a nuisance to her daughter, the rapturous welcome she received from her two grandchildren consoled her It was true that Ada looked with mixed feelings upon the small shabby figure, in her old-fashioned button boots and jet-trimmed bonnet, which ambled up the gravel path, always, it seemed, when she had a party of genteel Caxley friends whom she was trying to impress.

Emily and Dolly found the Saturday morning buses very useful too They frequently met in Caxley to shop and exchange news over coffee Edgar was never mentioned, but Dolly knew that the marriage was successful and that he had two small children. How Emily felt about it she could only guess They were both in their thirties now, and often spoke good-humouredly of 'being on the shelf' Chances of marriage were very small, they knew, for their generation and Dolly counted herself lucky in having Ada's children in the family and all the young fry of Fairacre to work among Nevertheless, her sense of loss was great, for other people's children are a very poor substitute for one's own, and there were occasions when, at that sad time of day between sunset and twilight, Dolly could not bear to think of the long lonely years ahead.

It was during Mr Benson's period of headship that Mrs Pringle was engaged as school cleaner. This dour individual, who was 'never so happy as when she was miserable', as the villagers said, had lived in Fairacre since her marriage and worked for Mrs Hope at the school house. The shortcomings of Mr Hope and the decline of his wife had furnished Mrs Pringle with ghoulish interest. She had wanted to take over the school cleaning for several years, for the two great black tortoise stoves which warmed the building exercised a strong fascination over her, and she longed to apply blacklead and elbow grease to their neglected surfaces.

'Fair makes my blood boil to see the state that Alice got 'em in,' she grumbled to Dolly on her first day in office. Alice was the poor toothless old crone who had been taken from an orphanage at ten, set to work as kitchen maid for fifty years, first here, then there, until she drifted to a hovel in Fairacre and earned a few shillings by scrubbing the school floors and lighting the stoves. In all the years that Dolly had known her she had only heard her speak about a dozen times. She bobbed and nodded when addressed, a skinny hand fluttering to her mouth.

She had been found dead in her little broken cottage, rolled up in a thin grey blanket before an empty grate, a week or two earlier, and the neighbour who had lifted her said that she was lighter than his own two-year-old.

Mrs Pringle would have made six of her. A squat, square figure clad in a thick skirt and jumper covered with a vivid flowered overall, she stumped morosely about the premises grumbling at the mess made by the children and the amount of coke consumed by the stoves. She was to be part and parcel of the Fairacre scene for many years and Dolly Clare found it best to turn a deaf ear to most of the lady's complaints.

As time passed Dolly sometimes thought that she knew every stick and stone of Fairacre School. The grain of her desk lid, the knots in the wooden partition, the clang of the doorscraper and the sound of the school bell above her were as familiar to her as her own face and voice. Only the children changed, and now she taught many whose parents had once sat in the same desks. Miss Clare was becoming an institution. Would she ever leave? she asked herself.

Mr Benson left after five years, his successor left after seven, but Miss Clare remained at her post.

'She won't never go,' the parents said to each other. 'And a good thing too. Taught us all right, she did, and teaches our kids good manners, as well as sums and reading.'

She was looked upon with affection and with much respect. The years added dignity and authority to Dolly's upright figure. Her fair hair was beginning to grey a little, but her blue eyes were as bright and kindly as ever.

'Pity she never married,' she overheard her headmaster say. 'A bit late now, I suppose,' he added and Dolly echoed the sentiment.

It was not only age, but circumstances that kept Dolly at Fairacre. In the early thirties Francis collapsed one day, while he was digging in the garden. Doctor Martin surveyed him gravely. Mary and Dolly watched the doctor closely from the other side of the bed. He was an old friend, but they rarely needed to call him in professionally. This was an alarming moment.

'I'll call again in the morning,' he said at last, leaving Francis in a heavy sleep.

The next morning he was moved to Caxley hospital, and Mary was inconsolable. Dolly was obliged to have the week away from school to comfort her mother. They went daily to visit Francis, who lay very quiet and still, but smiled at them and occasionally spoke. He seemed very weak, and from Doctor Martin's manner Dolly guessed that this was her father's last illness.

One May evening she went alone, cycling along the scented lane. It had changed little since the first time she had driven along it behind Bella's massive bulk, but sometimes a car passed her now, where there was none before, and the main street of Caxley had more cars and lorries than horse-drawn vehicles these days. Her dislike of Caxley had changed over the years to affection. So much had happened to her there that it now seemed as much a background to her life as Beech Green and Fairacre.

Later, sitting beside her father's bed, holding his hand in hers peacefully, the feeling that she was part of Caxley stole upon her. How many other people had sat as she did now, or lay as her father did, gazing upon the trees outside that sheltered the nearby alms-houses? Caxley was the mother town to which all the surrounding villages turned. Here they came to work, or sent their children to school. Here they gathered when war broke out, or a queen died, or peace was celebrated. Here were the offices which dealt with rents and rates and other irksome matters which concerned them. And here was the hospital which took them into its shelter and restored them to health, or eased their going when life ebbed.

When she left her father that evening she made her way down a quiet by-road leading from the back of the hospital to the centre of the town. She felt curiously at peace, still sustained by the feeling of being at home in the town. A motor hearse overtook her and waited to slip into the main road ahead, leading to the market place. Four men, in sober clothes, sat beside the coffin on its way to the town undertakers. There was a decent restraint about their quiet bearing which Dolly admired. A right and proper way, she thought, to make one's last journey through familiar streets, flanked by companions, slipping along unobtrusively with schoolboys on bicycles and vegetable vans, as unremarked as any other part of the moving stream. If that was what fate had in store for Francis then she felt she could face it all the more bravely from having seen the passing of that unknown one who had walked the ways of Caxley as her father had done.

He died that same night and was buried three days later beneath a giant yew tree in Beech Green churchyard not far from little Frank. Mary was braver than Dolly had dared to hope. She went to stay for a few days with Ada, and the children's chatter and affection seemed to comfort her.

When she returned she seemed her old self. She sighed with relief at being back again, lonely though it was without the dear presence of Francis.

'Ada's is lovely,' she said to Dolly. 'Full of fine things, and hot water straight from the tap and that – but it don't seem homely to me. I'm happier here.'

Later that evening she looked across the table at Dolly, who sat sewing a shirt for John Francis.

'When you was born,' she said slowly, 'the old dame that was helping said you'd be a lucky child. She said: "That child be blessed and the day will come when you'll remember what I told you." Those were her very words, Dolly, and they've come true. You've been a real blessing to me – all my days '

Dolly was deeply moved. Her mother rarely showed emotion, and when, soon after, she kissed her good night, she felt that they had never before been quite so close.

Francis left very little. Almost all his money had gone to the buying of the cottage, but his thatching tools and those of his father were carefully stored in the garden shed. It was Emily who discovered a young man in Springbourne who wanted to take up a thatcher's craft, and to him Dolly and Mary gave the tools. He was a handsome lad, with a look of Frank about him, and it gave both women much happiness to think of Francis's tools being used again, on the same familiar roofs, by one of the next generation

19

Looking back upon those twenty years between the wars Miss Clare realized how great a change had taken place in the lives of her neighbours.

Very few of her mother's generation had been to London, or had seen the sea, although both were within seventy miles of the village She herself had not seen either until she was in her twenties. But with more and more cars pouring into the roads and with buses and charabancs increasing their services weekly, there were very few children in Miss Clare's class of babies who had not seen both before they were five or six years of age.

It made life much more wonderful and exciting. When you have been bounded by the limits of your legs, or bicycle wheels, there is something deeply thrilling about boarding a coach which will take you a hundred miles away. Dolly Clare never completely lost her sense of wonder at the miracle of modern speed. Holidays away from home were not possible on her small salary, but occasionally she took her mother on a day's outing to the coast, during the school vacations, and this was a rare joy for them both.

The children's annual outing was equally exciting. When Dolly was at Fairacre School as a pupil, and in her early teaching years a brake pulled by four horses had taken them all to Sir Edmund

Hurley's park just beyond Springbourne, and there five miles from home, they had felt that they were in a foreign land.

Another new joy was the occasional visit to the theatre at the county town. To be sure, the scenery was sometimes a little shabby and some of the acting mediocre, but to Dolly and her unsophisticated friends it was always an evening of enchantment.

Even more miraculous was the wireless. In its early days, soon after Mr Benson's coming to Fairacre, the children besieged Dolly's desk each morning to tell her what the invisible uncles and aunts in Children's Hour had told them the day before. And when, one unforgettable day, they heard 'Hello twins!' boomed forth in unison, for a pair who lived at Beech Green, their excitement knew no bounds. Sometimes, Dolly thought wryly, they seemed to learn far more from the wireless than they did from her. Would lessons ever be broadcast to the schools, she wondered?

In the little cottage in the evenings Dolly listened to concerts and satisfied that love of music which had first been fired by Arnold's wheezy phonograph. Mary's pleasure in it increased as the years went by, for her eyes soon tired of reading and sewing, and she found this new invention fascinating. There was no doubt about it, she told Dolly, life was richer by far than when she was a girl at the farm, creeping to her attic bedroom, lamp in hand, soon after darkness fell.

But despite the new wireless sets in cottage homes, and the new excitement of modern travel, things were still difficult for those employed in agriculture. Many of the children who clamoured round Dolly's desk, eagerly trying to tell her of last night's wireless programme, were thin from lack of proper food. The lot of the farmer, and, worse still, of the farm labourer, was as hard as it had ever been, and Dolly often wondered how long the land could support a fast-growing population. It was not enough to expect industry to pay for the foreign food that packed the little village shop at Beech Green and the rest of the shops in England. The farmer must be given hope and help to be able to contribute his share. It grieved Dolly to see the heritage of the countryside, held in trust for generations to come, being so sadly neglected.

For women a new interest sprang up during these years. The Women's Institute had a thriving membership at Beech Green and at Fairacre. Mary Clare was a keen supporter and acquired many new skills. Dolly was amused to see her proficiency at upholstery, and acted as unskilled assistant when her mother boldly re-stuffed and covered the ancient sofa and matching armchair. It was Dolly's job to pull the tough strings which drew the buttons into their allotted dimples, and very hard work she found it. But Mary seemed inspired by her new ability and from upholstery she progressed to making loose covers, going from strength to strength.

The years passed tranquilly. The spring term, bedecked with primroses and violets and loud with cuckoo song outside the school, and the remains of winter coughs inside, gave way to the pinks and roses of the summer term, arrayed in 'Virol' jars along the window-sills. Hips and haws and trailing bryony welcomed the autumn in, and new babies faced Miss Clare for the first time in their young lives. And always the highlights of the year remained the same – Christmas, Easter, Harvest Festival and the school outing and the church fête, held, as always, in the grounds of the vicarage.

To some women this familiar cycle would have proved stultify-ing. Dolly Clare saw nothing monotonous in it. She liked order, she liked knowing the pattern ahead. Within the framework of seasons' and terms' events she found variety and excitement enough. For one thing, no child was like its neighbour. More fascinating still to the elderly teacher, no child was exactly like its parents. There was something infinitely satisfying in comparing the generations of the families she knew so well. There were hereditary tendencies in looks or behaviour which were interesting to study. She knew too the background of the homes from which they came, which child went to bed too late, and which was frightened of its father and for what reason. She knew which child was jealous of a newly born brother, which one pined for one, which one resented being the youngest. There was nothing hidden from Miss Clare, as both children and parents knew, and better still, she could be trusted to keep confidences to herself. In a village a silent tongue is rare, and much respected. Dolly Clare heard many secrets, gave advice when it was asked of her, and found the study of character endlessly ab-sorbing. Life in Fairacre, she discovered, grew richer every year, and the slow measure that she trod there pleased her more than the giddy whirling of the world outside

★

The news from abroad, during the mid-thirties, was disturbing to say the least of it. The domination of Austria by the Germans, and Ethiopia by the Italians were ugly reminders to Dolly Clare of the happenings of twenty years before. Surely such appalling things could not happen again in a lifetime? She pondered on the spirit of hope which had transfigured the world at the end of the first war. Surely the League  of Nations could not fail? It had the support of all right-thinking men and women. It seemed stupid to worry over the childish posturings of Hitler and Mussolini when one considered the forces ranged against them.

So Dolly tried to comfort herself, but she was not completely successful. There was something terrifyingly insane about the statements made by the two dictators and Dolly trembled to think what might happen if they were allowed the time to gain further military strength. Arrogance unchecked becomes megalomania, and it is impossible to reason with a madman. Would the dearly-bought peace be shattered yet again?

That harbinger of doom, Mrs Pringle, prophesied war for many months before Munich, and at the time of that event spoke scathingly of the hopes of peace makers.

Dolly came across her before school one morning early in the autumn term of 1938. She was spreading newspaper round the newly whitened stone at the base of the stove in the infants' room. Crouched on all fours, in an unlovely toad-like position, she stabbed vehemently with a podgy forefinger at a photograph of Mr Chamberlain waving a piece of paper.

''Opeless!' announced Mrs Pringle. 'Just 'opeless, trying to deal with that Hitler fellow. My mother, God rest her, would have called this a sop to Cerebos. Mark my words, Miss Clare, we'll 'ave to pay for this all right!'

All through that uneasy year, when a nation's conscience grew more and more troubled as one German coup followed another, Mrs Pringle's dire prognostications were cast like black pearls before the surfeited swine. The headmaster at that time, Mr Fortescue, goaded beyond endurance one hot day in the summer of 1939, sharply told her to hold her tongue.

Dolly, washing a child's sticky hands in the lobby, heard the swift intake of Mrs Pringle's outraged breath. Then the floorboards resounded to the limping gait of Mrs Pringle's substantial frame. It was obvious that her leg, always combustible in times of affront, had 'flared-up' with unusual ferocity. She stumped through the lobby, looking neither to right nor left, mouth compressed and nostrils flaring.

Dolly put her head round the classroom door. Mr Fortescue was alone, scribbling a fierce note to a dilatory publisher who had failed to send some promised inspection copies.

'We shan't see Mrs Pringle again this term, I suspect,' she said.

'That'll suit me,' replied the headmaster grimly. 'It's only another fortnight anyway. At last we shall have some peace.'

Dolly was right. Mrs Pringle sent a stilted note which said that her leg was too inflamed to use, and she did not know when she would be back.

'That means,' said Dolly, construing the letter to her colleague, who had not the same experience of Mrs Pringle's warfare, 'that we must woo her back if we want the school scrubbed out during the holidays.'

'Oh, dammit!' expostulated Mr Fortescue. 'What an old vixen she is!' He looked doubtfully at Dolly.

'Yes, I'll go,' she offered, reading his thoughts, and on the last day of term she made a treaty with the enemy.

'It's only because his lordship's going away,' announced Mrs Pringle. 'Wild horses wouldn't drag me back inside that school if he was going to be prying about. You can tell him from me, Miss Clare, I'm coming to oblige you and because I knows my duty to the children!'

Dolly promised to deliver the message, wondering privately why Mrs Pringle's strong sense of duty to the children had remained quiescent for the past fortnight.

And so this petty storm, just one of many made by Mrs Pringle, passed over, while the storm that was to darken the whole world swept closer and closer.

At the end of August, a few days before Fairacre School, freshly scrubbed and polished, was due to reopen, the evacuation of children from London began, and Caxley and the villages around it awaited the newcomers.

Dolly and Emily went to Caxley station to help. As the long trains drew in to the platform, with heads and arms sprouting from the windows, Dolly remembered that other war, so tragically near, it seemed, when she had watched her own generation on its way to annihilation. Now these younger casualties of a new war emerged into the shimmering heat, pale-faced and heavy-eyed, clutching one another's hands and weighed down with gas masks and cases.

All through the long hot day Emily and Dolly helped to sort out the children, and returned to their own cottages with two apiece. Dolly had chosen two small sisters, June and Dawn Milligan, both tearful and bewildered. Emily, as bold as ever, had returned to Springbourne with a pair of black-haired twin boys of twelve who looked as tough and unmannerly as any among the hundreds who arrived. Dolly had no doubt that Emily would win any future battles. Her own family background and many years of teaching had given Emily a rare resilience.

On the next Sunday the Prime Minister was to speak to the nation. War looked inevitable, and Dolly and her mother sat down with heavy hearts to listen to the broadcast. The cottage door was propped open. Outside, the two little girls dressed and undressed the doll they had brought with them, and the ghostly Emily that Dolly had unearthed from the trunk in the loft. She was sadly shabby and her stuffing had shifted so that her figure was badly deformed, but the Milligan children took her to their hearts, and Dolly was glad to see poor Emily beloved once more.

The sunshine bathed the children playing by the door, and warmed the brick floor by Mary Clare's feet. The scent of tobacco plant stole into the room as they listened to Mr Chamberlain's voice. At last it came to an end. Mary and Dolly looked silently at each other, both fearful of breaking down before the unheeding children.

At that moment, the distant wailing of Caxley's air-raid sirens began to be heard, and close at hand the banshee clamour of Beech

Green's began too. The two children looked up at the cloudless sky with such pathetic terror in their faces, as they clutched their dolls to them, that Dolly's own fears were transformed to fury. It was insupportable that innocent children should have to suffer in this way – torn from their homes, set down among strangers and then forced to live in constant fear! Brave with the wrath that burned within her, she brought the two little girls indoors and calmed them, and when at last they were busy in the kitchen and the all-clear had sounded, Dolly's anger cooled.

In the last war, she thought, she had seen many men go into battle. This time the battle came to them – to all of them, women and children too. Everyone would be taking part in this war, Dolly suddenly realized, and with this thought fear was inconsequently replaced by infinite relief. Somehow, it was comforting to be in it with the men this time.

Dolly had never known anything like the term that began so soon after. A London school shared the building, and overflowed into the modest village hall nearby, a building which had been put up in memory of the Fairacre men who had died in the 1914–18 war.

Fairacre School had never been so tightly jammed. Half a dozen long desks, which had not been in use since Dolly was a child there in Edwardian days, were pulled from their resting place in the playground, scrubbed and polished, and put back into use. Kitchen chairs were set by collapsible card tables, the nature table was stripped and furnished accommodation for six more children, and every inch of space, it seemed, was occupied by the children. At first, the teachers had wondered if it would be better to let the London children and their teachers take over the building in the mornings, and the Fairacre children in the afternoons, but this presented many difficulties. Thus for the first few weeks of the war, Dolly Clare shared her room with two teachers from London, twenty of their pupils, and her own normal class.

It did not last long. The weeks slid by with no expected air raids, and the children gradually drifted back to town, followed eventually by their thankful teachers. Fairacre was left with a mere sprinkling of visitors, the Milligan children among them much to Dolly's delight, and the year slipped away with very little incident.

It was a good thing that there had been this rehearsal, for when, in September 1940, the onslaught began in earnest, the children came flocking back, and this time they stayed. No bombs fell in Fairacre throughout the war, but two were dropped at Beech Green one clear night in 1942, and Mrs Pringle knew why.

'It's the solemn truth,' said that lady, folding her arms majestically across her cardigan. 'As sure as you're standing there, Miss Clare, it was Ted Prince's bakehouse as led them Germans to Beech Green.'

Dolly began to protest, but was overborne. Mrs Pringle, in spate, swept everything before her with awful might.

'He says 'isself as 'e opened up the oven to see if it was all right for the loaves. Twenty to five that was. *Twenty to five!*' repeated Mrs Pringle thrusting her face belligerently towards Dolly. 'And what 'appens?'

'I don't know,' admitted Dolly weakly.

'I'll tell you. Up goes the glare from Ted's oven! Down comes the bombs at *exactly nineteen minutes to five!* That's the answer. And lucky Ted Prince might think 'isself to have no innocent deaths laid at 'is door!'

She stumped away before her argument could be taken up, and the children who had been listening enthralled to this exposition stored up the pleasurable story of Ted Prince's villainy for future telling.

Mary Clare had been in bad health for the whole of that winter, and early in 1943 Dolly sent for Doctor Martin, despite her mother's protests. Mary was in bed with a severe cough and a temperature, and Doctor Martin closed the door of the box staircase carefully when he returned from visiting the patient.

'Sit down, Dolly,' he said. They faced each other across the table, Dolly more frightened than she cared to admit.

'Can you stay at home, do you think? Or get someone in?' he asked. 'What about Ada?'

Dolly thought quickly. She hated the idea of leaving her teaching, but her mother would never tolerate Ada about her if she were ill. There was no one that she could ask. Everyone in war time was busy.

'I think I could manage it,' she answered as calmly as she could.

'Good girl,' said the doctor, patting her hand kindly. 'If you keep her warm and on a light diet, she should be up and about again in a month or so.'

'A month?' cried Dolly. 'Is she as ill as that?'

'She'll probably see us both out,' answered Doctor Martin heartily, 'but she wants cosseting through the winter. Now, don't worry yourself too much. See if the school can run without you, and settle here with your mother and have a rest yourself.'

And so Dolly made her plans and nursed her mother for a month. Mary was an unusually good patient, delighted to see friends and fonder of her wireless set than ever. But to Dolly's anxious eyes she did not look robust, and her appetite grew smaller and smaller.

'"Tis sticking in this old bed,' said Mary cheerfully one spring evening. 'Now it's getting warmer I'll sit outside in the garden and the fresh air will soon put me right.'

Dolly lifted the untouched supper tray and went towards the door.

'Bring your sewing up here tonight,' said Mary. 'I reckon that old dame knew a thing or two when she said you'd be a blessing to me. How would I have got on without you this winter?'

'Ada would have had you,' answered Dolly reasonably.

'She ain't worth the half of you,' said the old lady dispassionately, 'and never was – for all Francis thought of her!'

Dolly laughed, but could not help a warm glow at the sincerity of her mother's remark. She returned with her sewing, and they talked for an hour or so, until Mary yawned and settled down for the night.

In the morning Dolly carried up a cup of tea, to find her mother in exactly the same position, with her hands clasped lightly upon the white bedspread and a look of utter contentment upon her face. But the room was uncannily still, and when Dolly touched her mother's enlaced hands, they were cold in death.

20

Dolly was glad to return to her crowded classroom a week after her mother's death. The cottage seemed bleak without her warm presence and Dolly was grateful for the return of the Milligan children

A neighbour had offered to put them up on the day of Mary's death, and they stayed there until after the funeral. Dolly had found her week of solitude profoundly depressing. Worn out with nursing, deprived now of both parents whom she had loved dearly, and low in health through meagre war-time diet, Dolly wondered if she were really fit to take charge of children again. All her instincts were to return to the cheering bustle of the schoolroom, but such weariness possessed her that she doubted if she could ever teach again.

She need not have feared. The comfort of the children's presence at school and the Milligans' at home did much to restore her spirits, though she often longed to have another grown-up with her in the evenings when the little girls had been put to bed.

Emily came over sometimes, but was tied with her own two evacuees and her ageing mother.

'One day we'll share a house,' Emily promised. 'And I'll give you your breakfast in bed one day and you shall do it for me the next!'

'Then it shall be in this house,' Dolly said, 'and you can choose your own bedroom – the one with the sparrows or the one with the house-martins outside.'

And so, half in jest, they made their plans for the future though each wondered secretly if circumstances would ever allow them the pleasure of sharing a home. It seemed as if the war would never end. The drone of bombers in the night sky, as they set off from an airfield to the west of Caxley, was the noise to which the inhabitants of that area fell asleep. There was a dour, business-like approach to this war, Dolly thought, quite different from the tragically idealistic outlook of the earlier one. It was a job to be done, as efficiently and as ruthlessly as possible, and though the young men possessed the same courage and endurance as their fathers, no poets sang them into battle. Dolly's generation had lived through a war to end war, followed by a period of hopes and dreams. There could be no glamour about this conflict which shattered the illusions of a quarter of a century.

Ada's son, John Francis, was a bomber pilot, and Dolly shared his parents' anxiety for him. He was stationed in Yorkshire, and occasionally Ada made the tedious journey northward to see him, staying at the local inn with other wives and mothers. Dolly marvelled at her bravery throughout the war years. Her robust good health and spirits seemed to thrive in adversity, and she never showed her fears before her friends. She had volunteered for driving with the R.A.F at the beginning of the war, and spent a large part of her time on the road.

The terms dragged by. After D-Day, in June 1944, some of the London children returned to town, as the war seemed to be nearing its end, but the Milligan children remained at Beech Green. Dolly wondered how she would feel when they too returned. She hoped they would stay for a long time.

At last, in May 1945, the long-awaited European peace came. Dolly's thoughts turned back to that earlier war as she listened to the joyous pealing of bells across the spring meadows around her. This time she mourned no lover. Her nephew, John Francis, remained unscathed, though many of his friends had gone, and Dolly was thankful for this mercy.

In the months that followed, while the world waited for fighting to end in the Pacific and the Far East, Dolly wondered what the future held. This war was not ending with the same firm conviction of an ever-lasting peace, as when the First World War came to an end. On the contrary, it seemed almost as if the thought of future wars was present in people's minds. Mr Willett voiced many people's feelings when he spoke to Dolly one morning.

'Got them Germans beat for a second time,' he announced cheerfully, 'and now I s'pose it's them Russians next.'

'But, Mr Willett,' protested Dolly, 'they're our allies!'

'Hmph!' snorted the caretaker disbelievingly, 'how long for, I'd like to know? Best by far polish 'em off while we're at it!'

It was not long after this conversation that the horror of Hiroshima's bombing burst upon the world. The frightening possibilities of warfare in the future clouded the rejoicing which accompanied the final stage of the war. Now, it seemed, not what kind of a world would we live in, but would there be a world at all, as mankind had always known it? Sitting before her innocent babes that summer, Dolly Clare wondered what hopes she could put before them. It had been much simpler at the end of the First World War. Then she and Mr Hope had honestly believed that the world would be built anew upon the ashes of the old, and that the sacrifice of thousands of young lives had not been in vain. They had been able to speak with conviction and hope to the children before them. But now those same children had experienced a war themselves, and many had made the same sacrifice. What could she say to their children now?

She could only pass on to them the philosophy which sustained her throughout her life. She could teach them to face whatever came with calmness and courage, to love their families and their friends with unswerving loyalty, and to relish the lovely face of the countryside in which they lived. It might seem a humdrum, day-to-day set of values, but Dolly Clare knew from long experience that they could carry a man bravely through a lifetime's vicissitudes.

In 1944 an Act of Parliament was passed which had an important effect upon the lives of Dolly Clare and those like her. This Education Act meant that almost all the older children in the villages around Caxley would leave the small schools after eleven years of age and be taught together in one of three types of secondary school, grammar, technical, or modern. Furthermore, the school leaving age was raised to fifteen, and this meant an extra year at school.

It was impossible to put this revolutionary idea into practice immediately. Beech Green School was to have a large extension to take the over-elevens from the small schools nearby, including those from Fairacre and Springbourne, and was to be called 'Beech Green Secondary Modern School'. Children who were assessed as intelligent enough to profit by a grammar school education would go to the ancient Caxley Grammar School, as had been the custom for generations. Those who seemed best fitted for a technical school were destined to share the secondary modern school's amenities, for no technical school was to materialize for many years.

The effect of this step was far-reaching. The children themselves much resented the extra year, Dolly found. Country children have traditionally been early wage earners, and those who were looking forward to leaving Mr Fortescue's care and launching out on their own in a year or two's time felt thwarted when they found that they must mark time for another twelve-month. For, despite the high-flown theories about the advantages of a further year's schooling, the truth of the matter was that there were very few schools equipped, either in apparatus or staff, to make the extra time of any real value to the last-year pupils. In time this would be altered, but immediately after the war, labour and materials were short, money was needed desperately for other aspects of national recovery, and the schools struggled to put into practice a project which was almost unworkable in the circumstances. Nevertheless, Dolly and her fellow teachers realized that it was indeed a step forward which should, in time, prove a wise move.

Another result of the Act was the transfer of some church schools to the County Education Committee, for the managers had to undertake to bear half the cost of improvements and maintenance. Springbourne was one of these schools. Fairacre's managers decided to continue as a church school, and undertook to find the money for its upkeep.

During the next year or two Dolly found teaching a difficult task. Mr Fortescue was due to retire in 1949. He was certainly ready for it. To Dolly's eyes, he looked twenty years older than he had at the outbreak of war, and the addition of a dozen or so resentful fourteen-year-olds to his normal class taxed him sorely. He did his best to contrive useful work of a more advanced nature for them but without equipment he could not undertake carpentry, metalwork or the electrical work which they would have enjoyed and profited from learning. He organized an occasional trip to Caxley to watch a council meeting or to visit factories there, but the children sensed that it was all a makeshift passing-of-time, and longed to be in a job where they could be earning money, as their older brothers and sisters had done at the same age.

Dolly was now approaching sixty, and though she was as upright as ever, her hair was snow white and she suffered from occasional twinges of rheumatism. She still cycled daily the three miles from Beech Green to Fairacre, and still looked out with fresh joy for the coming of each year's violets and wild roses along that well-loved route. During the war school dinners had come, to stay for ever it appeared, and this extra duty taxed Dolly's strength more than she realized.

Twice, during the last few years of Mr Fortescue's rule, Dolly suffered a momentary black-out, all the more alarming because she had no warning of the sudden attack. On both occasions she was in her own classroom, the children appeared to notice nothing, and she did not mention either occurrence to her headmaster, dismissing the incidents as the result of being rather over-tired, as indeed she was.

Life alone at the cottage was very quiet without June and Dawn. Dolly had grown accustomed to their chatter and the pounding of their young feet overhead in the little bedroom. She had always prepared an evening meal while they were there, but now that she was alone she could not be bothered to cook, after a day's teaching, and took a glass of milk and a biscuit to an early bed. She hated to think of the empty room next door where first she and Ada and then the two Milligan children had slept. She herself now slept in the room which had been her parents', and very lonely she found it as autumn gave way to the cold of winter.

One windy January evening Emily came to see her. They sat by the fire and Emily told Dolly some surprising news. Springbourne School was to be closed as its numbers had fallen steadily and it now boasted only sixteen pupils.

'And what about you?' asked Dolly.

'I'm to be transferred to a school in Caxley. That dreadful old place by the gasworks that's now called "Hillside Secondary Modern School". Not much modern about that ancient monument,' said Emily, poking the fire vigorously.

'But where will you live?' persisted Dolly. The thought of Emily leaving the nearby village was shocking.

'With Joe,' said Emily. 'It all works out very well. His housekeeper gave up at Christmas and he's glad to put me up in exchange for looking after things. I shall enjoy it.'

Dolly said nothing, but she wondered if Emily really would enjoy it. Her mother had died a few months earlier so that she was free to go to Joe, but the two had never got on very well. He was the youngest of the Davis brood, and a bachelor of about fifty years of age. By trade he was a plumber, and, by the Davis's standards, a well-to-do man. Natural shyness had kept him from marriage, though it was well known in the family that a personable widow in the same Caxley road pursued him relentlessly. So far he had resisted her enticements.

'You must come into Caxley and see me often,' continued Emily, busy with the poker. 'Joe was always fond of you.'

It would not be quite the same, Dolly felt, to visit Emily in someone else's home, but she promised to go frequently, and begged Emily to spend as much time as she could at Beech Green. She looked at her friend in the firelight. Her hair was sprinkled with silver threads but was still, in the main, the crisp dark crop she had known since they were children. Emily had altered little over the years, and still had the power to give the same comfort to Dolly as the first unforgettable Emily had done in her infant years. This was a sad moment for them both. Life in a Caxley street, no matter how comfortable Joe's home was, could not be as happy for Emily as her own rural independence.

'When must you go?' asked Dolly, at last.

'I start there next term,' said Emily. 'I shall move in the Easter holidays.'

She looked at the clock upon the mantelshelf and uttered a cry of horror.

'So late! Never mind, I've only myself to think of,' she said, putting on her coat. 'When I'm a housekeeper I shall have to take more care!'

Dolly walked to the gate with her through the windy night. The light of Emily's bicycle wavered along the brick path, and the moon emerged from scudding clouds for a brief moment. By its gleam Dolly caught sight of Emily's face. It was sad, but had the dogged look about it with which she had always faced misfortune.

She watched her old friend mount her bicycle, called farewell, and watched the brave little light until a bend of the road extinguished it. Dolly went to bed that night with a heavy heart.

It was a relief to everybody when Beech Green's new buildings were ready and the long-awaited transfer of the older children took place. Fairacre's parents had been vociferous about the scandal of moving their offspring at first. Later, they said it was 'a crying shame they never learnt nothing in their last year' at Fairacre, and it was high time they went on to Beech Green's superior instruction at eleven.

Mr Fortescue had just retired, and as Fairacre was now a primary school only, a woman head was appointed. Dolly Clare liked Miss Read from the first, and the two worked well together. It was much more peaceful with the bigger children absent. Playground duty was far less arduous, and fewer numbers in the classroom meant that it was easier to give the children individual help in a quiet atmosphere.

Dolly was grateful for a less busy working day. She had been obliged to go to Doctor Martin's surgery one day and confess that she had had 'a turn'. The old doctor listened gravely to her heart and shook his head.

'Feel like retiring?' he asked.

'No,' said Miss Clare composedly.

'I thought not,' replied the doctor. He surveyed his old friend with a gleam of amusement. 'Well, take one of these tablets once a day, and try to rest more. I suppose I might just as well talk to that table there, but that's my advice, Dolly.'

It was soon after this encounter that fate struck again. One autumn afternoon, the children were engrossed in making bunches of corn to decorate St Patrick's Church next door for Harvest Festival. It was a time that Dolly always loved. She loved the clean floury smell of the grain, and the sight of the busy children preparing to garland the sombre old church. She sat at her desk watching their solemn faces as they arranged the heads of corn evenly together.

It was warm and close, and suddenly the room began to tilt alarmingly. Her heart began to beat so loudly that she felt the children must hear it. She struggled to rise from her chair to open a window, but the last thing she was conscious of was the stream of water which flowed across the desk top from an overturned vase of pink dahlias.

Later she found herself in the school house with Doctor Martin gazing steadily at her.

'I'm sorry,' she whispered.

'Nothing to be sorry about,' he replied cheerfully. 'You can't control your heart's antics, you know.'

Dolly heard his voice as he made his farewells to the headmistress. She knew suddenly, with devastating clarity, that this was the end of the life she loved at Fairacre. She was no more use to the children if these attacks were to become frequent. She must have frightened them to death by this afternoon's collapse. It was not right to stay in her condition.

The room swam before her tear-filled eyes, but her voice was steady when her headmistress came in to see her.

'I shall go at Christmas,' she said, and felt as though her heart would break.

Retirement was something which Dolly had dreaded. To be idle, to be useless, to be laid aside, seemed appalling to her. But when it actually happened, and she had made the sad farewells to the school she had known all her life, and had put a generous cheque from the managers in the bank and a presentation clock upon her bedside table, she found that there were compensations in this time of enforced leisure.

At first she looked at her new clock and thought of what they would be doing in the classroom at that time. Now they would be out in the playground, now they would be at arithmetic, now washing their hands ready for school dinner. But gradually other activities engaged her attention and she found it wholly delightful to potter in the garden when she would have been marking a register or collecting savings money.

Emily retired very soon after, for she was a little older than Dolly, but still she kept house for Joe and the two seemed to get along very well together. Once or twice she suggested to him that he might find another housekeeper, and that Dolly could do with her company, but he seemed so distressed by the idea that she did not pursue the subject. The friendly widow called as often as ever, and played cards on two evenings a week. On these occasions Emily and Dolly usually met.

To augment a tiny pension, Dolly Clare occasionally took in a lodger. Her first was a redoubtable young woman called Hilary Jackson, who taught her own infants' class at Fairacre School. It began as a happy relationship, for Dolly looked forward to the girl's return at the end of each day, and to hearing the school news. But she soon found that Hilary Jackson's love affairs were too tempestuous to endure, and when at last the girl decided to leave the district Dolly Clare was relieved to see her go.

One or two temporary lodgers followed, but Doctor Martin decided that his patient was doing too much, and finally forbade her to take more.

'Better to have less money than too much worry,' he told her.

See how it goes, my girl. You'll manage, I expect. Pity you and Ada don't get on better. You could share a house with her.'

'Never!' said Dolly forthrightly, thinking of HARADA in all its ostentatious glory. It now had a billiard room, two tennis courts and a swimming pool, and Ada was in the throes of choosing the third car for the establishment. Dolly felt that she could never fit into such grandeur.

Doctor Martin had been right, she discovered. She went gently on her way with only a beloved cat for company in the house. She was not lonely now, for in a village there are always people to call and be called upon, and everyone was fond of old Miss Clare. Her garden was one of the loveliest in Beech Green, and the little thatched house always as gracious and serene as its owner. The furniture might be old, but it shone like silk; the rugs might be threadbare, but they were spotless, and everywhere there were flowers from the garden to add colour and fragrance to the cottage rooms

And always, more precious with every passing year, was the friendship of Emily.

21

Old Miss Clare stirred in the hot sunshine. Whilst she had dozed among her memories, the June sun had slid round the sky and now fell fully upon her head. It was too much even for Miss Clare's thin blood, and she rose and made her way towards the house.

Heat shimmered across the silvery thatch, and the great pink poppies had fallen wide open in the heat. A bumble bee fumbled up and down the blue spire of a lupin, and the cat lay stretched at full length in the shade of the hedge.

Stepping down into the cool twilight of the living-room was like entering a shady wood from some bright open meadow. The clock said four and Miss Clare spread the table with a white cloth for which Mary had made the lace edging long ago.

Humming happily to herself she went gently to and fro between the kitchen and living-room as she had done ever since she was a little girl of six. Soon Emily would arrive by bus, for this was market day in Caxley and an extra bus drove the villagers back in good time for their husbands' home-coming.

She set out her best china, a dish of plum jam, a plate of wafer-thin bread and butter, and a freshly-made sponge cake. The kettle was beginning to sing as she heard the bus stop obligingly at her gate.

'Must be Bill Prince driving,' said Miss Clare aloud. He had once been a pupil of Emily's at Springbourne and would look after his old teacher well, she knew.

The two friends met in the path and kissed affectionately.

'Come inside, where it's cooler,' said Miss Clare. 'I'll make tea at once, if you like to put your bag upstairs.'

Emily paused at the foot of the box staircase, her grey eyes sparkling.

'Doll, I've got the most wonderfu new fo₁ you' At that moment the shrill whistle of the kettle shattered the peace of the room, and Dolly Clare hastened to the kitchen. 'Tell me when you come down!' she called.

A few minutes later, with the tea cups steaming and the bread and butter on their plates, Miss Clare looked across at her friend. Emily was obviously bubbling with excitement. Her clear grey eyes were as mischievous as a kitten's.

'Joe's given in at last,' she announced. 'On Tuesday he said he'd marry Caroline.'

Miss Clare put down her cup with a crash, and stared dumb-founded.

'1 can't believe it!' she cried at last. 'After all these years!'

The full significance of the disclosure suddenly dawned upon her. She put a thin hand upon her friend's.

'And you're free? You can come here?' she asked, with a quiver in her voice.

Emily nodded, smiling.

'If you still want me,' she said.

As soon as you like,' said Miss Clare thankfully. The little room seemed lit with more than sunshine. A great happiness suffused her. At last the little house would be a shared home again. The empty bedroom would be occupied, and her companion for the last years of her long life would be the dearest and most constant friend of all. There were no words to express her joy at this sudden blessing.

Later, in the evening, they sat in the quiet garden and discussed plans. The wedding was to be as soon as possible. Caroline obviously had the sense to act swiftly after years of waiting, and she and Joe proposed to live in his house as soon as they were married.

'I ought to be able to come next month,' said Emily. 'In nice time to help with the bottling and jamming.'

'And to think,' sighed Dolly happily, 'that you'll be here to enjoy it next winter! I still can't believe it's happened!'

They sat there until the white owl from the elms nearby swooped out on his nightly affairs, and the moths began to flutter in the twilight. Then the two old friends walked slowly indoors and prepared for bed.

'This has always seemed like home to me,' said Emily, when Dolly came to say good-night. 'It's lovely to be in Beech Green again. I started my life here, and I hope I'll end it here, Dolly. It's funny when you think of it — the furthest I've been is Dorset, and the furthest you've been is Norfolk. I suppose some people would think our lives have been narrow, and would feel sorry for us. But I think we've been two of the luckiest women alive — to have lived all our lives in this dear small place and to have watched the children grow up and have children of their own, and always to have had our friends about us.'

'I thank God daily,' answered Dolly simply, 'for the same things.'

Half an hour later, Miss Clare, in her nightdress, leant from her window to take a final look at the sleeping garden. The scent of the tobacco plant floated from below, a bat rustled on its erratic way, and in the distance the white owl hooted over Hundred Acre Field.

There was still a lightness in the sky and the splendid whaleback of the eternal downs was visible. Dolly Clare looked up to them with affection. How many thousands of men and women, she wondered, through countless centuries had lifted up their eyes to those great hills and there found help as she had done throughout her long life?

Beside her, a few feet along the roof her father had thatched so well, Emily's dormer window glowed companionably. It was good to know that through summer sunshine and winter storm they would share the same roof and the same view for the rest of their time on this earth. It might not be for long, but, no matter how long or how brief their allotted time, it would be a blessing shared.

Dolly Clare took one last look at the night's beauty and then, with a thankful heart, crept softly to bed.

OVER THE GATE

For
Kit and Ivor
with love

1. The Portrait

If you walk down the village street of Fairacre you will come before
long to 'The Beetle and Wedge' on the left-hand side. It is a long,
low public house, sturdily built of brick and flint, and so attractive
to the eye that it is easy to miss the narrow lane which runs between
its side and the three cottages, also of brick and flint, which stand
next to it.

This lane leads to the downs which shelter our village from the
north-east wind. It begins, fairly respectably, with a tarred and
gravelled surface, but after a quarter of a mile such refinement ends;
the road narrows suddenly, the tarmac finishes, and only a muddy
track makes its way uphill to peter out eventually on the windy
slopes high above the village.

Here, where the hard surface ends and the rutted lane begins,
stands a pair of dour grey houses which bear no resemblance to the
cheerful brick-and-thatch architecture of most of Fairacre. They are
faced with grey cement which has fallen off, here and there, leaving
several scabrous patches. Each has a steep gable terminating in a
formidable spike, and the roofs are of cold grey slate. Even on a day
of shimmering heat, when the small blue butterflies of the chalk
downs hover in the still gardens before them, these two houses
present a chilly visage to the passer-by.

They were built in the latter half of Queen Victoria's reign by a
well-to-do retired ironmonger from Caxley. At the same time he
had built a larger and more imposing residence in the village street
for his own use. This was called Jasmine Villa and boasted a black
and white tiled path, an ornate veranda of iron trelliswork, and was
magnificently out of keeping with the modest dwellings nearby.

Laburnum Villas, as the two were called, had housed the iron-
monger's aged mother and two spinster sisters in one, and a married
couple with two sons, all of whom worked for the family, in the
other.

When I first took up the headship of Fairacre village school, some years ago, the property belonged to a descendant of the iron-monger's, and was pathetically shabby. The owner lived in Caxley, but Jasmine Villa became familiar to me, inside and out, for the tenant, Mrs Pratt, played the church organ and sometimes invited me in to hear one of my pupils practising his solo part in an anthem. At one time too she let a room to one of the school staff so that I became well acquainted with the chill of the late ironmonger's drawing-room and the gloom of his stairway.

But Laburnum Villas remained a mystery. The windows of one were shrouded in dirty lace, and inside, I heard, dwelt an old lady of ninety, who supped innumerable cups of strong tea and dozed between whiles. The tea was made when she rose in the morning and the pot kept hot on the hob all day, the kettle steaming comfortably beside it, ready for refilling. Sometimes, when the children and I walked past on our way to the downs, I thought of that somnolent room murmurous with the humming of the kettle, the gentle snoring of the old lady and the purring of her great black cat which was sometimes to be seen sitting in the window sunning itself.

Next door seemed a little livelier. The windows were clean, the curtains fresh, and a trim lawn sloped down to the front gate. Occasionally we saw a middle-aged man and woman working in the garden, but we rarely met them in the village street, a bare two hundred yards away. They seemed to lead a retired life tucked away from the main street of Fairacre and, like all curious country people, I was interested to hear more about them from Mrs Pringle, the school caretaker.

'A very respectable pair,' was Mrs Pringle's dictum when I asked. This was high praise from my curmudgeonly school cleaner and she must have noticed my surprise.

'I always speaks fair of folks when I can,' continued Mrs Pringle self-righteously, putting down her dustpan and settling herself on the front desk for a good gossip. The desk groaned under her thirteen stone but knew better than to let the lady down. 'There's mighty few these days as can be spoke fair of in Fairacre – a proper lazy, shiftless, godless, money-grubbing lot as they be. As I said to Mr Pringle only last night: "If this is the age of flatulence," I says, "then there's something in being poor but honest!"'

'But tell me about Laburnum Villa,' I urged, steering Mrs Pringle back to the point. Once launched on a sea of invective she will sail on for hours, as well I know. The great clock on the wall, ticking ponderously, already said ten minutes to nine, and very soon the children would be called in from the playground.

'Well, these Hursts,' said Mrs Pringle dismissively, 'have only been here two or three years; but before that the Fletchers were there. As nice a family as ever come to Fairacre,' boomed Mrs Pringle, warming to her theme, 'despite their old grandad being a byword in Caxley for pinching things he never had no need of off the market stalls. A real affliction he was to them – everlasting having his name in the *Caxley Chronicle* for all to see.'

'But the Hursts –' I persisted, one eye on the clock.

'Highly respectable,' replied Mrs Pringle, inclining her head graciously. 'Chapel goers, but none the worse for that, I daresay.' The parish church of St Patrick's has Mrs Pringle's support and the choir stalls there reverberate to her powerful contralto lowing, so that this was magnanimous indeed.

'Both been in good service,' continued the lady, 'and was with Sir Edmund over Springbourne way for donkey's years. When the old gentleman passed on they went to one of his relations, I seem to recall. Some long way away it was. Let me think.'

There was a pause while Mrs Pringle frowned with concentration. New Zealand, I thought, or the Argentine, perhaps. The sound of children's voices stirred my conscience and I rose from behind my desk.

'Leicester!' said she triumphantly. 'I knew I'd get it in the end! That's right, it was Leicester they went to –.'

At this point a small girl appeared dramatically between us.

'Please, miss, Ernie made me give him half of my toffee bar and now his tooth's come out in it,' she gabbled agitatedly, 'and what's more he says it's all my fault.'

'Rubbish!' I said, advancing to the door. 'It's nothing more or less than rough justice.'

'I was about to tell you,' boomed Mrs Pringle's voice behind me, heavy with outraged dignity.

'Sorry!' I called back above the rising din. 'It'll have to wait!'

Slowly, Mrs Pringle collected her paraphernalia together and limped heavily from the room, her back expressing outrage in every

sturdy line. Mrs Pringle's bad leg 'flares up', as she puts it, whenever
anything goes wrong. It looked as though I should have to wait
some time before she would be in a fit state to tell me more about
the mysterious Hursts.

But, before long, I had occasion to call at Laburnum Villas. The
leg of a small brass trivet came off in Mrs Pringle's massive hand
whilst she was polishing it. As she explained: 'When things are let
get that filthy they needs a bit of purchase put on them.' It was
apparent that the purchase this time had been too much for my
elderly trivet. I looked at it sadly.

'I'd take it to Fred Hurst,' advised Mrs Pringle. 'I daresay Mr
Willet would have a go if he had a soldering iron, but he hasn't, so
there you are.'

'How do you know Mr Hurst has one?' I asked.

'Because he fixed the twiddly-bits up to the chapel pulpit real
lovely,' replied Mrs Pringle proudly. 'Mr Lamb told me at the Post
Office, and what's more he says he likes doing soldering jobs any
time he's asked.'

I must have looked a little diffident for Mrs Pringle's normal
bellow rose to a crescendo of hearty encouragement.

'You pop down after school and see him,' she advised. 'Better
than taking it to Caxley. You won't see it again this side of Christmas if it gets in there.'

There was some truth in this remark. Urged by Mrs Pringle's
exhortations and my own curiosity I decided to walk down the lane
after tea carrying my trivet with me.

It was one of those bell-like May evenings described by Edmund
Blunden. A sharp shower had left the village street glistening and
the bushes and trees quivering with bright drops. Now, bathed in
evening sunlight, the village sparkled. Scent rose from the wallflowers and polyanthuses in the cottage gardens, and blackbirds
scolded from the plumed lilac bushes. Our village of Fairacre is no
lovelier than many others. We have rats as well as roses in our back
gardens, scoundrels as well as stalwarts ploughing our fields, and
plenty of damp and dirt hidden behind the winsome exteriors of
our older cottages. But at times it is not only home to us but heaven
too; and this was just such an occasion.

As I waited in the porch, cradling the trivet, I wondered if there would be the usual delay in answering a country front door. A back door is usually open, or quickly answered, but I knew from experience that rusty bolts and heavy chains are often involved in front-door transactions in Fairacre. Only on formal occasions do we call at front doors, but this, I felt, was one of them.

To my surprise, the door opened quickly and quietly, showing an elegant white-painted hall and staircase. Mrs Hurst greeted me politely.

'I wondered if your husband –' I began diffidently.

'Come in,' she smiled, and I followed her into the drawing-room on the right-hand side of the corridor. The sight that greeted me was so unexpected that I almost gasped. Instead of the gloomy interior which I had imagined would match Laburnum Villa's unlovely exterior I found a long light room with a large window at each end, one overlooking the front, and the other the back garden. The walls were papered with a white-striped paper and the woodwork was white to match. At the windows hung long velvet curtains in deep blue, faded but beautiful, and a square carpet echoed the colour. Each piece of furniture was fine and old, shining with daily polishing by a loving hand.

But by far the most dominating feature of the room was a large portrait in oils of a black-haired man dressed in clothes of the early nineteenth century. It was not a handsome face, but it showed strength of character and kindliness. Surrounded by an ornate wide gold frame it glowed warmly above the white marble fireplace.

'What a lovely room!' I exclaimed.

'I'm glad you like it,' replied Mrs Hurst. 'My husband and I got nearly everything here at sales. We go whenever we can. It makes a day out and we both like nice things. Our landlord let us have the wall down between these two rooms, so that it's made one good long one, which is a better shape than before, and much lighter too.'

I nodded appreciatively.

'Sit down, do,' she continued. 'I'll get Fred. We live at the back mostly, and I'll tell him you're here.'

I waited in an elegant round armchair with a walnut rim running round its back, and gazed at this amazing room. What a contrast it was, I thought, to Mrs Pratt's counterpart at Jasmine Villa! There the room was crowded with a conglomeration of furniture, from bamboo to bog oak, each hideous piece bearing an equally hideous collection of malformed pottery. That was, to my mind, the most distracting room in Fairacre, whereas this was perhaps the most tranquil one I had yet encountered.

Fred Hurst returned with his wife He was short while she was tall, rosy while she was pale; and certainly more inclined to gossip than his dignified wife. He examined my trivet carefully.

'Nice little piece,' he said admiringly. 'A good hundred years old. I can mend it so as you'll never know it was broken.'

He told me that he could get it done in a week, and we talked generally about our gardens and the weather for a little while before I rose to go.

'I envy you this room,' I said truthfully. 'The school house has tiny rooms and furniture always looks so much better with plenty of space for it.'

'Pictures too,' added Fred Hurst. He pointed to the portraits 'One of my ancestors,' he continued. I heard Mrs Hurst draw in her breath sharply.

'Fred!' she said warningly. Her husband looked momentarily uncomfortable, then moved towards me with hand outstretched.

'We mustn't keep you, Miss Read,' he said politely. 'I'll do my best with the trivet.' I made my farewells, promised to return in a week, and walked to the gate. There I turned to wave to Mrs Hurst who stood regally still upon her doorstep. She wore upon her pale face such an expression of stony distaste that I forbore to raise my hand, but set off soberly for home.

What in the world, I asked myself in astonishment, had happened in those few minutes to make Mrs Hurst look like that?

A week later, in some trepidation, I called again. Somewhat to my relief, only Fred Hurst was at home. He took me into the charming drawing-room again and lifted my mended trivet from a low table. The repair had been neatly done. It was clear that he was a clever workman.

'My wife's gone down to the shop,' he said. She'll be sorry to miss you.'

I murmured something polite and began to look in my purse for the modest half crown which was all that he charged for his job

'She doesn't see many people, living down here, he went on.

'Bit quiet for her, I think, though she don't complain. I'm the one that likes company more, you know. Take after my old great-great-grandad here.' He waved proudly at the portrait. The dark painted eyes seemed to follow us about the room.

'A very handsome portrait,' I commented.

'A fine old party,' agreed Fred Hurst, smiling at him. 'Had a tidy bit of money too, which none of us saw, I may say. Ran through it at the card table, my dad told me, and spent what was left on liquor. They do say, some people, that he had some pretty wild parties, but you don't have to believe all you hear.'

It was quite apparent that Fred Hurst's ancestor had a very soft place in his descendant's heart. He spoke of his weaknesses with indulgence, and almost with envy it seemed to me. Certainly he was fascinated by the portrait, returning its inscrutable gaze with an expression of lively regard.

I could hear the sound of someone moving about in the kitchen, but Mr Hurst, engrossed as he was, seemed unaware of it.

'I should like to think that I took after him in some ways,' he continued boisterously. 'He got a good deal out of life, one way and another, did my old great-great-grandad.'

The door opened and Mrs Hurst swept into the room like a chilly wind.

'That'll do, Fred,' she said quenchingly. 'Miss Read don't want to hear all those old tales.' She bent down to pick an imaginary piece of fluff from the carpet. I could have sworn that she wanted to avoid my eyes.

'Your husband has mended my trivet beautifully,' I said hastily. 'I was just going.'

'I'll come to the gate with you,' said Mrs Hurst more gently. We made our way down the sloping path to the little lane.

'My husband enjoys a bit of company,' she said, over the gate. 'I'm afraid he gets carried away at times. He dearly likes an audience.' She sounded apologetic and her normally pale face was suffused with pink, but whether with shame for her own tartness to him or with some secret anger, I could not tell. Ah well, I thought, as I returned to the school house, people are kittle-cattle, as Mr Willet is fond of reminding me.

'A pack of lies,' announced Mrs Pringle forthrightly when I mentioned Mr Hurst's portrait. 'That's no more his great-great-grandad than the Duke of Wellington!'

'Fred Hurst should know!' I pointed out mildly. I knew that this was the best way of provoking Mrs Pringle to further tirades and waited for the explosion.

'And so he does!' boomed Mrs Pringle, her three chins wobbling self-righteously. 'He knows quite well it's a pack of lies he's telling – that's when he stops to consider, which he don't. That poor wife of his,' went on the lady, raising hands and eyes heavenward, 'what she has to put up with nobody knows! Such a god-fearing pillar of truth as she is too! Them as really knows 'em, Miss Read, will tell you what that poor soul suffers with his everlasting taradiddles.'

'Perhaps he embroiders things to annoy her,' I suggested. 'Six of one and half-dozen of the other, so to speak.'

'Top and bottom of it is that he don't fairly know truth from lies,' asserted Mrs Pringle, brows beetling. 'This picture, for instance, everyone knows was bought at Ted Purdy's sale three years back. It's all of a piece with Fred Hurst's goings-on to say it's a relation. He starts in fun, maybe, but after a time or two he gets to believe it.'

'If people know that, then there's not much harm done,' I replied.

Mrs Pringle drew an outraged breath, so deeply and with such volume, that her stout corsets creaked with the strain.

'Not much harm done?' she echoed. 'There's such a thing as mortal sin, which is what plain lying is, and his poor wife knows it. My brother-in-law worked at Sir Edmund's when the Hursts was there and you should hear what went on between the two. Had a breakdown that poor soul did once, all on account of Fred Hurst's lies. "What'll become of you when you stand before your Maker, Fred Hurst?" she cried at him in the middle of a rabbit pie! My brother-in-law saw what harm lying does all right. And to the innocent, what's more! To the innocent!'

Mrs Pringle thrust her belligerent countenance close to mine and I was obliged to retreat.

'Yes, of course,' I agreed hastily. 'You are quite right, Mrs Pringle.'

Mrs Pringle sailed triumphantly towards the school kitchen with no trace of a limp. Victory always works wonders with Mrs Pringle's bad leg.

In the weeks that followed I heard other people's accounts of the tension which existed between volatile Fred Hurst and his strictly truthful wife. It was this one regrettable trait evidently in the man's character which caused unhappiness to Mrs Hurst. In all other ways they were a devoted couple.

'I reckons they're both to be pitied,' said Mr Willet, our school caretaker one afternoon. He was busy at the never-ending job of sweeping the coke into its proper pile at one end of the playground. Thirty children can spread a ton of coke over an incredibly large area simply by running up and down it. Mr Willet and I do what we can by exhortation, threats, and occasional cuffs, but it does not seem to lessen his time wielding a stout broom. Now he rested upon it, blowing out his ragged grey moustache as he contemplated the idiosyncrasies of his neighbours.

'They've both got a fault, see?' he went on. 'He tells fibs. She's too strict about it. But she ain't so much to blame really when you know how she was brought up. Her ol' dad was a Tartar. Speak-when-you're-spoken-to, Dad's-always-right sort of chap. Used to beat the livin' daylights out o' them kids of his. She's still afeared that Fred'll burn in hell-fire because of his whoppers. I calls it a tragedy, when you come to think of it.' He returned to his sweeping, and I to my classroom. I was to remember his words later.

Time passed and the autumn term was more than half gone. The weather had been rough and wet, and the village badly smitten with influenza. Our classes were small and there were very few families which had escaped the plague. Fred Hurst was one of the worst hit, Mrs Pringle told me.

It was some months since the incident of the trivet and I had forgotten the Hursts in the press of daily affairs. Suddenly I remembered that lovely room, the portrait, and the passions it aroused.

'Very poorly indeed,' announced Mrs Pringle, with lugubrious satisfaction. 'Doctor's been twice this week and Ted Prince says Fred's fallen away to a thread of what he was.'

'Let's hope he'll soon get over it,' I answered briskly, making light of Mrs Pringle's dark news. One gets used to believing a tenth of all that one hears in a village. To believe everything would be to sink beneath the sheer weight of all that is thrust upon one. Seeing my mood Mrs Pringle swept out, her leg dragging slightly.

At the end of that week I set off for Caxley. It was a grey day, with the downs covered in thick mist. The trees dripped sadly along the road to the market town, and the wet pavements were even more depressing. My business done, I was about to drive home again when I saw Mrs Hurst waiting at the bus stop. She was clutching a medicine bottle, and her face was drawn and white.

She climbed in gratefully, and I asked after her husband. She answered in a voice choked with suppressed tears.

'He's so bad, miss, I don't think he'll see the month out. Doctor don't say much, but I know he thinks the same.'

I tried to express my shock and sympathy. So Mrs Pringle had been right, I thought, with secret remorse.

'There seems no help anywhere,' went on the poor woman. She seemed glad to talk to someone and I drove slowly to give her time.

'I pray, of course, she said, almost perfunctorily. 'We was all brought up very strict that way by my father. He was a lay preacher, and a great one for us speaking the truth. Not above using the strap on us children, girls as well as boys, and once, I remember, he made me wash my mouth out with carbolic soap because he said I hadn't told the truth. He was wrong that time, but it didn't make no difference to dad. He was a man that always knew best.'

She sighed very sadly and the bottle trembled in her fingers.

'He never took to Fred, nor Fred to him; but there's no doubt my dad was right. There's laws laid down to be kept and them that sin against them must answer for it. 'As ye sow, so shall ye reap," it says in the Bible, and no one can get over that one.'

She seemed to be talking to herself and I could do nothing but make comforting noises.

'Fred's the best husband in the world,' she continued, staring through the rain-spattered windscreen with unseeing eyes, 'but he's got his failings, like the rest of us. He don't seem to know fact from fancy, and sometimes I tremble to think what he's storing up for himself. I've reasoned with him – I've told him straight – I've always tried to set him an example –.'

Her voice quivered and she fell silent. We drove down the village street between the shining puddles and turned into the lane leading to the misty downs. I stopped the car outside Laburnum Villas. It was suddenly very quiet. Somewhere nearby a rivulet of rainwater trickled along unseen, hidden by the dead autumn grasses.

'You see,' said Mrs Hurst, 'I've never told a lie in my life. I can't do it – not brought up as I was. It's made a lot of trouble between Fred and me, but it's the way I am. You can't change a thing like that.'

She scrubbed at her eyes fiercely with the back of her hand, then opened the door.

'Can I come and see him?' I asked impulsively. She nodded, her face expressionless.

I followed her up the steep wet path to the forlorn house. Its ugly exterior, blotched with damp, was more hideous than ever. Inside, in the lovely room, Fred Hurst lay asleep on a bed which had been brought from upstairs. He faced the portrait above the mantelpiece.

The sleeping man woke as we entered and tried to struggle up, but weakness prevented him. I was aghast at the change in him. It was apparent that he had very little time to live. His eyes wandered vaguely about the room, and his breathing was painful to hear. His wife crossed quickly to his side and took his hand. Her face softened as she gazed on him.

'Fred dear, it's me. And I've brought Miss Read to see you,' she said gently.

A flicker passed across his face and the dull eyes rolled in my direction.

'Come to see me?' he asked slowly. 'Me, or my great—' he took a shuddering breath, 'or my great-great-grandad? He is my kin, ain't he, my love?'

There was a terrible urgency in the hoarse voice as he turned to his wife. Across his wasted body her eyes met mine. They had become dark and dilated as though they looked upon hell itself, but her voice rang out defiantly.

'Of course he's your kin,' she cried, tightening her grip on his hand. 'Miss Read can see the likeness, can't you?'

I responded to the challenge.

'A strong family likeness,' I lied unfalteringly, and felt no regret.

2. Strange, But True?

Poor Fred Hurst died a fortnight before Christmas, and Mr Willet, who is sexton of St Patrick's as well as caretaker of Fairacre School, had the melancholy task of digging his grave.

We could hear the ring of his spade as it met sundry flints embedded in the chalk only a foot or so below the surface of the soil.

It was a dark grey December afternoon outside, but within the classroom was warmth, colour and a cheerful hum as the children made Christmas cards. Above their bent heads swung the paper chains they had made. Here and there a pendent star circled slowly in the keen cross draughts which play constantly between the Gothic windows at each end of the school building. A fir branch, cut from the Vicarage garden, leant in a corner giving out its sweet resinous breath as it awaited its metamorphosis into a glittering Christmas tree.

Crayons stuttered like machine guns as snow scenes were created. Reindeer, with colossal antlers which took up far too much room, tottered on legs – inevitably short – across the paper. Robins, fat as footballs, stood on tiptoe; Father Christmas, all boots and whiskers, appeared on every side at once; holly, Christmas puddings, bells and stars flowed from busy fingers throughout the afternoon. And every now and then, during the rare quiet pauses in their activity, we could hear the distant sound of Mr Willet at work, in the desolate solitude of an empty grave.

The winter afternoon was merging into twilight when the children shouted and skipped their way homeward from Fairacre village school. Mr Willet, coming from the churchyard next door, propped his spade against the lych gate and paused to light his pipe. In the murk, his wrinkled countenance was illumined, standing out against the dark background like a Rembrandt portrait. Hands cupped over the bowl of his pipe he squinted sideways at me.

'Finished your day, I s'pose,' he commented. 'Nice work being a school teacher,' he added mischievously.

'What about you?' I retorted. Mr Willet flung back his head and blew a fragrant blue cloud into the mist around him.

'Got your plaguey coke to sweep up now I've dug poor old Fred's last bed,' he answered equably. He reached for the spade with a massive muddy hand.

'My kettle's on,' I said. 'Come and have a cup of tea before you start again.'

'Well now,' said my caretaker, eyes brightening, 'I don't mind if I do, Miss Read. I'm fair shrammed. Grave-digging be mortal clammy work this weather.'

We strolled back together, across the empty playground, to the school house.

'Here, I can't come in like this!' protested Mr Willet at the kitchen door. 'All cagged up with mud! What'll old Mrs Pringle say when she comes to wash your floor?'

'No more than she says every week. This house is the dirtiest in the village, so she tells me.'

'Miserable ol' faggot!' Mr Willet smiled indulgently. 'How she do love a good moan! Still, this mud's a bit much, I will say. Give us a bit of newspaper and I'll 'ave it under me boots.'

We settled in the warm kitchen, the tea tray between us on the table. We were both tired and cold and sipped the tea gratefully. It was good to have company and Mr Willet always has something new to impart. He did not fail me on this occasion.

'Poor old Fred Hurst,' he mused, stirring his cup thoughtfully. 'I've got him right at the end of a row next to the old bit of the churchyard. Funny thing, he's lying aside Sally Gray. Two fanciful ones together there, I reckons.'

'Sally Gray?'

At the querying tone of my voice the spoon's rotation stopped suddenly.

'You don't tell me you ain't heard of Sally Gray! Been here all this time and missed Sally?'

I nodded apologetically, and pushed the fruit cake across to him to atone for my short-comings. Mr Willet waved it aside, his eyes wide with amazement.

'Can't hardly credit it. She's about the most famous person in Fairacre. Why, come to think of it, we had a young chap down from some magazine or other writing a bit about her. Before your time, no doubt. Nice enough chap he seemed, although he had a beard.'

Mr Willet checked himself, blew out his own thick walrus moustache, and resumed his tale.

'Well, *beard*, I calls it. 'Twasn't hardly that. More like one of those pan cleaners, the bristly ones, and much the same colour. For two pins I'd have advised him to have it off, but you knows how touchy young fellers get about their bits of whisker, and I was allus one for peace. "Civility costs nothing," my old ma used to say. She were full of useful sayings.'

I began to see where Mr Willet got his own fund of maxims. No matter what the occasion, tragic or farcical, our caretaker-cum-sexton at Fairacre always has some snippet of homely wisdom to fit the case.

'And what did he write?' I prompted, edging him back towards the subject.

'Next to nothin', when it come to it!' Mr Willet was disgusted. 'I thought at the time, watching him put down these 'ere twiddles and dots and dashes and that –'

'Shorthand,' I interpolated.

'Maybe,' said Mr Willet dismissively, 'but I thought at the time, as I were saying, that he'd never make head nor tail of that rig-marole, and I bet you a quid that's just what happened. You know why?'

Mr Willet raised his teaspoon threateningly.

'After us talking to 'im best part of a January afternoon, up the churchyard there, with an east wind fit to cut the liver and lights out of you, all 'e 'ad to show for it was a measly little bit in the corner of a page. And most of that was a picture of the grave-stone, what you could make out through the fog, that is. Proper disappointing it was.'

'Which paper?' I asked.

'Some fiddle-faddling thing they brings out the other side of the county. Not worth looking at. All about flowers, and old ruins and history and that. Waste of time really, and not a patch on *The Caxley Chronicle*.'

Mr Willet drained his cup and set it carefully down on the saucer.

'Well, must be off to me coke-sweeping, I s'pose.' He began to push back his chair.

'Not yet,' I begged. 'You haven't told me a word about Sally Gray.'

'Well, now –' began Mr Willet, weakening. 'I daresay the coke'd keep till morning, and it don't seem hardly right that you don't know nothing about our Sally.'

He watched me refill his cup without demur, rearranged his muddy boots on the newspaper and settled, with evident relish, to his task of enlightenment.

Sally Gray, Mr Willet told me, died a good ten years or more before he was born, in 1890 to be exact, and as her grave-stone bore testimony, 'in her 63rd year'. Consequently, as he pointed out, he was not speaking at first hand, although he could vouch for this strange story, for his mother and grandmother had both heard it from Sally's own lips during her last illness.

Evidently she had always been 'a funny little party', to quote Mr Willet. She was the only child of elderly parents and was brought up in the end cottage of Tyler's Row. Her father was a carter, her mother took in washing, and the child grew up used to hard work and little reward for great labour. Nevertheless, she was happy

enough, although the other children in the village found her prim
and shy and tended to tease her. She was small of stature, so that she
was called 'Mouse' by the boys, and dressed in cut-me-downs of
her mother's which gave her a ludicrous dowdiness which invited
the ridicule of the girls. No doubt her primness and shyness were
the outcome of this treatment.

Her greatest joy was in reading, which she mastered at an early
age. Books were scarce, but tattered volumes cast out from the
vicarage nursery came her way and gave her endless pleasure.
Sometimes a newspaper became available and she read the account
of Victoria's coronation to her parents, to their wonder and pride.

When she was twelve or so she entered into service at the Parrs', a
well-to-do family who lived in a Queen Anne house at the end of
the village. She was quick and neat, obedient and dutiful, and gave
satisfaction to the mistress of the house and more important still, to
the housekeeper who ruled the staff with a rod of iron. She lived in
as a matter of course, although only five minutes' trot from her
own home, but was often allowed to slip along the village street to
see her family. Sometimes the cook gave her a bowlful of dripping,
or a stout marrow-bone for the stock pot, to eke out the meagre
commons of the Grays' diet. Sally was always careful to hide these
titbits under her cloak, safe from the eyes of the housekeeper or
village gossips who might be encountered on the brief journey.

Time passed. Housemaids came and went at the Parrs' house, but
Sally remained. Girls who had worked beside her, dusting, brushing
stair carpets, carrying interminable cans of hot water to bedrooms,
married and left. They showed their fat offspring to Sally, in the
fullness of time, and commiserated with her about her state of
spinsterhood. Sally did not appear to mind. She was as spry and
nimble as ever, although a few grey hairs now mingled with the
dark ones, and she continued to trot briskly about Fairacre.

One bitterly cold winter the two old Grays fell desperately ill,
and Sally asked leave to sleep at home and to work part-time at the
Parrs. Mrs Parr, who was an autocratic person, did not care for the
idea. By now, Sally was senior housemaid. It was she who carried
in the early morning tea, pulled back the heavy curtains on their
massive brass rings, and announced the weather conditions prevail-
ing, to her comatose mistress. She disliked the thought of someone
else taking on these duties and told Sally that she must give it

much consideration'. However, Mrs Parr knew full well that if she wished to keep Sally in her service then there must be some slackening of the reins whilst the old people were in need, and graciously gave her consent. 'But understand,' added the lady severely, 'you are to bring in the morning tea whenever it is *humanly possible.*' Sally promised, obedient as ever, to do all in her power.

For the next few months she scurried between the great house and the little thatched cottage and more often than not was early enough to take up the tea to her mistress and prepare her for the return to consciousness.

One summer morning, just before seven o'clock, she hastened by the dew-spangled shrubbery and was amazed to see the doctor's carriage outside the front door. In the kitchen a woebegone staff, sketchily dressed and with hair in curlers, poured forth the dramatic news. The master was dead! A heart attack, said the doctor, and mistress must be kept lying down to get over it!

Within a month poor Mr Parr was buried, his widow was settled in France, and his son was directing the decoration and alteration of his heritage. To Sally's stupefaction she found that she had been left the fabulous sum of one hundred pounds by her late employer. Young Mr Parr took her into Caxley and deposited it for her in the safety of a bank.

The village was agog with the news. Sally's parents were beyond understanding her good fortune. Their days and nights were spent in fitful dozing, hovering between life and death, stirring occasionally to sup a bowl of gruel before sliding down thankfully upon the pillows again. In the thick of harvest time, as Fairacre folk sweated beneath a blazing sun, they slipped away within three days of each other and were buried together not far from Mr Parr's newly-erected marble angel.

Although she mourned her parents sincerely there was no doubt that Sally's life now became very much easier. She still worked for the new master, but lived at home enjoying being mistress of her own small domain. Always an avid reader, she now had more time to indulge in this pleasure, and often took a book in one hand and her candle in the other and made her way to bed before nine o'clock, there to read until St Patrick's great clock struck midnight and the candle must be blown out.

She had been given a pile of books from her dead master's library when things were being sorted out, and these were to keep her occupied in her leisure moments for many years to come. Contentment of mind, more rest, and plenty of good country air and food began to show their effect on Sally. Hitherto small and rather skinny, she now began to put on flesh and soon became a little dumpling of a woman, albeit as quick on her feet as ever despite a certain breathlessness. She was now well on in her forties and her neighbours gave her no comfort.

You be bound to put it on at your age,' said one.

'Better be fat and happy,' said another, 'than a bag o' bones.'

'You won't lose it now, my dear,' said a third smugly. '"Tis on for good when 'tis put on at your time of life.'

Sally was secretly nettled at this embarrassment of flesh. She let out seams, moved buttons and unpicked waistbands hoping, in vain, that one day she might revert to her former size. But the months grew into years and Sally's bulk grew too.

One sunny evening she sat in her back porch with a very strange book in her hand. It was one of those bequeathed to her by her late master, a leather-covered exercise book which she had not troubled to open before. In it she found a number of recipes written out in a crabbed angular hand, in ink which had faded to a dull brown. They were not particularly interesting to Sally. Cooking was not one of her major interests and such household hints as: 'A Useful Polish for Ebonised Mahogany', or 'A Valuable Amelioration for Children's Croup', which were also included in the book, did not stir her imagination. She yawned widely, and was about to put the book away and prepare her simple supper, when a heading caught her eye. It said: 'An Infallible Receipt for Losing Weight'.

Tilting the book to get the maximum light from the setting sun, Sally read with growing excitement.

To be sure, some of the ingredients sounded perfectly horrid. A basinful of pig's blood beaten with a pound of honey, some goose grease and a plover's egg was bad enough, thought Sally, but when an impressive list of ground herbs, moistened with cuckoo-spit, was to be added to it, then the concoction would surely be nauseating.

'Seal Top of Paste with Pig's Lard to Exclude Air,' said the recipe, and added in capital letters: 'PARTAKE SPARINGLY'.

Sally considered the page. Revolting it might be, but it was supposed to be infallible. The title said so. Would it be worth trying?

She read the list of ingredients over again with close attention. The herbs would be easy to obtain, either from her own garden or the Parrs'. Cuckoo-spit glistened in all the meadows of Fairacre, honey stood ready in its comb on her pantry shelf, pig's blood and goose-grease could be obtained fairly readily. The plover's egg would be the most difficult article to procure, but somewhere on the flanks of the downs which sheltered Fairacre a boy's sharp eyes would be able to find a plover's nest, she felt sure.

The biggest problem was the assembling of all these ingredients without arousing suspicion. There are no secrets capable of being hidden in a village, as Sally well knew. It was not that she feared ridicule alone. Within her time she had seen old women ducked in the horse pond because their neighbours had suspected them of dabbling in witchcraft; and although the exercise book purported to be a straightforward recipe book there was something suspiciously sinister about the weight-reducing recipe. Sally decided to go about her task with the greatest circumspection. Who knows, in a few months' time she might have the trim slim figure of her youth? It was worth the trouble.

All went well. Even the plover's egg was obtained with comparative ease from a shepherd boy who, carrying six eggs to her cottage in his cap, was glad to earn a silver sixpence. One evening, after work, Sally prudently drew the curtain in her kitchen against prying eyes, and set about making the paste.

It smelt terrible and looked worse. It was yellowish-grey in colour, and speckled abominably with the ground herbs. Sally felt that she could not bring herself to taste it that evening, but would hope for strength in the morning. She retired to bed, with the reek of the concoction still in her nostrils.

It looked singularly unattractive by morning light, but after breakfast Sally put the tip of a spoon into the jar and bravely swallowed a morsel.

'I must do as it says and partake sparingly,' she told herself as she washed the spoon.

All that week she continued with the treatment. There seemed to be no result, but Sally was patient, and in any case expected to wait some weeks before her bulk began to diminish. Sometimes she felt a slight giddiness a few minutes after swallowing the stuff, but when one considered the nature of the ingredients this was hardly surprising.

One morning she decided to take a slightly larger dose. The clock on the mantel shelf told her it was later than usual, so that she flung the spoon in the washing-up bowl and set off at a brisk trot to the big house at the end of the village. She was perturbed to find that her gait was impaired. It seemed almost impossible to keep her heels on the ground, and Sally found herself tripping along on her toes, scarcely touching the ground at all. At the same time the giddiness occurred with some strength.

'Very strong stuff,' thought Sally to herself. 'Small wonder one's bid to partake sparingly!'

She took care to reduce the dose during the next week or two. By now it was high summer. Plumes of scented meadowsweet tossed by the roadside, and the bright small birds kept up a gay clamour as they flashed from hedge to meadow and meadow to garden. Sally tried on her summer print gowns with growing despair. They were as tight as ever. Buttons burst from the strained bodices and waistbands gaped as Sally strove in vain to ram her bulk into the protesting garments.

'Dratted stuff!' panted Sally. 'Never done me a 'aporth of good!' She surveyed herself in the small mirror which she had tilted forward in order to get a better view of her figure. Exasperation flooded her bulky frame. It was no good. She would simply have to make new dresses. These had been let out to their furthest limit.

She struggled out of the useless frocks, dressed in her former gown, and went sadly downstairs. The offending pot stood on the kitchen shelf.

'For two pins,' exclaimed Sally aloud, 'I'd throw you where you belongs – out on the rubbish heap!'

She was about to bustle about her household chores, when a thought struck her.

'Maybe I ain't been taking quite enough,' thought Sally. 'It's worth trying.'

Today was the perfect day to make an experiment. It was Sunday, and she need not go out anywhere. If a giddy attack followed the taking of too much medicine, then she could simply lie down until she recovered.

'And if it do make me giddy, but it works, then 'twill be worth it,' said Sally aloud. 'I can always take it at nights afore going to bed and sleep the giddiness off afore morning '

She took a large spoon, dipped it deeply into the reeking mixture, and bravely downed it.

For a moment, nothing happened, apart from a slight feeling of nausea which taking the stuff habitually gave her. And then, to Sally's horror and alarm, her feet left the ground and she began to rise steadily to the ceiling. She bumped her head against the central rafter with some violence, and was about to scream loudly with combined pain and terror, when prudence checked her.

'A fine thing if the neighbours saw you now,' she told herself severely. 'Look a proper fool, you would.' She tried to quieten her panicky heart; and the fear of ridicule, as well as being suspected of witchcraft, helped to keep her tongue silent.

It was uncomfortable and strange bobbing loosely about the ceiling trying to dodge the iron-hard rafter and the hanging oil lamp suspended from it; but Sally had always been of a philosophic strain and decided to make the best of a bad job.

' "What can't be cured must be endured," ' quoted Sally, running a finger along the top of the white china lamp shade. It was thick with dust, and Sally clucked disapprovingly at such filth in her house.

'No doubt about it: "Out of sight is out of mind." I must take this lot down and give it a real good wash in some suds.' A pang seized her.

'If I ever do get down,' she added despairingly. She propelled herself by pushing her hands against the ceiling until she was level with the high shelf where she stored bottling jars and preserving pans. To her horror she saw a large black beetle, dead and on its back, in the pan she kept for making pickles and chutney.

' 'Tis really shameful,' Sally scolded herself. 'If it hadn't been for this misfortune I'd never have realized what a slut I am.'

Below her the potatoes waited in a bowl of water to be peeled. The cat mewed by his empty saucer, and the big black kettle on the oil stove began to hum.

'Lawks!' thought Sally. 'How long do I have to stick up here, I wonder? Them dizzy turns went over in ten minutes or so. With any luck I'll be down in half an hour.' Would the kettle boil over before then, she thought agitatedly? Really, it was too bad! It would teach her a lesson to go dabbling in things she didn't understand!

She had realized, as soon as her head cracked against the beam, that she had misconstrued the heading of the recipe. She had indeed lost weight, but not size. It was only now, in the first half hour or so of her bizarre imprisonment, that she began to foresee the possibilities of her discovery. As a short woman, she had always found difficulty in reaching shelves and cupboards put into the cottage by her tall father. A stout stool accompanied Sally on many a job in the house such as window-cleaning, or storing preserves, or the winter blankets, in high little-used cupboards.

'If I takes just the right amount,' pondered Sally, picking a particularly thick cobweb from the top of the curtains, 'I can float just where I need to.' She began to dally with the idea of picking apples and plums without needing to borrow a ladder, but reason told her at once of the dangers.

'Too many prying eyes,' decided Sally sagaciously, 'and dear knows how high I might go if the wind got me! It's got to be faced. I'm more like a balloon than anything else when I've that stuff inside me.'

At that moment she heard footsteps. Her front door stood open, as was its custom in fine weather, and this gave direct access to the living-room. Luckily, the door between that room and the kitchen was securely shut. Sally edged her way, silently and painfully, to a shadowy corner of the ceiling. Her heart pounded. Would she be discovered?

'You in, my dear?' called her neighbour. Sally preserved a frozen silence.

'Be you upstairs?' went on the voice. Sally heard the clang of the metal door scraper. Lawks a mercy, what if she came in? Sally's throat dried at the very thought. She clung to the pan shelf with trembling fingers praying with all her might. The kettle began to bubble steadily, and the cat jumped noisily on to the table among the dishes.

'You home, Sal?' said the voice, a little louder. The door scraper clanged again; then silence fell. At last, there was the sound of muttering and the slow fading of footsteps along the brick path to Sally's gate. Sally covered her face with her grimy hands and wept with relief. Ten minutes later, her body began to feel more solid and manageable. She found she could control the direction of her legs and arms with growing accuracy, and slowly she sank groundwards.

The first thing she did was to make a good strong pot of tea and carry it into the living-room to recover. A fine cabbage, obviously brought by her neighbour, waited on the threshold. She must go and thank her, when her legs stopped trembling, and explain that she must have been 'down the garden' when she called.

Meanwhile, sipping and thinking, Sally regained her composure and turned over in her mind the best way of making use of the secret and surprising accomplishment with which she was now endowed.

There now began, for Sally, a period of engrossing interest and pleasure. After her duties at the big house, she hurried home to experiment with her essays in levitation. She found that by taking a small amount of the concoction she could hover about a foot above the ground for a period of roughly ten minutes. This gave her ample time to tidy shelves, wash out high cupboards, dust the picture rail and so on, tasks which had always been irksome to one of her low stature.

She found it wholly delightful to be without weight, and became skilled at balancing herself, with one hand touching a wall, whilst the other performed its task. Naturally, she did not indulge in this secret practice every day. For one thing, she still feared that it might be discovered by her neighbours in Fairacre, and she had no intention of giving them cause for gossip. She found it prudent to keep her 'floating periods' for Thursdays. Market day in Caxley was on a Thursday, and usually the other inhabitants of Tyler's Row spent their Thursdays hunting for bargains, meeting their friends and catching up with their news amidst the market-day bustle. Alone in her cottage, Sally felt safe from unexpected visitors, and experimented with the mixture.

One day she noticed that both the plum tree and the ancient Bramley Seedling apple tree were heavy with fruit. She had wondered for some time if she might dare to practise floating out of doors, and this seemed the time to experiment. There was much to consider before she began.

Of course she must remain unseen by the neighbours. That was the first consideration. It would be wise, therefore, to wait until nightfall to make her first attempt. Then she must be careful to leave a considerable amount of fruit to be picked in the normal way or her neighbours would wonder why she had not borrowed a ladder as was her usual practice.

Then, of course, there was the question of staying in her own garden. She shuddered at the thought of floating out into the blue, as well she might, if she did not take care. It was not so much the *danger* that worried Sally as the *impropriety* of such a mode of travelling. After considerable thought she decided to tie a stout length of clothes line round her waist and to tie a brick to the other end. She would carry the brick, already tied, up in the basket with her. On attaining the correct height she would throw the brick to the ground, remain safely tethered level with the fruit, pick it and place it in the basket, and so get the job done.

Of course there was more to it than the general plan. For one thing Sally had to calculate the height of the fruit from the ground, how much the brick would weigh and how much of her mixture she needed to take to balance all these factors. But she was determined to try her luck, and one moonless night she crept from the cottage to embark on this adventure.

It was very still and quiet. The windows in the row of cottages were dark. Not a soul stirred. St Patrick's clock had struck one as Sally tip-toed down her stairs, and all Fairacre slept the dreamless sleep of those who live and work in the bracing air of the downs.

A spoonful and a half of the revolting brew was doing its best to settle in Sally's affronted stomach as she approached the plum tree. Already her feet were skimming the grass and she had hardly reached the gnarled old trunk before she began to rise swiftly. For a moment Sally was torn with panic. She felt horribly vulnerable out here in the open and would have welcomed the painful crack of the kitchen rafter on her head, at that moment. She clawed frantically at a substantial branch, as she floated by, and paused to get her breath. Taking a tight grip with one hand, she groped inside the basket on her arm, found the brick and cast it downward.

It seemed to make the most appalling shindy and also jerked Sally cruelly round the waist. Breathless, she listened. Supposing the neighbours were disturbed and looked out of their windows? Supposing the rope broke? Sally gripped the tree even more desperately in her agitation. But the silence engulfed her, and only the distant yelping of a stoat stirred the blackness, as a falling leaf might ruffle the satin smoothness of a still pool.

Emboldened, Sally turned to her task. It was not easy, but it was wonderfully exhilarating to be at large in the tree tops and her basket was soon full. Weight returned to her in roughly half an hour, and Sally crept back to the cottage, basket in one hand, brick in the other, and went, highly elated, to bed.

Time passed. A pot of the mixture stood permanently on Sally's larder shelf and she began to take her ability to levitate almost for granted. She was wonderfully lucky in preserving her secret, although over the years she had one or two dangerous moments. One day, for example, she was cleaning her bedroom window inside, floating about eight inches above the rush matting, when her neighbour appeared on the garden path below her and asked if she might borrow some sugar.

'I'll be down in a minute,' Sally replied, doing her best to keep her feet hidden from sight below the window sill.

'Shall I take a cupful myself?' suggested the woman 'Save you leaving the windows, like?'

'No, no,' answered Sally, trying to sound airy, as indeed she felt. 'I'll bring it round the minute I've finished.'

If she gets in here, thought Sally frantically, she'll be upstairs in double quick time and I'm aloft here for a good five minutes yet. The woman watched her closely, as she undulated from one pane to the next.

'What you standin' on, gal?' she asked suspiciously.

'My little old stool,' responded Sally, tightening her hold on the curtain and concentrating her attention on one pane. 'Don't you trouble to wait,' she added hastily. 'I'll be round in two shakes.'

To her infinite relief the woman departed, but the incident left Sally severely shaken. It was several weeks before she dared to take another dose.

Under cover of darkness she often repeated her first outdoor experiment and picked fruit for pies and puddings, jamming and bottling. On one occasion the landlord of 'The Beetle and Wedge' had asked her curiously how she had picked her apple tree so clean, and she had said quickly that she had 'given it a good old shake' and the wind had done the rest. He seemed to believe her.

One late October day, when Sally was almost sixty years of age, she gazed with a speculative eye upon her walnut tree. This was a lofty beauty, of great age, and heavy this year with magnificent nuts. Sally decided to lengthen her rope and to make an assault upon it.

''Tis Thursday,' said Sally aloud, 'and they all be safely at market. By teatime it'll be dark enough to try.' She made her preparations and made her way to the tree as dusk began to fall. The neighbours' cottages were empty and would remain so for a full hour, as well she knew. What she had not reckoned with was a freshening wind and the enormous collie puppy which came from the farm.

The brick lay at the foot of the tree, half hidden in wet grass. Higher than she had ever been before Sally plucked swiftly at the green walnuts, staining her fingers brown as the basket filled. The wind made things difficult, tugging at her skirts and lifting the boughs from her reach. It grew more boisterous each minute and Sally began to feel alarmed.

'I'll be downright thankful when this lightness wears off,' she said to herself, clinging to a sturdy branch. At that moment she became conscious of a rhythmic tremor running up the rope. There, busily gnawing at it, just above the brick, was the collie puppy. Caution thrown to the winds, Sally screamed at him.

'Be off, sir! Get away, you rascal!'

The puppy wagged a delighted tail and continued his gnawing. His strong white teeth, busy at their task, seemed to grin at her. Sally began to pelt him with walnuts, but he was unperturbed. Slowly but surely the strands were severed, until a particularly fierce gust of wind caught Sally unawares, broke the rope completely, and jerked her violently from the walnut tree. Still screaming, Sally rose abruptly another twenty or thirty feet, and began to twirl this way and that as the wind blew her on an erratic course clean across the village.

Over and over Sally rolled, like an escaped balloon, and soon she felt sick as well as frightened. But her innate common sense began to assert itself, and just as she had accepted the first ridiculous position against her own kitchen ceiling so, in this present predicament, she did her best to come to terms with the situation.

First, she stopped screaming. On no account would she draw attention to herself. She'd got herself in this pickle, and she'd get herself out of it. Luckily, dusk was falling fast and with luck her progress through the sky would pass unnoticed. The roaring of the wind would distract people's attention from unusual sounds above them. Heads down against the onslaught, they would probably be intent on getting home, Sally comforted herself.

Her own travelling arrangements next occupied her thoughts. The rope trailed behind her like an unwieldy tail. She hauled it painfully in towards her, rolling the end loosely round one arm. This steadied her a little, and by gripping it between her feet, a few inches below her billowing skirts, she was more likely to stay upright, she discovered. True, she still twirled and bobbed in a highly distracting fashion, but at least she was travelling with a little more decorum and her skirts were hanging in approximately the right direction. Her bun had come down and her locks streamed in the wind, but Sally found this remarkably refreshing. It was years since she had felt the wind blowing through her loose hair.

She floated dangerously close to the spire of St Patrick's and noticed how remarkably dirty the weather cock was at its tip. Below her she could see the new village school and the little playground, now mercifully empty. The village street wound its way beneath her, and she was thankful that it too appeared to be empty. Her pace was brisk, for the wind was now a gale and the noise from the topmost branches of the elms beyond the school almost deafened her. She looked down upon the untidy rooks' nests swaying dizzily at the top of the trees, and then swirled onwards towards the open fields between Fairacre and Springbourne.

At last, she began to lose height. Her weight began to return and she braced herself for the descent to earth. Alas, by this time she was in the great park of Springbourne Manor and heading at incredible speed towards the avenue of lime trees which bordered the drive to the house. Closing her eyes and gripping the rope tightly, Sally awaited the crash. It came with a vast rending of boughs and garments. Dazed and bruised, Sally came to rest a good thirty feet above ground, securely enmeshed in lime branches and the remains of a squirrel's drey.

She was discovered by a cowman, who was making his way home after milking. By that time she had thrown the rope off and descended carefully as low as she could. The last twelve feet, unfortunately, consisted of trunk alone and it was while she was trying to brace herself to jump that the man arrived.

To Sally's relief he was a man of few words.

''Old on,' he said. 'I'll get a ladder.' He returned in a few minutes and helped her down. They walked part of the way to Fairacre together in silence. At length he turned in to his cottage gate.

'Good night,' he bade her and then added: 'How d'yer get up there?'

Sally began the tale she had already manufactured. It involved being chased by a bull, and was the best she could manage under the trying circumstances. She was aware, as she came to a faltering halt, that her rescuer was not impressed.

'Must be a dam' good leaper,' he observed drily, and went indoors.

Sally, bruised and weary, dragged herself homeward, took the pot from the larder shelf and threw it resolutely on to the rubbish heap.

Later that evening she thrust the exercise book into her fire, and holding it resolutely down with the poker, she watched it burn to ashes.

She had flown for the last time.

'Well, there it is, Miss Read,' said Mr Willet, rising from his chair. 'Take it or leave it. That's what Sally told my mother a year or two later, just afore she died.'

'I don't disbelieve you,' I said slowly. 'It's a wonderful story. It's just that – somehow –'

'Well, what?' asked Mr Willet, blowing out his moustache fiercely. 'Proper doubting Thomases, some people be!'

'It's just that it seems extraordinary that no one ever saw her. Particularly on the last journey, I mean.'

'Ah, but they did! There was two little boys, brothers they were, as had been sent down to the "Jug and Bottle". They saw Sally, and rope and all, skidding along over "The Beetle and Wedge", and tore 'ome to tell their mum and dad.

'"Course, all they got was a clump on the ear-'ole for being such a pair of liars, so they never said no more. And years later, when the poor ol' girl had gone, the landlord at the pub said he'd seen her picking plums two or three times, but never liked to say so.'

'I wonder why not?' I exclaimed. Mr Willet sighed patiently.

'You a school teacher and you don't know 'uman nature yet!' he commented. 'Why, people don't mind being thought downright evil and wicked, but they fair hates to seem fools. Ain't you learned that yet, Miss Read?'

He opened the kitchen door and looked out into the windy darkness.

'That coke'll have to wait till morning now. Goodbye, miss, and thanks for the tea. See you bright and early.'

And he vanished into the night.

3. Jingle Bells

Mr Willet was as good as his word, and next morning, 'bright and early', I had my breakfast to the accompaniment of the brushing up of coke in the distance.

❀ He was still at it when I crossed to the school, wielding the broom vigorously in his capable hands, his breath wreathing his head in silvery clouds.

'Nasty cold morning,' I called to him, scurrying towards shelter.

'This keeps me warm,' he replied, pausing for a moment to rest on his broom. 'But I s'pose I shan't be doing this much longer.'

'Only three days,' I agreed. 'And then it's the lovely Christmas holidays!'

'You should be ashamed!' said Mr Willet reproachfully. 'Young woman like you, wishing your life away.'

But it was too cold to argue, and I only had time to wave to him before whisking into the shelter of the lobby.

The last day of term, particularly the Christmas term, has a splendour of its own. There is an air of excitement at the thought of pleasures and freedom to come, but there is also a feeling of relaxation from daily routine made much more acute by the deliciously empty desks. Books have been collected and stacked in neat piles in the cupboard. Papers and exercise books have been tidied away. All that remains to employ young hands in this last glorious day is a pencil and loose sheets of paper which have been saved for just such an occasion.

Of course, work will be done. There will be mental arithmetic, and some writing; perhaps some spelling lists and paper games, and stories told to each other. And today, the children knew, there would be Christmas carols, and a visit to the old grey church next door to see the crib recently set up by the vicar's wife and other ladies of the village. The very thought of it all created a glow which warmed the children despite the winter's cold.

They entered more exuberantly than ever, cherry-nosed, hair curling damply from the December air and wellingtons plastered with Fairacre mud. I began to shoo them back into the lobby before our virago of a caretaker discovered them, but I was too late.

Mrs Pringle, emerging from the infants' room where she had just deposited a scuttle of coke on an outspread sheet of *The Times Educational Supplement*, looked at them with marked dislike.

'Anyone 'ere seen fit to use the door-scraper?' she asked sourly. Don't look like it to me. What you kids wants is an hour or two scrubbing this 'ere floor like I 'ave to. That'd make you think twice about dirtying my clean floorboards.'

She cast a malevolent glance in my direction and stumped out to the lobby. The children retreated before her, observing her marked limp, a sure sign of trouble.

The clatter of the door-scraper and the bang of the heavy Gothic door announced Mrs Pringle's departure to her cottage, until midday, when she was due to return to wash up the school dinner things. The children's spirits rose again and they sang 'Away in a Manger' with rather more gusto than perhaps was necessary at prayer time.

The infants departed to their own side of the partition and my class prepared to give part of its mind to some light scholastic task. Multiplication tables are always in sore need of attention, as every teacher knows, so that a test on the scrap paper already provided seemed a useful way of passing arithmetic lesson. It was small wonder that excitement throbbed throughout the classroom. The paper chains still rustled overhead in all their multi-coloured glory and in the corner, on the now depleted nature table, the Christmas tree glittered with tinsel and bright baubles.

But this year it carried no parcels. Usually, Fairacre School has a party on the last afternoon of the Christmas term when mothers and fathers, and friends of the school, come and eat a hearty tea and watch the children receive their presents from the tree. But this year the party was to be held in the village hall after Christmas and a conjuror had been engaged to entertain us afterwards.

However, the children guessed that they would not go home empty-handed today, I felt sure, and this touching faith, which I had no intention of destroying, gave them added happiness throughout the morning.

The weather grew steadily worse. Sleet swept across the playground and a wicked draught from the skylight buffeted the paper chains. I put the milk saucepan on the tortoise stove and the children looked pleased. Although a few hardy youngsters gulp their milk down stone-cold, even on the iciest day, most of them prefer to be cosseted a little and to see their bottles being tipped into the battered saucepan. The slow heating of the milk affords them exquisite pleasure, and it usually gets more attention than I do on cold days.

'It's steaming, miss,' one calls anxiously.

'Shall I make sure the milk's all right?' queries another.

'Can I get the cups ready?' asks a third.

One never-to-be-forgotten day we left the milk on whilst we had a rousing session in the playground as aeroplanes, galloping horses, trains and other violently moving articles. On our return, breathless and much invigorated, we had discovered a sizzling seething mess on the top, and cascading down the sides, of the stove. Mrs Pringle did not let any of us forget this mishap, and the children like to pretend that they only keep reminding me to save me from incurring that lady's wrath yet again.

In between sips of their steaming milk they kept up an excited chatter.

'What d'you want for Christmas?' asked Patrick of Ernest, his desk mate.

'Boxing gloves,' replied Ernest, lifting his head briefly and speaking through a white moustache.

'Well, I'm havin' a football, and a space helmet, and some new crayons, and a signal box for my train set,' announced Patrick proudly.

Linda Moffat, neat as a new pin from glossy hair to equally glossy patent leather slippers, informed me that she was hoping for a new work-box with a pink lining. I thought of the small embroidery scissors, shaped like a stork, which I had wrapped up for her the night before, and congratulated myself.

'What do you want?' I asked Joseph Coggs, staring monkey-like at me over the rim of his mug.

'Football,' croaked Joseph, in his hoarse gipsy voice. 'Might get it too.'

It occurred to me that this would make an excellent exercise in writing and spelling. Milk finished, I set them to work on long strips of paper.

'Ernest wants some boxing gloves for Christmas,' was the first entry.

'Patrick hopes to get –' began the second. The children joined in this list-making with great enthusiasm.

When Mrs Crossley, who brings the dinners, arrived, she was cross-questioned about her hopes.

'Well now, I don't really know,' she confessed, balancing the tins against her wet mackintosh and peering perplexedly over the top. 'A kitchen set, I think. You know, a potato masher and fish slice and all that, in a nice little rack.'

The children obviously thought this a pretty poor present but began to write down: 'Mrs Crossley wants a kitchen set,' below the last entry, looking faintly disbelieving as they did so.

'And what do you want?' asked Linda, when Mrs Crossley had vanished.

'Let me see,' I said slowly. 'Some extra nice soap, perhaps, and bath cubes; and a book or two, and a new rose bush to plant by my back door.'

'Is that all?'

'No sweets?'

'No, no sweets,' I said. 'But I should like a very pretty little ring I saw in Caxley last Saturday.'

'You'll have to get married for that,' said Ernest soberly. 'And you're too old now.' The others nodded in agreement.

'You're probably right,' I told them, keeping a straight face. 'Put your papers away and let's set the tables for dinner.'

The sleet was cruelly painful on our faces as we scuttled across the churchyard to St Patrick's. Inside it was cold and shadowy. The marble memorial tablets on the wall glimmered faintly in the gloom, and the air struck chill.

But the crib was aglow with rosy light, a spot of warmth and hope in the darkness. The children tip-toed towards it, awed by their surroundings.

They spent a long time gazing, whispering their admiration and pointing out particular details to each other. They were loth to leave it, and the shelter of the great church, which had defied worse weather than this for many centuries.

We pelted back to the school, for I had a secret plan to put into action, and three o'clock was the time appointed for it. St Patrick's clock chimed a quarter to, above our heads, as we hurried across the churchyard.

I had arranged with the infants' teacher to go privately into the lobby promptly at three and there shake some bells abstracted earlier from the percussion band box. We hoped that the infants would believe that an invisible Father Christmas had driven on his sleigh and delivered the two sacks of parcels which would be found in the lobby. At the moment, these were in the hall of my house. I proposed to leave my class for a minute, shake the bells, hide them from inquisitive eyes and return again to the children.

This innocent deception could not hope to take in many of my own children, I felt sure, but the babies would enjoy it, and so too would the younger ones in my classroom. I was always surprised at the remarkable reticence which the older children showed when the subject of Father Christmas cropped up. Those that knew seemed more than willing to keep up the pretence for the sake of the younger ones, and perhaps because they feared that the presents would not be forthcoming if they let the cat out of the bag or boasted of their knowledge.

I settled the class with more paper. They could draw a picture of the crib or St Patrick's church, or a winter scene of any kind, I told them. Someone wanted to go on with his list of presents and was readily given permission. The main thing was to have a very quiet classroom at three o'clock. Our Gothic doors are of sturdy oak and the sleigh bells would have to be shaken to a frenzy in order to make themselves heard.

At two minutes to three by the wall clock Patrick looked up from drawing a church with all four sides showing at once, and surmounted by what looked like a mammoth ostrich.

'I've got muck on my hand,' he said. 'Can I go out the lobby and wash?'

Maddening child! What a moment to choose! 'Not now,' I said, as calmly as I could. 'Just wipe it on your hanky.'

He produced a dark grey rag from his pocket and rubbed the offending hand, sighing in a martyred way. He was one of the younger children and I wondered if he might possibly half-believe in the sleigh bells.

'I'm just going across to the house,' I told them, squaring my conscience. 'Be very quiet while I'm away. The infants are listening to a story.'

All went according to plan. I struggled back through the sleet with the two sacks, deposited one outside the infants' door into the lobby, and the other outside our own.

The lobby was as quiet as the grave. I withdrew the bells from behind a stack of bars of yellow soap which Mrs Pringle stores on a lofty shelf, and crept to the outside door to begin shaking. Santa Claus in the distance, and fast approaching, I told myself. Would they be heard? I wondered, waggling frantically in the open doorway.

I closed the door gently against the driving sleet and now shook with all my might by the two inner doors. Heaven help me if one of my children burst out to see what was happening!

There was an uncanny silence from inside both rooms. I gave a last magnificent agitation and then crept along the lobby to the soap and tucked the bells securely out of sight. Then I returned briskly to the classroom. You could have heard a pin drop.

'There was bells outside,' said Joseph huskily.

'The clock's just struck three,' I pointed out, busying myself at the blackboard.

'No. *Little* bells!' said someone.

At this point the dividing door between the infants' room and ours burst open to reveal a bright-eyed mob lugging a sack.

'Father Christmas has been!'

'We heard him!'

'We heard bells, didn't we?'

'That's right. Sleigh bells.'

Ernest, by this time, had opened our door into the lobby and was returning with the sack. A cheer went up and the whole class converged upon him.

'Into your desks,' I bellowed, 'and Ernest can give them out.'

Ernest upended the sack and spilt the contents into a glorious heap of pink and blue parcels, as the children scampered to their desks and hung over them squeaking with excitement.

The babies sat on the floor receiving their presents with awed delight. There was no doubt about it, for them Father Christmas was as real as ever.

I became conscious of Patrick's gaze upon me.

'Did you see him?' he asked.

'Not a sign,' I said truthfully.

Patrick's brow was furrowed with perplexity. 'If you'd a let me wash my hand I reckon I'd just about've seen him,' he said at length.

I made no reply. Patrick's gaze remained fixed on my face, and

then a slow lovely smile curved his countenance. Together, amidst the hubbub of parcel-opening around us, we shared the unspoken, immortal secret of Christmas.

Later with the presents unwrapped, and the floor a sea of paper, Mrs Pringle arrived to start clearing up. Her face expressed considerable disapproval and her limp was very severe.

The children thronged around her showing her their toys.

'Ain't mine lovely?'

'Look, it's a dust cart!'

'This is a *magic* painting book! It says so!'

Mrs Pringle unbent a little among so much happiness, and gave a cramped smile.

Ernest raised his voice as she limped her way slowly across the room.

'Mrs Pringle, Mrs Pringle!'

The lady turned, a massive figure ankle deep in pink and blue wrappings.

'What do you want in your stocking, Mrs Pringle?' called Ernest. There was a sudden hush.

Mrs Pringle became herself again.

'In my stocking?' she asked tartly. 'A new leg! That's what I want!'

She moved majestically into the lobby, pretending to ignore the laughter of the children at this sally.

As usual, I thought wryly, Mrs Pringle had had the last word.

4. Mrs Next-door

One of the most exhilarating things about the holidays is the freedom to wander about the village at those hours which are, in term time, spent incarcerated in the classroom. There is nothing I relish more than calling at the Post Office, or the village shop, in the mid-morning, or afternoon, like all my lucky neighbours who are not confined by school hours.

A few days before term began I set off to buy stamps from Mr Lamb, our postmaster. It was a sharp, sunny January morning, with thin ice cracking on the puddles, and distant sounds could be heard exceptionally clearly. A winter robin piped from a high bare elm. Cows lowed three fields away, and somewhere, high above, an airliner whined its way to a warmer land than ours.

Nearer at hand I could hear a rhythmic chugging sound. As I turned the bend towards the Post Office I saw that it came from a cement mixer, hard at work, in front of a pair of cottages which were being made into one attractive house.

A group of my school children hovered near by, gazing at the operations. Some trailed shopping bags, and I could only hope that their mothers were not in urgent need of anything, for it was obvious that the fascination of men at work was overpowering. Patrick was among them, gyrating like a dervish, as an enormous scruffy dog on a lead tugged him round and round.

''Ello, miss,' he managed to puff on his giddy journey; and the others smiled and said 'Hullo' in an abstracted fashion. The work-men seemed to be getting far more concentrated attention than is my usual lot, I noticed.

As I waited my turn to be served, I looked through the window at the scene. I had ample time to watch, for this was Thursday, pensions day, and several elderly Fairacre worthies were collecting their money. Mr Lamb had a leisurely chat with each one, and as we all had a word with each other as well, it was a very pleasant and sociable twenty minutes, and we all felt the better for it.

The cottages had been stripped of their old rotting thatch, and the men were busy making a roof of cedar shingles. Watching them run up and down ladders I suddenly remembered that it was in one of these cottages that Mrs Next-Door had lived. Miss Clare had told me her story soon after I arrived as schoolmistress at Fairacre School.

It happened to be the first time I had visited Miss Clare's cottage at the neighbouring village of Beech Green. She had lived there since she was six years old. When I first met her she was in charge of the infants' class at Fairacre, a wise, patient, white-haired teacher who had taught there for half a century.

It was a gloriously hot August afternoon when I set out to walk to Miss Clare's, and I very soon found that it was much further than I realized. I toiled up a short steep hill, and leant thankfully upon a field gate near the summit. Cornfields spread before me, shimmering in the heat. Scarlet poppies dropped a petal or two, and high in the blue a hawk hovered motionless for a while, and then painted in-visible circles with its wing-tip, slipping languidly and elegantly round the sky.

I resumed my travels, but determined to catch the bus home. Luckily it was market day, and a bus would leave Caxley just before six o'clock, passing Miss Clare's cottage about half past.

After one of Miss Clare's sumptuous teas, and a great deal of chatter, we walked together to her white gate. Two hawthorn trees flank it, and have met above to form a thick archway. In its welcome shade we waited, she on her side of the gate, and I on the other, ready to dart to the edge of the road when the bus came in sight.

An old lady, very upright on an ancient bicycle, pedalled slowly past, and wished us 'Good evening'. When she was out of earshot, Miss Clare said: 'That's Mrs Next-Door. At least, she's really Mrs Wood, and my nearest neighbour, but I think of her as Mrs Next-Door.'

She began to laugh, and then noticed my puzzled air.

'Of course, I forgot. You don't know the story of Polly, who was the original Mrs Next-Door. It happened years ago in Fairacre and was as good as any serial story to us in the village.'

She leant comfortably upon her gate in the shade of the leafy archway and embarked on a gay snippet of Fairacre's history. A few years after the Great War of 1914–1918, when Fairacre was doing its best to settle down again to peaceful village affairs, two young couples moved into the pair of thatched cottages opposite the Post Office, within a few weeks of each other.

The first pair were named Leslie and Bertha Foster. They were both big, fair and rather slow, with one boy, Billy, who was almost five years old. When they arrived, soon after Michaelmas Day, Bertha was again in an interesting condition; or, it might be more correct to say, in a condition interesting to the village. Fairacre speculated upon the possible date of the unknown's arrival, its sex, and the many vicissitudes it would cause its mother before, and during, birth.

Leslie Foster was the newly appointed cowman to Walnut Tree Farm, and as he had an aunt in Fairacre his history was fairly well known. But his wife was a Caxley girl and the village watched closely to see how she would settle down.

On the whole she was approved. She was friendly and hard-working. By the evening of the first day her house was clean and tidy, and new curtains hung at the windows. To be sure, Fairacre was not at all certain about the curtains. Most people had lace ones, a few rose to flowered cretonne, and the gentry seemed to go in for damask or velvet as they had done for years. But Bertha's curtains were of plain cream cotton, and she had stitched five rows of coloured braid along the bottom. The braid was a deep blue, exactly the same colour as the one cushion in the room, which was placed squarely upon the seat of Leslie's wooden armchair. Some thought the curtains were 'a bit far-fetched and arty-crafty', but one or two younger people thought them 'real pretty and up-to-date'.

A few weeks later the second cottage became occupied. Mike Norton was also going to work for the same employer as his neighbour, for these were tied cottages. They had not moved in earlier because a faulty chimney had needed attention. His wife Polly was thin and dark. It was noticed, by keen eyes around them, that their house was not put in order as quickly as the Fosters' had been, and that Polly's curtains were extremely shabby and obviously makeshift.

There were no children, but many a wife told another that Polly Norton looked a bit peaky and as they had been married now for six months (so they had heard) perhaps she had good cause.

The two families became friends. The men did not have the same opportunity to exchange confidences, obstetric and otherwise, which their wives had, for they only saw each other briefly on the farm and were both glad to rest indoors when they reached home in the evening. But the two women spent a great deal of time in each other's houses and often took Billy for a walk in the afternoon together.

Within a fortnight Bertha had told Polly that her second was due in January and that she wanted a girl, and Polly had coyly mentioned her hopes for the following June. She had set her heart on a boy and was already trying to decide between the names Mervyn and Clifford. Bertha's girl was to be called Maria, after Leslie's mother, and Polly secretly thought it a very common name indeed.

Thus began a halcyon period of exchanging knitting patterns, comparing the discomforts of early and advanced pregnancy, and shopping frugally in Caxley for all those things incidental to a new baby's arrival. Despite Bertha's slowness, her greater experience and her upbringing made her the leader of the two. She had been brought up in a respectable home in Caxley, had been taught well at one of the town schools and enjoyed the advantage of a mother who was an excellent cook and dressmaker. Bertha's few shillings went a good deal further than Polly's. Polly was one of a large, and somewhat feckless, family from Beech Green. This was her first home and she was anxious to make it as splendid as she could without taking too much time and trouble in doing so. As soon as Mike brought home his first week's wages she clamoured for money for new curtains.

'Can't be done this week,' said her husband ruefully. 'You'll 'ave to put a bit by regular.'

Polly saw the sense in this and reckoned that she should have enough to buy the material before Christmas. She discussed the matter eagerly with Bertha, and this was her neighbour's first shock.

'If you don't mind,' said Polly brightly, 'I'd like 'em just exactly like yourn.'

Bertha was seriously taken aback.

'Well,' she began doubtfully, in her slow voice, 'I don't truthfully know as —'

Polly cut in swiftly.

'I reckons they're the prettiest curtains as I've ever seen. And another thing, the two houses'd look much nicer with matching curtains in the front. Dales had some real nice cream material in their sale last week, and I can get the braid there too.'

It was quite apparent to Bertha that the matter was as good as settled. Nettled though she was, she did not protest. After all, there was really nothing to stop Polly from having similar curtains, she told herself, and for the sake of the coming baby she tried not to feel upset.

But for the rest of the day resentment smouldered in Bertha's breast. When Leslie came home she poured the tale into his ears.

Leslie, cold, tired and busy with his rabbit stew, did his best to smooth things over.

'I shouldn't fret about it. Don't hurt you if the curtains are the same. My ma says: "Imitation is the best form of flattery." Come to think of it, Bertha, it's a compliment really. Shows she likes your choice.'

Bertha was somewhat mollified by this aspect of the matter. In any case, she did not want to fall out with her neighbour, and nothing more was said. Nevertheless, the incident rankled, and when the curtains were hung, at last, she felt crosser than ever when she saw that the braid was the identical width and colour, and arranged in exactly the same five rows.

'Should have thought she could've had red or green, or summat different,' exclaimed Bertha to her husband. 'I should be ashamed to be such a copycat.'

Bertha's placid countenance was quite pink with wrath and Leslie again had to act as a soothing agent. The baby was now due, and whether the curtains next door had anything to do with the arrival of a fine daughter that night, no one could tell. The birth was easy, and Leslie was able to set off to work at his usual time, leaving Bertha and Maria in the capable hands of the local midwife.

'Ain't she just lovely?' breathed Polly admiringly, when she came round to see the baby. Her sharp eyes fell upon the cradle. It had been dressed in yard upon yard of spotted muslin, by Bertha's mother, and caught at the top with a splendid pink satin bow.

'You never showed me the cradle,' she said reproachfully. Bertha, sleepy and content, smiled upon her.

'It was at my ma's. She only brought it over yesterday. What's more, she made two bows, one pink and one blue, so's we'd have the right one.'

Polly was full of admiration. United in baby-worship, the two neighbours were in happy accord.

But this blissful state of affairs was not to last long. Spring arrived, and a double row of purple crocuses bordered Bertha's path. Behind them stood a fine row of polyanthuses heavy with buds. In Polly's identical border, there were also purple crocuses, and behind hers grew an equally fine collection of polyanthus plants.

''Tis too bad!' exclaimed Bertha to Leslie, thoroughly vexed. 'She knew I'd put them in. And I wouldn't mind betting her spring flowers come out yellow, same as ourn!'

They did, and Bertha's wrath grew. The tart comments which hovered on her tongue she managed to restrain, however, although she wondered at times if a bit of plain speaking would be a good thing.

Her baby was now a few months old, a big, fair, placid child like her parents. Billy had started school and Bertha was free to attend to her neighbour when she felt the onset of birth pangs. Polly was unduly fearful, clinging to Bertha in much agitation.

'Don't'ee leave me till Mrs Drew comes!' she begged, naming the local midwife.

'Don't fret,' answered Bertha soothingly. 'I'll stay with you; but I think you'd be better upstairs.'

'No, no,' responded Polly. 'I'll walk about down here and get

Mike's dinner ready atween whiles. Keeps my mind off it a bit, to have summat to do.'

Bertha saw the sense in this and did not press the matter. She was greatly relieved, though, when the midwife came and hustled her patient upstairs.

The baby was a long time arriving. Bertha and Leslie could hear muffled activity in the bedroom next door to their own.

'I do feel downright sorry for Polly,' murmured Bertha, the memory of her own experiences still fresh in her mind. 'It must be over soon, that's one comfort.'

But the baby had not arrived when the Fosters rose next morning. Mike came round, haggard and unshaven, to ask Leslie to take a message to the farm.

'She's about all in,' he said. 'Dammit all, that's the last baby we're having. Never thought it'd be such a set-to.'

Bertha and Leslie made light of it, teasing him, but he was too tired to appreciate badinage, and returned moodily to his home.

At midday the child was born. The midwife called in to tell Bertha it was a girl.

'They're both asleep, and can do with it,' declared the old woman who had brought half Fairacre into the world.

'I'll look in tomorrow,' promised Bertha, 'when she's feeling better.'

The next morning, a posy in her hand for Polly and a freshly-made pie for Mike's supper in her basket, Bertha went next door. She called, but there was no reply. She mounted the stairs and gently pushed open the bedroom door.

What Bertha saw, before the opening had widened enough to include a view of mother and child, made her grip the posy in a furiously clenched fist. For there, beside the bed, stood a cradle which was the replica of her own, even to a splendid pink satin bow.

Bertha swallowed her rage and tiptoed into the bedroom. The creaking of the old boards awakened Polly.

'Oh, Bertha!' she said, with such affection and relief that Bertha's anger melted. ''Tis lovely to see you. Take a peep at the baby. Fancy me having a girl, just like you!'

Bertha could have said that it caused her no surprise, but this was hardly the time to be so uncharitable. In any case, the new-born infant quite won her heart with its red puckered face, cobwebby black hair and skinny fingers.

'Ain't she a real beauty!' she exclaimed with sincerity. A thought struck her.

'What are you going to call her?'

'Mildred,' replied the mother. 'It begins with M, just like yourn.'

Bertha was thankful that the child was not to be another Maria, and turning her eyes from the ribbons and flounces of the hated cradle, she settled the posy in water, made Polly some tea, reiterated her congratulations and returned next door.

Billy arrived home from school and was told the news. He took it stolidly. Babies did not mean much to Billy. If anything, he disapproved of them. They drew attention to themselves, he knew, to the detriment of their older brothers' welfare. But he brightened at the thought of telling Miss Clare, his teacher, all about it when he went to school next morning.

Miss Clare was as impressed with the news as he had hoped she would be, but Billy's eyes did not miss the flicker of amusement which crossed her kind face when he said:

'And it's a girl! Just like ourn!'

At playtime Miss Clare told the news to Mr Benson, the headmaster. In common with the rest of Fairacre, he had watched the doings of the pair of cottages with amusement and considerable sympathy for the much-tried Bertha Foster.

'Isn't that typical?' he commented. 'Poor Mrs Foster! I wonder what Polly will call it. Maria, no doubt, and it will have an identical pram.'

The village hummed with the news.

'Give Polly her due,' said one fair-minded neighbour, 'she couldn't help it being a girl. Now, could she?'

'She could help her curtains and the flowers in the front and this 'ere new cradle she's got,' answered a less charitable listener. 'Bertha must be a proper angel to stay friends with a copycat like Polly.'

Time passed. It was a long hot summer and both babies flourished. Bertha's polyanthuses were succeeded by sweet williams and then asters. So were Polly's. Bertha whitewashed two large stones and set them one each side of her doorstep as ornaments. So did Polly. Leslie bought Bertha a canary in a cage for her birthday. Mike, under pressure, did the same for Polly.

By now, relations were decidedly strained between the two women, although they maintained a surface civility. Billy, over-hearing many a tart comment at home, often told a tale to Miss Clare who did her best to discourage him. She found this compara-tively easy. It was not so easy to stem the flow of confidences which Bertha began to pour into her unwilling ear when she came to meet Billy from school. It was at this stage that the name 'Mrs Next-Door' began to be used in a fruitless attempt to veil Polly's identity from the young listeners milling round them.

'That Mrs Next-Door,' Bertha would whisper, 'has done it again. Pink asters, same as mine. It do fairly make my blood boil at times!'

'Ignore it,' Miss Clare used to answer. 'It really doesn't matter, you know.' But secretly she had every sympathy with poor pro-voked Bertha. How long, she wondered, would her patience last?

The children added fuel to the fire by teasing Billy.

'Your Mrs Next-Door's got a hat with daisies on, just like your mum's!'

'I see Mrs Next-Door's got a canary now!'

'Mrs Next-Door's got a pink bedspread on the line this morning. Looked like the one your mum had out last week!'

At last the storm broke. The immediate cause, as Fairacre had foretold, involved the two babies. Christmas was now at hand, and as usual, a teaparty for the whole village was to be held in the school. Anyone was welcome to this festivity, whether a parent or not, and it was usual for all the women, and one or two old retired men, to foregather on this village occasion. The school children, dressed in their best, looked upon themselves as hosts.

Bertha took considerable trouble with her own appearance and even more with Maria's. The child was dressed in a white silk frock, embroidered with forget-me-nots on the bodice, and over this crea-tion wore a blue coat edged with swansdown and a bonnet to match. Bertha had seen this delicious set in a Caxley shop window and had been unable to resist it. This was the first time that Maria had put it on, and very beautiful she looked.

Bertha pushed her daughter proudly towards the school. The after-noon was cold and foggy, but Maria's face glowed from the becoming blue bonnet. She was much admired by the throng at the school.

About twenty minutes later Polly arrived, carrying Mildred. To the amusement of some, the resentment of others, and the speechless

fury and astonishment of poor Bertha, the child had on exactly similar garments to Maria's. Bertha pointedly turned her back towards the newcomers and did her best to appear unconcerned, knowing that she was the centre of all eyes.

The party appeared to be as gay as it always was, but for Bertha it was sheer misery. She was one of the first to leave, pushing Maria in her finery, with Billy clinging to the pram, at a pace which taxed the strength of all three.

It was now dark. Maria was strapped into her high chair and Billy was told to look after her. Before Leslie came home, Bertha intended to confront her infuriating neighbour She returned to the gate to await Polly's homecoming.

'Now she's going to have it!' Bertha told herself fiercely. 'I been too meek all along, sitting down under her impudence. I'll settle her!'

The sound of footsteps and the familiar squeak of Polly's pram wheels heralded her approach. Bertha advanced like some avenging fury.

'I'll thank you,' she began ominously, 'to step inside here a minute, Mrs Norton.'

This was the first time that Polly had been so called by her neighbour, and she was at once on her guard.

'What's up?' she inquired, trying to sound at ease, but her voice trembled.

'You knows, as well as I do, what's up!' breathed Bertha menacingly. 'You dare to dress up that kid of yours just like my Maria and parade it in front of all Fairacre! Trying to make me a laughing-stock! I've had enough of you and your copying ways!'

Polly tried to laugh, but she was very frightened. There is nothing more terrifying than a calm woman suddenly aroused. She had no idea that placid Bertha could feel such venom, or express it with such menace.

'No law against buying a coat and bonnet for my baby, I suppose?' queried Polly.

'No, nor curtains, nor flowers, nor hats, nor bedspreads, same as mine,' burst out Bertha, 'but you're not going to do it any longer, my girl, or you'll be in trouble! Take it from me, Polly Norton, if I ever sees any more copying from you I'll be round at your place and black your eye for you! I've just about had enough, see?'

She thrust a red furious face close to Polly's startled one and slammed the gate between them. Polly, much shaken, moved slowly towards her own.

'I'll tell—' she began truculently.

'You'll tell no one,' Bertha cut in. 'All the village is on my side. You've branded yourself as a plain copycat. I ain't saying no more to you. *Not ever*. But just you mark what I've said to you!'

Still pulsing with righteous indignation, Bertha returned indoors to attend to the children and Leslie's tea.

'I feels all the better for that,' she told herself. 'It's cleared the air. Come to think of it, I should've done it months ago.'

Now that battle was joined, Bertha found life much more straightforward. She simply ignored her neighbour. If she met her

in the garden, or in the village street, she had the exquisite pleasure
of looking clean through her. Polly retaliated with a toss of the
head or a muttered aside. The village watched with avid interest.
There were a few who maintained that Polly was not as bad as she
was painted, but the majority felt she had got off lightly in the
affair and that Bertha had every justification for cutting off relations
with her neighbour.

The two husbands found the whole thing very trying. At work,
they talked normally to each other, each being careful to leave his
wife's name out of the conversation. At home, they did their best to
soothe their wives and keep out of trouble's way. It was not easy.
Both women were expecting again, Bertha in October and Polly a
month later, and tempers were frayed all round.

However, Polly had seen reason in Bertha's tirade that dark evening, and although she would not admit that she was in the wrong,
she took care not to rouse her fire again by any obvious copying.
Unfortunately, much remained that had been done before the split
occurred. The canaries still sang and fluttered in the two front
windows. The white stones flanked the two doorsteps, the curtains,
the bedspreads and the babies' coats still remained identical, for
neither would give way.

Even worse was the simultaneous ripening of the two rowan
trees in the front gardens. Bertha's had been planted soon after their
arrival, Polly's a month or two later. This year Polly's was covered
in bright red clusters of berries. Bertha's was decidedly inferior.
Bertha, now near her time, a massive unwieldy figure venturing no
further than the garden, watched her neighbour picking sprays to
take indoors. It gave her no comfort to see that Polly was wearing a
blue flowered smock over her bulk exactly like the one she had on.
They had been worn during their earlier pregnancies and one could
hardly expect Polly to throw hers away. Nevertheless, Bertha found
the sight annoying. Would she never be free from Polly shadowing
her?

A week later Bertha was brought to bed. Mrs Drew arrived in
the morning confidently expecting to be back in her own cottage in
time to cook her midday dinner. But the day wore on, Bertha
continued her labours, Leslie ate bread and cheese for his dinner, the
same for his tea, and went post-haste for the doctor at six o'clock
when Mrs Drew clattered down the stairs in a state of urgent alarm.

Fairacre watched with some agitation. What could be happening to Bertha? Always had her babies as easy as shelling peas! Could Mrs Drew have bungled things? Not like her to send for the doctor! Mind you, she was getting on a bit; perhaps she was a shade past it!

So the tongues wagged. Doctor Martin was seen to enter the cottage at a quarter to seven. No one saw him leave. Of course it was dark, but the doctor's old Ford car made enough noise to rouse the dead. What could be going on?

As St Patrick's church clock struck eleven Dr Martin was drying his hands in Bertha's crowded bedroom. He was smiling broadly, but his eyes were on his patient. Her eyes were closed, her hair, damp and dishevelled, clung to her forehead. Mrs Drew was busy with baby clothes. Leslie Foster, summoned from his vigil below, had just approached the bed. He looked thunderstruck, as well he might. Beside his exhausted wife lay three tightly-wrapped snuffling bundles.

He stroked the hair back from his wife's hot forehead.

'Bertha?' he whispered questioningly.

Her eyes opened slowly. She gazed at Leslie and then at the three small faces beside her. A look of intense joy lit her face.

'Let Mrs Next-Door copy *that*!' cried Bertha triumphantly.

5. A Tale of Love

The alterations to the pair of cottages where Polly and Bertha had once lived took many weeks. The children's interest in all that went on continued unabated. The four workmen who were engaged on the job became their friends and heroes, and I became more and more annoyed as the children arrived late for school.

'You can miss your playtime,' I announced to a little knot of malefactors who entered noisily, bursting with good spirits, at a quarter past nine. 'I'm tired of telling you to be punctual.'

They looked at each other with dismay.

'But we was only givin' the workmen a hand, like,' said Richard, assuming an air of injured innocence. 'They had an ol' bucket they was pulling up to the top windows, see, on a bit of rope –'

'On a little wheel, sort of—' broke in Ernest, his eyes alight at the happy memory.

'A *pulley*, he means, miss,' said John, sniffing appallingly. 'They has cement in this 'ere bucket and it's heavy to lug up the ladders, so they has this wheel thing called a *pulley*, miss, as pulls it up. That's why it's called a *pulley*,' explained John patiently, as though to a particularly backward child.

'I daresay,' I said shortly. 'And nine o'clock is not the time to stand and watch it. Get to your desks at once, and for pity's sake blow your nose, John.'

There followed a great fuss of pocket searching, feeling under his jersey, exploring sleeves, looking in his desk and so on, accompanied throughout by sniffs and exclamations of surprise and dismay.

'Don't seem to have one, miss,' said John at length.

'Get a Kleenex from the cupboard,' I said ominously, 'and don't let me hear another squeak, or sniff, from you for the rest of the morning!'

This sort of thing went on intermittently throughout the early part of the spring term and I should be heartily glad, I told myself, when the workmen had vanished and the new house was occupied. Mrs Pringle agreed with me.

'Bad enough sweeping up honest Fairacre mud,' boomed the lady, after school one afternoon, 'without bits of cement off their boots, and shavings and nails and that out of their pockets. And when it comes to *this*,' added Mrs Pringle opening a massive fist and thrusting it before my nose, 'it's time to *speak*!'

In her palm lay some glutinous grey matter which I recognized as putty.

'Stuck on the lobby wall, if you please,' said Mrs Pringle, disengaging the stuff with a squelch and putting it, unasked, on my desk. 'I thought it might be that chewing gum again when I first saw it, and then I thought: "Not likely. Not that sized lump. No one could get a lump that big in his mouth. Not even Eric Williams, and dear knows his mouth's big enough, on account of his poor foolish mother feeding him with a dessertspoon at six months." So I looked closer and saw it was this 'orrible putty. Them workmen want sorting out, Miss Read, letting the children have such stuff.'

'I believe they've nearly finished,' I answered, trying to soothe the savage breast. I glanced at the clock. Amy was coming to tea and it was already past four. Mrs Pringle grunted disbelievingly.

'I knows workmen,' she said darkly. 'Got no sense of time. I feel downright sorry for that couple waiting to move in. They'll be lucky to close their own door behind them before Easter, at this rate.'

This was the first I had heard of the future occupiers and though, as any normal villager, I should dearly have loved to hear more, I did not intend to probe Mrs Pringle for details, and, in any case, it was time I put on the kettle for Amy. I made my way to the door. Mrs Pringle, who can read my thoughts much too easily for my comfort, sent a parting shot after me.

'Name of Blundell,' trumpeted Mrs Pringle. 'Could tell you more, but I can see you're not interested.'

I caught the glimpse of smug triumph on her unlovely face as I closed the door.

Amy and I were at college together many years ago. We lost touch with each other and only met again when I came to Fairacre. She had moved to Bent, a village a few miles south of Caxley, when she married, and so knew more about the Caxley neighbourhood than I did.

Amy is a dynamic person, full of good works and good ideas. I only wish I had half her energy. It is always exhilarating to have a visit from her and I looked forward to an hour or two of her company on this particular afternoon.

The car arrived as I set tea. Amy, elegant as ever in a new suit, emerged with a bunch of daffodils and a new hair style. We greeted each other warmly and I complimented her on her looks.

'Do you like it?' she asked, patting her variegated locks and preening herself.

'Very much,' I answered truthfully. 'I like all those stripes, like a humbug.'

Amy looked at me with distaste.

'Like a humbug!' she echoed disgustedly. 'What a dreadful way of putting it!'

'What's wrong with it?' I asked. 'I'm very fond of humbugs, and those auburn streaks remind me of the treacly ones.'

Amy bit delicately into a sandwich.

'It cost a fortune,' she said sadly. 'And took hours to do, with all

the strands sprouting through a bathing-cap affair. I thought James
would like it, but he hasn't noticed yet.'

I inquired after James, her husband, and learnt that he was away
for the night at a conference in the north. To my mind, James has a
suspiciously large number of overnight engagements, but it is no
affair of mine, and Amy is wise enough not to discuss the matter
with me.

'You know,' said Amy, looking at me closely, 'I think you could
take this high-lighting effect. It would do something for you.'

'Now, Amy,' I begged, seriously alarmed, for I have had many a
battle with my old friend about my mousy appearance, 'please don't
start on me again! I am a plain, shabby, middle-aged woman with
no pretensions to glamour. I like being like this, so leave me alone.'

Amy waved aside my pleading and took another sandwich.

'A few glints in your hair, some decent make-up, and a good
strong pair of corsets would work wonders for you,' said Amy.
'Which reminds me – I want you to come to the Charity Ball at the
Corn Exchange next month!'

'Never!' I cried, with spirit. 'You know I can't keep awake after
eleven o'clock. And I don't like dancing. And I haven't got a frock
to wear anyway.'

Amy sighed.

'Then it's time you bought one. You simply can't waste the whole
of your life in this one-eyed village. You never meet a soul –'

'I do,' I protested. 'Every day. I meet far too many souls. There
are thirty-odd to be faced every morning.'

'I mean *men*,' snapped Amy with exasperation. 'There's no reason
why you shouldn't get married, even at your age, and it's time
someone took you in hand and made you see reason.'

'But I don't *want* to get married!' I wailed. 'I should have done it
years ago if I'd intended to do.'

'And who,' said Amy coldly, 'ever asked you?'

I began to laugh.

'Well there was that neighbour of yours who was in a constant
state of inebriation and wanted someone to keep him from drinking –'

'You can't count him,' said Amy firmly. 'He asked everyone.'

'I can't think of anyone else at the moment,' I said.

'I can tell you one thing,' said Amy, 'if you take up this attitude, and refuse to make the Best of Yourself, then you are doomed to be an old maid.'

'Suits me,' I said comfortably. 'Have some more tea.'

Amy stirred her second cup thoughtfully.

'There's still time,' she assured me. 'Look at Elsie Parker. Blundell, I mean. She's managed it.'

'Blundell?' I queried. 'Not the Blundells who are moving to Fairacre?'

Amy looked interested, and ceased stirring.

'It's quite likely,' she said slowly. 'They are having a pair of cottages knocked into one house somewhere or other.'

'It's here,' I assured her feelingly. 'I should know. The children spend most of their time watching the workmen. It was Mrs Pringle who mentioned the name Blundell, only this afternoon.'

'That must be Elsie,' said Amy, 'and her newly caught husband. Well, well, well! So they're settling in Fairacre!'

Amy produced a beautiful gold cigarette case, a present from James after a week away, lit a cigarette, and settled back in a cloud of blue smoke.

'Well, go on,' I urged. 'Tell me about my neighbours to be!'

And, smiling indulgently, Amy began.

It was generally agreed, in the little village of Bent, that Elsie Parker was an uncommonly pretty girl. She was the only child born to Roger and Lily Parker a year or two after the First World War. Her father returned from his arduous, if undistinguished, duties as an army baker to start afresh as part-owner of a small general store on the southern outskirts of Caxley.

At first, he cycled the few miles to work on a venerable bicycle, but as the business prospered he changed to a small second-hand van with which he began to build up a modest delivery round. People liked Roger Parker. He was hardworking, honest and utterly reliable. If he said that he would bring the pickles in time for Monday's cold lunch, then you could be quite sure that the jar would be with you before the potatoes had come to the boil! He deserved to prosper, and he did.

By the time Elsie was six, the shabby delivery van had been changed for two larger new ones which spent the day touring the district and the night safely locked up in the new shed at the rear of the general stores. Roger now owned a bull-nosed Morris tourer which he drove to work each morning. At the week-ends he polished it lovingly and then took his wife and pretty little daughter for a drive.

Elsie was the apple of her parents' eyes. She had a mop of yellow curls, lively blue eyes with exquisitely long curling lashes, and a smile that disarmed even the most curmudgeonly. Needless to say, she was the belle of the infants' class at Bent village school and was accompanied to and from that establishment by a bevy of small admirers.

Her first proposal of marriage came when she was seven. It came from the shabbiest of her escorts, whose nose was constantly wet, despite a rag pinned to his dirty jersey, and whose attentions had long been deplored by Mrs Parker. Elsie turned him down promptly, but gave him one of her heart-turning smiles as she did so, for she was a kind child.

It was an experience which was to occur many times in the future, and as time went on Elsie was to learn many refinements in the art of rejecting a suitor. But, as a first attempt and for one of such tender years, the present rejection was commendable – a blend of firmness and gentleness, lit by a certain light-hearted awareness of an honour received, which many an older maiden could not have bettered. The young man ran ahead to school, and after shedding a few hot tears in the blessed privacy of the boys' lavatory, recovered his good spirits and continued to accompany his goddess as before – without hope, certainly, but also without rancour.

Hard on the heels of this proposal came another, from an urchin almost as disreputable as the first. He too was turned down, and in an unguarded moment Elsie mentioned both incidents to her mother. She was much distressed.

'I can't think why such *dirty* boys like you!' exclaimed poor genteel Mrs Parker. 'You mustn't encourage them, Elsie. It won't do! It really won't do at all!'

If Mrs Parker had been capable of giving the situation a moment's clear thought she would have realized that it was the very difference in her daughter's appearance and nature which acted as a magnet to the rough rumbustious boys. Those glossy curls, the freshly-starched voiles and the enchanting scent of Erasmic soap created a being of such sweet cleanliness that she was well-nigh irresistible to the lesser washed.

'Why don't you play with some of the other boys?' asked Mrs Parker. 'There's Jimmy Bassett and Stanley Roberts,' she went on, naming the firstborn at the flourishing new garage on the main road to Caxley, and the vicar's son who would be going on to his preparatory school next term. Mrs Parker had a nice regard for the social ladder.

'Jimmy lisps,' said Miss Parker, speaking truly. 'And Stanley Roberts dropped a dead rat in old Mrs Turner's well last week.'

'*Stanley* did?' exclaimed Mrs Parker, much shocked. 'The vicar's son? A dead rat?'

'Mrs Turner's chapel,' explained Elsie succinctly.

The matter was dropped.

At the age of ten Elsie was taken from the village school and travelled daily into Caxley to attend a larger establishment run by some charming and hard-working nuns. She wore a cornflower blue uniform which enhanced the beauty of her colouring and very soon the schoolboys who travelled on the bus with her were jostling for the place beside her. Elsie treated them with happy impartiality, bestowing conversation, smiles and sympathy upon whichever escort had been lucky enough – or rough enough – to gain the seat next to her.

On more than one occasion during her time at the convent school Elsie was drawn quietly aside by one of the sisters and given a few words of mild reproof. It was not fitting, she was told, to be seen at the centre of a crowd of the opposite sex day after day. It gave the school a bad name. She was advised to be polite but distant, kind but not too kind. Dreadful dangers, it was hinted, could attend too great an interest in the male sex.

It was all rather hard on Elsie. She did not encourage the young men, they simply gravitated towards her as wasps to a sun-ripe pear. Her father, made aware of his daughter's attractions by a dulcet word or two from Sister Teresa, decided to take Elsie to school with him in the car and collect her again in the afternoon. But this state of affairs did not last long. It was most inconvenient for Roger to leave the business. Sometimes lacrosse or tennis kept Elsie late, sometimes a half-holiday meant that she was out early. Gradually the arrangement fell through, and Elsie returned to the bus and the adoration of her swains.

At seventeen, still unscathed by love, Elsie left school and began training to be a nurse. She was at a hospital in London but spent as many week-ends as possible at Bent. By now Roger was what is known in the north as 'a warm man'. A wing had been built on to the small four-square house where Elsie had been born, and a field next door had been acquired to ensure future privacy. Roger, who as a young man had voted Liberal, bought his ready-made suits from a Caxley outfitters, and enjoyed mustard with mutton, now helped himself to mint sauce instead, had his suits made in London, and voted Conservative. He worked, if anything, harder than ever, was much respected in Caxley, and continued to give the same never-failing service which had built up the business.

Mrs Parker, too, rose with her husband. Her hopes were centred on Elsie with more concentration than ever before. In London, she felt sure, there must be many eligible bachelors. Elsie could have whomsoever she wanted, of that she was positive, for she was now at her most beautiful and the stimulation of work and life in London had given her added gaiety and poise. At week-ends Mrs Parker combed the neighbourhood for likely young men, and the field next door was transformed into a tennis court, set about with the very latest garden chairs and a dashing swing seat with a canopy and cushions covered in wisteria-entwined cretonne. Delicious snacks were eaten in the gnat-humming twilight, laughter set the tall lemonade glasses tinkling and the young men feasted their eyes on Elsie Parker, cool, adorable and completely untouched by love.

Of course, it was inevitable that when Elsie fell in love the affair would be disastrous. As might be expected, Elsie's heart was first touched by a married man. He was a doctor who visited the hospital, an unremarkable man, running to fat, and so swarthy that he needed to shave twice a day. He had occasion to speak to Elsie, now and again, and had no idea of the emotion which he unwittingly aroused. His presence alone affected Elsie. Her legs trembled, her hands shook, her throat grew dry and her head grew dizzy. She found it almost impossible to take in his orders.

'That Nurse Parker,' the doctor commented to one of his colleagues, 'is practically an imbecile. Talk about a dumb blonde!'

'It's love,' said the other laconically. He was sharper-eyed than most.

'Rubbish!' snorted Elsie's hero, and dismissed the whole conversation from his mind. He had a perfectly good wife, four children, a house with a mortgage, and no intention of getting entangled with a silly chit of a nurse, even if she was as handsome as Nurse Parker.

Elsie's love grew as the months went by, although it was given no encouragement. At week-ends her mother noted the abstracted air, the paler cheek, the slight, but becoming, loss of weight. She longed to be taken into her daughter's confidence, relishing her role as understanding mother, but Elsie said nothing. In an earnest desire to cheer the girl Mrs Parker began to plan a small party for her nineteenth birthday.

'Oh, mum!' protested Elsie, when the project was broached. 'Let's skip my birthday this year. Honestly, I just don't feel like a lot of fuss.'

'You'll thoroughly enjoy it,' said Mrs Parker firmly. 'You've been moping long enough – about what I can't say, though I can guess – and it's time you pulled yourself together. I'll make all the arrangements.'

'I'd much rather you did nothing,' replied Elsie shortly. She had no energy or time for anything else but her preoccupation with the adored. Her mother, however, was undeterred. Invitations went out, food and drink were ordered, the local dressmaker was summoned to take Mrs Parker's ever-increasing measurements, and one Saturday night in June was appointed as the time of celebration. Scarcely aware of what was happening, Elsie acquiesced listlessly in the plans.

Work at the hospital seemed doubly hard in the warm weather. There was, too, an air of profound disquiet hanging over the whole nation, for this was 1939 and the threat of world war came closer daily.

On the day before Elsie's birthday party the weather was close and thundery. Patients complained in their hot crumpled beds, nurses' tempers were short and the doctors' were even shorter. Shortest of all, it seemed, was the temper of Elsie's beloved. He was a sorely tried man. One of his children had mumps, his wife was prostrated with a migraine which could well last a week, his mother-in-law, whom he detested, was advancing plans to make her permanent home with theirs, the cat had been sick in full and revolting view of the breakfast table, and he had had considerable difficulty in starting his car that morning.

On arrival at the hospital he found that one of his cases in the men's surgical ward had developed alarming complications, and it was this that Elsie overheard him discussing with the sister on duty. Elsie was busy sluicing rubber sheets but could hear the beloved voice above the splashing of the water.

'Keep a nurse by him for the next hour,' he was saying, his words clipped with anxiety. Sister's reply was inaudible.

'Anyone you like,' responded the doctor. 'Anyone but Nurse Parker. She gets worse as she goes on.'

Elsie dropped the sheet she was washing and ducked her head as though she had received a physical blow. She felt stunned with shock. As from a great distance, she surveyed her submerged hands resting on the bottom of the deep sink. The clear cold water acted as a magnifying glass, and every hair and pore looked gigantic. Elsie observed the tiny bubbles on the fleshy part of her thumb, uncannily like the seed pearls her father had given her on her confirmation day.

Her mind seemed to dwell, with unusual clarity, on many things long forgotten. The terrible words, uttered a second before, and all that they implied, had as yet no real meaning for her. She remembered the beads of sweat on the hairy upper lip of one of her sixth-form admirers whom she had not met, or thought of, for years. She remembered bright hundreds and thousands, scattered on plates of junket, which she used to love as a child. She dwelt with compulsive intensity on the visual memory of a spider's web spangled with drops of dew. And all the time her gaze was fixed upon the tiny bubbles clustering on her thumb.

She was roused from her trance by the sound of sister returning. All that day she went automatically about her duties, oblivious of the world about her. Late that night, lying straight and cold in her bed at the nurses' hostel, the tears began to flow, running down the side of her temple and dripping silently into the pillow. She wept noiselessly at first, and then, as the treachery and cruelty of those dreadful words began to burn into her, the paroxysm increased in intensity until she was choking with tears, her head throbbing and her chest aching with pain.

When dawn came she was red-eyed, swollen-faced and in a state of complete exhaustion.

'A cold,' she told her fellow nurses. 'I'm going home this after-noon anyway. I'll get over it during the week-end.' She was

reported sick, took the two aspirins handed to her, and fell to weeping again. In the early afternoon she rose, dressed, packed her case
and went to the station. She felt like a very frail old lady just recovering from a serious illness.

The sight that met her eyes on her return home brought her
almost to a state of collapse. In the long room of the new wing she
found her mother. The blond parquet floor, the pride of Mrs
Parker's heart, was stripped of its rugs and shone with much polishing. Against the wall stood tables already dressed in virgin-white
cloths. Flowers were banked on window sills, lamps were wreathed
with garlands. The room awaited young company, music, laughter
and, above all, the gay presence of the daughter of the house.

Elsie put down her case very carefully. She felt that she might
overbalance or even faint dead away. Her mother looked at her
with a smile. She seemed not to notice anything amiss. Her mind
was too occupied with ices, cherry sticks, blanched almonds and
wine glasses to register much else.

'I'm ill,' announced Elsie. Her voice seemed to sound a long way
off. She tried again, intent on making herself understood.

'I'm not well,' she said a little louder. 'I can't be at the party.'

'Elsie!' breathed Mrs Parker incredulously. She advanced towards
her, her poor face working. 'Can't come to the party? But, Elsie,
you must – you simply must!'

She gave a small despairing gesture with one hand indicating the
preparations. Elsie leant against the wall and closed her eyes. Inside
her eyelids was imprinted the face of the man she loved. She studied
it intently. Her mother was speaking again. Now her voice was
firmer, her resolution returning.

'A nice lay-down,' she was saying. 'Slip under the eiderdown for
an hour or two. I'll bring you up your tea and an Aspro. You'll
soon be as right as ninepence.'

As if in a dream, Elsie found herself being propelled upstairs, her
clothes removed, and her unprotesting body thrust into her bed.
Still concentrating on her beloved's swarthy face she dropped instantly into a heavy sleep.

Her mother roused her at seven. The anxiety in Mrs Parker's face
brought all Elsie's misery flooding back. She longed to turn away
and abandon herself again to grief, but her mother, she knew, could
not be disappointed. She rose and dressed, automatically making-up

that lovely face which seemed recovered from its earlier ravages, and going at last to take her place in the hall to welcome her guests. She felt as though some part of her had died, and that she dragged it with her, a cold heavy weight, draining strength from her.

To outward appearances she seemed much as usual, lovely, smiling and as desirable as ever. Halfway through the evening, the vicar's son engineered a trip into the garden with his hostess, and there poured out his heart whilst offering his dank hand. With all her habitual skill Elsie extricated herself and contrived to leave the young man tolerably resigned. During the last waltz, she received her second proposal of the evening, but was cool-headed enough to realize that claret-cup had inflamed this suitor as much as her own looks. He was thanked, refused and mollified, all within the time it took to dance from the French windows to the dining table. Grief, it seemed, had not dulled either Elsie's wits or her attractions.

She returned to work, her passion still raging. Elsie thought bitterly that those who say that unrequited love soon dies know very little of the matter. In the face of her beloved's impatience, and even dislike, despite the torturing memory of those chance-heard words, Elsie adored him more as the weeks went by. It was enough to walk the same corridors, to touch the same door-handles, to read the same hospital notices. When, on September the third, war was declared and a week later she heard that he had gone into the R.A.F. and was to be posted almost immediately as medical officer to a windswept station in Scotland, she felt that she could not live without his presence.

But work, with all its blessed urgency, drove complete despair away. There were patients to be evacuated, wards to reorganize and a hundred and one matters to attend to. Only at night, before she fell asleep, did Elsie have any time to mourn her beloved, and then the pain was almost more than she could bear.

On Christmas Eve she heard terrible news. The doctor and two other officers had been killed in a car accident as they returned to the station late one foggy night. After the first few days of shock and grief, an extraordinary change came over Elsie. It was as though released, at last, from the bondage of her infatuation, she found freedom. It was over. Nothing could hurt him now, and nothing could hurt Elsie for that reason. She could look around, begin to live again, welcome kindness, affection and admiration and, perhaps, one day, return it.

During the years of war Elsie Parker was the cause of much head-shaking in Bent.

'A fast hussy!' declared one righteous matron, with three plain unmarried daughters. 'A proper flibbertigibbet, always running after the men!'

'No better than she should be, I don't doubt, up there in London where her parents can't see her!' quoth another.

There was certainly a hard gaiety about Elsie these days. She was now Sister Parker, conscientious and hard-working in the hospital. But off-duty Elsie craved excitement. The admirers were more numerous than ever. Americans, Poles and Norwegians joined Elsie's village wooers, and she parried their advances with the same skill, if not perhaps quite the same endurance, as before.

When the war ended Elsie was twenty-five. There was a spate of weddings as the young men returned home. The villagers of Bent smiled kindly upon the newly married couples and welcomed with genuine joy the offspring who were born into a world full of shortages, inordinately tired, but at least at peace.

And still Elsie remained unattached. The years slipped by. Roger Parker died one winter. His wife followed him two years later. Elsie, as sole heir, found herself in control of the house, a flourishing business and a comfortable sum of money in the bank. She was now thirty-eight. Her hair was untouched by greyness; in fact, its golden hue was rather brighter than it had been. Her teeth, though much-stopped, were her own. Her figure was as trim as ever, her blue eyes as devastating. Level-headedly, Elsie took stock of her position.

The business could carry on, as it was doing, under its reliable manager. She would give up nursing, return to her home at Bent, and get married. Without her parents she might well be lonely. A husband was the thing and, with luck, there might still be time for children. Elsie set about putting these practical plans into action.

Within three months she was ensconced in the house, had joined the Caxley Golf Club and the Caxley Drama Group. She gave a handsome contribution to Caxley Cottage Hospital in gratitude for the kindness extended to her parents and was made a member of the hospital board. Her garden was lent for various local functions, she visited and was visited, and generally took her place in the gentle whirligig of Caxley's social life. People were genuinely glad to see her so engaged. The Parkers had always been liked, and Elsie deserved a break after those years of nursing, they told each other.

Unfortunately, Elsie's aims were only too apparent and soon became the object of derision by the less charitable. She had never been a very subtle person. One of her charms was her openness. Now that time was running short for Elsie, she became alarmingly direct in her hunt for a husband. Naturally, eligible men were scarce. In Caxley society, at that time, there were half a dozen elderly bachelors, about the same number of widowers, and a few middle-aged men separated from their wives for an interesting variety of reasons.

They were not a very inspiring collection, but Elsie was a realist, and did not expect to find anyone who could compare, even remotely, with her first and only love. She looked now for kindness, companionship and protection. If humour and some physical attraction were added, she would count herself lucky, she decided. Financial stability was not essential, for her own position could comfortably support a husband, if need be.

Her first choice fell upon one of the widowers, a childless man in his forties, who was a partner in one of Caxley's firms of solicitors. She had known him slightly during her years of nursing and knew him to be liked by the little town. He played golf and took leading parts in Caxley plays Elsie pursued him resolutely and charmingly, to the surprise of the flattered man and the intense interest of the neighbourhood. But, before long, the hunt was off. Elsie, to her dismay, found that her intended had one small, but unforgivable, fault. He did not wash – at least, not enough.

After this set-back, Elsie began to wonder if *cleanliness* perhaps should take precedence over *kindness* on her list of desirable qualities. She had not reckoned to be troubled by such elementals, and was not impressed by excuses put forward by well-meaning friends who seemed to have guessed the cause of her withdrawal.

'Poor dear Oswald,' they said. 'So terribly cut up by Mary's death, you know. Seemed to go all to pieces. You can see that he really needs a woman to look after him.'

Maybe, thought Elsie privately, but not to the extent of washing his ears for him or cleaning his teeth. Personal fastidiousness, heightened by a nurse's training, did not condone greasy collars, black fingernails and the same filthy handkerchief for a week. Oswald, in his expensive, well-cut and smelly suits, was rejected.

Others, observing Elsie's aims and aware of her comfortable circumstances, made themselves pleasant. Elsie earnestly did her best to see them in the role of husband, never blinding herself to the true aim of their attentions but willing to ignore it if other less ignoble qualities were present. Too often there were none.

Time passed. Elsie continued her search, an object of pity to some and derision to others. She was still lovely, though now in her forties, and her energy seemed unimpaired. But at heart she was beginning to despair. Was marriage never to be her lot?

One bleak December afternoon she made her way to the churchyard at Bent bearing a bright-berried cross of holly for her parents' grave. She walked slowly between the mounds, reading the well-known inscriptions yet again.

'*Loved and Loving wife of John Smith*,' said one. '*A beloved wife and mother*,' said a second. '*This stone was erected by a sorrowing husband to the memory of his much beloved wife*,' said a third.

All wives, all loved, all missed, all mourned, thought Elsie bitterly. Of what use was beauty, health, a loving heart and worldly possessions, if marriage never came? What would be written on her own tombstone for others to read?

Elsie Parker, Spinster? What a hateful word that was! She hastened her steps at the very thought, and reached her parents' resting-place.

'*And Lily, his dearly-loved wife*,' read Roger's daughter. '*In death they are united.*'

Controlling an impulse to rush away from the spot, Elsie set the cross gently against the headstone, stood motionless in the biting cold and offered up a small prayer for her parents, and for their only child.

She made her way quickly to the gate, carefully averting her eyes from the inscriptions around her. There was only one other person in the churchyard, and he too was setting a holly wreath upon a grassy mound. As she came near him he stepped forward into her path. He was a big dark man, much about her own age, and unknown to Elsie.

'Elsie Parker?' said the man gently. She nodded.

'I'm John Blundell,' said the man. 'I'd have known you anywhere. But you've forgotten me.'

Elsie felt a warm surge of recognition.

'John!' she exclaimed. 'My goodness, how many years is it since we saw each other?'

'I left Bent to join up in 1939,' he said. 'I don't think we've met since then, though I've heard about you.'

Elsie looked at him. John Blundell, the little dirty boy who had been her very first suitor! Undoubtedly he had prospered. His air was quiet and authoritative, his appearance immaculate. He had come a long way from the ragged child with the handkerchief pinned to his jersey who had been such a faithful admirer all those years ago.

She remembered, in a flash, that she had heard of his marriage during the war, but no further details. Lily Parker had risen above the station of the Blundells and had not passed on news of this family to Elsie.

'I'm still living at the old house,' said Elsie. 'Where are you now?'

'Near Southampton,' said John Blundell, falling into step beside her. 'I've a small shipping business there.'

'Alone?' asked Elsie, probing gently.

'No, I've got two sons, both married now. They help me to run it. They're good boys.'

They emerged from the yew-flanked gateway into the village square. A beautiful glossy car was waiting near the railings of the village school which they had both attended so long before.

'I'll run you back, if I may,' said the man. They drove at a sedate pace to Elsie's home.

'Do have some tea with me,' said Elsie. 'You don't have to hurry back, do you?'

He must not be too late, but he would love some tea, he said. They talked until it was half past six, and during that time Elsie learnt that he had married an Italian girl whose father was in an Italian shipping line and was a man of some substance. Their two sons were born in Italy. They had come back to England for the boys' schooling. The climate had not suited his wife but she refused to leave him during the winters to run the business alone, and had contracted Asian 'flu, five years before, which had proved fatal.

It was apparent that he had loved her dearly. His voice shook as he told the tale in the shadowy firelit room and Elsie was reminded

of his early tears when she had so light-heartedly turned him down at the tender age of seven.

This was the first of many meetings. Elsie knew, before a month had gone by, that this would end happily. Despite local tales to the contrary, Elsie did not pursue John Blundell. There was no necessity. There was mutual attraction, affection and need. Before the end of February they were engaged, and the marriage was arranged to take place after Easter. To Elsie it seemed wonderfully fitting that her first suitor should also be her last.

'And so, you see,' said Amy, lighting another cigarette, 'it all ended happily. Elsie adores the boys and the first one is going to live at the old house at Bent with his wife and children. Elsie and John want something smaller, and I think they both want to be at a little distance from Bent. Everyone says they're tremendously happy, even though they are, well – somewhat *mature*.'

Amy eyed me speculatively. I returned her gaze blandly.

'Funnily enough, I said, 'I had my first proposal at the age of seven. I was fishing for frogs' spawn at the time. Not a very glamorous pursuit, when you come to think of it.'

Amy leant forward with growing interest.

'What happened to him? Do you ever hear?' Clearly, she was hoping that history would repeat itself.

'I heard only the other day,' I told her. 'He's doing time for bigamy.'

6. Black Week

I suppose everyone encounters periods when absolutely everything goes wrong. The week after my friend Amy's visit was just such a one, and left Fairacre village school and its suffering headmistress sorely scarred.

On Monday morning I awoke to find that there was no electricity in the house. I am not a great breakfast-eater and can face a plate of cornflakes with cold milk as bravely as any other woman on a bleak March morning. But it is very hard to go without a cheering pot of tea, and this I saw I should have to do, for the clock stood at twenty to nine – inevitably, I had overslept – and the oil stove would not boil water in time.

A wicked north-easter cut across the playground. A few wilting children huddled in the stone porch.

'Go inside!' I shouted to them, as I bore down upon them.

'Can't get in!' they shouted back. I joined the mob. Sure enough, the great iron ring which lifts the latch failed to admit us.

'Mrs Pringle's inside, miss,' said Ernest.

'Well, why didn't you knock?' I asked, mystified.

'She don't want us mucking up her floor, she says.'

'What nonsense!' I was about to exclaim, but managed to bite it back. Instead I hammered loudly with the iron ring. After some considerable time, during which icy blasts played round our legs and blew our hair all over our faces, there was the sound of shuffling footsteps, the grating of a key, and Mrs Pringle's malevolent countenance appeared in the chink of the door. I widened the crack rapidly with a furious shove and had the satisfaction of hearing a sharp bang occasioned by the door meeting Mrs Pringle's kneecap.

'Can I have a word with you?' I said with some asperity, ignoring her closed eyes and martyred expression. The children surged past us to their pegs in the lobby, and I went through to my room followed by Mrs Pringle. As I guessed, her limp was much in evidence. I hoped that this time the affliction was genuine. Judging by that crack on the kneecap, it might well be.

'I have asked you before, Mrs Pringle,' I began in my best schoolteacher manner, 'to leave the door open when you arrive so that the children can come inside. It isn't fit for them to be out in this weather.'

Mrs Pringle arranged a massive hand across her mauve cardigan and gasped slightly. She replied with an air of aggrieved dignity.

'Seeing as the lobby floor was wet I didn't want the children to catch their deaths in the damp atmosphere,' began the lady, with such brazen mendacity that I felt my ire rising.

'Mrs Pringle,' I expostulated, 'you know quite well that you locked the door because you wanted to keep the floor clean.'

Mrs Pringle's martyred expression changed suddenly to one of fury.

'And what if I did? Mighty little thanks I gets in this place for my everlasting slaving day in and day out. What's the good of me washing the floor simply to have them kids mucking it up the minute it's done, eh?'

Fists on hips she thrust her face forward belligerently. 'And what's more,' she continued, in a sonorous boom audible to all Fairacre, 'you've no call to give me a vicious hit like you done with the door. My knee's almost broke! I could have you up for assault and battery, if I was so minded!'

'I'm sorry about your knee,' I said handsomely. 'Of course, if you'd left the door unlocked there would have been no need to push our way in.'

'H'm!' grunted Mrs Pringle, far from mollified. 'No doubt I'll have to lay up with this injury, and with the stoves drawing so bad as they are with the wind in this quarter *someone's* going to find a bit of trouble!'

She limped heavily from the room, wincing ostentatiously.

For the rest of the day she maintained an ominous silence.

I can't say I let it worry me. Mrs Pringle and I have sparred for many a long year and I know every move by heart. Now I confidently awaited her notice, and was rather surprised when it was not forthcoming.

The wind was fiendish all day. Every time the door opened, papers whirled to the floor. The partition developed a steady squeak as the strong draught shook it, and the door to the infants' lobby made the whole building shudder every time an infant burst forth to cross to the lavatory.

During afternoon playtime, when my back was turned for three minutes, Patrick, trying to shut the windows with the window pole, lost his balance and broke an upper pane, bringing down a shower of glass upon the floor and a shower of invective upon himself. Now we had an even fiercer draught among us, accompanied by banshee wailing among the pitch pine rafters. We were all glad when it was time to go home.

Mrs Pringle, black oilcloth bag swinging on her arm, stumped into the lobby as I went out. She stared stonily before her and did not deign to answer my greeting. Past caring, I fled through the wind to the haven of my little house, craving only peace and tea.

On Tuesday I woke to hear the hiss of sleet on my bedroom window. The playground was white, and the branches of the elms swayed in the same wicked north-easter. Luckily, the electricity was functioning again, and after breakfast I made my way back to the school to see if the stoves were doing well.

They were not going at all. Mrs Pringle, with devilish timing, was going to give in her notice this morning, I could see. Meanwhile, sleet and snow blew energetically through the broken pane, and the usual cross-draughts stirred the papers on the walls.

Mr Willet arrived as I was lighting the stove in the infants' room. His face was red with the wind's buffeting, and his moustache spangled with snowflakes.

'Here, I'll do that,' he said cheerfully. 'They tell me her ladyship's gone on strike again.'

'I'm not surprised,' I said, and told him about yesterday's fracas.

'She's a Tartar,' commented Mr Willet. 'But never you fear, we'll manage without her. Soon as these 'ere stoves is drawing I'll paste a bit of brown paper over that there broken window. Best tell the Caxley folk to come and do a bit of glazing, I suppose. That's too high for me to manage this time.'

The children arrived. Ernest handed me a note. The handwriting was Mrs Pringle's.

Am laid up with my damaged knee [it said]. Doctor is coming today and may say give in my notice. Will let you know. Matches is short.
Mrs Pringle.

Matches were not short, they were non-existent, as I had discovered, but by now the stoves were going, in a sullen black mood, and little puffs of smoke occasionally escaped from them. Mrs Pringle had been correct about their dislike of a north-east wind. The stoves resented it as much as we did. As the fuel grew warm the smoke increased, and we worked throughout the morning amid lightly-floating smuts and eye-watering fumes.

Mr Willet, working perilously on an inadequate ladder as he

blocked up the hole in the window pane, left his lofty perch now and again to survey the stoves.

'Beats me,' he said, scratching his head. 'I'll bet Mrs P. put the evil eye on 'em before she left!'

It seemed more than likely.

In the afternoon Eileen Burton complained of a stiff neck. I was about to dismiss this as a result of the draughts, but observing her flushed appearance I took her temperature. It was over a hundred, her neck glands were painful and she had not had mumps. I surveyed her anxiously.

'But my cousin's just had them,' she told me. 'And we often plays together.'

There was nothing for it but to wrap her up warmly, put her in my car and run her home at playtime. How many more, I wondered, peering through the gloom of the smoke-filled room on my return, would succumb in the next few days?

The sleet had changed to heavy snow by Wednesday morning, but mercifully the wind had dropped and the stoves behaved themselves.

The relief was tremendous, and I began to enjoy school without Mrs Pringle's presence. But the snow brought its own problems. The children were excited and fussy, quite incapable of working for more than three consecutive minutes, and standing up to look out of the windows whenever it was possible to see 'if it was laying'.

'Eggs or bricks?' I asked them tartly, but, quite rightly, they did not rise to this badinage and I was forced to give an elementary grammar lesson, in the middle of a spirited account of Moses in the bulrushes, knowing full well that neither would bear much fruit.

The snow was certainly 'laying'. It was coming down thick and fast, large snowflakes whirling dizzily and blotting out the landscape as effectively as a fog. It was nearly six inches deep by midday and the dinner van was remarkably late. Surely there were no drifts yet, I thought to myself, to hold up Mrs Crossley on her travels? She was usually at Fairacre between half past eleven and twelve, having only Beech Green's dinner to deliver before returning to her depot.

At twelve the children who go home to dinner departed. There was still no sign of the van and I was beginning to wonder if I should telephone the depot when Patrick came running back to school, followed by the rest of the home-dinner children, all in a state of much agitation.

'Mrs Crossley's slipped over,' shouted Patrick.

'And spilt all the gravy,' shouted another. He seemed to think that the loss of gravy was more important than Mrs Crossley's accident.

'She's hurt her leg,' volunteered a third.

By this time all my pupils, clad and unclad, were out in the snowy waste of playground. I made a valiant attempt to restore order, banishing the unclad indoors and telling the others to accompany me to the scene.

The dinner van had pulled up just out of sight of the school, and Mrs Crossley had started to walk bearing a pile of large tins propped against her chest. When we reached her she had struggled back to the van and was sitting sideways in the driving seat, massaging an ankle. I could see by the look of pain on her face, and the swelling of the joint that she had a severe sprain.

A pool of brown gravy stained the snow, but that was the only culinary casualty. Two of the bigger boys carried Fairacre's food into school while poor Mrs Crossley hobbled to my house supported by half a dozen anxious children and me. She lay on my sofa looking very woebegone.

'So silly of me,' she said, near to tears. 'I must have stepped awkwardly on a hard lump of snow. I couldn't see over the tins.'

'You stay there,' I said, 'and I'll give you first aid in two shakes. In the meantime, drink this.'

I poured out a tot of brandy. Mrs Crossley shuddered.

'Knock it back!' I said firmly, tucking a rug over her. 'I'll just see that the children aren't throwing the dinner all over each other and I'll be back.'

As is so often the case in a crisis, the children were behaving in an exemplary manner. They had served themselves, said grace, and were eating with the utmost decorum when I called in. I gave them much well-deserved praise, begged them to keep it up, and left them smug with self-righteousness.

'I simply must get Beech Green's dinner to them,' was Mrs Crossley's greeting on my return.

'I'll ring Mr Annett,' I assured her, 'and he can come and collect it. But let me see to this ankle.'

'Oh please,' begged Mrs Crossley, 'do ring Mr Annett and the depot! I shan't have an easy moment till it's done!'

You won't have an easy moment for some time with that ankle, I thought, watching it turn from red to mauve as I listened to Beech Green School's telephone bell.

Mr Annett answered promptly. Yes, he would come at once. Could he take Mrs Crossley to her doctor or her home or fetch her husband? I was full of admiration for Mr Annett's rapid grasp of the situation and practical help. But Mrs Crossley, from the sofa, preferred to rest for a little and to stay where she was.

I then rang the depot who promised to send someone to collect the van, and only when that was done would Mrs Crossley put her poor swollen ankle into my amateurish hands. By the time I had strapped it firmly, made her some tea, and promised to run her back after school, it was time to go back to school.

The classroom was beautifully quiet. The dinner things had been cleared away; but on the tortoise stove stood a dinner plate, carefully covered by another.

Ernest lifted it from the stove with the folded duster and placed it reverently before me on my desk.

'Bin keepin' it hot for you, miss,' he said. And it was only then that I realized that I had missed my meal.

I lifted the lid. The gravy had dried to a papery skin, and the slices of meat were curling with the heat. It all looked horribly daunting, but touched by the children's kindness I bravely took up fork and knife.

Watched by their solicitous eyes I ate my dinner thankfully.

The snow did not cease all day, and I drove Mrs Crossley home after tea through a positive blizzard. Luckily the roads were passable and I was soon home again. There was still no word from Mrs Pringle and I could hear Mr Willet manfully filling the coke buckets as I put the car away. What would Thursday hold? I wondered, as I ploughed through the snow to my front door.

It held, I discovered next morning, three more cases of mumps and no word from Mrs Pringle. It was still bitterly cold but the snow had stopped during the night. I crunched it underfoot as I crossed the playground and could imagine the snowballing that would delight the children at playtime.

The stoves had resumed their sulky behaviour and filled the two classrooms with smoke. We tried the damper open, shut, and half-way open with exactly the same result. At length we resigned our-selves to the inevitable and resumed our interrupted work on fractions in the midst of an acrid blue haze.

The vicar called during the morning. The Reverend Gerald Partridge is as near a saint as it would be possible to find in any village. His mild sweet face usually wears a vague benign smile, but today he appeared much agitated. At the sight of the smoke, his alarm grew.

'Good heavens!' he cried aghast. 'Are you on fire?'

'I wish we were,' I replied. 'We're only smouldering. The stoves object to a north-east wind.'

'It all looks very uncomfortable,' said the vicar, approaching the tortoise stove warily, as though expecting it to explode. 'I gather that Mrs Pringle is not with you at the moment,' he added delicately. I told him why.

'Yes, yes; I heard that there had been a little upset,' nodded the vicar understandingly. He is much too wise and diplomatic to take sides; and in any case I suspect that he thinks 'our little upsets' are six of Mrs Pringle's making and half a dozen of mine. And he is probably right.

The vicar now began to twist his leopard-skin gloves together unhappily.

'I have a really dreadful confession to make, Miss Read,' he began. 'I simply cannot put my hand on that pamphlet you lent me about religious books for the young from the Oxford University Press.'

'It doesn't matter in the least,' I assured him. 'I had quite finished with it.' But he seemed too sunk in self-mortification to hear.

'You see, I put it most carefully on the hall table, and this morning my wife and the two girls began spring-cleaning.' The two girls, incidentally, are two buxom Fairacre matrons of sixty-two and sixty-five.

'And not only had the pamphlet gone,' continued the poor man, 'but the hall table and the rugs and chairs – and to tell you the truth, every room in the house is completely upside down.'

Knowing his wife's vigour and the matching energy of 'the two girls' I could imagine the state of the vicarage only too clearly. This visit, I suspected, might be in the nature of a brief escape.

I did my best to calm his fears and accompanied him out to his car.

'Just look at that splendid bullfinch!' exclaimed Mr Partridge, his face lighting up.

'Splendidly picking off my plum buds,' I responded grimly, though I had to admit that the vivid little creature was a cheerful sight on that bleak day.

The vicar climbed into his car, and looked at me anxiously through the window.

'Don't hesitate to close the school, my dear, if the stoves prove too intractable. It can't be good for your lungs, or the dear children's, to inhale those fumes. What a pity Mrs Pringle is away! She is the *tiniest* bit difficult, I realize, but she has a wonderful way with stoves.'

Before I could reply, he gave me a disarming smile, let in the clutch and shot erratically away down the lane.

During the dinner hour I consulted Mr Willet about my little cat.

For several days he had been off his food, and I had supposed that a diet of local mice had been preferred to the delicacies offered by me. But this morning he looked wretched, sitting four-square with paws tucked under him, and his eyes half-closed.

'Fur balls,' pronounced Mr Willet.

'I'll get the vet,' I said at once.

'Ain't no need to get him out from Caxley,' said Mr Willet. 'You give ol' Tib a spoonful of liquid paraffin to oil the works. He'll be as right as rain tomorrow.'

'Are you sure?' I asked doubtfully.

'Positive!' Mr Willet assured me. 'This time of year they loses their winter coats, see, and keep all on a-licking theirselves tidy, and swallering great 'anks of 'air. It all gets twizzled up inside em. Liquid paraffin's the stuff.'

I thanked him and watched him return to his daily coke-sweeping. What a tower of strength and information Mr Willet was!

I poured out a dessertspoonful of liquid paraffin and approached the unsuspecting cat. It is not easy to open a cat's mouth in order to administer medicine, as everyone knows It is harder still when you are attempting it alone, and particularly when you have been foolish enough to pour out the dose beforehand and are trying not to spill it. Somehow or other I got most of it into the side of Tibby's mouth, and was just beginning to congratulate myself, when he gave his head a violent shake and ejected at least half the oil over my beautiful new suede shoes.

I returned, growling, to afternoon school, recounting my luck to Mr Willet en route.

'I'll give you a hand after school,' he said cheerfully. 'You allus wants two to cope with a cat, and then the cat nearly allus wins.'

He looked at my stained shoes sadly.

'It do seem to be one of those weeks, don't it?' he observed. And I agreed, with feeling.

There was still no word from Mrs Pringle on Friday morning. Although it was delightful to be without her presence, the school was beginning to look a little worse for wear despite my own efforts and Mr Willet's.

The snow, luckily, was melting fast, but plenty managed to find its way into the building. With it were the usual flotsam and jetsam of school life, and a plentiful sprinkling of additional matter from the workmen at the Blundells' new home.

'If anyone brings any more nails, putty or shavings into this school,' I said threateningly, 'I shall ring up the builders and tell them what is happening.'

The putty in particular was a sore trial. It seemed to be the thing to have a small lump under one's desk, or about one's person, and the children's hands had never been so filthy. By dint of constant nagging I was beginning to make a little headway against this infiltration.

We were all glad that it was Friday. It had been a trying week for everyone. By the afternoon I was beginning to feel a little more hopeful. The stoves were emitting only half as much smoke as before, only one more case of mumps had occurred overnight, Tibby appeared to be on the mend, a new pane of glass had replaced the broken one, and I had decided to find a substitute for Mrs Pringle if I did not hear from the lady during the week-end.

But Fate still had one more blow in store for us. Jimmy Waites, on returning from play, set up a wail.

'I bin and lost my half-crown!'

'Where was it?' I inquired.

'Under my desk. Someone's pinched it!'

Now if anything makes me cross, it is this kind of glib accusation. I spoke sharply.

'Rubbish! And in any case, you know you should have given it to me to mind. What was it for?'

'Half of cheddar, two boxes of matches and a pricker for the Primus,' gabbled Jimmy. Obviously he had been repeating this to himself all the afternoon.

Then began the search. We turned the whole place upside down. We shifted desks, turned out likely cupboards, and completely wrecked the room. It was not to be found.

Our Friday afternoon story had to go by the board. By now I was beginning to wonder if someone perhaps had succumbed to temptation. The half-crown had been seen by Jimmy's neighbours. It was there at playtime. Jimmy had been in and out of the room himself during that time.

It was a mystery that must be solved.

'We'd better look in our clothes,' I said. It is a job that I hate doing, but things looked suspicious. Pockets were turned out, socks rolled down, children jumped up and down to see if any coins would emerge from jerseys and trousers. But nothing was forthcoming.

By now it was time to say prayers and go home. In the middle of the hubbub the door opened and in stumped Mrs Pringle, complete with black bag.

She surveyed the chaos grimly.

'Seems this place wants a bit of doing-up,' she boomed, but made no move to discard her coat and hat.

'Sit down for a moment, Mrs Pringle,' I said. 'We're in rather a pickle.'

'*That*,' said the lady with emphasis, 'is plain for all to see!'

She folded her arms across her capacious bosom and watched the scene majestically.

'We'll have one last look,' I said desperately to the children. 'It must be somewhere in this room. If it doesn't turn up now I shall have to think about keeping you all here until it is found.'

There was something in my tone that made them realize the

seriousness of the occasion and they began to look frenziedly about them, bending under desks, running their hands along the high window sills and scrabbling in the dusty corners of the classroom. Quite rightly, they resented being suspected, and I hated, just as much, the feeling that I was suspecting them.

It was Mrs Pringle who discovered the half-crown. The only calm person in the room, she had perhaps a clearer eye than the rest of us.

'If it's a *coin* you're looking for,' she shouted above the din, 'it's there!'

She pointed at the back view of Jimmy Waites himself. The child was kneeling under his desk, and cleaving to the instep of his wellington boot was a glutinous lump of the ubiquitous putty. There, embedded in it, was the missing half-crown.

After we had congratulated Mrs Pringle and each other, I improved the shining hour by pointing out the absolute necessity of leaving putty severely alone, and then dismissed them.

There was genuine relief in their farewells. The dark shadow of distrust was lifted, the half-crown was restored and Fairacre School could relax again.

'The vicar told me you was in trouble,' said Mrs Pringle austerely, when the children had gone. 'And though I doubt if my knee will ever be the same again, I knows where my duty lies.'

She advanced, limping, towards the stove.

'Been letting it smoke, have you?' she said. I felt that this was hardly the correct expression, but was not given time to reply. To my amazement, Mrs Pringle lifted a mighty hand and smote the pipe about a foot above the stove itself. The smoke, which had been dribbling gently from the crack in the lid, ceased emerging immediately.

'Gets a bit out of true sometimes,' observed Mrs Pringle with satisfaction. 'Well, I'll get the place to rights while I'm here, so's we can be straight for next week.'

'Thank you, Mrs Pringle,' I said meekly, bowing my head, with secret relief, to the inevitable.

7. The Fairacre Ghost

The Easter holidays are probably more welcome than any other, for they mark the passing of the darkest and most dismal of the three school terms and they herald the arrival of flowers, sunshine and all the pleasures of the summer.

At this time, in Fairacre, we set about our gardens with zeal. Potatoes are put in, on Good Friday if possible, and rows of peas and carrots, and those who have been far-sighted enough to put in their broad beans in the autumn, go carefully along the rows, congratulating themselves, and hoping that the black fly will not devastate the young hopefuls in the next few months.

We admire each other's daffodils, walk down each other's garden paths observing the new growth in herbaceous borders, and gloat over the buds on plum and peach trees. We also observe the strong upthrust of nettles, couch grass and dandelions, among the choicer growth, but are too besotted by the thought of summer ahead to let such things worry us unduly.

It is now that the vicar gets out his garden furniture – a motley collection ranging from Victorian ironwork to pre-war Lloyd-loom – and arranges it hopefully on the vicarage veranda. Now Mr Mawne, our local ornithologist, erects a hide at the end of his lovely garden in order to watch the birds. He weaves a bower of peasticks, ivy-trails and twigs, upon the wood and sacking framework, as intricate as the nests of those he watches.

Now the cottage doors are propped open with a chair, or a large stone, and striped cats wash their ears or survey the sunshine blandly through half-closed eyes. Tortoises emerge, shaky and slower than ever, from their hibernation, and sometimes a grass snake can be seen sunning itself in the dry grass.

This is the time for visiting and being visited. For months we have been confined. Bad weather, dirty roads, dark nights and winter illnesses have kept us all apart. Now we set about refurbishing our friendships, and one of my first pleasures during this Easter holiday was a visit from my godson Malcolm Annett, and his father and mother

It was a perfect day for a tea party. The table bore a bowl of freshly-picked primroses, some lemon curd made that morning, and a plentiful supply of egg sandwiches. Mr Roberts, the farmer, has a new batch of Rhode Island Red hens who supply me with a dozen dark brown eggs weekly. These are lucky hens, let me say, garrulous and energetic, running at large in the farmyard behind the house, scratching busily in the loose straw at the foot of the ricks, and advancing briskly to the back door whenever anyone emerges holding a plate. No wonder that their eggs are luscious compared with the product of their poor imprisoned sisters.

After tea we ambled through the village, greeting many old friends who were out enjoying the air. Mrs Annett used to teach at Fairacre before she married the headmaster at our neighbouring village Beech Green so that she knows a great many families here. Mr Annett is choirmaster at St Patrick's church at Fairacre, so that he too knows us all well.

We walked by the church and took a fork to the left. It is a lane used little these days, except by young lovers and Mr Roberts' tractors making their way to one of his larger fields. A dilapidated cottage stands alone some hundred yards from the entrance to the lane.

We stopped at its rickety gate and surveyed the outline of its ancient garden. A damson tree, its trunk riven with age, leant towards the remaining patch of roof thatch. Rough grass covered what once had been garden beds and paths, and nettles and brambles grew waist high against the walls of the ruin.

The doors and windows gaped open. Inside, on the ground floor, in what had once been the living room of the cottage, we could see hundredweight paper bags of fertilizer propped against the stained and ragged wallpaper. They belonged to Mr Roberts and were waiting to be spread upon his meadows any day now. Upstairs, the two small bedrooms lay open to the sky. The thatch had retreated before the onslaught of wind and weather, and only the frame of the roof stood, gaunt and rotting, against the evening sky.

'It must have been pretty once,' I said, looking at the triangle of garden and the rose-red of the old bricks

'The vicar told me it was lived in during the war,' said Mr Annett. It housed a family of eight evacuees then. They didn't mind it being haunted, they told Mr Roberts.'

Haunted? we cried. I looked at Mr Annett to see if he was joking but his face was unusually thoughtful

'It is, you know,' he said with conviction. 'I've seen the ghost myself. That's how I came to hear the history of the place from the vicar.'

'Is that why it stays empty?' I asked. It was strange that I had never heard this tale throughout my time at Fairacre. Mr Annett laughed.

'No, indeed! I told you people lived in it for years. The evacuees said they'd sooner be haunted than bombed, and spent all the war years here. I think Roberts found it just wasn't worth doing up after the war, and so it is now in this state.'

We looked again at the crumbling cottage. It was too small and homely to be sinister, despite this tale of a ghost. It had the pathetic look of a wild animal, tired to death, crouching in the familiar shelter of grass and neglected vegetation for whatever Fate might have in store.

'When did you see the ghost?' I asked. Mr Annett sighed with mock impatience.

'Persistent woman! I see I shall have no peace until I have put the whole uncomfortable proceedings before you. It was a very frightening experience indeed, and, if you don't mind, I'll tell you the story as we walk. Even now my blood grows a little chilly at the memory. Brisk exercise is the right accompaniment for a ghost story.'

We continued up the lane, with young Malcolm now before and now behind us, scrambling up the banks and shouting with the sheer joy of living. With the scents of spring around us, and the soft wind lifting our hair, we listened to the tale of one strange winter night.

Every Friday night, with the exception of Good Friday, Mr Annett left the school house at Beech Green and travelled the three miles to St Patrick's Church for choir practice.

Some men would have found it irksome to leave the comfort of their homes at seven in the evening and to face the windy darkness of a downland lane. Mr Annett was glad to do so. His love of music was strong enough to make this duty a positive pleasure, and although his impatient spirit chafed at times at the slow progress made by Fairacre's choir, he counted Friday evening as a highlight of the week.

At this time he had much need of comfort. He was a young

widower, living alone in the school house, and ministered to by a middle-aged Scotswoman who came in daily. The death of his wife, six months after their marriage, was still too painful for him to dwell upon. She had been killed in an air raid, during the early part of the war, and for Mr Annett life would never be the same again.

One moonlit Friday evening in December, some years after the war had ended, he set out as usual for Fairacre. It was so bright that he could have driven his little car without headlights. The road glimmered palely before him, barred with black shadows where trees lined the road. He was early, for he had arranged to pick up some music from Miss Parr's house and knew that the old lady would want him to stop for a little time.

A maid opened the door. Miss Parr had been invited to her nephew's, but the music had been looked out for him, Mr Annett was told. He drove to St Patrick's, and went inside It was cold and gloomy. No one had yet arrived, and Mr Annett decided to use his time in taking a stroll in the brilliant moonlight.

There was an unearthly beauty about the night that chimed with the young man's melancholy. He made his way slowly along a little-used lane near the church, and let sad memory carry him on its flood. It was not often that he so indulged himself. After his wife's death, he had moved to Beech Green and thrown himself, almost savagely, into school life. He had filled his time with work and music, so that he fell asleep with exhaustion rather than the numbing despair which had first governed every waking hour.

He passed a broken down cottage on his left, its remnants of thatch silvered with moonlight. Just beyond it a five-barred gate afforded a view of the distant downs. Mr Annett leant upon its topmost bar and surveyed the scene.

Before him lay the freshly ploughed fields, the furrows gleaming in the rays of the moon. Further away, a dusky copse made a black patch on the lower flanks of the downs. Against the clear sky their mighty bulk looked more majestic than ever. There was something infinitely reassuring and comforting about their solidity, and the young man, gazing at them, let the tranquillity about him do its healing work.

It was very quiet. Far away, he heard a train hoot impatiently, as it waited for a signal to allow its passage westward. Nearer, he was dimly conscious of the rustling of dead leaves at the foot of an old crab apple tree which stood hard by the gate. Some small nocturnal animal was foraging stealthily, wary of the silent man nearby.

Sunk in his thoughts, he was oblivious of the passage of time, and hardly surprised to notice that a strange man had appeared in the lane without any noise of approach.

He came close to Mr Annett, nodded civilly, and leant beside him on the gate. For a moment the two men rested silently side by side, elbows touching, and gazed at the silvered landscape before them. Despite the stranger's unexpected advent, Mr Annett felt little surprise. There was something gentle and companionable about the newcomer. The schoolmaster had the odd feeling that they were very much akin. Vaguely, he wondered if they had met before somewhere. He shifted along the gate – the stranger seemed excessively cold – and turned slightly to look at him.

He was a loosely-built fellow, of about Mr Annett's age, dressed in dark country clothes which seemed a pretty poor fit.

He wore an open-necked shirt and a spotted neckerchief, tied gipsy fashion, round his throat. He had a small beard, light in colour, which gleamed silver in the moonlight, and his fair hair was thick and wiry.

'Full moon tomorrow,' commented the stranger. For such a big man he had a remarkably small voice, Mr Annett noticed. It was almost falsetto, slightly husky and strained, as though he were suffering from laryngitis.

'So it is,' agreed Mr Annett.

They relapsed again into contemplation of the view. After some time, Mr Annett stirred himself long enough to find some cigarettes. He offered the packet to his companion.

'Thank'ee,' said the man 'Thank'ee kindly, but I don't smoke these days.'

The schoolmaster lit his cigarette and surveyed the man

'Haven't I seen you before somewhere?' he asked.

'Most likely. I've lived in Fairacre all my life,' answered the man huskily.

'I'm at Beech Green,' said Mr Annett. The man drew in his breath sharply, as though in pain.

'My wife came from Beech Green,' he said. He bent his head forward suddenly. By the light of the moon Mr Annett saw that his eyes were closed. The use of the past tense was not lost upon the schoolmaster, himself still smarting with grief, and he led the conversation from the dangerous ground he had unwittingly encountered.

'Whereabouts in Fairacre do you live?' he asked. The man raised his head and nodded briefly in the direction of the ruined cottage nearby. Mr Annett was puzzled by this, but thought that perhaps he was nodding generally in the direction of the village. Not wishing to distress him any further, and realizing that his choir must be soon arriving at St Patrick's, Mr Annett began to stir himself for departure. It was time he moved, in any case, for he had grown colder and colder since the arrival of the stranger, despite his warm overcoat. The stranger only had on a long jacket, but he seemed oblivious of the frost.

'Well, I must be off,' said Mr Annett 'I'm due to take choir practice at seven thirty. Are you walking back to the village?'

The man straightened up and turned to face the schoolmaster. The moonlight shone full upon his face. It was a fine face, with high cheekbones and pale blue eyes set very wide apart. There was something Nordic in his aspect, with his great height and wide shoulders.

'I'll stop here a little longer,' he said slowly. 'This is the right place for me. I come most nights, particularly around full moon.'

'I can understand it,' said Mr Annett gently, scanning the sad grave face. 'There is comfort in a lovely place like this.'

A burst of laughter broke from the stranger's lips, all the more uncanny for its cracked wheeziness. His wide-open eyes glittered in the moonlight.

'Comfort?' he echoed. 'There's no comfort for the likes of me – ever!' He began to tear savagely at the neckerchief about his throat.

'You can't expect comfort,' he gasped painfully, 'when you've done this to yourself!'

He pulled the cloth away with a jerk and tore his shirt opening away from the neck with both hands.

By the light of the moon, Mr Annett saw the livid scar which encircled his neck, the mark of a strangling rope which eternity itself could never remove.

He raised his horror-filled eyes to those of the stranger. They were still wide open, but they glittered no longer. They seemed to be dark gaping holes, full of mist, through which Mr Annett could dimly discern the outline of the crab apple tree behind him.

He tried to speak, but could not. And as he watched, still struggling for speech, the figure slowly dissolved, melting into thin air, until the schoolmaster found himself gazing at nothing at all but the old gnarled tree, and the still beauty of the night around it.

The vicar was alone in the vestry when Mr Annett arrived at St Patrick's.

'Good evening, good evening,' said the vicar boisterously, and then caught sight of his choirmaster's face.

'My dear boy, you look as though you'd seen a ghost,' he said.

'You speak more truly than you realize,' Mr Annett answered soberly. He began to walk through to the chancel and his organ, but the vicar barred his way. His kind old face was puckered with concern.

'Was it poor old Job?' he asked gently.

'I don't know who it was,' replied the schoolmaster. He explained briefly what had happened. He was more shaken by this encounter than he cared to admit. Somehow, the affinity between the stranger and himself had seemed so strong. It made the man's dreadful disclosure, and then his withdrawal, even more shocking.

The vicar put both hands on the young man's shoulders.

'Poor Job,' he said, 'is nothing to be frightened of. It is a sad tale, and it happened long ago. After choir practice, I hope you will come back to the vicarage for a drink, and I will do my best to tell you Job's story.'

The younger man managed a wan smile.

'Thank you, vicar,' he said. 'I should be glad to hear more of him. I had a strange feeling while we were together –' He faltered to a stop.

'What kind of feeling?' asked the vicar gently.

Mr Annett moved restlessly. His brow was furrowed with perplexity.

'As though – it sounds absurd – but as though we were brothers. It was as if we were akin – as if we shared something.'

The vicar nodded slowly, and sighed, dropping his hands from the young man's shoulders.

'You shared sorrow, my son,' he said as he turned away. But his tone was so low that the words were lost in a burst of country voices from the chancel.

Together the two men made their way from the vestry to the duties before them.

The vicarage drawing-room was empty when the vicar and his guest entered an hour or so later. A bright fire blazed on the hearth and Mr Annett gratefully pulled up an armchair. He felt as though he would never be warm again.

He sipped the whisky and water which the vicar gave him and was glad of its comfort. He was deathly tired, and recognized this as a symptom of shock. Part of his mind longed for sleep, but part craved to hear the story which the vicar had promised.

Before long, the older man put aside his glass, lodged three stout logs upon the fire and settled back in his chair to recount his tale.

★

Job Carpenter, said the vicar, was a shepherd. He was born in Victoria's reign in the year of the Great Exhibition of 1851, and was the tenth child in a long family.

His parents lived in a small cottage at the Beech Green end of Fairacre, and all their children were born there. They were desperately poor, for Job's father was a farm labourer and times were hard.

At ten years old Job was out at work on the downs, stone-picking, bird-scaring and helping his father to clear ditches and lay hedges; but by the time he was fifteen he had decided that it was sheep he wanted to tend.

The shepherd at that time was a surly old fellow, twisted with rheumatism and foul of tongue. Job served a cruel apprenticeship under him and in the last year or two of the old man's life virtually looked after the flock himself. This fact did not go unnoticed by the farmer.

One morning during lambing time Job entered the little hut carrying twin lambs which were weakly. There stretched upon the sacks stuffed with straw which made the old man's bed, lay his master, open-eyed and cold.

Within two days Job had been told that he was now shepherd, and he continued in this post for the rest of his life. He grew into a handsome fellow, tall and broad, with blond wiry hair and a curling beard. The girls of Fairacre and Beech Green found him attractive, and made the fact quite plain, but Job was shy and did not respond as readily as his fellows.

One day, however, he met a girl whom he had never seen before. Her family lived in Beech Green but she was in service in London. Job's sister worked with her and the two girls were given a week's holiday at the same time. She walked over to see Job's sister one warm spring evening and the two girls wandered across the downs to see the lambs at play.

Job watched them approach. His sister Jane was tall and fair, as he was. Her companion was a complete contrast. She was little more than five feet in height, with long silky black hair coiled in a thick plait round her head, like a coronet. She had a small heart-shaped face, sloe-dark eyes which slanted upwards at the corners, and narrow crescents of eyebrows. Job thought her the prettiest thing he had ever seen.

Her name was Mary. To Job, who had a deep religious faith, this seemed wholly fitting. She was a queen among women. Job had no doubts this time and no shyness. Before Mary's week of holiday had ended the two young people came to an understanding.

It was Christmas time before they saw each other again, and only a few letters, written for them by better-schooled friends, passed between Mary and Job during the long months of separation. They planned to get married in the autumn of the following year. Mary would return to London and save every penny possible from her pitiful earnings, and Job would ask for a cottage of his own at Michaelmas.

He was fortunate. The farmer offered him a little thatched house not far from the church at Fairacre. It had two rooms up and two down, and a sizeable triangle of garden where a man could grow plenty of vegetables, keep a pig and a few hens, and so go more than half way towards being self-supporting. A few fruit trees shaded the garden, and a lusty young crab-apple tree grew in the hedge nearby.

The couple married at Michaelmas and were as happy as larks in their new home. Mary took work at the vicarage and found it less arduous than the living-in job in London. She was a quick quiet worker in the house and the vicar's wife approved of her. She was delighted to discover that her new daily was also an excellent needlewoman, and Mary found herself carrying home bundles of shirts whose collars needed turning, sheets that needed sides to middling, and damask table linen in need of fine darning. She was particularly glad of this extra money for by the end of the first year of their married life a child was due, and Mary knew she would have to give up the scrubbing and heavy lifting for a few weeks at least

The coming of the child was of intense joy to Job. He adored his wife and made no secret of it. The fact that he cleaned her shoes and took her tea in bed in the mornings was known in Fairacre and looked upon as a crying scandal, particularly by the men. What was a woman for but to wait upon her menfolk? Job Carpenter was proper daft to pander to a wife in that namby-pamby way. Only laying up a store of trouble for himself in the future, said the village wiseacres in 'The Beetle and Wedge'. Job, more in love than ever, let such gossip flow by him.

The baby took its time in coming and as soon as Job saw it he realized that it could not possibly survive. His experience with hundreds of lambs gave him a pretty shrewd idea of 'a good do-er' or a weakling. Mary, cradling it in her arms, smiling with happiness, suspected nothing. It was all the more tragic for her when, on the third day, her little son quietly expired.

She lay in a raging fever for a fortnight, and it was months before she was herself again. Throughout the time Job nursed her with loving constancy, comforting her when she wept, encouraging any spark of recovery.

In the two years that followed, two miscarriages occurred and the young couple began to wonder if they would ever have a family. The cottage gave them great joy, and the garden was one of the prettiest in the village, but it was a child that they really wanted. Everyone liked the Carpenters and Job's demonstrative affection for his wife was looked upon with more indulgence by the villagers as time passed.

At last Mary found that she was pregnant yet again. The vicar's wife, for whom she still worked, was determined that this baby should arrive safely, and insisted on Mary being examined regularly by her own doctor. She engaged too a reputable midwife from Caxley to attend the birth, for the local midwife at that time, in Fairacre and Beech Green, was a slatternly creature, reeking of gin and unwashed garments, whose very presence caused revulsion rather than reassurance to her unfortunate patients.

All went well. The baby was a lusty boy, who throve from the time he entered the world. Job and Mary could hardly believe their good fortune and peered into his cot a hundred times a day to admire his fair beauty.

One early October day, when the child was a few months old, Mary was sitting at the table with a pile of mending before her The boy lay asleep in his cradle beside her,

It was a wild windy day. The autumn equinox had stirred the weather to tempestuous conditions, and the trees in the little garden flailed their branches in the uproar. Leaves whirled by the cottage window and every now and again a spatter of hail hit the glass like scattered shot. The doors rattled, the thin curtains stirred in the draught, and the whole cottage shuddered in the force of the gale. Mary was nervous, and wondered how poor Job was faring outside in the full force of the unkind elements.

As the afternoon wore on, the gale increased. Mary had never known such violence. There was a roaring noise in the chimney which was terrifying and a banshee howling of wind round the house which woke the baby and made him cry. Mary lifted him from his cradle to comfort him, and walked back and forth with him against her shoulder.

There was a sudden increase in the noise outside – a curious drumming sound in the heart of the fury. To Mary's horror she saw through the window the small chicken house at the end of the garden swept upward and carried, twisting bizarrely, into the field beyond. At the same time a great mass of straw, clearly torn from a nearby rick, went whirling across the garden, and, as it passed, one of the apple trees, laden with golden fruit, snapped off at the base as though it were a flower stem.

Mary could scarcely believe her eyes. She stood rooted to the spot, between the table and the fireplace, her baby clutched to her. The drumming sound grew louder until it was unendurable. Mary was about to scream with panic when a terrifying rumble came near at hand. The chimney stack crashed upon the cottage roof, cracking the rafters like matchwood, and sending ceilings, furniture, bricks and rubble cascading upon the two terror-stricken occupants of the little home.

When Job arrived at the scene of the disaster, soaked to the skin and wild with anxiety, he found the whole of one end of his house had collapsed. No one was there, for the neighbours were all coping with troubles of their own, and there had been no time to see how others were faring in the catastrophe that had befallen Fairacre in the matter of minutes

He began tearing at the beams and sagging thatch with his bare hands, shouting hoarsely to his wife and son as he struggled. There was no answer to his cries. A ghastly silence seemed to pervade the ruined house, in contrast to the fiendish noises which raged about it.

An hour later, when neighbours arrived to help, they found him there, still screaming and struggling to reach his dead. Sweat and tears poured down his ravaged face, his clothes were torn, his battered hands bleeding. When, finally, the broken bodies of his wife and child were recovered, Job had to be led away, and only the doctor's drugs brought him merciful oblivion at the end of that terrible day.

In the weeks that followed, while his house was being repaired, Job was offered hospitality throughout Fairacre, but he would have none of it. As soon as the pitiful funeral was over, he returned numbly to his work, coming back each night to his broken home and sleeping on a makeshift bed in the one remaining room.

Neighbours did their best for him, cooking him a meal, washing his linen, comforting him with friendly words and advice. He seemed scarcely to see or to hear them, and heads shook over Job's sad plight.

'There's naught can help him, but time,' said one.

'''Tis best to let him get over his grief alone,' said another.

'Once he gets his house set to rights, he'll start to pick up,' said a third. Fairacre watched poor Job anxiously.

The men who had been sent to repair the cottage worked well and quickly. Their sympathy was stirred by the sight of the gaunt young man's lonely existence in the undamaged half of his tiny house.

At length the living room was done. The bricks which had crashed on that fateful afternoon had been built again into the chimney breast. The broken rafters had been replaced, the walls plastered and whitewashed afresh.

Job met the men as he trudged home from work. They called to him with rough sympathy.

'It's ready for you now,' they shouted through the twilight.

'We've finished at last.'

A kindly neighbour had gone in to replace his furniture.

'There now,' she said, in a motherly burr, 'you can settle in here tonight.' But Job shook his head, and turned into his old room.

Sad at heart, the good old soul returned home, but could not forget the sight of Job's ravaged face.

'I'll go and take a look at him,' she said to her husband later that evening. 'If the lamp's alight in the room then I'll know he's settled in, and I'll go more comfortable to bed.'

But the window was dark. She was about to turn homeward again when she heard movements inside the cottage and saw the living room door open. Job stood upon the threshold, a candle in his hand. Breathless, in the darkness of the garden, the watcher saw him make his way slowly across the room to the chimney breast. He put down the guttering candle, and rested his fair head against the brickwork. Before long, his great shoulders began to heave, and the sound of dreadful sobbing sent the onlooker stealthily homeward.

''Tis best by far to leave him be,' comforted the neighbour's husband, when she told him what she had witnessed. 'We'll go and see him in the morning. It will be all over by then.'

But there was little comfort for the woman that night, for the spectacle of Job's grief drove all hope of sleep away.

Next morning they went together to the house. Her heart was heavy with foreboding as they walked up the little brick path. Inside the silent house they found him, with a noose about his neck, hanging against the chimney breast which had crushed his wife, his child, and every hope of Job himself.

There was an uncanny silence in the sunny lane as Mr Annett finished speaking.

'And that,' he said soberly, 'is the tale of poor Job, as the vicar told it to me.'

Suddenly, a blackbird called from a hazel bush, breaking the spell. Despite the sunshine, I shivered. We were alone, for Malcolm and his mother had gone ahead to pick primroses from the steep banks, and though we were surrounded by the sights and scents of spring I remained chilled by this strange winter's tale.

'You're sure it was a ghost?' I asked shakily.

'Other people have seen Job,' answered Mr Annett, 'and the vicar knew all about him. But I believe I am the only person that Job has spoken to.'

'I wonder why?' I mused aloud.

'Perhaps he felt we had much in common,' said Mr Annett quietly.

I remembered suddenly Mr Annett's own tragedy. He, too, had adored a young wife and had lost her in the face of overwhelming violence. He too had watched a broken body removed to an early grave. There was no misery, no depth of hopelessness which Job had known, which was not known too to young Mr Annett.

We were summoned abruptly from the shadowy past by the sound of young Malcolm's excited voice.

'There's a nest here,' he called, 'with eggs. Come and look!'

'Coming!' shouted Mr Annett, suddenly looking ten years younger. And he ran off all grief forgotten, to join his wife and child.

8. Mrs Pringle's Christmas Pudding

One of the pleasures of school holidays is the opportunity to join in the village affairs more fully than is possible in term time. When I was asked if I would help the Women's Institute to prepare a party I agreed with alacrity.

Once a year the members of Fairacre W.I. invite a coachload of Londoners for the afternoon. Many of the visitors were evacuated to this area from the East End during the last war. Some had their schooling, during the war years, at our village school. Their mothers, now elderly women, lived in our midst, made friends, worshipped at St Patrick's, shared our pains and pleasures, and generally forged bonds which will last a lifetime. It is always a gay afternoon, with much reminiscing about shared memories and much gossip about new babies, marriages, good fortune and bad, which have been experienced since the last meeting.

The visitors were due to arrive at two o'clock. The custom is to greet them at the village hall with the tea urns ready. The main tea – a gargantuan meal – is prepared for five o'clock, but the two o'clock cup is considered the right welcome after their long trip from London, and their lunch-time stop on the way.

At one time we used to prepare our offerings in our own kitchens, converge upon the village hall about two and deposit sandwiches, sausage rolls, cakes and so on upon the dishes provided for the main meal. As anyone who organizes these things knows, the results could be chaotic. Four people who had offered sausage rolls would decide to provide chocolate sponge instead. The six who had promised sandwiches found that the local baker had no sliced bread, and so had opted to provide rock cakes instead, and the carefully prepared lists pinned up in the hall became covered with indescribable scribblings as the two people in charge tried to sort out the muddle.

After a few years of such crises it was decided to leave the matter in the hands of the committee, ably headed by Mrs Partridge, the vicar's wife, who is our President. These noble and efficient ladies ordered the bread, butter and fillings for the sandwiches, and every other necessity, and detailed squads of underlings to prepare the food under their vigilant surveillance in the hall. It worked much better that way, we found.

Consequently, at ten o'clock on the morning of the great day I made my way to the rendezvous, carrying my basket with a knife for buttering, a knife for cutting bread and some tea and sugar as my fool-proof contribution to the festivities.

The hall was buzzing like a beehive when I entered. The card tables which are used for local whist games had been placed at intervals round the hall and covered with bright cloths ready for the visitors. At one end, two long trestle tables were the scene of much activity. Here the noise was at its greatest for about twenty women cut and buttered bread, wielded salt and pepper pots, stacked sandwiches, arranged cakes on plates and generally made as much hubbub as my own schoolchildren.

I joined the throng and found myself between Mrs Mawne and Mrs Willet. Mrs Mawne has lived in Fairacre only a year or two and is the wife of our local ornithologist. His other claim to fame is his wonderful grasp of the church accounts which used to drive the vicar to distraction before Mr Mawne's coming. Mrs Mawne has the happy knack of upsetting everyone in the village by much forthright and tactless comment.

Her remark about the general incompetence, and probable dishonesty of the clergy in money matters, spoken directly to the vicar's wife in the presence of several speechless parishioners, has long been remembered. However, as we all have to live cheek by jowl in the village here, we push such memories to the back of our minds as best we may, and get on with day to day living.

Mrs Willet, the wife of our school caretaker, is a small mouse-like creature who looks meek and frail. In fact, she is a dynamic person who gets through more work in twenty-four hours than I do in a week. Her washing line on a Monday morning flies a multiplicity of spotless linen, long before her neighbours have pegged theirs out. Her store cupboards bulge with jams, jellies, pickles and chutneys of her own making. Puddings and pies, batches of scones, roast joints, and a thousand other delicacies stream from her oven to nourish sturdy Mr Willet three times a day. Besides this, she makes her own clothes, sings in St Patrick's choir, enters all the W.I. competitions, knits, crochets, makes rugs and generally leaves one feeling quite useless and incorrigibly lazy.

Now her hands flew briskly back and forth from potted meat to bread and butter, working at twice the pace and with twice the deftness of my own. Mrs Willet's sandwiches were models of square exactitude. Mine gradually grew more and more rhomboid as the loaf went down. Mrs Willet's crusts sliced away cleanly. Mine broke away raggedly despite my best endeavours. The only comfort was that Mrs Mawne's were, if anything, rather more dilapidated than mine.

We shouted amicably to each other among the din.

'The new people are moving in,' Mrs Willet told me. 'The Blundells. I knew her as a girl. Very pretty, she was then.' I remembered Amy's story, and waited for more. Mrs Mawne added her usual contribution with her usual tact.

'Looks rather a rackety type now,' was her comment. 'Hair very obviously dyed, and in trade, I hear.' Mrs Willet began to bridle.

'A very flourishing business in Caxley,' I put in placatingly. If trade is flourishing enough, I notice, there seems to be less antagonism towards it. Mrs Mawne, however, was not particularly moved. She sucked a buttery finger and continued to arrange her sandwiches. It would have made a sanitary inspector's hair curl, but we are tough in Fairacre, and one of our favourite maxims is: 'You have to eat a peck of dirt before you die,' which we quote as we sketchily dust the tomato that has rolled on the floor, or take in the loaf that has been lodged on the outside window sill.

'I shan't bother to call,' said Mrs Mawne, filching my bread knife shamelessly, and making the handle horribly buttery, I observed.

Mrs Willet muttered something which sounded like: 'Fat lot she'll care!' but was unheard by Mrs Mawne. Mrs Willet's neck was growing rosy with suppressed anger and feeling rather nervous with so many knives flashing about, I attempted to be a little peacemaker once again.

'I believe Mrs Blundell used to sing very well,' I began.

'Oh, she sung lovely!' replied Mrs Willet, with enthusiasm. 'Used to come out here with the Operatic during the war, and we had rare old times!'

She gazed round our dingy village hall with affection. The walls are covered with sticky gingery-brown matchboarding and upon its surface hang lop-sided photographs of football teams of long ago, faded brown with age. Stern country countenances, many of them wearing fine moustaches, peer from among the clouds which the damp has drawn over the group. Here and there are pinned such notices as 'Scouts' Rules', 'The Resuscitation of the Drowned' (though we are miles from any water), and 'Suggestions for W.I. Programme – PLEASE HELP!' By the door there is a dilapidated piece of cardboard on which is printed: PLEASE SWITCH OF THE LIGHT and that missing F has been a thorn in my flesh ever since coming to Fairacre.

Dusty plush curtains, on a sagging wire, screen the minute stage from sight, and the wood is of splintery bare boards with here and there a knot of wood, polished by friction, projecting like a buttered brazil. There is nothing truthfully to gladden the eye in our hall, and yet Mrs Willet looked upon it now with all the doting tenderness of a mother gazing upon her firstborn. Such, I observed, is the power of association.

'A lot went on here during the war,' continued Mrs Willet. 'We used to have canning sessions in here twice each summer – soft fruit time, and then later when the apples and plums were ready. The W.I. used to bring the canning machine and we spent all day up here. Had some fun, I can tell you!'

'I always bottled mine,' said Mrs Mawne. 'Much more wholesome.'

'Sometimes there'd be as many as thirty of us up here canning,' continued Mrs Willet, ignoring the interruption. 'With the evacuees, and that. Some of 'em will be here this afternoon. You ask 'em, Miss Read, about this hall in the war. Fairly hummed with life it did! We had the clinic here, and First Aid classes, and no end of concerts and whist drives. And when we won the war, we had a proper beanfeast for the Welcome Home!'

'I suppose most of the evacuees had gone home by then,' I said.

'Nearly all,' agreed Mrs Willet sadly. 'We missed 'em, you know. Never really wanted 'em to begin with, as you can guess, but somehow, sharing everything, we got fond of one another – and then, well, they was a larky lot, real mischieful, some of 'em! You couldn't help laughing! There was one – her name was Mrs Jarman – she'll be coming this afternoon, she was a caution. We all reckoned she was the larkiest of the lot. And I'll take my oath,' said Mrs Willet solemnly, turning earnestly towards me, 'that she was at the bottom of that Christmas pudding affair.'

'The Christmas Pudding Affair?' I echoed. 'It sounds like a detective story.'

'Well, it was one what never got explained,' said Mrs Willet. 'I'll tell you what happened – some time.'

And she returned to her sandwich stacking.

When our preparations were completed we all trooped home to a midday meal and to exchange our pinafores and working attire for more elegant *ensembles* in honour of the visitors.

Efficient and hardworking married women, like Mrs Willet, returned to their kitchens to dish up such succulent dishes as beef casserole or steak and kidney pudding which had been cooking themselves gently since nine or ten o'clock that morning. Scatter-brained spinsters, like me, with no hungry husbands to consider, had a piece of cheese, three biscuits and a cup of coffee, while they propped up their aching feet on a kitchen chair and read the paper. It was a good thing Amy couldn't see me, I thought, as I dusted the crumbs from my lap to the floor. This was Letting Myself Go in the way which caused her such heart-burning. Amy, my censorious college friend, when she lunches alone, sets one place at the dining room table, complete with glass, side plate, table napkin and so on, and eats her meal as decorously as any memsahib.

'And just think of the washing-up!' I said to Tibby, offering him a cheese rind. The disdainful creature took one sniff, flirted his tail and walked away.

'Thousands of poor cats,' I told him severely, retrieving the cheese rind for the birds, 'would give their eye-teeth for a delicious piece of cheese rind like that!' I tossed it through the open window. It was followed immediately by Tibby who devoured it instantly, and I sipped my coffee meditating on the maddening, but absorbing, ways of cats in general.

At ten to two we were all back in the hall awaiting the arrival of the coach. Our hair was freshly brushed, our noses powdered, our handkerchiefs sending out wafts of lavender water or Chanel Number 5 according to taste and income. The sun had come out, the tea urns hissed merrily, rows of blue-banded tea cups covered the trestle tables, and the air was filled with happy expectancy. When the coach drew up in the lane the tea ladies rushed to the urns, and those with less responsibility surged out to meet the visitors.

They were a cheerful crew and dressed much more gaily than we country mice were. Little hats with eye-veils, mauve coats and pink coats, stiletto heels, lots of patent leather, green and blue eyeshadow, flashing earrings and, above all, the high-pitched rapid twang of racy Cockney voices, made us feel that a flock of some exotic birds had suddenly descended upon us, and that we were as drab and unremarkable as our Fairacre hedge sparrows.

There were hugs and kisses, and much bonhomie and badinage as they were ushered into the hall. Over their tea cups the voices rose higher and higher. The noise was deafening. Carrying cups and saucers back and forth to the trestle table I marvelled at the snippets of conversation that came my way.

'Rosie got married last May and they've got a lovely flat at Ruislip, so he's a computer.'

'And our Janice – what was born here, you remember – well, a gentleman's got a very good job for her up the West End, with a flat and all. Makes anything up to sixty pounds a week, she does.'

'Dad's retired now, of course, and all for buying a bungalow at Peacehaven, but I say: "What's wrong with Hackney? Done us all right all these years, and you do see a bit of life!"'

Mrs Willet pointed out Mrs Jarman to me. She was a tiny bird-like woman with sparkling eyes. Her face was as wrinkled as an old apple, but her lips were a vivid orange and her crêpy eyelids were thick with blue eye shadow. A tiny black velvet hat was lodged jauntily on her yellow hair, and a cigarette dangled between her fingers. She was telling a tale with great animation, her Fairacre audience registering half-shocked delight. She certainly looked 'a larky sort', as Mrs Willet had described. She seemed to epitomize the very spirit of Cockney effervescence and one could guess at her courage and example during the dark days of war.

As I watched her, Mrs Pringle passed bearing a tray. Mrs Jarman's face lit up with devilment and she called out some quip which was drowned in the general hubbub. It was not lost upon Mrs Pringle however, for that lady's face grew redder than ever and an expression of deep disgust curved her mouth downward. She cast a look

of outraged dignity towards the gay party and continued majestically with her tray. Mrs Willet nudged me.

'No love lost there,' she hissed behind her hand. 'There's no
forgiving and forgetting about Mrs P. They fair 'ates each other –
she and Mrs Jarman.'

Before long we all set out for a walk round Fairacre in the sunshine, and I had no chance to hear more. But when the massive tea
was over, and the coach was packed again with visitors bearing
daffodils and farm eggs and hundreds of messages to those left
behind in London, and Fairacre W.I. had cleared up the debris,
'switched of the light', and locked the hall door, my chance came.

Wearily, Mrs Willet and I walked down the village together and
paused by my gate.

'No, I won't come in,' Mrs Willet said, shifting her basket from
one arm to the other. 'I've got some flower seeds to put in before it
gets dark; but I just wanted to tell you about Mrs Pringle and Mrs
Jarman now you've seen 'em together.'

We propped ourselves amicably one on each side of the school
house gate. A clump of nearby narcissi sent up wafts of fragrance
into the evening air, and Tibby rubbed himself round my tired legs
as Mrs Willet unfolded her tale of a wartime feud.

Mrs Jarman and her family arrived in Fairacre in the early summer
of 1941. They had endured the air raids which had made their days
and nights hideous from September 1940 onwards, sleeping most of
the nights in a Tube station and doing their best to carry on a
normal life during the day. In May, however, their home was demolished, Mr Jarman was killed, and Mrs Jarman brought her four
children to the comparative peace of Fairacre.

The eldest, Clifford, was fifteen, a tousle-headed lad whose rubbery lips seemed constantly glued to a mouth organ. Doreen, known
as Dawreen, who was twelve, already ogled the boys, and was affronted when she was made to wash off her lipstick at Fairacre
school. Nigel, two years younger, spent his time machine-gunning
with outstretched fingers, and Gloria, aged six, was the baby. All
four had their mother's blonde hair, but none had quite the vivacity
of that irrepressible widow.

The family was billeted in the cottage next door to Mrs Pringle.
It was owned by an elderly woman, now dead, called Jane Morgan.

Mrs Morgan's husband, like his neighbour, Fred Pringle, was serving overseas. Mrs Morgan looked upon the Jarman family as the price one has to pay in wartime, and was unhappy about their presence, but resigned to it. Mrs Jarman, for her part, thought Jane Morgan 'a stuffy old party, dead from the neck up, but never meaning no harm'. They shook down together fairly well.

It was Mrs Pringle, of course, who really caused the trouble. Her evacuees were an elderly couple who did for themselves in one room of her house. They were a self-effacing pair and were careful to give no cause for annoyance. They crept in and out like mice, giving scared little smiles to their formidable landlady and offering her such small tributes as clothing coupons or morsels of margarine in order to 'keep her sweet', as Mrs Jarman said.

Before long, the Jarman children fell foul of Mrs Pringle. It was their habit to retire to the end of the garden, climb upon the roof of the empty pig sty and there watch the activities of their next door neighbour.

They had a foreign Cockney impudence which Mrs Pringle abhorred. Fairacre children might have called names or even thrown a clod or two of earth over the hedge. The Jarman children were much more subtle.

'You ever seen anyone what's as broad as she's high?' one would shout to the next. The result would be tempestuous giggles on one side of the hedge and much bridling on the other. The children watched their neighbour pegging out voluminous nether garments on the line and made rude comments to each other in voices calculated to carry well.

'Never knew Fairacre'd got a barrage balloon, did you?' and so on.

To give Mrs Jarman her due, she corrected the children whenever she found them at fault, administering a brisk cuff or letting fly with a vocabulary as lively as their own. But she needed to work long hours charring at various large houses in the neighbourhood, and the children had a good deal of time on their own.

Mrs Pringle brought matters to a head one day by making a formal call next door to complain. She had donned a hat and gloves to add more dignity to the occasion, and registered majestic disapproval from the cherries nodding on her brim to the steel tips on her war-time heels. Mrs Jarman, just home from work, frying chips on an oil stove and enduring the clamour of four hungry children around her, was not in any mood to be conciliatory.

'What did you say to Mrs Pringle?' she demanded of her innocent-eyed offspring.

'Never said nothin',' said Dawreen glibly.

'Never said a word,' quoth the two younger ones, raising limpid blue eyes to their mother. Mrs Jarman, brandishing a fish slice, turned to the massive figure in the doorway.

'That's your answer,' she said flatly. 'My kids don't tell lies. Take yourself off!'

Mrs Pringle drew in a long outraged breath.

'They not only tell lies, they're rude, pert little monkeys. And if they was mine they'd get a jolly good hiding for it.'

'Say that again!' yelled Mrs Jarman, advancing menacingly, much to the delight of the juvenile onlookers. Mrs Pringle took a step or two backward, but did not retreat completely.

'Not that they've had any chance,' boomed the lady, 'as anyone with half an eye can see, looking at you. But if I has any more of their old buck, Mrs Jarman, I shall go to the police – and *the Caxley police*, at that!'

Mrs Jarman, eyes blazing, now rushed upon her neighbour and would have dragged the fruit-laden hat – and the hair beneath it – from her adversary's head, but Mrs Pringle, with a dexterity surprising for one of her bulk, nipped smartly down the garden path and put the gate between them. Mrs Jarman's furious shrieks, punctuated by Mrs Pringle's booms, caused several curtains to twitch in neighbouring windows. Mrs Pringle had just managed to shout something about 'East End scum!' above the din, when the four children, who had been watching the fun from the doorstep, screamed in unison: 'Fat's on fire! Mum, the fat's on fire!' and this diversion brought the ladies' immediate hostilities to a close.

From then on a state of constant warfare existed between Mrs Pringle and the Jarman family. If the children's ball went over the hedge, Mrs Pringle impounded it with smug satisfaction. When Mrs Pringle's tea towel blew off her line, into the next door garden, it ended up flying like a flag from the topmost branch of the Jarmans' greengage tree, a position for which the gale was not responsible, despite the assurances of the children.

'We can't reach that, Mrs Pringle,' they said with mock regret, and dancing eyes. 'Ain't it a shame? Must have blowed there in the wind, see?'

And there it fluttered, for several weeks, before being ripped to pieces by the elements and an inquisitive pair of jackdaws who used strips for the adornment of their nest.

The two women never let the opportunity of a verbal brush pass, without making full use of it. In a way, each enjoyed the situation. They were well-matched. Mrs Jarman might be quicker and more prolific of vocabulary, but Mrs Pringle had a native malice, and an incalculable capacity for taking umbrage, which stood her in good stead. She moved like a tank into battle, heavy, slow and apparently indestructible. But, now and again, a burst of deadly fire came from that implacable front to score a hit upon Mrs Jarman, the resilient sniper.

One Saturday a jumble sale was arranged in Fairacre. It was to take place, as always, in the Village Hall, and on the morning of the day in question a few women went there to set up the tables and sort the jumble into the time-honoured categories of Men's, Women's, Children's, Hats and Shoes, and General Junk.

Mrs Pringle set out laden with a large bundle. All was held together with a faded mackintosh, tied securely round the bulk by the sleeves. Mrs Jarman watched her struggle up the road in a high wind before collecting her own parcel and setting forth.

'Don't want to catch up with that old tartar,' she said to Dawreen, who was dreamily picking at the flaking paint of the mantel shelf. 'And give over that lark, will you?' she added ferociously, giving the girl a swift box on the ear.

'Don't forget,' she continued, as she whirled about the room for her possessions, 'spuds on at eleven, two large whites from the baker, tell the milkman it's six and fourpence and none of his old buck, keep the cat off the custard and expect me when you see me.'

The door slammed behind her and, despite her desire to let Mrs Pringle arrive first, she found herself entering the narrow doorway with her. Mrs Pringle drew aside with marked distaste.

'Don't mind me breathing the same air, I hope?' commented Mrs Jarman tartly, pushing in first. Mrs Pringle maintained an affronted silence.

About half a dozen women were already at work sorting a mountain of assorted garments on the floor. Back and forth hurried another two taking the articles to the right table. Mrs Pringle, by ancient custom, was in charge of 'General Junk'. As Mrs Jarman had never been forgiven for saying on an earlier occasion, 'it seemed just right, somehow, to see Mrs P standing by that label!'

Hers was a comparatively simple task. Saucepans, chipped vases, lidless casseroles, faded pictures, lop-sided toast racks, stone hot water bottles, riding boots stuffed with beautiful boxwood trees, archaic lawn mowers, and many unidentifiable objects found their way to Mrs Pringle's table. Sometimes large pieces of furniture flanked her counter; wash stands, fireguards, sagging wicker armchairs, and dilapidated bamboo tables. Once there was the ugliest three-piece suite in Christendom among 'General Junk'. Competition for this had been fierce, as well I knew, for on that occasion I had been Mrs Pringle's feeble assistant and had watched her masterly handling of the sale. It had gone eventually for two pounds to Mrs Fowler of Tyler's Row. She was going to present it to her mother in Caxley, and I must say I felt the greatest sympathy for that unsuspecting old lady.

Now Mrs Pringle deposited her mackintosh bundle with the other clothes and made her way to her stall. Mrs Jarman fell on her knees with the other sorters and began to work with spirit.

'Lor'!' she cried, holding up a moth-eaten moleskin waistcoat. 'Who'd buy this stuff? Talk about "Granny's little old skin rug"! Gives you the creeps, don't it?'

'My husband's,' said one of the helpers shortly. Mrs Jarman seemed not a whit abashed. She was rummaging in the bundle which Mrs Pringle had brought, making disparaging comments on her discoveries, much to the embarrassment of the Fairacre women who knew full well how important it was to guard one's tongue on such occasions.

'Look at this,' cried Mrs Jarman, 'three shirts and never a button among 'em! Who's pinched the buttons, eh?'

Mrs Pringle, wreathed in sea-grass from the unravelling footstool she was carrying, paused by the group and replied loftily.

'I took the trouble to remove those shirt buttons. They'll do for another day.'

'How's that for meanness!' commented Mrs Jarman, twinkling at the others. 'The poor chap who buys this will have to go about with his shirt flapping, I s'pose.'

'Some people,' began Mrs Pringle, 'knows their duty to their country in war time, and saves every possible penny, not like some I could mention, not a hundred miles from here, as buys pineapple chunks when there's rhubarb in the garden.'

This side-swipe simply had the effect of bringing Mrs Jarman's usual high spirits to bubbling point. Her blue eyes flashed with the joy of battle joined. The onlookers were half-fearful and half-delighted to see Mrs Pringle in combat with such a worthy adversary.

'Well, I never!' crowed Mrs Jarman. 'Ain't we high and mighty? But I wouldn't stoop to pinching shirt buttons and then giving the rest to the jumble. About as low as you can get, I reckon.'

'It's nothing short of *patriotism*, I tells you,' boomed Mrs Pringle, her neck flushing an ugly red. '"Save all you can!" they keeps telling us. Well, I'm saving shirt buttons!'

She marched heavily towards her stall somewhat impeded by the strands of sea-grass trailing behind her. Mrs Jarman let out a peal of derisive laughter, and continued with the sorting. But she did not forget Mrs Pringle's last remark.

The jumble sale itself passed off without further incident between the two antagonists. In fact, Mrs Jarman covered herself with glory at the men's stall by her shrewd bargaining with customers. Her clients were kept in spasms of laughter by her barrage of raillery and Cockney patter. At the end of the sale it was discovered that her stall had taken by far the largest amount, and it was generally acknowledged that Mrs Jarman's cheeky approach to the customers was the reason.

'Not much good living near the Caledonian Market all your life, if you can't pick up a few tips!' was Mrs Jarman's reply to those who congratulated her. Needless to say, Mrs Pringle was not among them.

Some months after the sale, at the beginning of November, the good ladies of Fairacre Women's Institute decided to make their Christmas puddings together. They worked out that the whole process would be much cheaper if they made the mixture in one batch and cooked all the puddings in the large electric copper.

The recipe, cut from a daily paper, made grisly reading to those used to the normal ingredients of pre-war puddings. No brandy, stout, fresh eggs or butter appeared in the 1943 recipe. Instead, such dreadful items as grated carrot, margarine, dried-egg powder and – the final touch of horror – 'a tablespoonful of gravy browning to enrich the colour', figured on the depressing list of ingredients. But times were hard, and years of privation had blunted the sensibilities of even the most fastidious. With much cheerfulness the ladies set about their preparations for making 'An Economical and Nutritious War-Time Christmas Pudding'.

Dozens of pudding basins, each bearing their owner's name on adhesive tape stuck on the base, waited on the long tables. Little paper bags bearing treasured ounces of currants and sultanas, mixed spices, breadcrumbs and two precious fresh lemons, jostled each other near the enormous yellow mixing bowl from the Vicarage. By ten o'clock the ingredients were being stirred zealously by half a dozen helpers, most of them elderly women, for the majority were doing war work of some sort or other. Mrs Willet busily greased the basins with carefully-hoarded margarine papers, listening to the chatter about her.

'We'll set the copper to *Very Slow*,' said the vicar's wife, 'and then it should be perfectly safe until tea time. Mrs Willet's staying until eleven-thirty, to make sure it's simmering properly and then the rota begins.'

It had been arranged that one or other of the W.I. members should look in every hour to see that all was well, and to top up the water in the copper if it was getting too low. Christmas puddings were too precious to be left entirely to themselves for such a length of time.

By eleven, the puddings were ready for immersion. Every household in Fairacre had one, and some had two or three, standing in the water. This was the Women's Institute's practical help towards Christmas, and very well planned the organization had been.

'Here's Mrs Pringle's,' said Mrs Willet, bearing a stout two-pounder to the copper. She peered underneath the basin to read the big black capitals on the tape, before letting it down gently beside the others.

'Then that's the last,' said the vicar's wife thankfully. 'Just time to have a cup of tea before we knock off'

★

It was very quiet when they had gone. Mrs Willet took out her knitting and sat by the humming copper. The clock said twenty past eleven and she had promised to stay until half past. As she knitted, she read the list of names pinned on the wall by the copper. During the afternoon she saw that Mrs Pringle and Mrs Jarman were due to call in. Both worked in the mornings and had been unable to stir their own puddings this year.

'2.30 – Mrs Pringle'

'3.30 – Miss Parr' – only that would be her maid, Mrs Willet surmised, and

'4.30 – Mrs Jarman' – who would no doubt rush back to her family in time to fry the inevitable chips on which that ebullient household seemed to exist.

'5.30 – Anyone welcome.' This was when the puddings would be lifted out and handed to their lucky owners. Mrs Willet had promised to help with this chore.

At twenty-five to twelve she lifted the lid, noted with relief that the water was bubbling gently, checked all the switches, wrote a note to the next pudding-minder saying:

> 25 to 12. Everything all right
> Alice Willet

and made her way back through the village.

At five-thirty a throng of women crowded the steamy hall collecting their basins and lodging them in shopping baskets, string bags or the baskets on the front of their bicycles.

'Got the right one?' called Mrs Jarman to Mrs Pringle, as she watched that lady peering under the basins for her name. 'Bet you've got more fruit in yours than the rest of us!'

Mrs Pringle sniffed and ignored the quip. Depositing her pudding in the black depths of her oilcloth shopping bag, she passed majestic-ally from the hall without deigning to reply.

The fantastic sequel to the pudding-making session might never have been known to Fairacre but for an unusually generous gesture of Mrs Pringle's.

As Christmas Day approached she heard that a large party of the Jarmans' friends were proposing to spend the day next door.

'My heart fair bleeds for poor Jane Morgan,' said Mrs Pringle lugubriously to her son John. 'She'll be crowded out of house and home, as far as I can see. I've a good mind to invite her round here for Christmas dinner.'

Neither Corporal Pringle nor Private Morgan were to be given Christmas leave. Mrs Pringle's sister and a schoolgirl niece, much the same age as John, were coming from Caxley for the day, and as the sister and Jane Morgan knew each other well it seemed a good idea to ask their neighbour to join the party. Jane Morgan was gratefully surprised, and accepted.

The pudding simmered all the morning, and most delightful aromas crept about the kitchen, for there was a duck roasting in the oven as well as the 'nutritious war-time' delicacy on top of the hob. Mrs Pringle and her sister had a good gossip, their children played amicably with their new presents, and except for the ear-splitting racket occasioned by the crowd next door, the benevolent spirit of Christmas hung over all. At twelve-thirty Jane Morgan appeared, thankful to be out of her noisy home, and they all sat down to dinner.

The duck was excellent. The pudding looked wonderful. Mrs Pringle plunged a knife into its gravy-darkened top and cut the first slice.

'Mum!' squeaked John excitedly. 'There's something shining!'

'Sh!' said his aunt. 'Don't give the game away! Perhaps it's a sixpence.'

Mrs Pringle looked puzzled.

'No sixpence in this pudding!' she said. 'In any case, I don't hold with metal objects in food. I always wraps up anything like that in a morsel of greaseproof.'

She put the first slice on a plate for Mrs Morgan. There was certainly a suspicious chinking sound as the pudding met the china surface.

'When I was little,' said Jane Morgan, 'we used to have dear little china dolls in our Christmas pudding. No bigger than an inch, they were! With shiny black heads. We used to put them in the dolls' house, I remember.'

But Jane Morgan's reminiscences were being ignored, for all eyes were on the pudding. There was no doubt about it, there were a great many shiny foreign objects among the other war-time ingredients. Mrs Pringle's breathing became more stertorous as the slices were cut. She sat down heavily in front of the last plate, her own, and then spoke.

'Just pick it over before you take a mouthful. I reckons someone's been playing tricks on us.'

Spoons and forks twitched the glutinous mass back and forth, amidst amazed cries from the assembled company. When they came to count up the foreign objects they found no fewer than two dozen mother o' pearl shirt buttons.

Mrs Pringle said not a word, but opened a tin of pineapple chunks instead.

Late that night, when the Jarmans' company had roared away and the children had been chased to bed, Mrs Jarman met her land-lady in the communal kitchen. Jane Morgan was in her husband's dressing gown, her wispy hair was in a small pigtail, and her teeth had been left upstairs in a glass of water. She was busy filling a hot water bottle.

'Had a good time?' asked Mrs Jarman boisterously. 'We have. Never laughed so much since I came here.'

'That'th nithe!' said Mrs Morgan politely. 'Yeth, I enjoyed it next door, but there wath thomething wrong with the Chrithtmath pudding.'

Mrs Jarman drew in her breath sharply,

'What was up with it?' she inquired.

'It wath abtholutely thtuffed with thirt buttonth,' said Mrs Morgan, wide-eyed. 'Mithith Pringle wath dumbfounded.'

'Shirt buttons!' echoed Mrs Jarman. She broke into peals of noisy laughter.

'Ah well,' she gasped, through her spasms, 'that should please the old trout! She told me once that she saved shirt buttons!'

Still laughing, she made her way upstairs, followed by her mysti-fied landlady.

Mrs Willet straightened herself and patted my garden gate.

'Well, Miss Read, that's the story. Of course, it was all over Fairacre before Boxing Day sunset. Jane Morgan let it out, in all innocence, and the village was fair humming with the news.'

'Did Mrs Jarman ever admit it?' I asked.

'Never! Swore she never knew a thing about it, but it was her all right. I should know – I remember the pudding list. "2.30 Mrs Pringle". It wouldn't be her. "3.30 Miss Parr". That was her Annie that popped in then, as law-abiding as they come, and wouldn't

dream of doing such a thing. "4.30 *Mrs Jarman*". And "5.30 All welcome". Don't need much working out, when you come to think of it.'

She bent to pick up her basket, and stroked Tibby affectionately.

'I will say though,' she continued, 'that Mrs Pringle minded her manners a bit more after that, when she and Mrs Jarman got together. Ah, she was real mischief, was Mrs Jarman. You couldn't help liking her.'

Mrs Willet gazed, with unseeing eyes, down the Fairacre lane, her mind on times long past.

'I still miss them, you know, them Londoners. I liked 'em – and always shall. It was good to see them again this afternoon. Took me back to the old days. Say what you like about 'em, Miss Read, Londoners are a larky lot! A real larky lot!'

9. Outlook Unsettled

As so often happens when term begins, the weather became idyllic. Great white clouds sailed indolently across pellucid blue skies, and warm winds from the south replaced the sneaky little easterly one which had harassed us throughout most of the Easter holidays.

One warm afternoon, in late April, we propped the door of the schoolroom open with an upturned flowerpot and did our best to turn our attention to learning Robert Bridges' poem 'Spring Goeth All in White'. It seemed an admirable choice in the circumstances, for white narcissi spilt their heady fragrance from the window sill, white daisies, gathered by the children, filled three paste pots on my desk, and an early cabbage white butterfly opened and shut its wings against the south-facing Gothic window.

Nevertheless, it was uphill work. Languor, born of unaccustomed heat, engulfed my class. Shirt necks were opened, sleeves rolled up, jerseys peeled off and stuffed in desks, and the sing-song country voices stumbled heavily through this most tripping of spring lyrics.

Sleepiest of all was young Richard, not yet five, who was spending the day with us while his mother paid a necessary visit to the hospital in our county town. It is not easy to get someone to mind a child in a small village, and I often get urgent requests asking me 'if our youngest can come along with his brother for an hour or two'. If it is possible – and it usually is – we all enjoy the newcomer's company, and it gives him an insight into school routine before he takes the plunge himself later on.

Richard lolled on the desk beside his brother Ernest, who nudged him occasionally and whispered severely to him, with no noticeable result. As we battled on, Richard amused himself by blowing large glassy bubbles from lips as red and puckered as a poppy petal. Ernest, scandalized, bent down to remonstrate.

'Leave him alone, Ernest,' I said mildly. 'He's tired. Perhaps he'll fall asleep.'

'In school?' cried Ernest, deeply shocked.

'Why not?'

Ernest, still looking affronted by my slackness, drew himself up, folded his arms and applied himself sternly to the task before him, ignoring the indolent and shameful child beside him.

Everywhere in the room were emblems of spring. The weather chart for April showed a number of umbrellas, depicting the rainy weather during the holidays, with arrows pointing fairly consistently to the north-east. But a row of triumphant suns, like yellow daisies, blossomed in the last six or seven squares, and the arrows were now happily reversed.

Across the back of the room ran a frieze of spring flowers. Crocuses, daffodils, tulips, and a large number of new species, as yet unknown to Messrs Sutton and Carter, had been cut out of gummed paper and affixed by every hand in the class. Many a fat thumb went home in the afternoon bearing an indented ring round it made by hard-worked school scissors. It was, as the seed catalogues say, 'a riot of bloom' and a very colourful addition to our dull walls.

A new spring poster to encourage savings, showing a bird and its nest, brightened the door between the two classrooms, and the nature table was laden with wood anemones, primroses, violets, sprays of young honeysuckle leaves, a few early coltsfoot and dandelions, and a splendid pot of horse chestnut twigs thrusting out green hands in all directions.

Hard by, the glass fish tank glimmered with shiny frogs' spawn, for all the world like submerged chain-mail. The tiny dots were already beginning to turn into commas, and before long the children's patience would be rewarded by the sight of a myriad thrashing tadpoles. Nothing could be more suitable, I told myself again, than 'Spring Goeth All In White' for such an afternoon.

But, there was no doubt about it, those eight exquisite lines were really more than the children could manage in the circumstances. I felt impatient and cross at their laziness, but was loth to spoil the poem for them by bad-tempered bludgeoning. In the midst of this impasse, young Richard raised himself, stretched short arms each side of his rumpled head, and said clearly:

'Let's go out!'

There was a shocked silence. The sound of a bee droning up and down the open door could be heard distinctly as the children waited to see what my reaction would be. Sometimes a remark like this will make me fly clean off the handle, and they shivered with apprehension. Ernest's face was scarlet at the effrontery of his young brother.

I looked at the expectant children.

'What about it? Shall we?' I asked.

There was a rapturous roar of agreement, and a general stampede to the lobby.

The air outside was wonderful, heady and honeyed with hundreds of unseen flowers. The elm trees at the corner of the playground were rosy with buds, and noisy with rooks at their building.

We straggled down the village street between the beds of velvety polyanthus and the neat kitchen gardens striped with vegetable seedlings. Birds flashed across our path, dogs panted on cottage doorsteps and a cuckoo's call see-sawed across the afternoon.

All this, of course, was what had held my class in thrall – the compelling imperious spell of spring. Of what use were the frieze, the crayoned sun, the poster, the laden nature table and the captive frogs' spawn? They were but substitutes for the real thing that exploded all around them. It was the babe among us, young Richard, still in touch with the vital stuff of living, who had led us unerringly to reality.

We made our way slowly up the sunny slopes of the downs before throwing ourselves down on the dry springy turf in order to revel to the full in the glory of a warm spring day.

Below us spread the village like some pictorial map. The trees were misted with young leaves, and here and there a flurry of white blossom lit up a garden. I thought of our poem left neglected, but felt no regret. Let us savour this now, and then come to Robert Bridges' poem, 'recollecting it in tranquillity,' was my feeling.

A row or two of flapping washing caught the eye, and a herd of black and white Friesians, belonging to Mr Roberts, looked like toys as they grazed peacefully in the field next to the school. I gazed at it all with particular interest this afternoon, for I had a problem on my mind. Would it, I wondered, be a good thing to leave Fair-acre?

I suppose that most people feel unsettled in the early spring. There must be something in the rising of the sap and the general urgency of the season that makes us long for change and movement. I read the 'Appointments Vacant' at the end of *The Times Educational*

Supplement with unusual fervour during March and April, and usually find that this pastime calms the fever in my blood. What about this job in Sicily? I ask myself. Would I really be able to 'TEACH ENGLISH by Direct Method'? Come to think of it, are *any* of my teaching methods direct? Is the teaching of 'Spring Goeth All In White' direct, when one abandons the task to scramble up the springy turf of the downs, for instance?

There is a wonderful post offered in Barbados and another in New Zealand, and several in Dar-Es-Salaam (I only consider those in a warm climate, you notice), but, alas, I am not a communicant member of the Presbyterian Church, nor am I qualified to teach practical brickwork or plumbing. I browse among these delights over my cup of tea, when the children of Fairacre have run home and only the voice of Mrs Pringle, at her after-school cleaning, is heard in the land. After half an hour or so of this mental dallying, I rouse myself, take stock of my nice little school house, the fun I have in Fairacre, and decide I am better off where I am. In any case, the thought of filling up forms and asking people to give references for me, if need be, is enough to dissuade me from any serious application, as a rule. By the end of April my spring fever has usually abated. Fairacre looks more seductive than ever. I find, surprisingly, that I am in love with all the children, and even look upon Mrs Pringle with an indulgent eye. Such is the power of warm weather.

But this year my feelings were stronger. If I really wanted promotion, as headmistress of a larger school, then it was time I stirred myself before I became too decrepit to be considered at all. As Amy, my old college friend, frequently tells me, and reiterated with considerable force the other evening when I mentioned a particular post I had seen advertised, I have been in Fairacre long enough. It might be better for the school, as well as for me, to have a change.

The job which had caught my eye was the headship of a junior and infants' school in south Devon. I knew the little town fairly well from visiting it at holiday times, and because I had friends in the neighbourhood. It was a market town, rather smaller than Caxley, about five miles from the coast, and situated away from the main roads which were so busy in summer time.

I remembered the school particularly. It was a pleasant old building, with a new wing recently added, and an attractive school house adjoining it. A peach tree spread its branches fanwise over its front wall, which faced south, and at the back there was a sheltered walled garden with some fine fruit trees and lawns. One could be very happy indeed there, I had no doubt, and when my friends wrote to tell me of the vacancy and to urge me to apply for it, I fell to thinking seriously of the matter.

The biggest attraction to me was the climate. Fairacre can be bitterly cold in the winter, and the number of gnarled rheumaticky old people in our midst constitutes an awful warning to those with a tendency to rheumatism and its allied diseases. Apart from an occasional bout of influenza I ailed nothing, but the last winter or two I had been having twinges of rheumatism which I did not like to think of as simply old age. Fairacre School, too, was renowned for its draughts and the inefficiency of its heating system, and latterly I had come to dread the winter months with their fierce blast of winter air from the sky-light above my desk, concentrated on the nape of my neck, and the particularly spiteful draught that hit one round the ankles and came from the icy wastes of the outside lobby.

It would be good to work in a snug building tucked into the side of a hill, and with most of its windows facing south. The very thought of that soft mild air made me feel hopeful. I read my friend's advice. I read the advertisement a dozen times. I looked out of my school house window – it was a blustery April evening with a spatter of hail now and again – and I bravely sent for the application forms.

That had been a week ago. The forms awaited my attention still, propped behind the coffee-pot on the dresser, my usual filing place. I must get them off this week if I really intended to apply. I looked again at Fairacre, spread below me, and sighed at the difficulties of making up one's mind.

'You got the belly-ache?' asked Joseph Coggs solicitously, sitting down beside me.

'No, no,' I assured him. 'I was just thinking how pretty the village looked from here.'

A few more children left their pursuits to join us.

'It's the prettiest place in England,' declared Ernest stoutly.

''Sright!' echoed young Richard loyally.

'My auntie,' said John, 'lives at Winchelsea and she says *that's* the prettiest place.'

'Maybe she don't know Fairacre,' suggested someone reasonably. 'What's it like anyway – this ol' Winklesea?'

'*Winchelsea!*' replied John, nettled. 'Well, it's a funny place, because it used to be right by the seaside and now there's a whole lot of flat fields between the town and the sea.'

> 'Below the down the stranded town
> What may betide forlornly waits,'

I quoted, with what I thought was rather a beautiful inflection. John looked startled.

'I dunno about that, but that's what my auntie told me. She said the sea was right up to the town once.'

'Likely, ain't it?' said Joseph Coggs scornfully. I rose to my feet. I was glad to have some interruption to my thoughts, and it was time we were getting back.

'I'll get the map out when we are in school,' I promised them, 'and you shall see for yourselves. First one to reach the lane has a sweet! Off you go!'

Shrieking and squeaking, they tumbled down the steep slope of the grassy hill leaving me to descend more circumspectly behind them.

In the lane, where the rough track ends and the tarmac begins, Dr Martin's car waited outside Laburnum Villas. As I approached the vociferous mob awaiting me – each claiming that he had arrived first – the doctor came out of one of the ugly pair of houses and watched, with some amusement, as I quelled the riot.

'Playing truant?' he asked. I said we were.

'Very sensible too. We none of us get enough fresh air these days. When I first came to Fairacre it was lack of decent food which gave me most of my patients. Now it's too much food, and not enough air and exercise.'

He climbed into his car with a grunt of exertion, then leant from the window and laughed.

'I need more myself,' he said. 'How's my old friend Mrs Pringle? Still suffering with her leg?'

'When it suits her,' I replied. There are no secrets to hide from Doctor Martin. He has known us all in Fairacre much too long to be hoodwinked. Forty or fifty years, I thought suddenly.

Doctor Martin has lived and worked in Fairacre! I had a sudden desire to ask him if he had ever felt like moving, but restrained myself.

'Are you feeling quite fit?' he asked, an observant eye cocked quizzically upon me.

'Yes, thank you,' I said hastily. 'Just thinking about something, that's all.'

'You look a trifle pale to me,' said the doctor, twinkling. 'Is it love?'

'No, indeed!' I said, with spirit. 'I'm too old for such capers. More likely to be advancing senility. I'm beginning to suspect that rheumatism's trying to infiltrate my old bones.'

'You aren't the only one in Fairacre,' said the doctor, starting his car. 'Let me know if it gets any worse, that's all. We get such plaguey cold winters here, that's the trouble.'

He waved cheerfully and drove off, hooting to shoo my children to the side of the narrow lane.

The memory of that south-facing Devon school returned to me with overwhelming intensity, as I made my way back to Fairacre School amongst my clamorous pupils.

'Can I get it out now?' asked John as we clanged across the door-scraper.

'Get what out?' I asked bemused.

'Why, the map! You said as you was going to show us Winchelsea, and all that!' He sounded aggrieved. I pulled myself together, and approached the map cupboard.

It is called the map cupboard, and does indeed house the maps, but that is not all. Somehow, everything that has no proper home gets thrown in the map cupboard. There are cricket stumps, old tennis shoes, a pile of china paint palettes which have not been used for years, some dilapidated *Rainbow Annuals* adored by the children during wet dinner hours, part of a train set, a large tin full of assorted pieces of Meccano, and a rusty hurricane lamp which, we tell each other, 'might come in handy'.

The maps jostle together in one corner, and ever since I came to Fairacre I have meant to label them properly and hang them in some sort of order. In practice, I go through *Muscles of the Human Body, The Disposition of the Tribes of Israel, The Resuscitation of those Suffering from Electrocution*, the tonic sol-fa modulator and a number of maps, ranging from Greenland's icy mountains to India's coral strand, until I find the one I am searching for

This afternoon was no exception. At length, however, the map of the British Isles was hung over the blackboard and I began my lesson on coastal erosion. Refreshed by their outing the children gave me quite flattering attention.

John bustled out to the map, full of importance, and pointed to Romney Marsh with his yellow ruler, and I did my best to explain the cause of the sea's retreat here. There are times when I wish fervently that I had more geographical knowledge. This was one of them. Mercifully, the children seemed to understand my halting explanations, and I was fired to go further.

'Sometimes,' I said, 'the opposite thing happens. The sea encroaches on the land, and then the bottom of the cliffs gets washed away.' I remembered childhood holidays at Walton-on-Naze, and gave a dramatic account of a garden, and then, finally, the house belonging to it, sliding down the cliffs into the hungry sea. Perhaps I overdid the drama. There was an awed silence when I finished.

John raised his ruler and put it shakily across the Wash.

'It's eaten in there all right,' he commented.

Patrick and Ernest now walked out, unbidden, to take a closer look at the map.

'Look how it's busted its way up here!' exclaimed Patrick, his eyes on the Bristol Channel.

'And here!' echoed Ernest, peering closely at the Thames estuary. 'Looks as though they could meet, real easy, and chop us in half.'

'How quick,' asked Joseph Coggs nervously, 'do the water come?'

'You remember at Barrisford?' queried John. 'It came in as quick as lightning, and terrible strong it was. Fair sucked us off our feet when we was paddlin' and I got my best trousers absolutely soppin'.'

I did my best to calm their fears. If I weren't careful I could see that I should have some very cross parents coming to see me on the morrow, complaining that their children had been having nightmares.

'Good heavens,' I said robustly, 'it only manages a few inches in a year, at the most. You've nothing to fear here, living in Fairacre. Why, we're safely in the middle,' I assured them, appropriating John's ruler, and pointing out *Caxley* printed in unflatteringly small letters.

These downland children see very little water, and the sea but rarely. There is a very healthy respect for it when they visit the coast, and their apprehension about inundation was understandable. Even today, some of their grandparents have never seen the sea.

St Patrick's chimes began to ring out through the warm limpid afternoon.

'Time to go home,' I said. 'Don't forget, there are miles of dry land between you and the sea, here in Fairacre. Stand for grace!'

Within five minutes the classroom was empty. I returned the map to the shameful cupboard and made my way across the hot playground. To my surprise, Joseph Coggs was swinging on the school gate. His face was thoughtful, his dark eyes fixed upon the horizon.

'What are you doing?' I asked.

He nodded towards the vast bulk of the downs, quivering in a blue haze of heat.

'I was thinking,' he said huskily, in his hoarse gipsy croak, 'it'd take a tidy long time for the sea to get through all that lot, wouldn't it, miss?'

'It would,' I agreed.

He sighed with relief, clambered down from the gate, and set off along the sunny lane towards his home.

The long envelope, containing the application form, was horribly noticeable, sticking out from behind the coffee pot. I resolved to tackle it later that evening, but first of all I made some tea.

Mr Willet was busy at the bottom of my garden, erecting a fine row of bean poles. He cannot bear to see a few yards of untilled soil, and had insisted on turning a miniature jungle of old gooseberry bushes, draped in dead grass, into a flourishing vegetable patch. The fact that I should never be able to consume a quarter of the crops he was so generously planting did not seem to occur to him, and I was too touched by his kindness to point it out.

I took two hefty blue and white striped mugs of tea down the garden path. Balanced on top of one was a plate bearing a large hunk of fruit cake for my gardener. The heat shimmered everywhere, and some of the polyanthuses were wilting slightly already My spirits rose at the thought of a possible fine spell.

'Well now, that do be real welcome,' said Mr Willet, grasping the mug in a mud-caked hand. He upturned a wooden box and motioned me politely towards it. I sat down, with a sigh, and let the sunshine soak into my bones. Little rainbows played round my half-shut eyes. This was the weather! They probably had it like this all the time in Devon, I thought.

The sound of steady champing told me that Mr Willet had found the cake.

'You makes a very good fruit cake,' he said indistinctly. 'Moist without being too heavy. And got your cherries well spaced. Takes a bit of doing, that. My wife has a rare job with cherries. Flours 'em, or summat, to keep 'em up. You done real well with this, miss.'

I wished I deserved his compliments but truth will out, so I replied dreamily, my eyes still closed:

'Marks and Spencer's!'

'Is that so?' said Mr Willet. 'Well, they does a good job then.'

There was silence except for the sound of mastication and the birds' singing around us.

'You feeling all right?' asked Mr Willet. 'You looks a bit peaky to me, and you ain't drinking your tea!'

I sat up hastily. He was the third person this afternoon to comment on my frail looks.

'I'm fine,' I assured him.

'Don't look yourself to me,' persisted Mr Willet. 'Got a sort of bilious look. You ever had the jaundice?'

'I probably need a change,' I said briskly. 'When we get some sunshine I begin to realize what I've been missing. Perhaps I'd better take a job in France or Italy,' I added lightly.

Mr Willet looked concerned.

'Don't you go flinging off to no foreign parts now!' he warned me. 'Full of mosquitoes and malaria, they tells me, and not a decent drop of water to drink, even if it do come out of a tap. And the food's a proper mess – oily and that – wouldn't do your biliousness any good, you can take my word for it!'

At this moment, Mrs Pringle appeared at the side of the house, and bore down upon us in all her black-clothed majesty. Her oil-cloth bag swung upon her arm, and from it poked a corner of the flowered cretonne overall in which she performs her cleaning duties. Obviously, these were now ended and she was on her way homeward.

'Cup of tea?' I asked. Mrs Pringle shook her head magisterially.

'I never drinks between meals,' she said. 'And I shall be dishing up our high tea in an hour's time.'

Mr Willet whipped a sack from the wheelbarrow and spread it, with a Raleigh-like flourish, on the grass. Mrs Pringle lowered her bulk cautiously upon it, and smiled graciously.

'Ah! Nice to have a set-down! Sometimes I wonder if this cleanin' job's too much for me.'

I wondered what was coming.

'Well, not so much the *cleaning*,' continued Mrs Pringle heavily, 'as the *danger*!'

This was mystifying, but was obviously leading to a grievance.

'Sweeping, I expect. Scrubbing, I expect. A certain amount of back-breaking bending and lifting, I expect,' said Mrs Pringle, rising to heights of rhythmic peroration which made me suspect Welsh blood somewhere among her forebears

'But *when*,' continued the lady, turning and fixing me with a glittering eye, 'I gets hit over the head through other people's carelessness. then I thinks it's time to *complain*.'

I was about to speak, but was overborne by Mrs Pringle in full spate. Mr Willet and I exchanged martyred looks, and resigned ourselves to more

'I don't say a word about slatternly goings-on, in the ordinary way. Some are born sluts, no matter how much schooling they've had, and if they cares to muddle along with dust under their beds and the same saucepan for soup as milk, not to mention a bread crock with mildewed crumbs in the cracks, then all I says is: "Well, let them wallow in their muck, and be forbearing." But when those slatternly ways bring damage to *others*, then plain speaking has to be done!'

'Cough it up then,' I said inelegantly. I could recognize the wallower-in-muck all right. 'What hit you?'

'Nelson's Column, by the sound of it,' commented Mr Willet, unimpressed. He dusted some grass from his corduroy trousers, and began to resume his tasks.

'I was sweeping gentle-like by the map cupboard,' said Mrs Pringle with dignity, 'when the broom knocked against the door. It flew open –' here Mrs Pringle flung her arms dramatically apart – 'it flew open, I says, and down crashed a good dozen maps. Gave me a cruel blow on the side of the head – most dangerous place, that is, near the temple!'

'I'm sorry,' I said. 'That catch isn't very reliable.'

'If the maps was hung up properly,' continued Mrs Pringle severely, 'as they always was in Mr Hope's time – and after – we shouldn't get accidents like this. Might have had Concussion. Might have been Disabled. Might have been Laid Out!' intoned Mrs Pringle.

'Pity you weren't,' said Mr Willet shortly. I looked away hastily.

'You're quite right,' I said nobly to the old harridan, 'I really must tidy that cupboard. Do you want something put on your head? Witch hazel, perhaps?'

'Very suitable,' muttered Mr Willet, who was beginning to enjoy himself. Mrs Pringle gave him a cold glance.

'Nothing, thank you,' replied the lady, with crushing dignity. 'I shall let Nature take its course.'

She began the herculean task of getting to her feet, swaying backwards and forwards and breathing heavily. I put both arms round one of hers and gave a mighty heave. Suddenly, she was erect, red in the face, but triumphant.

'Thank you, Miss Read,' she puffed.

'Here, you don't want to lift great weights like that!' cried Mr Willet, who had only just seen this manoeuvre. 'And you not very well!'

Mrs Pringle looked at me suspiciously.

'Not well?' she echoed truculently.

'I'm perfectly well,' I said. Mr Willet, no doubt seeing a means of paying out his old enemy, shook his head vehemently.

'She's just been talking about having a change. Can't blame her, either, with folks like you to plague her!'

'A change does us all good,' conceded Mrs Pringle. She looked at me warily as though remembering something. 'As long as it don't last too long. I wouldn't think about a *permanent* change, if I was you. Taking it all in all, you could jump from the frying pan into the fire, and Fairacre ain't a bad place, when all's said and done.'

She fished inside her oilcloth bag and produced a brown paper one.

'Six eggs,' said Mrs Pringle, thrusting them upon me. 'I brought 'em up when I come, expecting you'd still be in school, but seems you packed up before time today. Good job the Office don't know what goes on!'

'It's very good of you,' I said, with sincerity. 'Especially after your accident.'

Mrs Pringle grunted and set off up the garden path.

'I'll do my best to put these away tidily,' I promised, patting the paper bag.

'Hm!' commented Mrs Pringle, with one hand on the latch of the gate, 'there's some – no matter how much schooling they've had – what never learns!'

Triumphant as ever, she continued on her way.

Back in the solitude of my house I found myself putting off the task of filling in the application form. I sorted the laundry, cleaned the dining-room windows, shown up in all their squalor by the bright sunshine, and generally fiddled about in a procrastinating mood.

Should I apply or not? Now that the sun shone again, I began to shilly-shally. I remembered the peaceful view from the top of the downs. Mrs Pringle was right when she said that Fairacre took some beating. She seemed to know an astonishing amount about my present proposals, I thought, remembering her advice about making a change. There was little doubt, in my mind, that the lady had been snooping at the contents of the long envelope in the course of her dusting. I had suspected this before. Looking at it in one way, I mused, it was really rather flattering that she advised me to stay. Perhaps she enjoyed my slatternly ways after all!

I paused in my window-cleaning and gazed at Tibby basking on the top of the rain-water butt, one of his favourite spots.

How would he react to a move, I wondered?

The chances of getting the job were one in a hundred, I well knew There would be a host of applicants for such a tempting post, and a house with it meant that there would be double the number, at least. Why not send in my application form, and let the gods decide? After all, if I were lucky enough to be called up for interview, I could make up my mind then.

I groaned in turmoil of spirit. How truly dreadful it is to have to make a decision! No, I was sure that I could not leave this to the gods. This was something I must settle for myself, here and now. Either I applied because I really wanted the post, or I would decide to stay on in Fairacre. Having got thus far, I went over the reasons for and against, all over again. It was a wearing business.

I should simply hate to leave the Fairacre children and all the friends in the village. There would be more children, and friends, in Devon, I answered myself. And this little house is extremely attractive! The Devon one is even better, said my second self. I should be leaving a job which I knew I could manage fairly competently. All the more reason for trying something more ambitious, commented my nagging half.

Perhaps this was the secret. Perhaps I should be more adventurous, stretch myself a little, climb out of my rut. I was too fond of clinging to the present, to the things I knew, the friends about me. Amy was possibly right to urge me to make a change. Fairacre was not the only place in the world. It was time I uprooted myself.

Now or never! I took out the application form from the envelope and spread it on the table. I must say it looked rather daunting. I whipped out my fountain pen before I weakened again, and at that moment the telephone bell rang.

It was Amy. I was glad to hear her voice. Now I should get some much-needed moral support, I felt sure.

'I'm just filling in that application form,' I told her, rather proudly, after the first civilities were over.

'Only just?' asked Amy. She sounded incredulous.

'It doesn't have to be in for a few days yet,' I answered defensively.

'But you've had it there over a week,' answered Amy severely. 'I quite thought it had been sent off long ago.' I began to feel rather hurt.

'I had to think about it,' I said, in an injured tone.

'Stuff and nonsense!' snorted Amy. 'We worked it all out together last week. In any case, it is your move that I've rung up about.'

'What do you mean – my move?' I asked. 'Aren't you counting my chickens for me rather prematurely?'

Amy brushed my tartness aside.

'I met Lucy Colgate at a party yesterday,' she said, 'and told her

about your plans. She's interested in Fairacre School, and I'm pretty sure she'll apply when you leave.'

Lucy Colgate! I was speechless. As if it wasn't bad enough to have Amy busying herself about my affairs, and bullying me into action, without adding the insult of Lucy Colgate. She had been at college with Amy and me, and try as I might – and I must admit I did not try very hard – I could not take to her. I found her domineering, utterly self-centred, and painfully affected. No doubt she considered me equally unpleasant. In any case, we met as little as possible, but Amy kept in touch. The very thought of Lucy teaching in my school and living in my house was enough to make me bristle.

'Amy,' I said firmly, 'you take too much upon yourself. At times like this you strain the bonds of friendship to snapping point.'

'Are you trying to tell me that you are *still* trying to make up your mind?' demanded Amy shrilly.

'No!' I said grimly. 'It's made up now!' And I slammed down the receiver.

Lucy Colgate, I fumed, pacing round the dining-room table. Lucy Colgate living in this house! I could well imagine its transformation, tricked out with the frilly lampshades, Regency stripes and Redouté roses beloved by my old fellow student. As for Mr Willet's vegetable patch, that would be turned into a lawn, sprouting a cretonne garden umbrella with gold fringe, before the first term was over!

The idea of Lucy Colgate queening it in my little school was even more distasteful. Fancy leaving Patrick and Ernest, and Joseph, and Linda − all the adorable and maddening hustle of them, in fact − to the mercies of Lucy! It simply could not be done.

I had a sudden vision of Mrs Pringle's face. How would the two get on?

'The meeting of the dinosaurs,' I told myself, with some relish, my fury beginning to abate. 'What a battle that would be!' I could see Lucy facing Mrs Pringle over the tortoise stoves. Lucy spilling coke, and as yet ignorant of the consequences. Lucy would face many a hazard if she ever found herself in Fairacre School. Why, with any luck, I thought suddenly, the map cupboard door might burst open again and project the contents painfully upon her!

At this uncharitable flight of fancy, I began to laugh. Lucy Colgate and Amy could connive until they were blue in the face! My mind was now made up. I advanced upon the unsullied form.

I hesitated for one moment. This news of Lucy was not the main reason for my decision. It was simply the final straw which weighted the scale in favour of staying. It had made me realize, with devastating clarity, how much Fairacre really meant to me. For that I should be grateful to Lucy always.

With infinite joy, I began to tear the application form into small pieces. Then − slattern to the last − I flung them in the direction of the waste paper basket, unmindful of whether they went in or not. I felt wonderful.

I bounded into the sunlit garden − *my* garden − and positively skipped down the path. As I passed the water butt I let out a joyous shout to the sleeping cat.

'Fairacre for ever!'

For two pins I would have run up the school's Union Jack.

10. The Wayfarer

Strangers are rare birds in the village of Fairacre and cause us as much interest as any hoopoes. We have our annual migrants, of course, and are always eager to see them each year, but they are only half-strangers.

These half-strangers come mainly in the summer. One really can't blame them. Winter comes with a vengeance here, with great roaring winds, cruel frosts and plenty of snow. As most of the visitors are townsfolk, they wisely remain where pavements, buses, indoor entertainment and central heating are available during the worst of the weather. But once spring begins, Mr Lamb, at the Post Office, recognizes the handwriting of friends and relatives of Fairacre natives and looks at the postmarks of London, Birmingham, Bristol and Leeds, and nods his head wisely.

'Asking to come again, no doubt,' he surmises. And, usually, he is right.

As well as these people, we look forward to seeing half a dozen or so regular tradesmen. In May, a small flat cart pulled by an ancient donkey appears in Fairacre. On board are dozens of boxes of seedlings. Alyssum and lobelia for neat border edgings, tagetes and African marigold, snapdragons and stocks, and best of all, velvety pansies already a-blowing in every colour imaginable. Sometimes there is a box or two of rosy double daisies. These I can never resist, and each year they are drawn to my notice by the two dark-eyed gipsies, who do the selling.

'Lovely daisies, dear. Better than ever this year. We got new seeds, see. They was more expensive, but we'll let you have 'em the same price as last year, dear, as we knows you so well.' And so I have a dozen or so, as they knew I would, and probably pay more, for I can't possibly remember what I paid the year before. And this they know too.

While the transaction goes on the children cluster round the donkey, stroking his plushy nose and murmuring endearments. Somehow, the donkey cart always manages to call on a sunny day, at about one-fifteen, when the school dinner is over and the children are free to enjoy the fun.

'Miss, have you got a lump of sugar?' they plead.

'Miss, the donkey likes carrots, the man says!' cries another.

'Miss, have you got a bit of ol' bread to spare?'

It always ends the same way. Bearing my damp little newspaper parcels, and my much lighter purse, I return to the school house followed by the children and the gipsy woman. I hand over sugar lumps, old apples, the end of a loaf and anything else which, at a cursory glance round my larder, will make acceptable donkey-fodder, and watch the children tearing across the playground with their largesse. But the gipsy woman remains. Her eyes have grown very large and sad, her voice pathetic. She speaks quietly, as one woman to another, on intimate matters.

'I'm not one to beg, miss, as you well know, but the fact is I'm expecting again and hardly a decent rag to fit me. I'm carrying low this time, and not a skirt will go round me.' I wonder, inconsequently, if 'carrying high' would mean that her upper garments would be too tight, but hastily dismiss the idea.

She shuffles a little closer, and looks furtively about her. The whisper becomes a whine.

'Don't matter how old, dear. Or a coat, now. Say you had a coat. Don't matter if it's torn or grubby. Do us a good turn, lady, and see what you can find, if it's only for the sake of the baby.'

I tell her to wait, whisk upstairs, collect a dear faithful old flannel skirt, which I know I shall mourn later, a tartan jacket which Amy unkindly but truthfully told me made me look 'like mutton dressed as lamb', and return.

The skinny dark hands grab them quickly and turn them inside out. The sharp eyes, I notice, are bright with approval.

'Thank you, dearie. God bless you! I've got no money to give you, with all we've got to feed, but I'd like you to have a pot plant off the cart.'

'No, really –' I protest. 'Just take the clothes.'

'You come on!' insists my caller. Meekly, I accompany her to the cart. The donkey, surfeited, is scraping the road with one neat little hoof. The scrunching of sugar lumps can be heard, but not from the donkey.

I choose a handsome pink geranium. We exchange civilities. The couple mount the cart. My skirt and jacket are stuffed under the wooden board that serves as a seat, in company with an assortment of other garments, I notice. We all wave until they are out of sight.

'Ring the bell, Ernest,' I say. 'It's time we were back to work!'

We install the geranium on my desk, as a happy reminder of one of our visitors. It will be a year before we see them again.

Later, the scissor-grinder comes, and we rush out to his Heath Robinson machine with shears and scissors, knives and bill-hooks. Sometime in June, a stocky figure appears pushing a light barrow full of assorted materials and tools. This is the chair-mender and mat-mender. He does rushing, caning and a certain amount of simple carpentry. Doormats are the things he likes mending best, and I remember the pride with which he told me one day that my back-door mat was 'one of the finest ever made in one of Her Majesty's prisons'. I have no way of testing the truth of this statement, but I like to think that I wipe the garden mud from my shoes on a decent bit of British workmanship.

Then, in high summer, more gipsies come, bearing gaudy flowers made of woodshavings and dyed all the colours of the rainbow. Sometimes they bring clothes pegs, clamped together in rows on long twigs, still green and damp from the hazel bushes where the wands were cut and peeled.

All these people are known and welcomed. They are as much part of the season as the daffodils or the Canterbury bells. In addition we sometimes have a visitor of more exotic caste. Once a tall turbaned stranger, with dusky skin and flashing eyes, called at our cottages. When we appeared, startled, at our doors he chanted:

'You lucky lady! Me, holy man from Pakistan!' And after these opening civilities he displayed the contents of a large suitcase for our delectation. Writing paper, soap, bright ties, hair ribbons, toothpaste – all jostled together to tempt the money from our purses. But I don't think he sold a great deal in Fairacre, for he never came again. Nor did 'the antique dealer' who offered Mrs Pringle ten shillings for her grandfather clock and Mr Willet a pound for the silver teapot left him by a former employer.

And another stranger, who called but once, was perhaps the most haunting of all our visitors. I see his face more clearly than many of my children's, and often wonder what happened to that shabby little figure who visited my house, long ago, and never returned.

It was a still, hot May morning when he arrived. The lilacs, tulips and forget-me-nots shimmered in a blue haze. It was a Saturday, and I had done my weekly washing. It hung motionless upon the line, but was drying rapidly, nevertheless, in the great heat.

I had dragged the wooden garden seat into the shade and was resting there, glorying in the weather, when I heard the click of the gate. A small man, carrying a battered suitcase slung over his shoulder with a leather strap, shuffled up the path. My heart sank. Must I rouse myself to face a jumble of assorted objects, none of which I really wanted, which no doubt awaited my inspection inside the case?

He did not stop at the door, but made his way across the grass towards me, slipped the heavy case from his back, with a sigh of relief, and spoke.

'Mind if I sit down, miss?' he asked. His voice had a Cockney twang and he sounded tired. I nodded and he sat abruptly on the grass, as though his legs would carry him no further.

We sat in silence for a few minutes, he too tired, I suspected, and I too bemused with the sunshine, to make conversation. A bumble-bee buzzed busily about the daisies on the grass. It seemed to be the only thing that moved in the garden. At length, I roused myself enough to speak.

'Don't bother to undo your case,' I said. The man looked faintly surprised.

'I weren't going to. Why should I?'

'I thought, maybe you were selling things,' I replied apologetically.

'Got nothin' to sell,' he said laconically. He lay back on the grass with his eyes shut, and I studied him.

He was quite old. He was a man in his seventies, I guessed, looking at the grey stubbly hair and his wrinkled forehead. A red band ran round his damp brow, where his cap had been, and a little trickle of sweat crept down his temple. He had a humorous look, and I guessed that he was a cheerful sparrow of a man, in the normal way. At the moment he looked utterly exhausted, and my heart smote me.

'Would you like a drink?' I asked. 'I haven't any beer, but there's cider or lemonade.'

He sat up slowly, his face creasing into a smile.

'I'd like a drop of lemon, miss, thank you,' he replied. He took a red and white spotted handkerchief from his pocket, and I left him wiping his face and neck, as I went towards the kitchen for refreshment.

It was a relief to leave the dazzling garden for the cool shade of the kitchen. I loaded the tray with a jug of lemonade, two glasses and the biscuit tin, and returned. The stranger struggled up at my approach, and took the tray from me.

He poured one glassful of lemonade straight down his throat, sighed, and put it back on the tray.

'I could do with that,' he said, thankfully, watching me refill it. 'I bin on the road since 'arpars six.'

'Have you far to go?' I asked him.

'Making for Weymouth,' he said.

'For a holiday?'

'For good!' he said shortly. He looked away into the distance, turning his glass round and round in his rough hands. There was sadness in his face, but a determination about the set of his mouth that made me wonder what lay behind his journey. I was soon to know.

'I got an ol' friend in Weymouth. We was in the army together. Went all through the war – Ypres, retreat from Mons, the lot. Name of Miller – Dusty Miller, of course.'

He gave me a quick sidelong smile.

'We 'ad some good times together. And some narrer squeaks too. "You come down anytime you like," Dusty says to me, whenever we met. "Always a welcome at Weymouth," he says, "for an old comrade!" So I'm going!'

He scrunched a biscuit fiercely. He looked a little defiant, I thought.

''Course I shouldn't say this,' he said, swallowing noisily, 'but poor ol' Dusty picked the wrong girl when he got wed. Worst day's work he ever done, in my 'umble opinion! Can't think what come over 'im!'

He ruminated for a moment, crossing one leg over the other, and contemplated his battered boots. His spirits were rising with rest and refreshment, and his natural loquacity became apparent.

'Ol' Dusty,' he assured me with emphasis, 'could 'ave 'ad 'is pick of the girls. Fine set-up feller always. Curly hair, good moustache, biceps like footballs. Always ready for a lark. Why, in France –' He stopped suddenly, coughed with some delicacy, and started again.

'After the war 'e 'ad a nice little packet of money saved up. His dad run a little confectioner-tobacco shop down the Mile End road, and when the old boy conked out in 1920 Dusty sold up and put the money into this caffy at Weymouth. Always bin fond of the sea, 'as Dusty, and I thought that's where 'e'd end up.'

'And so he's been there for a long time,' I observed.

'Ever since. Married a local girl too. Great pity really.'

He sighed, and helped himself to another biscuit.

''Course, you can understand it,' he continued. 'With this 'ere caffy to run, and that, you need a woman to lend a hand. And I must say, she could make two pennies go as far as three. A real 'ead for figures. It's thanks to Edie the place 'as done so well, but she weren't the woman for Dusty. No fun. Never one for a laugh. One of them stringy women, with a sharp nose. A bit white and spiteful, if you know what I mean.'

I said I did. St Patrick's clock began to strike eleven, and my visitor cocked an eye at me.

'Suppose I'd best be getting along,' he said, but with a questioning inflection. 'You must be busy.'

This was the opportunity which I should have seized, but it was so warm that I dallied. I knew that I ought to take my basket and go shopping. There were bedrooms to dust, and a salad to prepare. There were two telephone calls to make and the laundry to sort out.

Let all these things wait, I decided.

'I'm not particularly busy,' I replied.

'Well, I'll have another five minutes, if you're sure,' said my visitor, propping himself against a handy tree. 'It's good to 'ave a bit of a chin-wag. I must say I've been a bit lonely since Thursday.' He checked suddenly, and then resumed in a quieter vein.

'Thursday!' he said slowly, as if talking to himself. 'It seems weeks ago! A different life – that's what it seems! Eh, a lot's happened to me since this time last week. Funny, ain't it, the way you go on, year after year, in the same ol' rut, and then, suddenly – phut? Everything's changed. You find yourself starting all over again. Queer, how things 'appen. If you're sure you're not busy, miss, I'll tell you about it.'

I assured him that I had all the time in the world, stretched my legs into the sunshine, and gave him my attention.

★

The year that Dusty Miller went to Weymouth, it appeared, his old brother-in-arms, Alf, got married, and set up home near the Elephant and Castle in South London. He and his wife occupied a ground floor flat consisting of a kitchen-living room, a bedroom, and a parlour, known as the front room. The front room was only used on Sundays, or when guests were invited, and housed most of their wedding presents on a large sideboard.

Alf had a steady job as a butcher's roundsman. He was at work at seven-thirty each morning, cutting up the joints for the orders and loading his van. This was his employer's first motor vehicle, and the pride of both men's hearts.

He enjoyed his work. He was quick and friendly, a favourite with his customers who liked his badinage and unfailing cheerfulness. At Christmas time he carried home as much in Christmas boxes from kindly clients as he did in his wage packet.

His wife Jessie was a round pink girl with a frizzy fringe and pearl ear-rings. She liked satin blouses, an evening at the music hall, or a lively sing-song with her friends in the front room. Alf adored her.

They had three children, Frank, Norman and Ursula. The first two were named after relatives, but Ursula derived her name from the pages of a novelette which her mother had been reading a few hours before the baby arrived. The heroine of the novelette had had a particularly affecting experience, at a château somewhere well behind the lines in the First World War, involving a wounded officer of unsurpassed valour and passion, and a great deal of heart-searching on Ursula's part before the final renunciation.

It was all excessively moving, and the baby was to be either Jocelyn – the hero's name – or Ursula. And, eventually, after a prolonged and painful labour, Ursula arrived.

The family thrived, despite cramped conditions. The children ran round the corner to the gaunt Board School, as soon as they were old enough. The classes were enormous, the classrooms dark, but the teachers were well-trained and energetic, and the children got on famously.

Occasionally, Alf met Dusty at a British Legion function in London. The families exchanged Christmas cards, and one summer the London family was invited by Dusty to spend a holiday at Weymouth. This was a real treat and the children looked forward to it for weeks. But disappointment was in store. It was quite apparent, when they arrived, that though Dusty was pleased to see them, Edie was not.

'Miserable ol' faggot!' was Jessie's comment, in the privacy of the tiny back bedroom to which they had been shown. 'Some holiday this is going to be, Alf! You should've had more sense than to accept Dusty's invitation. He's properly under her thumb, poor soul!'

It was indeed a most uncomfortable time. The children were scolded if they brought in sand on their shoes, or shells in their pockets. Jessie, bridling, did her utmost to keep silent for the sake of poor shame-faced Dusty, as much as for her own family. But everyone was relieved when Saturday came and they could return home.

The two women pecked at each other's cheeks through their veils. The men shook hands a shade too heartily, and avoided each other's eyes. The children smiled more freely than they had done all the week, as they hung out of the train window.

'Never again!' exclaimed Jessie, as the train left Weymouth station. She withdrew two long hatpins from her straw hat, threw it on the rack, fussed up her fringe, and leant back with a sigh.

'That's the last I want to see of Edie Miller!' said Jessie flatly.

It was, in fact, the last that she did see of Edie, or Dusty For before the year was out, jolly lively Jessie was operated on for cancer, and died under the anaesthetic. Alf was inconsolable.

Ursula was ten at the time of her mother's death. The boys were twelve and thirteen. Jessie's mother, a widow who lived near by, took over the running of the house and the upbringing of the children. For Alf, it seemed as if the sun had gone for ever. For months he went about, looking like a shadow of his usual jaunty self, but gradually he recovered. His customers were glad to see his return to cheerfulness. He threw himself with renewed fervour into his work and into such activities as the British Legion's affairs. He and Dusty met often, but never spoke of the holiday which had been Jessie's last.

Years passed, and the two boys went out to work in New Zealand, where they married and settled. Ursula took over the housekeeping when their grandmother died, and Alf and his daughter rubbed along fairly well together.

She was nothing like her mother, Alf used to think, watching her at the other side of the hearth. She was thin and angular, with a sharp tongue and a way of tossing her head, when crossed, which Alf recognized as a danger signal. He was secretly relieved when she became engaged to a young man from Northampton, and he gave her away without a pang.

Then began for Alf some of the happiest years of his life. He was free to do as he pleased. His work ran smoothly, his health was good, his spirits remarkably gay now that he had the house to himself. A neighbour cleaned the flat once a week, and for the rest of the time the dust gathered gently, the oven remained cold, and only the frying pan and kettle were in general use. Life was very simple.

He began to see more of Dusty Miller. Both men were now in their sixties and had plenty of reminiscences to share. During the Second War Dusty had been to the forefront in Civil Defence at

Weymouth. Alf had been in the Fire Service, and both had experienced hair-raising episodes. Somehow, they did not talk of these. It was always the First World War which engrossed their attention. They relived the flight from Mons, the tedium and terror of trench life and the horror of that day when L Battery was wiped out beside them. They reminded each other, too, of lighter moments. Did Alf remember the time when his horse wheeled smartly into the pub yard as was its wont, leaving the colonel, whom he was accompanying, looking thunderstruck on the highway? Did Dusty recall the occasion when he played the piano in the pub, and generous comrades filled his tumbler with Benedictine, so that he began to think that he was playing a two-manual organ?

Time passed all too quickly when the old soldiers met. Dusty now ran a small car and frequently took Alf out. Sometimes, Alf stayed a day or two at Weymouth. Edie was civilly welcoming, but it was Dusty who did the real entertaining. The Millers had no family, and all Edie's energy seemed to go into the running of the flourishing business. The two men seemed to see very little of her.

'Don't forget, old boy,' said Dusty on many occasions, 'there's always a home here for you, if you get tired of your own company. Just say the word. Plenty of room for one more.'

Alf was grateful, and failed to notice that on these occasions Edie was either absent, or silent.

When Alf was seventy he had the first real illness of his life. It had been a miserable December, cold and foggy. Mists from the Thames hung over the area where Alf lived and worked, making life doubly difficult at the busy time before Christmas. Handling frozen meat, his hands numb and aching, Alf began to feel his age. The round seemed to take twice as long as usual, hampered as he was with fog and extra orders. Customers were short-tempered, the traffic was frustrating, and Alf looked forward to the Christmas break with more fervour than he had ever felt before.

One night, a few days before Christmas, he returned home late and tired. His chest was unusually painful. To breathe was difficult; to cough was agonizing. Reluctantly, after a night of wakefulness, he dragged himself to the local doctor's surgery.

'Bed for you,' was the verdict. 'Who is there to look after you?'

'No one,' said Alf. 'Well, I've a daughter, but she's in Northampton.'

'See if she can come down,' said the doctor, handing him a prescription. 'I'll be in tomorrow morning.'

Ursula, with a martyred expression, arrived the next evening. She made it quite clear that her duty really lay with her husband and children, that it was most inconvenient to leave home with so much to do, and that only her filial devotion had brought her so swiftly to her father's bedside. Alf thought, yet again, how different she was from her warm-hearted mother. If only his Jessie had still been alive! A tear, born of weakness, crept down his cheek, and Ursula, noticing it, was glad to see how grateful the old fellow was to her.

Two wretchedly uncomfortable days followed, while Ursula grew steadily more dictatorial and her father grew steadily weaker. The doctor, summing up the situation, removed Alf to hospital, warning Ursula that he might not be fit to live alone when he was well enough to be discharged.

'I don't need to be reminded of my duty,' said Ursula, bridling. 'Dad's got a home with us at Northampton whenever he wants it.'

'He'll want it very soon,' the doctor assured her.

It was a sad day for Alf, some weeks later, when he left the flat which had been his home for so long. A few treasured pieces of furniture travelled ahead to Northampton, the rest went to local auction rooms.

One windy March day of blinding rain, Alf took the train to the Midlands, with a very heavy heart.

He knew, as soon as he crossed the threshold, that it would never work. There was something about the angular light wood hat-stand in the hall, and the overpowering aroma of floor polish that met him, which seemed to epitomize the unwelcoming quality of Ursula's abode.

He had been allotted the front room, a bleak, north-facing apartment, sparsely furnished. An iron bedstead, with a thin mattress and frosty white counterpane, took up the space by the window. The lino, printed to look like parquet blocks, shone like a mirror. A skimpy rug slid about the polished surface whenever anyone was rash enough to step on it. A small one-bar electric fire did its best to cast a little warmth into the room, but failed miserably.

Alf's two grandchildren came into the room to greet him. They were an unprepossessing pair. Sandra was a lumpy, sandy-haired eight-year-old, and Roger a skinny, rabbit-toothed boy of eleven. Both had adenoids and breathed habitually through their mouths. As they ate almost without cessation, the spectacle of his grandchildren did not encourage Alf's affection for them.

Their father was a lorry driver, a man of few words, but enormous appetite. It seemed to Alf, in the months that followed, that Ursula spent most of her time peeling great saucepans full of potatoes to assuage his hunger. He did not see much of his son-in-law, as he worked long hours, and Alf regretted this. It would have been nice to have a man to talk to, now and again. With every week that passed, Alf realized, with increasing despair, how bitter it is not to have a home of one's own.

He did his best to remain equable. Indeed, with his unquenchable Cockney spirit, 'cheerfulness kept breaking in,' whether he would or no. Ursula resented this. She would have liked to see a proper humility, an appreciation of all her hard work. The gay quip, the sardonic aside, any sort of ironic levity, beloved of Alf, smacked of insurrection to Ursula. It was obvious that the old man would rebel one day; and before long, things came to the boil between Ursula and her father.

The row began, as might be expected, over the children. It was a hot May day, so hot, in fact, that for once Alf was grateful for his cold room. He sat, reading a letter which had come from Weymouth that morning, and looking forward to his tea when the children returned from school.

Dusty wrote as affectionately as ever. He knew, well enough, that his old friend was unhappy although he had not said so in black and white.

'Don't forget, what I've said before,' wrote Dusty, 'that you are welcome here any time you like to come.'

Alf found great comfort in that sentence. He read it several times before returning the letter to its envelope on the table, and then settled back for a doze.

Before long he awoke. The two children were in the room, the boy gazing out of the window, and Sandra – Alf's anger rose as his senses returned – Sandra was reading Dusty's letter.

He struggled to his feet and made towards the table.

'Don't you dare meddle with my things!' stormed the old man.

The child looked sideways at him and contorted her face, by the lift of one nostril, into a contemptuous sneer. Just so, many years before, Ursula had looked at him, and received a resounding box on the ear.

Without thinking further, Alf repeated the process, and had one moment of unalloyed pleasure as his palm clouted the sandy head.

The piercing shrieks that followed brought Ursula hurrying from the kitchen.

''E 'it me, mum! I wasn't doing nothin', mum! 'E just 'it me!'

Ursula's face and neck grew red with wrath.

'You keep your hands to yourself,' she yelled. 'I can remember your bullying ways when I was her age! Don't you think you can knock my kids about the way you knocked us!'

'She was reading my letter–' began Alf, but was brushed aside.

'As though it's not bad enough having you here all the time, burning the firing and the lights, eating us out of house and home–'

'I pay my own way!'

Ursula gave a derisive snort.

'Pay your way?' she echoed. 'And how far do you reckon your bit of pension goes these days?'

Sandra, seeing attention slipping from her, set up a further bout of snivelling.

'Mum, I believe I've got mastoid. I do, really! My ear 'urts somethin' awful where 'e 'it me!'

Ursula threw an arm protectively round her daughter.

'We'll take you down to the hospital after tea.' She rounded again on the old man.

'And if she's got a broken ear drum and is deaf for the rest of her days, she'll have you to thank! The ingratitude! That's what gets me – the ingratitude! Here I am, slaving day in, day out, with never a word of thanks for my trouble, and how am I repaid?'

'Stop play-acting–' began Alf.

'Play-acting!' screamed Ursula. 'Don't you dare insult me after all the harm you've done. I've just about had enough of you and your ways!'

She flung out of the room, dragging Sandra with her. The boy, who had watched the proceedings with sly enjoyment, slid after them. At the door he turned, poked out an impudent tongue, and vanished. Alf was left alone.

He was more shaken than he cared to admit. He shouldn't have hit the girl, he told himself. He was enveloped in a hot wave of guilt and shame. It receded, leaving him shivering with shock. God, what a hole, he thought, looking round the room! To think of spending the rest of his days in this place, with the added misery of Ursula and the children!

His eye fell upon Dusty's letter. In all that bleak room it was the only spot of comfort. Why should he stay? Why should he endure the humiliation of living with Ursula? He had his pension. He had a true old friend – a friend, moreover, who offered him a real home.

With growing purpose he went to his bed, reached beneath it for his battered suitcase, and set it open upon the white counterpane.

Methodically, with the exactitude of an old soldier, he began to pack his possessions. He was off.

'That was Thursday,' said the old man, reaching for his glass. He sounded bemused. 'And now it's Saturday. Seems a lifetime ago, miss – a lifetime.'

He gazed into the distance towards the towering downs, but I guessed that he was looking beyond them to the life that he had left behind in Northampton. He looked very old, very vulnerable, to be alone and with no home. I felt uneasy.

'And your daughter?' I inquired. 'You told her where you were going?'

I could imagine the remorse which might well be gnawing at any woman in her position, despite the portrait of flinty-hearted indifference the old man had drawn of her.

'Left a note,' said the stranger perfunctorily. 'Just told her I'd had an invitation from Dusty, and this seemed a good time to go down there.'

'So she'll expect you back some time?' I said. It was a relief to know that he had not burnt his boats completely.

'Never!' he shouted, sitting bolt upright. 'Not if she begged and prayed of me! I've had more'n I can take there. Never again!'

He scrambled to his feet, still looking belligerent. His gaze flickered over the sunny garden as though he saw it for the first time, and he turned to look directly at me. The anger faded into a smile.

'You bin good to me, miss, letting me run on like I have. I must be getting along.'

He fished inside his jacket and brought out a small creased map. He unfolded it carefully, and I noticed that his fingers shook. Across its grubby surface a thick ruled line ran from Northampton to Weymouth.

'There's my route,' he said proudly, holding up the map. 'Always like a bit of map work ever since my Army days. I'm a bit off true here, but no matter. Reckon if I make for Salisbury Plain I shan't be far off.'

He stuffed the map back in his pocket and began to hoist the case across his shoulders again.

'You're not walking all the way?' I asked anxiously.

'Not me!' he said. 'I've hitch-hiked most of it so far, but took a fancy to a walk this morning. Haven't seen the country on a summer day − not to notice it, I mean − ever since Jessie died. Brought her back to me somehow, being alone and peaceful, out in the fresh air.'

'Make for Caxley,' I said. 'But wait here a minute.'

I returned to the house and looked in my purse. As usual it was remarkably light, but there was a pound note. Why, I wondered, was it always the end of the month when such emergencies arose? I hastened out again and pressed it upon him.

'No, miss,' he protested. 'I got a bit by, you know.'

'If you don't get a lift, go by train,' I urged him. 'You don't want to arrive absolutely knocked up.'

He pocketed the note and we walked together to the gate. He was smiling now, as though at some pleasurable secret.

'Can't wait to see ol' Dusty's face when I turn up,' he said, over the gate.

'You haven't told them?' I asked, my heart sinking.

'Why should I?' he replied reasonably. 'I know ol' Dusty means it when he says I can go any time.' His tone was warm and affectionate. His wrinkled old face glowed at the thought of the welcome ahead. He straightened himself up and gave me a smart salute.

'Thanks for everything, miss, bless you! Think of me paddlin' in a day or two!'

Within two minutes I watched the little figure disappear round the bend of the lane. Despite the sunshine, I shivered, for I could not help thinking of the woman that Dusty should never have married, the stringy one with the sharp nose, who was 'white and spiteful'.

Poor Alf, I mourned, poor Alf!

Yes, some of our Fairacre visitors are lively birds. The gipsies, in their clashing colours, look as exotic and gay as any parrot from the East. But I remember Alf as a wren, perky and completely English but somehow infinitely pathetic in his smallness.

I think of him often, the stranger who called but once. Will he ever return?

I can't be certain, but I have a feeling that Alf was on his last flight that summer day.

11. The Old Man of the Sea

'It's my belief,' announced Mrs Pringle, as she baled boiling water from the electric copper into the washing-up bowl, 'that they over-ate themselves.'

'I thought they were rather more abstemious than usual,' I replied. 'Usually they start eating as we reach the end of the lane, and continue until we get to Barrisford.'

'Shameful!' ejaculated Mrs Pringle, flinging a trayful of sticky cutlery into the water. The noise was deafening.

'Then it's a quick dash into the sea, out again, and time for a solid lunch. This time they didn't appear to eat so much on the journey. Unless I'm getting used to it,' I added.

We were trying to probe the mystery of the many absences from school on this particular Monday morning. Almost a third of the desks were empty, and I suspected that general inertia was the common complaint after a long day at the sea on Saturday. Mrs Pringle argued for gluttony alone, but I have never found Fairacre children suffering from delicate digestions. Their appetites, quickened by the winds which sweep the downs, are enormous, and their digestive tracts are quite accustomed to coping with a steady supply of ices, sweets, fruit, fizzy drinks, as well as four hefty meals a day.

'Could be typhoid, of course,' said Mrs Pringle chattily. 'There was a bit on the telly about the sewage going into the sea. Fair gives you the creeps! I said to Pringle: "The way folks live! Thank God we've got a nice wholesome cess-pit!"'

She plunged her hands into the steaming water and withdrew a fistful of dripping dessert-spoons, lately used for gooseberry pie.

'But can't do you no good, say what you will, to go bathing when that sort of thing's goin' on. As well as dumpin' this atomic rubbish they don't know what to do with. The sea must be proper un'ealthy these days. Me heart bleeds for those poor fish, it do indeed!'

She was now drying the spoons and setting them rapidly in rows. She counted them hissingly, stopped, scrabbled again in the cloudy water, drew blank, and turned to me. Her unlovely face was made even unlovelier by dark suspicion.

''Ere!' said Mrs Pringle truculently. 'You bin featherin' your nest again?'

This charitable remark referred to an unfortunate incident a few weeks earlier when Mrs Pringle had come across a school dessert-spoon in the kitchen drawer at the school house. I had not been allowed to forget this lapse. Mrs Pringle guards the school cutlery – as battered and dingy a collection of plate as one could find any-where – as if it were the Crown Jewels.

'I find that remark offensive,' I said coldly, moving off to ring the school bell.

'So's stealing!' shouted Mrs Pringle after me, above the clatter. With what dignity I could muster, I pulled the school bell-rope to summon my depleted pupils to afternoon school.

The outing on Saturday had started in brilliant sunshine. By ancient custom, Fairacre Sunday School and Church Choir Combined Outing takes place on the first Saturday in July. Evidently, many years ago, the schools in this area used to have a fortnight's holiday at the end of June to enable the children to pick the soft fruit crop. At the end of that time their wages were paid and there was money, as well as the longing, for a jollification. Somehow, the first Saturday in July still remains as the only accept-able day for the annual outing.

Two coachloads set off at eight o'clock, packed with parents and friends as well as the vociferous children. It was a sparkling morning. Bright drops glittered on the fresh hedges, sunshine glinted on cottage windows, the village pond, and the glossy backs of Mr Roberts' herd of Friesians as they ambled back from being milked. It was most exhilarating.

'Won't last,' said Mr Willet morosely, following his wife into the coach.

He was dressed in his best blue suit, and his boots shone like jet. No gaudy beachwear for Mr Willet when he accompanies us to the sea! He is sexton of St Patrick's, a public figure, and he shows himself to the world as a man worthy of the dignity of his office. He now rammed a small case containing their lunch upon the rack and then bent down to whisper conspiratorially in my ear.

'Where's old misery sitting?'

'Right at the front,' I whispered back, knowing at once to whom this referred.

'Thanks, miss. I'll make for the back,' said Mr Willet, pulling the case from the rack, and departing. I heard him settle with a satisfied sigh, as Mrs Pringle entered, took her place in the front and intimated to the driver that it was now in order for him to proceed.

'Old 'ard, ma,' said the driver irreverently. 'Just gotter check we're all 'ere.'

He hoisted himself from the wheel and turned round to count us.

'All aboard?' he cried at length.

'All aboard!' we echoed cheerfully, and set off for Barrisford.

Mr Willet, as a weather prophet, is usually right, and by the time we had driven through Caxley, the sky was overcast, and remained so for most of the day. Not that this dimmed the spirits of the Fairacre children. They tore along the famous sands, rushed into the waves – but not too deeply, I noticed, for the sea is not really trusted by us landlubbers – and wielded buckets and spades energetically for most of the exciting day.

Their elders enjoyed themselves more sedately, walking along the short pier, scanning the distant horizon through the penny-in-the-slot telescope, and studying the photographs outside the miniature theatre at the very end of the pier. It was a pity, we told each other, that we had to set off for home so early, otherwise we could have seen the variety show. Twelve acts – and all spectacular – it said so!

The air was wonderful, despite the lack of sunshine, tangy and salt upon our faces, and we all had prodigious appetites when we foregathered for high tea at Bunce's, the famous restaurant on the front.

The vicar counted heads earnestly. Were we all assembled? Would someone else check the numbers with him?

Thereupon half the company rose to count the other half, and confusion reigned. Order was eventually restored, but we were, it was agreed, one missing.

'Joseph Coggs!' shouted Patrick. 'I saw him mucking about under the pier. Shall I run and fetch him?'

'I think,' said Mr Partridge, the vicar, in his gentle voice, 'we'll wait for five minutes and then send out a search party if he hasn't arrived. No doubt he will be along.'

At that moment, Joseph wandered through the brown and gold swing doors. He was excessively grubby and looked pale and bewildered. No adult from the Coggs' family was present so I took charge of him. He was remarkably quiet during tea, but ate his way steadily through a plate of ham and salad, three iced cakes, a butterscotch sundae and two cups of tea. I was not perturbed by his taciturnity, as I watched his eating prowess. He obviously had enough to engross him, at the time, and was, in any case, a somewhat uncommunicative child.

Just before six we said a sad farewell to lovely Barrisford for another year, and mounted the coach. Still the skies were sullen. At nine we were back in Fairacre, and at ten o'clock I, for one, was in bed.

Now, on Monday afternoon, it all seemed a very long time ago. Confronting my depleted class I mentally rearranged the timetable. The song, which I had proposed to teach them, must wait until the others returned. A spelling test, and then some revived memories of Barrisford, in words and pictures, should fill our afternoon very usefully and happily.

The spelling test was greeted with groans. Perhaps because they are unbookish children, as a whole, and do not see the printed word as often as I should like, spelling is a weak point at Fairacre. Even their names, when they are first in my class, at the age of seven or so, give some of them trouble, and I silently curse the parents who saddle their poor spellers with 'Penelope', 'Francesca' or 'Reginald'.

Perhaps the worst one is 'Ronald'. It has been my lot, for many years, to wrestle with 'Ronlads', 'Rondals' and even 'Ronslads' and very exhausting I have found it.

This afternoon I bullied them through such necessary exercises as the days of the week – 'Wednesday', of course, is the stumbling-block – the months of the year – all, with the possible exception of 'March' and 'June', fearfully hazardous – and a brisk revision of local place names which are invariably written awry. They tottered out to play, quite done up.

Ten minutes in the boisterous air of the school playground soon restored them to their usual vivacity, however, and they settled down to write and draw their impressions of the day at Barrisford. I wandered round the busy classroom, admiring their efforts.

They were much as I expected. Sand castles topped with flags, sailing boats, rowing boats – even a steamer, though I am positive no steamers come to Barrisford – and unflattering portraits of fellow pupils paddling in zig-zag waves. But Joseph Coggs' picture roused my curiosity.

Beneath a framework of black-crayoned girders stood two figures. One, from the blue striped tee shirt, I recognized as a self-portrait. The other, about half the size, wore scarlet bathing trunks and a crown on its head. A certain amount of scrawling with a pale blue crayon indicated that water was near by, and in the distance it looked as though there were a fairytale palace with the conventional spiky towers. I began to wonder if Joseph was remembering the pantomime rather than the trip to the sea.

'Who's this little boy with you?' I asked.

''S'man!' said Joseph

'But he's only half your size,' I protested. Our art at Fairacre is pretty pedestrian. We make the sun circular, and grown-ups are usually twice the size of children in our pictures.

'So he was!' persisted Joseph. 'But he were a man, all the same.'

I was about to pass on and let him enjoy his fantasy, when he pointed out one or two other features.

'This 'ere's the pier, see. I met this man under there. He was only up to my shoulder.'

'Sounds likely, don't it!' scoffed Ernest who had come to see the picture, and was rapidly joined by half a dozen others who felt like stretching their legs.

'Bet you dreamt it, Joe!' said John.

Joseph's dusky face grew red with anger. His dark eyes smouldered.

'He was a man,' he repeated mulishly. 'He told me. He said he was The Old Man of the Sea and he lived in a palace. That's it there!'

He thrust a black forefinger upon the spiky towers. There was a burst of derisive laughter from the onlookers which I hastily quelled. Joseph was very near to tears and I was not going to see him taunted, inexplicable though his garbled story sounded.

'Ten minutes to finish!' I announced, 'and we'll have a quiet ten minutes, please. I'm looking for someone sensible to help me clear up at home time.'

This, as usual, worked like magic, and peace descended while they finished their scribbling. Partly to keep Joseph from being teased on the way home, and partly because I was intrigued with what lay behind his account of the stranger, I chose him to remain behind after school.

The rest of the children ran off, their voices dying away in the distance.

The classroom seemed unnaturally quiet. We could hear the birds cheeping on the guttering, and the whispering of the leaves outside the Gothic window.

Joseph stacked the papers carefully. His own, I noticed, was placed lovingly on top. He brought them to my desk, put them down, and remained gazing at me.

'I ain't lying,' he said abruptly.

'I know you're not,' I answered.

There was silence for a moment, a silence which I did not intend to break first.

'I really did see him under the pier,' said Joseph slowly. 'That's why I was late for tea. That's why –'

He faltered, took a deep breath, and began again. In bits and pieces, fits and starts, the astonishing story came out. To an adult it was both pathetic and comic. To a small boy, it was quite apparent, the encounter had been terrifying and miraculous.

As far as I can gather, Joseph stayed with his younger twin sisters, as he had been bidden to do by his mother, until they had eaten their sandwiches at midday.

The three children had played blissfully with the sand and the shells for which Barrisford is famous, but in the afternoon Joseph began to get restless. The two little girls had started a mammoth earthworks, with which they were entranced. Joseph found the business of digging remarkably boring. After all, he could dig any time in Fairacre. What Joseph wanted to do was to explore.

Mr and Mrs Willet, propped comfortably in the shelter of a breakwater nearby, saw his predicament.

'You go and 'ave a look round, Joe,' said Mr Willet. 'We'll be 'ere for a bit, reading the paper. We'll keep an eye on your sisters.'

Joseph scrambled eagerly to his feet, his dark eyes sparkling, and set off in the direction of the pier.

'Don't forget tea's at half past four,' bellowed Mr Willet, in the voice that carries across the mighty winds of Fairacre. 'Keep your eye on your gold wrist-watch!'

Mr Willet gave a mighty chuckle at his own wit. Mrs Willet smiled wanly, and the two little girls looked at him open-mouthed.

''E ain't gotter wrist-watch!' explained one slowly.

'Tch! Tch!' said Mr Willet testily, and shook out the newspaper.

Joseph made his way diagonally across the sand towards the sea. His feet were bare, and he gloried in the feel of the wet ribs of sand under his insteps. The tide was out, leaving pools of every imaginable shape. Here and there were outcrops of slaty black rock. These Joseph found particularly fascinating. Slimy bladder-wrack covered many of them, and he squatted happily on the rubbery mounds popping the salty blisters one after another. There were limpets too, grey, ribbed and conical, that he tried in vain to prise from the rock. He was intrigued by the way he could move them a trifle, and then no more, as they put out their defences.

He wandered nearer and nearer to the pier. Here the pools were deeper, and he discovered, for the first time, the brown jelly-like anemones that waved their tentacles and sucked at his finger.

There were a number of people walking along the pier, hanging over the railings, gazing at the sea. Joseph recognized some of the Fairacre party among them. But he was not particularly interested in what went on aloft. It was the great sub-structure of criss-crossed iron girders which Joseph intended to explore.

They were very cold, wet and rusty, he discovered. Brown streaks and green slime coloured their gaunt shapes, and where the water lapped the legs, green fringes swayed to and fro rhythmically.

Joseph made an attempt to climb up one of the girders, but the iron-work was cruelly hard to hands and feet. Little flakes of metal came off at a touch, and the salty roughness made his finger-tips sore. He abandoned the attempt and stood listening to the strange noises around him.

Above his head came the thudding of people's feet as they walked the planks of the pier. Around him came the constant sound of trickling water as it ran down the girders, or dripped into the rock pools. The wind made a little whistling sound in the iron lattice-work, and always, as a bass accompaniment, there was the rushing and booming of the swirling sea.

It was particularly rocky under the pier. Great flat plateaux of rock overlapped, forming wide irregular steps. At their edge were deep pools, almost black in the dim light beneath the pier. Joseph, stepping into one, caught his breath as the water came high above his knees. He scrambled out of the slippery hole, and walked in a more gingerly fashion, peering at this strange and frightening element.

He was now almost at the end of the pier. Above him he could hear people walking round the little theatre. There was a distant sound of tea cups, for a small refreshment room adjoined the theatre. Sometimes a child called. Sometimes a gull wheeled and cried. It was difficult to tell which was the human voice. Joseph found it all wonderful and strange.

At length he came to a large pool. It was overhung by an outcrop of rock and was as dark as ink. Something large, coloured red and white seemed to be floating in it. Cautiously, Joseph approached, knelt upon the slippery rock and peered over.

To his horror he saw that it was the motionless body of a boy. Surely, he must be dead! His eyes were closed. His legs and arms floated gently away from the body and his hair moved as rhythmically in the water as the tentacles of the anemones had done.

Fearfully, his throat aching with suppressed screams, Joseph put out a shaking finger and prodded the body. 'Give over!' said the corpse, opening its eyes suddenly.

Joseph flinched away, startled, scraping his knee painfully on the sharp rock. There was a wild thrashing in the pool, the red trunks and legs were submerged and only the top half of the body confronted Joseph.

'Whatcher think you're up to?' demanded the bather. 'Poking people about like that?'

Joseph, never very voluble, found communication more difficult than usual. For one thing, he was in a state of shock. And for another thing, he was extremely puzzled. The stranger was very small. He had believed him to be a boy, possibly two or three years younger than himself, but as soon as he spoke he realized that, despite his small stature, the bather was a grown man.

Somehow it all seemed part of the fantastic world immediately around Joseph. Anything could happen here, among the faintly menacing shapes of the girders and rocks. The cold, salty air was as far removed as it could be from the pollen-laden winds that blew around Joseph's native village. The music of birdsong and rustling trees was exchanged for the queer atonal sound of dripping water and surging sea. He felt as though he had strayed into an unknown world, where colours, shapes, sounds, and now people themselves, were strange and sinister.

Despite his aching throat he managed to swallow and find his voice.

'I'm sorry, sir,' he said tremulously.

Immediately he was glad that he had added that last word to his apology. The little man's face softened. A look of gratification passed over the pudgy countenance, and he wiped the wet hair away from his forehead.

'That's all right, boy,' he said grandly. 'Now you're here you can give me a hand out.'

He presented a cold wet hand to Joseph. It was as small as those of Joseph's little sisters, but on the back were the hairs of a grown man. Joseph tugged with all his strength. There was a good deal of puffing and blowing and then the little man bounced from the pool on to the rocks.

'Get my towel, boy, will you?' asked the stranger, waving towards the direction of a nearby girder at the outside edge of the pier. Joseph saw a bundle propped between the angle of two girders, out of the wet, and made his way carefully across the slimy rocks to do as he was bidden. There was something imperious about the man which awed Joseph. He was glad to be of service to him.

When he came to withdraw the rolled-up towel from its resting place, Joseph was surprised to see that a few yards of rope ladder were tucked in with it. One end was obviously fixed aloft, and Joseph stepped out beyond the pier to see where it went. He could see it lashed securely to the bottom stay of the pier railings. From there it hung down against the girders, flapping gently in the breeze. Joseph guessed that at its full length it would easily reach the sand. Tucked up as it was, a little higher than his head, it was unnoticeable at a cursory glance.

'Come on! I'm dam' near freezing!' shouted the man.

Joseph hurried back with the towel. The stranger, jumping up and down with remarkable agility, was covered with goose-pimples.

He snatched the towel from Joseph's arms and began to rub himself energetically Joseph surveyed him with interest.

Now that the water had drained from his hair, Joseph could see that the man was fair. He was thickset and very muscular. His chest and legs were faintly hairy and he had the suspicion of a moustache. His eyes were very blue, his ears very red. Joseph wondered how old he was. It seemed strange to think that he might be as old as his father, and yet he was no bigger than one of his twin sisters!

The man gave his head a final rub, threw the towel round his waist, and turned to look at Joseph.

'Perishin' cold under here,' he said. 'Let's sit outside for a bit.' He indicated the sand beyond the pier. A little faint sunlight was struggling through the clouds, and chasing the shadows across the bay.

The two picked their way across the rocks. At the edge of the pier the man stopped.

'Anyone about?' he asked. Joseph looked up and down the beach. There were a number of people further along, but no one at hand. The most popular beach, where the Willets were already beginning to think of packing up and making their way to Bunce's, lay behind them.

'Can't see anyone,' said Joseph, wondering at the man's sudden desire for privacy. They emerged into the open. It was a relief to feel flat sand again underfoot.

'I'll show you how to warm up after a bathe!' cried the little man, whose spirits seemed to have risen rapidly. He flung off the towel, and did a backward somersault before Joseph could draw breath.

'Cor!' said Joseph, full of admiration. 'Who learnt you that?'

'Never you mind!' answered the man. 'Watch out now!'

He flexed his muscles, stood on his toes, took a deep breath, and then turned three backward somersaults in a row. After the last he stretched his arms above his head, looking this way and that, as though acknowledging applause. Joseph thought he looked just like the acrobat he had seen in the pantomime last Christmas. If anything, he was better, because he was so small and neat. Joseph was entranced.

'That's chicken feed,' said the man. He swaggered slightly, thrusting his thumbs into the top of his red trunks. 'Look at this!'

He stretched his arms again and began to turn cartwheels, with extreme dexterity and rapidity. He wheeled so steadily, that his red trunks and white torso seemed to blur before Joseph's admiring eyes. He must have turned almost twenty times before he ceased and became upright again.

'Ain't you a marvel!' breathed Joseph, awed.

The little man laughed, but was obviously pleased with the boy's admiration. He smote him cheerfully across the shoulders and they sat down together in the shelter of a rock. Joseph compared their outstretched legs. His own were thin and brown, marked with many an ancient scar on the shins, and the fresh scrape across one sore knee. The stranger's were several inches shorter than his own, but twice the thickness, and bulging with muscles.

'D'you live in Barrisford?' asked the stranger.

'No,' said Joseph. 'Do you?'

'Not likely! Not in this one-eyed dump! Do I look as though I live here?' He cocked a blue eye upon Joseph. Anxious to please this superman, Joseph hastened to apologize, although he himself could see nothing wrong with Barrisford. Indeed, to someone whose home was in the modest confines of Fairacre, Barrisford seemed a splendidly sophisticated place.

'What's your name, sir?' ventured Joseph.

'Ah now! That's telling!' said the little man teasingly.

He leant back against the rock, clasping his hands behind his head, and gazed quizzically at the boy with half-closed eyes.

'I think you'd better call me "The Old Man of the Sea",' he said lazily. 'That's where you found me, wasn't it?'

'The Old Man of the Sea,' echoed Joseph, not completely understanding. 'Do you mean you live there?'

The man nodded, grinning at the boy's mystification.

'That's right,' he said. 'I live in the sea. In a palace, in fact. I'm a sort of King, you know, got a crown and that when I'm at home.'

Joseph pondered this. It sounded a bit far-fetched, but why should a grown-up man want to lie? And the whole affair was odd – the queer, dark, under-pier world, the tiny man, the cartwheels! He wanted to know more.

'Where is this palace?' he asked suspiciously.

'If you're not going to believe me,' said the man, suddenly looking sulky, 'I shan't waste my time telling you.'

'Oh, but I do!' cried Joseph, aghast at upsetting this godlike creature yet again. The stranger appeared mollified.

'Well, if you must know, it's way out beyond the end of the pier, on the sea-bed.'

'What's it made of?' asked Joseph.

'Oh, rocks and stones, and that!' said the man airily. There was a short silence, as though he were thinking heavily, and then he began again.

'Sea shells, too, of course. It's sort of decorated with shells. And we have sea-weed trees in the garden. It's a pretty place. Fish swim in and out the windows. We always keep the windows open. I like a bit of fresh sea-water in the rooms myself.'

Joseph sat contemplating this picture of royal life beneath the waves. He found it wholly enchanting, and only a fragment of his former doubt remained.

'What d'you eat?' he inquired.

'Fish, of course,' replied the little man, opening his blue eyes very wide. 'What fool questions you ask! We've got nets from the garden, straight through the kitchen window, to the larder where we keep 'em.'

'I like fried fish,' said Joseph warmly. This talk of food was beginning to make him hungry.

'Oh, we don't fry ours,' answered the man casually. 'Too wet, you know. Makes it difficult to keep the stove alight.'

'Ah! It would!' agreed Joseph. Somehow, the difficulty of keeping the stove going underwater, seemed to make sense of the whole, slightly improbable, situation.

'No, we eat 'em raw,' said the man. 'Very nutritious too.' He suddenly gave a gigantic yawn.

'Ah well, my boy, wish I could stay longer with you, but I'd best be getting along.'

'Back to the palace?' asked Joseph. He half-hoped that he would be invited to accompany him.

The man rose to his feet and began to shake out the sand from his towel.

'Not just yet,' he said, smiling. 'I've got some friends to call on first.' He wrapped the towel round his shoulders.

A distant yelling caused the two to look round. Leaning over the pier railings, just where the rope ladder was fastened, was a small figure. To Joseph it looked like a little girl.

'Come on, Bill!' she shouted. 'It's half past four. Your tea's ready!'

'Coming, Katy!' the little man shouted back, and set off towards the rope ladder with incredible speed. Joseph ran beside him.

He watched him untangle the lower rungs and begin to mount aloft. The strong little arms and legs twinkled over the criss-cross rope, like a monkey in a ship's rigging. Halfway up he stopped and looked down at Joseph's upturned face.

'Hey, boy,' he said, grinning. 'You cut off to your own folk. And don't believe all you hear, son!'

He nipped smartly up the rest of the ladder and through the railings. Joseph watched him untie the rope, his face suddenly solemn and intent. He slung it across his towelled shoulders, with never a backward glance at the boy below, and vanished towards the theatre.

Disconsolately, with the words of his hero echoing in his ears, Joseph obediently retraced his steps, seeking – tardily and reluctantly – his own folk, who were already ensconced amidst the solid worldliness of Bunce's restaurant.

'And you knows the rest, miss,' said Joseph, fiddling with the brass lid of the Victorian ink stand which dominates the teacher's desk at Fairacre School. His dark eyes were downcast, crescents of thick lashes brushing his dusky cheeks.

'And I 'ad my tea with you, and then we come 'ome,' he continued.

'I remember,' I said. I also remembered Mr and Mrs Willet's conversation at the tea table, of which Joseph was obviously unaware.

'A pity we have to go back so soon,' Mr Willet had said. 'They say there'a a good show on at the end of the pier.'

'Someone told me there's a juggler that keeps six bottles moving,' said Mrs Willet, 'and a dog, dressed up like a nursemaid, pushing a monkey in a pram!'

'There's twelve acts altogether,' said someone further down the table. 'I looked at the posters. Top of the bill is the midgets. Acrobats they are – six of 'em. Call themselves The Mighty Atoms, or some such name. "Appeared before all the crowned heads in Europe," the poster said. I bet they'd have been worth seeing!'

'I'm partial to midgets myself,' Mr Willet had agreed, before the conversation took a different turn.

I looked at the little gipsy boy before me. What was going on under that black thatch of tousled hair? I wondered. Did he really believe the yarn spun him by the fanciful midget? Or did he merely want to believe it?

And what should be my reaction to Joseph's disclosures? I doubted whether this was the time to tell him the cold truth – whether, in fact, he would ever want to know the truth. It seemed wiser, I decided, to say as little as possible at this stage. Joseph's feelings were still too raw to stand rough handling. If he ever wanted to know more, I felt that he would ask me, and then I should answer him with the truth.

At this moment the problem was settled, or at least shelved, by the appearance in the doorway of Mrs Pringle. In one hand she held an upturned broom, in the other a dustbin lid. She looked, at first glance, like some squat Britannia, with trident and shield.

'You done?' she inquired glumly.

'Yes, indeed,' I said. Under the present trying circumstances Mrs Pringle's appearance was almost welcome. I put the stack of papers on top of the ancient walnut piano, anchored them safely from the cross-draughts with *Hymns Ancient and Modern*, locked the drawers of my desk, and made my way out into the playground.

Joseph followed me, still looking thoughtful. Outside, by the doorway, Mr Willet was perched on a pair of rickety steps. He was drawing a bent stick along the guttering, collecting dead leaves, an old nest or two, twigs and odd slivers of slate, all of which impeded the flow of rainwater to the butt behind the school.

I stopped to hail him.

'Run home now, Joseph,' I said to my shadow. 'You shall pin your picture on the wall tomorrow morning. It's one of the best.'

His countenance became more animated, and he began to move off. Suddenly, as though remembering something, he turned again to confront us.

'And there *was* a little man!' he said earnestly. 'Honest, there was!'

'I know,' I assured him. We looked at each other for a moment. Then he smiled, and he set off at a brisk trot through the school gates.

'What's up with young Joe then?' inquired Mr Willet, when the child was out of earshot. 'He bin in trouble?'

'Not trouble exactly,' I answered. 'I'll tell you all about it some day. Let's say he's finding life a bit of a puzzle at the moment.'

Mr Willet snorted, and dropped a noisome handful of muck into the bucket at the foot of the steps.

'Who don't?' he demanded.

12. *Harvest Festival*

There are a number of people in Fairacre who maintain that far too much importance is given to Harvest Festival in our village. Mrs Mawne, our local ornithologist's wife, is one.

'I find something abhorrently bucolic about Harvest Festival,' she announced one day, looking round the chancel of St Patrick's church where the ladies of the village were busy festooning ledges and pillars with the fruits of the earth.

Miss Jackson too, I remember, voiced much the same sentiments. She came among us – mercifully for a short time – as infants' teacher at the school, and had a very poor idea of rural festivals, church or secular.

'Simply a survival of primitive superstitions,' was her comment. 'An act of propitiation to malevolent tribal gods, bound up with fertility rites and other ceremonials of earlier civilizations.' Miss Jackson's dicta were always couched in high-flown language of this sort, and very tedious it became.

Luckily, such people are in the minority. For most of us in Fairacre our Harvest Festival is a well-loved and well-supported institution. It is, after all, a public thanksgiving for the fulfilment of a year's hard work in the fields and gardens, and a brief breathing space before tackling the next year's labours.

Mr Roberts, the local farmer, gives a mammoth Harvest Home supper in his biggest barn, at this season, but naturally it is the farm workers and their friends who attend this jollification. The service at St Patrick's caters for the whole village, for chapel-goers join church-goers on this occasion, and the church is always crowded.

'Far more crowded, in fact,' sighs the vicar, 'than for any other of our church festivals. I sometimes wonder why.'

I think I could tell him. Here is something tangible, something vital, the fruits of the earth – in turn, the fruits of man's labour – lying in splendid array, as living witness of God's and man's work together. A good harvest means food, security, life itself. A poor one, not so long ago, could mean starvation – and memories are long in the country. It is easier to comprehend the things of the flesh than the spirit, and although one can sympathize with the good vicar's attitude, it does not mean that the praise and honour rendered to the Almighty at Harvest Thanksgiving are any less meritorious.

On the Friday afternoon before Harvest Festival Sunday, I took the schoolchildren across to St Patrick's as usual. Every year we decorate the pews and other allotted portions of the church, and we guard this privilege jealously. On Saturday the ladies of the village come with armfuls of flowers and greenery to do their share, but they always find that the Fairacre children have done their part first.

Usually we tie little bunches of corn to the pew heads, and arrange marrows, shiny apples, onions, giant potatoes, and any other contributions which will not wither or fade, along the ledges and window sills which we know by ancient custom are 'ours'.

It was a bright windy afternoon as we made our way across to the church. Somewhere in the village an energetic gardener was having an autumn bonfire, and great billows of blue smoke hung gauzy veils between us and the distant downs. The smell of the burning leaves had that whiff of sadness which an autumn bonfire always brings; a reminder that summer is over and that soon we shall be head-bent against the gales of winter. I thought briefly of that Devon school, but this time with no regrets. This, I thought, looking at my straggling flock bearing their harvest tributes, is the place for me!

On the south side of St Patrick's the creeper was glowing scarlet and bronze against the grey flints. On the graves chrysanthemums and Michaelmas daisies made a brave show, and over the lych-gate, where Mr Willet began his story of Sally Gray last winter, a many-berried bryony trailed its bright loops and coils. In the vicarage garden, adjoining the churchyard, I could see dahlias, pink and yellow, as big as soup plates; and on the telephone wire, which stretched from the lane to the chimney stack of the vicar's study, a row of swallows chattered together – no doubt of the journey so soon to be undertaken.

St Patrick's was very peaceful after the wind outside, and very soon the children had decked the pews, the steps of the font, and the allotted window-sills. They wandered about admiring their efforts.

'I reckons it looks real good,' said John, squatting down at the foot of the font. 'Tidy and careful!' He gazed with appraisal at the neatly spaced apples before him.

''Twould look better with a marrer in the middle,' said Ernest, surveying it.

'A marrer!' echoed John, shocked. 'Much too big! Them apples is *exactly* the same size, and four inches apart!' He whipped from his sock a yellow school ruler to prove his point. His expression was scandalized.

'A marrer!' he repeated, with infinite disgust. 'That'd properly put the kibosh on it!' He gave Ernest a withering glance, replaced the ruler in his sock, and moved away in high dudgeon, every inch an outraged artist.

We returned to the school, wind-blown and much refreshed. Mrs Pringle had already arrived to clear up the mess. To give her a surprise we had already swept the floor clean of bits of straw and other debris from our harvest preparations. If we expected praise from our curmudgeonly cleaner we were to be disappointed.

'Hm! And so I should think!' was Mrs Pringle's comment, when an innocent infant drew her attention to the unusually clean floor. 'Pity it ain't done every day!'

She limped heavily across the room towards the infants' class room, and did not hear Ernest's regrettable, but justified, remark to his neighbour.

I did. But I don't mind confessing that I turned a deaf ear.

On Saturday afternoon I made my way across the churchyard again. This time I was carrying an armful of foliage for the ladies of the village to use in their part of the church decorations.

Luckily, I am not required to assist on this occasion. It is considered that I have done my share with the schoolchildren the day before, so that my visit is usually brief.

Mrs Partridge, the vicar's wife, and Mrs Mawne were standing back surveying two large stone vases which flanked the altar. Doubt was writ large upon both faces.

'It isn't so much the *form*, dear, as the *colour*,' said Mrs Partridge earnestly. 'That mass of peony leaves near the base looks far too dominant, to my mind.'

'Rubbish!' retorted Mrs Mawne, who had obviously put the peony leaves there. 'It's just a good splash of colour, repeated, if you notice, in the left hand top of the set. Personally, I feel it is perfect for *form*. I just rather wondered if that spray of yellow golden rod which you've just added, isn't the tiniest bit jarring.'

Mrs Partridge looked hurt. She is one of the keenest members of the Caxley Floral Society, and has won several diplomas for flower arrangements of a somewhat sparse and austere nature. A few spiky leaves, and one or two tulip heads, balanced in five stones from the vicarage rockery, were much admired last year by those who know about such things.

'Such economy of line!' breathed the judge, making a little box of his fingers and peering at the arrangement through the gap. And Amy, who was present on that occasion, said that it well deserved first prize for 'inspired asymmetry'.

'She deserves first prize for keeping the thing upright, I said. 'One good cross-draught and the lot'd capsize.'

Amy informed me coldly that I lacked the right approach to flower arrangements, and regretted my mundane outlook on Beauty and Higher Things. I was unrepentant.

Mrs Partridge, on this occasion, rose to the defence of the golden-rod.

'It is freely acknowledged, she told Mrs Mawne, 'by both Eastern and Western authorities on Floral Art, that a touch of yellow, in any arrangement, adds the vital spark of life and sunshine to the whole. It is closely connected with the fact that yellow is one of the primary colours – and the most dominant one at that!'

She advanced militantly upon the stone vase with yet another spray of the offending plant. Mrs Mawne's mouth took on a grim line, and I deposited my armful thankfully on the chancel floor and fled outside.

I get quite enough sparring with Mrs Pringle from Monday to Friday. On Saturdays and Sundays I like a little peace.

Mr Willet was working in the churchyard. He was armed with a bill-hook and was taking vigorous swipes at the long grass which grew beneath the hawthorn hedge dividing the graveyard from the vicarage garden.

He straightened up as I approached, resting one horny hand on the small of his back.

'Not so young as I was,' he said, puffing out his stained walrus moustache. 'Bending double, after three helpings of my wife's treacle pudden, don't seem as easy as it used to.'

The sun was warm. It was a mellow September day, with the elm trees turning a pale gold against a pellucid blue sky. Mr Willet's ruddy face was beaded with sweat. He had rolled up his shirt sleeves, and his muscular hairy arms were smudged with grass stains and blotched with pink where the nettles had stung him. Nevertheless, he appeared unperturbed.

He seated himself on the low flat lid of a tomb, and I sat down beside him. It was comfortable and warm with the sunshine which had been pouring on it since daybreak. Among the moss and lichens which covered the stone was the inscription: 'Jno Jeremy – Gent of this Parifh.' I felt sure that he would have no objection to our presence.

'Fred Hurst's grave's coming on a treat,' said Mr Willet approvingly. He had put the bill-hook on the stone beside him, and his two tired hands drooped between his knees. His eyes, however, were bright as they surveyed his domain.

I followed his gaze. Certainly, a fine strong growth of green grass, neatly clipped, covered poor Fred's resting place. But it was the older grave beside it that caught my eye.

'What's that on Sally Gray's mound?' I asked.

Mr Willet looked a trifle shame-faced.

'Well, to tell you the truth, it's a little rose-bush – one I took as a cutting from ourn in the garden. Seemed a pity for it to go to waste, and the poor old dear hasn't got nothing growing along her. I put it in soon after I told you the tale about her. Remember?'

I nodded. The tale of Fairacre's flying woman had certainly intrigued me.

'Funny how we all likes a story,' ruminated Mr Willet, watching a red admiral butterfly settle on some Michaelmas daisies. 'Don't matter if you really believes it or not – as far as I can see. I mean, half of you believes, let's say, but the other half doubts, and in the end it's the half that wants to believe in the story that wins.'

'What's put this in your mind?' I asked lazily. A pigeon cooed from a tree nearby, and the air was so soft that I found the two together peculiarly soporific. If Mr Willet's sturdy bulk had not been beside me, I should like to have stretched out flat upon Jno Jeremy's warm stone, and had a gentle doze.

'That business of Joe Coggs,' answered Mr Willet. 'I bet he really knew that little chap under the pier was a midget. Yet you see, he sticks to it it was the Lord of the Seas, or some such.'

'It's difficult to know,' I murmured.

When you're that age,' continued Mr Willet, 'these 'ere fairytale ideas get hold of you real strong. Witches and that.'

He stopped suddenly and there was a pause. I felt myself slipping from reality to the world of sleep. The pigeon's cooing sounded fainter and fainter.

'We 'ad one in Fairacre,' said Mr Willet's voice, startlingly close at hand.

'A pigeon?' I asked, struggling to sit upright.

'Tch! Tch!' tutted Mr Willet. 'A pigeon! Who was talking about pigeons? What I said was – we 'ad a witch once in Fairacre. At least they said she was.'

'And when was this?' I asked, now fully awake.

'When I was a nipper. Same age as young Joe, come to think of it. Proves what I was saying. You want to believe anything out of the ordinary when you're a kid. Take me, for instance.'

'Did you believe she was?' I queried, scenting a story.

'Me? I was positive. And I went out to prove it, what's more.'

He took out a short-stemmed pipe from his trouser pocket, and a small tin of tobacco.

'May as well 'ave one as I tell you the tale,' said Mr Willet, with a mischievous sidelong glance. 'You ain't busy, I suppose?'

'Never too busy for a story,' I assured him, watching him fill his pipe.

Within two minutes, with the fragrant blue smoke wreathing his head, Mr Willet began.

Mr Willet was about seven at the time, he told me. He and his brothers and sisters lived in a cottage on the way to Springbourne, and walked daily to school at Fairacre.

There were four children of school age, and a baby of two at home. The four Willet children carried a rush basket with them, containing a substantial midday meal. A large proportion of it was bread and butter, but a finger of cheese apiece, a hard-boiled egg, or a slice or two of cold fat bacon, added relish and nourishment and old Mrs Willet made sure that fruit in season and a mammoth bottle of buttermilk accompanied her little family daily.

The schoolmaster at that time was Mr Hope. He was a clever, rather sad fellow, who wrote poetry, and occasionally read it, too, to his pupils. They were not, it seemed, particularly appreciative, and, in fact, looked upon their headmaster as 'a bit loopy'. Tragedy touched the Hope family when their only daughter, much the same age as young Willet, died at the age of twelve. After that Mr Hope found consolation in drink, and before long was asked to leave the district.

But while young Willet was in his class, Mr Hope taught well. He read many stories to them, chiefly the classic tales of adventure, the myths of Greece and Rome, some stirring passages from Scott or Henty, and so on. But now and again, conscious that the younger members of his class were finding difficulty in following some of the excerpts chosen, he took down the fairy books of Andrew Lang and read them a tale of enchantment and fantasy.

It was thus that young Willet – Bob to his family – became acquainted with the supernatural. He had heard of ogres and giants, of wizards and witches, before, but now they became much more real to him. He entered, it seemed, into a knowledge of their ways, became conscious of their powers and of the infringement of such powers upon an ordinary mortal's life. He began to look at grown-ups with a slightly suspicious eye. Could it be that among them was a wizard? Or a witch? Circumstances combined to persuade him that there was such a one – and very near at hand.

About a quarter of a mile from the Willets' cottage, the road to Springbourne dropped suddenly downhill into a hollow. The ground here was marshy, and trees and flowers, foreign to the surrounding downland, made it seem a strange and slightly eerie place. Here, at the foot of the hill, was a small ramshackle cottage known as 'Lucy's'.

Lucy had lived there for many years. At the time of the story she was a bent old woman in her eighties, a fearsome sight with sparse grey locks and one formidable eye-tooth which had grown so long that Lucy had difficulty in accommodating it comfortably in her mouth. It protruded over her lower lip and gave the poor old crone a most sinister appearance.

Fairacre was not at all sure about Lucy, and never had been. She and her husband, Seamus Kelly, had been brought from Ireland by Sir Francis Hurley who lived at Springbourne Manor. The Kellys had been brought to his notice one day when he was visiting friends in Ireland. He had mentioned that he was in need of a coachman with a real understanding of horses, and Seamus Kelly was warmly recommended.

The couple were duly installed in rooms above the coach house at Springbourne and gave great satisfaction until one sad day when Seamus was involved in an accident. He had taken the carriage and pair to Caxley Station to meet Sir Francis who was returning from London, when one of the magnificent bays took fright as the train drew in, and bolted. Seamus was thrown, the wheels passed over his back, and his spine was permanently damaged.

Everyone agreed that Sir Francis behaved with the utmost generosity. All medical care was lavished upon the unfortunate man and he spent many months in a convalescent home by the sea, at his employer's expense. Finally, he was given a pension and the small cottage in the hollow for the rest of his days.

Lucy, who had been a somewhat scatter-brained lady's maid, also had to retire from service to look after her crippled husband. Luckily, she was a strong woman, more than able to tend the garden and look after hens and two goats, as well as running the house and acting as nurse.

Seamus's temper, always violent, grew worse as he grew older. Lucy gave as good as she got, her Irish tongue uttering the most blood-curdling oaths, which scandalized the Fairacre worthies whose swearing was limited to a paucity of curses of Anglo-Saxon origin. Lucy, they agreed, was a wild one! To hear the way she went on made you wonder if she was right in the head! I mean, they said, we know she's *Irish*, but even so –.

One winter's day, when the mist from the hollow shrouded the little house, Seamus gave a great cry from his bed. Lucy, milking the goat in the nearby shed, set down her pail and ran in. There, his face tipped towards the smoky ceiling, lay her husband, his blue eyes wide open in death.

After that dreadful day, Lucy had lived alone, with only her pets for company. Three cats had lived inside the cottage, and their numerous progeny had been dealt with by Seamus, keeping the numbers within bounds. Many a Fairacre cat had started life at Lucy's, and very fine specimens they were.

Now, with Seamus gone, Lucy did nothing about the kittens, and the number grew to a score in no time. It was true that she still gave one away, now and again, to anyone in need of a cat, and gratefully received the basket of plums or bowl of chitterlings which might be given in return, but the fact remained that there were far too many cats in the house.

Lucy did not seem to worry. She did not seem to worry about anything after Seamus's death. It was as though, with her sparring partner gone, she lacked the will to live. She neglected the house and her person, and Fairacre tongues wagged even more feverishly about Lucy's feckless ways.

'A dirty ol' saucepan on the kitchen table, as large as life, and her

eating out of it with a wooden spoon! It's the truth, my dear! I saw
it with my own eyes!'

'And it's my belief she hasn't had a good wash since her poor
husband went. She don't waste much on soap, I'll be bound!'

'As for that black skirt she wears, it's time it was burnt. She
bought it up the Jumble a good eight years ago, that I do know,
and she's had it on, day in and day out, ever since!'

So spoke the good wives of the village, and among them was
young Mrs Willet. As Lucy's closest neighbour she particularly felt
the shame of such a slut in the neighbourhood. Newly married,
with a cottage as spruce as endless scrubbing and polishing could
make it, Mrs Willet was already spoken of as a paragon of cleanliness. She was to be honoured as such all her days.

Time passed. Lucy continued to exist on the pension granted by
Sir Francis, and now administered by his heir Sir Edmund. Only
the minimum repairs were done to the cottage to keep it weather-
proof. Lucy neglected the property to such an extent that it was
hopeless to do more.

She was seen very little in the village. She now began to mutter
to herself and her animals, emerging when dusk began to fall and
when she would not be bothered by the sight of any neighbours or
casual passers. It was at this stage of Lucy's decline that young Bob
Willet became convinced that she was, without any doubt, a witch

He had said as much to his older brother Sidney as they walked
home from school one summer's day. Mr Hope had read them a
Russian folk tale with a description of Baba Yaga, the witch, which
seemed to young Bob a faithful portrait of Lucy Kelly who lived so
perilously near them.

Perhaps he half-hoped for a decisive denial from his brother. If
so, he was disappointed.

'Might be,' was Sidney's perfunctory comment. At that moment he
was engaged in swishing the heads from a bed of stinging nettles, and
was clearly too engrossed to give the matter of Lucy Kelly much
attention. Bob did not press the point, but it seemed to him that Sid
too considered it a possibility. It was alarming, to say the least of it.

In the days and nights that followed, Bob listened with growing
terror to any conversation about their elderly neighbour. He did
not like to speak of his fears to Sid, but he did mention it, as casually
as he could manage, to another boy of his own age.

Ted Pickett, Bob was relieved to find, took his remarks quite seriously.

'She might be,' said Ted slowly. 'You see you can't tell, unless you know she flies on a broomstick.'

'Well, she don't do that,' said Bob flatly.

'Or has a black cat.'

'She's plenty of they,' said Bob, feeling a little shaky.

They sat in silence for a little while. Then Ted began again.

'The way to find out is to go down her place when the moon's full. That's when witches fly. I know that for a fact, Bob. I read it in a school book.'

'What time?' asked Bob practically.

'Any time it's real bright,' replied Ted, 'on the night it's true full moon.'

'Come with me?' asked Bob.

'Not likely!' answered his friend. 'I'm real frightened of anything like that,' he added with disarming honesty. A playfellow rushed up at this point, carrying the limp body of a long-dead grass snake. In the pleasurable few minutes following, Ted forgot the witch for ever.

Not so Bob. He could think of nothing else. He was frightened of the idea, but none the less fascinated. In school, when his mind should have been on the intricacies of punctuation or the problems of fractions, it roved instead to Lucy Kelly's cottage. What spells could she weave? Could she really fly? How could he find out if she really were a witch or not? Was Ted's test the true one?

As the month wore on towards the night of the full moon, the boy's tension mounted. He had made up his mind that he would go alone, if the night were fine and bright, to see for himself just what went on at Lucy Kelly's cottage.

Full moon, according to the almanac pinned on the kitchen wall, was on September 17th. The day was cloudless and still. From the hot schoolroom young Bob could hear the harvesters working away under ideal conditions. Already many of the corn fields bore rows of stooks, the sheaves sagging together with the weight of a fine harvest.

The boy half-hoped that the weather would change, and that nightfall would bring such rain or tempest as would mean a postponement of his plans. But the weather held. At half past eight, he mounted the creaking stairs to the bedroom under the thatch, which he shared with his brother Sidney. Outside, the world was still bathed in golden light, and the swallows and swifts dived joyously through the air, snatching the flying insects that hung in the sunshine.

Bob had intended to stay awake until all the household was abed, but fresh air had made him drowsy and he was asleep before he knew it. Luckily, he was roused by the sound of his father and mother going to bed. It was nearly dark, but a great golden moon, low on the horizon, gave promise of a bright moonlit night.

Bob's heart thumped at the thought of the adventure ahead. He was not quite sure what he was going to look for. Certainly a broomstick, and perhaps evidence of actual flight by old Lucy. If she did fly, as Ted Pickett had said, then this was just the sort of night for her jaunting.

He listened to the sounds of the household. Sidney lay on his back, as always, snoring slightly. Bob knew that he had nothing to fear there. Once Sid was asleep, nothing – short of screaming in his ear – would wake him. The two girls, in the tiny slip room at the back of the cottage, slept as heavily as his brother. Only the youngest child roused occasionally. He slept in his parents' room, and if he should wake up, it was reasonable to suppose that his parents would calm him without having to leave the bedroom. Bob reckoned that he could leave the house and return without much trouble.

He heard the clock at St Patrick's, across the fields, strike eleven, and waited a little longer. Midnight was supposed to be the time that witches chose for their flying operations, as Bob well knew. Then he slipped from his warm bed, dressed with shaking fingers, and crept fearfully downstairs.

The creaks and groans from the ancient staircase brought his heart into his mouth, but no one stirred. He made his way through the kitchen and let himself out by the back door.

The night was mysteriously beautiful. It was scented with corn, warm earth and garden flowers. The moonlight was so bright that young Bob could have read by it, had he been of such a mind.

He slipped through a gap in the back hedge, out of sight of his parents' bedroom window, and gained the lane. It was white in the moonlight, and dropped away to the hollow which was his destination.

His boots seemed to make a dreadful amount of noise on the gritty road. A cat shot across his path – one of Lucy's, he guessed – and frightened the wits out of him. By the time he reached Lucy's, he was bathed in sweat.

There was no gate. Bob crept on tip-toe up the overgrown path with one wary eye upon the upstairs window. It was tightly shut, as indeed were all the others downstairs, Bob noticed. It was as quiet as the grave, and in the light of the moon, the little grey cottage seemed to merge into the crepuscular background of the silvery willows and rank dead grass surrounding it.

At the side of the house was a lean-to shed made of wood, which had once been tarred, but was now weathered to a ghostly grey. If Lucy really had a mount then this would be its stable, Bob decided. He crept quietly towards it, intending to enter, but froze in his tracks long before he gained the lean-to. For there, propped outside the door, as large as life, was a stout broom, or besom, made of birch twigs.

Bob was almost sick with fright. Was it waiting there for Lucy to ride shortly? Or was it simply an innocent garden besom, such as his mother used to sweep their garden path? Who could tell?

He decided to creep right round the cottage, listening for any movement of Lucy's within. He passed by the broomstick, almost expecting to see it pulsing with hidden life, and was relieved to gain the shelter of the side wall. Here was crouched a tabby cat, sitting sphinx-like and motionless – only the glittering of its moonstone eyes showing that it was alert and wakeful.

The boy padded along the back of the house where the shabby thatch was so low that it pricked him through his jersey as he grazed by the edge. Stinging nettles and docks made a rank and painful jungle here, and he was glad to reach the side of the house where the hens had pecked a bare patch. A little window looked out on this side and Bob peered within.

As far as he could see, it was Lucy's primitive larder. A dish or two stood on the shelves, and some onions were hanging from a hook. There seemed to be little more, except for cobwebs.

The front of the house was in full moonlight. Two small windows, cracked and grimy, glinted in the moon's brilliance. Through one Bob could see little, for a tattered curtain obscured his view, but he heard the sound of a cat jumping to the floor, as though he had been observed, and the cat was making for cover.

All around him was silence. His heart had ceased to thump so dreadfully, but he still sweated with fright and the nape of his neck felt tight with terror. As he edged along to look into the remaining window, the clock of St Patrick's struck twelve, and the boy froze with renewed horror. Now was the witch's hour!

As the last clear note died away into the warm stillness, Bob looked into Lucy's living room. Moonlight lit the dishevelled apartment, and at first sight it appeared empty. Then suddenly, in the shadow beneath the window, Bob saw a dark figure roll from a low couch or mattress hard against the wall. He shrank back, out of sight, his mouth dry with fear.

Lucy was clad in her daytime black, her grey hair looked wilder than ever in the light of the moon. Her crazy eyes and one long tooth glinted from the shadows as she stumbled, muttering, about the room.

She snatched a black shawl from the tumbled bed and flung it round her shoulders. From a peg on the door she clawed an old black trilby hat of the long-dead Seamus's, and clapped it on her eldritch locks. Then, with purposeful haste, she emerged from her door and made her way towards the lean-to.

But before she reached the broomstick, Bob Willet had fled.

'So you never found out,' I commented, as Mr Willet finished.

'I found out one thing,' said Mr Willet grimly. 'And that was not to go scaring folk at night. My dad heard me coming in and caught me on the stairs. I got a cuff on the ear as made me see stars as well as moon that night, I can tell 'ee.'

He paused for a moment, contemplating that distant night encounter.

'Looking back now, I'd lay a wager the poor ol' gal was making for her privy in the lean-to, but that warn't in my mind at the time, as you can guess.'

He rose stiffly from the gravestone and picked up the billhook.

'Well, best get back to work, I s'pose. But it makes you think, don't it? You see, I reckons I was as keen to believe in my witch, as little ol' Joe is to believe in his King of the Sea. It's a sort of *hunger*, if you takes my meaning.'

'More things in heaven and earth, Horatio",' I quoted. Mr Willet looked a little startled.

'I wouldn't know about Horatio,' said Mr Willet reasonably. 'I'm only telling you my opinion.' And he resumed his onslaught on the long grass.

The next day Amy came to tea. She was elegant in a new brown and white dog-tooth check suit which I much admired.

'You could have bought it for yourself,' said Amy. 'It's been in the window of Bakers in Caxley High Street for over a week.'

'I haven't been to Caxley for three weeks,' I said. 'Nor anywhere else, come to think of it.'

Amy pursed her lips impatiently.

'Are you ever going to get yourself out of this rut?' she demanded. 'You were excessively naughty about that Devon job, and all because you didn't want poor little Lucy Colgate to come here.'

'Poor little Lucy Colgate,' I pointed out with some warmth, 'weighs over eleven stone, and is the last person on this earth needing anyone's pity – great, smug, insensitive lump of self-congratulation that she is!'

'Now, now!' warned Amy. 'You see what I mean? You are getting positively *warped* living alone here – a mass of neuroses – coveting my suit, and now picking poor Lucy to bits.'

'Let's have some tea,' I said. 'It might sweeten me.'

She followed me into the kitchen, and watched me stack a tray.

'My cousin tells me,' she said, 'that there is an excellent post going at a comprehensive school in her town. I think she said there are four thousand pupils and two swimming pools.'

'Good luck to them!' I said. 'But I prefer thirty-six pupils and two buckets of drinking water. And who knows? I may live long enough in Fairacre to see water laid on to the school! No, Amy, "I won't be druv!"'

Later, we walked across to our Harvest Festival. It was a perfect evening of mellow September sunshine. Through the west window the golden sun lit the nave and burnished the sheaves of corn and all our offerings of fruit and flower.

Mrs Pratt was bumbling happily at the organ, improvising a voluntary until such time as the vicar and choir entered. As this was an important festal day in Fairacre, and the church was suitably

crammed, there would be a procession from the west door down
the nave.

Suddenly there was a scuffling noise behind us, the west doors
were thrown open, and the sunlight streamed in. Bathed in its
golden light the choir and the vicar slowly made their way eastward
while we scrambled to our feet.

> Come, ye thankful people, come!
> Raise the song of harvest home!

we sang fortissimo.

Mrs Pringle, foremost among the contraltos, swayed past me
lowing powerfully. Mr Willet was not far behind, holding his own
among the basses. Ahead, several of my pupils, unnaturally clean
and holy, raised their voices in song.

It was good, I thought suddenly, to be taking part in something
which had happened in this church for many years, without fail, an
act of thanksgiving for the harvest which surrounded this ancient
building on every side. Just so did Sally Gray, Fred Hurst, poor Job
the Fairacre ghost, Mrs Next-Door and a host of others who now
lay so quietly outside these walls, rejoice together, as we did, for
mercies received. I looked about me. Amy, friend of many years,
stood by my side. In front of me I could see Elsie Blundell and her
husband. Two pews ahead were Mr Annett, from Beech Green,
and his wife Isobel with Malcolm, my god-child, and dear Miss
Clare. My eye roamed to the chancel where the choir was now in
place and still singing lustily. Mr Willet's honest face was red with
his exertions, and I remembered, with affection, the story of his
midnight adventure.

How right he was, I thought! We do all need a story, as he said.
There is a hunger in us which needs to be assuaged. With what
avidity I have listened to my neighbours' accounts of tales of long
ago, and with what unfailing curiosity I observe the happenings of
today!

Here, around me, are all the folk of Fairacre, both the quick and
the dead. The story of the village goes back a long, long time; and
it still goes on. Every hour that we live the story unfolds, now
tragic, now comical, but always and everlastingly absorbing.

Can you wonder that we are never dull in Fairacre?

THE FAIRACRE FESTIVAL

For Anne,
with love from her godmother

On the first night of October a mighty wind arose and smote the countryside around Fairacre. The violence of that wild night took almost all by surprise. Only the exceptionally weatherwise, such as Mr Willet, had any inkling of the devastation which lay in store, and even they admitted, as they surveyed the wreckage the next morning, that it was 'a durn sight worse'n they'd thought it would be'.

We had enjoyed a week of mellow sunshine at the end of September. Butterflies clung decoratively to the Michaelmas daisies, wasps lurched drunkenly from ripe pears to ripe plums, and the schoolchildren at Fairacre School were more comfortable in their cotton frocks and thin shirts than they had been on many other occasions during a changeable summer.

Harvest Festival was celebrated on the last day of September and, as usual, we helped to deck the ancient church of St Patrick's with 'all things bright and beautiful'. Coral-berried bryony from the school hedge wreathed the font. At the foot lay mounds of apples, pears and marrows. Carrots, parsnips and onions lined the ledges, and two fine sheaves of corn gleamed and rustled in their time-honoured place, one on each side of the chancel steps. The ladies of the parish had put their natural talents, and the expertise learnt at the local floral society, into the handsome flower arrangements, and it was generally maintained by the congregation that the church had never looked so magnificent.

Monday morning dawned as benignly as ever. I watched the children, summer-clad and relaxed, as they drank their morning milk, and congratulated myself on postponing the lighting of the two tortoise stoves. Far too often, in the autumn term, I have asked my curmudgeonly school cleaner, Mrs Pringle, to light these monsters, only to experience a spell of humid weather in which we have all sweltered in the classrooms. Mrs Pringle never lets me forget these unfortunate errors.

'Remember last year?' she demands belligerently, massive jaw out-thrust. 'You would have it. Said the children was cold, and up I come with paper, with sticks, with matches, although my leg was not what it should be—'

'But it *was* cold,' I begin, but am swept aside.

'I fetches the coal, fetches the coke, goes down on me hands and knees for a full quarter of an hour to get the stoves to draw – and what happens?'

I don't bother to answer. This, I know from experience, is a rhetorical question. Sometimes I think what a wonderful actress the stage has lost in Mrs Pringle. Her looks are definitely a drawback, but she has a fine sense of drama and puts plenty of punch into her lines.

'We gets a hot spell. All my work's for nothing, and the coke's got to come out of us ratepayers' pockets. What's more, the children's pores are left hanging open for all the germs to get in as soon as they goes out into the cold playground!'

This year, I told myself, on that fair Monday morning, I had behaved in an exemplary manner. Tomorrow would be October the second, and after that the lighting of the stoves must surely be considered acceptable by my task mistress.

But, by midday, I was beginning to have doubts. The sun went in, the temperature dropped sharply, and the children began to rub their goose-pimpled arms. By the time they ran home in the afternoon, a cold wind had sprung up, snatching the yellow leaves from the plum tree in my garden and sending me scuttling to light my sitting-room fire.

As darkness fell, the force of the wind increased. It roared in the elm trees towering above the school. It screamed round the school house, spattering leaves against the window and sending the dustbin lid clanging across the garden. The little house shuddered at its onslaught. Safe by the leaping fire, with a pile of exercise books to mark and the cat asleep by my feet, I gave the elements scant attention.

But later, in bed, I became anxious. Never before had I heard the wind quite so violent in Fairacre. I remembered the doleful tales about elm trees which Mr Willet never tired of telling me. If one of those hefty branches fell across my roof it could be pretty damaging. And what about the roof tiles? It seemed incredible that anything could withstand the fury of the wind tonight. Strange creaks and groans seemed to come from the loft above me and an ill-fitting window let in a piercing draught accompanied by an ear-splitting whistle.

I pulled the bedclothes up round my ears, thanked heaven that I was a schoolteacher and not a sailor, and slept amidst the uproar.

Throughout the night the wind wreaked destruction. In the streets of Caxley it wrenched slates from roofs and toppled a dozen chimney-pots into the gutters. A flying tile broke the plate-glass window of Howard's restaurant in the market square, and a poor unfortunate man, cycling head down against the onslaught on his way to night shift, was blown from the towpath into the cold waters of the Cax, and there drowned.

Just outside Caxley station a telegraph pole fell across the line throwing all into confusion, and on the road to Beech Green a tree had crashed, tearing down the telephone wires in its fall. But Caxley, tucked in its hollow, came off comparatively lightly. It was the windswept villages on the downs which bore the full brunt of the wind's savagery and it was Fairacre which suffered the most shattering blow.

On a little knoll of high ground between the vicarage and St Patrick's a cluster of ancient elms stands, cradling a rookery in the topmost boughs. We, in Fairacre, admire the way that these lovely old trees form a background to the church. Rosy-purple in spring as the buds swell, providing dense shade in full summer, turning to clear gold in the autumn and spreading a black lacy tracery against the winter skies, they are a constant pleasure to the eye.

But Mr Willet has never been one of their admirers.

'One of these days,' he has said, on many occasions, 'them dratted elms is going to cause trouble. Got no proper root growth, has elms. All spread out too near the surface for my liking. A good wind up top and over they goes.' And he was to be proved right.

About two o'clock the fury of the wind was at its height. Its screaming woke me. The loose window shuddered and thudded, and the roaring outside was terrifying. It must have been this particular gust which caught the tallest of the elms nearest the church and sent it toppling. The topmost branches swept St Patrick's stubby spire, and bent the proud weathercock until it drooped head-down from its twisted stay. The heavy branches came to rest across the nave, scattering tiles and damaging the roof for which the church is famed. The massive trunk lay athwart the graveyard and the old roots, torn from the turf, writhed above a huge gaping hole.

I did not hear the crash; nor do I think anyone else did. The noise was so continuous that it was impossible to pick out any particular incident. But the vicar said later that he awoke at that time and was conscious of some extraordinary commotion at the heart of the storm, and confessed frankly that he had felt frightened.

When light returned, the damage was discovered, and in no time at all a bevy of villagers came to survey the wreckage. Mr Willet was first on the scene, and with commendable magnanimity forebore to say: 'I told you so!' It was he who broke the news to Mr Partridge, the vicar, who was shaving when the bell of the back door rang.

'Bad news, sir,' Mr Willet shouted up to the frothy face which appeared at the bathroom window.

'The greenhouse?' queried the vicar, holding the window against the wind.

'No, sir. The church. Tree across it, sir.'

'Oh, my dear Willet!' cried the vicar, his face puckering in distress. 'What a terrible thing! I will be with you directly.'

The window slammed, and within five minutes the vicar and his wife joined Mr Willet at the scene of the disaster. Several workmen, on their way to their labours, had propped their bicycles against the flint churchyard wall, and stood shaking their heads at the confusion.

'We must get help from Caxley,' said Mrs Partridge decisively. 'There's no one in Fairacre with the equipment to shift that enormous thing.'

'We must indeed, my dear,' agreed the vicar distractedly. There were tears in his blue eyes as he paced from one position to another assessing the appalling damage to his beloved St Patrick's. 'I suppose a crane or some such piece of machinery will be necessary, Willet? I can't bear to think of the wreckage we shall discover when the tree is lifted. I must go inside at once and make sure that everything is safe.'

I'll come inside with you,' said Mr Willet. 'You wants to watch out that none of them timbers is busted.'

They entered the church while more villagers arrived to inspect the night's work. Here was drama in plenty! The schoolchildren were pleasurably excited by it all, and to a certain extent so were their elders, but there was in addition a shocked solemnity in the face of this tragedy, and thin-lipped Mrs Fowler from Tyler's Row put into words the unspoken thoughts of all when she asked of the villagers at large:

'And who's going to pay for this lot, may I ask?'

It was a question which was to perplex Fairacre for many a long month.

Meanwhile, the work of clearing up the mess began. It was impossible to telephone to Caxley as the Post Office men were busy all the morning repairing the line at Beech Green, but Mr Mawne, churchwarden and member of the Parochial Church Council, set off for Caxley at the vicar's behest.

Henry Mawne is a comparative newcomer to Fairacre, a retired schoolmaster and a keen ornithologist. He and his wife take their fair share of responsibilities in village matters and the vicar, in particular, relishes the friendship and support of this quiet man. His competent handling of church accounts is a source of great comfort to the vicar whose grasp of financial details is hopelessly vague. Mrs Partridge confided once to me that her devout and erudite husband is under the impression that ten pennies make a shilling, and that this fundamental misapprehension is at the root of his difficulties. Certainly parochial affairs have been much more businesslike under Henry Mawne's administration.

As Mr Mawne expected, the plant hire firm had most of its equipment spread about the country that morning, but a crane was promised for the afternoon and two men set off at once from Caxley to start cutting away branches and to clear the site for the rescue operation. He returned to find the vicar in conversation with his Bishop at the county town, the telephone lines in that direction having miraculously escaped damage. He had already been in touch with the Rural Dean, he told Henry Mawne, when he replaced the receiver, and the diocesan architect would be along as soon as possible to look at the damage.

'But the best news of all, my dear Henry,' cried the vicar, 'is from Jock Graham, who arrived just after you had gone, to say that he will act as our architect without any payment. Isn't that a magnificent gesture?'

'It is indeed,' agreed Mr Mawne. He did not care for this elderly Scot, recently retired, but realized how much this generous offer would mean to the parish.

'You see,' went on the vicar, 'I gather that all the expenses will have to be found by Fairacre. The diocesan people have just made it clear that there can be no money forthcoming from them. It's a parish responsibility. I suppose we must expect a bill of a hundred pounds or so?'

'I should prefer to wait until the diocesan architect has had his look,' said Mr Mawne cautiously, 'but from what I saw this morning, I should say we'd be lucky to get away with anything less than two thousand.'

'*Two thousand?*' quavered the vicar. Horror and stupefaction showed in his face. 'It's impossible, Henry!'

Henry Mawne rose from his seat and patted the vicar's shoulder kindly.

'Cheer up, Gerald,' he said. 'I'm probably hopelessly wrong, but I don't want you to get a shock later on. I think you'll find the bill is going to be a great deal more than a few hundred pounds, that's all.'

But we can't pay it,' protested the vicar helplessly. 'Fairacre can't possibly raise anything more than a hundred at the outside!'

'I'm aware of that,' said his friend.

'And even that amount,' went on the vicar despairingly, 'means a succession of whist drives, fêtes, jumble sales, coffee mornings and all those terrible, terrible affairs. You realize that, Henry?'

'Only too well, Gerald,' replied Henry Mawne, doing his best to suppress a shudder.

The vicar rose from his chair and began to pace distractedly round his desk, his hands clasped behind his back and his brow furrowed. Mr Mawne watched him sympathetically from the doorway. It seemed hard to leave his stricken friend in his present distress, but there was much to be done.

Gerald Partridge stopped suddenly and faced him.

'It is a challenge, Henry! This is something sent by Providence to test us, to strengthen our faith. We must, and shall, restore St Patrick's!'

'That's the way to take it,' agreed Mr Mawne, touched by this brave display of resolution. Closing the study door gently behind him, he returned home through the wind.

When school dinner was over, I made my way to the church to see the extent of the damage. The men were busy clearing the worst of the mess from the churchyard, and I went inside by the west door.

Several people had volunteered to tidy up. Mr and Mrs Willet were there, the two sisters, Margaret and Mary Waters, and various other women.

'Got my washing on the line and come straight up,' said one.

'Had to find my poor hens first,' said another. 'The hen house blew clean off their backs, and they was everywhere from the fir tree to the coal-hole.'

Tales of the night's wrecking flew back and forth as they plied brooms and dustpans.

'The top half of Mr Roberts's hay stack went whirling by our roof.'

'Our Nelly lost three tea towels off the line. And the cat! He *would* go out and it's her belief he's been blown out of the parish.'

Somehow, I suspected, listening to these exchanges, the damages grew at each recital. We enjoy a bit of excitement in Fairacre, and the drama of this wild night would certainly go down, suitably embellished, in local history.

There was a great deal of plaster on the floor of the nave, and the pews were white with dust. Mr Willet was collecting the rubble in a wheelbarrow in the aisle. A dark patch gaped above, in the beautiful hammer-beam roof, but no daylight showed through. Hopes were running high that the damage was only superficial, but more would be known when the surveyor had inspected it.

The pulpit was badly scratched and one of the chandeliers had bounced from its hook, at the time of impact, and lay shattered on the floor.

'No loss!' remarked Mrs Mawne to me in an aside audible to all. 'Hideous Victoriana! Pity the rest didn't come down too!'

Afternoon school was a somewhat distracted affair. The children are always excitable in windy weather, and this fascinating disaster added to their general fidgetiness. Hoping to channel their feelings into some positive and useful work – as exhorted to do by all good educationists – I set them to write an essay on the night's storm.

'And you can illustrate it too,' I added, hoping for a prolonged period of peace in the classroom.

'With crayons?'

'Yes, with crayons.'

'Won't be much good. 'Twas all dark. Shan't want no colours.

'Then you can simply use your lead pencil,' I retorted loftily. Disgruntled muttering from the malcontent's desk I ignored pointedly.

An unusual quietness fell upon the room, broken only by laboured breathing as the pangs of composition gripped them, and the stutter of crayons depicting rain. I wandered to the window and gazed out. A drift of dead leaves rustled against the foot of the school wall, and a mat of ivy flapped loosely above it, wrenched from its anchorage by the gale.

The vicarage garden seemed bare of leaves, and through the gaps in the denuded shrubbery I could see several of the helpers making their way home. This, I told myself, certainly brings people together – nothing like a common foe to unite a community.

At that moment, young Tom in the front row raised his hand. His parents are fiercely evangelical, and he is uncomfortably well behaved and a trifle smug.

'How do you spell "Wrath-of-God"?' he inquired earnestly.

'How do you intend to use the phrase?' I asked guardedly.

He turned his attention to the paper before him and read slowly.

' "Our chapel was not hit in the night, but the church was. My mum said it was –" ' He paused and looked up hopefully.

I spelt out the desired phrase. My sympathy went out to those working for Christian unity, and I made a mental note to have a lesson on 'loving thy neighbour as thyself', before the end of the week.

It looked as though Fairacre might profit from it.

2

Before Monday came round again, much had happened in the village.

In the first place, Fairacre had put itself to rights as best it could. Broken branches were sawn up into neat logs and stacked inside wood-sheds. Shrubs and standard roses were lashed to new stakes. Slates and tiles were hung again, thatch patched and hen-house roofs replaced and weighted with sizeable flint stones, in case of future gales.

Nelly Potter's cat returned, none the worse for a night out. Mr Roberts, the farmer, retrieved some of his scattered hay, and Mrs Pringle, discovering a child's apron blowing on the hedge, recognized it as one of little Vanessa Emery's and returned it graciously to the child's scatter-brained mother.

'Nearly tore to shreds it was by the time the wind had done with it,' said Mrs Pringle to me, before school one morning, 'but I don't suppose it'll ever see needle and thread in that house. Proper muddler that woman is! Half-past nine when I called in, and she still in her dressing-gown!' Mrs Pringle drew an outraged breath at the very thought, and picked up a cinder which was marring the glossy jet of the stove's surround.

'Still, I will say,' she conceded, as she straightened up with an ominous creaking of whalebone stays, 'that she give me a very nice smile and thanked me for my trouble.'

'Good,' I said absently, rummaging in my drawer for a paperclip.

'*Which*,' boomed Mrs Pringle pointedly, 'is a lot more than some people do!'

And with a pronounced limp she made her way to the lobby.

Mr Willet had cleared up the mess in the school playground, and had continued the good work, in his capacity of church sexton, in the graveyard next door. Luckily, the ancient headstones had escaped injury, for the tree which caused most of the trouble had lodged against the roof of the church, and had been lifted clear by the crane without much difficulty.

The damage to the fabric of the church was Fairacre's most serious problem. Providentially, it was less than had been feared at first. The stout ancient roof beams had stood the blow well, and only three or four would need to be replaced. But much retiling needed to be done to the spire and the nave, and the belfry wanted a stone-mason's attention.

'And can you give us any idea of the expense?' asked the vicar anxiously as he, Mr Mawne and Jock Graham accompanied the diocesan architect and his young assistant on the tour of inspection.

The architect peered over his half-glasses and looked solemn.

'Mr Graham will go into figures of course, but I should say, at a rough estimate –'

'A *very* rough estimate,' chimed in the assistant, speaking as one

who has often been caught out and hoped to miss the unpleasant experience this time.

'As a *very rough* estimate,' agreed the architect, looking coldly at his colleague, 'somewhere in the region –'

'Only *in the region*,' interjected the assistant sternly.

'Of about one thousand eight hundred pounds to two thousand.'

'*About*, of course, *just about*,' echoed his companion. 'One can never be sure what one will find once the work is in hand, as I am sure Mr Graham will agree. One doesn't want to be too hasty in suggesting a figure.'

'So I noticed,' observed Mr Mawne drily.

His face wore a small satisfied smile. This was the sum he had suggested in the first place to his friend, the vicar, and it was some comfort in this bleak hour to know that he was not far out in his estimation.

The vicar's rosy face, however, showed no sign of pleasure, simply stupefaction and distress. He was quite beyond speech.

'We'll go back and report our findings,' said the architect kindly, tucking his half-glasses into a splendid gold-tooled case. 'And, if Mr Graham wishes, I'll send you the names of some reputable contractors who specialize in church repairs who will, of course, give you a detailed estimate when they have had a look at your little bit of trouble here.'

The vicar opened his mouth as though stung into speech, thought better of it, and said nothing. They crossed the churchyard to the black Humber at the gate.

'I shouldn't worry too much, my dear sir,' said the architect with misplaced heartiness. 'Could have been much worse, you know. Think of Coventry Cathedral. Now there *was* some damage!'

The car drove off, watched by Mr Mawne, Mr Graham and their stricken friend. As it rounded the bend to the village street, the vicar found his voice.

'I don't like to seem uncharitable, but I hope that I may never see that man again! "Our little bit of trouble" indeed!'

'Take no heed of his havering,' rumbled Jock Graham.

The vicar's lips quivered suddenly.

'But what are we to do? What are we to do?'

Henry Mawne rose to the occasion.

'We will call an emergency meeting of the Parochial Church Council and put on our thinking caps,' he replied firmly. Together they shepherded Gerald Partridge to the haven of his vicarage, and a much-needed cup of coffee.

The Parochial Church Council, all twelve of us, turned up in full force on Friday evening. We met in the vicarage dining-room which was still faintly redolent of the curried lamb and baked apples on which Mr and Mrs Partridge had recently dined.

There were present the vicar, in the chair, Mr Mawne and his wife, Mr Roberts, the other churchwarden and our local farmer, Mr Graham as honorary architect, Mr Willet and myself, all from the village. Mr Basil Bradley and Major Gunning represented Springbourne, which is also in the living of Fairacre's vicar, along with three rather prosperous younger men, who commute daily to the City, thus making up our full complement.

Basil Bradley produces a novel each year and is much thought of in the district. He is called upon to open bazaars and fêtes, and is much in demand as a speaker at various functions, twice rising to the dizzy heights of chief speaker at local Women's Institute group meetings. Since the death of his formidable mother, who guarded his goings-out and comings-in zealously, he has lived alone in a pretty cottage enjoying his freedom. He is a remarkably handsome man, with the ashen fair hair which slips imperceptibly over the years into silver, and the gentle manners born of many years of willing servitude to his tyrant. Men dislike him. Women dote on him, and do their best to get him married. Somehow, I do not think that they will ever be successful.

Major Gunning is as martial as his name, and has a garden full of well-disciplined plants as upright as himself. His paths are straight. His standard roses line them like a guard of honour. A row of poplars stands sentinel upon his skyline. No daisies spangle Major Gunning's lawns, no groundsel mars the beds. And should any pink or poppy droop its pretty head out of its appointed place, then summary execution must be expected.

It was he who spoke first after the vicar had explained the dilemma.

'Open an Appeal Fund. Stick up a good bold board outside the church, and send notices to every man-jack in the parish.'

'Humph!' snorted Mrs Mawne beside him. 'That won't bring in much!'

'And have you any suggestions?' asked Major Gunning, bristling.

'Plenty,' snapped Mrs Mawne, slapping her gloves down on the table challengingly. 'First of all—'

'Address the chair,' put in Mr Mawne.

His wife twitched round exasperatedly and faced the vicar.

'Mr Chairman, I think determined and regular money-raising efforts should be started at once. A weekly whist drive, a weekly dance, a weekly raffle, a weekly coffee morning—'

'But, my dear Mrs Mawne,' pleaded the vicar, 'where is the money to come from?'

'I'm telling you. From all these activities!'

Basil Bradley took upon himself the thankless task of explanation.

'But where, I think our Chairman means, will *the people* get the money? Their wages will remain at the same level. They can't afford to go to so many weekly functions.'

'Thank you,' said the vicar simply. 'That is the position exactly. We must try to think of attracting outside help. The parish itself has no riches.'

A gloomy silence fell while we all pondered this sad fact.

'D'you mean that there is no help at all from some body or other?' demanded Mr Roberts at length. 'You know — Ecclesiastical

Commissioners or the Diocese, or Friends of Friendless Churches? Something o' that?'

'St Patrick's isn't a *friendless* church,' said the vicar defensively. 'It's a very much-loved church.'

'Yes, indeed. Yes, indeed,' agreed Mr Willet warmly.

'But I'm afraid we have only ourselves to rely on,' went on the vicar. 'The Bishop was deeply sympathetic, but made it quite plain that the parish is solely responsible for these repairs.'

'I think Mrs Mawne's suggestions are on the right lines,' I volunteered. 'If all the village organizations make a particular effort it means that we shall raise quite a decent part of the whole by our own exertions.'

'We could map out a programme,' said Mr Roberts. 'What about a traction engine rally in my big meadow?'

'And a folk-dancing display by the village school?' said Mrs Mawne. I could have made a tart retort, but forbore.

'And a bumper Fur and Feather Whist Drive this autumn?' said Mr Willet.

'I should be very pleased to open my garden next summer,' offered Basil Bradley. 'And provide tea. I've just mastered Chelsea buns.'

'How very clever!' cried Mrs Mawne turning towards him. 'Now they are things which I simply *cannot* manage. Cream horns, almond slices, Victoria sandwiches, gingerbread – I flatter myself I can cope with anything like that, but yeast cookery is my Waterloo. How much sugar do you put in with your yeast?'

The chairman, seeing his meeting dissolve, as is so often the case in village affairs, banged loudly on the table.

'Please, please, ladies and gentlemen! Miss Read and Mrs Mawne have both made the suggestion that we see how much can be raised by superhuman efforts in the village by traditional methods. Can anyone add to this idea?'

A rumbling noise from under Mr Willet's tobacco stained moustache gave warning of wise words to follow. Little did we think, as we waited, that we were witnessing the birth of a momentous brainchild.

'What's wrong with having all these things – or most of 'em, say – in one week next summer? A Festival, like. We hears a lot about the Edinburgh Festival and all their goings-on up there. And there's that chap, Britten, at the Aldwych –'

'Aldeburgh,' put in Basil Bradley.

'Same thing,' said Mr Willet airily. 'He has a Festival by the seaside. Mr Annett's been. He said 'twas a real slap-up affair. Well, what I'm getting at is this. Why can't we have a Fairacre Festival?'

We all gazed at Mr Willet with respect.

'It's a wonderful idea, Willet,' said the vicar. 'Quite wonderful! But do you think people would come?'

'Why not?' demanded Mrs Mawne. 'If they go to Edinburgh, to that perishing cold climate, not to mention the reeking smoke which they admit themselves, then why on earth shouldn't they come here?'

'Perhaps not quite in the same numbers,' said Basil Bradley. 'After all Edinburgh has wonderful concerts and ballets and what-have-you – but I'm sure we could have a Fairacre Festival which would be successful on a more modest scale.'

'Dam' good idea,' announced Mr Roberts. 'One great glorious burst of fête, jumble-sale, concert, whist-drive, bingo, dancing and everything else. If we advertise it well, the money will come rolling in.'

We might have *Son et Lumière*,' said Major Gunning, 'with St Patrick's as the background. Tell the parish story, you know.'

'Not all of it,' said Mr Willet cautiously. 'There's some things best kept quiet. Take that affair of Ted Grimble's grand-dad now –'

'Yes, well–' the vicar broke in hastily. 'Perhaps we are getting away from the point. Could we have a show of hands for Mr Willet's excellent proposal?'

We were all agreed. It was decided to meet again to plan not only the Fairacre Festival for next summer, but also to arrange other money-making efforts, starting immediately.

It was while we were congratulating ourselves, and Mr Willet in particular, on our cleverness, that Henry Mawne spoke up.

'Before we go, I think we should be realistic about these ideas. They will raise a few hundred, I feel sure, and we might raise a few more by donations. But I don't think we can hope to raise even half by these methods.'

'But what else can we do?' pleaded the vicar.

Mr Mawne screwed his propelling pencil slowly, making the lead emerge further and further. He studied it intently as he spoke.

'You said earlier that the parish had no riches. It's not quite true. I hardly like to suggest this but I'm going to. We have, as you all know, locked in the bank and used only at the great church festivals, a valuable old chalice of solid silver and impeccable workmanship. One recently fetched over two thousand pounds. It was not as fine as ours.'

We gazed at Henry Mawne in silence. We were all, I think, a little shocked by his suggestion. To tell the truth, I had not realized the value of the chalice, and had certainly forgotten its existence whilst we had been debating ways and means. The vicar looked horrified and Mrs Mawne surveyed her husband with as much disgust as she would have displayed had he suggested slaughtering her dachshund for lunch.

'Impossible!' she exclaimed.

'Unthinkable!' cried Major Gunning.

'That's not ours to give away,' observed Mr Willet austerely. ''Twas given to the church to celebrate Queen Anne's reign. Some relation of old Miss Parr's, so they told us at school, gave it over two hundred and fifty years ago. It belongs to the parish.'

The vicar found his voice.

'Willet is quite right, Henry. The chalice is beyond price, and is in any case only ours on trust. It belongs to St Patrick's.'

'So did its roof,' said Henry Mawne. 'I know the idea is distasteful, but there you are. Is it right to keep such a valuable object locked away, while rain comes through the roof and the church deteriorates? St Patrick's also belongs to the parish. Which is of more use?'

Surprisingly, it was Basil Bradley who came to Henry Mawne's support.

'It has been done before. My uncle's church in Cumberland sold a most beautiful silver paten some years ago. It went to a new church somewhere in Massachusetts where it is very much prized, I can assure you.'

'I daresay,' replied the vicar, a shade frostily. 'But I cannot entertain the thought of selling our own silver.'

'I'm only suggesting,' said Basil Bradley steadily, 'that it may be some comfort to know that if the appeal and the Festival do not raise the money then at least we have the chalice behind us, as it were.'

'Quite wrong!' said Mrs Mawne forcefully, jamming on her gloves. 'The chalice must remain here for future generations.'

'Absolutely!' growled Major Gunning.

'Let's hope it won't come to that,' said Mr Roberts. 'We'll do our best to get the cash in every other way possible.'

And on that note, the meeting ended.

Later that night, the vicar lay sleepless, watching the moonlight wavering upon the ceiling above his head. Somewhere, far away, a stoat yelped shrilly. The leaves of the Virginia creeper rustled by the open window, and near at hand his big silver watch ticked companionably from the bedside table.

All was as usual in the peaceful room, but still sleep evaded him.

His thoughts turned again and again to Henry's appalling suggestion. How could he have conceived such an idea? It amounted almost to betrayal. The whole idea was monstrous. He simply could not think what Henry meant by putting forward such an outrageous scheme. It was bad enough to have had such thoughts. To put them into words made the matter even worse! The poor vicar tossed restlessly, and remembered the beauty of the ancient chalice with piercing clarity.

How heavy and smooth it was to handle! How comforting was the sturdy stem, the beautiful moulded base! How warm and glowing the red wine looked in its polished depths! To the vicar, and to his flock, Queen Anne's chalice, as it was known, was a precious part of the Christmas and Easter communion service. And had been, the vicar reminded himself, for generation upon generation of Fairacre folk. Lips, dusty-dead two hundred years and more, had sipped the wine from this cup. Squire and servant, man and maid, the virtuous and the villainous had knelt beside each other awaiting pardon and peace from the chalice.

And they would do so still, the vicar told himself resolutely. They would do so still!

He turned over his pillow, thumped it soundly as though he trounced the Devil himself, and was asleep in three minutes.

3

The autumn was wet, windy and unseasonably warm. The children squelched into school from muddy lanes and the puddle-filled playground, incurring the wrath of Mrs Pringle daily.

Scaffolding was beginning to shroud the stumpy spire of St Patrick's and the damaged area of the nave, and the Appeal Fund board made a new feature in the village. So far the hand of the clock on the board stood only at one hundred and twenty-three pounds, but as we all pointed out to each other, it was a wonderful beginning.

The weathervane had been removed and the cock awaited regilding. On the day it was brought down to ground level Mr Willet put his head round the school door.

'If you've got a minute to spare,' he said deferentially, 'you might like a close look at the 'ol weathercock. He's come to roost in the churchyard, afore he gets a new lick of paint.'

The children began clamouring at once, only too glad to leave their English exercises.

'We'll come straightaway,' I told Mr Willet, rising in readiness to quell the stampede to the door. When we had attained some semblance of order we made our way decorously to the churchyard. Near the south door, propped against a convenient flat tombstone, stood St Patrick's weathercock. It was surprisingly large with an expression of great ferocity.

'It's bigger'n our baby,' breathed Joseph Coggs with awe, stroking its cold head with a grimy hand.

'Weighs a fair bit, too,' said one of the workmen. 'Plenty of good metal in him.'

The children surveyed it admiringly and a few of them seated themselves on the damp tombstone beside it.

'Get up! Don't sit there!' I said a trifle sharply, more concerned with internal chills than irreverence, I must confess.

'Old Tom wouldn't mind, miss,' said Mr Willet peaceably. 'A loving sort of man by all accounts, specially to children – or so his stone do say.'

I stood rebuked in the face of such tolerance. A few yellow leaves fluttered down upon the sodden grass, and a wren skittered up and down the hawthorn hedge by the lych gate. Sunshine, so seldom seen in the last few drenching weeks, flooded the scene with amber light.

'We'll go for a walk before going back to school,' I announced, amidst general rejoicing. Thanks were given to Mr Willet and the workmen, affectionate pats to the weathercock, and then we set off to profit from sweet country air and exercise, in the forlorn hope that they would sharpen our wits for the work awaiting us in the schoolroom.

★

As Christmas approached, the money-raising activities increased in the village. The Fur and Feather Whist Drive was well attended, and the usual display of turkeys, ducks, hens, pheasants, and hares adorned the platform in the village hall. Almost thirty pounds was raised by this mammoth effort, and only the collapse of the trestle table bearing the coffee cups marred the success of the evening.

'And it's my belief,' Mrs Pringle told me the next morning, 'that Mrs Emery's ugly great dog pushed the legs along. No business to let an animal into the hall at all. Nothing but a bag of fleas and smelling worse nor Mr Roberts's pigs! As I told her straight.'

Mrs Pringle is a great one for 'telling people straight' and makes much trouble in doing so. Sometimes I feel like quoting to her a prayer learned in childhood which says: 'Let me not mistake blunt-ness for frankness,' but I doubt if such a frail dart would penetrate my school cleaner's rhinoceros' hide. And as she herself is so fond of saying: 'You can't teach an old dog new tricks.' I have learnt to leave well alone whenever possible, for Mrs Pringle makes a formidable foe, and I have to meet her daily.

We spent the latter weeks of the term preparing a school play, in which every child from the smallest five-year-old to Ernest, a hefty eleven-year-old, had a part. Miss Clare, who once taught the infants' class at Fairacre, emerged from her retirement at Beech Green to help to dress the children and to play the accompaniment to their songs. The parents packed the school to overflowing, and apart from such expected crises as a measles suspect, two sore throats, a burst knicker elastic and a hitch in the curtain-pulling equipment, it all went splendidly. Two performances of our masterpiece netted ten pounds for the fund, and we were well content.

'A Gigantic Christmas Bazaar' widely advertised by posters on barns, trees and gateposts, as well as a notice in the *Caxley Chronicle*, was perhaps a trifle larger than the usual Christmas Bazaar which Fairacre organizes, and we all bought knitted tea-cosies and gingham aprons for each other's Christmas presents, and little boxes of home-made fudge which we fully intended to give away too, but ate ourselves as it was quite irresistible and, as we told ourselves, might not keep. The Appeal Fund was larger by twenty-six pounds at the end of the afternoon.

Nevertheless, the hand moved very slowly towards the target of two thousand pounds. After morning service on Christmas Day a little knot of us stood outside the church, in the bleak east wind, exchanging Christmas greetings and discussing the progress of the Appeal. The hand pointed to a little under four hundred pounds, and with the best will in the world it was hard to be very optimistic.

'I suppose it's not too bad for a beginning,' said Miss Margaret Waters to her sister Mary. 'After all, it's only a few weeks since it happened.'

'I'd like to see it nearer the thousand,' said Mr Willet, standing next to her. 'We've had in the best part of the donations, from all accounts. Once we gets into the New Year, somehow it won't seem so urgent. People soon forgets, you know.'

Mrs Pringle, emerging after her stentorian boomings in the choir, heard the last part of Mr Willet's remarks.

'"Forgets" is the word, Mr Willet. Why, in the old days, this money would've been found in next to no time. The gentry – who *was* gentry then, let me say – would have put their hands in their pockets and settled it at once.'

'There ain't the money about,' agreed Mr Willet. 'At least, not to the same extent. It's spread over a few more, that's all, and them as earns it sticks to it. You can't blame the gentry. The tax man gets it off of them, and there's nothing left for things like the church spire.'

We gazed dolefully aloft at the roof, now bristling with scaffolding. No bells had rung a Christmas peal this year, because of the damage in the belfry. St Patrick's wore a forlorn and battered air. Without its golden weathercock the little spire looked unusually truncated.

'Ah well!' said Mr Willet, turning up his coat collar against the wind, 'mustn't lose heart, you know, specially on Christmas Day! Maybe, the New Year will bring us all a bit of luck. And there's always the Festival to look forward to!'

'Yes, indeed,' said Mary Waters, snatching at this comfort. 'There's always the Festival!'

We set off on our several ways determined to be of good cheer, despite the nagging little doubts which pierced our defences as keenly as the bleak east wind about us.

The Christmas holidays slipped away with their usual speed and the spring term began in a flurry of snow. The children, of course.

greeted it with rapture. Mrs Pringle looked upon it as yet another cross to bear. She went about her duties tight-lipped and with the limp which becomes more marked when she feels more than usually 'put upon'.

Luckily, the snow was light, nothing more than a shower here and there, powdering the black branches of the elms and the roofs in the village. But the weather was bitterly cold and even I, a poor weather prophet, knew that we should get more snow before long.

On one freezing evening the Festival Committee met in my sitting-room. Thanks to Mrs Pringle's administrations it presented an unusually tidy appearance. Piles of exercise books, test papers, infant apparatus and the general flotsam and jetsam found in a school-mistress's room had been carted up to the spare bedroom, and although I despaired of ever finding any of it in order again, it was wonderful to entertain my guests in such immaculate splendour.

The Committee was formed by most of the Parochial Church Council and one or two other energetic people who had some organizing ability and bright ideas. I must confess that I had envisaged an evening making a list of the usual entertainments known only too well to Fairacre, and possibly deciding on the days on which to present them. It was exciting therefore to have Basil Bradley's bombshell exploded at the outset.

'This is really Major Gunning's idea,' he began, glancing across at that upright figure. 'You remember that he suggested that we might have *Son et Lumière* with St Patrick's as the background. Well, I've been talking to a friend of mine who has helped to produce this sort of thing, and he's willing to stage it and produce it for us.'

Congratulatory murmurs broke out on all sides.

'And if you would allow me,' went on Basil Bradley, looking modestly at his fingers, 'I should really love to write the story and – er – record it for you.'

'That is indeed most generous,' said the vicar. 'Most generous.'

We all agreed warmly. It was Mrs Mawne who rushed in where angels feared to tread, and said:

'But all that wiring and amplifiers, and setting up seats and things in the churchyard – surely that's going to be horribly expensive?'

'I thought, if the vicar agreed, it would be much more practical to have it inside the church, with the lights changing on the chancel and altar. Then, of course, we should be independent of the weather.'

'And have seats,' cried Mrs Mawne, seeing the light.

'And have seats,' agreed Basil Bradley gravely.

'I can see no objection to having the performances inside,' said the vicar. 'After all, the churches were always used for the early miracle plays, and it seems fitting that the story of our parish should be told in the building which has seen almost all its history. I think it is a splendid idea.'

'The only thing is,' said Basil Bradley, warming to his theme in the midst of such general approval, 'it is hardly worth setting up all the paraphernalia for less than a week. Do you think we can expect enough support?'

'Why not?' asked Mr Mawne. 'We'll advertise it well. People can bring parties from miles away. They're much more likely to come if they know it will be inside the building.'

'Oh, I do agree,' said his wife firmly. 'What with gnats, and the wind, not to mention the odd thunderstorm, outdoor evenings are more of a penance than a pleasure.'

It was at last agreed that the *Son et Lumière* arrangements would be for every evening of the Festival Week, and would, in fact, be the major part of the whole project which would take place in July.

'And do you really think we shall cover our expenses?' persisted Mrs Mawne.

'There will be no expenses,' said Basil Bradley. 'My friend John is giving his services, and the electrician's bills and so on will be my own contribution to the Fund.'

'It is uncommonly generous,' repeated the vicar. 'A really wonderful gesture. I am sure we are most deeply grateful.' And with this we all concurred.

Major Gunning cleared his throat so martially that we all jumped to attention, or as nearly as we could in a sitting posture.

'I've taken the liberty of speaking to a young cousin of mine ... by way of being a singer. You may have heard of her. Jean Cole.'

'Jean Cole!' exclaimed Mrs Mawne, looking at Major Gunning with new respect.

'Jean Cole!' echoed Basil Bradley, turning pink with excitement. 'I'd no idea she was related to you. The most beautiful contralto voice in existence today! She was superb in *Aida* at Covent Garden last year.'

'I have all her records,' said the vicar. 'The Bach arias are my particular favourites.'

Major Gunning bowed his head politely in acknowledgement of the adulation, but his tobacco-stained fingers, drumming on the edge of the table, showed his impatience.

'Yes, well ... top and bottom of it is that she would be willing to give us a tune ...'

Basil Bradley winced.

'To come here? To Fairacre?' breathed Mrs Mawne incredulously.

'As I was saying,' continued Major Gunning with a touch of asperity, 'Jean said that she could come and sing in the church during, or after, the *Son et Lumière* performance, if it would help. Not the Monday, though. She's flying back from Berlin that day, after a tour.'

There were delighted cries from the company. The vicar broached the delicate subject which was in all our minds.

'It is indeed the most generous offer. It would mean a great deal to our efforts. But your cousin is – er – much in demand. We must offer her some – er – recompense for the honour she is doing us. Can we ...?'

'She'll come,' said the major briefly, 'for nothing. I'll see to that.'

If this sounded a trifle ominous, it was soon forgotten in the general delight.

'It's too good to be true,' cried Mrs Mawne. 'The most encouraging news of the evening!'

And with that we all agreed.

The rest of the programme was settled provisionally. The *Son et Lumière* would take place after dark each evening, beginning about nine. The Festival would begin with a splendid service in the church on the Sunday, at which the Bishop had promised to come and bless our endeavours.

'And all denominations in the area will be invited,' said the vicar.

'Bet they don't all come!' whispered Mr Roberts to me in a horribly penetrating whisper.

'They will be invited,' repeated the vicar reprovingly.

Various functions would take place during the week, a mammoth jumble sale, a gargantuan whist drive and so on, organized by various bodies in the village, and the week would culminate with a magnificent fête in the vicarage garden on Saturday afternoon, to be opened by someone who would be 'a real draw', as Mr Willet said, followed by a dance in the evening.

'Shall we have enough going on to warrant a *whole week*?' asked Mr Willet doubtfully.

'The *Son et Lumière* will be the main thread,' explained the vicar, 'and our other festivities will be hung like jewels, as it were, upon this chain.'

'Very nicely put,' commented Mr Mawne, a trifle drily.

'Yes, it turned out rather more poetically than I intended,' replied the vicar, rather surprised and pleased with his flight of fancy. 'I really should make a note of it for a future sermon.'

By this time the hands of the clock stood at ten o'clock. I went into the kitchen to prepare coffee, and the meeting ended with much animation and hope, on the part of the Fairacre Festival Committee, before they set off to face the wintry night.

4

'No, I never!'

'Yes, you did then!'

'I never, I tell you! I never done it!'

'We knows you done it all right, don't us?'

A chorus of self-righteous voices greeted this ungrammatical exchange which floated through the schoolroom window one bright morning. Sometimes I wonder why I trouble to correct the children in the classroom, knowing full well that they will relapse into their mother tongue as soon as they escape from my clutches.

The accused appeared to be Joseph Coggs. I could recognize his hoarse, husky croak easily above the manifold sounds from the playground. He is fairly popular with the other children who do not seem to be bothered by his poor clothes and his gipsy background. What he had done to deserve their united attack I was soon to know.

''Twas there all right yesterday,' said one, belligerently.

'Funny thing you havin' a wooden dagger the same evenin',' shouted another mockingly.

'My cousin from Caxley give it to me,' growled Joseph. 'He got it off of some kid up the street.'

'Likely, ennit?'

'What, same colour an' all?'

The voices grew shriller, and I was in half a mind to leave my marking to investigate when I heard Mr Willet's hearty voice.

'What's going on then?'

A dozen voices clamoured together, and the gist of the story was that the hand of the clock had vanished from the Appeal Fund and Joseph Coggs 'had bin and pinched it'.

'You want to watch your tongues,' announced Mr Willet sternly. 'And stop picking on Joe. I took the hand away, if you must know, to put another coat o' paint on it. Put that in your pipes and smoke it, you young know-alls.'

His heavy footsteps passed on, leaving an uneasy silence.

'See?' cried Joseph triumphantly.

'Well, how was we to know?' muttered one of the crowd. 'Your dagger was the spittin' image of that hand.'

'Always on at us to look out for folks breakin' the law,' grumbled another, 'and what thanks do us get for trying?'

'Come on up the coke-heap,' shouted someone cheerfully. 'The bell'll be going before we've had a game.'

And the drama ended in a wild confusion of yells and scrunching coke, enjoyed by accusers and accused alike.

*

The hand of the clock which had been the cause of this fracas was moving far too slowly towards the target for Fairacre's peace of mind.

The most dramatic leap forward, in these last months, had been caused by an anonymous gift of one hundred pounds. Naturally, rumours as to the identity of this generous benefactor were legion.

'I wouldn't put it past the vicar himself,' said one.

'Or Mr Mawne?' queried another.

'That'll be the day,' said Mrs Pringle sourly, when she heard this suggestion. 'Them Mawnes don't part with money that easy. Best end of neck served up as chops in their house, so my niece Minnie tells me.'

One of the infants thought it might be 'a fairy'. This pretty fancy was soon dispelled by the realists who were slightly older.

'Don't talk soft!' implored her brother Ernest, shamed before his fellows in the playground.

'No such thing as fairies,' added Patrick scornfully. 'And if there was, how d'you think they'd lug a hundred pounds up to the vicar's? They ain't no bigger'n my thumb.'

This irrefutable argument settled the matter, in this instance, but the anonymous donor still remained a fascinating mystery. It was one which was never solved.

Even more exciting than the anonymous gift was that Peter Martin, the pop star and idol of the young, had agreed to open the fête on the Saturday and to sing at the dance in the evening, accompanying himself on the famous guitar. He was going to prove a tremendous draw.

'The weather really won't matter,' said the vicar, beaming. 'People will come from miles around just to see him. A very *personable* young fellow, I believe.'

Mrs Pringle's niece Minnie expressed the general reaction to the news.

'Ain't it just wonderful? We'll be breathing *the very same air*! To think of him coming to this place! All Caxley'll be there. You ever seen him, miss?'

I said that I had not had that pleasure yet.

'Beautiful hair, he's got. Long and that, all thick down to his shoulders. And his clothes costs a fortune, and he don't drink nothin' but champagne!'

She sighed ecstatically. A visitation from the entire heavenly host, I thought somewhat tartly to myself, could not occasion more reverent adoration than this one glamorous star. Nevertheless, I too rejoiced. Think how it would swell the funds!

Work on the roof progressed steadily, and the sound of hammers and saws formed the background to our own school activities. These included now, in the last weeks of the spring term, preparations for the entertainment which was to be our contribution to the Fairacre Festival.

Only teachers, who have dealt with these affairs, can truly assess the heart-burnings and headaches which accompany something which the outsider considers a simple, and even a pleasurable, undertaking.

The only other member of the staff is the infants' teacher. For years Miss Clare, now retired and living at Beech Green, ruled the infants, and most of the adults in the village learned to read, write and calculate under her benevolent eye. Miss Gray followed Miss Clare, but left to marry our neighbouring schoolmaster, Mr Annett, who also acts as choirmaster and organist at Fairacre. Then came Miss Jackson, a stormy young woman straight from college whose departure I viewed with relief.

Since then we have had a succession of 'supply' teachers, some good, some ghastly; but for the last year the infants have been in the charge of Mrs Bonny, a buxom widow, who manages them very well. All goes swimmingly if she is able to work in her own way, and I interfere as little as possible. Unfortunately, any sort of mild suggestion throws the lady into a defensive and resentful mood, as if one were casting a slur on her abilities. Coming to an amicable arrangement about the concert was an operation fraught with hazards, I found.

My first idea of a play in which the whole school could take part fell upon stony ground.

'Why can't the babies sing their nursery rhymes?' demanded Mrs Bonny plaintively. 'I've spent hours teaching them, and their mothers would love to hear them.'

Both facts were true. The daily chorus – one might be forgiven for saying 'caterwauling' – had penetrated the partition between our classrooms with painful clarity. And the mothers of these young choristers would dote on Mrs Bonny's efforts with them. I agreed resignedly.

'But nursery rhymes won't take very long,' I said, trying not to sound too relieved. 'We'd better have some other items.'

Mrs Bonny promised to consider the matter, and within two days the floorboards of the infants' room were reverberating with one of those galumphing folk dances from mid-Europe which involve much clapping and stamping. The clapping and stamping are no doubt performed in unison in the country of the dance's origin, but it certainly was not in Fairacre's infant room. Next door we were sorely tried. It was almost a relief to return to the nursery rhymes, and to listen, wincing, to:

> 'Ickory, dickory dock
> The mou-house run up the clock
> The clock struck ONE
> The mouse run down –

Here there followed a succession of claps as each child took its time to register the need for action, and then, triumphantly they would bellow:

> 'Ickory, dickory, dock.

Mrs Bonny would then praise them loudly, point out the aspirate at the beginning of 'Hickory' and the necessity of singing 'ran' instead of 'run', and the same thing would be repeated *ad nauseam*.

Our own efforts were little better. I had dramatized *The Princess and the Swineherd*, which gave everyone a chance of appearing on the stage, and doubted if the words would ever be learnt. Ernest, the only possible swineherd-cum-prince, became so sheepish about performing a courtly bow that I threatened to demote him to a courtier, although we both knew that there was no one else really capable of taking the part. Sometimes I despaired of ever getting Fairacre School to take part in the Festival, and wondered gloomily if the sale of Queen Anne's chalice might not, after all, be a better way of raising the money.

I did not, of course, voice these treacherous sentiments, but Mr Lamb, our village postmaster, spoke about it when I went to buy the school's savings' stamps one afternoon, some weeks later.

'Of course, it's not plain sailing, this selling the church silver. Has to be a Faculty or something, the vicar tells me. A lot of chit-chat goes on evidently before permission's given. I can't see us being allowed to part with it. And, to tell the truth, I don't think anyone in Fairacre wants to see it go.'

He handed me the stamps and with them three or four photographs in colour.

'Your brother's family?' I asked, looking at them. Mr Lamb's brother George left Fairacre for New York after the war and runs a catering business there. He left before I took over the school but regularly corresponds with our Mr Lamb who shows us the photographs, and tells us all about his brother's successes, when we visit the Post Office. He is very proud indeed of this younger brother, now the father of three husky boys who beamed from the photographs.

'Just a chance he may be over,' said Mr Lamb, taking back the photographs and inserting them carefully into his wallet. 'Some business trip, he says. They're chartering a plane, it seems, and if he can manage it, he'll be over here for a fortnight.'

This was good news. As I sauntered down the village street, enjoying the sunshine, I hoped, for Mr Lamb's sake, that his brother would be able to return to Fairacre. It was my guess that he would not find it much changed even though he had been absent now for over twenty years.

The question of the sale of the chalice was in everyone's mind None worried quite as deeply as the vicar. He woke, on these bright summer mornings, to the chorus of the birds in his garden and then, after the first few moments of pleasure, the familiar little cloud cooled the sunshine of his waking moments and was with him for the rest of the day. He refused to do anything about negotiations for the sale of the precious chalice. He steadfastly hoped and prayed that enough would be raised by the Festival, and that this step, so repugnant to him, might never be necessary.

Mr Mawne did his best to make his friend change his mind, but he remained obdurate.

'I refuse to discuss it,' said the vicar one evening, pink with rare impatience.

'But, my dear Gerald, you simply can't bury your head in the sand like an ostrich. At least find out the facts. Let's see if we can try for permission. Time's running out, you know. The bills are going to be pretty formidable, and can you honestly believe that the Festival will raise enough to pay them?'

'I have no doubt that the Lord will provide,' repeated the vicar stubbornly. His friend raised his eyebrows, looked helplessly at Mrs Partridge, but forbore to reply.

The chalice had last been used at Whitsun, and not one touching the ancient mellow silver and gazing into its gleaming depths failed to feel a pang. Would this be the last time that Fairacre's treasure, with its blessed contents, would be offered to them? The service was a paean of praise. Red and white roses nodded on the altar. Sunshine poured through the windows, gilding the arum lilies at the chancel steps. Country voices had made the glittering brass vibrate with Whitsun hymns and Mr Annett, at the organ, had pulled out all the stops and flooded the church with mighty splendour. The thought of the possible loss of the chalice was the one touch of frost among the bursting glory of Whit Sunday.

As the Festival drew closer our fears for the chalice became sharper. Somehow we simply must make the Fairacre Festival a success, we told each other! We did not say, in so many words, that Queen Anne's chalice was at stake, but the unspoken thought was constantly with us.

It was Mrs Pringle, usually the harbinger of doom, who brought a rare touch of comfort to Mr Partridge, the vicar, at about this time. He had called at the school with the list of hymns which he hoped I would teach the children, when Mrs Pringle clattered in

bearing a battered pail in one hand and a scrubbing brush in the other.

'Bit late leavin', ain't you?' she remarked sourly. 'Clock wrong then? I was going to give the lobby a scrub out but no use doing it till the children have cleared off. Love's labour lost, that'd be!'

The vicar, who is used to this sort of thing, smiled benignly.

'You're going to have a churchful on the Tuesday then. You was lucky to get that Miss Cole to sing,' she continued conversationally, setting down the bucket with a clang. 'My sister's girl, what works at the coach station in Caxley, says there's three coach loads booked already to come over,'

The vicar's smile grew wider.

'What splendid news, Mrs Pringle!'

'And no end of Women's Institutes have rung up about it, and the Mothers' Union and some Young Farmers.'

'A really *wide* audience!' commented the vicar rapturously.

'It takes all sorts to make a world,' conceded Mrs Pringle graciously. 'But it do look hopeful, I must say.'

'It does indeed,' replied the vicar, gazing affectionately upon my school cleaner. 'It does indeed.'

She bent to pick up the bucket and then took up her customary militant stance.

'Well,' she demanded, with a return to her usual truculence, 'do them children go now or not? This 'ere water's getting cold.'

'I'll send them through the other way,' I said meekly. 'We won't hold up your scrubbing any longer.'

This was no time for petty warfare, I felt. Mrs Pringle, messenger of hope, should have her way.

5

The posters were up everywhere in the countryside. They blazed from barn doors, from gateposts, from tree trunks and in the windows of many a village shop. One made a bright blue corner on the Appeals' board. Across the village street, between 'The Beetle and Wedge' and the Emerys' house, a banner fluttered, bearing the words:

FAIRACRE FESTIVAL
JULY 9–15

Bunting was draped across our house fronts, and those of us who owned a flag had it in readiness to hoist on the Sunday which was to be the first day of the Festival. The cross of St George, freshly laundered by Mrs Willet, would soon be flaunting itself above the church spire upon which the regilded weathercock perched again.

Inside the church the electricians were putting the final touches to the wiring and lighting. Jock Graham, the retired architect who had so nobly offered his services, became extremely agitated by the ladders lodged among the timbers of the hammerbeam roof. He was unduly sharp with Mr Mawne who had dropped in one morning to see how things were progressing.

'I'll not be responsible,' he rumbled, rolling his r's in Doric splendour, 'for any damage to that historic roof. A lot of tomfoolery to rig up lights so near the timbers. Those men have no idea of the pricelessness of the work around them.'

'Oh, come now,' protested Mr Mawne. 'They are used to this sort of thing. I believe they were employed at Winchester Cathedral. Or was it Salisbury?'

'It wouldn't be allowed in Scotland,' Mr Graham assured him.

'That I can well imagine,' remarked his companion drily. The hint of sarcasm inflamed Jock Graham still further.

'A decent God-fearing kirk would be ashamed to turn itself into something no better than a theatre. I'd no idea, when I offered my sairvices, that this sort of thing would be countenanced.'

'I see nothing offensive about it,' retorted Mr Mawne. 'It is an act of praise.'

'It's commaircial!' boomed Mr Graham, his sandy eyebrows bristling. 'It wouldn't happen in Scotland, I tell ye!'

'I really can't think,' replied Mr Mawne, with maddening detachment, 'why so many of you Scotsmen bother to come south if you dislike it so much. Personally, I'm all for Scottish nationalism, and I'd rebuild Hadrian's Wall for good measure, once I'd got all you immigrants back on the right side of it.'

'Ye'd no get far without a stiffening of good Scots' blood among ye,' thundered Jock Graham. 'A weakly unprincipled set of shilly-shallyers, lacking pairpose and integrity!'

The workmen, high above, had ceased their labours and were watching this passage of arms with intense interest.

The two men faced each other. Mr Mawne's pale face wore a supercilious smile. Mr Graham's, suffused to an unbecoming shade of purple, was thrust close to his antagonist's. At this dramatic moment, Basil Bradley arrived on the scene.

'I can't tell you how relieved I am that I've already recorded the script,' he croaked huskily. 'My tonsils are absolutely aflame. I can't think why I've succumbed so easily at this time of year. I swear by orange juice for breakfast – nothing more – just fresh orange juice!'

'Ye'd do better on a braw fresh herring and a plate of salted porridge,' thundered Jock Graham. He brushed past the two men and marched, head erect, down the aisle to the west door.

'Whatever's got into him?' asked Basil Bradley, bewildered.

'Scotch blood,' said Mr Mawne cryptically. '"Scotland for ever!" I mean "Scotland for aye!"'

'Oh dear,' croaked Basil Bradley, extracting a small tin from his pocket. 'Ah well, it makes one quite glad to have been born in humble Bayswater, doesn't it? Have a blackcurrant lozenge, Henry.'

Jock Graham was not the only Fairacre resident to be in a state of tension at this time. The vicar, facing the Bishop's visit, was anxious about the service, and also about the safety of the church fabric. What a terrible thing it would be if something should fall upon that stately figure! Despite reassurances, the vicar was not wholly at ease. Mrs Partridge, whose privilege it was to entertain the Bishop to lunch, and possibly to tea, was busy planning a meal which would do honour to their distinguished visitor and yet be simple enough to prepare and serve single-handed. Cold salmon and salad had seemed a good choice until she remembered that the Bishop was extremely short-sighted and far too handsome a man to relish wearing glasses at lunch time. And just suppose that a fish-bone appeared? It would, without fail, be on the guest's plate. Perhaps cold beef? Or leg of lamb left in a slow oven during the service and mint sauce made beforehand?

Mrs Partridge continued to cudgel her brains, and to long for the days when the vicarage had a resident cook and two kitchen maids.

Mr Annett, the choir master, was worrying about the new anthem. The choir of St Patrick's had left him in no doubt that he had bitten off more than they could chew.

'This 'ere modern stuff ain't got no tune to it,' protested Mr Willet. 'What's wrong with a bit of Bach or Handel?'

'It's a very good thing to make a change,' Mr Annett snapped back, secretly conscious that the new anthem was beyond their powers, but too proud to admit it. 'As Browning said:

A man's reach should exceed his grasp.'

'Browning never 'ad to tackle this lot,' pointed out Mr Willet, peering closely at the sheet of music. 'If there's anything I 'ates it's five flats.'

They had struggled on with their unfamiliar burden, but no matter how often they practised, Mr Annett realized that the anthem would turn out to be a hesitant dirge rather than the outpouring of praise which the composer had intended. Too late to do anything now, he told himself, as the great Sunday approached. But the thought gave him little comfort.

Basil Bradley, afflicted with his feverish cold, was suffering agonies of self-consciousness about the script which he had written, and his recording of it. He had checked all his facts most carefully, but there was always the possibility of a mistake. How dreadful if he had made some blunder! There was that episode about the nun being given shelter in the vestry during the eighteenth century. Should he have omitted it, perhaps? There were some very dubious rumours about the incumbent at that date, and the Bishop might take exception to the publicity, guarded though Basil's account had been of the affair. Really, creative work was terribly exhausting, thought poor Basil, as he gargled hopelessly before the final rehearsal.

A spell of unbroken sunshine preceded Festival week and we in Fairacre prayed that it might continue. It grew so hot that the children took many of their lessons outside, in the shade of the elm trees. Rehearsals of the infants' contributions also took place in the playground, which afforded some relief to our class, when it was working inside, and considerable interest to proud mothers who clustered at the gate to watch their offspring bounding around in the folk dance.

The Princess and the Swineherd still had many faults. Ernest had overcome his shyness with such success – terrified of handing over the part to someone else – that he now played the Prince with a swashbuckling impudence which was, to my mind, quite as offensive as his former interpretation of the part. However, I was now resigned to the shortcomings of my production and simply concentrated on getting the cast word-perfect, which was no light matter.

Mr Willet, as sexton, was concerned about the tidiness of the church and the churchyard.

'Slummocky lot, them builders,' he told me. 'Drops their paper bags everywhere. Bread crusts and cheese rinds and old potato crisps scattered all over the churchyard. Them mice are getting as big as foxes.'

'It will look splendid on Sunday,' I assured him. 'Especially if this weather lasts.'

We looked across my garden to the meadows at the base of the downs. A heat haze veiled the distance, but nearer at hand a herd of black and white Friesian cows, the pride of Mr Roberts, stood knee-deep in tall grass. Not one moved. They might have been painted there, against the hot motionless beauty of hills and empty sky, so still they stood.

'Well, let's hope it does,' agreed Mr Willet. 'Don't want it to break yet awhile. It'll end in thunder, or my name's not Willet.'

He turned to look at St Patrick's. The scaffolding had been removed from the spire but still clad the square tower containing the belfry and part of the nave.

'Wish we could have rung in the Bishop with a fine peal,' he said regretfully. 'But there it is. All six o' they bells is up against the church wall waiting to go aloft again as soon as it's safe for 'em. I likes to go and look 'em over now and again. I've got a soft spot for them bells, particularly Old Bess. They say she was cast in the field behind "The Beetle and Wedge", sometime in the 1560s.'

'The children don't want the bells to go back again. They've been over to see them – under my eagle eye, let me say – lots of times, and they've copied the inscriptions.'

' "Sanctus, sanctus, sanctus",' gabbled Mr Willet, swatting a gnat on his freckled forearm. ' "In piam memoriam Caroli Fowler. Requiescat in pace". Fowler, notice? Still a good few Fowlers in Fairacre. Wonder if any of them cast Old Bess?'

He bent to pull up a dandelion from my border, and straightened up with a sigh.

'I do truly hope this Festival puts the old church on its feet. There's a lot at stake, Miss Read. A lot at stake!'

Sunday dawned bright and beautiful. I took my breakfast tray

into the garden among the dewy pinks and roses. A robin perched hopefully on the lilac bush nearby, a beady eye cocked for crumbs.

The Union Jack hung motionless from the school flag pole. High above it, on St Patrick's church the cross of St George waited for a breeze to spread it out in its full red and white magnificence.

It was already blissfully hot although the clock said only nine. By ten to eleven, when I made my way to church, the heat was almost oppressive. We were all in our best summer finery and I felt quite sorry for the Bishop, magnificently accoutred in a splendid gold and white cope which must have been uncomfortably warm.

We sang the most exultant hymns, beginning with 'Praise my soul the King of Heaven' as the choir processed from the west door up to the chancel. Several of my pupils had undergone their weekly metamorphosis from scruffy urchins to well-scrubbed cherubs, and with hair plastered down with a wet brush and their eyes modestly downcast upon the polished boots peeping demurely from beneath their cassocks, they gave an impression of youthful sanctity which did not deceive those of us who knew them during the rest of the week.

The new anthem was tackled with dogged effort and Mr Annett gave noble support not only with his hands and feet at the organ, but with a resonant voice which led his struggling choir valiantly.

When it was over, I noticed Mr Willet mopping his brow and moustache with obvious relief.

The Bishop gave the sermon and spoke of the part the church played in parish life, the disaster which had befallen it, and praised the efforts of our small community to repair the damage.

'God will bless your work,' he promised us. 'This is a Festival in every sense. It is an expression of praise for past mercies and a re-dedication of ourselves to service.'

He made a brave and unforgettable figure in our ancient pulpit, and his words were as inspiring as his presence. When the benediction had been said, and Mr Annett broke into a triumphant voluntary, we all felt that Fairacre was embarked upon a venture which was bound to succeed.

We emerged into the hot sunshine, blinking like owls in the dazzling light. Around us the rose bushes gave out a voluptuous fragrance. Above us an aeroplane left a white trail in the cloudless sky. Bumble bees lumbered from clover-head to clover-head on the grassy mounds of our Fairacre forefathers. It was indeed high summer.

'And real Festival weather!' said Miss Margaret Waters, gazing happily about her, beneath the brim of her old-fashioned straw hat.

'After all this looking forward,' said her sister, 'it's hard to believe that it's actually started.'

It was a thought we all shared as we made our various ways homeward to Sunday dinner.

At last, the Festival had begun!

6

Amy my old college friend, drove over from Bent to the first performance of the *Son et Lumière*.

It was to be a very grand affair. Several local landowners were bringing parties of guests and we humbler folk were busy looking out our best evening attire. It was not easy to find something splendid enough for the occasion, decorous enough for churchgoing and warm enough to counteract the chill of an evening in St Patrick's draughty pews. I had plumped for safety in my plain black frock, and had looked out my one fur piece, a useful stole, for despite the heat of the last few days, which had degenerated into an ominously still stuffiness, the age-long coolness of the church's interior would take some combating.

Amy, *soignée* in a most beautiful frock of blue silk, looked me over critically.

'You really *shouldn't* wear black, my dear, with your skin. It kills any sort of glow you have. Why not wear a deep red dress, or a brown?'

'Because I haven't got one,' I said flatly.

Her eye travelled, without relish, down my full length and lingered sadly at my feet.

'Those heels are definitely out,' she pronounced.

'Not in Fairacre,' I replied with spirit. 'In fact, they've only just *come in*! I paid a great deal of money for these shoes, my girl, and I intend to get plenty of wear out of them.'

Amy shuddered delicately, and fingered her one splendid adornment, a glittering diamond brooch on her shoulder. It was, I knew, a present from James, her husband, and marked his return from a particularly protracted business trip to the Bahamas. There are many such absences from home, about which I have my private suspicions, as no doubt Amy has too, but they certainly result in the most beautiful presents for his wife, and she has enough sense not to cross-question James too closely.

We sat down to my carefully prepared meal of cold chicken and salad. I was secretly rather proud of the salad for I had remembered to cut the radishes into water-lily shapes in the dinner hour and had left them soaking all the afternoon. The tomatoes and cucumber had come from Mr Willet's greenhouse, and the lettuce from my own garden. The hard-boiled eggs, winking goldenly from among the greenery, had come from Mrs Pringle's hens and the fine chicken was lately one of the members of her flock.

Amy ate heartily, I was glad to see.

'All so deliciously fresh,' she commented, and I preened myself at this unaccustomed compliment – prematurely, as I might have known.

'But I really think the latest way of dishing up a salad is better. Just a bowl of green stuff tossed in the very best olive oil and

vinegar, and tomatoes freshly sliced in a separate dish salted and peppered and with a *soupçon* of chopped chives or parsley, of course – for those who like *coloured* salad mixed with green. I find that most people these days consider radishes rather too coarse a flavour, and there's so much medical argument about hard-boiled eggs that I don't serve them, I must admit.'

'You'd better bring your own nose-bag next time you come,' I told her. I've known Amy too long to worry about her criticisms and can well recall the hearty relish with which she attacked college bread and margarine spread with thick-cut Scottish marmalade, not to mention a truly repellent dish of minced meat in a suet crust which, with juvenile flippancy, we christened 'Boiled Baby'.

However, she approved graciously of my coffee, and as soon as we had finished we set off to the church.

'Looks like thunder,' commented Amy, eyeing the darkening sky. There was a sullen coppery look about the piled clouds, and not a leaf stirred in the airless heat.

'Let's hope it waits until we're safely home again,' I answered, as we joined the queue at the south door.

It was good to see St Patrick's so full. Seldom had the ancient hammerbeam roof looked down upon such a glittering assembly. We had all done our best to make this a splendid occasion. I studied the

attire and coiffures around me. There were several new hats, worn by
those who felt unable to attend church unless so crowned, and among
them was one upon Mrs Pringle's locks. It was entirely new to me.
Where was the faithful old number adorned with dangling
cherries? Where was the navy-blue, decorated with white feathers,
which had first seen the light at her niece Minnie's wedding? No
doubt safely lodged on top of the wardrobe at home. I hoped so. I
missed those two old friends, but studied the new creation with
interest. It was of green straw, formidably brimmed, and garlanded
with plastic anemones which looked suspiciously like those given
away recently with packets of soap powder. It was exceedingly
handsome, I thought, and proof of Mrs Pringle's support of the
Festival.

In the front pews sat our local gentry, elegant in silks and velvets,
their hair blue-rinsed, silver-streaked, or discreetly tinted Occasionally, wafts of delicious perfume floated back to us, as a stole was
rearranged or a handbag was opened.

The nave was shadowy, but a shaft of golden light illuminated
the chancel and altar. Mr Annett, at the organ, played some gentle
melody, vaguely familiar, which I guessed must be by Haydn or
Mozart.

St Patrick's clock struck nine. The music stopped and the vicar
appeared at the chancel steps

'You are about to hear the story of Fairacre,' he told us, 'and in
particular the story of this lovely old church. But before it begins
let us pray that we may see it restored to its former beauty, so that
those who come after us may cherish it as we have done.'

We slipped to our knees and listened to the simple prayer. Then,
with a susurration of silks and satins, we resumed our seats, eager
for what might come

The golden light which suffused the chancel changed to a dim
blue. The cross glimmered upon the altar amidst the ghostly
shadows. We shivered in awe. It was very quiet. Only, far away, a
faint rumbling could be heard It could have been distant thunder,
or a farm vehicle out late upon its lawful business.

There was a faint crackling sound and then Basil Bradley's voice
echoed strongly through the church.

'Long, long ago, so learned men tell us, the Romans may have passed this way. They did not settle here as far as we know. Among our downs water is scarce, and there are few natural defences against the elements or the enemy. The Romans left no signs of occupation here.

'But centuries later, when the next invaders came to Britain, they left their mark upon this place. Upon this spot, where now we are gathered, the Normans built a small, strong church of which parts still remain.'

At this point the chancel arch was thrown into prominence, a mellow golden light illuminating the angular stone carving. Few of Fairacre's parishioners had realized until this dramatic moment what unsuspected richness had lain in the shadowy chancel arch so high above them.

'The work was begun probably about the middle of the twelfth century –' A crackling noise interrupted the mellifluous voice, and was immediately followed by a burst of thunder which broke around us like machine-gun fire. We ducked involuntarily at the report, then, remembering ourselves, sat up and looked polite and attentive.

The church was plunged in darkness and the voice had ceased. A little agitated whispering rustled round the congregation.

'Lord Almighty!' boomed Mr Roberts whose voice is as large as his generous heart. 'We've been and got struck!'

At this, commotion broke out on all sides. There was nothing panic-stricken about us. We are all used to storms, which can occur with horrifying ferocity, but they are soon over in Fairacre. What really worried us was the breakdown of the performance and the bitter disappointment of all those who had spent so long in preparing it.

The vicar, rising from his seat to direct and comfort his flock, suddenly saw, with amazing clarity, in his mind's eye Queen Anne's chalice. It seemed to float in mid-air, brilliantly clear at first, but gradually fading, as if it were passing away from him to distances unknown. The vicar's heart beat uncomfortably loudly, his throat grew constricted, but he put his fears from him and addressed his flock.

'Please remain seated, dear people. Candles will be lit at once, and would Mr Roberts be so kind as to step across to the vicarage and telephone the Electricity Board to see what can be done?'

'I'm on my way, sir,' called Mr Roberts, and the crash of strong footsteps confirmed this.

'Mark my words,' said Amy beside me. '*The Caxley Chronicle* will tell us that this power cut was caused by a swan flying into the cable.'

'Perhaps it was,' I replied.

'Fiddlesticks!' snapped Amy. 'It was the storm!'

A jagged flash split the sky, to be followed by another reverberating thunder clap.

'It's farther off,' said someone hopefully.

'You wants to count, one, two, three, four, see? As soon as the lightning comes you starts counting and sees how many you gets to afore the thunder bangs out. That'll tell you how many miles off the storm be!'

I recognized the voice of this young know-all as Ernest, my Swineherd-Prince.

'You speak when you're spoken to,' said his mother, in a scandalized whisper. 'Piping up like that, and in church, too!'

A few scurrying figures flitted about the shadows bearing candles. There was a medieval beauty about their downbent heads and their curved hands sheltering the precious tiny flames from any draught, which was poignantly in keeping with the ancient building.

'Mr Annett,' announced the vicar, 'will play some music by Bach while we wait.'

We settled back against the hard pew-backs and let the sonorous chords flow over us. How many of our Fairacre forebears, I wondered, had listened to Bach by candlelight, as we were doing now? My mind began to wander. There was something wonderfully comforting in the thought that we shared so much in this building with those long-dead and those yet unborn. We were, after all, simply a link in a long chain stretching back for centuries and forward into eternity.

The candle flames stretched and wavered in the draught. A rumble of thunder rattled over the roof.

'I told you so,' whispered Ernest defensively. 'It's going away.'

At that moment, Mr Roberts reappeared.

'The power will be back at any minute,' he announced. 'A swan has flown into the cable, they say.'

Amy nudged me with such vigour that my side was quite sore.

'Thank you, Mr Roberts,' said the vicar 'Let us sing a hymn together while we wait.'

After some whispering with Mr Annett, the vicar proclaimed:

'*Pleasant are thy courts above*' and we all dutifully arose in the twilit church and raised our voices. As we reached the last line, the lights came on again, and we sang 'Amen' with undue fervour.

We resumed our seats expectantly and Basil Bradley, looking slightly careworn, appeared at the chancel steps.

'I think we had better begin again from the beginning, ladies and gentlemen. We are so very sorry for this breakdown. Please bear with us, and let us hope that all is now plain sailing.'

There were sympathetic murmurs from the congregation, the lights went out and the blue spotlight lit up the altar once more. There was a preliminary crackle and then Basil Bradley's voice as before.

'Long, long ago, so learned men tell us, the Romans may have passed this way.'

We settled back, like children hungry for a story, and gave ourselves up to enjoyment.

It took a little over an hour for the tale to unfold, and so well had Basil Bradley told it and so beautiful had the lighting been, that we emerged from the experience filled with unbounded admiration tinged with awe.

Even Amy was impressed.

'*Remarkably* good,' she said as we walked home. 'Really *outstandingly* good! It ought to bring hundreds of visitors.'

'Let's hope it does,' I replied. 'Two thousand pounds takes some finding.'

'I wonder if the national press will write it up,' mused Amy. 'It deserves it. You'll get people from all over the place if it's widely advertised.'

'We've done our best,' I assured her. It's been in all the local papers, I know.'

'I think I shall send a letter to *The Times*,' said Amy, climbing elegantly into her car. 'We want to cast the net *really wide*.'

She drove off and I returned to the school house. Distant voices in the lane and the sound of cars starting on their homeward journeys formed the epilogue to Basil Bradley's moving production.

A star, bright as a jewel, hung beside St Patrick's spire. It looked hopeful, I thought, as I prepared for bed. If the rest of the Fairacre contributions matched this evening's in splendour, our Festival must surely succeed, and more important still, Queen Anne's chalice would remain among those who loved it so well.

7

Next morning I began to realize just how far-flung the news of our Fairacre Festival had been.

There was a hearty banging on the classroom door during our history lesson and in walked a thickset man wearing a crewcut and a broad smile. The likeness to our Mr Lamb at the Post Office was unmistakable.

'Miss Read?' he began.

'George Lamb,' I said. 'How nice of you to look in!'

'Well, you see, I was raised in this place and I felt I just had to take another peek at this old schoolroom. Don't appear to have changed much since my time. Bit cleaner, perhaps.'

'You'd better repeat that to Mrs Pringle,' I told him. 'It'll make her day.'

I turned to the class.

'Stand up and say "Good-morning" to Mr Lamb, who was once a pupil here.'

There were welcoming cries and smiles, all the warmer because any interruption to lessons is a pleasurable one.

'That's a Coggs,' exclaimed our visitor, pointing delightedly at Joseph in the front row.

'Quite right,' I said. 'He's Arthur Coggs's son.'

'Oh, I know *Arthur*,' replied George Lamb with some emphasis. I had no doubt that he knew a great deal about his old schoolmate's fondness for liquor and the resultant shindies in our village.

I settled the children to some work and accompanied our guest on a tour of the room.

'Not the same piano! Sakes alive, that must be going on for a century.'

'Eighty, anyway,' I agreed, fingering the walnut fretwork front, and the ivory keys, yellow with age.

'And still the same gaps in the partition,' he went on, bending down to squint through a crack into the infants' room. 'The things we poked through there you'd just never credit, Miss Read.'

'Mr Willet's told me,' I assured him. 'Stinging nettles, knitting needles, dozens of notes – yes, I can well imagine. It happens still, you know. Children don't change much.'

He ambled appreciatively round the room, touching the walls, peering from the windows, and ruffling the children's hair as he passed.

'I hear Miss Clare's still at Beech Green. I'm paying her a visit before I fly home.'

'She'll be so pleased,' I said truthfully.

'I owe a lot to her,' he said, suddenly grave. 'Taught us all proper manners and to think for others. She used to say grace before we went home at night. It went: "Bless us this night and make us ever mindful of the wants of others." I always liked that. "Mindful of the wants of others." Good words those.'

He gazed through the window as he spoke, his eyes fixed upon the men working upon St Patrick's belfry.

'They're getting on very well. They've almost finished,' I said, intending to release the tension a little. George Lamb shook himself into the present again.

'Ah! Looks pretty tidy now. You been to the show there yet?'
I said that I had.

'I'm taking some of the chaps who flew over with me tomorrow night. All helps the funds. I owe a lot to Fairacre, and it'll give the fellows no end of a kick to see a building that's over eight hundred years old, and to hear Jean Cole too.'

He glanced at the square gold watch upon his wrist and grimaced.

'Best get back to the Post Office for my lunch, or I'll catch it,' he said. 'Goodbye, Miss Read. Goodbye children. Hope you'll look back on your days at Fairacre School with as much pleasure as I do.'

I accompanied him to the gate. Above the elm trees the rooks were circling high.

'Sign of rain, eh?' he said. ' "Winding up the water," we used to say as kids. You know one thing, Miss Read? Everything seems a lot smaller in Fairacre than I remember it except St Patrick's spire and them old elm trees! Maybe they've both been growing since I left here.'

Chuckling at his own fancies, he made his way back to the village.

On Tuesday evening came the eagerly awaited visit of Jean Cole.

Halfway through the recorded story of Fairacre there was an interval. A spotlight lit the chancel arch and the vicar led in the majestic figure of Major Gunning's cousin. She was resplendent in a long glittering black gown, and her appearance alone was enough to awe her country admirers, but when that glorious voice wrapped us in its warmth and beauty we were touched as never before.

She sang the aria from Handel's *Judas Maccabaeus*, to Mr Annett's accompaniment on the organ. It was a felicitous choice for it celebrated the restoration of the Sanctuary of Jerusalem. We sat in wonderment as the lovely voice soared and fell, and when finally she bowed and left us, we still sat silent and spellbound, whilst through my mind ran Shelley's lines:

> Music, when soft voices die,
> Vibrates in the memory –

I heard later that George Lamb was as good as his word, and that eight of his business friends had been among that evening's congregation.

After the performance was over, it appears, the vicar found them looking round the church in the company of the honorary architect, Mr Graham. He was busy pointing out the particular beauties of the building, and had a fascinated audience. The vicar joined the party and was moved to see the awed admiration with which the strangers viewed the ancient building.

'Back home,' said one, 'we reckon two hundred years as mighty old. It takes your breath away to touch a wall or a doorway this ancient.'

They wandered from vestry to belfry, from altar to sidechapel, and finally emerged from the west door and accepted the vicar's invitation to coffee at the vicarage.

'I can offer you Drambuie with it,' said the vicar with pleasure, as he handed round the steaming cups, 'or a liqueur called aurum, distilled from oranges, and brought from Italy as a present by some friends in the village.'

'Not for me,' said Jock Graham austerely   but I'll no refuse a good Scots liqueur like Drambuie.'

He was in a remarkably mellow mood. To have such an attentive audience was a joy to him. The villagers of Fairacre took their church very much for granted, but these strangers were perceptive and appreciative. Jock Graham's tongue wagged all the faster, as the Drambuie diminished sip by sip, and he extolled the unique attributes of the building he loved so well.

It was almost half-past eleven when at last the party broke up.

'I'd no idea it was so late,' said the vicar. 'Have you far to go?'

'We're booked in at Caxley,' said one. Two of us have business there tomorrow. The others are off to London on the early train, rustling up some more customers we hope.'

Farewells were made, and the vicar and Mrs Partridge turned back into the hall.

'What very nice fellows!' exclaimed Mr Partridge. George Lamb seems to have found some good companions.'

'And a wife who's interested in cooking,' added Mrs Partridge. 'He's going to ask her to send me a recipe for almond cookies.'

'Cookies?' repeated the vicar, his brow furrowed with perplexity.

'*Cookies!*' said his wife firmly. 'Biscuits to us. Really, Gerald, at times you are hopelessly insular.'

'I suppose so,' agreed the vicar rather sadly. Then his face brightened.

'But we've broadened our horizons tonight, my dear, haven't we? With our American friends, and prima donnas!'

Amicably, they mounted the stairs to bed.

The day came when Fairacre School presented its contribution to the Festival. We had decided to give two performances, one in the afternoon when mothers with young children could come, and one in the evening when fathers could attend.

We chose Wednesday for the simple reason that it is early closing day in Caxley and that the people of Fairacre would not be tempted to go there to spend their money. Thursday is market day, and three buses run from our village into Caxley on that busy day. We could not hope to compete with Caxley's magnetic pull on a Thursday. Besides, as Mrs Bonny pointed out reasonably, they would have more money to put in the silver collection *before* market day.

Excitement had mounted steadily during the Festival week and by the time Wednesday came it was at fever-pitch. The costumes and simple properties had been stacked on desks at the side of my room and Mrs Bonny's, for want of any other place to put them, and mighty little work had been done by the children with such attractions lying near by. Pens in hand, arithmetic exercises neglected before them, the children's bemused gaze turned constantly to the glamorous heaps of clothes. Here was a glimpse of another world. Our country children rarely go to the theatre. An annual visit to the pantomime is about all that comes their way. Here, close at hand, were all the trappings of magic, the means of slipping from the everyday world of school to one of enchanting fantasy. It was little wonder that I had very few sums to mark each day. But a wise teacher knows when she is beaten, and I forbore to scold.

As soon as school dinner was demolished we set about arranging the seating. The partition was pushed back, the desks removed either to the playground or to one end to form the basis of the stage. Mr Willet, Mr Roberts the farmer, and Jim Farrow his shepherd, arranged the long planks across the desks, tried the curtains we had rigged up, and pronounced the stage ready.

Meanwhile, the children were putting the chairs in rows for the audience. These were new stackable beauties from the village hall, and we had been threatened with all sorts of penalties if any damage were done.

The din was appalling. The metal frames of the chairs clanged like an iron foundry. The men's voices, raised above the racket, were thunderous. The thud of their mallets as they knocked the planks into place reverberated among the pitch-pine rafters above. When at last the work was done, and the men had departed, Mrs Bonny and I took an aspirin and a cup of tea apiece in the hope of curing our headaches.

At two-thirty the schoolroom was packed tight. In the front seats were the vicar and the managers and a number of illustrious friends of the school. Parents, aunts and uncles, little brothers and sisters and numerous distant relations, whom I had never seen before, kept up a cheerful hum of conversation while panic grew steadily behind the stage curtain.

The first item was a collection of folksongs sung by the whole school. It was a tight squash to get all sixty-odd children on to the stage, and one scaremonger among the infants told everyone that 'them planks ain't safe', thus causing widespread terror.

'Anyone who wants to get off the stage can do so,' I said fiercely. 'But don't forget your mothers have come to see you.'

This quelled the riot a trifle, but Mrs Bonny and I had the usual fears to calm.

'S'pose us forgets the words?'

'S'pose there's a fire. Which door does we go for?'

'I feels a bit sick.'

'I forgets how the tune goes.'

'John Todd shoved me!'

'I never then!'

'Miss, there ain't enough room for us up this end. The wall's all coming off on my sleeve, miss. My *best* sleeve.'

At this moment, Mrs Bonny was obliged to take three of her youngest to the lavatory – an inevitable hold-up at any school function – whilst I applied my eye to the crack of the curtain to watch the audience. It really was a wonderful house, kindly and enthusiastic, and I only hoped we should not disappoint all those present.

At last all was ready. Mrs Bonny took her seat at the piano. United in the face of their common ordeal, the children grew suddenly silent. I hauled on the curtain rope, and we were off to a flying start.

The deafening applause which greeted every item was most gratifying. The infants, naturally, won the palm, and every time the curtain rose upon them there were loving cries of: 'Oh, aren't they sweet?' 'Look at our Billy!' 'The pretty dears!' 'Don't they sing lovely?' and the like. They certainly went through their paces magnificently, after initial bashfulness, and the folk dance nearly brought the roof – and the stage – down with energetic clapping and stamping.

This number ended the first half and we could hear the infants hard at it as my class prepared for *The Princess and the Swineherd* in the lobby. Ernest, usually so stolid, had become hilariously excited and was clowning about in his finery, reducing the girls to a state of helpless giggling.

The princess's skirt had been trodden on, and given way drastically at the gathers, so that I was obliged to do last-minute repairs with safety pins, with my hand inside her waist-band.

'Oh, miss, you tickles!' giggled Elizabeth, wriggling about like an eel. 'Oh, miss, your hands is cold!' Then a squeal.

'Oh, miss, you've bin and *pricked* me!'

'Stand still then,' I begged, snapping the last pin home. 'There, now you'll do!'

'It's pinned to my vest, miss.'

'And that's how it will have to stay,' I assured her flatly. 'We're on in five minutes.'

These words had a dual effect. Some children were, mercifully, struck dumb. Others became panic-stricken and fussed even more vociferously. Luckily, applause and cheers broke out from the schoolroom at this stage, the infants came trooping back, flushed with success, and we were obliged to collect our senses ready for our big moment after the brief interval.

'The magic saucepan's bin and gone!' exclaimed Patrick dramatically. This was the highly necessary property round which the Princess and her ladies gathered to discover the meals being cooked all over the town. There was a frenzied scattering of costumes, searching under chairs and general confusion until one of the infants, flown with success, was discovered with it on his head from whence it was wrenched by one of his enraged elders.

'You might have had his ears off,' observed an onlooker dispassionately, but relief was so general that no one took much notice of this true statement.

After all the excitement I was prepared to find the cast both agitated and wordless, but all went well. Ernest's courtly bows were marvels of grace, and the only slight slip was the addition of 's' now and again, in true Fairacre fashion.

'We knows who's going to have sweet soup and pancakes! We knows who's going to have porridge and chops!' chanted the ladies exultantly. At least, I told myself philosophically, they did not say· 'Us knows', as they might so easily have done.

The applause at the end of the performance was deafening, and augured well for the repeat programme in the evening.

By the time the children and their parents had gone home, Mrs Bonny and I were dog tired. We tottered across to my house, and revived our strength with tea, tomato sandwiches and shortbread.

'Mr Willet says we've taken over seven pounds this afternoon, and it should be as much again this evening,' said Mrs Bonny, surveying her stockinged feet at the other end of the sofa. 'It should help the funds quite a lot.'

'It should,' I agreed. We lapsed into exhausted silence, and I guessed that her thoughts were running on the same lines as mine. Should we ever, in this small village, even with the herculean efforts we were making, ever come anywhere near the target we had so hopefully and bravely set ourselves?

Three hours later, much refreshed, we crossed the playground for our second house. Against a ravishing blue sky, the newly gilded weathercock flamed triumphantly on the pinnacle of St Patrick's spire. It was a heartening sight.

Resolutely we thrust our doubts from us, pushed open the heavy school door, and were engulfed once again by our teeming mob.

8

Our School Concert, which finally netted sixteen pounds for the funds, was one of the more modest efforts in Festival Week. It was on a par with the Mammoth Whist Drive, the Giant Draw and the Fabulous Flower Show. The *Son et Lumière*, with the added attraction of Jean Cole, was the backbone of the week, of course, and was so successful that it was decided to carry on for the next week as well, much to everyone's joy.

It was fortunate that it had done so well, for calamity hit Fairacre the day before the fête. Peter Martin, whose advent we had all awaited so eagerly, was involved in a car crash on Thursday evening, and was taken to hospital with two broken ribs and concussion.

We heard the news on radio and television that evening and were plunged into gloom. The vicar, good Christian that he is, forbore to express what was in most of our minds, simply saying: 'Poor young fellow!! It is a mercy that his injuries are no worse!'

Jock Graham was more outspoken.

'This'll make a difference to the takings,' he observed dourly, reading the headlines in Friday's *Guardian*.

'He won't die, will he, miss?' asked a bevy of little girls round my desk. Peter Martin's injuries and the cruelty of Fate in thus snatching him from us were the playground topics of the day, and in fact, of the whole neighbourhood.

Lady Sawston, who lives locally, nobly agreed to step into the breach and to open the fête, but it was quite apparent that fewer people would attend now that our star attraction had gone.

It was a sore blow indeed to our efforts.

But the final item in the Festival's programme was the Gala Dance which was held in the Village Hall on Saturday evening and at which Peter Martin was to have sung. It was the culmination of our efforts, and the ladies of the Floral Society excelled themselves with shower arrangements on every wall bracket and a bank of massed flowers, contributed from Fairacre cottage gardens, across the width of the stage.

Homemade refreshments had been billed as one of the chief attractions, my own modest contribution consisting of two dozen sausage rolls and a rather handsome set of small savouries in aspic jelly, so ravishingly pretty – at least, in my own eyes – that I hoped that Amy might drop in unexpectedly and be impressed. Needless to say, she did not, and the only comment which I heard on their appearance came from Mrs Mawne, who remarked disparagingly to one of her helpers: 'Probably sent by the vicar's wife. She dabbles in aspic.' *Dabbles in aspic indeed*, I thought, smarting in silence. It is hardly surprising that Mrs Mawne is so generally detested.

I looked in during the last hour of the event. Faces were flushed, skirts whirling, you could have cut the air with a knife, and 'The Dizzy Beat' from Caxley lived up to its name, with enough tympani to drown the other three instruments.

It was a huge success, and I joined with zest the great circle for 'Auld Lang Syne', and wrenched other people's arms from their sockets with enthusiasm matching my neighbour's. After 'God Save The Queen', the company drifted away to the sound of car engines, roaring motor bikes and farewell cries, and I helped to wash up the debris.

Mrs Willet accompanied me home. It was lovely to be out in the cool night air. Someone had night-scented stocks growing in his front garden, and the fragrance was delicious. A half-moon lay on its back, cradled in the tree-tops, and an owl hooted from the vicarage cedar tree.

'A beautiful night,' said Mrs Willet. 'And a successful one. Do you think the vicar will know the result of the Festival Week tomorrow? Everyone's praying we'll have made enough to save the chalice, though they don't say much.'

'We'll live in hope,' I replied, opening my gate. 'We couldn't have done more anyway. That's one comfort.'

The vicar did not make an announcement the next day, but the hand on the Appeal's board shot round to one thousand and seven hundred pounds.

'Getting along now!' said the parishioners excitedly, as they made their way past the board. 'It's coming on, isn't it?'

'But not fast enough,' was Mr Mawne's comment to the vicar, after the service.

'I agree with you there,' said Jock Graham soberly. 'I've kept a tight eye on the money all the way along the line, and give Christie's their due, they've done a fine job at a reasonable price.'

'What is still outstanding?' inquired the vicar, leading the two to the vicarage for a glass of sherry.

'My estimate, a generous one, was two thousand. Christie's have had two lots of four hundred so far, the rest to be paid when the job is finished. That's twelve hundred to find. With luck we'll find the total is something under two thousand, and the rest can go into the Fabric Fund. We must have something behind us in case of further disaster.'

'God forbid!' exclaimed the vicar, his mouth working piteously. He poured a sherry with a shaking hand, and they sipped in silence. Mr Mawne broke it at last.

It's no good, Gerald. You must go into this business of the sale of the chalice. It's all very well to be sentimental –'

'*Sentimental!*' cried the vicar, but his friend swept on.

'But the fact is that the chalice could be our salvation. Not only now, but as a hedge against future crises. After all, we could always have a replica made.'

'*A replica?*' echoed the vicar in anguish. 'But it wouldn't be the same!'

'Of course not,' agreed Mr Mawne soothingly, as if addressing a fractious child, 'but it would do as well.'

The vicar, too stunned to explain, shook his grey head sadly. Jock Graham, unusually perceptive, spoke gently.

'It's a sore blow, I know, vicar, but it would be prudent to find out the possibilities. With any luck, it may never be needed, but it's only fair that the parish should know the position. We need another five or six hundred pounds to pay for this damage and to put the Fabric Fund on a sound footing. The Festival may bring in another sixty to seventy. There are the sums from the guarantors and the covenantors which will bring in another hundred or so, over a period of time. But it just isn't enough.'

The vicar put down his sherry glass carefully and looked from one to the other.

'Let me sleep on it,' he said. 'I'll give you an answer, one way or the other, early next week. It's a step I can hardly bear to contemplate.'

'Good man!' said Mr Mawne encouragingly, slapping his old friend painfully on the back, and the two men left the vicar to his own troubled thoughts.

'Simply pecking at your food, Gerald,' commented his wife, briskly removing the plates at lunch-time. 'You worry far too much. You'll have another of your dizzy spells, if you're not sensible.'

'I'll have a walk this afternoon,' said the vicar meekly. 'Fresh air always calms me.'

The road to the downs above Fairacre peters out into a grassy track. Birds darted across the vicar's path, with cries of alarm. Rabbits bounded away with a flourish of white scuts, and at least four larks vied with each other high against the blue and white dappled sky. It looked so peaceful, so unchanging, much as it looked, thought the vicar, with a pang, when the silversmith had finished his masterpiece, in the reign of Queen Anne, over two hundred and fifty years ago.

He sat himself heavily on the springy turf and plucked a nearby harebell, twisting its wiry stem this way and that as he gazed at the village spread out below.

What should he do? He had had faith that his prayers would be answered, but God in His wisdom had seemed to withhold the easy way. There, below him, the villagers rested after their wholehearted efforts in Festival Week. The response had been wonderful, the village united as never before. There could be very little more expected from them. Henry Mawne was right. More help must come from another source, and the only possibility was the chalice. He must bring himself to approach the Bishop and to seek his advice. He owed it to his church and to his villagers. He had been selfish and weak in refusing to face the facts.

He sighed heavily, and the view below him grew suddenly blurred. Sad at heart, he struggled to his feet and made his way home.

The vicar slept little in the nights that followed. He had met Mr Mawne and Jock Graham and agreed reluctantly to consult the Bishop. It had taken him a week to compose a letter, and now he awaited a reply in an agony of spirit.

One morning he sat leaden-eyed before his breakfast egg, survey-ing the pile of letters. There was no word yet from the Bishop, but among the bills, receipts and circulars was a long blue air mail en-velope, as gaudy as a peacock among sparrows. The vicar took it up first, savouring this rare foreign treasure.

'George Washington had a fine face,' he observed, studying the stamps closely. 'And what a good idea these little address tickets are! So much more legible than some unknown hand-writing at the head of a letter.'

'Who's it from?' asked Mrs Partridge, cutting to the heart of the matter.

'Oh, now let me see. "G. D. Lamb," it says. Lamb,' said the vicar ruminatively. 'Do we know a Mr Lamb in America, my dear?'

'Of course we do,' exclaimed his wife impatiently. 'George Lamb who was here during the Festival. That's probably the recipe for almond cookies he promised me. Do open it, dear, and *please* eat your breakfast. I want to clear the table. I'm having a coffee morning here today to raise more funds.'

The vicar obediently took a bite of toast and then slit the en-velope. The letter was written in a firm hand in good copperplate which owed its beginnings to Miss Clare's guidance, many years earlier

Mrs Partridge watched her husband's eyes widen and his face grow pinker as he perused the paper in his hand. At last, bemused, he put it down, and rummaging in the envelope produced a cheque which he studied with stupefaction.

'Is my recipe there?' asked Mrs Partridge. The vicar shook his head slowly, as if to clear it, rather than in answer to his wife's query. He seemed beyond speech.

'Has he sent something to the Fund?' asked Mrs Partridge, her glance falling on the cheque. 'How very, very kind of him!'

The vicar opened his mouth, and shut it again. He took a sip of coffee, and then found his voice.

'He has sent us a cheque for two thousand dollars.'

'*No!*' said his wife, thunderstruck. He *can't* have done! Not even Americans are as rich as that, and George only has a catering business which he built up himself!'

Without a word, the vicar handed the cheque across the table.

'It must be two thousand, because it's got it in words as well as figures,' said Mrs Partridge, studying the cheque earnestly, and speaking with great care as though she were explaining matters to herself. 'I simply can't take this in, Gerald.'

'It's not George alone, my dear. It appears that his good friends on the trip were most concerned to hear of our plight, and contributed very generously, and also got other people to do so. George says in his letter that two old ladies, whose parents came from these parts originally, gave a considerable part of the money, and so did some relatives of George's wife. Can you believe it, my dear? We have been wonderfully blest.'

'It is absolutely wonderful!' said his wife huskily. 'In the face of such generosity one hardly knows whether to laugh or cry. Oh, Gerald, this will save the chalice, won't it?'

'It was my first thought,' confessed the vicar. 'I must telephone Henry immediately, and Jock, and then we must get in touch with the Rural Dean and the Bishop.'

He pushed back his chair and came round the table to kiss his wife. He looked, she thought, as though twenty years had fallen from him in the last five minutes.

She watched him affectionately as he gazed once again at the cheque.

'How does one translate it into pounds?' he asked.

'Divide by three,' said Mrs Partridge promptly. 'That's somewhere near. Henry will know exactly.'

'But that means this is worth almost seven hundred pounds! It is quite incredible! To think that people who have never seen us or our little church should be so overwhelmingly generous! It does one's heart good.'

'The same sort of thing happened at Dorchester Abbey,' his wife reminded him. 'And there was a simply lovely service of thanksgiving with lots of Americans there. Remember?'

'Yes, indeed,' nodded the vicar. 'And there will be one here in Fairacre before very long, I can promise you.'

He picked up George Lamb's letter and put it carefully, with the cheque, into his wallet.

'I shall do my telephoning, and write this morning to George and all his kind friends,' he said. 'But what I shall say, I really don't know. My heart is too full.'

The joyous news flashed round the Fairacre grapevine within hours, helped considerably by the partakers of coffee at Mrs Partridge's morning meeting. Villagers were incredulous at first, and then genuinely touched by the unexpected benefaction. Even Mrs Pringle seemed moved by the magnificence of the present, though she was grudging in her first pronouncements to me.

'That George Lamb must've done well for himself in New York. Been fleecing the customers, I shouldn't wonder.'

I was roused to wrath and told her that the idea may certainly have been George's, but the bulk of the money was from Americans who had never even seen St Patrick's, which made the gesture even more wonderful. Mrs Pringle had the grace to look a little sheepish as she spread a tea towel over the hot boiler to dry.

'Yes, that's true,' she conceded. 'I've always understood the Americans – for all their funny ways – had a feeling heart. And say what you like, Miss Read, it's a feeling heart that matters when you're in trouble. They tell me the vicar's already planning a thanksgiving service as soon as the repairs is done.'

'We'll all be there,' I promised her.

Epilogue

Exactly a year after the fateful night which wrecked the roof of St Patrick's, the bells were rehung in the repaired belfry.

Now all was completed. The spire and the roof presented their usual tidy aspect to the village. At last the scaffolding had gone. The workmen's huts had vanished, and the trodden grass of the church-yard was fast returning to its velvety greenness under Mr Willet's tending. The hand on the Appeal Fund board stood triumphantly at well over two thousand pounds thanks to the efforts of the folk of Fairacre and their friends near and far.

In his study, the vicar was composing the sermon he would be giving the next Sunday at the great thanksgiving service. On his desk stood Queen Anne's silver chalice reflecting the autumn sun-shine in its mellow curves. The vicar touched its ancient beauty with loving fingers. In a few minutes it would be in the kitchen being cleaned by Mrs Partridge in readiness for its part in the festivities of the great day.

What hopes and fears had centred round this lovely thing during the past year, he thought! What a year it had been for them all in Fairacre!

He pushed aside his papers and went into the garden for a breath of air. It was a quiet, gentle day with no breath of wind, a contrast indeed with the fury of the first of October last year when disaster had struck.

He thought with gratitude of all the blessings which had

followed – the united efforts of all in the village, the bravery, the generosity of everybody, particularly of those American friends who had forged an unforgettable link with this small unknown village, as a result of last year's storm. What friends Fairacre had made! What fun it had been!

He stooped to pick up a shred of paper which was lodged among the button chrysanthemums in the border. He smoothed it out and surveyed the lettering with a smile of intense happiness. Crumpled, rain-washed and faded, it was the final triumphant scrap of

The Fairacre Festival

EMILY DAVIS

And some there be, which have no memorial; who are perished, as though they had never been . . .

But these were merciful men, whose righteousness hath not been forgotten . . .

The people will tell of their wisdom, and the congregation will show forth their praise.

ECCLESIASTICUS, XLIV

1. Two Old Friends

One golden September evening, Dolly Clare and her friend Emily Davis set out on a walk at the edge of Hundred Acre Field, which lay behind the hawthorn hedge of their cottage home.

It was a leisurely progress; more of a potter than a true walk. There were frequent stops to admire the scarlet rose-hips in the hedge, or to pick a spray of late honeysuckle, or simply to stand, eyes shaded against the declining sun's dazzle, to gaze across the great field to the hazy blue of the downs beyond.

But then both ladies were in their eighties, slight and silver-haired, and the track was rough going even for the young and sure-footed.

Besides, why hurry? Their time, after years of teaching in the village schools near Caxley, was their own, and had been ever since retirement some twenty years earlier. Their days were as serene and cloudless as the evening air which they were now enjoying. The clock, once their stern task-master, had no power over them now.

The two had met at Beech Green village school when Emily Davis was seven, and Dolly Clare, then a timid newcomer, was six years old.

'You can sit by Emily,' the teacher had said to the bewildered Dolly. 'Emily Davis will look after you.'

The dark little girl had shifted along the desk seat obligingly, and given Dolly a wide smile, made more endearing by the gap left by the loss of her two front teeth.

From that moment they had been friends, and Dolly grew to love Emily even more deeply than she did her own older sister Ada.

The little house which Emily shared with her six brothers and sisters became a second home to young Dolly. Somehow, there was always room for one more child to tumble about in the crowded living room at the Davis' cottage.

The two little girls had shared their schooling at Beech Green School and later had travelled almost three miles together each morning to attend Fairacre School in the next village.

They knew every foot of the road intimately. They knew where a robin had his nest, where white violets were hidden, where there were blackberries to quench a child's thirst and the first primroses to carry proudly home. Their love of nature's treasures was doubly deep because it was shared. It was to be a never-failing source of happiness to them throughout their lives.

They both became pupil teachers, attending evening classes at Caxley, the local market town, and trying out their skills with the younger children at Fairacre.

Their ways later divided, but were never far apart, and weekly letters held the bond between the two friends. The Great War of 1914–18 brought tragedy to them both. Dolly Clare's fiancé, Arnold Fletcher, was killed at Ypres, and Emily had, perhaps, an even harder blow to bear. Edgar, whom she loved dearly, lay ill in a war-time hospital for many months. Week after week, Emily made the difficult journey to see him, sustained by the hope of his progress to health and their future happiness.

It was a bitter day for Emily when she received a letter from him confessing that he had fallen in love with his nurse, and all was over.

Later, he brought his wife to live near Fairacre, and it was Emily's painful lot to witness the progress of the marriage.

She was careful to keep out of the way of Edgar and his family, but she heard from many neighbours that the marriage was an unhappy one. The nurse had proved a nagger, and Edgar, once so gay, had become sullen with the years. The knowledge distressed Emily but she said nothing.

The two friends never married. There were very few eligible men left in their generation, and they filled their days busily with work for other people's children. When the time came to retire, Dolly Clare left Fairacre School, and continued to live in the same little cottage, thatched by her father Francis Clare, at the foot of the downs.

A few years later, Emily came to join her, and a period of perfect companionship began for the old friends. Their ways fell together as sweetly as the two halves of an apple, and every day brought its own simple joys.

This evening walk was one of them. They had walked this track watching the corn sprout, grow, turn from green to gold, and had listened to the clamour of the combine harvester as it gathered the grain. The baler had been at work during the past few days, and neatly stacked piles, seven bales to each, stood among the glistening stubble awaiting collection.

Overhead the rooks flapped slowly homeward uttering their raucous cries, and, in the distance, pin-points of flame on the hill side showed where a farmer was burning his stubble, with thoughts of ploughing to come already in his mind.

The pair walked to the oak tree which stood in the hedge. Soon the acorns would be ripe enough to fall.

'We shall soon see the pheasants gathering round here,' observed Dolly.

'I've always loved the autumn,' said Emily. They stood in the oak tree's shade, gazing up into its gnarled branches.

Emily shivered, and Dolly noticed it.

'It's chilly here,' she said. 'Let's go home. There begins to get a nip in the air when the sun goes down.'

They turned to face the silvered thatch above the hawthorn hedge and, like the rooks above them, made their way home.

The evening was spent sitting one each side of the fireplace. Dolly had put a match to the paper and sticks which always stood ready in the hearth, and a small fire of logs now crackled cheerfully

'It seems extravagant,' said Emily, lowering her knitting and gazing at the flames. 'And only September! But what a joy a fire is, Dolly, isn't it? Thank goodness, we've still the strength to bring in a bit of firing.'

They listened to a little music on their ancient radio set, knitting the while, and basking in the warmth from the fire.

At eight o'clock Dolly fetched their modest supper on a tray. Thin brown bread and butter, a little cottage cheese, and two bowls of blackberries, dappled with the cream from the top of the milk, made their meal, with a glass of warm milk apiece to wash it down.

'We're like the good rabbits, Flopsy, Mopsy and Cottontail,' commented Emily, laughing, 'with our "bread and milk and black-berries for supper".'

'I wonder how many hundreds of times we've read that,' said Dolly.

'Recited it,' corrected Emily. 'We certainly never needed to look at the pages.'

They fell to reminiscing, as they did so often, while the meal was in progress. Their memories were prodigious, and their enjoyment of the follies and foibles of their neighbours, past and present, was as keen as ever.

The meal over, they washed up together in the little kitchen. Emily gave a great yawn.

'I can't think why I'm so sleepy tonight. I feel just as I did after a ten-mile walk as a girl. A lovely feeling really – but just dog-tired.'

'Go up to bed early,' urged Dolly. 'Shall I help you upstairs?'

'No, no!' cried Emily robustly. 'There's nothing wrong with me. But I think I will go up, as you say.' She took her book and made her way up the short staircase. Dolly, below, heard the creak-ing of the old floorboards as she made ready for bed, and the gentle squeak of the springs as Emily settled herself.

Dolly knitted for a little longer. The logs were almost burned through, black and zebra-striped with silvery ash. The cat had taken advantage of Emily's absence to establish itself in her chair. There, curled up luxuriously, it would stay until morning, unless the mys-terious noises of the night tempted it through the window left ajar for its convenience.

The sky was clear when Miss Clare made her way to bed at ten o'clock. A great full moon silvered the sleeping world. From her bedroom window Dolly noted the luminous beauty of the field of stubble, besides which she had walked with Emily a few hours earlier. She was reminded of Samuel Palmer's pictures of the countryside. He had caught exactly that eerie moonlight transfiguring an everyday world.

In the distance a sheep coughed, rasping and rhythmic, like an asthmatic old man.

It was very still. The perfume of night-scented stock came from the garden bed beneath the window. Emily, who loved the scent, had planted the seeds that spring.

Reminded of her by the fragrance of the flowers, Dolly went softly across the landing.

Emily had put out her light, but lay awake, gazing at the bands of moonlight across the rafters.

'All right, my dear?' asked Dolly gently.

'Perfectly,' answered Emily. 'What a heavenly night!'

'Can I bring you anything?'

'Nothing, dear, thank you. I've all I want.'

'Then sleep well,' said Dolly.

She kissed her friend's forehead briefly, and closing the door behind her made her way to her own room.

She was asleep within twenty minutes, but Emily, next door, was not. Tired though she was, sleep seemed to evade her.

She plumped up her pillows and sat up in bed. Now she could see the tops of the trees in the garden, the cornfield and the distant downs. Somewhere at hand a night bird rustled among leaves, and in the thatch above her there was a tiny scratching noise. No doubt a mouse was out upon its foragings.

The peace of the countryside enveloped her. Had it ever been so beautiful? Lit by the full moon, scented with stocks, the familiar view was enhanced by the mystery of night.

Emily sat there entranced for almost an hour. She had known that scene for eighty years, and still it had power to move and delight her, to present a different aspect with every changing season, and with every changing hour.

At last, with a sigh of pleasure, she sank back upon her pillows and closed her eyes.

She was never to look upon her lovely little world again.

2. Dolly Clare Alone

Miss Clare woke early. The hands of the china clock pointed to six o'clock, as she sat up in bed to survey the day.

The sun was slowly dispersing the light mist which veiled the distant downs. The beech hedge was draped with filmy cobwebs, and the grass was grey with a heavy autumn dew.

'There should be mushrooms about,' said Miss Clare aloud.

The shadow of the cottage, elongated absurdly, stretched across the cornfield. The chimneys were just like rabbits' ears, thought Dolly Clare, with amusement.

The croaking cry of a pheasant came from the distance. No doubt he was searching for a few early acorns from the oak tree. There had been another picking of ripe blackberries close to the tree, Dolly remembered. She would take her basket there later in the morning when the sun had dried the long grass a little. Emily enjoyed a dish of blackberry and apple meringue, and there were plenty of apples and eggs in the larder.

She wondered if Emily were awake, but decided not to disturb her so early. Countrywomen both, they were usually astir by seven o'clock, but Emily had seemed so tired, it would be a good thing if she slept on, thought Dolly.

She rose, and dressed as quietly as possible, but no matter how lightly she trod, the ancient floorboards creaked and squeaked, and the staircase was equally noisy as she crept downstairs.

She opened the windows and doors, letting in the fresh morning air scented still with stocks and damp grass. It was Dolly's favourite time of day, when the world was cool and quiet, and the day was full of hope.

She fed the purring cat which rubbed about her legs, and then set the breakfast table. Next she filled the kettle and switched it on. To have an electric kettle which boiled within five minutes, was still a wonder to Dolly Clare, who well remembered the lengthy process of lighting the kitchen fire and waiting for the black iron kettle to boil above it.

She thought she heard a sound above. Emily might be stirring. She made the tea, and found an unusually pretty porcelain cup, given long ago to her mother, for Emily's tea.

The tea was just as Emily liked it, not too strong and with only a little milk. The steaming fragrance whetted Dolly's own appetite as she bore it gently upstairs.

She tapped upon the door, but there was no answering call. The cat, which had followed her upstairs, hoping for a comfortable bed, mewed by the closed door.

'I've brought some tea, dear,' called Dolly, opening the door.

Emily was turned away from her, her face towards the window, and the bed-clothes drawn round her motionless figure. Dolly put the cup carefully upon the bedside table, and walked round the foot of the bed to survey her sleeping friend.

She knew, before her trembling hand touched Emily's cold forehead, that she had been dead for some hours.

Slowly, Dolly descended the staircase and fumbled her way to a chair. Suddenly, the full weight of her eighty-odd years seemed to crush her. Her heart fluttered in her breast like an imprisoned bird H - head throbbed dully, and she rested it upon the table before her.

She lay there, felled by the blow, for ten minutes or more. Gradually, her heart quietened and she raised her head Tears, of which she had not been conscious, had made a damp patch upon the polished surface of the table, and when she raised a hand to her cheek she found it wet with tears which still were running.

She let them flow unchecked, while her strength slowly returned. There was much to be done, but the day was still so young that few people would be astir. For this Dolly was thankful. Her private grief would be unseen, and the last services, which she intended to render her friend, could be undertaken alone.

Dolly Clare had seen death many times in her long life and had prepared her parents for their last journey. She did not flinch from the practical duties which must now be done.

Still trembling, but with quiet courage, she filled a bowl with warm water, collected snowy linen cloths, and returned to the bedroom

An hour or so later, she locked the house, and walked along the lane to the school house where her friends Mr and Mrs Annett lived

The leaves were beginning to fall, bright as new pennies on the surface of the road. The mist had gone, and the warmth in the sun was welcomed by Dolly's thin blood.

There was no telephone at the cottage. It was too expensive an item for the two old friends to install. A public call box was nearer than the Annetts', but Dolly disliked the idea of transmitting her news whilst someone might be waiting outside, an interested witness to her grief.

The school house was peaceful, for the headmaster had just gone across to his duties and was at that moment taking morning prayers, and the two children of the house were also at school.

Mrs Annett took one look at the tall figure, the tear-stained face, and the ineffable air of grief which surrounded the old lady.

'Emily?' she asked swiftly.

Dolly Clare nodded, her lips quivering.

'Sit down, and I'll fetch coffee,' said practical Mrs Annett. But Dolly preferred to follow her hostess into the kitchen. Now that the first shock was wearing away, she felt the need for company.

'I wondered if I might use your telephone,' she said diffidently. 'I should ring Doctor Martin, and then I must make the funeral arrangements.'

'We'll do all that,' said Mrs Annett swiftly. 'Now drink your coffee, and I'll send a message over to the school.'

'You mustn't disturb the time-table,' replied Miss Clare, years of school discipline coming to her aid. But she was overborne.

'It was all very peaceful,' said Dolly. 'I'm sure it was just as Emily had hoped to go. We'd had a perfect last day together, and she went to bed rather tired, but very tranquil and happy.'

'I'm thankful to hear it,' said Mrs Annett, watching the old lady's frail hands twist and turn in her lap, far more poignant than any spoken expression of grief.

'I'm thankful for *everything*,' replied Dolly soberly. 'Our lives have been bound together for so long that we both dreaded prolonged pain and disability for each other Emily was spared that.'

She rose to go.

'Do stay, please.'

'If you don't mind, I'd sooner be alone. I shall feel better at the cottage, and if you will be so very kind and make all the arrangements I shall be so grateful, my dear. Tell Doctor Martin I shall be waiting for him. No doubt he'll be along after surgery.'

Mrs Annett insisted on walking back with her. She saw her safely installed in her armchair, promised to call again during the day, and returned to make the telephone calls from the school house.

'I wonder,' she thought, as she rustled through the dead leaves at the roadside, 'how long she will survive poor Emily?'

The day passed for Dolly as if in a dream. Doctor Martin, that wise old friend, called in the latter part of the morning. He made his examination, noted the tidy body, the brushed hair and the clean linen enfolding Emily's thin frame. This, he knew, was Dolly's handiwork, and his respect for the old lady's courage grew deeper still.

He surveyed Dolly now as he put his certificate upon the mantel-shelf. Her face showed the ravages of grief, but she was as calm and dignified as ever.

'Any good advising you to stay with your sister for a bit?' he queried.

'No good at all,' answered Dolly, with a small smile. 'This is my home. I need it more than ever now.'

'Very well,' said the doctor. 'Go to bed early, and take two of these pills to make sure that you'll sleep.'

She gave him a quizzical look, but did not take the pills from him.

He put them beside the paper on the mantel-shelf.

'Stubborn girl!' he said. 'Well, there they are, anyway. I promise you, they wouldn't hurt a two-year-old.'

'I'll take them if I can't sleep,' said Dolly. 'You're very kind to me.'

'You wouldn't like me to run you along to the Annetts?'

'No, indeed. I must stay here until Emily is taken into Caxley.'

She put her hand upon his arm and smiled at him.

'My dear, I'm not in the least frightened. Only sad — and then only selfishly, because I shall miss her so. For her, I don't grieve. She always hoped to go first, and I'm glad things fell out so rightly for her. But I must stay with her until she goes. You understand?'

The doctor nodded, patting the frail hand upon his coat sleeve, then went his way. She might be old, she might be frail, but she had a strength of spirit which out-matched his own, and this the doctor recognized.

In the afternoon, the great black car arrived from the Caxley undertaker's, and four dark-clad men carried Emily down the little staircase and out into the mellow September sunshine. Mute, dry-eyed, Dolly watched them go.

Neighbours called, unhappy and diffident, seeking to help and to offer sympathy. Dolly met them all with sweetness and dignity, but refused to be led from her cottage. Compassion she appreciated: companionship, as yet, she must refuse.

At last, as the sun sank behind the downs, she found herself truly alone. Who would have thought that so much could have happened in the course of twenty-four hours?

This time yesterday, she and Emily had walked back from the oak tree to the shelter of their shared home. She thought of that evening – aeons ago, it seemed – when they had knitted and talked, and shared the company of the crackling fire and the purring cat.

It was another world – shattered by the cruel hand of Death She took a deep breath, and walked to the window.

The rooks were flying home. The downs were deep blue against the gold of the sunset. Emily's stocks were already beginning to scent the evening air, and in the distance Dolly could hear the coughing of the one afflicted sheep.

Life went on. No matter what happened, life went on, inexorably, callously, it might seem, to those in grief. But somehow, in this continuity, there were the seeds of comfort.

Dolly returned to the table, took out writing paper and began to draft an entry for the *Caxley Chronicle*.

DAVIS: *On September 20th, at Beech Green, Emily, aged 84. Funeral 2.30 p.m. Beech Green, Saturday, September 25th.*

She looked at it carefully, checking the notice for any mistakes as meticulously as she had corrected her pupils' work for so many years.

She put it into an envelope, stamped it, and put it on the window sill for the postman to take in the morning.

The house was deathly quiet. She looked about her automatically before mounting the stairs. Doctor Martin's two pills remained untouched, and she ignored them now. She had no heart to warm milk for herself, as she usually did at this hour, and could not trouble to put on a light.

In the darkness she ascended the stairs, comfortless and friendless. She undressed, shivering, and crept into her cold bed.

She had never felt so alone and forlorn, and the night stretched before her, black, bleak and hopeless Could she go on. she asked herself? Without Emily?

3. Manny Back's Marrow

Without Emily!

The words still beat in Dolly Clare's mind as the dawn broke, and she rose thankfully, glad to leave behind the wretchedness of a sleepless night.

She went about her early morning tasks automatically. She felt unusually weak and, grief apart, realized that lack of nourishment was partly the reason. She had been unable to eat the day before. Now she boiled an egg for herself, and cut a thin slice of brown bread and butter for her breakfast. She must look after herself.

There was no trace of self-pity in this observation. Sensible, as always, Dolly now faced the fact that she was quite alone, and if she wished to maintain her independence, which was so dear to her, then she must take care of herself, both in body and mind.

Emily was in her thoughts constantly during the day. Memories of Emily came flooding back. Small incidents, long forgotten, swam into her consciousness, as if to compensate her for the loss of Emily's physical presence.

The name itself had been dear to her for as long as she could remember, for the first Emily in Dolly's life had been a heavy, cumbersome, rag doll, stuffed hard with horse-hair, and much battered about its painted face.

It had been Dolly's companion from babyhood. The doll Emily was lugged about the little house in Caxley where Dolly was born, bumped upstairs, thrown down them, taken in Dolly's high wicker-work pram on the shopping expeditions in Caxley High Street, and accompanied her young owner to bed each night.

When Dolly was six, the family moved to Beech Green, to the cottage in which she was to live for the rest of her life. Of course,

Emily was put into the waggonette which carried their furniture. But a dreadful misfortune occurred on the way.

Emily, who had been propped up in an armchair, the better to see the passing landscape on this great adventure, was jogged by the rough road, fell out, and lay for many days hidden by bushes.

Young Dolly was heart-broken. Even her joy in the new home was dimmed by this catastrophe.

Francis Clare, her father, who was the local thatcher, discovered Emily at last and, full of relief, handed her back to his tearful daughter.

But, somehow, Emily had changed. Rough weather had faded her beauty. Her paint was washed away here and there, and the battered face had become more battered still, so that there was a sinister wryness about Emily's looks which chilled Dolly's ardour.

It was true that Emily was still looked after. She was dressed carefully, and put to bed at night time, but now she slept in a doll's bed and not in her mistress's. Emily had changed, and Dolly mourned for the old Emily she had loved and lost.

Doubly heartening was it then to encounter the second Emily – the small dark girl with eyes as bright as a squirrel's, who took timid Dolly under her wing and made sure that no school bully approached her charge. From that first meeting the friendship had flourished, growing in strength as the years passed.

Dolly was always the quieter of the two. There was a tomboy element about Emily, encouraged no doubt by her lively brothers who dared her to face exploits which she would not have essayed on her own. It was a high-spirited family, dominated by their mother, a busy little Jenny-wren of a woman.

Dolly found the boys' society overwhelming at first. At home, there was only Ada, her senior by two years, as playmate. She was a sturdy headstrong child, with a healthy beauty which Dolly envied. Ada was soon elected as queen of the school playground. For her, the boys were creatures who must pay homage.

Dolly looked upon them differently. It was not long before she came to appreciate the humour and honesty, first of the Davis boys, and later of most of her male school fellows. Later still, when she began to teach, she found she had to guard against this secret sympathy with the boys' point of view. She liked their directness of response. If she had occasion to reprimand a boy, there was usually a posy brought the next day as a peace-offering, and then the whole affair was over.

When a girl needed correction Miss Clare often found that the results were far more complex. There might be no sign given of resentment or guilt. Very often there was a show of bravado instead. But sometimes a mother would appear, with tales of nights spent weeping, or a daughter reluctant to attend school. Certainly, Dolly Clare soon learnt that boys and girls often react differently to the same treatment, and the Davis' household was a sound training ground for her future experience.

All the Davises had a strong sense of justice and fair play. In Emily this quality was allied to an impish sense of humour which led her into many an escapade.

The case of Manny Back was one of them. Although it had occurred more than seventy years ago. Dolly Clare recalled it clearly, and with amusement.

Manny Back had been christened Mansfield Back by his loving parents because Mansfield was the town where their courtship had taken place. Manny was the only pledge of their union, and hopelessly spoilt.

He was a big child. When Dolly Clare first met him at Beech Green School, he sat in one of the senior pupils' desks which had been moved to the junior section of the big schoolroom to accommodate his bulk.

He was not bad-looking in a florid, massive fashion, and his clothes were superior to those of his raggle-taggle neighbours. In the latter years of good Queen Victoria's reign, large families were normal, and clothes were passed down from big brother to the next in line, or cut down from father's, for money was short and, in any case, thrift and ingenuity were looked upon as virtues. A neat patch here and there, or an exquisite darn, were signs of industry as well as poverty. There were plenty of both in Beech Green.

But Manny, as an only child, fared better than most. His father was a boot-maker, and although he did not actually supply all the beautiful riding boots worn by the horse-riding gentlemen of the district, he was generally entrusted with their repair which he did very satisfactorily.

His wife had been laundry maid in good service. Together they saw to it that their only sprig was well shod and his clothes immaculate.

As much care was lavished on the boy's diet, which was unfortunate for Manny. Whereas the village children carried a home-grown apple, a plum or two, or even a couple of young carrots or some radishes as the seasons supplied them, for their morning 'stay-bit', young Manny would produce a bar of chocolate or a slice of plum-cake for his.

Like most of his fellow-pupils, he ran home for his midday meal and there received much larger and much richer helpings than they could afford. The results were predictable.

Grossly over-weight, Manny soon became the butt of his school-fellows' teasing. A strong streak of savagery runs through every child. Beech Green children, at the end of the last century, could be particularly cruel when roused. After all, it was only the toughest that survived in those days. Weaklings died in infancy, or soon fell prey to consumption, diphtheria and other diseases as yet unconquered by medical science. Those who remained were further toughened by a constant fight against poor food, poor housing, and the stark necessity of competing for work.

Jealousy, no doubt, added to the children's dislike of Manny Back. It is hard to watch a luscious slice of cake vanishing into an already over-sized face when one has only the heel of a stale loaf to satisfy the gnawing pains of youthful hunger. It is hard to see one's fellow-pupil sitting at ease in warm well-fitting boots whilst the damp chill of worn-out soles inflames one's own chilblains.

Manny took his teasing fairly well in the playground, but it was asking too much of human nature for the insults to be ignored completely. Consequently, he vented his outraged feelings on younger children on the way home.

It was unfortunate for Dolly that Manny's house lay beyond her own and that she soon became one of his favourite victims. Fearful of violence, and bewildered by this surprising animosity, poor Dolly began to dread the passage homeward. She watched the great clock on the schoolroom wall with increasing agitation as the hands crept round to four o'clock.

When they stood to sing their grace before leaving, Dolly's folded hands trembled.

Lord, keep us safe this night,
Secure from all our fears,
May angels guard us while we sleep,
Till morning light appears.
Amen.

She sang desperately, longing for the angels to be on guard on the homeward way. After all, she reasoned, her parents and Ada could guard her while she slept. Far better to have some assistance, heavenly or otherwise, to withstand Manny's attentions.

If the older Davis boys accompanied her, then Manny did not dare to approach, but more often than not they joined forces with others of their age and vanished on their own ploys in the woods and fields. Emily's presence was a comfort, but no real safeguard from attack. She put up a good fight, using fists, feet and even teeth if necessary, but Manny's bulk could easily overpower her.

Not that Manny took to fighting very often. His methods were more subtle. He was cunning enough to realize that parents would dismiss tale-telling about teasing on the way home. Actual physical harm – a bruise or scratch – might bring a furious parent to his door.

His ways were sly. He would tweak off a hair-ribbon, and hold it too high to be reached by a tearful little girl dreading a mother's wrath. He would threaten the two with stinging nettles. Once, on a hot summer's afternoon, he stirred a wasps' nest, deep in the bank, sending an enraged swarm to follow the girls whilst he escaped over the fields to his house.

He had managed to collect a number of filthy and blasphemous epithets which would have made his devoted parents' hair rise, had they heard him using them. Dolly and Emily found them shocking, and said so. Manny, needless to say, was only encouraged by his success, and used them all the more.

All in all, Manny Back was a menace to Dolly's happiness and, short of telling tales, which she had no intention of doing, there seemed to be no way in which she could take action.

But Emily did.

A day or two after the incident of the wasps, and while her arm still smarted with the stings, Emily vowed vengeance.

'It's not fair!' she said indignantly to Dolly. 'Not fair!'

'But what can we do?'

'I've thought of something to pay him back.'

'Oh Emily,' quavered Dolly, 'it will only make him worse.'

Emily's face took on a look of grim determination, but her eyes sparkled.

'I'll teach him,' said Emily.

'What will you do?' asked Dolly fearfully.

Emily surveyed her timorous friend.

'I shan't tell you,' she announced, 'because you'd be upset, and maybe tell your mum.'

'I *wouldn't!*' shouted Dolly, much hurt by this slur on her integrity.

'Well, all the same, I'm keeping it to myself,' said Emily, a trifle smugly. 'You'll know in good time.'

She began to laugh, and danced dizzily about the playground, her dark plaits bouncing. Dolly, recognizing defeat, watched her friend rejoicing in her secret, and trembled for her future downfall.

It was the custom at that time at Beech Green School, for the boys to cultivate a large kitchen garden.

It was worked communally, under Mr Finch's keen eye, and the vegetables were bought very cheaply by the boys. By the side of the communal patch lay a narrower strip, divided into a dozen or so small plots, for any boy who wanted to till a little garden of his own, providing his own seeds or plants.

Manny owned one of these, and had devoted the entire plot to the growing of marrows. Perhaps it was the affinity between the bulbous marrows and his own stoutness which made Manny's marrows grow so remarkably well. They certainly throve, and Manny plied them with manure and rainwater and watched them swell into sleek striped maturity.

The pick of the crops from the school garden went to the Beech Green flower show in September. The school had a special display, and it was considered a great honour to have something on show for parents and friends to admire. Manny was determined to put in his largest marrow.

There was one in particular which was his pride. It was dark and glossy, with a sheen on it like satin, and it was destined to be a perfect beauty. Beside its splendour, its striped brothers looked positively peaky although, in truth, they were very fine specimens as marrows go.

Early in its life, Manny had taken a stout darning needle and scratched his name neatly along its side.

MANSFIELD BACK it said in tidy capitals, and as the weeks passed the letters grew larger and plainer as the marrow increased in girth. Manny had no doubt that it would be chosen for display, and the thought of his signature emblazoned there for all Beech Green to see and admire gave him the keenest satisfaction.

After the show, the school's produce was carried to the church for Harvest Festival which always took place on the Sunday following the show day. With any luck, thought Manny, his marrow would be placed in the porch, or perhaps below the pulpit, there to dazzle the eyes of the devout.

Later still, the produce would be taken to Caxley hospital, there to be devoured by properly grateful patients. The thought of his marrow being assailed by a sharp knife, plunged into boiling water, and finally eaten, gave Manny acute pain. He turned his mind from the marrow's ultimate fate and concentrated instead on the glory which was to be his.

One evening, just as dusk was falling, a small figure might have been seen, entering the school garden through a hedge at the rear. It advanced stealthily through the gathering gloom and knelt down among Manny's marrows.

A small hand, bearing a penknife, lifted the vine-shaped leaves beneath which the prize beauty lay hidden. For three or four breathless minutes, dreadful work went on in the silent garden.

Then, back through the hedge crept Emily, revenged and unrepentant.

A week of heavy rain followed, and Manny had no need to pay much attention to his marrow bed. It 'was some ten days later that he went to water the beauties and, as he was in some hurry, on that occasion, he did not disturb the leaves which covered the prize exhibit. The dark glossy end protruded like the polished barrel of a cannon. At this rate of growth, it should be the largest marrow in the whole show, let alone on the school stall. Manny's spirits were jubilant.

Four days later, whilst he was digging with his fellows on the communal patch, two breathless children rushed up to him.

'Seen yer marrer, Man?'

Manny looked at them with distaste. There was a gloating excitement about them which made him apprehensive.

'What's up with it?'

'Someone's bin and written on it.'

'I know that,' said Manny huffily. 'I scratched my name on it weeks ago.'

'It ain't just yer name,' retorted one of the boys. He waved his arm expansively, beckoning the group to come and see for themselves.

Mr Finch had gone into school for a few minutes leaving the boys to get on alone. Carrying forks and hoes, the boys now drifted across the private plots.

The more vociferous of the two discoverers knelt down by Manny's marrow and lifted the leaves aside.

There, plain for all to see, were the words:

MANSFIELD BACK

and below in smaller capitals the one word:

BULLY

Grins split the faces of the watching boys as they observed Manny's face. It changed from pink to scarlet. then faded to a greyish pallor. And then, to everyone's horror, Manny burst into tears.

'And what,' said Mr Finch, returning, 'is the meaning of this? Get back to your work.'

'Please, sir,' said the vociferous one, 'somethink's happened to Manny's marrer.'

Mr Finch's sharp eye fell upon the tearful owner

'Let me see, boy.'

Snuffling, shaken with sobs, Manny parted the leaves and displayed the outrage. Mr Finch looked stern. He then bent down to finger the added word BULLY.

'Done recently,' he said. 'Within the last week or two.'

He straightened up and surveyed the little crowd around him.

'Well, come along, boys,' he said peremptorily. 'Own up now. You are the only people to come in this garden. Who's to blame?'

There was an unhappy silence and much foot-shuffling. Manny's sniffs grew more frequent.

Blow your nose, child,' snapped Mr Finch. Manny unfolded a beautifully clean handkerchief and did as he was bid.

'At once, boys. Who's done this mean thing to Manny?'

'I never,' said one quaking red-head, known as Copperknob.

'Not me,' whispered several more.

Mr Finch's experienced eye travelled over them all. There seemed to be very few guilty looks among them.

'Who's away today?'

Only Jim Potts, sir. He never done it.'

'And how do you know what Jimmy Potts done? Did?' Mr Finch snapped, correcting himself briskly.

Silence fell again. Mr Finch's moustache was bristling, a sure sign of danger.

'File into school as soon as you have cleaned your tools and put them back,' ordered the headmaster. 'We'll get to the bottom of this.'

Twenty minutes later, after ruthless interrogation, Mr Finch had to admit to himself that the mystery was unsolved. He could only be certain of one thing. These boys, for once in their lives, were innocent.

Most of the schoolchildren had gone home by the time Mr Finch's class were dismissed.

'We'll see about this after prayers first thing tomorrow,' announced the headmaster. 'You may dismiss. But I want you to stay behind, Manny.'

The schoolroom was very quiet as Mr Finch asked a few searching questions. He had heard rumours about Manny's behaviour, but had had no definite evidence of bullying. What he learned from Manny's faltering replies gave him some sympathy with the unknown malefactor. But justice must be done, and would be done in the morning.

Manny, still tearful, made his solitary way homeward, leaving Mr Finch to think about the incident.

What a simple way of getting one's own back, thought the headmaster, as he locked up the cupboards! Manny would be powerless to hide the incriminating word. Any attempt to disguise it would ruin the marrow's beauty. Oh, yes, this was indeed a subtle blow!

Nonetheless, thought Mr Finch, the culprit must be punished. To deface Manny's marrow, on which so much loving care had been lavished, was a cruel trick.

The next morning the whole school remained standing after prayers and heard the sorry tale. There were a few titters which Mr

Finch quelled instantly. It was pretty plain that Manny had few supporters.

'Will the boy who did this despicable thing come forward,' said Mr Finch, his eye raking the back rows where the tallest and oldest pupils stood.

'At once!' thundered Mr Finch. 'Or the whole school stays in this afternoon until we get to the bottom of this!'

From the front row, where the smallest children stood, the neat figure of Emily Davis emerged. Her dark head was on a level with the headmaster's watch chain. Her clear grey eyes looked up into his astonished face.

'I cut the word,' said Emily. Her voice was steady.

There was a stir of amusement in the ranks behind her

'Silence!' roared Mr Finch, and there was.

'Go to your classes,' he ordered. 'And you, Emily Davis, will come with me.'

He led the way into the lobby where the children hung their clothes. Dolly Clare watched Emily's small figure following the headmaster's portly one, looking like a diminutive tug following a liner. What would happen to her in the privacy of the lobby? Dolly trembled for her friend.

She need not have suffered so. Mr Finch was a just man and, after hearing Emily's side of the story, he realized that there had been provocation.

Emily's punishment was to have no play for a week. Whilst the others rushed about the playground, she was to stand by the headmaster's desk contemplating the fearful ends of those who took the law into their own hands. Alas, it was a lesson which Emily Davis never completely learned in life, and injustice was always quick to prick her into action.

As for Manny Back's marrow, it was never displayed. A lesser giant from his marrow bed gained third prize, and with this he had to be content. Dolly Clare and Emily Davis were not molested again by the biggest boy in the school, on their homeward journeys. Mr Finch saw to that.

Years later, looking back on the incident, Dolly Clare wondered if they had not under-estimated Mr Finch's sense of humour which was so successfully hidden under his stern manner.

For could it have been coincidence alone that caused the headmaster to read the story of David and Goliath at assembly next morning?

4. Wartime Memories

It was not only Emily's keen sense of justice that Dolly Clare remembered, as she moved slowly about the cottage, trying to accustom herself to the numbing sense of loss. Emily had always had courage in abundance.

It had needed courage to step forward and confess to the crime of defacing Manny's marrow. It had needed courage to stand by the headmaster's desk, dry-eyed, whilst the rest of the school played outside in the sunshine. But, to Dolly's mind, Emily's courage was supreme when she faced the darkest hour of her life as a girl in her twenties.

Dolly and Emily, as they grew up, made very few friends. The furthest they went from home was Caxley, where they went to evening classes as part of their teacher-training, or sometimes to shop for things which were unobtainable at the village stores.

Most of the young men had been known to them all their lives, had shared desks with them at the village school, and stirred them no more than a brother would. No one could accuse either Emily or Dolly of being flirtatious: many, in fact, thought them too prosaic and unromantic. Certainly, the flamboyant novelettes, so beloved by some of their contemporaries, did not interest them, and older women, gossiping by the village pump, looked sourly at the two friends when they passed.

'Heads too full o' book-learnin' to find them a husband,' said one, when the girls were out of earshot.

'They'll find themselves on the shelf, them two,' agreed another

'Too hoity-toity to go out with my Billy as asked 'em to the fair,' added a third. 'Gettin' above themselves with all this teaching nonsense '

Jealousy was at the root of such remarks. Most of their daughters were in service at twelve years old, or soon after, and to see Dolly and Emily aiming at higher things aroused maternal resentment.

It was not that the two girls were blind to male attractions. They discussed the pros and cons of the young men around as keenly as the other girls of their own age, and probably more wisely. But, whereas most of the girls talked of nothing else but their conquests and their intention of marrying, Emily and Dolly had many other equally absorbing interests. The children they taught, the books they read, the lovely natural things around them which gave them constant joy, engrossed them quite as much as the thought of marriage. Luckily for them, their work was fascinating, not something to escape from, as it was for so many of their over-worked young friends, at the mercy, very often, of dictatorial employers. If Emily and Dolly married, as they calmly assumed that they would do some day, then it would be for a positive cause, not as an escape from tedious or intolerable conditions.

It so happened that the two friends became engaged within a few weeks of each other. Dolly Clare was attracted, at first sight, by the tall young man with red hair who came to be under-gardener at the big house at Beech Green. His name was Arnold Fletcher, and his home was in Norfolk.

There was something exciting about this young man from far

away. He was quicker and gayer than the friends of Dolly's youth, and the mere fact that he found his new surroundings stimulating made Dolly look at the old familiar places with a fresh eye. He shared Dolly's love of books and music, and he brought with him a breath of the salty wind which blew so refreshingly about his native Norfolk. Their engagement was considered an excellent thing, even by the most curmudgeonly of the village folk.

Emily's choice was a local farmer's son. His name was Edgar Bennett and his father and grandfather had been tenant farmers at Springbourne, a neighbouring village, for many years.

Edgar was as tall as Dolly's Arnold, but his colouring was pale. He had ashen-fair hair, and the clear grey eyes which so often go with it. He was a quiet, gentle fellow, and the general feeling was that Emily's drive and vivacity would 'put some life' into him.

He was the eldest son and it seemed likely that he would carry on the farm when his father gave up. Two younger sons were in business in Caxley, and it looked as though Emily would live eventually in the sturdy four-square Georgian farm house set in a hollow on the flanks of the downs.

But to begin with, the young couple were to make their home in a cottage near the boundary of the Bennetts' farm and that of Harold Miller who owned the Hundred Acre field hard by the Clares' cottage.

Dolly and Emily planned to have their weddings in the autumn of 1914. By that time, Edgar would have helped to bring in the harvest and there would be a break before winter ploughing began.

But these plans were made in the spring, a few months before the outbreak of war with Germany shattered their hopes.

'Better postpone it,' said Arnold to Dolly sadly.

'We'll all be back by Christmas,' said Edgar to Emily, consoling her.

The two young men went to Caxley to enlist, one bright August day, waving from a farm wagon, crowded with fresh-faced country boys going on the same errand.

Dolly and Emily were heavy-hearted, but saw the sense of a postponement of their plans. Far better to continue steadily with their teaching while their men were away. Everyone said it would be over before long. Perhaps a spring wedding would be better still?

They were false hopes indeed. Far from being over by Christmas, as the confident had boasted, it was quite apparent, by that time, that the war could drag on indefinitely.

In February, when the year was at its coldest and most cheerless, Dolly came home from school one day to find a tear-stained letter from Arnold's parents, telling her that they had heard of his death in action. Dolly's first reaction was complete disbelief.

Someone as loving and alive as Arnold could not possibly be snuffed out like a candle flame! This was some cruel mistake. It could not be right.

It was the stricken look on her parents' faces which finally brought home to her the awful truth. Even then she could not cry, but went about her affairs, numbed with grief, in a dreadful strange calm which frightened those about her.

It was at this time of her life that Dolly felt the full strength of Emily's support. Her sympathy took a practical turn. She brought her a bunch of violets to smell, or a bottle of homemade wine to tempt her listless appetite. She persuaded Dolly to accompany her on quiet walks where the gentle sounds of trees and birds could act as a balm to her friend's torn spirits.

Emily said little about Arnold's death, unlike so many neighbours, meaning well, who poured sympathy into Dolly's ears but only succeeded in torturing the girl and distressing themselves. The fear that Edgar too might die, was constantly with Emily, but she gave no sign of it to Dolly. Outwardly, she remained cheerful and loving, and Dolly, looking back later, realized just how bravely and generously Emily gave all her strength to comfort her. There was an unselfishness and nobility about Emily, at this time, far beyond her years.

A more cruel blow was in store for Emily. One spring day, when the high clouds scudded across the blue sky above the downs, and the lambs skipped foolishly below, an urgent message came from Edgar who was fighting in France. It said simply: 'For God's sake send me a gas mask.'

The two bewildered girls had done their best with cotton wool and tape to design some poor defence against this unknown method of warfare. Together they had taken the precious parcel to Caxley, cycling through the balmy evening air filled with the music of the blackbirds' song, so that it should go by the quickest possible post from the main office in Caxley High Street.

They heard that Edgar received it, but the gas attacks continued relentlessly. Some weeks later, Edgar returned from France, a victim of gas, and was sent to a hospital, not far from Bournemouth, for long months of recovery.

Emily took the blow well. She was now headmistress of the tiny school at Springbourne, for the headmaster had enlisted as soon as war broke out. Despite the hard work which this involved, Emily made the long journey to see Edgar every weekend, staying overnight in cheap lodgings near the hospital gates.

Edgar was a wraith of his former self. His eyes looked huge in his pale wasted face, and the terrible coughing attacks, which tore his damaged lungs, tore just as cruelly at Emily's heart-strings.

But Edgar's welcome and his joy in her presence were worth every minute of the long journey. She stayed with him until the last train each Sunday, and it was often past midnight when she reached home to fall exhausted into bed.

Throughout the dismal winter Emily continued to make her journeys, and now it was Dolly's turn to be comforter. Once or twice she accompanied Emily, but she could not afford to make the trip very often. Emily herself had forgone a new winter coat and boots to pay the fare each weekend, and Dolly had insisted on giving her money as a Christmas present, so that she could visit Edgar as often as possible.

Gradually, Edgar improved. They made their marriage plans anew. Now they would have a summer wedding.

Edgar was moved to a convalescent home not far from the hospital. It was an easier journey for Emily, with one less change by railway.

She was as blithe as a summer bird as the days grew longer. She and Dolly set about preparing the cottage which had been waiting empty for so long.

The two girls spent the long light evenings distempering the walls and scrubbing out cupboards and floors. There were wide serene views from the cottage windows, looking down over the sloping downs dotted with the sheep of Edgar's farm. They would perch on the wooden window seat or on upturned buckets in the porch, and revel in the last rays of the sun as they rested from their labours. Sometimes, they took a simple meal of cheese and biscuits and would sit outside, their hair lifted by the soft breeze, gazing at the view which would soon be Emily's daily one.

These busy, but tranquil, hours did much to restore Dolly's spirits, and her own sense of loss was lessened by Emily's bubbling happiness. It was plain that Edgar would never be fit for active service again. As soon as he was released from the convalescent home he would return to the farm to work as best he could. His future, it seemed, held no more war-like excursions, and Dolly rejoiced for her friend.

Doubly bitter was it then when the blow fell. One evening of golden sunlight, only a few weeks before the appointed wedding day, Dolly arrived at the cottage to find Emily with a letter on her lap, and tears rolling down her ashen cheeks.

She handed the letter to Dolly without a word. It was a short note from Edgar stating baldly that he had fallen in love with one of the nurses and that they planned to marry as soon as possible.

'I don't deserve you anyway,' the letter ended. How true that was! thought Dolly, putting her arms round Emily's shaking frame.

They sat thus for hours it seemed, while the sun grew lower and the sheep's distant cries came to them through the open windows.

At last, Emily rose and left the house, followed by Dolly. She locked the front door and put the key and the letter together into her belt.

'Emily?' questioned Dolly, searching her friend's resolute face for an answer.

'He's made his choice,' said Emily, taking a deep breath 'I'll abide by it.'

'But won't you try and see him?' asked Dolly.

'Never!' said Emily. 'It's her house now. I can't bear to look at it ever again.'

From that day Emily Davis had done her best never to look upon the little cottage where she had dreamed of happiness. It was Dolly and Mrs Davis who had removed Emily's curtains and the few pieces of furniture which were already put into the downstairs rooms.

It was they who disposed of them, for Emily would have nothing to do with this bitter clearing-up. The wounds were too fresh and raw to bear this added salt rubbed into them. For a time, she spoke to no one about the tragedy, but gradually she brought herself to say a little to Dolly, and as the months and years passed, Emily faced life without Edgar with a courage which was typical.

Only Dolly guessed how deeply Emily was wounded by this affair. Edgar married his nurse one July day of thunderstorms and torrential rain. Maybe it was augury, thought Dolly, for the years that followed were stormy ones indeed for Edgar. He had married a virago, it turned out, and despite three bonny children there was little happiness in the cottage on the downs, and later in the farm-house which they took over at his father's death.

There was no doubt in Dolly's mind that Emily's tragedy was far more difficult to bear than her own. Edgar lived in the same small community, his marriage under constant scrutiny by his neighbours. Emily was forced, throughout her long life, to keep a still tongue and a calm face when informed of Edgar's doings.

Her love for him never wavered. It was the kind of love, Dolly often thought, which one read of in old ballads, where the woman was called upon to endure all manner of humiliations and tests before her lord would acknowledge her. But in ballads, this faithful love was rewarded. Emily's was not.

The fact that Edgar's marriage was a miserable one added to her unhappiness. Her spirit was too fine to find consolation in the 'I-told-you-so' attitude of many of her neighbours. It was no comfort to Emily to know that Edgar had chosen wrongly, but only an added tragedy.

She did her best to avoid meeting him, sometimes going some distance afield to miss him at work on the farm. Never, if she could help it, would she pass the cottage. But, one day, some eight or nine years after his marriage, she met him face to face unexpectedly, and they spoke a few words. She told Dolly about this encounter many years later.

She was walking up a rough cart track which led to the top of the downs. Spindleberries grew at the edge of a little copse on the chalky lower slopes, and she was on her way to collect some for a nature study lesson next day. Suddenly, there was a crackling of twigs from the copse, and Edgar emerged, holding a gun. He drew in his breath sharply.

'I'm sorry, Emily. Hope I didn't scare you. I'm after jays.'

Emily, speechless, shook her head.

He leant his gun against the green-rimmed trunk of an elder tree and came towards her. She looked steadily into his face, and what she saw there made her start to run.

He caught her arm, and looked sadly and longingly into her eyes.
'Oh, Emily,' he said, 'what a mess I've made of it!'

'Edgar, please,' protested Emily. 'This will do no good.' She struggled to get away but he held her arm firmly.

'Hear me for one minute.'

Emily stood still. She was more stirred than she could believe. That steadfast love, which had never wavered, was now mingled with pity for the unhappy man before her.

'I made the mistake of my life when I chose Eileen. Life's hell I'm not complaining – I brought it on myself. But when the gossips tell you tit-bits about our cat-and-dog life, Em, you can multiply it by a hundred.'

'So bad?' whispered Emily, shaken.

'So bad,' repeated Edgar. He released her arm and turned away.

'I'm sorry – *truly* sorry,' said Emily. 'You deserve happiness after all you went through in the war. But, Edgar, try not to speak to me again.'

Her lips quivered, and the elder tree, and the gun, and the man were blurred by the tears which filled her eyes.

He turned towards her, and Emily saw that tears too were on his cheek.

'*Please*,' cried Emily, 'because – can't you see? I just can't bear it!'

And, weeping, she stumbled back the way which she had come, leaving him there, forlorn.

Poor brave Emily, thought Dolly Clare, standing now in Emily's room which she would enter no more. She had carried the memory and the love of that man to the grave with her. Courage such as hers could never completely die.

And Edgar, now an old, old man, how would he face the news of Emily's death? Did he still remember the girl whom he had once loved, so many years ago?

5. Edgar Hears the News

Edgar Bennett sat in the September sunlight and surveyed his gnarled old hands ruefully. The dratted joints were more swollen than ever! Fat lot of good that doctor's muck had done him!

He had once been proud of those hands, now mottled with the brown stains of old age. They had held a plough steady all day long, wielded a scythe, harnessed scores of horses, and used a cricket bat, with such skill, that at least one century from Edgar Bennett, each season, was celebrated at Beech Green in the old days.

Now they were fit for nothing but pulling on his clothes each morning, and then with pain, or peeling the confounded potatoes that Eileen put before him every day.

'No need to sit idle,' she said sharply to him. 'Just because you can't get about as you used to, it don't follow that you're helpless.'

He looked at them now, swimming about in a bowl of muddy water on the bench beside him. He sat in an old wooden armchair which had been his father's, close by the back door of the farm house.

It was a sheltered spot, and whenever the weather was fine, Edgar struggled out there with the aid of his stick and looked across the fields which he had sown and tended until ill-health had forced him to retire, two or three years ago.

His son John ran the farm now, and lived in the main part of the farm house. Edgar and Eileen had the old kitchen and two other rooms downstairs for their quarters, and the old dairy had been turned into a bathroom.

One way and another, thought Edgar, listening to the distant combine churring round the farm's largest field, they were pretty lucky. No stairs to worry about, for one thing, but no one knew how much he missed the glorious view of the downs from the window of the main bedroom. It had never failed to hearten him – in good weather or bad.

The fruit trees in the garden obscured the vista, and now Edgar's horizon was bounded by the hawthorn hedge which enclosed the farm garden. It was all pretty enough, he supposed, looking with lack-lustre eye at the dahlias and early Michaelmas daisies which John's wife Annie tended so zealously; but it was not a patch on the rolling downs, undulating as far as the eye could see, filling a man with wonder and awe.

He sighed, and fished in the bowl of water for the first potato His right hand held an ancient steel knife with a horn handle. It had been new when he and Eileen married at the end of the First World War. Now, the blade was broken short, and it had come down to kitchen work. Edgar found it comfortable to manage with his twisted fingers.

He peeled carefully, getting the parings as thin as possible. Eileen was a stickler for wasting nothing. Even the eyes must be gouged out with the least possible waste. It was a ticklish job, thought Edgar, bending over his task in the sunlight.

And one which Eileen had always hated, he remembered. When she had given up her nursing to marry him she made it clear that cooking was a penance to her. Housework she enjoyed. Her training as a nurse made her standards of cleanliness uncommonly high – too dratted uncomfortably high, Edgar said – and the farm house gleamed from every surface capable of being polished. The place reeked of cleaning materials. If it wasn't bees-wax on the furniture, it was methylated spirits from the rag which cleaned the windows, or the breath-catching pungency of the bleaching liquid which Eileen liked to use for the sink and drains.

Now that the house was mainly in Annie's hands, it smelt less like an institution and more like a home, thought Edgar. The smell of baking pervaded the house. Vases of roses or narcissi, or wallflowers – or whatever fragrant blooms were in season in the garden – gave out their own sweetness. It did not please Eileen.

'Everlasting petals all over the place,' she grumbled to Edgar. 'Messy things, flowers. Spoil the polish.'

'I like 'em,' said Edgar mildly. 'And in any case, Annie's entitled to do what she likes in her own home. Some young women would have turned us out. In-laws don't make the best house-mates, you know.'

Eileen snorted. There was small chance of getting Edgar to take her side, as well she knew. From the very first days of marriage she had discovered that, despite his gentle ways and apparent submissiveness, there was an obstinate streak in Edgar's character. She, who loved to rule, found that there were some occasions when her husband stood fast. Her temper was fiery, her voice shrill. Neither improved with age, but Edgar had grown used to these outbursts, treating them with a stubborn silence which drove Eileen to even greater fury.

Luckily, the three children had inherited their father's nature. In some ways, it made matters even worse for Eileen, for there was no one to answer her with equal fire. Her sharp tongue met little verbal resistance. John, the eldest, went so far as to laugh at his mother's tantrums as he grew to manhood, and his easy attitude did much to help his wife Annie to be philosophical about the old people's presence in the house.

'I'd put up with anything for the old man,' John said. 'He bears the brunt of it, poor old chap. Don't hurt us to have 'em here, if we act sensible, and I'm not seeing my mum and dad turned out of their home at their age.'

The two younger boys, equally mild-mannered, worked in Caxley and were both married. Sometimes they came out on a Sunday afternoon to see the old people, but they did not visit very often, and as neither enjoyed letter-writing, Eileen and Edgar heard little of them, despite their presence within five miles of the farm.

'All the same, children,' Eileen said tartly. 'Ungrateful lot. You brings 'em up and gets no thanks for it.'

'Didn't ask to come, did 'em?' replied Edgar. 'You be thankful they ain't turned out jail-birds or worse. We've got three fine boys, all doing well. What more d'you want?'

Looking back, turning the wet potato in his swollen fingers, Edgar wondered how many days of his marriage had passed without some outburst from Eileen. God, she was a nagger, if ever there was one! What madness had made him take her on in the first place?

A shadow fell across his armchair, and he looked up to see Tom More, the postman. He held out a letter.

'Shouldn't bother to open it,' he remarked. 'Looks like a bill.'

'You been through 'em all?' asked Edgar jocularly. 'Any good news?'

'No,' said Tom, settling on the bench near the bowl of potatoes. 'Got a bit of bad, though.'

'Oh? What's up?'

'Poor old Emily Davis.'

Edgar drew in his breath sharply. Tom More was too young to know what Emily meant to him, but he bent over the knife in his hand so that his face was hidden.

'She's gone,' continued Tom. 'Saw Dolly Clare half an hour back. She said they took their evening toddle up the field, had some supper and Emily was as right as rain at bed-time. Next morning she found her dead in bed.'

'I'm sorry,' said Edgar huskily. 'Very sorry. She was at school with me.'

There was a pause. From a distance the hum of the combine continued. Close at hand, one of the farm cats came round the corner of the house, mewing plaintively.

'How's Dolly Clare taken it? She got anyone there with her?'

'Seems all right. Looks a bit pale-like. I heard she was asked to go up Annetts' place, but she said "No".'

'Home's best at times like that,' agreed Edgar. His voice was shaky, and Tom More noticed that his hands shook too. These old people never liked to hear of their generation dying. Brought it too near home, no doubt. Maybe he shouldn't have told the old boy.

He shifted uneasily, and gave a gusty sigh.

'Ah well, must be getting along. You're looking very fit, Edgar. See us all out, you will. 'Morning, now.'

He ambled off towards the gate, hoping that he had made amends with his last remarks. Must be rotten, getting old, thought Tom, turning for a final wave at the gate.

Edgar was still bent over his task. But the shaky hands were not working, and Edgar's gaze was not upon the potato he now held, but upon a vision of Emily Davis, a life-time ago, as he remembered her.

The first time that Emily had come to Edgar's notice was on the occasion of her confession at school assembly. Edgar had been standing in the back row, among the oldest boys at Beech Green School, due to leave in a few months for the waiting world of hard work.

The affair of Manny's marrow had amused them. Mr Finch's threat of keeping in the whole school did not. He was a man who kept his word, and Edgar and his school-mates had too many activities to attend to after school to welcome any restriction of their liberty.

It was with relief then, as well as amusement, that the bigger boys saw little Emily Davis step out to take her punishment.

'Got some spunk, that little 'un,' one boy had commented, as they filed out.

'All them Davises have,' said another. It was something which Edgar was to find out for himself years later.

Emily Davis did not cross his path again for some time. He saw her occasionally about the village, usually in the company of Dolly Clare, but she meant nothing to him. He was busy on the farm, and his only relaxation was the cricket which he played on summer Saturday afternoons whenever the work on the farm allowed.

But one autumn evening, when the beech trees were ablaze on the road to Caxley, and the blue smoke of autumn bonfires drifted through the village, Edgar encountered Emily.

It had been a good harvest that year, and Edgar had taken a wagon laden with sacks of wheat to Caxley Station. When the wagon was empty, he had reloaded it with sacks of coal, ready for the winter, and set off on the return journey. He was pleasantly tired after the heavy work, and looking forward to an evening meal and early bed.

Perched high on the plank seat at the front of the wagon, he had a fine view of the surrounding countryside.

The fruit trees in the cottage gardens were weighed down with apples and plums. In one garden, a cottager was bent over his rows of bronze onions, turning the tops for final ripening. In another, a woman was tending a bonfire of dead pea-sticks and dried weeds.

Everywhere there were the signs of the dying year, and the nutty fragrance of autumn hung in the air.

'Soon be Harvest Festival,' said Edgar aloud to the massive haunches of Daisy, the old cart-horse, moving stolidly along between the shafts. She snorted in reply, and shook her shaggy head. She was a companionable animal, and liked the sound of a human voice.

The thought of Manny's marrow, destined never to be the centre-piece of a Harvest Festival, flashed back to Edgar. It was the first time he had remembered it for years, and he savoured the memory now, as Daisy descended the steep hill leading to distant Beech Green.

At the bottom, there was a sharp bend, and as Daisy rounded it, she pulled suddenly to one side.

'Whoa there!' said Edgar, startled. 'All right, old girl!'

On the verge, at the side of the road, knelt Emily Davis beside a bicycle. Her small hands were black, her hair dishevelled, and her hat hung from a spray of yellowing hawthorn in the hedge.

'What's up then?' asked Edgar, leaping down.

'The chain's come off,' said Emily.

'Here, you hold it upright,' ordered Edgar, 'and I'll have a go.'

Emily struggled to her feet, and did as she was told; Daisy wandered towards the grass and browsed happily, tearing great mouthfuls and munching noisily.

'Funny thing,' said Edgar. 'I was thinking about you.'

'Honest?' said Emily surprised. 'What about me?'

'Manny's marrow.'

Emily flushed and looked disconcerted.

'Oh that!' she said discomfited. 'I try and forget that. It was a mean trick really, but that boy got my dander up.'

'You did all right,' said Edgar robustly. He lifted the back wheel from the gritty road and spun it swiftly.

'This chain's pretty slack,' he observed. 'Tell you what. You climb up with me and we'll put the old grid on the back. Can't do much to that chain without some tools, and if you ride it like it is, then ten to one it'll be off again in a hundred yards.'

'Thanks,' said Emily. He watched her climb up to the front of the wagon, as nimbly as a monkey despite her long skirt. He heaved up the bicycle, lodging it securely between two sacks of coal, and clambered aloft beside her.

'Come up, Daisy!' he commanded, and the old horse left her meal reluctantly and clip-clopped steadily towards home.

'Where've you been then?' asked Edgar, making conversation.

'Caxley. At evening class. You have to, you know, while you're a pupil teacher.'

'D'you like it?'

'Teaching? Yes, I do – better now than when I started. Are you still with your father?'

'Yes. And I'll stay that way, I reckon. I'll take over the farm gradually, I expect, when he gets past it. Not that there's any sign of that yet. He's a tough old party, thank God.'

They jogged along peaceably. The air was growing chilly as the sun slipped down behind the downs.

'Do you go to Caxley much?' asked Emily, pulling her jacket round her.

'Next trip'll be to the Michaelmas Fair,' said Edgar. He looked at her suddenly. She'd grown into a nice-looking girl, small and neat, with dark hair piled untidily on top of her head. True, she had a black grease mark from the bicycle chain on one cheek, but it didn't detract from her charms, to Edgar's appraising eye.

'What about coming with me?' urged Edgar. Emily turned wide grey eyes upon him.

'Well, I *was* going with Dolly and my brother Albert,' she began uncertainly.

'Tell you what,' said Edgar. 'Dad'll let me have the little cart, and I'll pick you three up. How's that?'

'That would be lovely!' said Emily, glowing with pleasure. 'You say what time and we'll be ready waiting.'

'Good,' replied Edgar. 'Let's say half past six. I'll be there.'

They drew up at the end of the lane where the Davises lived. Their thatched roof was visible a few yards down the road.

Edgar jumped down and released the bicycle from its lodging place.

'I'll wheel it down for you,' he offered. 'Old Daisy'll wait for me.'

'No, don't you bother,' said Emily hastily. 'It's no distance. Albert'll be home now, and I'll get him to make the chain safe. And thank you *very* much, Edgar, for the lift, and for helping me.'

'No trouble,' said Edgar. 'I'll look out for you on Saturday week then.'

'It will be lovely,' said Emily, giving him a dazzling smile. My word, thought Edgar, she's getting quite a beauty, is little Emily!

She waved goodbye and set off down the lane. Edgar watched her until a bend in the road hid her from sight.

'That's a real nice little maid,' observed Edgar to Daisy.

Daisy snorted in agreement and quickened her pace, advancing towards her stable and a good feed. There had been enough dallying — that was her opinion.

6. Edgar and Emily

Old Edgar put a peeled potato carefully in the saucepan and straightened his legs in the sunshine. He had been to many Michaelmas Fairs since that one with Emily over half a century ago, but it was that particular occasion which stayed so clearly in his memory.

How slowly the days had passed after that first encounter with Emily on the road from Caxley! He had been surprised by the strength of his desire to see her again, and looked forward eagerly to the Saturday evening.

It had gone well, right from the start, he remembered.

His father had given permission willingly for the little cart to be used on the Saturday evening, and had come upon his son, during that afternoon, polishing the brass work on cart and harness with unusual industry. The long black cushions, buttoned and horse-hair stuffed, which ran along each side of the cart were dusted, and the bottom of the cart swept clean.

'Who's the girl?' asked Edgar's father, with a smile.

'I'm picking up Albert Davis and Dolly Clare,' said Edgar, trying to sound casual, and failing utterly.

'And who's to be your lady for the evening?'

'Well,' said Edgar, studying a brass stud closely, 'Emily Davis is coming too.'

'Look after her then,' replied the old man. 'I like the Davises. You treat that girl right, mind.'

'Of course, dad,' said Edgar shortly. The old man continued on his way.

The three were waiting for him at the end of the lane where he had dropped Emily after the bicycle incident. She was dressed in a bright scarlet coat, which showed up her dark hair to advantage. What Dolly wore, Edgar had no idea. His eyes were only for Emily.

The roundabouts and swingboats were close by the statue of Queen Victoria in the market square at Caxley. She looked faintly disapproving, standing there among the cheerful vulgarity of the fair.

Naphtha lights flared, music blared away, children screamed as they careered round and round on the galloping horses, and the stall-holders shouted their attractions with lungs of brass.

The din was unbelievable. After sampling all the side-shows, and having taken two trips on the roundabout and switchback, Emily begged to be allowed to stand still for a few minutes to calm her whirling senses. Dolly and Albert were high in a swingboat above them.

'Come down to the river for a minute,' said Edgar, leading the way, and Emily was glad to obey.

After the tumult of the market square, the riverside was cool and quiet. A little breeze rustled the autumn leaves, and Emily welcomed the refreshing air on her hot face. They leant companionably, side by side, on the bridge, and watched the placid Cax slipping gently along below them, gleaming dully like pewter in the night light. Somewhere nearby, a splash told of a moorhen or water-rat going about its business. The distant racket of the fair was muted and the native sounds of water and trees in harmony made the age-old music of the night.

Emily sighed happily.

'Enjoying yourself?' asked Edgar, putting one hand on hers as it rested on the wooden rail.

Emily nodded, and did not remove her hand.

Emboldened, Edgar put his disengaged arm round the red coat.

'Emily –' he began urgently, but Emily wriggled away

'Oh, Edgar, don't spoil it!'

'What d'you mean – spoil it? I was only going to say, won't you come out with me again soon?'

Emily came to rest again, and looked down upon the Cax for a time before answering.

'I'd like to, Edgar, I really would. Only—'

'Only what?'

Emily turned to face him.

'Only this. I don't know if you take out lots of girls – but – well, I don't want to be one of a lot. That's all!'

Edgar laughed, and put his arm round her again. This time she did not wriggle away.

'Oh, Emily! You're a plain speaker, and no mistake. I can tell you truly – if you're willing to be my girl, then you won't have no others to worry about. You're the only one for me.'

'But, Edgar, don't say that! How d'you know how you'll feel in a month or so? We hardly know each other.'

'I know how I feel well enough,' said Edgar soberly.

'Well, I don't.'

'You'll get to know,' said Edgar comfortably. 'What about coming to the dance next week?'

'Thank you,' said Emily, in a small voice.

Edgar bent to kiss her cheek, but Emily, shying away, caused him to land a rather wet one on her brow.

They laughed together, and Emily moved away.

'Let's go back,' she said. 'We haven't tried the swingboats yet.'

Together, hand in hand, they returned, like happy children, to the bustle of the market square.

Theirs had been an easy courtship, thought Edgar, looking back. There were no lovers' quarrels, no misunderstandings and no parental obstacles to overcome.

That auspicious Michaelmas Fair was in 1913, and throughout that winter and the following spring the young lovers were happy making plans for a wedding the following year.

'Better be October,' said Edgar practically. 'Have the harvest in nicely by then.'

'So I take second place after harvest!' quipped Emily, teasing him.

'As a farmer's wife, you always will,' replied Edgar. 'You know that without being told.'

Emily spent her evenings crocheting yards and yards of lace to edge tablecloths and towels. She still taught at Springbourne School during the day, and most of her earnings now went on linen for her bottom drawer

Dolly Clare and Arnold Fletcher were also engaged, and the four friends had many outings together. Edgar grew less shy as their social circle widened, but there were one or two people whom he disliked and with them he had great difficulty in making conversation.

Dolly Clare's sister Ada was one of them. She and her husband Harry Roper ran a thriving greengrocery business in Caxley, and she invited the four to supper on several occasions.

There was a boldness about Ada which Edgar found highly distasteful. He hated boastfulness and pretence, and in the Ropers' establishment he found both in abundance. What Harry Roper called 'ambition' or 'getting on in the world', Edgar, with his solid country background, called 'doing down your neighbour', or 'cutting a dash'. Edgar felt fairly sure that Harry was not above using some doubtful methods of making a quick profit – all in the name of good business – and he did his best to avoid mixing with Ada and Harry.

Luckily, Emily was as distrustful of the two as Edgar himself.

'She was always top dog at home,' Emily told him, 'though Dolly's worth ten of her. She did some pretty mean things at school that I could tell you about, but won't. I never took to her.'

In the early summer of 1914, Ada's first baby was born, and Dolly was delighted to be godmother to John Francis.

It so happened that Emily and Edgar encountered Ada in Caxley one Saturday afternoon, pushing the baby in a very fashionable pram. Of course, they stopped to admire him.

The child was plump and pink, his dark head resting on a pale blue satin pillow decorated with lace and ribbons. He was asleep, and in his mouth was a dummy.

'Shall I take it out now he's asleep?' asked Emily, bending over the child. Ada gave her a cold glance.

'No, thank you. I can look after my own baby, I hope.'

'I'm sorry,' said Emily, discomfited. 'I know lots of babies use comforters, but our doctor told me that they can cause adenoids when the child's older. Lots of my children at school breathe through their mouths instead of their noses – and he says comforters may be the cause.'

'Maybe he's a busybody,' said Ada pointedly. 'I must be getting along.'

She swept away up Caxley High Street, and Edgar pulled a face at Emily.

'You copped it then,' he remarked. 'And you know, you did ask for it.'

'I don't care,' said Emily stubbornly. 'That baby didn't need it when he was asleep, and I don't mind betting he'll get adenoids, and probably protruding top teeth as well, if Ada lets him go on with it!'

It so happened that the years were to prove that Emily Davis was correct. Needless to say, it did not endear her to Ada Roper.

'The cheek of it,' she had said to Harry later that day. 'A spinster like her – telling a mother what to do with her own child! I fairly froze her, I can tell you. Adenoids indeed! She and that doctor of hers want their heads seen to!'

Edgar and Emily were never invited to the Ropers' house again. They were not surprised – only mightily relieved.

★

They had been happy days, old Edgar mused, leaning back in his wooden armchair and closing his eyes against the dazzle of the warm sunshine.

No one, least of all young lovers, bothered about the political happenings across the Channel. The course of the seasons rolled steadily onward. Ploughing, harrowing, drilling, planting – the long days in the fields and farmyard passed swiftly away, and their wedding day was only two or three months ahead. The two were as blithe as nesting birds, when the blow fell.

War with Germany was declared on 4 August 1914, and within a month Edgar was training in Dorset with other young men from the Caxley area. He and Arnold Fletcher had leave at the same time in November, and both came to Beech Green to see their girls. For Arnold, it was the last time, for he was killed by a hand-grenade thrown into his trench near the Ypres Canal, one cold and cruel February day in 1915.

The months which Edgar spent fighting in France were like a nightmare to him. Remembering them now, in the September sunlight, so many years later, they still seemed unbelievable.

The constant noise, the habitual grip of fear, the stench of rotting corpses, the rats, the sea of grey mud broken only by the stark splinters of shattered trees, were so alien to the young Edgar's home background of quiet green beauty that he was in a constant state of horror and shock.

Some men managed to keep up a stout heart, even addressing their dead comrades with cheerful badinage as they passed up and down the trenches. This ghastly bonhomie Edgar found callous and macabre. His gentle nature was crushed and appalled by the sights and sounds around him.

When the gas attacks finally caused his collapse, and he was invalided out of the army, he returned to England with a thankful heart.

A thankful heart, indeed, remembered old Edgar, stirring uncomfortably in his armchair, but a changed one too.

What went wrong with his love for Emily in those dreadful months that followed? To say that his war experience had unsettled him was to make the whole affair seem too slight and uncomplicated. But, nevertheless, that was the root of the matter.

Lying in his white bed at the Bournemouth hospital, he had gazed at the green trim lawns and the leafy trees, remembering his comrades in that grey, shattered landscape overseas.

On some days the English soil trembled with the thunder from the distant guns in France. Edgar rolled his aching head from side to side in sympathetic anguish.

It was as though his mind were split in two. One half was here, with his suffering body, in this quiet room with birds and flowers outside. The other half, writhing and tortured, still inhabited that nightmare world of dying men and hopelessness. Perhaps there was an element of guilt in poor Edgar's mind at this time. Other men were in danger. He was safe. But should it be so? He tortured himself with thoughts of Arnold Fletcher, and other young men who had been his friends at Beech Green, sharing his background, his work and his play – men who had ploughed, sown and threshed with him, batted and bowled on Beech Green's cricket pitch, shared his laughter and his hopes. Where were they now? And could he ever return, to face those who had loved them, seeing the sadness – and perhaps the resentment – in their eyes?

When Emily came on her weekly visits, the first flood of joy at her approach gradually ebbed away in the face of these secret fears. Outwardly, Edgar seemed calm, but Emily sensed that all was not well with him. There was a barrier now across the easy passage of their affection. She put it down to general physical weakness, and to the horrors which a sensitive spirit like Edgar's would find hard to overcome. She never doubted that all would be well in time.

Remembering that steadfast trust, old Edgar groaned aloud, and buried his face in his hands. He should have waited! He should have waited! All would have come right for them both if he had been patient – as patient as poor Emily was!

He rocked himself to and fro. To think that something which happened nigh on sixty years ago could still give such pain!

He remembered his terrible tears when Emily had gone each week to catch the last possible train back to Beech Green. It was not her going which upset him so dreadfully, but the knowledge that he would never be able to face life with her. For in his present state he never wanted to see Beech Green again, or those who lived there.

He wanted to run away from all that had happened, to start afresh, where no one knew him, where he could make a new beginning, leaving the pain and heartbreak behind.

The Irish nurse, Eileen, had comforted him during these outbursts. She was kind and motherly, it seemed to Edgar, ready to hold his hot head against the starched bib of her apron. Later, he realized, she never spoke of Emily or his return to her.

In his weakness, he clung to her for support and advice. She gave both freely, never displaying the quick temper and sharp tongue which made her so heartily disliked by the other nurses.

In truth, Eileen Kennedy was looking for a husband, and in Edgar she thought she had found one who would suit her very well. She liked the idea of being a farmer's wife. She knew that Edgar would follow his father one day, and she enjoyed country life. Also, she was tired of nursing. She was twenty-five and was determined to marry. The fact that Edgar was already engaged weighed with her not at all. Emily she considered a poor thing. Victory should be easy.

She conducted her side of the campaign with ruthless subtlety. Circumstances were on her side. She was with him constantly, and he was dependent on her for all his comforts. She was careful to keep out of Emily's way, when she paid her visits, so that her rival's suspicions were not aroused. Edgar, weak in body and torn in spirit, gave way with little resistance. Eileen, as a young woman, had physical charms which faded after a few years of marriage, but in her nursing days she was trim and comely, with fair hair neatly waving under her flighty starched cap.

By the time Edgar's convalescence came, and he was moved a few miles away, there was a firm understanding between them. Now there was a dream-like quality, for Edgar, when Emily visited him. It was as if she were a ghost from the past – that past he wanted so desperately to forget.

He was too weak to tell her about his plans. This cowardice was to colour his whole life. It haunted him whenever he was unable to sleep, in the long years which lay ahead. He never forgave himself

Eileen encouraged him to keep silence.

'You aren't up to a scene,' she persuaded him. 'Write her a letter. You can put it all so much better in a letter.'

The little she had seen of Emily made her realize that she would accept the situation more readily with a letter before her. She recognized Emily's pride, and suspected rightly that she cared enough for Edgar to abide by his decision, no matter how cruel it might seem.

The scheme worked. Edgar was freed from his engagement, and he turned to a triumphant Eileen. Emily, her life broken, continued as best she could. No other man came into her life. For Emily, Edgar was her only love, both then and for ever.

It was a week or two after his engagement to the nurse, that Edgar first had an inkling of her true nature.

He broached the subject of where they should live when he had quite recovered.

'Why, Beech Green, surely? You say there's a house there for you,' said Eileen briskly.

Edgar gazed at her in dismay.

'But you know how I feel about going back. I want to start somewhere quite new.'

'Who'd have you, except your father?' asked Eileen flatly.

'I expect I could get a job with another farmer,' began Edgar, much shaken.

'Another farmer would want a full day's work from you,' said Eileen. 'Your dad will let you go your own pace for a bit. And there's the house. It sounds just right for us.'

Edgar roused himself.

'But surely, you wouldn't want to go back there, where everyone knows about me and Emily. You'd feel uncomfortable.'

Eileen gave a hard laugh.

'It'd take more than Emily Davis and a parcel of gossipers to make me uncomfortable. She had her chance, and lost it. It's our life now, and we'd be fools to throw away a house and a job ready-made for you.'

'But, Eileen –' protested Edgar, tears of weakness filling his eyes.

'No buts about it,' said Eileen ruthlessly. 'It's Beech Green for us, so get used to the idea.'

She whisked out of the room, leaving Edgar to his melancholy thoughts. For the first time, he began to realize that he had made a mistake, and one which was to cost him dear.

★

Old Edgar sighed, and reached for the last potato.

Humiliation, self-reproach, gnawing remorse and a lifetime of bitterness had been the result of a few vital months of sheer cowardice. God knows he had paid heavily for his mistake! Worse still, he had made innocent, loving Emily suffer too. The encounter by the wood had told him clearly all that he had suspected – that Emily's love remained constant, and that his did too. It had been his lot to see the finest woman he had ever known tortured, year after year, on his account.

And now she had gone.

He bent his grizzled head over the last of his task, and a tear rolled down his cheek.

'What's up?' snapped his wife, appearing suddenly, throwing a shadow between him and the sunshine.

'Sun in my eyes,' lied Edgar.

But he knew that, for him, the sun would never be as dazzling again.

7. Ada Makes Plans

The news of Emily's death spread rapidly when *The Caxley Chronicle* made its weekly appearance. Most readers turned fairly quickly, after reading the headlines, to the column headed 'Births, Marriages and Deaths', choosing the one of the three divisions most appealing to them, according to the age of the reader.

Ada Roper, widow of the prosperous greengrocer Harry, and sister of Dolly Clare, naturally looked first at the 'Deaths'. When one is in one's eighties there is a certain macabre pleasure in reading about those whom one has outlived.

She sat in her sunny drawing room on this shimmering September morning, a cup of coffee beside her, and a magnifying glass in her hand the better to read the small print.

The house, 'Harada', which Harry had built in the twenties, weathered the years well, and though her son John had once tried to persuade her to move to something smaller, Ada was resolute in her refusal.

'Why should I?'

'Because it's so expensive, for one thing. Fuel, rates, furnishings – and so much housework. I could easily find you a nice little flat –'

'I don't want a nice little flat. And anyway, I shan't need to buy any more furniture, and if I did move into a poky little place some-where, what should I do with all these nice pieces your Dad and I collected over the years?'

'You could sell them,' suggested John.

'Never!' cried his mother. 'No, John. This is my home and I'm stopping here. I've quite enough money to see me out, thanks to the business, and with Alice to help me the work is very light.'

Alice was the companion who had come to live with Ada soon after Harry's death. She was a gentle soul, herself a widow, but a penniless one, and glad to have a comfortable home and pocket money in return for an amount of work which would have daunted many a younger woman.

John, seeing the position pretty clearly, was sensible enough to insist on plenty of reliable daily help. Alice, he knew, was worth her weight in gold as a companion. She was genuinely devoted to his mother and took her somewhat over-bearing ways with cheerful docility.

If she left, it would be impossible to find another person so amenable. John had no desire to have his mother living at his own house. His wife and children were positively opposed to the idea when he had once broached the subject tentatively.

'No fear!' said his wife flatly.

'Grandma? Live here? Oh no!' cried his children. And though he had upbraided them with their selfishness, secretly he was very relieved. If his mother was happy to squander her money on that great house, then he would see that things were arranged to keep her there in contentment. But, now and again, a little secret resentment clouded John's thoughts. What would there be left, when the old lady died, if she continued to live in this way?

John's good business head always ruled his heart, which is why his parents' shop continued to thrive under his management.

At the time of Emily Davis's death he was a man in his late fifties with the dark florid good looks of his father.

A fine moustache and an expensive dental plate improved his looks as he grew older. As a young man, the slightly protruding top teeth had given him a rabbity look. Whether the comforter, abhorred by Emily, and the subsequent thumb-sucking had anything to do with it, one could not be sure. His mother, rather naturally, thought not. But Emily's words rankled for many years, nevertheless.

John took infinite pains with his clothes, going to London for his suits, which did not endear him to the local tailors. He presided over the shop in well-cut tweeds or worsteds, his dark hair carefully brushed, his expensive shoes as glossy as horse chestnuts.

His wife looked across the breakfast table, on this September morning, and thought how remarkably young he looked as he read *The Caxley Chronicle*.

'I see Aunt Dolly's Emily has gone,' he said, eyes fixed upon the paper.

'Poor old thing,' said his wife perfunctorily. 'But she must have been terribly old.'

'About the same age as mother, I should guess. They were at school together, I know.'

'What will happen to Aunt Dolly?'

John lowered the paper thoughtfully.

'I don't know. I really don't know.'

He rose, tugging at his jacket and smoothing his hair.

'She really shouldn't be alone there,' said his wife solicitously. 'Anything might happen.'

'I might drive over and see her,' said John, kissing her swiftly. 'It's rotten getting old. This'll cut up Aunt Dolly badly.'

During the day he turned over in his mind the possibilities for Dolly Clare.

Could she be persuaded, he wondered, to leave the Beech Green cottage and make her home at 'Harada'? There were points in favour of such a move.

For one thing, it would be further company for his mother, and if anything happened to Alice then Dolly, presumably, would still be there. It was another hedge against the possibility of his mother having to live in his own house some day.

Again, Dolly's little cottage, humble though it was, was exceedingly pretty, and just the sort of place which was being snapped up by Londoners looking for a weekend cottage. A similar one at Fairacre, John remembered with a glow of pleasure, fetched five thousand pounds last month. The money could be invested and add to Aunt Dolly's tiny pension, thought John solicitously.

Besides, it would be keeping the money in the family.

He spent much of the day working out little sums – the possible interest that Dolly Clare would get on her problematical gains, if invested wisely – and it was almost time to leave the shop before he faced the cold fact that Dolly might not wish to sell, and that his mother might prefer to have 'Harada' to herself.

He determined to go and see his mother that evening and to make a few delicate inquiries.

Meanwhile, Ada too had been thinking. This death of Emily created some problems. She was honest enough to admit to herself that she did not feel any grief on Emily's behalf. There had never been any love lost between the two.

Even now, Ada felt resentment at the way Emily had usurped her own place in young Dolly's affections. As little children in Caxley, Dolly had always followed Ada's lead. She adored her elder sister, and had been content to do her bidding without question.

But things had changed under the influence of the Davis family, and particularly with the growth of the friendship between Emily and Dolly. Now Ada was not always right. Dolly began to question some of her decisions, and to ask Emily's opinion before her sister's. Ada considered Emily a subversive influence, and, as she grew older, she found no reason to change her views.

Then there was the affair of Manny's marrow which had made young Emily a minor heroine. The boys' attention had been diverted from Ada, the queen of the playground at Beech Green School, and although it was only a temporary defection, it gave Ada further cause to dislike Emily.

Later still, when Ada was a young mother, and not long after the little contretemps of the baby's dummy, Emily played a more important part in Ada's life. It was an episode which she remembered with shame for the rest of her life, and Emily's attitude at the time did little to assuage Ada's guilt.

Even now, over half a century later, she shied away from the remembrance, although she knew from experience that it would return before long to haunt her. Did Emily ever tell? Did Dolly ever know?

The anxiety pricked her as keenly now as it had so many years ago. And she would never know the answers! Sometimes the old Jewish God of Retribution seemed very real to Ada.

The thought of Dolly brought more practical problems to her mind. She would be left alone in the little house at Beech Green, and would be worse off without Emily's financial help in the partnership they had so much enjoyed.

It was all very tiresome, thought Ada with exasperation. She supposed she ought to invite her to 'Harada'. It would be expected of her, by her local friends, she had no doubt, and when one was so well respected in the church, and particularly in the Mothers' Union, it behoved one to act correctly.

But why should she alter her comfortable way of life to accommodate a sister who really meant very little to her? They had gone their own ways for so long, that, despite a proper sisterly warmth when they met, they had little in common.

Would Dolly mix comfortably with the prosperous widows who still came occasionally to play bridge in Ada's drawing room? She was far more likely, thought Ada, to sit in a corner, like a death's head at a feast, while the chatter went on, making everyone self-conscious.

And how would Alice like it? After all, she must consider Alice's feelings. She might very well feel hurt at another person coming to live at the house, on intimate terms. And, of course, it would make more work. There would be another bed to cope with, more laundry, more heating in the bedroom, more vegetables to peel, more meat to buy. Really the more one thought of it, the greater the problem became.

She was restless and irritable throughout the day wondering what to do. She wanted to appear generous in the sight of the little world of Caxley, but she very much resented the discomfort and expense it might put her to.

So like Emily, she thought distractedly, to go first, and leave such a muddle for others to tidy up!

Perhaps John might be of help. She determined to telephone him, as soon as he returned from the shop. After all, Dolly was his godmother, as well as his aunt. He should give her some attention at this difficult time. It was all too much for Ada alone.

Really, she felt quite faint with worry about it. She went to the drawing room door and called Alice.

'Could we have tea early, dear? My poor head's throbbing. Jam and cream with the scones, Alice dear.'

But there was no need to make a telephone call, for John appeared very soon after the meal had been dispatched, and broached the painful subject with masculine frankness.

'Bad news about Emily Davis. You saw it, I expect, in the paper?'

'I don't know what's bad about dying in your eighties,' said Ada tartly. 'Surely it's only to be expected. I know I feel very near my end often enough.'

John sensed from this reply that his mother was in one of her difficult moods. The dash of self-pity in her last sentence was always a danger sign.

He patted her hand kindly.

'You're a wonderful old lady' he assured her 'Lots of happy years ahead for you.'

She allowed herself to be slightly mollified

'Yes, well – I suppose I do keep pretty bright, considering. But it's always a shock when one of your own generation goes.'

'Aunt Dolly will miss her,' said John, approaching the subject of his schemes warily.

'Bound to,' agreed Ada. She brushed a scone crumb from her lap and considered how best to put her difficulties to John.

'She shouldn't be alone,' said John. 'Not at her age.'

'No,' said Ada. 'Not at her age. And she's never been really robust. She was always the weakling of the two of us.'

'It's a problem.'

'It certainly is.'

'I take it she'll be pretty hard up?'

'No doubt about it. They shared expenses, of course, which helped them both.'

John stood up and balanced himself first on his toes and then on his heels. It was a habit he had had since childhood, and indicative of mental unrest. Ada found it irritating.

'Don't keep rocking, John.'

'Sorry, mother,' he said, standing stock still. 'It's just that I'm a bit worried about poor Aunt Dolly. She is my godmother, you know.'

'I know well enough,' snapped his mother, resenting the reproachful note in John's voice. 'And you're not the only one to be worried. I've been almost distracted, wondering what to do for the best, all day today.'

John felt that some progress was being made.

'What had you in mind?'

'Well, naturally, as she's my only sister, my first thought was to invite her here.'

'That's very generous of you, mother. But do you think you are up to it?'

Ada sighed heavily.

'We all have to make sacrifices at times like this. And no doubt Dolly would appreciate it.'

'I'm sure she would be most grateful.'

'But then – I don't know. It would be such a complete change in her way of life, wouldn't it? And we're so far here from the shops and things. Have you considered having her at your house? She is your godmother, you know.'

John, though taken aback at this surprise attack, rallied well.

'Out of the question,' he replied swiftly. 'No spare room, for one thing, and then I think Aunt Dolly would find the children too much for her.'

'Humph!' snorted Ada, thwarted. A short silence ensued.

'If she *did* leave Beech Green, I think she would get a very good price for the cottage,' said John at last. His mother's love of money was as strong as his own. He could have found no surer way of diverting her attention.

'Would she now?' said his mother speculatively. 'How much should you think?'

'Somewhere in the region of five thousand.'

Ada nodded slowly.

'She'd need some of that to see her fixed comfortably for the rest of her life, of course –' Her voice trailed away.

'Naturally, naturally,' agreed John hastily. 'Properly invested it should bring in a nice little sum for the next few years.'

He cleared his throat fussily.

'How old is dear Aunt Dolly now?' he asked in a would-be casual tone.

'Eighty-four,' said Ada shortly.

'She's made a will, I hope?'

'I believe so. I know if she went first, the house was to be Emily's.'

'Really?' John sounded startled. 'And now what happens?'

'I'm not sure, but I've an idea it might go to a niece of Emily's.'

It was John's turn to sigh.

'Ah well, she must do as she likes with her own property, of course, but I do hope she isn't making a mistake. Well, mother, how do you feel about inviting her here? Would you be happy about it?'

'I must think it over. I'm sure poor Dolly would enjoy the greater comfort she'd get here, and she'd have company, of course, but it would mean a lot of extra work. Not that I'd mind that – I've worked all my life – but I shouldn't like to place a burden on Alice.'

'Of course not,' agreed John. 'You think it over, my dear, and give me a ring, before you write to Aunt Dolly.'

He kissed her cheek and departed, leaving her to her thoughts.

★

Five thousand, thought Ada. It was worth keeping in the family. She reviewed the situation anew. There were arguments for and against inviting Dolly to 'Harada'. She pondered on the problem in the gathering dusk.

At last she came to a decision. She would write to Dolly expressing sympathy, and telling her that she could make her home in Caxley should she wish to do so. Then, in all truth, she could tell her friends that she had invited Dolly to live with her, and any money would be wisely invested for her maintenance. John would see to that.

She went to her writing desk and wrote swiftly in her large, bold hand.

Dear Dolly,

I was most distressed to hear about poor Emily and hasten to send my deepest sympathy.

You can guess how worried I am to know you are quite alone now. Should you care to come and stay here with me, you know you would be most welcome. For a short visit, if you prefer it, to see how you like it here, but with a view to living here permanently, I mean.

The back bedroom is very comfortable, although it is facing north, and the little box room next door could be turned into a snug little sitting room, if you like the idea.

I know you wouldn't want to be idle, and Alice and I would welcome your help in running the house.

Do think it over. I know John would be very happy to give you any help in disposing of your furniture and so on, if the need arises.

With love from,

Ada.

She glanced at the clock. If Alice hurried, she could catch the last outgoing post at the main office in the High Street.

She stuck on a stamp with an energetic banging, and called imperiously for Alice.

When she was safely dispatched on her hurried errand, Ada rang John to tell him what she had done.

He was a trifle annoyed that she had written without consulting him again, but he was resigned to his mother's high-handed and impetuous methods.

'Well, we'll have to wait and see now, won't we?' was all he found to say.

But as he put the receiver down, he had a strong feeling that Aunt Dolly's cottage would never be his.

He was right.

Two mornings later, he called to see his mother, who handed him Dolly's reply in silence.

My dear Ada,

Your kind sympathy is very much appreciated. I miss dear Emily more than I can say, as you may imagine, and because of that I am doubly grateful for your kind suggestion of sharing your home with me.

It is a very generous gesture, Ada dear, and I have thought about the matter seriously. However, I am determined to stay here, where I am so happy, and I am lucky enough to have good neighbours who will always help me, I know.

Perhaps John would bring you out to tea one day when things are more settled, and I can thank you both properly for all your concern for my welfare.

Your loving sister,

Dolly.

'That's that then,' said John, returning the letter. They both sighed. John for the loss of a dream; his mother with secret relief.

8. Did Emily Tell?

Ada's relief was genuine. There would have been many drawbacks to Dolly's presence in the house. Perhaps the most irksome would have been the constant nagging query in her own mind: 'Did Dolly know?'

What was this guilty memory which worried Ada so unduly

after so many years? And what part did Emily Davis play in it?

It was the age-old story of a boy and a girl, and it all began when Ada went, as a young girl, to live with her grandparents in Caxley.

She had a job in a flourishing draper's shop in the High Street, and her bright good looks and flirtatious ways brought many a young man into her department.

She had many admirers, and among them was the younger son of Septimus Howard, whose baker's shop stood in the market square.

Leslie Howard was dark, gay and a lady-killer. He worked hard with his father and brother Jim, and drove a smart baker's cart on the rounds outside Caxley. Leslie Howard was known well in the neighbourhood. He was a great favourite with the young of both sexes; a charmer who had inherited the dark looks of his gipsy mother.

The older generation, particularly those sober chapel-goers who respected his father Sep Howard, shook their heads over Leslie's goings-on, and warned their daughters about trusting such a flighty-minded young man. If anything, this increased Leslie's fascination in their eyes.

It was not long before bold Ada caught Leslie's eye, and he took to meeting her as soon as the shop closed. Ada was careful to say nothing about the meetings to her aged grandparents but, of course, in a town of Caxley's size, the word soon went round.

In the meantime, however, the two young people enjoyed each other's company. Sometimes, Leslie made an excuse to take the baker's cart out in the evening, on the pretext of a forgotten de-livery. He would pick up Ada, waiting in a quiet lane, and they would spend a blissful few hours before returning.

They attended several local dances held in the Corn Exchange. They were both fine dancers, and grew accustomed to much open admiration on the floor.

It was on one of these occasions that Ada's quick temper betrayed her. Another market square family, the young Norths, were present at the dance. Bertie North had brought his younger sister Winifred, whose pale blue frock and silver ribbons were more splendid than any other gown to be seen at the dance.

Leslie turned his attentions to his old friend Winnie, and danced with her far more frequently than Ada thought suitable. It was true that kind-hearted Bertie had taken pity on her, but Ada, becoming crosser as the evening wore on, decided that Bertie was simply patronizing her.

Her anger grew. The Norths were a prosperous family. The father, Bender North, had a thriving ironmongery business in the square, and Hilda North, his wife, could afford to dress well and to see her children beautifully clothed.

Ada considered the family 'stuck up'. In those days of class consciousness, she felt that the Norths were above her. The Howards were poorer, and with Leslie she felt comfortable. Bertie's good clothes and gentle manners made Ada feel rebellious and discomfited.

It was the beginning of the end of the affair between Leslie and Ada, but although they rarely met after the dance, there was a strong personal bond between them. They both possessed outstanding vitality, and the attraction they felt for each other did not grow less by being pushed underground.

Ada heard of his subsequent marriage to Winnie North with secret envy, although by that time she too was married to Harry Roper, and was the mother of a baby son.

Leslie came into Ada's life again during the 1914–18 war. She met him, quite by chance, one bright October evening as she walked along the tow path by the gently flowing Cax.

Baby John was safely in bed, looked after by a little maid-of-all-work who lived over the shop with Ada. Harry was serving in Italy, and from his boisterous letters seemed to be happy in the army.

Ada was bored and lonely. She worked hard in the shop all day, but when she had locked its door, and she had shared a meal with the little maid and kissed young John 'Good night', she took a brisk walk before darkness fell. Partly she felt the need for exercise and fresh air, but even more strongly she needed to pass away the long hours of evening time.

In war-time in Caxley, there were very few social occasions. With the young men gone, there were no dances or socials – nothing to give Ada the stimulus she loved.

She had a wardrobe packed with pretty clothes, for Harry was a generous husband, but no occasion to wear them. There were long ankle-length gowns trimmed with lace insertion and rows of diminutive buttons. There were smart fitted coats with fur at the hem and frogging across the front. There were several muffs to match the coats; and in a separate cupboard stood a dozen or more beautiful hats, some trimmed with feathers, or laden with silken flowers, or edged with fur or swansdown. Perched above Ada's bright gold hair, well-skewered with hat pins for safety, they crowned Ada's beauty with added glory. She mourned the fact that in war-time there were so few times when she could dazzle Caxley with such finery.

She met Leslie face to face as she took her walk along the towpath, and her heart leapt at the sight of him. He looked even more dashing than usual in uniform.

He held out both hands, and she put hers into them. They stood looking at each other, without speaking for a full minute.

Beside them the Cax gurgled. A few leaves fluttered down upon its silky surface and were borne away. The dry reeds whispered as the slow current moved them, and near by a moorhen piped to its mate.

'Ada,' said Leslie, at last, very low, 'I've been longing to see you again.'

'I've missed you,' replied Ada simply.

She turned to walk beside him. It was as though no rift had ever occurred between them. In that one short minute, they were once again in complete accord.

'I've ten days leave,' said Leslie, matching his step to hers. 'Can I see you again?'

'I usually come here for a walk about this time,' said Ada.

Neither said a word about wife or husband. There were no inquiries about their respective families, no polite small talk about the town or general matters.

Both knew instinctively that the feeling between them was too strong to be denied, and time was short. To be in the presence of the other was all that mattered.

For the next few days, Ada lived in a state of feverish excitement which she found difficult to conceal. She met Leslie each evening, sometimes by the Cax, sometimes in a quiet lane where prying eyes would not see them.

Leslie's leave ended at the weekend, and he persuaded Ada, with very little difficulty, to go away with him on the Saturday before he reported to his unit on the Sunday night.

'But Winnie?' said Ada, speaking at last of his young wife.

'She thinks I have to be back on Saturday. We can go to Bournemouth. No one knows us there. I know a decent hotel.'

Ada's heart leapt. Here was excitement, a change from stuffy Caxley and the dreary round of keeping the shop going. The thought of the neglected gowns in the wardrobe, now to see the light of day again, made her eyes sparkle.

Leslie kissed her swiftly.

'We can go on the morning train, travelling separately until we change at the junction, in case there are any old codgers who might tell tales.'

They laughed together. They were like two children, plotting mischief. To neither of them occurred the possibility of wrongdoing or disloyalty to their partners. They were perfectly matched in selfishness and animal vitality.

The plan worked smoothly. Ada left little John with his doting grandparents, on the pretext that an ageing aunt of Harry's wanted to see her in Sussex, and she felt that she must make the journey for Harry's sake.

As arranged, Ada made her way to the head of the platform, assiduously avoiding looking at the further end where a soldierly figure waited, his eyes, apparently, gazing down the line.

Leslie had made his farewells to Winnie at home, begging her not to upset herself by saying farewell in public. Winnie, touched by his thoughtfulness, had agreed to his plan.

The train arrived in a flurry of steam and smoke. Doors banged, porters shouted, the guard blew his whistle shrilly and waved his flag.

At that moment, a small figure hurtled from the booking office, wrenched open the nearest third-class door, and leapt inside.

Emily Davis had caught the train by the skin of her teeth yet again.

She was on her weekly pilgrimage to see Edgar in hospital at Bournemouth. At this time, she was acting headmistress at the little school at Springbourne, for her headmaster was in the army, and as it happened, was fated never to go back to Springbourne. On his safe return at the war's end, he moved to a larger school, and Emily continued as headmistress in her own right.

Running the school while he was away in the army was a heavy task for Emily, but one which she tackled with her customary energy. The hardest part was the journey back and forth each weekend to see poor Edgar.

His progress was so pathetically slow. The gas attacks had affected his lungs, and a painful cough persisted. He seemed to live for the weekends, and Emily travelled on Saturday morning and returned on the last train on Sunday.

This meant that all her domestic work had to be fitted in during the evenings or very early on Saturday morning. The school house at Springbourne was small but inconvenient. Water had to be wound up from a well in the garden. The bath was a zinc one which hung at the side of the garden shed, and had to be carried into the kitchen, there to be filled from hot saucepans and kettles bubbling on the kitchen range.

Emptying the bath was almost as great a labour as filling it.

Emily overcame all these difficulties effortlessly. After all, this was the way in which she had been brought up as one of a large and cheerful family. But she wished, sometimes, that Edgar were nearer, for the journey was tedious and involved precious money as well as precious time.

On this particular morning, she changed as usual at the junction, and whilst she was collecting her hand luggage together, she saw Ada, exquisitely wrapped in a fur-trimmed coat, with a hat and muff to match, moving swiftly towards a waiting figure. They linked arms and, heads together, made their way to the waiting train.

Emily recognized Leslie Howard. It was plain from their behaviour that they were completely engrossed in each other.

Emily hung back out of sight, and quickly climbed into an empty carriage at some distance from the couple. She did not want to embarrass them, and she also needed to mark some tests of the children's which she had brought with her in her bag.

But as she put the ticks and crosses automatically against the answers, Emily's bewildered brain tried to take in the full import of this meeting.

At Bournemouth she waited until the couple had gone through the barrier, and then gave in her ticket and made her way straight to the hospital.

Edgar's eyes lit up when he saw her walking down the ward. She kissed him gently and let him tell her all his hospital news – what the doctor said that morning, what meals they had been given, the excitement of a visiting soprano who had made their heads ache with patriotic songs.

Emily gave him the Springbourne news and the little presents of farm butter, brown eggs and late roses from his family. But she said nothing of Ada and Leslie.

She stayed near by in a shabby house which supplied bed and breakfast for a small sum. The woman was kind, but too busy to take much interest in her lodgers. There was nowhere to sit, and Emily was accustomed to walking along the promenade or looking at the windows of the shut shops on Sunday morning, until it was time to visit Edgar again.

This Sunday morning was clear and sunny. The sea air was heady, the sea-gulls cut white zig-zags across the blue sky, screaming the while. Emily gulped down the salty air, revelling in the fresh breeze on her face. A bright October day had a flavour all its own. Here, by the sparkling sea, everything was extra sharp and beautiful.

She went at a brisk pace, but presently slowed up. In front of her strolled Ada and Leslie. His arm was round her waist. Her head was almost upon his shoulder. They might have been a honeymoon couple. Passers-by looked at them fondly and with some sympathy. So many young men in uniform came here for their leave, and many of them never returned to England again. Let them enjoy life, said their indulgent smiles, while they can!

Emily was about to turn round and escape when, to her horror, they turned too. She was conscious of Ada's eyes upon her – eyes which widened in surprise. Emily bolted towards the rail of the promenade and, leaning over, gazed out to sea. She did not dare to move for a full five minutes.

When at last she turned, she saw the pair far away in the distance. They were as lovingly entwined as ever.

Emily made her way thoughtfully to see Edgar.

★

Ada was perturbed by the encounter.

'That was Emily Davis,' she told Leslie when they were out of earshot.

'And who's she?'

'Dolly's friend. Teaches at Springbourne.'

'I don't believe it,' said Leslie stoutly. 'You're getting fanciful.'

'I'd know that ghastly old hat of hers anywhere,' replied Ada, tossing her own furry beauty proudly.

'What does it matter anyway?'

'Supposing she tells somebody?'

'She won't. Why should she? It's none of her business what we do.'

'She doesn't like me. She might feel like making mischief.'

'Rubbish!' cried Leslie. He stopped by the end of a shelter, where they were hidden from sight, and took Ada in his arms. His kisses were not returned as ardently as before.

'Ada! Don't let this silly business upset you.'

'I bet she tells Dolly anyway,' said Ada spitefully. 'They never keep anything from each other.'

'Forget it,' said Leslie, drawing her close. She struggled free.

'It's all right for you. You're going away. I've got to go back and face them all. Suppose Harry gets to hear of it?'

'And suppose he doesn't!'

'Or Winnie?'

'They won't! Come back to the hotel and calm down.'

He guided his love back to the privacy of the hotel, and there they stayed, very happily, until it was time for Ada to catch the train home.

Emily, of course, had to catch the same train. She was careful to get into it early, and to busy herself with her books.

There was no sign of the couple and she began to think that they must be staying in Bournemouth when, at the last moment, they hurried on to the platform.

Ada climbed into a carriage only two from Emily's. There was little time for farewells for the train was about to move off, but Ada leant from the window and clung passionately to Leslie's neck for a brief moment, crying his name.

The train chuffed off, leaving Leslie, hand upraised, on the platform. Emily heard the window pulled up with a bang, and before she had time to wonder if she could slip down the corridor to a carriage further away, Ada herself appeared in the corridor.

She stopped dead, her chest heaving beneath its smart frogging, and tears still wet on her cheeks. She cast a look of venom upon poor Emily, who gazed back transfixed, as an innocent rabbit might when hypnotized by a stoat.

Ada turned and re-entered her compartment. Emily, sorely troubled, did her best to read a paper by the meagre light afforded by war-time illuminations.

At Caxley Station they reached the ticket-collector side by side.

Ada thrust her ticket into his hand and spoke in a vicious whisper to Emily.

'You keep your mouth shut,' she hissed.

She never forgot the look which Emily gave her from those clear grey eyes.

Emily said no word, but the look expressed loathing and contempt. In that moment, Ada was forced to face the truth that little Emily Davis, poor, shabbily dressed, a humble inky-fingered school-teacher was her peer in all that really mattered. There was no dis-guising the fact that Emily had every right to despise her.

When, in later times Ada looked back upon that mad weekend, which was never repeated, she realized that it was that look of Emily's which brought home to her the wickedness and cruelty of her behaviour.

It was the first step towards Ada's heart-searching, and her first true encounter with the feeling of guilt.

And now Emily Davis was dead, thought Ada, the old woman. She had kept silence. She had carried Ada's secret to the grave with her. Of that, Ada had no doubt. She would have heard soon enough, in Caxley, if Emily had ever breathed a word.

There had been many moments of panic for Ada in the years that followed. Harry was a loving and generous husband, but he would never have forgiven infidelity, Ada knew well. She trembled when she thought how completely she was at the mercy of Emily Davis. It made her dislike of Emily stronger than ever, for now it was allied to guilty fear.

Yet, in her heart, she felt sure that her secret was safe. That look which Emily had given her at Caxley Station expressed not only contempt, but also her own shining goodness. Emily Davis would not stoop to anything as shabby as tale-telling.

The old lady sighed, and picking up the poker, stirred the fire.

'Well, at least she made me take a look at myself,' she said aloud.

'Who, dear?' asked Alice from the other side of the hearth. She lowered her knitting and looked in bewilderment at her employer.

'Emily Davis. She made me look at myself. What's more, she made me see plenty to dislike when I looked.'

Alice studied the wrinkled face with some concern. For the first time, she saw humility written there.

9. Jane Draper at Springbourne

Among those who read the brief notice of Emily's death in *The Caxley Chronicle* was Jane Bentley, who had started her teaching career, many years before, under Emily's guidance at Springbourne School.

She was now a woman in her late fifties and lived in a village to the south of Caxley, some fifteen miles from Springbourne. She had not kept in touch with her old headmistress, but occasionally they had met by chance in Caxley, and were always glad to see each other.

As a child, Jane Bentley, then Jane Draper, was delicate, the type of child who spends a large part of the winter in bed, the prey of every epidemic in season.

Luckily, she was intelligent and fond of books. The youngest of four, she became an aunt in her teens and had plenty of experience with children. She decided to become an infants' teacher.

The Draper family lived in a respectable London suburb. Money was short, but with wisdom and thrift the family managed adequately. It was a sacrifice to let Jane go to the training college of her choice, for although she received a grant, and a loan which had to be repaid in the first three years of teaching, in the normal way she would have been earning at the age of eighteen, and able to augment the family income.

She was a conscientious girl doing well at college and, honouring her pledge to return to the authority which had financed her, she started her teaching career, in the bleak early thirties when posts were so scarce, at a large infants' school in her native borough.

She found the work tough going. Nervous and apprehensive, she discovered that she was expected to teach a class of fifty six-year-olds to read, to write, and to imbibe the rudiments of arithmetic. These three Rs in some form or other, and with a break for physical training, made up the morning's time-table. The afternoons were given over to such infant delights designated as Art, Music, Handwork, Free Expression, and the like.

Her headmistress was a forceful woman, over endowed with thyroid and the relentless energy which goes with it. She did her best to be patient with the succession of young teachers who passed through her hands, but it was plain that their slowness and lack of class discipline, allied to some vague and high-faluting clouds of Child Psychology which they trailed behind them from college lectures, drove the poor woman to distraction.

Miss Jolly – for that was her unlikely name – came into Jane's classroom one day to see what all the hubbub was about. She found Jane sitting at her table with half a dozen children round her, holding reading books. One of the books was upside down.

The rest of the class seemed to be wandering restlessly about the room, some children holding pieces of equipment, some gazing through the window at another class in the playground and others enjoying themselves by sweeping their fellow pupils' work from the tables with happy cries.

'What are they doing?' asked Miss Jolly in a voice of thunder.

'They're Working At Their Own Pace,' replied Jane, rising to look over the heads clustered about her.

'Half of them aren't working at all,' rejoined Miss Jolly truthfully. 'Get them to their desks.'

Poor Jane did her best by clapping her hands ineffectually and crying, in a voice faint with nervousness, for order. A few, who had noticed Miss Jolly's presence, had the good sense to obey, and sat, smiling smugly, at the chaos around them.

For almost two minutes, agonizingly long to Jane Draper, she did her best to make herself heard. At last Miss Jolly came to her aid.

'SIT DOWN!' commanded that lady, in tones which set the windows vibrating. Children scurried to their chairs.

'HANDS IN LAPS!' ordered Miss Jolly. They obeyed to a man. Even Jane's particular problem child, Jimmy Lobb, who had frequent fits – some of them quite genuine – subsided into his chair and sat mute and wide-eyed. They knew the voice of authority well enough, and most of them unconsciously welcomed it.

'You are making far too much noise,' Miss Jolly told them sternly. 'How can Miss Draper hear this group read?'

Rightly, the subdued class assumed that this was a rhetorical question and remained suitably mute.

'Has everyone got work to do?' asked Miss Jolly.

'Yes, Miss,' came the meek reply.

'Very well. You get on with it, and you STAY IN YOUR DESKS until the clock says half-past.'

She pointed to the enormous electric time-piece on the wall which jerked the minutes along in staccato fashion.

'When that big hand gets to 6,' she continued, improving the shining hour, 'you may CREEP from your desks to change your apparatus. NOT BEFORE! You understand?'

'Yes, Miss,' came the dulcet whispers.

'Those who were reading come quietly to Miss Draper's table,' ordered Miss Jolly. 'And I want to see every book the right way up.'

A demure half-dozen tip-toed politely to their former positions. Jane found the whole exercise unnerving, and hoped that Miss Jolly would soon leave her to her usual muddle.

But for a full five minutes, Miss Jolly prowled about the room, whilst work went on in an unnatural hush. Jane found herself trembling with anxiety.

At last, Miss Jolly departed, requesting Jane to meet her in her room as soon as school dinner was over.

By the time the meeting took place, Jane was in a state of panic. She entered the well-polished room, blind to the Della Robbia plaques, the cut-glass vase of roses, the silver desk-calendar (a parting gift from another school) and the hand-tufted rug on the floor.

Miss Jolly was kind but firm. She began by praising Jane's conscientious approach to teaching, her punctuality, her neat Record Book of Work to be done weekly, and did her best to put the dithering girl at ease.

She did not succeed, for in Jane's bewildered brain the phrase 'Damning with faint praise' beat about inside her head like an imprisoned bird, as she tried to listen to Miss Jolly's controlled commendations.

'You see,' said Miss Jolly at last, approaching the heart of the matter, 'we set ourselves certain aims in this infant school – aims of *attainment*, I mean. Ideally, each child should go forward to the junior school able to read – the most important thing – to write, and with a working knowledge of the four rules, at least in tens and units, preferably with hundreds too. Then, of course, they should have some idea of common measurements, be able to tell the time –'

'But there are *so many* of them!' wailed poor Jane.

'Unfortunate, I know, but there it is. What you have to learn, my dear, is to get them to do as they are told W H E N they are told. You saw what happened this morning.'

'But they really *were* working,' protested Jane. 'They must move about to fetch the next piece of apparatus. It shows they are keen to get on when they get one card done quickly and hurry out for the next.'

'It could show that they are bored with the piece of work in front of them,' said Miss Jolly. 'As far as I could see, quite a number of them couldn't be bothered to finish one job before trying their luck with the next. It's no good letting them get slack. You must check their progress. The bright ones will get on whatever happens. It's the idle ones who need prodding.'

'But if they're *interested*,' began Jane, 'they'll *want* to work. At college –'

Miss Jolly, with one eye on the clock, and patience sorely tried, let herself be told about Self-Determination, A Child's Natural Thirst for Discovery, and Working At One's Own Pace.

'Yes, well –' she said, when Jane had come to a faltering halt. 'Don't forget that a very small percentage are paragons. The rest, like most of humanity, are bone idle.'

Jane, horrified by such heresy, was about to argue, but Miss Jolly raised the capable right hand which had slapped so many infant legs.

'Keep the aims in mind, my dear. We want to send these children along to the junior school well equipped. If you can get the results by the methods shown you at college, well and good. But they won't work unless you have control of the class. Without that, nothing will work.'

She rose, and Jane made her way to the door.

'You're doing very well,' said Miss Jolly kindly. 'I think I shall be able to give you a good report at the end of this probationary year.'

'Thank you,' said Jane huskily. 'If only there weren't so many in a class, I think I'd manage better.'

'Wouldn't we all?' said Miss Jolly, with feeling. She gazed speculatively at Jane for a moment, and spoke again.

'I could offer you *forty backward* children next year, if you like the idea. Think it over, dear. Think it over!'

Jane did think it over. She thought a great deal in that first gruelling year, and many a time she despaired of continuing in the career she had adopted.

Would she ever become a fully-certificated teacher at the end of this probationary year? Did she want to be one for the rest of her life? And what could she do, if she wanted to change her job?

There were plenty of long queues outside the Labour Exchanges. Some of her college contemporaries were on the dole. It was a dispiriting situation.

She was not sure that Miss Jolly was right in her attitude to the children. She seemed to be far more concerned with the school's record of achievement than with the children themselves. Jane felt that she demanded too much of them, and of her staff. Not all of them were possessed of the self-assurance and drive which had swept Miss Jolly into a headship at a relatively early age.

On the other hand, she had the sense to realize that Miss Jolly did not ask anything of her teachers which she could not do herself. She might not conduct a class as Jane's college lecturers had recommended, but she certainly got results, and the children seemed to thrive. It was all very confusing.

At the end of the year, she was relieved to know that her work had been considered satisfactory. She was asked again if she would take the 'small' class of forty backward children, and agreed.

And so it came about that one September morning she faced her new class. Most of the six-year-olds were backward because of absence from school through illness. Some were mentally unsound and a few of these children would become certifiable at the right age. Some were incorrigibly lazy and would always lag behind, and a few were rebels by nature against any sort of discipline and authority, and likely to remain so for the rest of their lives.

Jane grew very fond of them. For one thing, they were grateful for any effort made for them. They were wildly delighted with such simple creations as a paper windmill or a lop-sided blotter, and carried these treasures home with far more care than their more brightly endowed fellows. They were affectionate and anxious to please. Jane found their goodwill exceedingly touching.

She also found them exceedingly exhausting, and returned home each evening tired to death. She had no heart for any sort of social life. Early bed was the thing she craved most, and her mother grew alarmed.

The family doctor prescribed iron tablets and sea-air. The iron tablets were taken regularly and seemed to do some good. Sea-air was more difficult to come by. The family had no car, and money was still short.

When, in February, Jane was forced to take to her bed with influenza and was unable to leave it for three weeks, the doctor spoke his mind to Mrs Draper.

'That girl of yours upstairs,' he told her frankly, 'is wearing herself out. She's no reserves of strength at all. See she gets a holiday by the sea, after this, and then a teaching post that's easier than this one. Don't you know any school that has small classes?'

The Drapers did not. But during the summer term, when Jane was back at school and still struggling feebly with her forty backward children, a post was advertised in *The Teachers' World* for an assistant mistress to take charge of eighteen infants at Springbourne School.

'Number on roll,' said the advertisement, 'forty-eight.'

A whole school, with only forty-eight, thought Jane longingly!

She looked up the village in the ordnance survey map. It was, she saw, a few miles from Caxley where one of her college friends lived.

She wrote to her, and asked for her advice and for any information.

'Come and see it for yourself,' was the answer, and with a glow of hope Jane went to spend the weekend with the Bentleys.

They were a happy-go-lucky family living on the northern outskirts of Caxley, some three miles from Springbourne. To reach the village the two girls cycled along a quiet valley beside a little river full of water-cress beds. It ambled along sedately beneath its over-hanging willows on its way to join the Cax.

It was a Saturday morning, warm and sunny. The school, of course, was uninhabited and so was the school house, for Emily had gone on the weekly bus to do some shopping in Caxley.

Emboldened, the two girls pressed their noses to the classroom windows and gazed at the interior. To Jane it seemed like a dolls' school after the enormous building in which she taught. She caught a glimpse of a large photograph of Queen Mary as a young woman, wasp-waisted in flowing white lace, with pearls in her hair.

The desks were long and old-fashioned, housing five or six children in a row. But there was nothing old-fashioned about the stack of new readers on the piano – Jane was using the same series herself – and she noted, with approval, the children's large paintings, the mustard and cress growing in a shallow dish, and the goldfish disporting themselves in a roomy glass tank, properly equipped with aquatic plants.

The playground was large, and shaded by several fine old trees. Elder bushes, turning their creamy flowers to the sun, screened the little outhouses which were the lavatories.

It all seemed cheerful and decent, a kindly spot where one could be happy, and could work without heart-break.

When Jane returned, she applied for the post and was accepted. Later that summer she met her headmistress-to-be for the first time.

She was in the playground carrying a tear-stained five-year-old in her arms. She kissed it swiftly before putting it down, and advanced to meet Jane. It gave Jane quite a shock. Would Miss Jolly do that?

'I'm so glad you can come and help us next term,' said Emily Davis, holding out her hand.

And, as Jane held the small warm brown one in her own, she felt that, at last, she had come home.

10. The Flight of Billy Dove

There began then for Jane a period of great happiness and refreshment which was to colour her whole life.

To begin with, she stayed with the hospitable Bentleys, for the

first few weeks of the autumn term, until she could find suitable lodgings nearer the school. After so much ill-health and strain, it was wonderful to be taken into the heart of such a cheerful family, and Jane thrived.

The bicycle ride to school and back brought colour to her cheeks, and an increased appetite. In those first few weeks of mellow autumn sunshine, Jane began to realize the loveliness of the countryside.

Harvest was in full swing, and the berries in the hedges were beginning to glow with colour. The cottage gardens were bright with Michaelmas daisies and dahlias, and the children brought sprays of blackberries and early nuts for the classroom nature table. Sometimes Jane received fresh-picked field mushrooms which the children had found on the way to school, or a perfect late rose from someone's garden.

She revelled in the bracing air of the downs and, encouraged by her headmistress, took the infants' class for nature walks round and about the village.

She found the children amenable and friendly. They might lack the sharp precocity of her former town pupils, but their slower pace suited Jane perfectly. Facing a class of eighteen, after forty or fifty, was wonderful to the girl. There was so little noise that there was no need to raise her voice. She could hear each child read daily – a basic aim she had never been able to achieve before – and found the children's progress marvellously heartening.

Of course there were snags. The chief one was the range of ages. The youngest was not yet five; the oldest – and most backward – nearly eight. But Jane was used to working with groups, and found that discipline was no bother with so few children who were mostly of a docile nature. Relaxed and absorbed, Jane's confidence in her own abilities grew steadily, and she became a very sound teacher indeed.

Emily Davis played her part in this process. Jane found her as quick and energetic as Miss Jolly had been, but with a warmth of heart and gentleness, both lacking in her former headmistress.

Emily was like a little bird, Jane thought, with her bright eyes and brisk bustling movements. The children loved her, but knew better than to provoke her. They knew, too, that a cane reposed at the back of the map cupboard. No one could remember it being used, but the bigger boys, who occasionally assumed some bravado, were aware that Miss Davis was quite capable of exerting her powers, if need be, and kept their behaviour within limits.

Emily's high spirits were the stimulus which these children needed. Mostly the sons and daughters of farm labourers, they were unbookish and inclined to be apathetic.

'Don't forget,' said Emily to Jane one playtime, as they sipped their tea, 'that most of them are short of food, and quite a number go cold in the winter. Times are hard for farmers and their men.'

'But they look well enough,' observed Jane.

'Their cheeks are pink,' answered Emily. 'If you live on the downs you soon get weather-beaten. And by the end of the summer they are nicely tanned. But look at their bodies when they strip for physical training! You'll see plenty of rib cages in evidence. There's just as much poverty in the country as in towns. The only thing is it's not quite so dramatic, and fewer people see its results.'

There were such families at Springbourne, Jane soon discovered. She saw too how Emily coped practically with the situation, supplying mugs of milky cocoa during the winter to those who needed it most. Those who did not run home for their midday meal brought sandwiches, for this was before the coming of school dinners. One family, in particular, was particularly under-nourished. When the greasy papers were unwrapped, they were usually found to contain only bread with a scraping of margarine.

Many a time Jane saw Emily adding a piece of cheese to this unpalatable fare, and apples from her store shed. It was all done briskly, without sentiment, and in a way which would not make a child uncomfortable.

It was small wonder, Jane thought, that Emily Davis got on well with the parents. There were exceptions, of course, and one incident Jane remembered for years.

It happened just before Christmas one year. Emily had arranged a school outing to a Christmas pantomime, put on by amateurs, in Caxley. A bus was hired, and the fare and the entrance fee together would cost five shillings. Parents could join the party, and there was a good response, despite the fact that five shillings seemed a great deal of money to find just before Christmas.

The fact that several Thrift Clubs would be paying out about that time may have accounted for the enthusiasm with which Emily's venture was received. The money came in briskly until only young Willie Amey's contribution, and his mother's, were outstanding.

The day before the outing, Mrs Amey appeared, in tears. Asking Jane to keep an eye on both classes, Emily took the weeping woman over to the school house and heard the sad tale.

'That beast of a husband,' Emily told Jane later, 'took the ten shillings from the jug on the top shelf of the dresser, where she'd hidden it – or *thought* she had, poor soul – and drank the lot at the pub last night.'

'What will happen?'

'I shall put in the money for them,' said Emily shortly, 'and I'll see Dick Amey myself. He'll pay up, never fear!'

Jane gazed at Emily in trepidation. Dick Amey, she knew, was a big, burly, beery fifteen-stoner. Jane was afraid of him under normal circumstances. Provoked, he could be dangerous, she felt sure.

'But he's such a great *bully* of a man,' said Jane tremulously.

'And like most bullies,' said Emily forthrightly, 'he's a great coward too. I shall square up to him tonight.'

She went about her duties as blithely as ever that afternoon, but

Jane was the prey of anxiety. She said goodbye to her diminutive headmistress that afternoon, wondering if she would see her unscathed next morning.

She need not have worried. Evidently Emily had put on her coat and hat as soon as she thought Dick was home, and had climbed the stile, crossed a field to his distant cottage, and tapped briskly at his door.

His frightened wife stood well back while the proceedings took place.

Emily had come straight to the point. Direct attack was always Emily's motto, and she got under Dick Amey's guard immediately.

'About as mean a trick as I've ever heard of,' said Emily heartily. 'But the money's in for both of them and they're going to enjoy the show. That's ten shillings you owe me. I'll take it now.'

Dick Amey, flabbergasted, demurred.

'I ain't got above two shillun on me,' protested Dick.

Emily held out her hand in silence. His wife watched in amazement as he rooted, muttering the while in his trouser pocket and slammed a florin into the waiting palm.

'When do I get the rest?' said Emily

'You tell me,' growled Dick.

Emily did.

'A shilling a week at least, till it's done,' said Emily. 'You keep off the beer for the next few weeks and you'll soon be out of my debt.'

Jane heard of this memorable encounter from Mrs Amey herself, long after the event. It must have looked like a wren challenging an eagle, thought Jane. But, no doubt about it, the wren was the victor that time.

Jane found permanent accommodation in a tiny cottage on Jesse Miller's farm at Springbourne.

It had been empty for some time, but was in good repair, for the Millers were always careful of their property.

It consisted of a living room and kitchen, with two small bedrooms above. The place was partly furnished and Jane had the pleasure of buying one or two extra pieces to increase her comfort. The rent was five shillings weekly and the understanding was that if Jesse Miller needed it for a farm worker sometime, then there would be a month's notice to quit.

She was now a near neighbour of Emily's, and frequently spent an evening with her headmistress and old Mrs Davis who now lived with her. Emily's father had died some years before and it had taken much persuasion to get her mother to leave the family cottage at Beech Green where she had reared her large family. But at last she consented, and had settled very well with Emily.

The two had much in common. They were both small, energetic and merry. Jane found them gay company, and often looked back, in later years, upon those cheerful evenings when the lamp was lit and stood dead centre on the red serge tablecloth, bobble-edged, which Mrs Davis had brought from her old home.

They knitted, or worked at a tufted wool rug, and chattered nineteen to the dozen. The school house living-room had an old-fashioned kitchen range with a barred fire and two generous hobs on which a saucepan of soup, or a steaming kettle, kept hot. It was all very snug, and Jane was always reluctant to leave the circle of lamp light to make her way home along the dark lane, following the wavering pool of dim light from her torch.

Often, she went to Caxley to see the Bentleys, for Richard Bentley, an older brother of her college friend, became increasingly attentive. He owned a little car and worked in a Caxley bank.

As the months passed, he came to fetch Jane from the cottage more and more frequently. When they became engaged, Emily Davis was the first to hear the news.

She was genuinely delighted, though not surprised, and kissed young Jane soundly.

'And don't have a long engagement,' urged Emily.

'But we must save some money,' protested Jane, laughing at her vehemence.

'Don't wait too long. I did, and I lost him.'

Her face clouded momentarily and, for the first time, Jane realized that this cheerful little middle-aged woman must once have been young and in love, and then terribly wounded.

It was the first she had heard of the affair, although she learnt more later.

'I'm sorry,' she said, taking the older woman's hand impulsively. 'I had no idea.'

'Well, it's over and done with,' said Emily, with a sigh. 'But take my advice. Marry soon.'

The two planned to marry in the spring of the next year, and at Easter 1939, Jane was married from her parents' house in London.

After the honeymoon, they settled at the Springbourne cottage, intending to move nearer Caxley when something suitable came on the market. Jane had resigned her teaching post, but still saw a great deal of Emily and her pupils.

When war broke out in September of that year, young Richard Bentley, who was in the Territorial Army, went off to fight.

Jane resumed her job as infant teacher at Springbourne School, and went to Caxley Station, with her headmistress, to collect forty or so evacuee schoolchildren who were to share Springbourne School for the duration of hostilities.

The war years had a dream-like quality for Jane Bentley. At times, it was more of a nightmare than a dream, but always there was this pervading feeling of unreality.

Had there ever been such a golden September, she wondered, as that first month of the war?

Day after day dawned cloudless and warm. Thistledown floated in the soft breezes. Butterflies, drunk with nectar, clung bemused to the buddleia flowers, or opened and shut their wings in tranced indolence upon the early Michaelmas daisies.

It was impossible to realize that just across the English Channel terror and violence held sway. At Springbourne one might have been swathed in a golden cocoon as the harvest was gathered and the downs shimmered in the heat haze.

Of course, at Springbourne School there was unusual activity as the newcomers settled down, amicably enough, with their native hosts.

Two teachers had accompanied the evacuees, one young, one middle-aged.

The middle-aged headmistress was a tough stringy individual with a voice as rough as a nutmeg scraper. She had run a Girl Guides troop for years, played hockey for her county and had the unsubtle team-spirit approach to life of a hearty adolescent.

She was billeted with Emily in the school house, and the two got on pretty well, both appreciating the other's honesty and concern for their charges. Miss Farrer, Emily discovered, was a whirlwind of a teacher, and a strict disciplinarian.

The younger woman, Miss Knight, was a different kettle of fish altogether, and poor Jane, whose spare bedroom she occupied, suffered grievously.

Molly Knight was one who thrived on emotion. She travelled from one dramatic crisis to another as a traveller in a desert moves from oasis to oasis. If the war could not supply enough material for sensation – and at that stage it was remarkably dull – Molly Knight created excitement from the little world about her. She was a mischief-maker, mainly because of this desire for sensation, and Jane found her particularly exhausting.

'What can I do?' she asked Emily one day, in despair. 'I try to look upon it as my contribution to the war effort, but I really can't face Molly breaking into my room at midnight to tell me how atrociously the Germans are treating their prisoners, and giving me a blow-by-blow account of her reactions to some stupid piece of propaganda.'

'I've been thinking about it,' replied Emily. 'If Miss Farrer's willing, I suggest they have your cottage, and you come here. How do you think that would work?'

Jane, despite a certain reluctance to leave the cottage, fell in with this plan, and for some time the two establishments were thus constituted. It made things easier in every way.

As the phoney war, as it came to be called, continued, a number of the children and their parents returned to London. One who did not, much to Emily's and Jane's pleasure, was a particularly attractive eight-year-old called Billy Dove.

He was a red-haired freckled boy, quick and intelligent. There was no doubt in Emily's mind that he would go on to a grammar school in time.

He was the only child of a quiet little mouse of a woman, and the two were billeted in a cottage not far from the school. The father was in the Navy, patrolling off the coast of Ireland, it was believed.

Mother and son were devoted. Mrs Dove was a great knitter, and young Billy's superb collection of jerseys was much admired. She did not mix much with the other women, although Billy was popular with the other children, frequently organizing their games.

One day in late November the tragedy occurred. By now the

weather had broken, and all day the wind had howled round Springbourne School and rain had lashed the windows. Playtime was passed indoors, in a flurry of well-worn comics on the desks among the milk bottles.

By afternoon, a fierce gale was blowing, ferocious enough to satisfy even Molly Knight's passion for excitement.

'Just look at the postman!' she exclaimed to Jane, as they watched the weather through the rain-spattered window. 'He can hardly walk against it!'

They watched him struggle up the path to Billy Dove's door, letter in hand. Water streamed from his black oilskin cape, and every step sent drops flying from his wellington boots.

The children were sent home at the right time, through the murky fury of the storm, with strict orders 'not to loiter'. Emily and Jane returned to the school house for tea, looking forward to a peaceful evening by the fire.

But at eight o'clock, an agitated neighbour arrived to say that Mrs Dove was in a dead faint across her table, with her wrists dripping blood, and that young Billy was nowhere to be found.

'You go and ring the doctor,' said Emily to Jane, 'while I run along to Mrs Dove.' They flung on their coats and hurried away on their errands.

The scene at Mrs Dove's, though frightening enough, was not quite as horrifying as the neighbour's breathless description had led Emily to believe.

There was blood upon the tablecloth, on the floor, and upon Mrs Dove's hand-knitted jumper, but the slashed wrists dripped no longer for, luckily, the poor woman's attempt at suicide had been unsuccessful. Emily had snatched up her mother's smelling salts on her way out, and now waved the pungent bottle before the pale face.

The neighbour found some rum in the cupboard, and when, at last, Mrs Dove came to, she and Emily made her sip a little rum and hot water.

'What ever made you do it?' asked the neighbour, bewildered.

Emily shook her head. This was no time to torture Mrs Dove with whys and wherefores. They must bide their time.

Although conscious, the woman said nothing, but sat, head sunk upon the bloodied jumper, in silence.

But when the doctor arrived, she stirred and pointed to a letter which had fallen to the floor. He read it, and passed it to Emily, without speaking.

It was a brief communication – that which Jane and Molly had seen the postman delivering that afternoon. It said that James Alan Dove was missing presumed killed.

'I'd like to have her in hospital overnight,' said the doctor. 'She's lost a good deal of blood, and is in a severe state of shock.'

'I understand,' said Emily. 'The boy is missing. I'll ring the police and start searching myself. He can stay the night at the school house when we find him.'

'By far the best thing, agreed the doctor. If only more women were like Emily Davis, he thought, turning to his patient!

The memory of that night stayed with Jane Bentley for the rest of her life. The two of them set out through the storm with only the faintest glimmer from torches, dimmed by tissue paper over the glass in accordance with black-out regulations, to guide them

'We'll stick together,' said Emily. 'And keep shouting his name Not that we stand much chance of being heard in this wind.'

'Which way?' asked Jane, at Mrs Dove's gate.

'Towards Caxley. He may have had some muddled idea of catching a train. Anyway, he wouldn't make for the downs in this weather. There's not a shred of shelter there.'

They splashed along the valley lane, past the school. The water gurgled on each side of the road, sometimes fanning across the full width where the surface tilted. Above their heads the wind roared in the branches, clashing them together and scattering twigs and leaves below. The elephantine grey trunks of the beech trees were streaked with rivulets of rainwater.

Jane's shoes squelched at every step. She could feel the water between her toes, and wished she had had Emily's foresight and had thrust her feet into wellington boots.

The little headmistress kept up a brisk pace Every now and again she stopped, and the two would cry.

Billy! Billy Dove! Billy!'

But their voices were drowned in the turmoil about them and Jane began to wonder if the whole venture would have to be aban-doned.

She followed in Emily's wake, envying the older woman's un-flagging energy.

'Are you aiming at anywhere particular?' she shouted above the din. Emily nodded.

'Bennett's barn and the chicken houses,' she responded. Jane knew that these buildings were Edgar Bennett's — that same Edgar, so she had recently learnt — who had jilted the indomitable little woman before her, so many years ago.

They splashed onward. Now the lane ran close by the little river. The watercress was now large and coarse, and swept this way and that by the torrent of water rushing through it. Who would have thought that the pretty summer trickle of brook, overhung with willows and long grasses, could become such a snarling leaping force, carrying all before it!

Emily turned left, and struck uphill along a rough track now streaming with chalky water from the downs. Some hundred yards up the hill, she left the track and beat her way, head down against the onslaught of rain, towards two large hen houses standing side by side in the field. Jane followed doggedly.

'Stand round here. There's more shelter.' said Emily. 'I'll only open the door a crack, otherwise the hens will be out. They're kittle-cattle.'

It was the first time Jane had heard this phrase. She savoured it now, watching Emily's small hand fumbling with the wooden catch of the door.

'Billy! Billy Dove!' she called through the chink. A pencil of light from the dimmed torch searched every cranny of the house.

There were a few squawks of alarm from the hens, and a pre-liminary rumbling from the rooster before taking suitable action against those who disturbed his rest. But there was no human voice to be heard.

'No luck,' said Emily. shutting the door, and squelching across the grass to the next.

They were just as unlucky here.

'We'll try the barn,' said Emily, tucking wet strands of hair under her sodden head scarf. 'Back to the road, Jane.'

Jane found herself stumbling along, almost in a state of collapse. She was not as strong in constitution as Emily, and this evening's tragedy had taken its toll. She longed for bed, for warmth for shelter from the cruel buffeting of the weather, and for the relief of finding the missing child.

She did not have to wait long. At the barn door, Emily motioned her forward. Together they moved inside, out of the wind and rain. It was quiet in here, and fragrant with the summer smell of hay.

Emily pushed aside the wet tissue paper from the torch, and a stronger light came to rest on a dark bundle curled up in an outsize nest in one corner of the barn.

Emily knelt down beside the sleeping child. His eyes were tightly shut, his red hair dark with moisture and clinging to his forehead. The cheeks were blotched and his eyelids swollen with crying. But he was unharmed.

'Billy,' whispered Emily. The child woke, and sat up abruptly. There was no preliminary stretching or yawning. Billy Dove was awake in an instant, and remembered all that had brought him to this place in blind panic. Emily knew how it would be.

'Mummy?' he asked, turning anxious eyes upon Emily. She took one of his grimy hands in hers.

'She's well again,' she told him. 'The doctor is looking after her.'

'And Daddy?'

'No one knows yet.' She gripped his hand more tightly. Obviously, the child had read the letter and understood his mother's action when he had found her slumped across the table.

'But what do *you* think?' said Billy, his bottom lip quivering piteously.

Jane, the silent spectator, never forgot Emily's reply, or the expression on her wet face as she made it.

'I think it would be wrong and wicked to stop hoping,' said Emily straightly.

The child sighed and struggled to his feet. Emily brushed the wisps of hay from his raincoat.

'You're coming to sleep in my house now,' Emily told him.

He managed a watery smile.

'Thank you, Miss Davis,' he said politely, holding open the door for her.

Jane Bentley put down the *Caxley Chronicle* slowly. Over thirty years had passed and yet she could remember that dimly-lit scene in every detail.

And now Emily Davis was dead!

Or was she, wondered Jane? What was that saying about those who lived in the hearts of others? Something to the effect that they never really died. If that were the case, then Emily Davis would certainly live on.

She herself owed much to Emily. She had gone to Springbourne a nervous, delicate girl with little to look forward to in the career which she had chosen.

Emily had given her strength and encouragement. She had sent her out into the healthy downland to regain her youthful spirits. She had taken in this apprehensive stranger and turned her into a happy confident member of the Springbourne family.

Whilst she was with Emily she had found health, happiness and a husband.

And more than that, she had found, by Emily's example, a way of living and a strength of character, both of which were to remain as guide-lines for the rest of her life.

Little Emily Davis's influence must have spread far, thought Jane, gazing into the September sunshine. Just as a small pebble, dropped into a still pool, spreads ever-widening ripples, so must Emily's impact have travelled through all the friends and pupils she had encountered.

What became of Billy Dove? she wondered. He certainly fulfilled the promise Emily foretold, and went on to Caxley Grammar School, then to a university, and was doing something quite important connected with mining, Jane believed.

There had been a happy ending to Billy Dove's war-time experience, Jane remembered, for his father had been picked up from the sea by a German ship and he spent the rest of the war, tediously but safely, as a prisoner. Billy's eyes had been like stars when he told Miss Davis the news, months after that never-to-be-forgotten night of storm and horror.

Dear Billy Dove! thought Jane, bestirring herself. He ought to know the news, but it wasn't likely that he took the *Caxley Chronicle* these days. He probably read the *Financial Times*, now that he was a prosperous man of nearly forty. No doubt he had done well for himself, but no doubt he often thought of Springbourne School and how much he owed to the guiding spirit who ruled it so wisely when he was young.

And in that, thought Jane Bentley, he would not be alone.

11. Billy Dove Goes Further

Jane Bentley was wrong.

Billy Dove read the *Caxley Chronicle* as well as the *Financial Times*. It arrived regularly each week, in a wrapper neatly addressed by his mother, wherever he might be in the wide world. The issue carrying the notice of Emily's death came to him in Scotland.

When his father, Petty Officer Dove, returned from prison camp at the end of the war, he found that his old London employer had died and the firm was no more. In a way, he was relieved.

He had had plenty of time for thinking in camp, and more and more his thoughts turned to the English countryside where he had been brought up Now he longed to return.

After leaving the village school, he had been bound apprentice, at the age of fourteen, to a family firm of cabinet-makers in London. He lodged with an obliging aunt in Mitcham, worked hard, and gained steady promotion with the firm as the years passed.

In one of the terraced houses opposite his aunt's home, he found his future wife, a pretty little auburn-haired girl, who caught the same train into the City as he did to work as a copy-typist in an insurance firm.

They married when he was twenty-five and she was twenty-three, and made their home in a tiny flat two streets away from their former abodes.

Jim Dove often thought of those early married days, as he went about his tasks in the German prisoner-of-war camp. They had been happy enough, for they were young and very much in love. Young Billy arrived within the year, and was an added joy – a good-tempered, healthy baby, with his mother's red hair and his father's cheerful disposition.

It was now that the Doves began to long for more room. Their flat was on the first floor. Their landlady lived below, a hard-bitten widow who resented the necessity of letting part of her home.

Billy's pram was left in her tiny hall with her grudging consent. Billy's napkins and other family washing were allowed to blow on a two-yard line near the garden rubbish heap, screened from sight by a large golden privet bush. Except for the purpose of hanging out the washing, the Dove family was not allowed in the garden.

Peggy Dove bore the restrictions patiently. Times were hard, and she knew that it would be several years before they could hope to move to a house of their own. Meanwhile, she took Billy to the nearby park for his daily outing, and did her best to keep on good terms with the landlady.

Jim Dove fretted far more. When war came, and settled their future for them willy-nilly, he was relieved to know that his wife and son would be settled safely at Springbourne. He knew the Caxley area fairly well, for he and his father had been great cyclists, and had camped many a time on the banks of the Cax, and had pushed their bicycles up the steep flanks of the downs nearby. At sea, and later in the prison camp, he had found comfort in the thought of Peggy and Billy enjoying the countryside he knew so well.

He was determined that he would not return to London to live.

It was no place for a boy to be brought up. Who knows? There might be more children, and a flat in London was little better than the prison he now inhabited, he told himself. He was tired of being cramped and confined. When he got back he would find a job in the country.

But would he? That was the problem. Would any other firm employ him? Peggy, cautious as a mouse, would tremble at the thought of any risk. She would try to persuade him to return to the old life, he felt sure.

Ah well! No use fretting about it whilst in German hands. He'd face that problem when the time came, Jim decided.

As so often happens, the problems resolved themselves by the time he was reunited with Peggy and Billy. The old firm had gone. Billy was now doing well at Caxley Grammar School, and Peggy had found a little cottage to rent on the edge of commonland within walking distance of Caxley. She wouldn't go back to London for a thousand pounds!

Jim found a post with a local firm of furniture makers, and the Doves settled down to make their life afresh. Jim and Peggy were destined to spend the rest of their long lives in Caxley, and to find contentment there.

Billy remained an only child, and a highly satisfactory one. He was almost thirteen when his father returned, and working well at the grammar school. He had found the transition from the little school at Springbourne to the large boys' school somewhat unnerving, but by the time his father came back he had settled down and was enjoying the work.

Eventually, he gained a place at Cambridge, obtained a good class Honours degree, and became a mining engineer. His work took him all over the world, but at the time of Emily Davis's death he was in Scotland with his wife and two children. His assignment there was for approximately two years, and the Doves had rented a house for that time. It stood among pine forests, on the edge of a sizeable village where the children attended the local school.

The job was an interesting one. On the site of a long disused coal mine, other mineral deposits had been discovered, but at a depth and angle which made them difficult to work. It was Billy Dove's job to overcome the problem.

He had been chosen expressly for it by his firm because he had done so well on a similar project for the Italian government. On the slopes of Mount Etna in Sicily, certain minerals had been discovered in the volcanic rock which were of great interest to the chemical industry. The deposits were at a considerable depth, in one particular stratum formed by lava ejected some hundreds of years earlier. Billy found the work arduous but fascinating.

He was at work there for six weeks, and there was a possibility of returning for a further month when the drilling had reached the second stage. It was a prospect which he viewed with mixed feelings. For, to his mingled delight and guilt, sensible, steady Billy Dove, devoted husband and father, regular church-goer and wise counsellor to those asking his advice, had fallen head over heels in love with a girl in Sicily.

It came about like this.

Billy's firm had booked a room for him at a modest but respectable hotel in Taormina, a few miles from the working site.

He lost his heart to the little town at once. Perched on the sunny hillside, tall cypresses towering like dark candles above the freshly-painted houses, the place had unique charm. It was at the end of April when he saw it first, and the public gardens, laid out in broad terraces, were fragrant with wallflowers, pinks and stocks. The orange trees added the warm scent of their blossom and the beauty of their golden fruit to the scene. Wistaria hung in swags from the pergolas, and, in the sheltered garden of the hotel next door, sweet peas were already in flower.

In all his wanderings, Billy Dove had never yet discovered a place which enchanted him so swiftly and so completely. He gazed at the vivid green-blue sea far below, at the craggy mountain which overhung the town, and at Etna against the blue sky forming a majestic backcloth to it all.

In his spare time he explored the town thoroughly. The ruined Greek theatre fascinated him, and the view from its heights across the Straits of Messina to the distant mainland of Italy was one which never failed to thrill him.

He enjoyed plunging down the steep steps from one level of Taormina to the next. He sampled all manner of places to eat and drink, from tiny cafés, murky with smoke and crowded with noisy Sicilians, to cosmopolitan hotels offering the accepted variety of French cooking found in every tourist centre.

It was not long before he entered the San Domenico Hotel. It had once been a monastery, and about its ancient courts and stairways still clung the gentle silence of earlier days. Here Billy Dove found hushed peace and rare beauty. He also found unexpected, and shattering, love.

The girl was small and golden. When Billy saw her first, she was clad in a brief white frock which contrasted with her glowing suntanned skin.

She was climbing up the steep slope from the swimming pool, carrying the bulky paraphernalia of an afternoon spent swimming and sun-bathing. Billy stood aside to let her pass, and the towel which was flung over one shoulder slid to the ground. Billy bent to retrieve it.

'Thank you,' said the girl, holding out a hand. Immediately, a Penguin book and one sandal clattered to the path.

The girl laughed as Billy bent again.

'I'm so sorry. It's like one of those circus acts, isn't it? You know, the clown drops one thing after another and then turns out to be an expert juggler.'

'And are you?'

'Does it look like it?' replied the girl. Her teeth were very white and even. Her eyes were a peculiarly light hazel which gave them a sunny look.

'Let me take some of the things,' offered Billy, genuinely concerned by the untidy collection of articles in her arms. 'Couldn't we put the small stuff in your bag?'

He squatted down and packed the book, two sandals, a spectacle case and a tube of skin-cream into the enormous beach bag. He then stood up and folded the towel neatly.

'You take that, and I'll bring the bag,' said Billy.

'No, really. I can manage perfectly now that you've tidied me up. You were going down to the pool, I expect.'

'I wasn't really going anywhere. Just savouring a perfect evening.'

More people began to descend the path, and Billy and the girl found themselves in the way.

'Well, thank you,' she said, moving on. 'I was going to have a drink before dinner. May I offer you one after all this porterage?'

'I should love it,' said Billy truthfully, following her nimble figure up the slope.

Over the drinks they introduced themselves and Billy told her about the work which brought him to Sicily.

'And you are on holiday, I expect,' he said.

'I have been. That's why I'm staying at the San Domenico. But I've come to a tremendous decision in the past fortnight. I'm hoping to settle here for good.'

'In this hotel?'

'Heavens, no! I should soon be broke. No, I've found a little house, higher up the hill. I've rented it for six months to see if life in Taormina is all I hope it will be. I've been looking for somewhere to settle ever since my father died last year.'

It appeared that her father had been a prosperous manufacturer in Yorkshire until a stroke had finished all activity for him Mary had left her job as almoner in the local hospital to nurse him. Her mother had been dead for some years.

On her father's death she found that everything had been left to her. He was 'a warm man', as they said locally, but a large house on the windswept moors, despite two old-fashioned hard-working maids to help in running it, was not what Mary wanted.

She was over thirty now, and longed to get away. Too long, she felt, she had been mewed up in the old home. She craved for sunshine and change.

She left the house in the maids' care while she set about her restless wanderings. Almost a year was spent in this way, and now she longed for a home, and somewhere to settle, as urgently as she had yearned for flight. In Taormina she believed she had found her goal.

'If I find it to my liking,' she told Billy, twirling her glass thoughtfully, 'I shall sell the Yorkshire place and stay here permanently. I've nothing to take me back – no relatives, no ties of any sort –'

Her voice trailed away, and she looked directly at Billy.

'Are you staying for dinner?'

'I ought to go back to do some work.'

'Do stay,' she said impulsively. 'It's lovely to talk to someone again, and you've been so very kind.'

Of course he stayed. And every minute that passed made her company dearer to him. He promised to come and inspect the little house on the morrow, and to help in any way he could with the move.

Billy Dove walked home, through the moonlit scented night, tingling with the most unusual sensations.

'My God!' said Billy, addressing a stone dragon on a gatepost, 'it's love again!'

In the days that followed, Billy felt himself the battleground of conflicting emotions, and very exhausting he found it. He had been a fairly uncomplicated character for almost forty years, distrusting violent emotion, and impatient with those who seemed to have no control of their feelings. He had met many philanderers in his travels, and had a hearty dislike of them. Those who boasted of their conquests he found doubly boring. They did not impress Billy Dove.

'Time you grew up,' he would tell them, yawning, and walk away.

And here he was, behaving in exactly the same way. The guilt he felt when he thought of his disloyalty to Sarah and the boys was overwhelming, but only momentarily so. It was swept away by this new wave of fierce, youthful, exulting happiness. Before its on-slaught he was powerless.

Mary's passion matched his own. It was as though, with so little time before them, their love had an added urgency. They spent every possible hour together, turning their minds away from the inexorable advance of the day of Billy's departure, like children who hide their eyes from a wounding light.

Taormina, and the golden girl, were heartrendingly beautiful when that last day came.

'You'll come back? Say you'll come back!' pleaded Mary, cling-ing to him.

'You know I can't promise that,' said Billy. She knew about Sarah and their two children, and he had been careful not to raise her hopes by telling her of the possibility of further work on the site. Cruel though it seemed, they must make the break unless their lives were to be wrecked.

They parted tenderly in the little house on the hillside, and Billy could not bear to look back as he strode away. He could have returned so willingly, so rapturously but, face averted, he walked on blindly while his heart plummeted

He flew from Catania that morning and he saw the green and golden island tipping beneath him through a blur of tears. He changed planes at Rome, and found he had to wait for three hours. He spent the time pacing restlessly up and down in the windy sun-shine, his mind in turmoil.

By the time he arrived at Heathrow, in pouring rain, he was calm enough to have made two decisions. This sweet mad interlude was over, and he would not see Mary again. Secondly, Sarah must never know anything about it

12. The Return of Billy Dove

It is easy enough to make good resolutions. Keeping them is another kettle of fish.

The decision to keep his guilty secret from Sarah was comparatively simple. He was deeply ashamed of his behaviour, although the remembrance of those few idyllic weeks would never fade, and would colour the rest of his life.

Billy was not the sort of man to unload his guilt on to another. What good would confession do to Sarah? No, he owed it to her to keep silent, and by his extra care of her, and the boys, to salve his smarting conscience.

But the decision to make a clean break with Mary was seriously undermined when a letter arrived from his firm asking him to return to the Sicilian site for the second stage of the work. Could he let them know how the Scottish project was moving? At a pinch, young Bannister could take over one or the other while he was away. He would need thorough briefing, of course, and it was to be hoped that Dove could arrange to carry on with both jobs. What did he feel?

What did he feel, echoed Billy! He put the letter to the side of his breakfast plate, and gazed out at the wooded Scottish hillside. In the garden John and Michael raced round and round pursued by a floppy-eared puppy. There were his two fine boys, full of roaring high spirits. He must do nothing to hurt them.

He looked across the table to Sarah, immersed in *The Caxley Chronicle* which had arrived with the morning letters. She looked very young and defenceless, despite her thirty-odd years, in her blue and white cotton frock. A little frown of concentration furrowed her smooth brow.

'There's an Emily Davis in the "Deaths",' she remarked. 'Could it be your old teacher?'

'I should have thought she'd died years ago,' remarked Billy absently. his mind on his problem.

Well, she was eighty-four,' said Sarah, her eyes still fixed on the paper. 'Died at Beech Green. Might well be, don't you think?'

She looked up. Billy was standing at the window, gazing into the garden. It was apparent that he had not heard her remarks. She was accustomed to his complete withdrawal from the world around him when his mind was perplexed, and was not unduly upset.

'Heavens, it's late!' she cried. She ran to the open window and called to the boys.

Billy shook his head, as though he had just emerged from deep water. He put his arms round her swiftly and kissed her with sudden fierceness.

Sarah laughed.

'Don't dally, darling,' she said, 'or the boys will be late for school.'

Within two minutes, the three were in the Land-Rover waving goodbye to Sarah at the window.

The road was steep, and wound its way downhill between dark fir woods which Billy found beautiful on a sunny morning, but sinister and silent at other times. Nothing grew beneath their shade, and Billy often thought longingly of the oak and hazel woods of his childhood at Caxley, starred in spring with primroses and anemones, and gay with the golden tassels of catkins.

The village school stood back from the road with a wide green verge before it. As Billy drew up, the bell was clanging from the little bell-tower, and the children were already forming lines ready to lead in. The two boys gave him hasty wet kisses, scrambled down, and raced to join their fellows. The schoolmaster was a stickler for punctuality.

He waited to see them take their places in the lines. John turned towards him and gave an enormous wink of triumph, as if to say: 'Done it!', just as the lanky form of the headmaster appeared at the school door.

Amused, Billy drove off slowly. There was a lot to be said for a village school education when one was eight, robust and cheerful.

He had been eight, he remembered sharply, when he was at Beech Green Village School. But, though he may have been robust, he had been far from cheerful at that time.

What would he have done without Emily Davis just then? At the same age as John, frightened and horror-struck, he had been rescued by her efforts He had never forgotten that night of storm and terror.

And she was dead? Is that what Sarah said this morning? Eighty-four, and at Beech Green? He mused as he wound his way towards work. That would be Emily Davis, without doubt.

He sighed deeply. She was a grand old girl! His thoughts strayed from the events of that wild night to another phase of his school life when, as a bewildered eleven-year-old, Emily Davis had come, once more, to the rescue.

The transition from the tiny world of Springbourne to the comparatively large one of Caxley upset the boy more than he would admit.

Instead of racing the few yards along the village street from his home to the school, he now had to rise much earlier and catch a bus into the town. His comfortable hand-knitted jerseys and flannel shorts, now gave way to a grey flannel suit with long trousers. Black laced shoes, polished overnight, took the place of easy well-worn sandals, and on his head he wore the familiar Caxley Grammar School cap, with much pride, but some irritation – for wasn't it just one more thing to take care of, and to remember to bring home at night?

At times, young Billy felt burdened with all these belongings. They weighed as heavily upon him as the shining new leather satchel which bumped against his hip as he walked.

He was bewildered too by the sheer size of his new school and by the hundreds of boys. When you have been one of forty or fifty children at school assembly, and one among only twenty or so in the classroom, it is unnerving to be cast among four hundred-odd boys, all larger than oneself.

To Billy, some of the prefects were men. Certainly, some of them looked quite as mature as some of the young masters. They filled the boy with awe with their tasselled caps, their gruff voices and their sheer size when they passed him in the corridors.

The standard of work, too, presented a problem. At Springbourne School he had held his own with little effort. Now he was among boys brighter than himself. There were new subjects to tackle, such as French, Latin and Algebra. At times, sitting at the cottage table, with his homework books spread out in the light of the Aladdin lamp, he came near to despair. Would his mind ever be able to hold all this mass of new knowledge?

But it was the affair of the conkers which brought all his troubles to a head. Billy had always loved the glossy beauties which tumbled from the Springbourne trees in the autumn gales. He collected them with the eye of a connoisseur, and Billy Dove was recognized by the other boys as a champion in the conker-playing field.

He owned a metal meat skewer which bored a hole beautifully. Only Billy's closest friends were allowed to borrow it. He was equally particular about the type of string he used to thread his collection. All in all, Billy Dove brought the care and use of conkers to a fine art.

He was delighted to find a stout horse-chestnut tree on the way from Caxley station to the school, and he filled his new jacket pockets with some splendid specimens. At playtime (which he tried, in vain, to remember to call 'break' now), he turned out his collection on the grass of the school field and, squatting down, began to sort them out for size. His metal skewer was in his inner pocket with his new fountain pen and propelling pencil. He produced it, ready for action.

At that moment, a shadow fell across him, and looking up he saw one of the prefects who was on duty.

'Whose are these?' said he disparagingly.

'Mine,' said Billy, blinking against the sunlight.

'Stand up when you talk to me.'

Billy obeyed briskly.

'What are these for?' continued the lofty one.

'To play with.'

'To play with,' mimicked the older boy. 'You'd better learn pretty smartly that we don't play kids' games like conkers here. Chuck them away.'

'But why –?' began Billy rebelliously.

'Don't argue. Throw them in the dustbin. And pronto!'

'Can't I take them home?'

The prefect took hold of Billy's left ear, and twisted it neatly.

'You talk too much, young feller. Do as you're told or I'll report you. And pick up every one. Understood? If they get in the school mower old Taffy'll murder you.'

His eye lit upon the skewer.

'And I'll confiscate that. Dangerous weapon, that is You can ask for it back at the end of term.'

There was nothing for it but to obey Furious at heart, Billy collected the shining conkers, grieving over the satin skins so soon to wither in the dustbin.

The prefect accompanied Billy to the dustbin and watched him deposit his treasures. He tossed the skewer nonchalantly from hand to hand as the disposal of the conkers went on.

Billy made one last bid for his property.

'If I promise to leave my skewer at home, can I have it back?'

The prefect stood stock-still, his eyes narrowing menacingly.

'Don't you understand the King's English? You'll get it back – IF you ever get it back – at the end of term. Clear off, and think yourself lucky not to be reported for disobedience!'

A dangerous weapon, thought Billy murderously, watching his enemy depart. That's what he'd called his beloved skewer. At that moment, in Billy's hands, it might well have been an instrument of fierce revenge.

This happened on a Friday. He returned home, moody and pale-faced, his satchel heavier than ever with weekend homework, and his heart heavier still. His mother was wise enough to refrain from questioning, but she watched anxiously as the boy fiddled about with his exercise books at the table, obviously unable to concentrate.

He slammed them together eventually, and spent the rest of the evening slumped in a chair with a library book. There was still a good deal of work to be done, his mother knew. Usually, Billy tried to get the major part of it polished off before the weekend began, but it was plain that he was in no mood to tackle it tonight.

He was little better next morning, and his mother sent him to the village shop for some goods. It was there that he met Miss Davis, also armed with a basket. Her quick glance noted the heavy eyes and unusually sulky mouth.

'How's school?' she asked amiably.

'All right,' said Billy perfunctorily.

'Lots of prep?'

'Too much. Much too much.'

Billy sighed. Miss Davis felt a pang of pity.

'Have you got time to help me saw some logs this afternoon?'

Billy's face brightened.

'Yes. I'd like to. What time?'

Any time after two. Ask your mother if she can spare you for a couple of hours. I'd be glad of a hand.'

She packed her basket neatly, smiled at Billy, and departed. Cheered at the prospect of some physical activity, Billy set about his shopping in better spirits.

Clad in his comfortable old jersey and shorts, Billy reported for work at a quarter past two. Emily was already hard at it, at the end of the garden, saw in hand.

'My poor old apple tree,' she told him, pointing the saw at the fallen monster. 'It's been rocking for two or three years, and last week's gale heeled it over.'

'We'll never get through the trunk with these saws,' observed Billy.

'No need to. It's just the branches we'll have to do. A man's coping with the main part next weekend.'

They applied themselves zealously to the smaller branches. Billy found the work wonderfully exhilarating. The smell of the sawn wood was refreshing, and a light breeze kept him cool.

He enjoyed stacking the logs in Emily's tumble-down shed, and made a tidy job of it. The rough bark, grey-green with lichen, was pleasant to handle, and his spirits rose as the stack grew higher and higher.

'It will probably be enough for the whole winter,' he said, sniffing happily. Emily straightened up and, hands on hips, looked at their handiwork with satisfaction.

'Easily, Billy.'

She gave a swift glance at the boy, now flushed and panting with his exertions.

'Have you had enough, or shall we finish the job?'

'Let's finish,' said Billy decidedly.

They worked on in companionable silence. Sawdust blew across the grass, as the saws bit rhythmically through the branches. By half past four the job was done, and only the twigs and chips remained to be collected into a box for kindling wood.

'I've got two blisters,' laughed Emily, holding out her hands.

'I haven't,' said Billy proudly, surveying his own grimy hands.

'We deserve some tea,' said his old headmistress, leading the way to the house.

It was over home-made fruit cake and steaming cups of tea that Billy told his tale. He had never felt any shyness in Emily's presence, and their shared labours that afternoon made it easier for him to speak, as Emily had intended.

There was little need for her to probe. The boy was glad to find someone to talk to, and the new problems came tumbling out. They were not new, of course, to Emily Davis. She had seen many children in the same predicament. There were very few, in fact, who went on to the large Caxley schools from Springbourne, who did not find the journey, the pace of work and the numbers surrounding them, as daunting as young Billy did.

And then came the sorry tale of the conkers. If Billy had expected sympathy, he was to be surprised. Emily took the account of his discomfiture with brisk matter-of-factness.

'If "no conkers" is a school rule – although I doubt it – you must just abide by it. Nothing to stop you enjoying a game at home anyway. And as for that prefect, well, you'll find people like that everywhere, and he was only trying to do his duty, poor young man.'

'Poor young man, indeed!' thought Billy resentfully. But he had the sense to remain silent.

Emily refilled his tea-cup and went on to talk, as though at random, of the difficulties of adjusting oneself to new situations.

Billy was soon aware that he was not the only person to have suffered growing pains. It was true, as Miss Davis said, that one's world grew bigger every so often. It was an ordeal to leave home for one's first school; it was a bigger one to change to a larger school, as he had just done.

'And then you'll plunge into a deeper pool still, if you go to a university,' said Emily, 'and probably nearly drown when you dive into the world of work after that! But you'll survive, Billy, you'll see, and be able to help a great many other young people who are busy jumping from one pool to the next and floundering now and again!'

It was all said so light-heartedly that it was not until many years later that Billy realized how skilfully the lesson had been imparted. At the time, he was only conscious of comfort and the resurgence of his natural high spirits, and put both down to energetic sawing in the open air, and Emily's excellent fruit cake.

At the gate, Billy turned and surveyed the old familiar playground next door.

'I wish I were back,' he said impulsively.

Emily shook her head, smiling.

'You don't really. You're much too big a fish for that little pond now, and I think you are beginning to know it.'

She looked at Billy thoughtfully.

'What was the name of that prefect?'

Billy told her. She was silent for a minute, and then seemed to come to a decision.

'I'm going to tell you something which you must keep to yourself, but I think you can do it, and I think it will help you.'

'I can keep a secret,' promised Billy.

'That boy went from Fairacre School to Caxley. The family moved later, but this is what I want you to know. Miss Clare told me that he was so upset in his first term that his parents thought he might have to leave. From what you tell me, he seems to be keeping afloat in his bigger pond now.'

'He's unsinkable!' commented Billy ruefully.

'Well, think about it. I've only told you because I believe it might help you to understand people. But not a word to anyone, Billy.'

'Not a word,' he echoed solemnly, and ran home with half a crown as wages in his hand, and new-found hope in his heart.

★

Wisps of white mist were drifting in from the sea as Billy Dove drove his Land-Rover over the rutted site to his office.

The sun was almost blotted out now, faintly discernible now and again, riding moon-like through the ragged clouds. Billy hated this sea-mist, which local people called 'the haar', which swept in unpredictably and wrapped the countryside in icy veils.

He shivered as he entered the small granite house where his office was situated on the ground floor. He was the first to arrive. His colleagues would be coming within the next quarter of an hour, but now he had the little house to himself, and had time to think.

He took out the letter and read it again. Taormina! And Mary! Gazing into the swirling whiteness outside, he longed to return to the sunshine, the flowers, the cypress trees – and, above all, to the warmth and love of Mary. It would be so easy to return, and have a week or two of utter happiness in the sun. The work here could go on under young Bannister's eye without much effort God, it was tempting!

He stood up suddenly, hands in pockets, and went to the window. Coins jingled as he turned his loose change over and over in his nervousness.

This was a situation he must face alone. No wise old Miss Davis to turn to now.

He gave an impatient snort of derision. What would Emily Davis know, anyway, of a man's feelings? Much use she would be to him with a problem like this. Her advice would come out ready-made, as automatically as a packet from a slot machine.

'Your duty, my boy, is to your wife and children! The rest is temptation. It is SIN, put before you by the devil himself.'

How simple life must have been to those old Victorians with their rigid rules of conduct! But how much they must have missed!

He faced about, turning his back upon the blank whiteness now shrouding the hill side in impenetrable clammy fog.

Nevertheless, it was the only course to take. He had made up his mind to stay in Scotland as soon as he read the letter. Temptation, the devil, Emily Davis and all the other faintly ridiculous issues which clouded his mind, at the moment, as confusingly as the mist outside, made no difference to his decision. He had made the break with Mary. He would not go back.

He had a sudden memory of Sarah that morning, laughing in her blue and white cotton frock, and of John's conspiratorial wink across the playground.

He smiled as he drew a piece of writing paper towards him. Young Bannister would see Sicily for the first time. He would remain in Scotland.

He banged on the stamp as his assistant's car drew up outside, and went outside to meet him. It was like stepping naked into a wet mackintosh. God, what a climate!

Some men, thought Billy Dove, would say he was out of his mind to turn down the opportunity of leaving it. Perhaps he was. Who knows?

Ah well, the decision was made and, bitter though it was, it was the right one. He began to smile.

'What's the joke?' said his assistant.

'I'm trying to decide if I've come to my senses – or lost them completely,' said Billy.

The assistant raised his eyebrows, and Billy laughed ruefully.

'One thing, Miss Davis would approve.'

He clapped his bewildered colleague on the shoulder.

'Come along, son. We've work to do.'

13. Mrs Pringle Disapproves

The village of Fairacre is some two miles from Beech Green but news – particularly bad news – travels swiftly in the country, and Emily's death was heard of within a few hours of its happening.

The people of Fairacre knew Emily well, but their first concern was for Dolly Clare who had taught them, and their children, for so many years at Fairacre School.

As children, Emily and Dolly had attended Fairacre School, and later had taught there as pupil teachers. Dolly had remained there for the rest of her teaching life, whilst Emily had gone first to Caxley and then to Springbourne. When Springbourne School closed, as a result of the 1944 Act, Emily was transferred to a Caxley School, and lived with a younger brother for whom she kept house.

She was glad when he married, and she was free to join Dolly Clare. In the last happy years of their shared retirement, the two old ladies had frequently visited Fairacre, and indeed they were as well known there, by young and old, as in Beech Green.

'I'd have taken a bet on Dolly Clare going first,' observed Mr Willet to Mrs Pringle. Mr Willet is a man of many parts. He is school caretaker, sexton, verger, local nurseryman and a pillar of strength to all needing practical advice on such matters as faulty plumbing, pruning roses, tiling a roof and coping generally with a householder's problems.

Mrs Pringle is as gloomy as Mr Willet is sunny. She acts as school cleaner, is the bane of her headmistress's life, and a terror and scourge to all those with dirt on their shoes. Mrs Pringle is one of this world's martyrs, but one who certainly does not suffer in silence.

On this mellow afternoon of autumn sunshine, Mrs Pringle encountered Mr Willet as she made her way homeward from washing up the school dinner plates and cutlery.

St Patrick's clock had struck two, and Mr Willet was perched on a ladder picking early black plums from a tree in his front garden. He was suitably impressed with the gravity of Mrs Pringle's news of Emily Davis's going, and dismounted the ladder to converse over the gate.

Mr Willet knew what was fitting. One could not carry on a conversation on such a serious matter when engaged on plum-picking, ten feet above ground. It would be disrespectful to the dead, and an affront to Mrs Pringle.

'Yes, I'd have taken a bet on Dolly Clare going first,' he repeated, pushing back his cap. 'She'll miss her, you know. Anyone with her?'

Flattered by his attention, Mrs Pringle launched into her narrative. It was not often that Mr Willet treated her words with such respect. She made the most of this rare occasion, and propped her black oil-cloth bag against the gate, at her feet, as if she intended to be some time imparting her news.

Mr Willet, anxious though he was to hear it, watched the gesture with some foreboding. He had some hoeing to do, after the plum-picking, and some seeds to water. Mrs Pringle, launched upon the tide of her story, could take an unconscionable time getting to its end, as he knew well.

'I thought, the last time I saw Miss Davis,' began Mrs Pringle lugubriously, 'as she was on the wane. Funny how you gets to know. There's a look about folks, as no doubt you've noticed, Mr Willet.'

'Can't say I have,' replied Mr Willet shortly, his eyes roving to the plum tree.

'Ah well!' conceded Mrs Pringle, with a certain ghoulish smugness, 'there's some of us more in tune with the Other World. You gets to recognize the Hand of Death, before it's even fallen. Miss Davis had that look – just as though she was seeing the Farther Shore.'

'Stummer-cake, more like,' said Mr Willet sturdily. He did not hold with morbid fancies, and in these realms of psychic fantasy Mrs Pringle could lose herself for a good ten minutes, if not checked. Dear knows when he'd get the seeds watered, at this rate!

Mrs Pringle ignored his coarse interjection. It was not often that she had such a valuable captive audience. She returned to her theme with all the concentration of a terrier with a rat.

'I saw the same look on my poor mother's face the night before she died. "She won't last another day," I told my husband. "She got that hollow-cheeked look."'

'You should have put her teeth in again,' observed Mr Willet.

'And next morning I found her cold,' continued Mrs Pringle undaunted. 'She looked a young woman. At Peace. We had them words put on her stone actually.'

'I might get my bike out later on and see if I can do anything for Dolly Clare,' said Mr Willet.

'With Emily Davis still in the house?' cried Mrs Pringle, scandalized. 'Where's your sense of fitness?'

'Dolly Clare might be glad of a hand. You can do with an old friend when you've taken a knock like that.'

'They say the Annetts are keeping an eye on her,' said Mrs Pringle. 'Very good thing too. She's none too strong, is Dolly Clare. A shock like this could be the death of her.'

There was a glint of pleasurable anticipation in the old terror's eye which riled Mr Willet.

'Don't start thinking of double funerals,' he said tartly. Mrs Pringle bridled. Her thoughts had indeed strayed into this delectable and dramatic field. She changed her tactics swiftly before

Mr Willet escaped from her clutches and returned to his plum-picking.

'The very idea!' she protested, her double chin wobbling indignantly. 'As a matter of fact, I was recalling how good Miss Davis was to my brother-in-law – the one at Springbourne. She often found him a little job when times were hard. You knows what a family he had.'

Mr Willet began to despair of ever getting his jobs done. He was about to make a firm break, and risk Mrs Pringle's displeasure, when he saw help at hand.

A large shabby pram, squeaking to high heaven, approached from the Springbourne direction. A slatternly girl, with dishevelled red hair, pushed it, a toddler clinging to her skirts.

Mr Willet's spirits rose.

'Here's one of the family now,' he said joyfully 'I'll get back to work.'

With remarkable speed for one so thickset, he remounted the step ladder.

It was Minnie Pringle who approached. She was still known to the neighbourhood as Minnie Pringle, although she was now a married woman. A feckless body, 'not quite all there', as people said, she had produced three children before marriage, and two since. Her husband was much older than she was, a dour widower with a number of young children of his own. The combined families occupied a dilapidated semi-detached villa on the outskirts of Springbourne and seemed to thrive under Minnie's erratic care.

The house reeked permanently of neck-of-mutton stew, which was the only dish which Minnie had mastered over the years. This, with plenty of potatoes, innumerable sliced white loaves from a Caxley supermarket, and pots of strong sweet tea, constituted the household's diet. They all seemed to thrive on it.

Their clothes were given to them by kindly neighbours or bought for a few shillings at local jumble sales. Minnie's husband reckoned that his wages as a road-sweeper paid the rent of their shabby house, provided the food and left him ten shillings a week for beer and cigarettes.

Minnie found the arrangement perfectly satisfactory. After her haphazard upbringing it all seemed a model of household efficiency.

She greeted her aunt boisterously, sniffing the while.

'We've bin in your place, but you wasn't there.'

'Not surprising, is it?' said Mrs Pringle.

Sarcasm was lost upon Minnie.

'Just going to the Post Office to get me family.'

Mrs Pringle rightly translated this as 'family allowances', and snorted. This was a sore point.

'It's people like you, Minnie, as keeps people like me *poor*! About time you stopped having babies and expecting us hard-working folk to keep 'em for you.'

'I don't ask 'em to come,' replied Minnie, tossing her unkempt head.

'You don't do much to stop 'em as far as I can see,' boomed her aunt. She looked with disfavour upon the toddler who was wiping his nose on his coat cuff.

'I'll drop in on my way back,' said Minnie cheerfully. She was not one to harbour grudges. Mrs Pringle sighed heavily, picked up her black oil-cloth bag, and faced the inevitable.

'I'll go and put the kettle on,' she said resignedly. 'Don't dillydally now, Minnie. I've plenty to do when I get home, so don't keep me hanging about.'

Mr Willet, high among the branches, echoed this sentiment, and watched Mrs Pringle's squat figure stumping homeward into the distance.

What a family! What a disgrace to decent people! thought Mrs Pringle, setting out the cups and saucers on a tin tray. Of course, they were only relations by marriage, but even so!

Mrs Pringle shuddered at the thought of her husband's younger brother Josh. Nothing but a byword, as far as Caxley, and further. The police of three counties had been after him, for one thing or other. If it wasn't petty thieving in the market, it was breaking and entering, or being picked up dead drunk. Or else it was poaching, thought Mrs Pringle, putting out a few broken biscuits for the children.

Yes, poaching. And Miss Davis knew a bit about that too, come to think of it. It wasn't the sort of story you would tell to Mr Willet, say, but it just showed you that Emily Davis had her head screwed on, and her heart in the right place too.

The sight of that dratted girl Minnie had brought back the memory very sharply. Mrs Pringle shifted the kettle to the side of the stove, picked up her crochet work, and sat down, with a sigh, to await her niece's coming with what patience she could muster.

It had all happened when Minnie was eight or nine years of age – the scruffiest and most scatter-brained pupil in Emily Davis's class at Springbourne.

The child's work was atrociously done. Her writing always appeared to have been executed with a crossed nib dipped heavily in black honey. The pages bore the imprint of dirty fingers, despite Emily's insistence on frequent washings in the lobby.

After super-human efforts by Emily, Minnie had begun to read. Figure work seemed to be completely beyond her. Numbers to five had some reality for the child, and Emily had hopes of her comprehending those up to ten in the future. A realist, Emily faced the fact that double figures would probably always be beyond Minnie's ken. In this she was to be proved right.

Emily concentrated on Minnie's newly-acquired reading ability, substituted a pencil for the pen with the permanently crossed nib, and began to see the child making some headway.

It was not surprising that she was so backward. Her father, Josh Pringle, was the black sheep of his family, constantly in trouble, easily led by his dubious companions, and a mighty consumer of beer whenever he could afford to buy it. Occasionally he obtained work as a labourer, but his income was mainly derived from petty thieving, or from keeping a watch for the police whilst his cronies were 'doing a job'.

Minnie's mother was a brow-beaten wisp of a woman, prematurely grey, who looked twice her age, and had long since given up the struggle to keep her home and children tidy.

Meals were erratic. Sometimes she cooked a rabbit stew for the family, or a simple pie or pudding. More often, the children were told to help themselves to bread and jam from the cupboard. There was no money to buy meat, but Josh's poaching supplied them with a certain amount of nourishment in the form of snared rabbits and hares. Now and again, he took his old gun and picked off a roosting pheasant on Sir Edmund Hurley's estate. Bob Dixon, the gamekeeper, was Josh's implacable enemy.

One night, in October, Bob Dixon sat in 'The Crown' at Springbourne. He had a pint of draught bitter on the table in the corner, and his companion was the local policeman, Danny Goss, off duty.

Bob was a taciturn individual, and made few friends. He was not particularly fond of Danny Goss, but at least they had a common enemy – poachers. And another thing, Danny Goss played a hard game of dominoes, and this Bob relished. They were in the middle of a game when old Tim Ryan came in and sidled up to them.

'Evening, Dan. Evening, Bob.'

They acknowledged his greetings with grunts, resenting interruption of the game.

Tim watched a few moves in silence, and then spoke in a low tone. 'There's some shootin' going on up Narrow Copse. Thought you should know.'

Bob stood up immediately. Danny finished his drink, put back the dominoes into their greasy box, and followed suit. Bob put a florin on the counter and nodded towards Tim.

'Give the old boy a drink,' he said to the barman.

The two men emerged into the cold night air. It was a light night, for it was full moon. Clouds covered its face, but a silvery diffused brightness made visibility easy. A shot rang out as they emerged, and without speaking they ran, one behind the other, along the grass verge which muffled the sound of their footsteps.

The small copse sloped at an angle to the road, and met it about a quarter of a mile from the pub. The two men entered the wood, and stood motionless for a minute or two.

They heard the cracking of twigs nearby and held their breath. From behind the oak tree which screened them they had a view of a small clearing. Across this, gun in hand, went the figure of a man, followed by another.

'Now,' whispered Bob.

He and the policeman ran into the clearing.

'Beat it, Arth!' shouted one of the men. They ran in opposite directions, crashing through the undergrowth, pursued by the game-keeper and policeman.

Bob Dixon caught his man within fifty yards of the clearing. But as he made a grab for his jacket, the man turned and smote Bob with such viciousness in the face that the game-keeper fell to the ground with a cry of pain.

The man ran off, as Bob was struggling to his feet. At the same time Danny Goss returned.

'He had a bike in the hedge,' he said bitterly. 'But I'd take a bet it was Arthur Coggs from Fairacre. Your chap called out "Arth", didn't he?'

Bob, staunching his bloodied nose, nodded.

'And I'm pretty sure mine was Josh Pringle. I'm going over there now.'

'I'll come with you,' said Danny grimly. 'They're a right pair, those two.'

Josh Pringle sped for home by a roundabout route, two fat cock pheasants thumping his thighs as he ran. He was in roaring high spirits. He had outwitted his enemy and he had paid off old scores with that satisfying crash on his nose.

Full of triumph, Josh did not fully realize the danger which he was in. The thought that Bob Dixon or Danny Goss might pursue him further that night did not seriously worry him. Tomorrow morning, perhaps, there might be a few awkward questions to face if they found him, but surely they'd had enough for tonight?

He was a little perplexed, though, as he ran, about the hasty disposal of the birds. He wasn't going to hide them in the woods or hedges. He'd been fleeced that way before by unscrupulous neighbours. Besides, Bob knew every hiding place as well as he did. Better by far to get them home and cooked as soon as possible. The gentry might prefer their game hung. Poachers could not afford the time.

'Get 'em under the crust,' he had told his wife often enough. 'No one can tell what's under the crust.' There would be pheasant pie tomorrow – enough for all.

He found his wife kneeling before the fire, poker in hand, when he burst in breathlessly.

'Don't rake that out, gal,' he told her roughly, tugging the birds from his poacher's pockets. 'We got to get these plucked straight away. Had a job gettin' away from Bob Dixon.'

'You ain't been seen, 'ave you, Josh?' quavered his wife, Agnes.

'He didn't 'ave no time to see anythink,' responded Josh, beginning to strip feathers expertly. He threw the second bird on to his wife's lap. 'Him and that great lump Goss come after us, but we give 'em the slip. You keep your mouth shut if they turns up tomorrow. Don't know nothin', see?'

Agnes nodded dumbly, her hands busy with the feathers. She took a sheet of newspaper from the table and spread it at her feet to catch the bronze plumage as it fell. Josh's bird lolled upon the table top, its long tail feathers brushing his jacket.

The fire whispered as they worked in silence. Josh raised his head suddenly.

'By gum, there's someone outside,' he whispered, gazing at the dirty drawn curtains. 'Nip upstairs with these while I burn the feathers. If it's Bob Dixon –'

His face was dark with fury. He thrust the two half-plucked birds into his wife's arms, and began to roll up the newspapers.

'Get on upstairs,' he told her in a fierce whisper.

'But where can I put 'em?' squeaked poor Agnes.

'Bung 'em under the bed clothes with the kids, you great fool,' hissed Josh, stuffing the bundles of papers and feathers to the back of the fire.

Agnes crept away, up the box staircase to the room above, on her errand. A strong smell of burning feathers floated about the room, and Josh cursed as he picked up a stray feather or two and added it to the blaze.

A thunderous knocking came at the door. Josh ignored it. By now the bundles on the fire were black and almost burnt through. He blew on the fire to hasten its work.

The knocking came again, and then a voice.

'Open up, Josh Pringle. Police here.'

Josh swore violently, and stirred the bundles until they disintegrated. He put on some chips of wood from a wooden box nearby, and watched them burst into flame.

He approached the door and opened it.

The sight of Bob Dixon's swollen and bloodied nose frightened him. One eye too was blackening fast. He had not realized that he had done so much damage. Too late now to worry about that, he told himself, putting on an innocent expression.

'What's all this about?' he asked truculently. 'Kicking up a fuss like this! We've got kids asleep, I'll have you know. And one's got spots — scarlet fever or summat, we reckon. Only just got off to sleep, he has.'

'We'd like to come in,' said Goss.

'I daresay,' responded Josh, with spirit. 'But I don't want you.' The longer he could keep them from the reek of burning feathers, the better.

'There's such a thing as obstructing an officer of the law in the execution of his duty,' said Goss ponderously. 'I want a word with you on one or two matters.'

'Such as?'

'Such as poaching,' broke in Bob Dixon warmly. 'And knocking me down, you ruddy swine.'

'Leave this to me,' said Goss, to his hot-headed friend. 'I've reason to believe,' he said to Josh, with a return to his official manner, 'that you have articles in this house which are not your property I'd like to take a look round.'

'Got a search warrant?' queried Josh. 'I knows me rights.'

'There'll be one tomorrow morning,' promised Goss. There was a menacing ring in his tone. 'If you've got nothing to hide, what are you hedging for?'

Josh appeared to waver. By now the feathers should have vanished. The smell too was practically non-existent He opened the door grudgingly.

'Come on in then, if you must. You won't find nothin' here, I'm warning you.'

Danny Goss made straight for the fire and stirred it with the poker. He saw at once that he was too late. But on the shabby mat he noticed two small brown feathers.

'Pheasant's, eh?' he said. Josh began to bluster.

'Don't make me laugh. Folks like us don't 'ave pheasants. We leaves that to chaps like Bob Dixon 'ere.'

At this point Agnes opened the door from the staircase and entered timidly.

'These 'ere feathers,' said Josh loudly, giving his witless Agnes time to sum up the situation. 'They're from that old hen your mum gave us. That's right, ain't it?'

'Yes,' whispered Agnes. Growing bolder, she added: ''Twas a Rhode Island Red. Finished laying. My mum give it to me to boil for the kids' dinner.'

'That's right,' agreed Josh, nodding approval. 'I told you, they've bin poorly. One's all over spots, ain't he, Ag?'

'Spots?' cried Agnes, her hand flying to her mouth. 'Who's got –?'

Josh broke in loudly Lord, was she thick? He'd have to get it through to her somehow, or they'd be upstairs in two shakes. 'Our Tommy. Just bin up to see him, you should know. I was telling these chaps we wondered if it was scarlet fever. Don't want them catching nothin'.'

'That's right,' said Agnes wonderingly.

'You have a look down here,' said Josh, throwing open his arms expansively. 'Look in the washus, out the back, in the privy – we ain't got nothing to hide here.'

'Take a look, if you've a mind,' said Goss to Dixon. The gamekeeper went through the kitchen to the ramshackle outbuildings at the rear of the house. They could hear him opening doors and stumbling among the heap of logs in the corner of the wash-house.

Danny Goss raked the living room with an experienced eye. There were few places to hide a pheasant here He'd lay a wager they were upstairs, but without a search warrant he was helpless Nevertheless, he tried

'I'd like a look upstairs I won't disturb the children

'You can wait then! Them kids is asleep I tell you Can't you take a chap's word?'

'No,' said Goss briefly.

'I lets you in,' protested Josh, with a fine show of affronted innocence, 'and shows you downstairs. I'll show you more!'

With a magnificent gesture, he wrenched open the door to the box staircase, displaying bare wooden stairs, much splintered, and the vanishing tail of a startled mouse.

'There! See anythink? Any pheasants, partridges, hares, or whatever old codswallop you reckons I've got here?'

'It's upstairs, Josh,' said Danny calmly.

'Don't talk so daft! When could I 'ave got it? I bin sittin' 'ere all evening. That's the truth. Eh, Ag?'

Agnes nodded obediently. She was wondering how soon it would be before the children awoke and discovered their gruesome bedfellows, and how loudly they would scream the news.

As if sensing her thoughts, Josh prudently closed the door. Bob Dixon returned, his discoloured face wearing a sullen look.

'Dam' all,' he said briefly.

Danny Goss, knowing he was beaten, prepared to leave, but not without a stern warning.

'Bob saw his assailant, you know,' he said. 'He'll give evidence in court.'

'Who else saw?' asked Josh pertinently.

'You should know,' said Bob hotly.

'I bin sittin' here all evening,' repeated Josh with emphasis.

'You'll have to prove that.'

'Me brother come up with the paper about nine, said Josh glibly. His brother would agree to anything Josh suggested. He was smaller than Josh. 'And Ag will vouch for me.'

'You'll need to do better than that,' observed Danny Goss, opening the door. 'We'll be back.'

Josh accompanied them to the rickety gate, and watched them until they were out of sight. He returned to hear the frenzied wailing of a child.

'Mum! Mum! There's chickens in our bed! Dead 'uns, mum, but they're pricking us something awful! Mum! Mum!'

Agnes started to climb aloft.

'Chuck 'em under our bed till morning,' advised her husband.

'We'll finish 'em off before his lordship comes back. All this bloomin' fuss,' he growled. 'It's enough to make a chap go straight.'

It so happened that no charge was made by the police against Josh on this occasion. Evidence was flimsy. No firm case could really be made. It would be Bob Dixon's word against Josh's. But both the gamekeeper and the policeman vowed to keep a sharp eye on Josh Pringle, and to make sure that next time he transgressed then justice would be done.

Rumours flew about, of course, but Josh played the injured innocent and weathered this particular storm with some skill. In the privacy of his own home he boasted of his triumph, but he kept a still tongue abroad, and congratulated himself on having deceived his neighbours. He would not have been so smug if he had known that Emily Davis knew all.

Some days after the poaching incident, Emily set her class an essay to write. She knew, from bitter experience, that it was little use to expect flights of fancy from the majority of the children. They were, on the whole, unimaginative and ploddingly prosaic As she wanted, on this occasion, as lengthy a piece of writing as they could manage, she gave them a simple, down-to-earth subject which all could tackle.

My Favourite Meal

she wrote in a fair copper-plate hand on the blackboard. There were murmurs of approval from the victims.

'And I want two or three pages,' said Emily briskly. 'Don't worry too much about spelling and writing this afternoon. Just show me how much you can do.'

After a few preliminary inquiries, such as: 'Must we draw a line under the heading?' and 'Is jam tarts all one word?' which Emily dismissed smartly, the class settled down to literary composition with all its accompanying sighs and groans.

The children worked well, and at playtime Emily collected their books. They were left in a pile on her desk, and were carried across to the school house for marking that evening.

Halfway through the pile she came across Minnie Pringle's effort.

'Well done, Minnie,' murmured Emily, surveying the laboriously pencilled page. 'The longest essay to date. If only I can read it—'

The spelling and the writing rendered Minnie's composition well-nigh incomprehensible. Minnie had no use for punctuation, so that the whole narrative appeared as one long breathless sentence.

Translated, it read as follows:

My Favourite Meal

Best of all I likes pheasant pie what mum makes with pastry to hide whats inside as my dad tells her with gravy my dad finds them up the woods they just walks about the other night some men come and my mum put them pheasants in us kids bed to keep them warm she said they tickled us and had fleas we had two pies one Wednesday one Thursday today it was bread and sauce pheasant pie is best

Emily, who had heard the rumours, smiled at this artless account. But it was Minnie's best effort to date. She was very pleased with the child. Taking out her box of gold stars, Emily stuck one securely at the end of the essay. 'For good work,' she wrote beside it.

Gold stars were rarely given. They were much prized by those who earned them. Emily usually allowed the child to take home the work to show the proud parents. In this case, Emily thought, it would be wiser not to do so. She could imagine Josh's reaction to his daughter's innocent admission.

Minnie was scarlet to the roots of her red hair when she found her star.

'Can I take it home, miss? Can I?' she begged.

Emily spoke gently.

'I've put a star on a piece of paper, Minnie. You can take that home to show them. Tell them it was for a good piece of writing.'

She wondered if she should warn the child not to mention the subject matter of the essay. It would seem rather hard to Minnie if Josh's leather belt greeted her success.

'Just for good work,' repeated Emily carefully. Minnie nodded, dumb with delight.

Emily need not have worried. The gold star was given a cursory glance by Agnes and no attention at all by Josh. Not that this worried Minnie. She expected nothing more at home. Her hour of triumph had been at school. But she would have liked to take her book home, nevertheless.

★

It had been Minnie's aunt, Mrs Pringle herself, Fairacre School's formidable cleaner, who had warned Minnie about disclosing the theme of the essay.

The child had shown her the famous star soon after it had been won.

'What was it for?' asked Mrs Pringle, and listened, aghast, as she was told. She had already heard the rumours about that fateful night, and suspected that they were true. This confirmed them.

'Have you told anyone else?' she asked.

'No, auntie.'

'Then don't. Your dad'll leather you if he finds out.

'Miss Davis knows.'

'Maybe. But Miss Davis won't tell.'

The child had seemed bewildered. Mrs Pringle often wondered if she realized the reason for keeping quiet. She doubted it. Minnie was as dim as a dark night, thought her aunt, but at least she'd kept her mouth shut after that, and Josh had got away with it.

But not for long, remembered Mrs Pringle, with satisfaction. A month or two later he had been caught with a carrier-bag stuffed with stolen silver. With a string of other cases taken into consideration, this escapade earned him six months in jail. Agnes and the children missed the rabbits, but the house was wonderfully peaceful

> Though mills of God grind slowly
> Yet they grind exceeding small,

Mrs Pringle hummed to herself, recollecting Josh's imprisonment with pleasure.

The squeaking of Minnie's pram became apparent and Mrs Pringle warmed the teapot. She must let Minnie know about poor Miss Davis. It ought to upset her nicely.

That is, if she remembered her at all, she thought, with some asperity. Knowing Minnie she wouldn't be surprised to find Miss Davis had been forgotten completely

Sighing deeply, she reached for the tea-caddy

14. Peeping Tom

Mr Willet filled his basket, stepped carefully down the ladder and went into the kitchen. His wife was ironing, a clothes horse beside her laden with Mr Willet's striped pyjamas and substantial underwear, and some snowy sheets and pillow cases. The comfortable smell of warm linen filled the air.

'Old Misery Pringle's just stopped by,' said Mr Willet disrespectfully. 'Got bad news as usual, and enjoying it.'

'What's that?'

'Emily Davis has gone.'

'No! Why, she was at church the Sunday before last!'

'She'll be going again, poor soul, said Mr Willet. 'And for the last time.'

He watched his wife sprinkling some water over the handkerchiefs.

'Thought I might pop up and see if Dolly Clare wants anything.'

'Oh, I wouldn't do that just yet!' protested Mrs Willet. 'Leave it a day or two.'

Women! thought Mr Willet. All the same, maybe she was right. He puffed out his stained moustache with a resigned sigh.

'Maybe that's best,' he agreed, and went off to his hoeing.

Emily's death had stirred memories for Mrs Pringle of her reprehensible brother-in-law. The event had stirred memories too for Bob Willet, memories which even now filled him with some shame. Both Mrs Pringle and Mr Willet kept their recollections to themselves with much prudence, but this did not render them any less painful.

It had all started when Bob Willet was at the impressionable age of seven. He lived then, with his four brothers and sisters, in a little house between Springbourne and Fairacre, and attended Fairacre School.

At that time the schoolmaster was a dreamy idealistic fellow called Hope. He was looked upon as 'a bit of a milk-sop' by the parents, but the children liked him. For one thing, he believed in reading them stories, which children always enjoy. Those who are attentive learn a great deal. Those who close their ears and daydream can get away with such behaviour with impunity. One way or another, storytime is universally popular.

Young Bob Willet was one of those who did attend. Mr Hope read them all manner of tales from the myths of Greece to passages from *Midshipman Easy*. He also read some of Andrew Lang's fairy tales, and it was these which impressed Bob particularly. He became fascinated by witches.

It so happened that a poor old crone called Lucy Kelly, then about eighty years of age, lived alone in a tumbledown cottage near the Willets' home. She was a fearsome sight, with one long eye-tooth overhanging her bottom lip, and tangled grey locks escaping from the man's black trilby hat which she usually wore.

Her clothes were deplorable, her cottage worse. Neighbours had long since given up trying to help her, for she was half-mad, muttering to herself constantly, and violent if provoked. Bob Willet had heard her called 'an old witch' by several people in the village. No doubt it was said in jest, but the boy believed it.

How could he prove it? Fearfully, he put his problem to Ted Pickett, a boy a little older than himself. Mrs Willet did not approve of the Picketts. She considered them dirty and untruthful, and wished her Bob had made friends elsewhere. But nothing could be done without giving offence, and Ted Pickett called for Bob, on his way to Fairacre School from Springbourne, and Mrs Willet could only hope that time would part them one day.

Ted Pickett was something of a hero to Bob. He was an intrepid tree climber and good at football. What more do you ask of a hero when you are a seven-year-old boy?

Bob half-hoped that Ted would give him some comfort when he told him about Lucy. It would have been a relief to have been laughed to scorn for harbouring such a wrong notion. But Ted Pickett did not laugh and Bob did not know whether to feel glad or not. According to Ted Pickett, Lucy might well be a witch. The only way to prove it was to catch her flying on a broomstick at the full moon. On that Ted Pickett was positive.

'Come with me?' asked Bob.

'No fear!' said his hero. 'I'm scared of anything like that!'

It was not very reassuring, but Bob's curiosity got the better of his fear, and one night of full moon he crept from the house and made his way to Lucy Kelly's cottage.

Everything seemed eerie in the silvery light. It was warm and still. The harvest had been gathered, and stooks of wheat stood in the stubbly fields, throwing sharp pointed shadows. The scents of the fruitful sun-warmed earth hung everywhere.

Bob approached Lucy's house stealthily, his heart in his mouth. The front of the shabby place was in full moonlight, and to Bob's horror he saw a stout besom broom lodged against the wooden lean-to at one end of the cottage.

So she had got a broomstick! For two pins, Bob would have run home, but having come so far he braced himself to investigate further.

The garden was full of waist-high docks and nettles, but by keeping close to the house he managed to make progress. Fearfully, he peeped into one grimy window. By the light of the moon he could see some ramshackle furniture. All was silent. Where was Lucy? Was she already preparing herself for a midnight flight?

He gazed spell-bound into the room, noting the battered kettle on the hob, the broken armchair with the stuffing oozing from its sagging seat, and the opened tin of condensed milk standing on the table with a spoon lodged in it.

There was something wholly fascinating in seeing a private life so plainly disclosed. Young Bob had never visited a theatre or he might have recognized the excitement which mounted in him, despite his fear. Here was a stage and although no actors could be seen upon it, a drama must take place.

Action was about to begin. The clock of distant St Patrick's began to strike twelve, each note floating clearly across the tranquil countryside. The boy grew cold with mingled terror and excitement. It was midnight – the time for witches' flights.

At that moment, a dark shape rolled from some low couch hard against the wall where Bob stood. It had been hidden from his sight as it was immediately below the window through which he was looking.

It was Lucy! Dry-mouthed, Bob watched her throw a black shawl round her shoulders and make for the door. It was enough for the terrified boy.

Lucy was off to her broomstick!

Bob Willet fled.

★

You may think that such an experience would scotch a boy's desire
for private investigation, but funnily enough, it seemed to whet
young Bob Willet's appetite for more. That glimpse into someone
else's life affected the boy deeply. He always loved a story, and was to
become a fine raconteur in later life, but this was something better than
a story. It was experience at first hand – real people occupying a real
place, an actual story unfolding while he watched.

He took to loitering past lighted cottage windows, and treasuring
the glimpses of life within. Here was a baby being bathed by the
fire. Here was a man setting down a foaming jug of beer on the
dresser. Here was an old woman, nodding by the fire, her head on
one side and mouth open, while the cat lapped milk from a jug on
the table. These little vignettes fascinated the child.

He did not speak about them for some time, knowing full well
that his mother would scold him for prying. But one day, he mentioned his new game to Ted Pickett.

By now it was winter-time and lamps were lit at tea-time. Children were told to be sure to be in by dark. Mrs Willet was a stickler
for obedience, and one Saturday afternoon young Bob was allowed
to go and play at Ted Pickett's only on the strict understanding that
he was home before dusk.

The two boys spent a blissful afternoon kicking an old ball about
a muddy field. Dusk began to fall and the cottage windows gleamed
golden as the lamps were lit. Bob Willet, seeing them, reminded
Ted Pickett of his game.

'Bet you wouldn't dare to look in Miss Davis's window,' chal-
lenged Ted. The village school stood near by, and the school house
adjoined it, surrounded on three sides by grass which Emily kept
shorn with a hand mower which frequently went wrong.

Bob's heart gave a jump. Emily Davis was someone to be respected, even feared. Supposing she saw him at the window?

On the other hand, Ted had dared him. And Ted was older and
bigger. If he did not take up the challenge, Ted might put an end to
the friendship. There were plenty of boys at school who would be
proud to take his place at Ted Pickett's side. Swiftly, the younger
boy made up his mind.

'Who said I wouldn't dare?' he boasted, his heart fluttering.
'Come on then. Let's go over now.'

In the grey moth-light between day and night, the two went stealthily across the road from the field. A light burned in the little sitting room of the school house. They could see the lamp quite clearly, standing centrally on the table, for the window was a low one.

'Get round the side,' whispered Ted, 'and creep along below the window level.'

Bob led the way, Ted following. They skirted a row of lilac bushes which grew between the school playground and Emily's garden. It grew darker every minute. The two crouched down in an angle formed by two walls, waiting for an opportune moment.

A farm labourer, with his dog, clumped along the lane, only a few yards from them. The dog raised its muzzle, sniffing the air, and for one awful moment Bob thought that they would be discovered. But the man was intent on getting home, and calling his dog to heel, he made off down the road.

Two small children then appeared, and took a long time to pass the school premises. Then one of their neighbours, who had been wooding, trundled an old pram piled high with dead branches along the lane. Bob was terrified that she might see him. His mother would soon hear about it, if she did.

The thought of his mother made him more nervous still. It was time he was home. It was cold squatting there, and getting dangerously late. Now he had taken up Ted's challenge he must get on with it – and the sooner it was over, the better.

Now the lane was clear, and Bob nudged Ted.

'Coming?' he whispered.

Ted nodded.

Bent low, young Bob crept along the front of the school house until he was squarely below the lighted window. Ted joined him, and they sat on their haunches side by side.

Bob listened. Not a sound disturbed the twilight. Face to the wall, he raised himself, inch by inch, until his eyes were level with the lowest pane of glass. Beside him, Ted Pickett followed suit.

There was only one person in the room, and that was Emily's mother. They could see the top of her white head above the back of the armchair. An open book lay on a stool beside the chair, and a large ball of white wool. They could see the old lady's right hand moving dextrously and rhythmically as she worked at her crochet.

At that very moment, just as the usual magic was beginning to work for Bob, a terrible blow smote him, and he banged heads with Ted Pickett violently. Both boys tumbled to the ground.

Through the stars born of this sudden assault, Bob looked up to see Emily Davis, who had approached noiselessly over the grass, standing over them.

'And what,' she said grimly, 'are you two doing?'

'Only looking,' quavered Bob, rubbing his ear.

'I call it *prying*,' said Emily. 'It's not only extremely rude, it could be very frightening to anyone inside the room. People's homes are private places. How dare you behave like that.'

Emily was very angry indeed. Looking back, Bob realized that she was anxious for her mother, as well as being affronted by such anti-social behaviour.

The two struggled penitently to their feet and apologized.

'Do you know what people like you are called? "Peeping Toms", that's their name, and pretty mean they are reckoned to be. The police look out for "Peeping Toms", so you'd better not do it again.'

The boys, thoroughly scared, promised fervently never to pry again.

'Then be off home with you. If I catch you at this again, there will be real trouble,' said Emily fiercely.

In silence, the two boys left the garden. In silence, they walked home along the muddy lane.

'See you Monday,' said Bob diffidently, when they reached the Picketts' gate. Ted grunted in reply.

Severely shaken, Bob Willet went on to his own home. It was the end, for him, of his secret game. Was it the end of his friendship, too, with Ted Pickett?

Mrs Willet was at the sink, washing up the tea things, when he entered. The table had been cleared.

'You're too late for your tea,' said his mother shortly. 'You should get home at the right time. You've been told often enough.'

She tossed him a tea-towel.

'Make yourself useful,' she said.

Dejected and hungry, wiping up the plates of those who had eaten, Bob Willet learnt his bitter lesson.

It didn't pay to be a Peeping Tom.

He never was again.

Mr Willet straightened his aching back and leant on his hoe.

Funny how fierce those little women can be when roused! Emily Davis could not have been much taller than he was, all those years ago, and yet the memory he had of her, on that distant evening was of a vengeful giant.

Well, she'd put the fear of the Lord into him sure enough! It had been the right thing to do, no doubt, but what pleasure he'd had while the game lasted! Pity it had to end like that, but Emily was the very person to make a boy see sense. He might have scared the life out of some poor old soul one day. As it was, Bob's shameful secret was known only to Ted Pickett and Emily Davis. And they never told.

Mr Willet plucked a piece of groundsel from the earth and put it tidily with the heap of weeds.

'Good old Emily!' he said warmly, to the robin perched on the runner bean sticks, waiting for worms.

It would have made a fitting epitaph.

15. Off to America

It was Mr Willet who passed on the news of Emily to Mr Lamb who kept the Post Office at Fairacre.

They were on their way to choir practice, prepared to tackle the usual Ancient and Modern hymns for the next Sunday, a fairly simple psalm, and a new anthem, which their choir-master Mr Annett, the Beech Green schoolmaster, called 'a refreshingly modern piece of music', and which the much-tried choir referred to privately as 'that hell-of-a-thing in E flat'.

'I'm sorry to hear it,' said Mr Lamb, entering the lych-gate. 'My brother George will be too. I'll mark the notice in the *Caxley Chronicle* when I send it on next week.'

'Does he find time to read the paper in New York?' asked Mr Willet, half-jokingly. George Lamb was known to be a prosperous restaurant owner there. His progress had been viewed with mingled admiration and envy by the Fairacre folk, but George's stock had risen considerably recently by his generous contribution to the repair of Fairacre's church roof. Those curmudgeonly souls like Mrs Pringle had been considerably sweeter in their attitude to George Lamb since that warm-hearted gesture of George's and his American friends'.

'He likes to keep in touch with things back home,' replied Mr Lamb. 'No friends like old friends, I always say. Emily Davis was one of them, come to think of it, though we never saw a lot of her. George would be the first to say so.'

They crunched up the gravel path to the vestry door. The sound of the organ greeted their ears.

'Lord love old Ireland!' exclaimed Bob Willet, 'Annett's started already! We'll cop it.'

Like two naughty schoolboys, the two middle-aged men slunk shame-faced into the choir stalls, and Emily Davis was temporarily forgotten.

It was a cold blustery day when George Lamb opened the *Caxley Chronicle* far away across the Atlantic.

'See p. 16' was written in his brother's handwriting on the top of the first page. He turned to page sixteen obediently, and read the brief notice of Emily Davis's death, marked by the pen of Fairacre's Post Office.

He lowered the paper to the counter, folded it carefully, and adjusted his coffee machine. His eyes strayed to the window. On the sidewalk the citizens of New York struggled against vicious wind and rain. In the shining road the traffic edged its way along, the windscreen wipers flicking impatiently.

But George saw nothing of the scene. He was back in time, back in Caxley, back in the Post Office living room at Fairacre, where his trip to the States had first begun, so long ago.

When George Lamb left Fairacre School at the age of fifteen, the Second World War had been over for almost two years.

Times were hard. Rationing of food was still in existence, and the basic necessities of life, houses, work, transport and even clothes were all in short supply.

Old Mrs Lamb still ruled at Fairacre Post Office, assisted by her older son. George, it was decided, should try for work at Septimus Howard's new restaurant in Caxley market-place. With any luck, he might be taught the bakery business too There was a double chance there to learn two trades. One, or both, could provide George Lamb with a livelihood.

The boy cycled daily to work in all weathers, and thrived on it At that time, Septimus Howard, respected tradesman and chapel-goer, was an old man, and within a year or two of his death. Mrs Lamb had a great regard for him, and was proud to think that George was in his care. Many a time she had listened to Sep's preaching, for she was a staunch chapel-goer herself, and Sep, as a lay-preacher, often came to the tiny chapel at Fairacre to give an address.

'If you do as Mr Howard tells you, and follow his example,' she told young George, 'you won't go far wrong.'

She had been widowed whilst George was still a small boy, and sound instinct told her that a man of Sep's worth could be of untold value to the boy in his impressionable years. He certainly influenced George's thinking, and gave him an insight too, into the way of running an honest business.

It was Sep's idea that George should learn the bakery business, first, and he began in the usual humble way of watching methods, weighing ingredients, checking the heat of the ovens, and so on, before proceeding to mixing and making himself. He was a conscientious lad, and Sep, always gentle with young people, took extra pains with the promising boy.

As time went on, he became skilled at decorating both iced cakes for the baker's shop and the enormous rich gateaux for which the restaurant was becoming famous.

He had his midday meal in the kitchen at the rear of the restaurant, with its view of the peaceful Cax through the window. This substantial meal was a great help to Mrs Lamb whilst food was still hard to come by. In the evening the boy ate bread and cheese, washed down with a mug of cocoa, with the rest of the family.

There were still contingents of United States troops stationed in the Caxley area. Howard's Restaurant was a favourite rendezvous for the men, and young George became friendly with several of them. One in particular, a blond young giant with a crew-cut was a frequent visitor, and he and George struck up a friendship.

He was the son of a restaurant owner in New York. His father, so George gathered, was another Septimus Howard, hard-working, teetotal, and a stalwart of the local chapel. His son was inclined to be apologetic about his father's somewhat rigid views but it was plain to George that Wilbur was secretly very proud of the old man and of his business ability.

'You want to come and see the place for yourself sometime,' said Wilbur.

'No hope of that,' responded George. 'No money for one thing. And I've got a lot to learn here yet.'

'My old man expects me to go into the business.'

'Well, you will, won't you? Lucky to have something waiting for you.'

Wilbur looked thoughtful.

'I guess I don't take to the idea, somehow. Been brought up among pies and cookies all my life. I kind of want a change.'

'Such as?'

'Well, now you're going to laugh. I've a girl back home who works in a dress shop. I reckon the two of us could run a shop like that pretty good.'

'Have you got enough to set up a shop?'

'Nope. That's the snag. But if my old man could put up the cash, we'd make a go of it, never fear. It's just that he's looking to me to take over some of his jobs when I get home. It'll take a bit of breaking to him.'

'And you want me to take your place?' queried George jokingly.

'Well now, who knows? You keep it in mind, George. You might do a lot worse than try your luck in the States. Plenty of scope there for a chap like you.'

George did not give much thought to the conversation. His present mode of life was full enough, and besides he doubted if his mother would approve of a son going so far away.

Mrs Lamb was a strongly possessive woman, and hard times had made her calculating as well. With the wages of both John and George she managed fairly easily. She had an eye for a bargain, went shopping regularly in Caxley market on Thursday afternoons, and took advantage of every cheap line offered by the shops. The thought of losing either son's contribution to the housekeeping was a nightmare to her, although she was better off than many of her neighbours.

At that time, John was courting a local girl, and having considerable trouble with his mother on that account.

'I've nothing against her,' said Mrs Lamb, mendaciously.

'Except her being in existence at all,' thought John privately, but keeping quiet for the sake of peace.

'But can you afford to get married? Where are you going to live? She's welcome here, but I don't suppose this place is good enough for her.'

'It's not that, mother –'

'I'm quite prepared to take second place hard though it is. I haven't had an easy time, as well you know. Bringing up two boys all alone, with mighty little money, is no joke. Not that one expects any thanks. Young people are all the same – take all, give nothing.'

This sort of talk nearly drove John Lamb mad at times. He saw quite clearly that self-martyrdom pleased his cantankerous old mother. He also saw the cunning behind it. As long as she could stave off the marriage, the better off financially she would be.

Things came to a head when his girl delivered an ultimatum. Her younger sister became engaged, and their wedding day was already fixed. This galvanized the older one into action. It was unthinkable that young Mary should steal a march on her!

'Well, do you or don't you?' demanded John's fiancée. 'If we have to live here for a bit, I don't mind putting up with your mum as long as we know we're getting a house of our own, in a few months, say. But if you can't leave your mother, then say so.'

'Don't talk like that,' pleaded poor John, seeing himself between the devil and the deep sea.

'I'm fed up with waiting. If you don't want me, there's another man who does. He's asked me often enough.'

'Who's that?' said John, turning red with fury.

'I'm not saying,' replied the girl, a trifle smugly. As it happened, John Lamb never did discover who the fellow was. Could he be mythical? John often wondered later on.

But the upshot was that John's wedding was arranged very quickly, and a double celebration took place in Caxley that autumn, much to the delight of the brides' father whose pocket benefited from 'killing two birds with one stone' as he put it bluntly. As the poor fellow had four more daughters to see launched, one could sympathize with his jubilation.

The atmosphere in the Lamb household, between the time of the girl's ultimatum and the wedding, was unbearable. Old Mrs Lamb went about her Post Office duties with a long face, and had the greatest pleasure in confiding her doubts and fears to all her customers. Most of their sympathy went towards John and his wife-to-be

'Miserable old devil!' was the general comment. 'I wouldn't be in that girl's shoes for a pension! If John Lamb's got any sense he'll clear out and let his old mum get on with it.'

It was at this unhappy stage that George began to think seriously of Wilbur's suggestion. He began to dread his return home, as he cycled back from Caxley each evening. Sometimes a brooding silence hung over the kitchen. Sometimes his mother was in full spate – a stream of self-pity flowing from her vigorously.

'How I shall manage I just don't know,' she complained one evening. 'It's bad enough keeping three of us going with what little comes in When there's a fourth to feed, it'll come mighty hard.'

George's pent-up patience burst.

'Maybe there'll be only three after John gets married. I'm thinking of leaving Howard's.'

There was a shocked silence.

'Leaving Howard's?' shrieked his mother. 'What's this non-sense?'

'I'd like to go to the States. Got an opening there '

This was not strictly true, but George was enjoying his mother's discomfiture.

'You'll do no such thing,' declared Mrs Lamb, recovering her usual matriarchal powers. 'You've got a good job with Mr Howard, and you're a fool to think of throwing it up.'

'I could do the same work in New York and get twice the money. Besides I want to see places. I don't want to stick in Fairacre all my life. If I don't go now, when I'm free, I'll never go. I'll be like old John here, married and stuck here for life.'

'And what's wrong with that?' demanded his mother. She looked at her younger son's rebellious face, and changed her tactics.

'And doesn't your poor mother mean anything to you?' she began, summoning ready tears. 'The sacrifices I've made, for you two boys, nobody knows. I've skimped and saved to feed and clothe you, and what do I get? Not a ha'p'orth of gratitude!'

She mopped her eyes.

'I only hope,' she went on, raising her eyes piously towards the ceiling, 'that you two never find *yourselves* unwanted by your family. A widow's lot is hard enough without her own flesh and blood turning against her!'

'Now, mother, please –' began soft-hearted John who could always be moved by tears.

But George was made of tougher stuff.

'Any children of mine will have a chance to do as they want in life,' he told his mother stoutly. 'What's the sense in keeping them against their will? We all have to leave home sometime. I'm thinking about it now That's all.'

'And what about the money?' said Mrs Lamb viciously.

George looked at her steadily.

'Let's face it, ma! That's all you're worried about.'

His mother turned away pettishly, but not before George saw that his shaft had struck home. He followed up his advantage.

'I'll get better opportunities in America After a bit, when I've got settled. I'll probably be able to send you a darn sight more each month than I give you now in a year '

An avaricious gleam brightened his mother's eye. Nevertheless, she clung to her martyrdom.

'And how do we manage until you make your fortune?' she asked nastily.

'As other mothers do,' said George. 'I'm going to talk to Mr Howard. He'll understand how I feel. I shan't let him down, but I intend to go before long.'

Knowing herself beaten, Mrs Lamb rose to her feet, reeling very dramatically.

'I shall have to go and lie down. All this trouble's made my heart bad again.'

John took his mother's arm and helped her upstairs in silence. Sitting below, at the kitchen table, George heard the bed springs creak under his mother's eleven stone.

John returned, looking anxious.

'D'you mean it?' he asked. 'Or are you playing up our mum?'

'I mean it all right,' replied George grimly.

As luck would have it, he came across Wilbur next day, and told him how things stood. Would he mind asking his father what the chances were for a young man in the trade?

Wilbur threw himself into George's plans with a whole-hearted zest which gave the boy encouragement when it was most needed. He was now quite determined to leave home. He would stay until John's marriage, but as soon as that was over he hoped to get away.

He did not intend to approach Sep Howard until he had heard from Wilbur's father. If he was discouraging he might just as well stay a little longer with Howard's, finding lodgings in Caxley. Whatever happened, he was not going to stop at home.

For one thing there would be little room for him when John married. For another thing, he foresaw that there would be trouble with the two women, and he was going to steer clear of that catastrophe.

But for all his determination, George suffered spells of doubt, particularly at night.

Lying sleepless in his narrow bed, he watched the fir tree outside the window, as he had done since he was a little boy. The stars behind it seemed to be caught in its dark branches, as it swayed gently, and reminded him of the Christmas tree, sparkling with tinsel, which he and John dressed every year. He would miss Fair-

acre, and his home. There would be no sparrows chirruping under
the thatch, close to his bed-head, in New York. There would be no
scent of fresh earth, or the honking of the white swans' wings as
they flew to the waters of the Cax.

And was he treating his mother roughly? In the brave light of
day, he knew that he was not guilty. At night, he became the prey
of doubts.

There was, too, so much to consider. Suppose he hated America
when he got there? Could he ever save enough for the return passage? He knew no one there – not a soul. Here he knew everyone,
and they knew him, and his mother, and his forefathers.

And that, thought young George, thumping his pillow, was what
was wrong! He felt stifled in this closed little world. He must get
away to live, to breathe, to be – simply – George Lamb, a man on
his own, not just a son, a grandson, a workmate or a neighbour –
but someone in his own right!

The letter from Wilbur's father was lengthy and full of good
sense. There were plenty of openings. He gave him a rough idea of
wages to be expected, and the cost of living. He pointed out certain
difficulties a country-bred boy might find in a foreign town, and
prejudices which might have to be overcome.

On the second page he came to his proposition. In a few months'
time his assistant was leaving to take over a new restaurant which
Wilbur's father was opening. If George's references were completely
satisfactory (this was underlined heavily), he would consider taking
him on when the vacancy occurred. If, at the end of a month, either
of them wanted to end the arrangement, well – fair enough. There
were plenty of caterers in New York who would give a steady
young man a chance.

Until he found suitable lodgings he was very welcome to stay
with Wilbur's family. Any friend of Wilbur's – and so on.

George's spirits rose as he made a note of the address. He would
write as soon as he had talked with Sep.

The frail old man listened attentively to the boy's tale. He had
lived in Caxley all his life, and knew something of Mrs Lamb's
possessiveness. He knew, too, that young George would prosper
wherever he went. Rarely had he had such a promising pupil. He
was a lad brought up on hard work, ambitious and adventurous and
with a strong sense of justice. It was this last, Sep surmised, which
had sparked off his revolt.

He advised the boy to talk of the matter, yet again, with his
family. He told him that he would be able to give him excellent
references, and he suggested that his own solicitor, Mr Lovejoy of
Caxley Market Place, might find out more about the proposed job
and his employer, so that the affair could be put on a business-like
basis.

Within a month it was almost settled. If only his mother would
bow to the inevitable, thought George! He would go so much more
cheerfully if she gave the venture her blessing, but she continued to
play the martyr.

It was at this stage that Dolly Clare and Emily Davis entered the
scene. They had called together in the late afternoon to buy stamps.
Dolly Clare, who had been button-holed many times to hear about
Mrs Lamb's woes, hoped that they would escape this time, but it
was not to be.

Emily Davis had not heard the tale first-hand, Mrs Lamb noted
with satisfaction, arranging her face into the drooping lines of suffering widowhood.

'And so, off he goes, in a few weeks' time, whatever happens, I suppose,' continued Mrs Lamb lugubriously, after ten minutes' brisk narration of George's unfilial actions.

'They're all the same, Miss Davis, aren't they? No thought for their parents. Everything taken for granted. What happens to us old folk, don't matter. They must do as *they* want, no matter who's hurt by it.'

'You don't expect him to stay here all his life, do you?' said Emily, smiling.

'John will,' replied Mrs Lamb.

'Then you are very lucky,' responded Emily. Mrs Lamb began to look even more disgruntled than usual. It was a fine thing when your own generation turned on you!

'I wouldn't mind so much,' said Mrs Lamb, changing her ground, 'if he was going to someone we knew. But to be thrust among strangers! Well, it's hard for a mother's heart to bear, I can tell you. To think of my boy, alone and friendless in that wicked city –'

'No worse than London, I expect,' said Emily mildly. Mrs Lamb ignored the interruption.

'With all its temptations – and we all know what those are for a young man! No, I wouldn't say a word against this trip,' went on Mrs Lamb, waxing to her theme, 'if I thought there was anyone there he could turn to, if he was in trouble. Just one, just one single person! It's all I'd need to set my mind at rest.'

'That's easy,' said Emily. 'I've a brother in New York. I'll give you his address.'

She put down her handbag and reached for a pen and paper. Mrs Lamb's jaw dropped. Here was a blow!

At that moment, she heard the sound of George's bicycle being lodged against the wall. The door burst open and there stood the young man, wind-blown and boisterous.

'I'm just telling your mother,' said Emily, still writing busily, 'that I hope you'll look up my brother in New York. He's a policeman there. Been there nearly twenty years. He's married with four children. He'd love to see you. This is his address.'

George held out his hand gratefully, and studied the slip.

'This isn't far from Wilbur's father's place from the look of it,' he said. 'I'm very grateful, Miss Davis.'

'Well,' said Emily, with a hint of mischief in her voice, 'your mother said she wouldn't mind you going one bit, if there were someone there you knew. So now you are settled.'

Mrs Lamb's face was a study in suppressed wrath. Her heavy breathing boded no good to George when the ladies had left, he knew well. He could have laughed aloud at the situation. This had taken the wind out of the old girl's sails all right!

'I'll write to my brother to tell him you are on your way,' promised Emily. 'How lucky that I called in! It must have been meant, mustn't it, Mrs Lamb? Good luck, George. I'm sure you're doing the right thing!'

Eyes sparkling, Emily Davis followed Dolly Clare through the door.

'Doing the right thing,' echoed Mrs Lamb, when the couple were out of earshot. 'That Emily Davis! Always was too fond of interfering in other people's business.'

'It pays off sometimes,' said George, tucking the address in his pocket-book.

He had such a grin on his face that for two pins his mother would have reached up and boxed his ears, but she forbore.

She would keep her recriminations for that meddlesome Emily Davis next time she saw her, the hussy!

'You look pleased with yourself,' said one of George's regular customers, offering a dollar bill. 'Had good news?'

'Not really. Heard of a death actually.'

'Gee, that's sad! Sorry I spoke.'

'That's all right. She was a very old lady – over eighty.'

'Don't suppose she's many friends left to mourn her then. Not at that age.'

'You'd be surprised,' said George, handing over the change. 'You'd be surprised! Emily Davis has got a lot in common with our John Brown.'

'Our John Brown?' echoed the man, puzzled.

'Sure. The chap whose body lies a-mouldering in his grave.'

'And whose soul goes marching on?'

'That's the lad. Emily Davis is right beside him, take my word for it.'

The customer nodded and made his way to the door. These English guys had the screwiest ideas, no matter how long they'd lived in a decent God-fearing country, he told himself.

16. Heatwave in London

The day of Emily's funeral was quiet and grey. No breeze stirred
the leaves or rustled the standing corn beyond the churchyard yew
trees. Only a wren, hopping up and down the stairway of the hedge,
added minute movement to the scene.

The church at Beech Green was small and shadowy. It was also
deathly cold, despite the warmth outside. The congregation shivered
as they waited for Emily to make her last journey up the aisle.

Dolly Clare sat in the front pew with several of Emily's nephews
and nieces. Doctor Martin, who had attended both friends, sat
behind her with Mr and Mrs Willet beside him.

Other Fairacre friends were near by. There were relations and
friends from Caxley, and a great many from Springbourne. But
very few were Emily's contemporaries, for she had outlived the
majority of them.

Among those from Springbourne was Daisy Warwick, whose
husband was a bank manager in Caxley. She represented Springbourne Women's Institute, on this occasion, for she was the President of that branch. But she was also there on her own behalf, for
she had been very fond of Emily Davis, and grateful to her for the
care and affection she had shown to her only daughter Susan.

Daisy Warwick contemplated her well-polished shoes as she
waited, and wished she had put on a thicker coat to withstand the
bone-chilling damp of the church. Her fore-arms, protruding from
the three-quarter length sleeves of the sober grey coat which had
seemed the most suitable garb in her wardrobe, were covered with
gooseflesh, and her hands grew colder and colder inside her gloves.

This would not do any of them any good, she thought practically;
particularly poor old Miss Clare, and the vicar, Mr Partridge, who
served the parish of Beech Green as well as Fairacre, and had recently
returned from hospital. At least he was warmer waiting outside for
the coffin to arrive.

At that moment, the sound of the bier's wheels on gravel was
heard, and the congregation rose as the voice of Gerald Partridge
fluted the unforgettable words at the west door.

'I am the resurrection and the life, saith the Lord: he that believeth in me, though he were dead, yet shall he live: and whosoever liveth and believeth in me shall never die.'

Later that evening, Daisy Warwick made a note on the telephone pad in her hall. It was the last of several such notes. The page now read:

> 1 yard black petersham
> Buttons or zip?
> Mary's baby
> Lunching at Aunt Bess's on Sunday
> Cushions?
> Miss Davis dead.

For this was the evening when she made her weekly telephone call to Susan in London, and unless she had a list before her she found that the precious minutes had slipped by, and the things which she really wanted to tell the girl had been forgotten.

The weekly list was always a source of great hilarity to her husband whenever he waited by the telephone. There was something surrealistic about the juxtaposition of such items as: 'Uncle John's asthma cure' and 'Try really ripe Stilton', or 'Theatre tickets' and 'Bed socks'. The present week, with its jumble of dress-making, births, deaths, lunches and cushions, was well up to standard, and he commented upon it to his wife.

'Well,' she said truthfully, 'life's like that.

And her husband was obliged to agree.

Susan Warwick shared a flat in Earls Court with four other girls. The rooms were large and lofty. The windows were the sash variety, of enormous size, and as the flat was on the first floor, it was light. This was one of its few advantages.

Susan shared a bedroom with Penny Way. The other three shared the second bedroom. The sitting-room, heated by an archaic gas-fire whose meter gulped down shillings at an alarming rate, over-looked the front garden. The kitchen and bathroom both small and dismal, were huddled together on a landing at the back of the house half a floor below. It was hardly surprising that the girls lived mainly on toast, made over the gas fire with various spreads upon it, or bowls of soup which could be heated easily on the kitchen gas stove and carried aloft to be drunk by the fire.

The house had been built in 1890 when three resident servants had been considered the absolute minimum for keeping such an establishment running properly. It was now owned by a gentleman who lived very comfortably in Switzerland, and whose interest in this house, and a number of others which he owned, was purely financial.

Susan's house was now divided into four parts. The ground floor and basement were occupied by two young men, one with a sable coat and a pink rinse, the other with a black velvet cloak and a blue rinse, who minced off at eleven each morning and returned long after midnight, invariably squabbling at the top of their high-pitched voices.

On the floor above lived two young couples, and a newly born baby who cried nightly, and wrung Susan's soft heart with its misery.

Up in the attics, where once the three maids had slept in more affluent days, lived a middle-aged artist who sometimes emerged with a portfolio of drawings, but more often sat in a haze of cigarette smoke, a bottle beside him, in his eyrie, and contemplated fame – preferably without working for it.

Of all the motley inhabitants, Susan found him the most repulsive. They occasionally met on the stairs. During the year in which she had lived there, she had watched him deteriorate from a slovenly, garrulous good-for-nothing into a shaking, morose wreck of a man. He had lost a great deal of weight, his eyes watered, his head trembled uncontrollably. His clothes, always stained and spotted, were now filthy and torn. Susan suspected, from the reek of the man, that he was now drinking methylated spirit. She flattened herself against the wall, and held her breath as he passed, praying that he would not engage in facetious conversation. She need not have worried. He now scarcely noticed her as he groped his way up and down the stairs.

After a year of London life under these conditions, Susan was beginning to have doubts. During her last year at school in Caxley, the thought of living in London in a flat, away from all who knew her in Springbourne, seemed the height of sophistication. Oh, to be free!

She was happy at home, and fond of her parents and brothers. The two boys were some years older than she was, and were already

out in the world. Susan envied them, and was rather sorry for herself, left behind, over-duly cosseted, in her opinion, by her father
and mother.

It was too much, she felt, to be obliged to be in by ten every
night. And why on earth, she asked herself privately, should she tell
her parents who she was with every time? Couldn't they trust her?
Heaven knows, at seventeen she was old enough to look after herself!

Or was she? In her less rebellious moments, Susan admitted that
her parents were only doing their duty. There were occasions when
Susan had found herself non-plussed – even frightened. There had
been that drunken youth at the bus-stop. Only Susan's speed and
natural agility had kept her from his unwelcome embrace. Then
there was that dubious party at Roger's where everything was
plunged in semi-darkness and everyone seemed remarkably gloomy
until mysterious tablets were passed round. Susan had had the sense
to make her way to the bathroom, throw away her tablets, and
creep from the house.

Her own home seemed doubly welcome after that incident. She
lay in bed and looked with pleasure at all her much-loved treasures.
There were her books, ranging from babyhood's Beatrix Potters to
last week's purchase – a Penguin edition of a pop-singer's auto-
biography.

The bedside lamp cast a cosy amber glow over the patchwork
quilt her mother had made. Normally, she considered it hideous
and rather sentimental. Her mother was given to fingering sections
here and there, saying: 'Isn't this sweet? Part of your first smock,
darling.' Or, 'Grandma gave me this. It came from a tablecloth she
bought in Lisbon.'

But after Roger's horrible party, even the patchwork quilt had
its charm, and her parents, looking up from their books when she
returned early, had seemed so sane and wholesome that she had
kissed them heartily, much to their surprise and pleasure.

After she left school, she took a secretarial course in London,
living in the hostel attached to it and going home thankfully most
week-ends.

She found the work gruelling, particularly shorthand. On the
other hand, the rudimentary French and German which she had
already taken at school was so slowly and so badly taught that she

sat through each class becoming more and more furious. She tried, in vain, to get her parents to cancel these extras.

'Oh, I'm sure it will come in useful, dear,' they replied vaguely. 'Just do your best and be patient.'

'But it's wasting your money!' Susan persisted.

'Well, that's our loss, isn't it? We want you to make the best of your time there.'

The greatest attraction of the secretarial college was Penny Way. Penny had been at school with her, but a form ahead. She was an attractive girl, dark and lively, and outstandingly good at acting. To Susan, she had always been something of a heroine. At college, Penny was still one jump ahead, for she was living in the Earls Court flat whilst Susan was incarcerated in the hostel.

Penny was kind, in an off-hand way, to her junior and Susan was suitably grateful for her condescension. Occasionally, they travelled back from Caxley to London on the Sunday evening train, but Susan was careful not to intrude if Penny happened to be accompanied by a young man.

In the last week of the last term, Susan obtained a post in an advertising agency in Kensington. She was talking about lodgings to a bevy of friends when Penny approached.

'We need another girl,' she said. 'Barbara's off to Geneva. Like to join us?'

Susan glowed with pleasure.

'Better come and see the dump,' said Penny, 'and meet the others. Then we can tell you about rent and so on, if you're interested. Come about eight. We usually eat at seven.'

If Susan thought this was rather cavalier treatment, the unworthy thought was instantly dismissed, and she presented herself at the shabby front door with its flaking paint, at eight o'clock promptly. No one answered the bell, and she stood at the top of the flight of dirty steps, surveying her surroundings.

They were not inspiring. The minute front garden had two jaded variegated laurel bushes as its sole adornment. On the sour black earth, which did its best to nourish this natural growth, were cigarette cartons, sweet wrappings, a saucepan lid, several grimy plastic bags and a child's plastic beach shoe.

On the steps, leading from this square yard of flotsam to the young gentlemen's basement, stood a posse of unwashed milk bottles, a small red dustbin with no lid, and an extraordinary number of screwed-up bags which had contained potato crisps. Presumably, the occupants consumed these as their main item of diet, thought Susan.

Having rung the bell a second time, with no result, she opened the door timidly. She was in an outer hall, once whitened daily with hearth-stone no doubt, but now grey and dusty. A door, with frosted glass in its upper half, led her into the main hall.

This, and the stairs leading from it, were covered in brown linoleum. Susan mounted the stairs, hardly conscious of the grime around her, so thrilled was she at the thought of emancipation ahead.

It was very dark on the first floor, but the sound of music thumping away behind one door must mean that someone was home. She banged loudly upon it, and Penny flung it open, looking surprised.

'Oh, hello! I forgot you were coming. Come in.'

The noise from the ancient gramophone was deafening, and the fumes from the gas fire were equally stupefying. Two girls lolled, one at each end of the vast broken-down couch, their trousered legs lodged on the back of it. They did not move as Susan was brought forward.

'Barbara,' said Penny, giving no hint of which one she was. 'And Jane. Dobby's out, and Pam's doing her face. This is Susan.'

Barbara and Jane nodded in a friendly way, but said nothing. They seemed to be attending closely to the music, in a stunned sort of way. Susan was not surprised.

'Well, this is it,' said Penny, waving a hand vaguely to indicate the amenities of the room. Susan looked about her, observing the frayed and dirty curtains, the sagging armchairs, the greasy rug in front of the fire, and the two enormous oil paintings of Highland scenes which occupied most of the wall space. But her spirits rose. She could settle here very happily particularly if Penny were here.

'Better see the bedroom,' said Penny, leading the way across the landing. 'This is ours.' Two single beds were lost in the vastness of what had once been the main bedroom of the house. In the enormous bay window, in front of the sagging net curtains, brown with London dirt, stood a small dressing-table *circa* 1935, with plenty of chrome fittings and a badly-spotted looking-glass. Apart from two cane-bottomed chairs and a rickety chest of drawers with grained marmalade paint, this seemed to be the only piece of furniture in the room. Here again was the ubiquitous brown linoleum, but beside each bed lay a thin strip of carpeting which had once been a stair carpet, judging by the worn stripes across it.

'The beds aren't bad,' said Penny, giving one a thump 'But you'd better bring your own sheets and blankets. Towels too, of course – and a few tea-towels would help.'

'I could do that,' said Susan, still besotted.

Penny went before her to the kitchen. If the rest of the accommodation had been disheartening, then this was down-right repellent, and even Susan's spirits quailed. An enormous black frying-pan, full of congealed fat containing pieces of burnt onion, potato and bacon rinds, dominated the gas stove. This itself was an ancient monster, furred with the black grease of many years.

The walls of the kitchen ran with small rivulets of condensation which had left lines of brown encrustations over the years. A naked electric light bulb, covered with a fine film of grease, hung over the stove. The one window was tightly shut, and papered with an oiled paper representing stained glass. It was not very convincing.

'Window won't open,' commented Penny laconically, observing Susan's glances. 'All the windows have the jim-jams, but there's such a hell of a draught from most of them I think we get all the fresh air we need.'

Susan nodded half-heartedly.

'Next door's the loo,' went on Penny, throwing open the door of a dismal room housing a vast peeling bath, encased in pitch-pine, and a regal-looking lavatory seat with tarnished brass fittings. A snarl of tangled water pipes, flaking generously, wreathed about the walls and gurgled.

'How do you heat the water?' asked Susan.

'There's a boiler down below, and an old dear is supposed to keep it going. She comes every morning – in theory, that is. Mostly the water's tepid. We chuck in a kettleful of boiling water to pep it up, and get a decent bath when we go home.'

'What about rent?'

'We pay thirty quid a week.'

'What? Each?' shrieked Susan, appalled.

'Don't be funny. Six quid apiece. Can't get anything for much under. The gas fire's extra, of course. And our grub. We usually buy our own.'

'I think that will be all right. I'll have a word with my parents next week-end and tell you then. Is that all right?' asked Susan anxiously.

'Fine,' said Penny carelessly. 'Start the first of next month, if you want to come. Barbara's off then.'

She closed the bathroom door after three resounding bangings. At the third, the brass door knob came away in her hand. She thrust it back expertly.

'Better say farewell now. I'm due to go out in ten minutes and my current young man swears like a trooper if he's kept waiting.'

Susan said goodbye, and made her way downstairs and into the street. A small Negro girl, her frizzy hair sticking out in a dozen small plaits, each ending in a flighty scarlet bow, was busy jumping up and down the steps. She looked up at Susan, bright-eyed.

'You live there?' she queried.

'I'm going to,' replied Susan, smiling.

'I wouldn't,' said the child, still jumping.

Susan went on her way, elated by this exchange. Later, she was to wonder if it had not been some sort of warning.

Her parents had been very understanding about the flat, although Susan's mother was shocked when she saw it, by the conditions under which Susan was going to live, and she said so.

'It's nothing but a slum. Will you really be happy there?'

'Of course I will. Hundreds of other girls live in far worse places than this. It only wants a good clean.'

'It needs blowing up, and rebuilding,' said Daisy Warwick. 'But if you are prepared to live here, my dear, we'll do all we can to make you comfortable.'

Sheets, blankets, towels, a chair, some saucepans and crockery were carried from Springbourne to Earls Court. A large box of useful tinned food and some jars of home-made jam and marmalade, as well as bottles of fruit from the Warwicks' garden made their way into the rickety store cupboard in the flat's kitchen. Susan prepared to enjoy life.

On the whole, she was happy for the first few months, although there were several things about sharing which annoyed her. During the first week she spent Saturday afternoon washing the paintwork and scrubbing the floor of their bedroom. She cleaned the windows as far as she could reach, and polished the battered furniture. Even if the room did not look much more attractive, at least it smelt clean.

It was as much as she could do to remain silent when she saw Penny flicking cigarette ash to the floor that evening. She realized before many days passed that Penny was hopelessly untidy, and thought nothing of borrowing anything in the flat without bothering to ask permission. Scarves, jewellery, tights, even coats were missing when Susan looked for them, and her opinion of Penny, once so high, now plummeted.

It was annoying too to see how the groceries, which she brought to the flat, were eaten readily by all and not replaced. She did not mind putting in her share, nor doing her part of the sketchy daily cleaning and shopping, but it soon became apparent that she was carrying most of the burden. Hating to quarrel, she did her best, but resentment began to grow.

The advertising job did not work out as she hoped, and she left after three months and took a post with a typing agency. This meant that she was sent out to different offices which were short-handed. The pay was good, and she thought that the varied experience would be useful.

She found that the experiences were varied all right. One of her temporary employers turned out to be a dipsomaniac, two were addicted to stroking her legs, and another – a hard-faced woman journalist – had such a vitriolic tongue that she reduced Susan to tears within half a day. But on the whole, she enjoyed the work and gloried still in her independence.

She went home less and less, and when her parents did see her they began to grow increasingly anxious. Hurried meals, late nights, stuffy offices and the slummy flat were taking their toll. Susan had lost weight, had a series of painful boils, and was so tired that she spent most of the week-end asleep.

'Why don't you come home for a time,' urged her mother. 'You can always go back if you want to, but whatever's the good of earning these large wages if they all go on rent and fares? And just look at you – all eyes, and as thin as a rail!'

'Lovejoys need a secretary,' added her father. 'They'd be decent people to work for. And I met Mallet at Rotary lunch yesterday.

He is looking for an assistant. There are plenty of openings locally. Do think about it. Your mother and I would love to have you at home.'

That had been in June, and very tempting Susan had found the offer. But she still clung to her independence. It would be a retrograde step, she felt, to return to Springbourne – almost an admission of failure. She turned her back on the garden, sweet with roses and strawberries, on the haymakers in the fields and all the joyous freshness of early summer, and went back to London.

It was harder to bear than ever in hot weather, and that summer was long and fine. The journeys across London by bus or tube were a nightmare in the rush hour. After a day at work, it was almost unendurable to squash among hundreds of other tube-travellers, all hot, perspiring, and as cross as she was herself. One evening of sultry heat, she fainted on her feet, but the crush was so great that she remained upright, supported by a kindly Jamaican giant who insisted on refreshing her from his hip flask, and poured most of it down her new cotton frock.

The flat was more squalid than ever. The windows refused to open, and the smell of stale cooking hung about the place revoltingly. By late summer, Susan was heartily sick of the whole sordid set-up. It was as much as she could do to speak civilly to the other girls. She was tired of having no privacy, no quietness – for the gramophone seemed to play endlessly – and no time in which to sit and rest, to mend her clothes, to read or to write letters.

On the day of Emily Davis's funeral, while her mother was shivering in Beech Green church, Susan was pounding her typewriter in an airless top-floor office. She sat immediately below a large sky-light, which would not open, and was hotter than she had been all the summer. She had elected to work through her lunch hour, as the letters upon which she was engaged were urgent. An apple and a glass of tepid water from the cloakroom tap were all that she had eaten during the day, and by the time she arrived at Earls Court station she was almost too tired to walk to the flat.

Everywhere seemed filthy. A hot breeze raised the dust, swirling pieces of paper across the pavements. Dogs lay panting in the scanty shade of porches. Children in bathing suits lolled on the steps of houses, too hot to play. Men, stripped to the waist, sat at open windows, their arms dangling across the sills, to catch what little air there was. Querulous babies cried in stuffy prams, turning their wet heads this way and that to try to ease their wretchedness.

The traffic rumbled and roared continuously, like some snarling monster. To sit in a moving vehicle was misery on a day like this. To sit in a stationary one, in a traffic jam, was more than human flesh and blood could endure. The blaring of horns added to the din.

Susan stripped, and had a tepid bath, then lay, exhausted, upon her bed. She must have fallen asleep for the telephone bell roused her. Bemused, she struggled from her bed to the sitting-room. For once, it was mercifully empty.

Her mother's voice sounded reassuringly near.

'And how are you?'

'Terribly hot.'

'Here too, dear. Thunder, I think. Mrs Smith is getting on with the suit and says will you get a yard of black petersham for the skirt top, and do you want a zip or buttons?'

'Buttons. I'll get them.'

'Right. Now the next thing. Mary Bell is having a baby at Christmas. Isn't that nice?'

Susan forbore to say that Mary had told her this some time before, so early, in fact, that Susan had felt it was tempting fate to mention it.

'And Aunt Bessie's asked us to lunch on Sunday, so bring a frock, dear. You know how she feels about trousers.'

'If it's as hot as this, I'll probably go nude.'

'Yes, well – I thought I'd let you know. And do you still want those two cushions? If not, they can go to the Scouts' jumble sale.'

'Can I tell you at the week-end?'

'Of course. And the last thing. I've been to a funeral this afternoon at Beech Green. Now, *there's* a place to get cool! That church is like an ice-well.'

'Anyone I know?'

'Miss Davis. Your old teacher at Springbourne.'

'I'm sorry. Poor old dear – but I thought she'd died years ago. She must have been a hundred.'

'Eighty-something, I believe. She'll be missed. She was always so kind.'

'She was indeed,' agreed Susan. The pips sounded peremptorily.

'Well, we'll see you on Friday night, dear. At the station. Good-bye.'

'Goodbye,' said Susan, putting the sticky receiver back in its cradle.

She must make a note about the petersham and buttons, and get them tomorrow in her lunch break. And the cushions? She looked about her, at the depressing airless room, and the broken couch which, she thought, the cushions might make more bearable.

To hell with the cushions! Why should she bother to make the place look decent! No one else did. She'd fought a losing battle long enough. She wished she need never set eyes on the dreary place again.

She went to the window and tried for the hundredth time to open it. A sash cord broke under her onslaught, but the window remained firmly closed, sealed tightly by the paint.

Panic seized her. She could have smashed the grimy glass at that moment, in her frantic longing for air. Oh, to be on the downs at Springbourne, to feel the wind lifting one's hair, or to feel the cold rushing breeze as the swing flew up and down from the beech tree in the garden. If you swung high enough, you could see over the hedge to the village school across the way.

The village school! And Miss Davis! Susan rested her hot forehead against the grimy window pane, and stared unseeingly at the traffic pounding below.

Miles and miles away. Years and years away. And now Miss Davis was dead. A different world – a quiet, happy world of light and air and sunshine – or so it seemed, thought Susan, looking back.

17. Snowdrops at Springbourne

Susan had known Miss Davis and the village school for as long as she could remember. The Warwicks had moved to Springbourne when Dudley Warwick was appointed to be manager of the Caxley branch of his bank, a few years after the war.

The house was a comfortable and solid building, put up between the wars. The first owner had made a fine garden, and the

Warwicks, who were keen gardeners themselves, were glad to find mature trees and hedges, settled pathways and well-tended flower beds, when they took over.

Susan was born at Springbourne, and her earliest memories were of her afternoon outings in the pram. The school was less than a quarter of a mile away, and the children were usually setting off for their homes, after school, when Mrs Warwick and Susan returned from their walks.

Miss Davis was often at the gate, seeing off the children safely, and always had a word with Mrs Warwick and the child. Emily's hair was greying by this time, but her eyes were as dark and sparkling as ever they were. They reminded Susan of the bright glassy eyes of her much-loved toy monkey. There was a humorous twinkling look about them both, which the child found irresistible.

At five years old she went to the school herself. It was the autumn term, and the beech tree in the garden was already beginning to drop leaves as bright as new pennies.

She was happy from the first day, for several of her friends were there, and she knew that home was only a short distance away.

As so often happens, the newcomer picked up measles as soon as it appeared in the village. She had it more severely than most, and Doctor Martin insisted that she stay at home for the rest of the term.

'It's not a thing to take lightly,' he told Mrs Warwick, who privately thought that the old man was making a mountain out of a molehill. 'It goes in cycles. At the present time, it's very severe. We don't want complications. She can go out, well wrapped up, as soon as she is out of quarantine, but I don't want to risk any further infection.'

Susan chafed at the delay in returning to school, but revelled in the short walks she took with her mother when she had recovered.

She loved to collect flowers and stones, or any other lovely treasure which she came across in the hedges or fields. In those few weeks was born the deep love of natural things which was to stay with her for the rest of her days.

When she returned to school after the Christmas holidays she seemed perfectly fit, but Mrs Warwick noticed that she still tired easily if she took too much exercise. Miss Davis promised to keep an eye on the child.

One morning in February, Miss Davis came into the infants' room and told them that they were going to have a treat.

Mrs Allen, the farmer's wife, who was also one of the school managers, had invited them to her garden to see the snowdrops. They grew in vast drifts in a small copse at the edge of the garden, and thicker still in a dell near the house which had once been a sawyer's pit, many years earlier. The garden was famed in the Caxley area for its profusion of snowdrops, and the children were excited at the thought of an outing to such a lovely place.

There was much bustling in the school lobby as the young children buttoned coats and wrapped scarves round their necks. The infants' teacher was left in charge of Miss Davis's class, while the headmistress shepherded her little flock through the village to the farm.

It was almost a mile distant, but the sun shone and their spirits were high. A thick frost still sparkled on the grass verges and the bare twigs, but some golden catkins told of spring at hand, and a blackbird sang from a thornbush as boisterously as if it were April.

Mothers at their dusting waved and called to them as they passed, and tradesmen gave them a friendly toot on their horns as they went by. Altogether, it was a glorious occasion, made even more splendid by the knowledge that normally they would have been closeted in the schoolroom.

Susan skipped along with the others joyfully, but was glad when the farm gates came in sight, for her legs had begun to ache. Miss Davis, noticing, offered to carry her, but Susan would have none of it. However, she held Miss Davis's warmly-gloved hand, and was secretly glad of this support.

The snowdrops were so unbelievably white and pure, so numerous and so far spread, that the children fell silent in wonderment for a moment. Susan thought how like snow they were – not only in their whiteness, but also in texture. There was something crystalline in the drooping heads, delicate and opaque in the morning sunlight. The greyish-green spears of leaves set off the purity of the flowers perfectly It was an unforgettable sight.

They were allowed, by kind Mrs Allen to wander about freely and to pick a small bunch each. What is lovelier than picking flowers, especially when they are the first after so many dark months of winter? The earth was moist and fragrant beneath the trees, and here and there the tiny leaves of the honeysuckle showed the first brave touches of spring.

When they had had their fill of these joys, the children walked back along the drive to the farm kitchen. On the way Mrs Allen picked ivy leaves to put with each bunch. Susan thought the dark glossy leaves, mottled like marble, were a perfect contrast to the white beauty of the snowdrops. Every year, she promised herself, she would have just such a February nosegay to remind her of this wonderful morning.

Beyond the back garden of the farm, a row of calves pressed against the low hedge. Their shaggy heads hung over it inquisitively. Their beautiful eyes, heavily fringed, gazed solemnly at the children, who gazed back just as solemnly.

The ground fell away gently into the distance, and then rose again to the swelling flanks of the downs, scarcely visible in the morning haze. To Susan, the distance seemed vast. She was suddenly conscious, for the first time, of the infinity of space about her, as she stood on the little hill in the shelter of the farmhouse.

The calves' breath floated up like steam, in the forefront of this picture, from their shiny wet noses Far away, the farm dog must have seen the children, and began to race down the slope of the distant hill towards them.

At first he was a dim black shape moving swiftly towards his home, but as he drew nearer Susan thrilled to the sight of his splendid movement as he stretched his legs as rhythmically and as proudly as a racehorse. His ears flapped, his white teeth were bared in a grin of ecstasy, and when he finally reached them, he was so warm and panting, so full of vigorous life and spirits that Susan felt her own strength and excitement rising at the sheer joy of being alive on this tingling day of early spring.

They went into the great farm kitchen, after much shoe-wiping supervised by Miss Davis.

There on the table stood two steaming jugs of milk and an array of mugs and glasses. There was also a yellow china bowl filled with ginger biscuits.

As she sipped her milk among her chattering companions, Susan was conscious of the sudden contrast between this warm room, full of colour and conversation, and the great empty airiness outside. Both were lovely, one in its cosy domesticity, the other in its limitless mystery.

Her physical tiredness made the child more sensitive to her surroundings than usual, and she suddenly became aware that, for her, she must always have both worlds – each was necessary and complementary. One was her nest. The other was the place in which she stretched her wings, and soared, as effortlessly as the lark outside, into a different dimension.

When elevenses were over, and the mugs had been put into the sink, and the beautiful ginger biscuits had all been eaten, the children thanked Mrs Allen individually and shook hands with her, as Miss Davis had told them to do earlier. When it came to Susan's turn she felt that such formality could only express part of her feelings. She put her arms round Mrs Allen's ample waist and gave her a loving hug, when the official handshake was over.

By the time the little crocodile had reached the end of the farm drive, Susan's legs refused to carry her further, and she looked up at Miss Davis in despair.

'My legs ache,' she began, but did not need to add any more, for Miss Davis swung her up on to a high bank and sat down in front of her.

'A piggy-back for you, Susan. Up you get!'

The child gratefully put her arms round Emily's neck. Her teacher's dark wiry hair tickled Susan's face, but this was pleasurable.

She enjoyed jogging along, her cheek against Miss Davis's scarlet coat. Below her the children bobbed along, their bunches of snowdrops clasped carefully in their gloved hands. Their breath rose in silver clouds, as they clattered along in their sturdy country boots, and reminded Susan of the adorable calves standing against the background of mistily distant hills.

There was something wonderfully reassuring and comforting about Miss Davis's small strong body which bore her along so steadily. Emily had given many a piggy-back to younger brothers and sisters, as well as her own pupils, and had the knack of carrying a child in a way which gave most comfort to them both.

Susan never forgot that welcome ride. The experiences of that shining morning culminated in the new bond forged between teacher and pupil as they made their way together through the village.

Standing listlessly at the stubbornly shut window of the flat, Susan noticed once again the small Negro girl sitting on the kerb opposite.

She was clad in a grubby elasticized white bathing suit. Her bare feet were thrust into a pair of silver evening sandals which might have been her mother's, so large were they. She rose to her feet lithely, and began to teeter along in the grotesque shoes, looking, for all the world, Susan thought, like Minnie Mouse.

Suddenly her amusement changed to pity. There she was, poor child, about the same age as she had been on that far morning of sparkling light and infinite airiness, but doomed to spend the day in a noisy prison of stone and brick. It was all wrong! No child should be forced to endure this claustrophobic squalor!

For that matter, no one – child or adult – should have to endure such conditions.

The memory of the snowdrops, the memory of Miss Davis, the memory of the calves and the emptiness beyond their endearing heads, flooded back to Susan. Why not go back?

She knew in her heart that these two worlds still existed side by side – the small and the limitless. Too long she had suffered from being penned. It was time to find her true self again, and for that she must have space and air and beauty.

It could be done. She could give in her notice tomorrow, telephone to her mother and ask if she could come for a week or two's holiday. She knew how joyously she would be welcomed. Who knows? She might find that job in Caxley after all.

But that was in the distance. All that mattered immediately was to escape – to put her affairs in order, in this swarming filthy ant-hill she had once thought so glamorous, and to find quietness and space for the survival of her body and mind.

Perhaps that had been the secret of Miss Davis's strength, she thought suddenly. She went at her own pace, and had time to relish all the lovely natural things in Springbourne and thereabouts. And when the occasion arose, that happiness, fed by inner serenity, could succour the weak and give, as Susan could so poignantly recall, strength and heart to those who needed it.

She went into the bedroom and began to pack in readiness for a longer stay at home than usual. She was not going to make up her mind one way or the other. No doubt London would pull her back before long, just as Springbourne tugged her now with an urgency her starved spirit must obey.

But she would go forward with her immediate plans. Her spirits rose as she moved about her work in the sultry heat. Soon she would be out on the windy hills above Springbourne, where the small happy ghost of Emily Davis had beckoned her.

Her mind raced ahead. She saw herself at the booking office in the deafening and dirty London terminus. Aloud, she rehearsed the words:

'Single to Caxley!'

18. Doctor Martin's Morning Surgery

A week or two after Emily's funeral, Doctor Martin sat in his surgery at Beech Green, awaiting the first of the day's patients.

The morning was warm and rather close for October, and the windows looking on to his garden were wide open. A bed of mixed roses stood immediately below the windows, and in the quietness the doctor could hear a blackbird busily scrabbling the earth for worms. Now and again a delicious whiff of the roses' scent wafted into the room, giving the old man much pleasure. His love of roses grew greater as the years passed.

He glanced at the silver clock on the mantelpiece. Nine-thirty. Time he opened shop, he told himself.

He smoothed his grey hair and opened the door into the little waiting room. Not many today, thank heaven. Fine weather cut his queue by half. It was in January and February that extra chairs had to be put in the waiting room.

'Good morning! Good morning!' said Doctor Martin cheerfully.

'Good morning,' replied his sufferers, with varying degrees of joy.

Doctor Martin consulted his list.

'Mrs Petty?'

A stout young woman rose, carrying a toddler, and followed Doctor Martin into the surgery. She was, in fact, Miss Petty, but the birth of Gloria, who now accompanied her, accounted for the change to a married title.

The Pettys were a large family, originating in Caxley. They ran to fat, were short-necked and inclined to respiratory diseases. They were also good-tempered, happy-go-lucky and quite incapable of keeping to any diet prescribed by their various doctors for weight reduction.

'Well now, what's the trouble?' asked the doctor kindly.

It appeared that Gloria's 'summer cold' refused to go. She complained of a sore throat, and had a stubborn cough which grew worse at night.

'Let's have a look,' said Doctor Martin, fishing the spatula from a glass of disinfectant.

Gloria began to wail.

'Give over, do!' begged her mother. 'And open your mouth.'

Doctor Martin expertly held down the child's tongue during one of the lulls in her whimpering.

'Tastes nasty!' whined the child when the instrument was removed.

'Maybe,' said the doctor amiably. 'I should think most things taste nasty with that throat.'

He pressed her neck glands, and then took out his stethoscope. After the examination, he sat at his desk and wrote the prescriptions.

'Now, this one is for tablets which she must suck slowly. Not more than six a day, mind you. Read the label carefully. You can read, Mrs Petty?'

The question was asked casually. There were still several people among Doctor Martin's patients who were unable to read despite a century of compulsory education.

'A bit,' replied Mrs Petty.

'Not more than six during the twenty-four hours. They should settle the infection.'

He held up the second slip of paper.

'This is the cough cure recipe. A teaspoonful when it is troublesome.'

She took the two papers almost reverently, and put them carefully inside a dilapidated patent leather handbag. She was about to leave when Doctor Martin motioned her to the chair again.

'This child's tonsils want attention. Bring her back in a fortnight. And her teeth have caries — are going bad. That means the second ones may be infected. She's having too many sweets, Mrs Petty. Cut them out.'

'But she likes a bit of chocolate! Her gran brings her a bar every day!'

'Ask her to bring an apple instead. Chocolate will rot her teeth and make her too fat. She's overweight now. You're storing up trouble for the future, if you don't feed her properly. We've talked about this before.'

'Well, I'll try,' said Mrs Petty grudgingly, 'but it's her gran you ought to talk to.'

'Are you still working?' asked the doctor, showing her to the door.

'Every afternoon,' said the woman, her eyes brightening. 'Down the new fish shop. It pays for me bingo, Mondays.'

'D'you take the child too?'

'No, Gran comes up. I leaves a bit of tea for 'em both.'

Doctor Martin had seen those teas once or twice. Bought pies, packets of crisps, sliced wrapped bread, glutinous shop jam and a pot of well-stewed tea. Not a ha'p'orth of nourishment in the lot! Even the milk was tinned. He had seen the opened tin standing on the table, with a large blow-fly in attendance.

'See the child gets eggs, fresh milk, some meat and plenty of fruit,' said Doctor Martin for the hundredth time. 'She needs building up.'

He opened the door, and Mrs Petty made her departure.

'Building up,' she echoed, when she gained the lane. 'He's gettin' past it. Says the kid's too fat and then, in the next breath, wants buildin' up.'

'Can I have an ice-cream?' cried the child, as the village shop came in sight. 'Can I, mum? Can I?'

'I'll see. Doctor only said: "No sweets." Yes, all right. I'll get you a lolly, love.'

She felt quite sure an ice-cream wouldn't hurt her. After all, mothers always knew best.

Doctor Martin worked his way steadily down the list of patients. There were a few unexpected visitors among them, such as Joe Melly the shepherd, who had nicked the top off a troublesome spot on his wrist, and now had a fat shiny hand which throbbed painfully, and a dangerous red line creeping up his arm.

There was seventeen-year-old Dicky Potts, with yet another boil to be lanced. There was garrulous Mrs Twist, who enjoyed fainting fits when life became too much for her – or she was getting the worst of an argument. Jane Austen would have diagnosed the vapours. Doctor Martin could do little more. There were the two youngest children of Minnie Pringle, smothered in spots, hot, flushed and tearful, with furred tongues and high temperatures, who were dispatched to bed promptly by the old doctor.

'And I'll call in on my rounds,' he told scatter-brained Minnie, who stood looking more like a bewildered hen than ever. 'They've got measles. You should have had more sense than to bring them out, Minnie.'

Might as well talk to a brick wall, he told himself, watching the trio depart up the lane.

'Who's next?' he asked of the two or three remaining patients. Mrs Barber, a comparative newcomer to Beech Green, rose with her daughter, a fair-haired schoolgirl, and the two followed Doctor Martin into his surgery.

'What's the trouble?' asked Doctor Martin of the mother. She gazed at him in silence and, to his dismay, her mouth began to tremble and her eyes fill with tears.

The doctor turned to the girl who was looking at her mother with mingled impatience and disgust.

'Are you the patient?'

'I s'pose so,' the girl shrugged.

Mrs Barber produced a handkerchief and blew her nose noisily.

'We think she's in trouble,' she said tremulously. There was only one condition which was described to Doctor Martin in these terms.

'Then I'd better ask you a few questions,' said the old man gently.

He put them simply, and the girl replied in an off-hand way. Obviously, the mother was more upset than the daughter.

'Lie on the couch,' directed Doctor Martin, 'and we'll have an examination. There's nothing to fear.'

When it was over, and the suspicions confirmed, the doctor told them that the baby would be born early in March, and gave them the address of the ante-natal clinic. He was kind and uncensorious, doing his best, by being completely matter-of-fact, to ease the tension of the unhappy situation.

'Perhaps you would wait outside a moment, while your mother has a word with me,' he said.

When the girl had departed, the mother's tears began to flow again.

'The shame of it! Only sixteen – barely seventeen when the baby comes – and no father! What will the neighbours think? We've given her everything she wants, tried to bring her up nice, and now **look what's happened!**'

Doctor Martin let her run on in this vein until she had had her outburst.

'Did you explain the facts of life to the child?'

'Well, no. It's so embarrassing, isn't it? You know, it never seems the right moment. Anyway, the school should teach her that these days.'

'These days,' said the doctor 'are much the same as any other days. Parents still have duties towards their children.'

'I blame her Gran,' said Mrs Barber, sniffing. 'She was supposed to go there straight after school on the days I was working. She never bothered if Audrey was late. I bet all this happened then.'

'And how old is her grandmother?' asked Doctor Martin mildly.

'Eighty – but very healthy.'

Doctor Martin felt some sympathy with this absent and elderly scape-goat, and said so.

'It's no good casting round for someone to blame,' he continued. 'You know the situation – it's all too common, unfortunately – and you must all make the best of it as a family.'

'That boy'll have to marry her,' said Mrs Barber fiercely.

'If he loves her, he'll want to,' agreed the doctor, 'but I can't see anyone benefiting from a shot-gun wedding, least of all your daughter and the baby.'

He patted the woman on the shoulder, and walked with her to the door.

'Say as little as you can to her until you've had time to cool down. You'll say things you'll regret all your life if you are too hasty now. Look after that girl of yours. She needs all the help she can get, silly child, and you're the one she'll turn to, if you'll let her.'

He watched the two depart, and beckoned his last patient into the surgery.

Elaine Burton was fifty-two, as Doctor Martin knew well, but she might have been sixty-two from her haggard looks. Her husband worked at a printer's in Caxley and her two children also worked there. They were unmarried and still lived at home.

Mrs Burton's main problem was her old mother, now nearly ninety, who lived with them. Brought up in a strict Victorian way, the old lady remained a martinet despite failing health. Her daughter, acting as buffer between the demands of the younger generation and the old, came off worst in the household, as Doctor Martin knew well.

'I think I need a tonic,' said his patient wearily. 'I'm tired all day, and when I get to bed I can't sleep. Mother needs seeing to at least twice in the night, and I think I've got into the habit of being on the alert all night. It's really getting me down, Doctor Martin.'

He surveyed the woman with an expert eye. She had been pretty once. He remembered her as a young woman with her first baby. She had been trim and lively, with soft dark hair, and a quick smile which revealed dimples.

Now she was running to fat, and was pale and listless. Blue smudges under her eyes bore testimony to lack of sleep. Her hair was lank, her neck decidedly grubby. Her whole bearing spoke of exhaustion and self-neglect.

'I'll put you on some iron tablets,' said the doctor, drawing his pad towards him. It was plain that the woman was anaemic and over-worked.

'How's your appetite?'

'I don't fancy much. By the time I've spooned mother's food into her, I don't want my own.'

'Do you have a cooked meal?'

'When the others get home, but I don't really want it then.'

'Milk? Eggs?'

'I could never take them, even as a child.'

The old doctor sighed. Here was yet another case of the dying sapping the living, but what could one do?

'And how is your mother?'

'To be honest, a terrible trial, doctor.'

'Can't your brother have her for a while? To give you a break?'

Mrs Burton snorted.

'He's under his Ethel's thumb, and she refuses point-blank to give any help with ma. Besides, ma hates her like poison. It would never do.'

She could have added that her own husband's attitude was much the same as Ethel's, but loyalty kept her silent.

'We might be able to get the old lady into a home, you know.'

'She'd never hear of it. And I wouldn't want to send her away, despite all the work. It's the washing and drying that gets me down.

I have to wash bedding and nightgowns every day – sometimes twice a day. It's far worse than having a baby to look after. Still, it's got to be done. I wouldn't have her moved. She's my mother, after all.'

'Do the young ones help?'

Elaine Burton gave a hard laugh.

'They take the tray up now and again, and switch on the radio for her, but that's about the lot. They nag me to send her away, and she nags me to keep them quiet, and tells me I've not brought them up respectful. You know how it is.'

Doctor Martin nodded sympathetically. He knew indeed.

He felt sorry for them all – the unhappy, cross old lady, confined to her bed; the exuberant young people criticized at every turn, the husband condemned to watch his wife's health slowly seeping away and, chiefly, Elaine Burton torn this way and that, by the demands of all, and fast becoming too tired to carry the heavy burden of the combined duties of daughter, wife and mother.

'You should get away with your husband for a holiday,' he told her seriously. 'If your brother won't have your mother, I can arrange for her to go into hospital for a fortnight. Now, talk it over. I know it won't be easy, but it's no good knocking yourself up. Where will the family be, if you have to give up?'

The woman was visibly moved and gave him a shaky smile, as she held out her hand for the prescription.

'I'll think about it, but I can't see it coming off,' she said honestly.

Doctor Martin showed her to the door.

'I'll drop in and see the old lady one day soon,' he promised. 'Meanwhile, take those tablets, and some good food.'

He watched her go sadly, then returned for his bag. Off to see two of his patients in Caxley Cottage Hospital, and then he must set about his rounds, he told himself.

He locked his desk, and the drugs cupboard, and went thoughtfully to his car.

19. Doctor Martin Looks Back

Caxley Cottage Hospital was a small building erected in the twenties, and opened by the Mayor of the day with considerable civic pomp.

It served the area well, but now there were rumours of its closure, much to the indignation of the local people. As they pointed out to each other, by the time you had been dragged all the way to the county hospital, twenty miles distant, and waited in the queues of traffic which had to be encountered on the way, you would probably be dead on admission.

'And who wants to go all that distance to visit relatives?' they demanded. 'And who can afford the fares there, anyway? A dam' silly idea shutting the Cottage. Hope it never happens.'

Doctor Martin agreed with them. He could quite see that a more modern operating theatre was necessary, and that the place was uneconomic to run, but there was still plenty of minor surgery and certain illnesses which could be dealt with in this little place, thus relieving pressure on the larger hospitals at the neighbouring towns.

His first patient was in high spirits when he went to see her in the children's ward. Mary Wood was seven years old, and had had her tonsils removed.

'Mummy's fetching me tomorrow,' she told him triumphantly. 'And I'm going to be home for tea. And I'm going to have a puppy.'

'What? For tea?'

The child smiled indulgently at this little joke revealing a gap where her two front milk teeth had vanished.

'I'm not a *cannibal*,' she answered, bringing out this new, half-understood word with considerable pride.

The remark amused Doctor Martin for the rest of the day.

His other hospital patient was less cheerful. Old George Smith was recovering from acute bronchitis, and was fearful of what the future might hold.

'My old woman ain't up to nursing me, sir and we can t abear the idea of living with our Nell, good girl though she be. They've got them two strapping boys, hollering about all day, and playing that electric guitar all night fit to blow yer 'ead off. Us old folks couldn't stand it, and they don't want us anyway.'

'Would she be able to look in to your home and give a hand? The district nurse could call each morning. We'll fix up something never fear.'

'We likes to be independent,' said the old man obstinately. 'And anyway, our Nell goes out cleaning every morning; she's got enough to do. No, let's face it, doctor, you keeps us old folks alive too long these days – and we're not wanted. Time was, this bronchitis of mine would've carried me off. Now I'm still 'ere, and a nuisance to everybody.'

Tears of self-pity rose to his eyes.

'Rubbish!' said Doctor Martin robustly, patting the wrinkled hand on the coverlet. 'You're just a little low in spirits. Wait till you're home again! You'll be as fit as ever.'

'If there's one thing I 'ates,' continued the old man, 'it's the work-house. I knows things is better now, but I can recall the time when 'usbands and wives were parted at the gate, and sometimes never saw each other no more. 'Twas a terrible thing that – to be treated worse than animals.'

'Things like that don't happen now,' the doctor assured him, but the old man rambled on, unconscious of interruptions.

'Seems to me the young people ain't got no respect for their parents today. They do say that in China the old folks are looked up to because they're reckoned to be the wisest of the family. Don't see much o' that in these parts. It's time I was dead, doctor, and that's the truth of it.'

Doctor Martin did his best to speak comfortingly to the old man, but it was clear that he was sunk too deeply in his own miseries and fears to heed much that was said.

Doctor Martin returned to his car and drove carefully through Caxley High Street. It was with a sigh of relief that he turned the nose of the car northwest and regained the leafy lanes leading to Beech Green, Springbourne and Fairacre.

'Thank God,' he said aloud, 'my practice is in the country.'

He pulled off the road, as he so often did, on the brow of a hill. Here there was a fine view of the countryside, backed by the splen-did whale-back of the downs

The doctor wound down the window and breathed in the fresh air, tugging a pipe from his pocket as he did so.

He filled it, meditating upon his morning's work, and the people with whom it had brought him in contact.

What problems people had! If one believed all one read in news-papers and magazines, or saw at the theatre or on the ubiquitous 'Box', the only problem besetting people these days was sex. Good grief, thought the doctor impatiently, that was a pretty minor problem, taking all ages of men and women into account! He'd put the problems of health, family and money, as being quite as important as sex – certainly from the age of forty-odd onward, which included a goodly proportion of the nation, after all.

His mind dwelt on poor old George Smith's worries. Here was the age-old difficulty of keeping the older generation happy and cared-for. Something had gone amiss with the pattern of family life today, making this problem even greater than it had been in earlier generations.

Yes, George had a point about being kept alive too long – but a doctor's first duty was to his patient, and he must do his best to prolong life. Nevertheless, it created problems for all.

He looked back upon his own memories. His grandmother had lived in a tall town house, four storeys high, and two unmarried daughters and an unmarried son lived with her. She had borne twelve children and eight had survived. The house always seemed full of nieces and nephews, of all ages, coming and going, bearing little presents, chattering about their families, showing Grandma their new babies, or pirouetting before the old matriarch as they displayed the latest fashions. There was a lot said against those large Victorian families, but at least there was a feeling of belonging – and even if there were battles now and again, a common enemy had only to appear to weld the clan into solid unity.

And then, there was always someone with time to spare. His maiden aunts seemed to be able to drop whatever they were doing to play shops with him. When Grandma's sight began to fail, one or other read out the items of news from the daily paper with real kindliness, it seemed to the child. No one seemed cross, or in a hurry, or resented serving the old lady, although no doubt there were times when they found her as tiresome as George Smith's grandchildren and poor Elaine Burton found their ancient relatives.

Of course, the burden had always fallen hardest on the unmarried daughters, and still did, for that matter. And then, so much depended on the old people's attitude to life. If they could keep busy, and avoid self-pity, it was half the battle against depression.

His grandmother, he remembered, always made herself responsible for the midday meal. She spent the morning preparing it, and the rest of the day planning for the next day's menu. She did little else in the house, but this one important chore eased the strain for everyone and, above all, gave her the inestimable reward of knowing she was useful.

He took out a match, struck it, and drew his pipe into life. Through the blue clouds, he gazed at the view spread out below him. The spire of Beech Green church pierced the surrounding trees, and his thoughts turned to his last visit there, when Emily Davis had been buried.

Now, there was a family which had managed its life well! he mused. When he first met them all, most of Mrs Davis's family were out in the world, and Emily went out to her teaching at Springbourne each day, but returned at night.

Every Sunday there seemed to be a family reunion. Sons and daughters from Caxley brought over their children for Sunday tea, and news was exchanged. They were a lively collection, Doctor Martin recalled, and there was plenty of laughter in the tiny cottage.

Perhaps that was the secret of happy family life – or one of the secrets. Nowadays people didn't seem to have time to laugh. All too busy rushing from place to place, like scalded cats, mused the old doctor, stirring the tobacco in his pipe bowl with a matchstick.

The Davises travelled very little. Poverty had its rewards sometimes. If one had to remain in the same place, then one made one's pleasures there. Certainly the Davis family created their own delights. They gardened, and saw the results of their labours in the fine string of onions hanging in the shed, the sack of home-grown potatoes, the jams and jellies ranged upon the kitchen shelf. They knitted and they sewed. Doctor Martin remembered the beautiful dolls' clothes which Mrs Davis made each Christmas for her grand-daughters' presents. He had admired tucks and feather-stitching on the minute petticoats – work which no modern parent would bother to do – but which would be prized by the owner of the lucky doll, and give pleasure too to the needlewoman.

The little cottage overflowed with the results of their handi-work. The walls were papered by one son, the paintwork done by another. Rugs, cushions, chair-covers, all were made at home, and most of their clothes, too, were hand-made. It was a way of life which had endured for centuries, but which was now fast vanishing.

Doctor Martin recalled one of his favourite characters who had lived in the eighteenth century and kept a diary Parson James Woodforde, although a fellow of New College, Oxford, did things with his own hands just as the Davises did. He brewed his own beer, he salted pigs, he kept his house to rights, he pruned and dug in his garden, as well as visiting his parishioners and serv-ing the church. He had a great deal in common with the country folk of Doctor Martin's earlier memories, and his sense of family duty was as keen. He was concerned about Brother Jack, the black sheep of the family, and considerate to his niece Nancy who lived with him.

The latest over-worked word 'involved' came into the old doctor's mind. Those earlier people really were involved. Emily Davis, a good daughter, cared for her mother until her death, and did it cheerfully, just as she did her duty towards the many school children who passed through her hands.

She had been a wonderful person – perhaps the finest character in that fine family. One did not meet many quite as selfless these days. That perhaps was one of the causes of Emily's strength.

She was completely devoid of self-pity, unlike poor Elaine Burton and George Smith.

She shouldered responsibility bravely, unlike Mrs Barber who thought that the school alone should tell her daughter the facts of life.

She had an unswerving sense of justice, based on her Victorian upbringing of recognizing right from wrong. It may have been too rigid a code, but it produced some good steadfast people who en-gendered those old-fashioned virtues of respect and duty.

Doctor Martin looked at the clock on the dashboard. It was time he moved on. His pipe was almost finished, and he had day-dreamed long enough. He must blame Emily Davis for much of it!

He wished he could tell her so. She would have enjoyed the joke. She always did.

He switched on the engine and drove gently down the hill to Beech Green.

20. Two Old Friends

As Doctor Martin slowly descended the steep, winding hill he caught a glimpse of the tall figure of Dolly Clare moving about in her garden. On impulse, he drew into the side of the lane, and made his way up the garden path.

Miss Clare was cutting a few late roses, and she held them up for the doctor to admire.

'For Emily's grave,' she told him. 'Now that all those lovely funeral flowers have gone, it is beginning to look rather bare.'

The doctor nodded. He approved of the way in which Dolly Clare talked so lovingly, and yet so calmly, of her dead friend.

'Mr Willet is going to plant a low bush of red roses for me on the grave. There won't be a headstone. Emily always set her face against any sort of permanent memorial.'

'She left her own memorial,' commented the doctor, 'she'll never be forgotten.'

Dolly smiled at him.

'Come inside. I've something for you.'

She led the way into the little cottage. It was as fresh and shining as ever. A vase of flowers stood on the polished table. The curtains stirred gently in the breeze from the open window. There was a delicious smell of something baking in the kitchen. It was quite apparent that Dolly Clare, old and bereft though she was, was still self-reliant, and still revelling in her independence.

'Do sit down,' she said, 'while I put these in water. I shall go up to the churchyard this afternoon, after my rest.'

He did as he was told and looked about him. It was obvious that

Dolly was busy sorting out Emily's effects, for a large suitcase, propped open, was filled with clothes, and on the little bureau by the window were some trinkets which the doctor recognized as Emily's.

Dolly Clare returned with the roses in a vase and put them on the window sill.

'Coffee?' she asked.

The doctor shook his head.

'Not for me, Dolly. I'm getting up an appetite for lunch. It's curried lamb today, I'm told.'

Dolly laughed, and crossed to the bureau.

'As you see, I'm sorting out Emily's things, and I've practically finished. The nieces and nephews were remembered, of course, but she asked me, several times, to give you this as a little remembrance of her.'

She brought over to him a silver pocket-watch on a silver chain.

'It was given to her brother when he retired. He left it to Emily, and she always kept it on the little table by her bed. It's an excellent time-keeper. She hoped you would find a use for it.'

The old doctor was too moved to speak for a moment, as he turned the beautiful thing in his hands.

'How generous of her,' he said at last. 'I shall always treasure it, Dolly. Always.'

He undid his jacket and patted his waistcoat.

'Help me to put it on now, Dolly. It's going to be my constant companion.'

Miss Clare helped him to thread the chain through a buttonhole, and the doctor put the watch very gently into his pocket. He stood up and surveyed himself in the mirror on the wall.

'Do you know, Dolly, I've always wanted a pocket-watch, and never felt that I could indulge myself. This is doubly welcome – a remembrance of dear Emily, though she would be remembered well enough without it, as you know – and something I've always longed for.'

Miss Clare smiled.

'It would have pleased Emily so much to know you like it,' she told him. She turned to the bureau and held up a gold locket for the doctor to see.

'I wish I had found this earlier,' she said seriously I should have **put it in the coffin with her.'**

She handed it to the doctor. It contained the portrait of a young man in uniform. He studied it for some moments, then looked questioningly at Dolly.

'Edgar,' she nodded. 'The only man she ever loved. Sometimes we used to say we'd both been unlucky in love. After all, we both lost our lovers – but we were wonderfully blest with all the affection we had from the children at school and all the friends about us here. It helped a lot, you know.'

'You both deserved happiness,' exclaimed the doctor.

Miss Clare sat down in the armchair by the fire.

'I was so touched by the dozens of letters I had. Some from as far afield as India and Australia – mostly from old pupils who had read the news in the *Caxley Chronicle* or in letters from home. And then there were a great many from people I scarcely knew – Jane Bentley, for instance, who taught with Emily many years ago, and Daisy Warwick. She wrote so kindly about Emily's care of her daughter.

'And the flowers, as you know, were unbelievably lovely. I'd no idea that Emily was so widely known. Even Mrs Pringle sent a beautiful heart made of Michaelmas daisies.'

'Well, that really is a tribute to Emily,' agreed Doctor Martin, laughing.

'And so many little kindnesses to me too,' went on Dolly. 'Mr Willet brought me a marrow – which I can't look at, incidentally, without remembering Manny Back, and Emily at her most mischievous. And I've been given enough fresh eggs by kind neighbours to keep me in omelettes for weeks.'

'I'm glad to hear it,' said the doctor. 'Mind you eat them, and look after yourself.'

He rose, and looked down at his new watch-chain proudly.

'I can't tell you how much I appreciate this,' he said soberly. 'This is a typical gesture of Emily's, generous and practical. I shall wear it always.'

He turned at the door.

'I'll call again, Dolly. Don't get over-tired. What are you doing for the rest of the day?'

'Finishing my sorting. I'm thoroughly enjoying looking through the old school photographs. I've recognized several Pringles and Billy Dove, and a host of others.

'Then I shall take the roses up to Emily's grave, and also plant a clump of snowdrops which I've dug up from this garden. Emily always loved them, and I went with her several times to see them at Mrs Allen's farm. What a glorious sight! Emily used to reckon it was one of the high-lights of the winter.'

'You're going to be busy, I can see,' commented Doctor Martin. 'Well, better to wear out than rust out, as my old grandmother used to say.'

He waved goodbye, and Miss Clare watched him drive along the lane into the distance.

That evening, as dusk was falling, Dolly Clare took her accustomed walk at the edge of Hundred Acre Field, behind her home.

All her little duties were done, and she felt free to enjoy the evening air before settling by the fireside.

She reached the oak tree, and stood very still, watching three fine pheasants searching for acorns at the foot of the gnarled old trunk.

Above her the rooks were flying homeward. The great field before her, gleaming with gold when last she walked there with Emily, was now freshly ploughed, the furrows dark and glistening. Within a few days the seed would be planted and she would watch, alone now, the first tender blades appear, then the ripening crop and, finally, its harvesting.

The comforting cycle of the seasons continued unchanged – the sowing, the growing and the reaping.

Dolly Clare turned, and made her way homeward with a grateful heart. Life went on and was still sweet.